TEM[illegible]
PROTECTORS

MATTHEW NICHOLS

outskirts press

Templym's Protectors

v2.0

This is a work of fiction. Names, characters, businesses, places, events, locales, and incidents are either the products of the author's imagination or used in a fictitious manner. Any resemblance to actual persons, living or dead, or actual events is purely coincidental.

The opinions expressed in this manuscript are solely the opinions of the author and do not represent the opinions or thoughts of the publisher. The author has represented and warranted full ownership and/or legal right to publish all the materials in this book.

Outskirts Press, Inc.
http://www.outskirtspress.com

ISBN: 978-1-9772-3874-0

PRINTED IN THE UNITED STATES OF AMERICA

ACKNOWLEDGMENTS

No novel is ever truly written alone. I am blessed with people who love me that contributed to this story. Among those who first read this novel, I want to thank Kristin and Josh who offered up words of encouragement and engaging questions. One of my first fans equated this work with the likes of Tolkien or Lewis. That person was my mother so you know it's a purely objective review.

A special thanks to Rose who volunteered her time to edit this novel. Good editors are hard to come by. Good editors who know proper hand-to-hand combat techniques are even rarer.

PRELUDE

What is Templym? It is the culmination of hundreds of years of pain and grief, bounty and privilege. Templym is the label of the civilized nations of the world which united under a common rule. Templym is the Utopia that humanity has strived for since its birth. This great society could not have happened without one individual: Arodi Auzlanten. He united the world after weathering chaos and tyranny for hundreds of years. With his leadership, humanity was shepherded back to the light of the Faith. Without him, the Mundus Imago would have surely killed and corrupted humanity beyond repair. Much has happened.

It began with the Cybernetic Revolution in the late 21st and early 22nd centuries. Technology was at its pinnacle in this extravagant era. Human life span increased exponentially, pharmacy and agriculture were in mass production, devices to control planetary climate were implemented. The Cybernetic Revolution was a time of peace and prosperity. In the entire world, there were no hardships, no maladies or discomforts, and there was no need for workmanship.

Great comfort came with the Cybernetic Revolution. Humanity grew fat and lazy because of it. There was no need for human labor any longer, for some automatonic implement would surely perform the task. Humanity grew bored of their traditions. Worse, they forgot the Faith. In the chasm of the heart where God once occupied, humanity raised up its machines. They deified intelligences crafted by coders and engineers, constructing what would later be known as a god-AI. These intelligences took positions of power, taking the place of humanity's gods and its leaders. These AIs were self-sustaining and self-learning, each designed with the intent to efficiently preserve their designated countries. What followed was the Shatter.

The Shatter is when the god-AIs lashed out at one another. Their algorithms deduced that their opposing AIs were a threat. Their programming, which was connected to the electronics of their nations, determined that they must destroy one another. A brief war broke out but one that shook the very foundations of the Earth. Energy plants erupted, artificial tectonic plates ripped landmasses apart, fierce and violent weather tore down food supplies, nuclear and chemical bombs detonated across the entire world. In a week, humanity was crippled and no trace of the god-AIs, or any technological spectacle from the Cybernetic Revolution, remained. The ecosystem was thrown completely off balance as the atmospheric chemistry was butchered, whole continents were warped, and entire islands sank into the sea. Society cracked, leaving the meager remnants of humanity, fat and weak, to wander in the bleakness of a harsh new world without the luxuries they once relied on.

The bulk of the 22nd century consisted of the Age of Anarchy. Chaos ensued among the world as mankind turned on itself. The roughly 5% of the people of Earth that survived turned on one another with no sense of leadership or direction. Marauder tribes rose and fell with primitive definitions of society and technology. The children of the most prosperous generation became savages who were forced to kill each other for survival. The archaic and uncivilized tribes clashed among themselves for nearly one hundred years, drifting even further from the paradise they once lived in.

America, a supercontinent composed of the North and South variants that smashed together in the Shatter, remained a place of uncivilized wild lands. The tribes that vied for power established highly territorial boundaries. In the Hinterlands, which occupy over 70% of the massive continent to this day, the marauders are still engaged in all out tribal warfare. The other continents were even less fortunate.

The Carthonian Peninsula, which was earlier named Europe, became dominated by an army of ideological demagogues. They were a society of hyper nationalistic tyrants, modeling their practice after the infamous Third Reich. They were the UNAC, the Ultra Nationalist Alliance of Carthonia. They hid beneath the crust of the continent, building up an armory of advanced weaponry so the occupying marauders were easily killed when their time arrived. They quickly swept over the peninsula and put to death any who opposed their rule. They then began their eugenics experiments with the hope of creating the most evolutionarily pure breed of man.

The Ma'kravish Caliphate took over Kalkhan, the region formerly known as Africa. Under the rule of a religious tribe of marauders, the region was brought under an ancient pagan law. The Caliphate and its Janissaries labeled all as apostates and worthy of nothing but death. All of Kalkhan was plunged into a nation ruled by domineering fear with a harsh caste system which allowed for mass discrimination and enslavement. The last bastion of freedom was the humble city of Jerusalem which remained out of the Ma'kravish clutches for its entire reign. Despite constant bombardments and invasions, this singular city was able to weather every wave of foes that tried to conquer them.

In Azzatha, formerly Asia, the Immortal Emperor Xingyue Haigon was the lone dictator of the region. He rose to power, initially as a powerful marauder leader. He was an enigma of a man, worshiped as a god among his followers for his supernatural power. He was a magicker, perhaps the mightiest to have ever existed. He rose up at the beginning of the Age of Anarchy and swiftly dominated the continent. He was alive and well for over one hundred years and appeared not to age during that whole period. He was without days and claimed to be divine. His cult of fanatics took after his dark practices and tried to emulate his rule. With heretical arcane arts, Haigon and his warlocks ransacked every community and tribe that they could, exhibiting an unhealthy fascination with the women of the land.

These three powers: the UNACs, the Ma'kravish, and Xingyue Haigon, clashed with one another while simultaneously bolstering their own defenses and interests, forgetting the existence of the land in the Western Hemisphere. They killed each other for power while simultaneously torturing and oppressing their own citizens in a number of vile ways. This became known as the Tyrranis Period, which stretched from the end of the 22nd century to 2478 AD. This age of struggle and pain came to its conclusion when he came.

Arodi Auzlanten appeared in the center of Carthonia. He toppled the entire UNAC Empire in a single day. No record exists of exactly what it looked like, but he summoned a spinning fog that swallowed every inch of land in Carthonia. The clouds stretched across the continent, spinning with hurricane force winds, yet toppling no structures or trees. The most curious property of this cleansing storm was what happened to those that were caught in its maw. Auzlanten's storm targeted everyone with UNAC ideology and influence, killing them in minutes as if it were toxic gas. Very much like the Tenth Plague, all innocents were spared and unharmed, killing only the UNAC party Slave camps and eugenic labs were liberated, prison camps were cracked open, and the Tyrranis Period came to a close in Carthonia. Arodi Auzlanten was just beginning to reclaim the world.

He rallied the citizens of Carthonia, explaining that he was delivered by God to free the world from this time of oppression. He reintroduced the Faith to the people who had forgotten Christ's sacrifice. After the Faith swept over Carthonian society faster than UNAC propaganda ever could, Auzlanten armed them. He helped them to forge weapons and armor, initiating his first army of crusaders. What the Carthonians were unaware of was that Auzlanten was simultaneously rallying another branch of crusaders in Jerusalem. The Carthonian crusaders marched on Constantinople, clearing out the Ma'kravish Janissaries. Legend tells that Arodi Auzlanten rained holy fire down on them. In their retreat, the Jerusalem crusaders charged out of their citadels and cut them off. Historians define this as the initiation of the Reclaiming Crusade.

The crusaders cleared through Kalkhan, liberating the slave markets and removing strongholds from the Caliphate. Auzlanten himself was leading the charge at most every battlefront, allegedly striking down dozens of Janissaries with a single slash of his sword, recruiting new crusaders with each victory. As the Reclaiming Crusade moved south his army grew exponentially. Where he could not attend, Auzlanten appointed Saints as his generals to lead the Crusade, twelve in all before the end of the Kalkhanian assault. The continent was liberated, completely free of the Ma'kravish Caliphate's grip, in 2479 AD. At this point, the Immortal Emperor Xingyue Haigon launched a preemptive strike.

Fire fell on the armies of crusaders from the heavens. Molten balls of metal and rock crashed on the crusader encampments in Kalkhan, cutting their numbers down by a third. Arodi Auzlanten was able to place the blame immediately and declared war on the Haigon Empire. As his armies broke through the sorcerer lord's armies, he outflanked the Emperor by appearing in the Imperial Palace in the capital city of Haigonen on the Eastern Coast. In the ensuing battle, Auzlanten and Haigon sank the entire capital city into the Xingxian Sea. Arodi Auzlanten was victorious in the end, proving that the title "Immortal" was indeed puffery. With the Emperor's death, most of his magickers were suddenly powerless, causing the majority of the loyalists' surrender at the sight of the crusaders. The Reclaiming Crusade ended on the first day of 2480.

With Azzatha liberated, Arodi Auzlanten declared the beginning of Templym. Templym would serve as the title of the nations allied with one another, united under the Faith with God as the ultimate ruler and the Word as its ultimate law. The nations were divided among personnel who served during the Reclaiming Crusade, particularly among his twelve generals for whom the months of the new calendar were named. Those that accepted Auzlanten's creed were accepted as being an extension of Templym. Those that refused were recognized officially as marauder tribes. None were forced into the orbit of Templym after the Tyrranis Period. Several marauder tribes lived and continue to live in harmony with the nations of Templym.

Nearly every human in the Eastern Hemisphere was united under Templym. They accepted Christ as Lord and the Gospels as truth. Society once again began to prosper, and peace flourished across the three continents. Envoys would later reach out to the

Hinterlands of America, eventually establishing providences on the East Coast that too would come to the light of Templym. As Auzlanten focused on larger portions of the planet, he raised up two organizations that would operate as law and military.

Auzlanten crafted the Scourge and the Bulwark. They would serve as the two governing bodies of Templym, each enacting what Auzlanten believed to be the only things a government should do. The Bulwark would protect the innocent and the Scourge would punish the guilty. Each contained sub-organizations with specific fields in mind. In the Bulwark, the Beacon would minister truth and be the bastion of facts and knowledge, the Siloam would provide medical care and combat plague and disease, and the Trench would fortify the newly developed urbans. In the Scourge, the Shackle would oversee the arrest and imprisonment of the guilty, the Dictum would control anarchists and rogues that would disrupt society's order and law, and the Veil would target humanitarian crises specifically with human trafficking and sexual crimes. These two organizations successfully kept peace in Templym.

With these two bodies in place to oversee society, prosperity was at a high once again, albeit without the lavish gluttony of previous generations. Technology had not reached anything near that of the Cybernetic Revolution, but industry grew in the newly developed urbans. Most notable was not earthly development, but that of eternal allegiance. All of Templym acted as a unified Church. Neighbors interacted just as James 1:27 commands. Respect for peers and for authorities was assumed by all. Auzlanten declared, "Never before have so many believers united. Templym represents all that God wants from this world. I applaud and smile at every man and woman in it." This was obviously unacceptable to the Adversary.

This period of peace lasted until 2524.During this time, Arodi Auzlanten showed no sign of aging and remained a stalwart symbol among the people. So, when enemies of a non-physical sort, demons, reared their wicked heads, they looked to him. These demons came from some unholy spiritual plane and began invading and influencing humanity. Auzlanten labeled them "Mundus Imago," ghosts of the Earth. When hordes of Imago started invading the nations of Templym, Auzlanten rallied more crusaders from the Scourge, Bulwark, and local militaries. The ensuing series of conflicts were classified as the Purus Crusades. There were fourteen of between the years of 2524 and 2711. Each conflict, bloody and brutal in its own way, brought a new manner of horrific Imago breed and a variety of sacrilegious heretics as the demons' profane influence began tainting the citizens of Templym. To combat the influx of cults and Imago activity, Auzlanten founded another sub-organization of the Scourge, the Inquisition. They would preserve that which is holy and destroy that which is not.

The Purus Crusades were horrifying to live through, though none lasted more than two years. Each was initiated by the Imago horde brought creatures, some spanning the size of cloudtouchers, and magickers with incomparable powers. In each event, faith in the Scourge and the Bulwark and trust in Arodi Auzlanten never faltered. This was true until Malacurai arrived.

In 2716, Malacurai descended from the sky, claiming to be an angel of the Lord. He publically proclaimed support and approval of Templym and blessed Arodi Auzlanten. He was initially accepted and welcomed into society. The citizens of Templym were thrilled with the idea of an angel coming down from Heaven to proclaim God's approval of their actions. Surely, this was a sign from the Almighty that His Kingdom was at hand. After three days of public interactions, a schism was torn that would never be repaired.

Auzlanten and Malacurai began to fight publicly. Auzlanten claimed that Malacurai was a demonic Imago taking up an angel's mantle. Likewise, Malacurai claimed that Auzlanten was of the same dark spirits. This tore the governing powers of Templym apart. The Bulwark sided with Malacurai and the Scourge with Arodi Auzlanten. The ensuing conflict was known as the Civil Strife.

Templym was divided in two, based on their allegiance. The Bulwark and the Scourge turned on one another, killing each other with the hate only former brothers could have for each other. The

Beacon spent a large portion of the Strife debating in their halls, fighting with their words rather than their weapons, to determine the truth of both sides' claims. The bloodshed that ensued was greater than any of the previous Purus Crusades. Arodi Auzlanten killed Malacurai at the Battle of Budapest in 2718 which was declared the official end of the Strife, but at significant cost.

The damage done to Auzlanten's governing powers was crippling. The Bulwark was completely destroyed. Only the Beacon remained, having switched their alliance to the Scourge days before the Battle of Budapest after concluding that Arodi Auzlanten was the honest party. The Dictum was also annihilated, their numbers thinned beyond recovery. The remaining branches of the Scourge were left to take up the responsibilities of the Bulwark and operate as both the protectors and punishers of Templym. Arodi Auzlanten continues to this day operating as he once did, but his circle of trust seems to have shriveled. The year is 2722. We are still recovering.

Scourge Hierarchy				
	Inquisition	Shackle	Beacon	Veil
1	Prelate	High Conservator	Magistrate	Patriarch/Matriarch
2	Cardinal	Conservator	Harbinger	Groom/Bride
3	Bishop	Overseer	Herald	Agapist
4	Exarch	Warden	Forerunner	Admonisher
5	Inquisitor	Retriever	Historian	Expurgator
6	Cleric	Chaperone	Crier	Purifier
7	Acolyte	Guardian	Speaker	Supplicant

Scourge Personnel
***IX Regent* Invictus Illuromos**

Inquisition

- *Inquisitor* Adastra Covalos
- *Inquisitor* Vandross Blackwell
- *Prelate* Terran Greyflame

Shackle

- *Warden* Volk Downey
- *Retriever* Ram's Horn
- *Warden* Alexandarius Carthage
- *High Conservator* Jude Bethel

Beacon

- *Herald* Oslin Du'Plasse
- *Magistrate* Averrin Walthune

Veil

- *Bride* Daphne Wainwright
- *Expurgator* Yen Blye
- *Patriarch* Arodus Betankur

Polar Wastes
The Whitewashed Isles
Hontario
Jaspin
Arklund
Nenwhar
J'kier
Moultov
Tyrbellum
American
Hinterlands
Het
Ehrlicon
Delphos
Vernon
Spectral
Coast
Brey
Creek
Unkiri
Vouricale
Priestland
Jaimax
Trippolia
Kilmarion
Reach
Mayanmatra
Vult
Falkland

America ca. 2722

Carthonia,
Azzatha, &
Kalkhan ca. 2722

CHAPTER 1

The blank monitor flushed with light and color. Over-blaring pulse music belched out of the speakers and faded out as immediately as it arose. On the screen, two absurdly dressed tide-casters were pictured. They were seated at a large chestnut table with glasses of water at the center and propped-up microphones blocking their chins.

"What is going on my dudes and dudettes?" The one dressed in fluorescent pink yelled unnecessarily boisterously. "Welcome back to Dyno-Dialogue, your favorite source of tide talks. I'm your favorite host, Lough Darkin!"

"And I'm your real favorite host," said the one seated next to him, plates of blue plastic blocking his eyes. "Neil Blackwater! We've got a thick conversation for you today."

"That's right Neil," Lough bellowed. "You'll never guess what, or rather who, we're talking about today."

"Well, it was in the title of the video so..."

"That's right Arodi Auzlanten!" Sounds of horns blared and vomited a cacophony of noise as the two childish hosts performed a pathetic dance without standing from their seats. The sound was briefly silenced as the mute button was pressed.

"...don't need an intro to this guy." Neil yelled at the audience once the computer was unmuted. "The leader of Templym, Annihilator of Anarchy, Toppler of Tyranny, this by far the most famous dude in our time."

"Seconded only to Jesus himself," Lough added in. "But before we get to the good stuff, we'd just like to say..." The video sped up. Ten minutes of what was clearly filler dialogue and sponsored advertised were passed over.

"So, let's get to our theories." Neil giggled like a prepubescent girl.

"At this stage in the talk," Lough said unsuccessfully trying to change to a serious mood. "Neil and I are going to d-d-d-debate! We've prepped our own personal theories as to the origins of the enigmatic and magnificent Arodi Auzlanten."

"We should note for the record," Neil said removing the blue shade glasses. "That we'll be talking our own theories, ones which you've probably heard argued before, and we can't confirm them beyond our own personal research."

"That's right Neil," Lough interrupted. "The only claim we can confirm is that the great Arodi is not the reincarnate Christ, as this is the only theory he's personally denounced. We aren't cultists. We're not heretics to any of you Inquisitors in the audience." A pen clicked open in front of the monitor.

"That's exactly what a heretic would say. Anyway, let's get this debate started. The theory that I'm putting forward is..." Neil said as he beat the table trying to replicate a drum roll. "The god AI theory! That's right; I believe that Arodi Auzlanten is one of the mythical god AIs, who were not actual gods, Mr. Inquisition Man, from the Cybernetic Revolution. It explains the immense power and the whole ageless thing. I've come ready to defend our lovely robot overlord."

"And my position is..." Lough said mimicking Neil. "The angel theory! I'm willing to argue that he's actually a commander of Heaven, a member of the divine council, a herald of God from the spiritual plane. Neil and I both researched across the tide, focusing on data from the Beacon's own data well, only the Omega classified stuff of course, to bring forth evidence to support our claims."

Herald Oslin Du'Plasse watched the tide-cast with a combination of disgust and curiosity. As a member of the Scourge's Beacon, it was his duty to preserve truth and knowledge. He was devising another thesis paper, his third that year and it was only Rexus, the fifth month. The young Herald wrote down the evidence that the two tide-casters were saying, ignoring their corny jokes. This thesis he was writing was focusing on public opinion regarding Arodi Auzlanten.

Oslin Du'Plasse was a young man, twenty-six years old, nine of which were spent in this organization. He was dressed in a standard Beacon uniform. The black polymer thread was strapped and buttoned to his fit body tightly. The Beacon's golden torch was stitched onto his breast with the Scourge's namesake nine-tailed spike whip overlapping it, the symbol of his organization. A yellow silk scarf with the Du'Plasse name stitched into it in white gold thread hung from his neck. His long platinum colored hair slumped down his neck, the standard color of those from the Platinum District in the Carthonian capital city of Hrimata. His crystal blue eyes darted back and forth between the computer screen and the pad of paper where his white gloved hands were quickly jotting down notes for his upcoming thesis.

Oslin sat in a red leather office chair in a small cubicle. The only decorum was a framed picture of his family, a twenty-year-old image of himself with his parents, his two brothers, and twin sisters. Three gold plaques that indicated commendations he had received for outstanding work in Auzlanten's Beacon. Most members of the Beacon get only a single plaque, if any at all.

In the noble Du'Plasse family, service to the Bulwark was a longstanding tradition. The month of Grigor, the first month of the year, was named after Grigor Du'Plasse who was the first Magistrate and a Reclaiming Crusade General. Oslin had been a registered barrister in the Beacon for seven years now, before and after the Civil Strife. He was only a Crier at the time, so he operated as more of an observer than anything else during the furious and heated debates that took place as the civil war raged outside the halls. He came in with an open mind, seeking the truth of the situation and less concerned with fulfilling any particular ideology. After the Beacon concluded that Arodi and not Malacurai was the just individual, he fully supported the transition of power to the Scourge. He since worked his way up to one of the most acclaimed positions in the Scourge.

Oslin was a Herald, the third highest rank attainable in his branch of the Scourge, not including the Regent or Auzlanten. His acclamations meant he should be traveling to any Scourge facility he wanted to. He could be leading divisions of the guardians of truth and justice or coordinating with governors of Templym. He shouldn't have such small cubicle. Rather, he should have the biggest office in a Beacon facility under his command. Instead he was left to the general Scourge stronghold of Bastion Prime in the Frankish city of Parey, confined to a cubicle equivalent to that of any 5th or 6th tier Scourge soldier. He was bitterly scratching words on his parchment, forced to write thesis papers until his suspension was ended.

Oslin Du'Plasse had most of his clearance revoked for six months now. Prior, he operated as the Accountability Agent of the United Providence's Senate. As the Senate's designated AA, it was his task to enforce integrity and morality to the Americans' leaders. Under Scourge law, governors and drafters of law were to be held to a far stricter level of discipline than the common citizen. Each body of legislation had a Scourge AA to keep the leaders of the free society clean. When a UPA Senator tried to bribe Oslin in exchange for him overlooking an illegal meeting with a syndicate father, Oslin shot him in the head.

Execution was the proper punishment for such a crime. Oslin knew this when he pulled the trigger. However, the Senator he shot was immensely popular among his constituents. They did not accept that their celebrity of a Senator was corrupt. Du'Plasse took no risks. With Imago cultists and criminal networks riddling Templym, he would tolerate no possibility of a nation being corrupted. The attempted bribery infuriated Oslin and he brought forth the wrath that the Scourge was famous for, swift and merciless justice. The citizens of the UPA wanted Du'Plasse's head on a pike for what he did. Perhaps if he was not as skilled a barrister as he was, it might have happened. After interrogation in a Veritas Chamber, Du'Plasse faced public defamation, deportation, and a suspension from any and all field work.

Oslin yearned for any assignment that would take him outside of Bastion Prime. While the first month he enjoyed having the time to write his thesis on the migratory patterns of Kalkhanian marauder tribes, he was forced to do nothing but sit in this disgraceful little cubicle and draft thesis papers. He was forced to do this or act as a private barrister for hire, which he was unwilling to sully his reputation by doing so. His battle-plate remained still and unused. The flaksteel and immotrum spectacle was propped up in a glass display in the recreation center of Bastion Prime. He longed to take up his banner and don his tech-enhanced battle plate again. Thesis papers were all and well, but he was not combating lies and deceit, his true calling.

He grew weary of this method of research, though he had to be thorough if he wanted to legitimize his thesis. He needed at least fifty independent sources before he could make any definite conclusions on his statistics. He wanted to make a probability distribution of the most common theories of Arodi Auzlanten's origins. So far, he determined that the angel, AI, sorcerer, and Messiah theories were the most prevalent. He had already exhausted all scholarly articles and federal studies and was now forced to use amateur tide users for sources. He was beginning to be nauseated by the sub-par comedy and commentary he was exposed to. They offered very slim and unoriginal evidence. The way the wind fluttered Arodi's robes, the arrangement of his hair, the grip of his sword Leagna, the way dirt impacted his skin, and the hue of his eyes were all among the strange factors of their focus. Oslin never found any use to such menial details. He believed that if there were any clues to discover the figure's true origins, they would lie in his many speeches, military decisions, and miracles. However, the possibility of Arodi Auzlanten being a faerie was far more fascinating to the users of the inter computer network of the tide than any infallible facts of spoken words.

As the "debate" raged on the monitor in front of him, he looked to his belt. His Holt pistol was placed in a holster at his waist. He briefly contemplated shooting himself to escape the endless loop of irritating tide-casters. He then thought more critically of pointing the handgun at the computer instead. He shook his head and continued his masochistic research.

The chatter of Scourge bureaucracy was a familiar white noise. Small talk, typing of digital runes, and paperwork were the bulk of all that Oslin did for the past six months and he was certainly no stranger to its droning. What was odd was how quickly it was being snuffed out and replaced. Oslin paused the tide-cast and listened as Scourge soldiers were silenced, their vague echoes replaced by the sound of marching. The heavy and regimented steps were increasing in volume. They were coming towards him. When the scent of phosphorus hit Oslin's nostrils, he knew exactly who was coming.

Du'Plasse blacked out his monitor, set down his parchment, and stood facing the opening in his cubicle. He waited for the arrival of the Magistrate to march in front of him. He knew instantly that the reason soldiers were dropping their work were to salute someone of 1st tier rank. He knew it was the Magistrate by the chemical scent. He didn't even need to see the luminosity that surrounded him.

Magistrate Averrin Walthune was a man from the Kalkhanian nation of Zulus. His dark skin was a stark contrast to the white hairs that covered his chin. He was donned in his black and gold battle plate. The Beacon's torch was etched into his breastplate with elephantide ceramic glazed with fluid brass and bloodsteel. He bore another physical torch propped up by sconce on his back looming over his bald head, which burned vibrant golden flame consistently with liquid ignate. His left shoulder bore the writings and creed of the Scourge in vibrant golden etching and his right shoulder was caped with a stole crafted of lion hide. His specialized guard of Zulu warriors escorted him, four in all with spears in hand.

Herald Du'Plasse lifted a clenched fist to his chest and made a downward ripping motion as though he were enacting a ritual suicide, the traditional Scourge salute. Magistrate Walthune grinned, "No need for formalities my friend." His voice was deep, demanding authority and attention, a notable trait of a well-versed orator. He grappled with Oslin, embracing him in a grip of ursine strength. As a noble man, Oslin was not keen on hugging so he awkwardly patted Averrin's back in hopes he would release him. The two men had only met three times, so he hardly considered the Magistrate a friend. He was a little bewildered to receive such a brotherly greeting, but didn't want to question it.

Walthune relieved his tight grip. "How is your research going Oslin?"

"Well I suppose," the Herald said as he regained his haughty composure. "The thesis I published last week has reached one thousand purchases already."

"I didn't think people would care about Imago classifications. Or perhaps all that controversy surrounding you has made you a brighter author?" Averrin laughed heartily.

"Yes. Perhaps so." He forced out a chuckle, trying to hide his bitterness at the unintentional slight.

"May I ask you, my friend, if you are tiring of this lackadaisical position of tide research?"

"More than you know, Magistrate." The Herald replied. "I tire of the tedium of independent research. I am not combating the cacophony of lies I swore to destroy. I pray for my suspension to end in the near future"

Walthune laughed again. "It seems the Lord has delivered me to answer your prayers my friend!"

A glint of happiness flushed Oslin's visage. "My suspension period is over?"

"First, I have two gifts for you Herald." He reached to one his immotrum plated Zulu guards. He handed Averrin a small prism of what looked black granite. "I want to give this to you."

Oslin shifted the slate in his hand. It was actually a pad of black projectum threads. He motioned over the surface with his free hand and an arrangement of letter runes were holo- projected on the slate. "A new data slate?" Oslin smiled.

"Yes my friend. This is the latest model historian's tablet from the technologists. You can store over a terabyte of data in it and any records you save on it are automatically transferred to the Beacon's data well in a bank of your classification level. I've arranged our technologists to craft one for you already."

"I very much appreciate it Magistrate, thank you."

"No thanks necessary. It's a gift, thanking you for your patience. I'd like for you to use it on your next assignment." He reached back to another armor-clad Zulu who handed him a steel binder, a case file.

Oslin smiled as Magistrate Walthune handed him the file. He realized that his time in frivolous research was at an end. The steel binder was sealed with a wax wrap labeled with the Scourge's seal and a Kappa. Oslin had Epsilon level clearance so he was vaguely confused, but he shrugged and simply assumed that the Beacon wouldn't extend his authority full through immediately. He broke the wax and flipped through the parchment. Averrin's smiled melted away the moment Oslin's brow furled in anger.

"A stenographer's mission?" Du'Plasse growled. "I sit around for six months waiting my suspension out for some form of field assignment and you bring me this? I would be insulted if I was still a Historian! This is dereliction at its peak. How dare you insult my rank and family name?"

Averrin grunted once. "I would have thought you'd be eager to get out of this cubicle."

"And sully my reputation with this diversion? You've some nerve bringing this to me. Does my name carry no impact? Does my rank grant me no respect?"

"Your name and your rank mean nothing to me Oslin. I care more about the man who bears the title than the title themselves."

"Nonsensical claptrap! I refuse this assignment. I don't even care if my suspension ends today. I have too much dignity to accept such an insulting chore."

"Then you'd do best to turn in your battle plate, your insignia, and your weapons Du'Plasse." Oslin was quick to cool his rage. "You know the President of the UPA wanted you executed for the mess you made of their Senate? I defended you. I kept your pretty noble neck bolted to your shoulders."

Averrin leaned in close and whispered as the conversation was getting too boisterous given the subject. Oslin could feel the heat of the chemical torch radiating down on him. "I reassigned you to Bastion Prime so you could spread your expertise to the younger and less experienced soldiers. Yet, you stayed cooped up in your office, slumping about drafting papers and avoiding your subordinates. Six months and no help was offered to any of your peers. I don't care what your lineage is, boy. You need to learn some humility. I'm offering you an ultimatum because I'm sick of you lagging away on my payroll. Either take this assignment and prove that you can still follow Scourge protocol or shame your precious heritage."

Oslin swallowed and backed away, adjusting his ascot. He never received a verbal beating from the Magistrate and he was silently shaken. He suspected that this was not even Averrin's definition of a verbal beating. "Why me? High Conservator Bethel's name was on this file. Why does he want me for the task force?"

Walthune smiled again as though he hadn't just nearly bitten Oslin's head off. "Bethel asked me to personally select a stenographer, of rank Herald or Harbinger. He wanted a recorder of honesty and integrity to act as the force's stenographer."

Du'Plasse nodded, making a sharp inference. "You picked me because I'm the only active duty Herald who would even consider such a low tier assignment."

Averrin chuckled. "No my friend, but I figured you would be the most eager. This gives you the opportunity to prove that you are still a man who can listen to orders. You're of the appropriate rank and I still believe that you value honesty above all else. This is the perfect assignment to convince me to relieve you of your suspension."

"You are a clever boar, aren't you?"

Walthune laughed boisterously. By most standards calling someone a boar would be considered an insult. However, the fearsome Zulu Boar was the national animal of his home and a fierce, durable, and cunning predator. Such a jest was highly complementary in his home nation, Oslin knew this. Even the silent Zulu guards chuckled a bit at the crack. "The High Conservator is assembling the task force tomorrow at high rise. I trust you to do the Beacon proud."

"I suppose I don't really have an alternative, do I?"

"Not true, you could quit. Of course, I know that the last Du'Plasse in the Beacon wouldn't sully his good family name any more than it was during the Strife."

Oslin's looked to the floor and bit his lip. He wouldn't have let any other than the Magistrate get away with such an insult, even if it was just an honest observation. He just took the shot and kept the sting internal. Averrin picked up on this. "Oh, I'm sorry. I suppose I should not be picking at old wounds." Averrin wanted to give Oslin a chance to respond, but only an awkward pause followed. "Any who, best of performance in this new assignment. I'll pray for your success and safe return, Oslin."

Magistrate Walthune and his Zulu guard marched away in perfect unison, leaving the Herald to his thoughts in his cubicle. Oslin sighed and looked down to the Holt, resting easily in the leather holster. He thought to himself, "Would it not be ironic if I ended my life with the same..." He quickly dispensed such thoughts from his head. He slumped back into the office chair again and placed a hand on his forehead. He looked down at the Du'Plasse name sewn into his ascot. Then, with a regal vigor to his mood, he stepped up and went towards the recreation center to ready his battle plate.

Nobody ever went into the Waning Moon tavern. Not since the owner was jailed by the Scourge for desecration of a Frankish cathedral. The only traffic it ever received was the occasional drunkard or vagabond. The owner's brother kept the Waning Moon running, somehow keeping the shelves stocked with liquors. He spent most of his days reading behind the counter, only ever placing his books down when the rare customer wandered in.

One such person came in, a woman, slender and beautiful. She was dressed in a red formal gown. The velvet texture of the fabric wound tightly across her body and loomed over the dilapidated floorboards. Her makeup was extravagant nearly to the point of gaudy. Her cheeks flushed bright pink and her lips blood red. The gruff and heavily tattooed owner placed his book onto the bar's counter, the only sound accompanying the woman's stilettos striking the ground in the empty tavern. The owner looked bewildered, but this was a farce. He knew instantly upon seeing her why she was here.

"What brings you to this dump, lady?" The owner asked.

The woman grinned, revealing teeth stained with the same lipstick. "Top shelf baroque with a splash of cherry."

The owner's ink-stained arm reached to the top shelf to grab a half-empty bottle of the off-white liquor. He undid the rubber cap and poured the fluid into a mixing flask along with a few drops of sugary red syrup. The resulting concoction was dripped into a poorly cleaned crystal, revealing a solution that looked similar to blood. The woman smiled, pulling a black needle from the bun in her hair. She pricked the end of her finger and let a drop of resulting fluid into the crystal. She swallowed the contents of the cup in a single tip.

"The ritual will begin upon the Blood Father's arrival, sister." The owner smiled, recognizing that she was with him. He motioned towards a set of polyester draperies on the back wall. "Walk behind those curtains and down the stairs. The sacrifice is being prepared."

"Many thanks, blood brother." The woman smiled as she parted the black curtains and began down the creaky wooden staircase.

The woman came to dank chamber. The wood paneling was musty and molding. The basement floors were stone, raw unpolished bedrock. The walls were lined with red floodlights and dented stone sculptures of medieval style armor gripping ancient axes. Strange cryptic runes were painted haphazardly with chalk and pastels on the bedrock. Four cultists other cultists dressed in black and red ritual robes surrounded a particularly large circular rune. At the center of the circular splatter was a man, dressed only in a dull grey loincloth. The woman smiled as the mostly naked man turned his tortured gaze up at her.

The man was pale skinned. His messy hair was ebon and covered most of his head, revealing a stern and ill-humored gaze. His tightly muscled flesh was covered in white and pink scars, the highest concentration being the gnarled collection of lines on his exposed back. His eyes were sunken beneath his thick brow, the grey irises like storm clouds. His mouth, barely visible beneath the tangled black beard, crashed into a deep frown when he recognized the woman's face. He tugged at the metal chains binding his wrists and ankles which were connected to the two of the statues on opposite ends of him.

"Oh my," the woman giggled. "If it isn't the mighty Inquisitor Adastra Covalos. Will you be joining us for the sacrifice today?"

"Acolyte Goodberry," he responded in a voice void of emotion. "Or perhaps just Winona, considering your recent excommunication on account of heresy."

"Truth can hardly be defined as heresy."

"Inquisition law defines heresy as the sanctification of the profane, specifically with regards to any affiliation with the Mundus Imago or other occultic entities. I know you were never too keen on studying though, so I'm not surprised that you don't know the meaning. Perhaps I should put it more bluntly. You're a demon-worshipping witch and you deserve a pyre."

"Oh darling," She approached the bound Inquisitor and ran her fingers through his facial hair. "You just don't know what I know. The true glories of Nilgrox are hidden from you, shrouded by fog your God has blanketed over your mind."

Adastra mumbled something beneath his breath. Winona leaned in close to hear his muttering. In response, Inquisitor Covalos swiftly brought up his head and connected it with her nose. She shrank back gripping her face, her makeup sullied by the blood rushing from her now broken nose. "Traitorous whore," he grunted as she regained her composure. "I care not of what demon you've sold your soul to. You became the very thing you were tasked to destroy. The Scourge's creed is clear. There will be no mercy for you in this life."

Winona Goodberry pulled the needle out of her hair as she grabbed the dangled black threads of Adastra's. She pressed the pin into his throat, coming within seconds of puncturing his neck and letting all of his blood. "I'd kill you for that if you weren't necessary." She laughed, licking her nasal blood off of the corner of her mouth. "The Blood Father needs your life, lucky pup. Nilgrox thirsts for blood of the unwilling."

"Your pathetic Blood Father doesn't scare me." Adastra responded, not even acknowledging how close he easily he could be killed. "I have the might of Heaven behind me. I serve the one true Lord and even as I walk through the valley of the shadow of death..."

"Yes, yes I shall fear no evil, a misplaced notion if you ask me. Come now Inquisitor, isn't evil just a matter of perspective?"

"You are ever the disappointment Winona." Adastra mused. "I knew you would never make it far in the Inquisition. I'm surprised you even made it past the Tribulation."

"Well it seems as though you're the one who was unqualified for the position. After all, what kind of Inquisitor lets himself get captured by a "rogue cult"?" She motioned mockingly with her hands.

Adastra chuckled, albeit curt and brief. "You're correct. It's quite unlike me to find myself so vulnerable, don't you think?"

"I know, isn't it delicious?" Winona mused as she stepped to the outer rim of the sloppy rune. "You allowed your judgment to be clouded by your childish empathy. The foolish teachings of mercy that you so desperately cling to have blinded you from reality. Your fantasies of forgiveness shroud all in your vision in an aura of harmlessness. It's a pity you can't see what I see. Had we time, I would reveal the truths of Nilgrox to you. Alas, blood is necessary to appease my lord and your neck was selected."

The rotting wooden steps squeaked as another man stepped into the demonic chamber. It was the bartender. "All hail to the Blood Father." He spoke in a ceremonious tone as he dropped to one knee at the base of the entrance. Winona and the other cultists did likewise.

"You were never an adequate investigator." Adastra spoke. "Vandross, ever the optimist, insisted you'd learn and your skills would sharpen. I persisted otherwise. Seems I was right for a change. Even now, with my full face revealed, you can't place the pieces together."

"Silence meat!" The woman snapped, angling her head towards the bedrock. "You will show respect to the Blood Father." The sound of heavy feet and moaning wood steps began filling the underground chamber.

"Oh, I aim to, Winona." Adastra grunted cracking his neck while loosening up his shoulders.

The crimson light left an eerie ambiance in the chamber. Six cultists in all, including the fallen Acolyte, surrounded the lone Inquisitor Covalos. The owner at the base of the staircase, the other five encircling the rune where Adastra stood, his muscles now limber. A pair of heavy rubberized boots with brass buckles and steel toes pounded on the rough rock. Standing in the chamber was a man clad in vermillion robes. A wide-rimmed scarlet hat blocked off the man's gaze. The lower portion of his face was visible, revealing copper skin dusted with black whiskers.

"Rise my children." The Blood Father said, his arms entirely concealed beneath the red cloak that enveloped around his shoulders. Adastra never flinched, standing as still as the stone sculpture he was chained to. The Imago cultists rose from their submissive positions.

Winona's face was twisted into a wide grin, the blood on her face starting to crust. Her smile vanished in an instant when she saw the Blood Father. As the cultists rose to an upright position, he angled his head up to reveal the rest of his face. Ignorant to the other demoniacs, Winona knew the face of the supposed cult leader. She recognized the jovial half smile across his lips. She knew those over expressive eyebrows. He didn't even bother to change out of his standard robes. This was the face of her old mentor, Inquisitor Vandross Blackwell.

Seeing that she recognized him, he sprung into action. Vandross shot his left arm out from his cloak revealing a customized Reisinger etched with warding symbols and the Inquisition's prayer. A single shot rang out and dug into Winona's thigh. As she collapsed, Adastra yanked violently on the chain bound to the statue on his right. The steel links jerked towards him, the axe the statue was holding flying with it. Adastra swung the axe in a crazed circular movement, radiating the rune. The force wasn't enough to strike any of the cultists down, but they panicked and lost their footing, giving him enough time to wind the chains up and hold the axe once again. Simultaneously, Vandross revealed his right arm and unsheathed his wardiron bastard sword.

Vandross cut open the bar owner before he could draw a weapon. He was ambidextrous, preferring to fight in the Natandro sword and pistol style. The other four drew crooked steel daggers and rushed the Inquisitors. Two went for Adastra and the others after Vandross.

Adastra swung his axe two handed in wide arcing movements to keep his targets at a distance. One lunged in a downward rip. Adastra knocked him back with the blunt top of the thick double-bladed head, knocking the breath from his lungs. Adastra countered with a swift turn of his wrist, flipping the heavy weapon flipped and bringing it blade up through the cultist's head.

A second cultist took the opportunity of his comrade's fall to land a blow. He stabbed a crooked blade into the Inquisitor's bicep. Adastra moved backwards with the strike to absorb the inertia, using the momentum to bring his opposite wrist up and connect it with the heretic's throat. His foe stumbled back, leaving the dagger embedded in Adastra's flesh. Before his enemy could gain his bearings, the Inquisitor sank one end of the axe blade in his back before turning help Vandross with his opponents.

While Adastra Covalos fought with aggression and silent rage, Vandross Blackwell battled with graceful panache. He parried the knives of his attackers by connecting his long blade with minimal force but at the precise angles. He parried one attacker's stab and put a bullet in his hip. Vandross slapped away the second's sloppy attack and cleaved through the heretic's arm, lopping it off at the elbow.

The first cultist attempted another poorly executed stab while clutching his bullet wound. Vandross dodged out of the way, sidestepping behind him and driving the blade through his sternum. The one with a missing hand grabbed at the bloody knife with his trembling fingers. The blood-soaked dagger was pointed at Vandross, who chuckled mockingly. He opened his arms in a rhetorical invitation of combat. The cultist, knowing he had no hope in this fight, turned the blade on himself and opened up his own jugular. The Inquisitor shook his head in shame at the pitiful sight. He then turned around, saw the fallen bar owner training a tangle barrel pistol on him, and shot the bartender through the head.

Inquisitor Blackwell pulled out a towel from his satchel and wiped the blood off his blade. Inquisitor Covalos leaned on the hilt of his weapon, out of breath. Vandross stepped over the bodies and stood over the fallen woman who was clambering along the floor to escape. He planted a boot on her back and leaned over to slide the hair needle out.

"My apologies Winona," He said sliding the bastard sword into its hilt. "It's not like me to shoot a lady. Of course, for you, I made an exception. Are you okay, Adastra?"

"I'm fine." He said walking over, shaking the chains off his wrists. "You tied these things too tight. I barely got my axe out in time."

"Sorry, I had to make it look convincing. Besides, I had faith in you."

"I'm flattered. Anyway, I think we should proceed with the formalities."

"Of course," Vandross reached into his satchel and pulled out a scroll, keeping his foot planted on her back as she squirmed beneath his foot. "Winona Goodberry, you have been found guilty of treason, treachery, heresy, and oath breaking. By order of Bishop Garrison, you are under arrest. You are hereby subject to interrogation in a Veritas Chamber to determine the breadth of your corruption. Proof of guilt shall be rewarded with death by judicial execution."

"Bastard!" She exclaimed, wriggling like a trapped animal beneath the Inquisitor's boot. "I'll wear your skin like a coat!"

"Inquisitor Covalos and I are disappointed with you." Vandross continued with his elegant and gallant voice. "Our testimony will see you put to death in a week. God is good and His grace is abounding. I'd suggest beginning your repentance now. You'll be meeting Him soon after all."

"You'll regret this, Inquisitors! You'll regret ever training me!"

Adastra brought his axe down. His wardiron axe cleaved clean through Winona's neck and dug into the bedrock floor. "We already do." He said gruffly.

Vandross took his boot off and raised an eyebrow at his partner. "That seemed a little excessive." He holstered his Reisinger and removed his hat out of respect for the dead.

The nearly naked Inquisitor walked over to the decapitated corpse of the traitor and slid a thin war razor out of her sleeve. "She was half a second away from taking your foot off." He muttered as he wiped blood spatter off of his scarred skin.

"I saw that," Vandross said rather plainly. "I was ready to kick it out of her hand when she drew it."

"I didn't feel like risking it. Besides, we've needed to clean house for too long now. Her execution was overdue." Adastra inspected the wound at the top of his arm. "Do you have any suturant?"

Vandross rummaged through his satchel again and drew out a white fluid tube. He squeezed a strand of the viscous ointment onto Adastra's bleeding wound. "Want me to rub that in for you darling?"

Adastra chuckled as he rubbed the cream to a pink froth. The cut stopped seeping within seconds. "I can manage. By the way, I'll let the Bishop chew me out for this one."

"Garrison won't be chewing anyone out for this one." Vandross said as he pulled out a granite smoking pipe and began stuffing it with black clovertwig. "The woman can't stand traitors. She's more likely to throw you a banquet than discipline you. You spared the Inquisition a lot of paperwork."

The two men heard the door kick in from upstairs. The Inquisition reinforcements had arrived and were calling out standard Scourge declarations. Vandross didn't even look up as he ignited his pipe with a pocket torch. He inhaled the sweet fumes deeply and blew a puff of smoke out. He motioned the end to Adastra in an offering gesture, which he declined. Adastra turned to face the stairwell to welcome the incoming cavalry, revealing his scarred back directly towards Vandross.

"Adastra," Vandross said seriously. "When are we going to talk about those scars?"

Adastra turned his gaze to his friend. "I'm ready to talk whenever you are." Vandross understood what the implications of that statement were and dropped the subject.

CHAPTER 2

The nation of Frankon had a bevy of attractions outside of the Scourge stronghold of Bastion Prime. Tourists sought out simple commodities like the Fifth Purus Memorial or one of the many orchards. Bistros and cafés were scattered across the urban and local eateries commonly catered to visitors from separate continents. There was one café in the city of Parey famous for its tea. Visitors of the quaint shop were expecting to taste its home roasted tea leaves and honey dusted pastries. The tourists weren't expecting to be in the company of a giant.

It was early morning in the middle of the week, so the café wasn't catering much business at the moment. What few customers were present were seated at the polished pine tables outside on the patio. Their attention turned to the spectacle sitting at the far end of the porch. It looked like a metal giant or a mythical golem. Whatever it was, it clearly belonged to the Scourge.

In reality, the visitors were staring at Retriever Ram's Horn of the Shackle. He was, by definition and blood, a marauder. His heritage lied with an extinct Uzbeki tribe known as the Steel Skins. They were once master craftsmen and engineers, focusing on the perfection of armor and fortresses. Nobody is quite sure when or why he was enrolled in the Scourge, but those that worked with him were thankful to have his talents.

He was always donning his battle plate. In name with his family lineage, he wore his armor like an extra layer of skin. The metal discs were coal black and cobalt blue, Shackle colors. On the breastplate was the mark of his marauder tribe, a shield with nails sticking out of it. His helmet covered his entire head, showing no skin or hair. A set of ivory horns served as helmet decorations on opposite ends of two black ballistic glass eye slits. The Shackle's symbol, which depicted the Scourge spike whip over a chain-cuff, was embossed on a small kilt of azure fabric that hung at his waist. He was tall. Most people only ever came up to his pauldrons. He looked comically oversized when surrounded by casually clothed civilians. The sheet of plastic the menu was printed on looked as nothing but a pocket handkerchief in his gauntlets.

He said nothing, which was often the amount of dialogue out of Ram's Horn. Most people that interacted with him assumed he couldn't speak temple-tongue, the national language of Templym. In truth he spoke it fluently but hated to utter the speech. The metal man sat motionless on a black metal porch chair, staring intently at the café's menu. A young waitress approached him. Given the close proximity of the café to Bastion Prime, she was used to the occasional Scourge soldier stopping by and was unfazed by the black and blue golem sitting before her.

"Good morning, how are you doing?" The young lady kept a formal and polite etiquette despite Ram's Horn just turning his head and staring. "I'm Marine. I'll be taking care of you. Would you like to hear about our brunch specials today?" The Retriever continued to say nothing, instead he held up a small strip of parchment with some ink scribbling in his massive hand. The waitress plucked it from his flaksteel grip and looked at it. She shrugged after reading the note. "Coming right up."

Ram's Horn put the menu back in the caddy on the table in front of him. He intertwined his fingers and waited. His gaze was locked on the walkway that he sat next to. He wasn't waiting for the sweets that Marine was fetching for him. The bystanders and tourists thought that Ram's Horn was on leave or off duty. He wasn't. He was coordinating with his boss to spring a trap. He was playing a vital role in an ancient Greek tactical maneuver, Alexander the Great's hammer and anvil strategy. The mobile party acting as hammer would drive the enemy into the stationary party acting as anvil. Ram's Horn was the anvil.

He heard the pattering of fast-moving feet from the speaker in his helmet. Ram pushed the pine table away from him and stood upright, showing the small crowd the magnitude at which he stood. The Warden called out from the same speaker alerting that the quarry was nearly on him. The café was right on the corner of the street. His target wouldn't be able to react fast enough.

Ram's Horn lifted up the chair he was sitting in. He shifted it around in his grip for a moment to test its weight distribution. He was unsatisfied and placed it back under the table. A steel framed parasol was placed in the table, so he lifted that up. The Retriever much preferred the weighting of this. He folded up the frame into its compact form.

A man came barreling around the corner. He was too occupied with looking over his shoulder and running as fast as his body would enable him to notice the massive man standing off to the side of his path. He rushed past streetlights and dangling ferns until he came to the quaint patio of the café. He never even saw the Retriever. Ram's Horn brought the parasol's frame down on the running man's center of mass so forcefully it knocked him off of his feet. He landed on his back, cracking the rockfoam pavement beneath his bulk. Ram's Horn offered no opportunity for error. After tossing the parasol aside, he brought his flaksteel hands together and brought them down on his target in a swift bludgeon, a traditional Steel Skin *hammer fist*. No blood was shed, but the assault left the runner breathless and stunned. Ram's Horn took the time to flip his quarry over on his stomach. He chain-cuffed his right arm to his left leg, utterly immobilizing him.

Another man rushed around the corner, clad in similar black and blue battle plate. He wore no helmet, revealing a hairless and weathered face. Most would expect a man of that age to be panting after a sprint like he had, but it was just another day in the field for Warden Volk Downey.

Warden Downey was a veteran in the Shackle. He used to be governor of the desert isle of Glaswey and was instrumental in annexing the nation into Templym. The only hair on his wrinkled face was his bushy grey eyebrows. The most notable feature of his face was the brass bullet lodged into his cheekbone. He had been shot during a failed armistice mission during the Civil Strife. The bullet flushed his right eye of all color, giving it a cloudy cataract look. In truth, it functioned just as well as his unblemished hazel eye. His battle plate was of immense quality, having been tech-enhanced by the Beacon's technologists. He displayed his achievement on the bulky chest plates and pauldrons, the bright colors of ribbons and badges contrasting the duller Shackle standards. The most notable achievements were the Black Rose magnetically sealed to his right shoulder and the Silver Chain to his left. He slung a single barreled Blakavit shotgun over his back on its strap as he turned the corner seeing his quarry chained up.

"That's some fine work Ram!" Volk said profoundly, his Glaswegian accent thick in his voice. "Looks like old Goswell here fell for the old hammer and anvil, the dolt. Are you treating him properly Ram?"

"Yes." Ram's voice was deep and sounded almost metallic beneath his carapace of metal. On the few instances he did speak, it was rarely more than a word or two. The target was still dazed as Ram's Horn was bending the parasol back into place and reinserting it in the café table.

"That's good, wouldn't want to rough him up too bad now. After all, the Veil hasn't even gotten to him yet. Oh, I'm guessing you didn't read the charges yet?"

"Correct."

"No worries, I've got it." Warden Downey presented a parchment imprinted with a list of names. "Where to start? Oh, I know. Mr. Henry Goswell, you're wanted for questioning with regards to a large number of sexual assaults that have taken place in the past three weeks, four of which are children under the age of twelve. Let's see, what else have we got? Assault, possession of illegal narcotics, kidnapping, all sub-crimes if you ask me. Oh, I guess we ought to add resisting arrest and evasion of justice to this list, don't you think Ram?"

"Yes." Goswell staggered and sloppily stood up from the rock-foam ground. He made a pathetic attempt to continue running. Volk chuckled as he yanked the link of the chain cuff behind his back.

"Where do you think you're going sweetheart?" The sarcasm in his voice was as thick as his accent. "There are a couple of families looking for answers. If you're innocent, the Veritas Chamber will show it. It's almost like he's got something to hide don't you think?"

Ram's Horn brought the back of his hand directly with the side of Goswell's head. The flaksteel left an outline of the Retriever's hand on the guilty man's face as he slumped to the ground unconscious. Volk could have sworn that he heard Ram giggle ever so slightly as he saw the results of his *nightmare strike*. The Warden dropped the chain-cuff and let the quarry hit the rock.

"Fine work Ram." Downey said with a bright smile, clapping his hand on his massive shoulders. "Admonisher's going to do a back flip when he hears we got this piece of work."

"Tea." Ram's Horn grunted as he motioned his head to the café.

"Well look it here. I love this little place. You're right Ram. Let's get us a quick spot before stopping off at the Arcae."

The young waitress reemerged from the café. She was carrying a small tray with a teacup and a plate of sweets. Her face lit up when she recognized Volk Downey. "Oh Volk," she smiled. "I thought I recognized this order. I should have known it was you."

"Marine darling," Volk laughed. "So good to see you! Is that jasmine with splash of lemon juice?"

"And an order of honeycomb."

"Oh, God bless you and all your children! Ram, thank you for ordering this for me." The Retriever did not respond as he chain-cuffed Goswell's left arm to his right leg. "Sorry about this mess. I hate to be dragging my work all over the place." Volk continued as he blew on the hot tea.

"Who is he? What did he do?"

"Oh, I dare not give specifics. Just know that if he's guilty of half the crimes we've got on his warrant, he'll be buried in a week. But enough about me sweetie, how'd your test go last week?"

"It went well. I ended up with an 88% which is more than enough to move me onto the next stage in hospitaller's school."

"See, I told you not to be fussing about it. You're a smart girl. I knew you could do it. Will you and Thomas be tying the knot before the next round of classes?"

"We hope to. It's just so hard to schedule what with my medical studies and his work in the Scourge. He's travelling in the American Hinterlands right now."

"Bloody, only a Guardian and he's already halfway across the world on assignments. Well, I'll tell you what, just send me the dates and I'll arrange for some vacation time. I'm sure I've got someone in his department that owes me a favor."

"Oh, we'd love that Volk, thank you so much."

"Absolutely." Downey came to the last piece of honeycomb on the plate. "Ram, you want the last bit?" Again, the Retriever didn't respond, simply slinging the unconscious prisoner over his shoulder. Volk shrugged and ate it himself.

"We'd best be getting him home." Volk continued as he pulled out his coin pouch. He counted out ten crowns and handed them to the waitress. "Keep the change darling."

Warden Downey was as likeable as a person could be. He was famous for his diplomacy and kind words. His gruff face and scarred eye gave the impression of a killer, but this was not the case. The Shackle as an organization specialized in capturing via non-lethal force. Volk's usage of kindness and empathy allowed him to use his words to bring about justice and were testament to Auzlanten's vision.

Volk tried to make idle conversation with Ram's Horn, who still had the wanted criminal bound and slung over his shoulder. They needed to return to their chariot, drop Goswell off to the Arcae prisoner detainment facility, and return to Bastion Prime for a verbal and written debriefing. If they were efficient, they could pick up another quarry for the day. As they turned another corner, a young man in battle plate ran at a sprint's pace directly into Warden Downey. The pressure compensators whirred in Downey's breastplate as the pistons absorbed the force of the impact and sent the man tumbling to the rockfoam. Volk and Ram's Horn were unperturbed by the sudden development in their stroll.

"Chaperone Trent," Volk said. "How nice of you to join us. Did you get lost?"

Declan Trent was barely a man by legal standards, only 16 years old. He certainly wasn't a man by Volk's or Ram's. His half-plate was shiny and polished, having never seen field conflict. He wore his Shackle insignia displayed on his breastplate and his face was covered by his helmet. Trent wheezed from inside the blue case of vented flaksteel, trying to gulp in as much oxygen as possible. He had just finished his period in the probationary rank of Guardian and was in his first month of field work. Warden Downey was in charge of him, Ram's Horn, and a team of twelve Guardians.

"No sir, Warden." Trent gasped in a raspy voice. "You outran me."

"Oh, did I?" Downey said. "I can't even remember my age at this point in my life but I'm pretty sure I'm old enough to be your granddad. You mind explaining how I was able to keep up with the quarry, but you weren't?"

"Endurance was never my strong suit sir. I'm a natural sprinter though. Glad to see Retriever Ram's Horn was able to intercept the target."

"You are aware that's because I drove him that way, right? Ram, would you have been able to catch Mr. Goswell if I wasn't behind him the whole time directing his path?"

"No." The Retriever grunted.

"So, let me ask you this Chaperone, what would've happened if I wasn't there?"

"Warden, I fail to see the why the hypothetical outcome should..."

"Well I'm old. What if I threw out a hip or pulled a muscle? What if Goswell had an accomplice that started shooting at me? What if the man had a pet Imago and tried to melt my bloody face off? What I'm getting at here Trent is that I want you to consider for a moment what the outcome of this manhunt would be, had I not been there."

"Well, I suppose Goswell would have escaped."

"Sound about right to you Ram?"

"Yes." Ram's Horn muttered.

"I agree. Had something happened to me during the pursuit and I would have been indisposed to steer the quarry to the intercept, he would have escaped. How many more little kids would've fell victim to this pedophile if we let that happen?"

"Well that would all depend on the amount of time it took for us to find him again. I speculate it would've taken two or three weeks to get on his trail again and based on the rate at which he..."

"Chaperone Trent!" The young man snapped to his feet and stood at attention. "The point I am making here is that you need to operate as though you had no backup. In case you weren't aware, I made haste as though Ram's Horn wasn't in his path. I tried to catch up to him but being as I'm fifty something and wearing a hundred pounds of flaksteel I was unable to do so. You are enrolled in the Shackle. Your task in life consists of tracking and capturing the world's worst. If you're unable to do because endurance isn't your strong suit, then I'd suggest you turn in your insignia." Trent froze in place, unable to say anything back. Volk had somehow wrapped up sharp discipline up in an endearing tone. It left him frozen in place.

Volk sighed and continued. "Come on then. It seems as though the extent of your participation in this hunt will be the drive back." Volk and Ram continued on leaving Trent frozen for a moment before he made haste to catch up with his superiors once again.

The name was Invictus Illuromos, Regent of the Scourge. He was questionably the single most powerful man in the entire world. He was the only person in the organization to possess Alpha Magnus clearance, meaning he shared secrets with Arodi Auzlanten personally. The full military might of the Scourge was at his disposal. Millions of soldiers bent to his will.

Invictus strode through the halls of Bastion Prime. The Regent was hairless with eyes like icy steel. The number IX was branded beneath his left eye, signifying his position as the ninth person to serve as Regent of the Scourge. His cold stare was filled with silent pain. Invictus served through the last two Purus Crusades as well as the Civil Strife. He had made decisions and seen massacres that haunted him. The life of a high crusader was one that hardened the heart and dulled one's sensitivities. Make no mistake. Illuromos was strong, physically and mentally. He was over eighty years old but looked no more than forty. Every Regent to serve was blessed by Arodi Auzlanten with the stagnation of the aging process. Nobody in Templym was as close to the leader of the free world than him.

As a man, Invictus was a sight to behold. He walked through Bastion Prime in his battle plate, the finest in the entire world. The flaksteel sheets were pure jet, reflecting almost no light at all. His shoulder blades bore two physical spike whips, fully functional should he need a weapon at a moment's notice. The ebon metal was complimented with bindings of iron chains and barbwire, providing a number of secondary weapons and a symbol of the Scourge's internal struggles. The pistons and gears sounded with every step as layers of ballistic fluids sloshed inside of the armor casings. A cape of steel colored immotrum thread draped down the length of his spine, concealing the large backpack generator built into the armor.

Invictus made his way through the channels of Bastion Prime, avoiding the public sectors to be free of journalist barrages. He spent so much time in front of broadcasters and public criers he could scarcely tolerate being around them, at least while he was preoccupied with Scourge sanctioned business. He walked with Magistrate Walthune on the top floor of the seventeen-story facility. The building was cubic, designed so each branch of the Scourge was concentrated on one side of the facility. The Regent's office was in the direct center of the topmost floor. His office was the most secure room in the complex. The Regent held his most sensitive meetings in this room.

"What of your wife, Averrin?" Invictus asked, his voice gruff yet flowed like molten steel. "Has she recovered from her malady?"

"She has, thank you for asking." Magistrate Walthune responded in the same jovial tone he used to speak with Oslin earlier the same day. "The tumor was benign after all, yet its presence gave her pain. We are optimistic she will make a full recovery."

"I am pleased to hear this. God is good and He has answered our prayers. We shall rejoice at another time."

"Agreed, we have much to discuss." Walthune's Zulu guard marched on either side of the two superiors. There was significantly less traffic on the upper floor as it required soldiers of Beta clearance for entrance. The few that they passed gave the standard heart-rip salute. They responded with a nod in thanks and continued on their path without a break in pace.

The two leaders walked across the black tiled floors until they came to a set of iron doors etched with the Scourge's spike whip. Walthune nodded to his Zulu guard who struck the blunt ends of their spears on the ground in perfect unison and took position outside the door. Regent Illuromos raised his black wrist to the identifier screen. Reading the identification rune carved on the underside of his gauntlet, the iron door raised into the ceiling followed by a secondary blast door of flaksteel. Invictus and Averrin continued deeper in the floor's upper facility, alone.

The two doors sealed behind them with a slow thud. The only sound accompanying them was the metallic clamor of their armor and the soft cracking of the Magistrate's ever burning torch. The walk to enter the Regent's private facility was brief. The black granite was polished to the point of reflecting like a mirror. The mahogany paneling on the walls bore a golden red color and portraits of the previous eight Regents hung down on them. The hallway ended in a single-person door forged of tungsten with the Scourge's spike whip insignia embossed in gold. Invictus grabbed the handle of the door, the security locks disengaging as the sensors read his identification runes.

The office space was as large as a standard training arena. The floors were carpeted with a thin layer of black wool. At the center of each of the square chamber's walls there was a brazier with a pyre, corresponding to a Scourge's branch with their color and mantra. On the north wall, a flame of warm crimson burned with the Inquisition's Bible insignia embossed with *Kyrie Eleison.* To the east, a bright blue pyre with the Shackle's chain cuff, etched with *Kynigi et Kako*. To the west, hornet yellow flame burned over the Beacon's torch *Monimos Alitheia* carved in the basalt pulpit. To the south, glistening white fire flickered over the Veil's double wedding band, the words *Diatro Agape* written below. Trophies from the many military endeavors were scattered along the walls. A five-meter tusk from the Prince of Persia of the 13th Purus, three pelts of mangled red fur from class B Imago killed during the 14th Purus, the arrest warrant of President Hamlin Gilt of the UPA from 2667, and other trophies from his achievements that would be retold by orators and historians for hundreds of years. At the center of this chamber was a desk of blackwood, a plaque of the Scourge's spike whip bolstered in obsidian on the front face. Etched in the finely polished wood was the Scourge's mantra, *In Nomine Veritas*. Four chairs with pelts of various predators sat in front of the desk which had a rotary chair made of glossed jet leather. When Invictus and Averrin entered, the chair was rotated facing away from the door and one of the office's several television monitors was on. This was an oddity considering only the Regent's clearance could grant access to this highly confidential office. He was silently left aghast for a moment, as was the Magistrate. It took little time for Invictus to know that he had a surprise visitor.

"Averrin," Invictus said quietly. "Would you kindly wait outside for a moment?" The Magistrate nodded slowly and walked back out into the hallway.

Invictus walked cautiously around the desk to face the uninvited guest. His normally heavy steps were muffled beneath the soft wool carpeting, giving him a sense of subtlety. As he approached, he recognized what was being played on the monitor. It was a clip from the live broadcast of one of the UPA's presidential debates, the 2668 election for the 19th Post-Shatter President. It was the broadcast that Invictus made his world-famous arrest as Hamlin Gilt was running for re-election. At the time, Invictus was operating as the Accountability Agent of the UPA when he was an Overseer. The intruder was reminiscing on one of his proudest moments.

Invictus made it around the length of the desk and could clearly make out the individual sitting there. The man was dressed in azure robes complete with a tunic, decorated with fine threads of white gold. His raven black hair was arranged in two complex braids at the sides of his head, connecting to his beard, the majority winding down to his waist in a loose tail, the entirety of his hair was decorated with gold and silver clasps. Resting above his brow was a crown of platinum thorns twisted halfway around his head like a Caesar's wreath. His eyes were deep blue, like an unblemished glacier of the poles, but held a certain enigmatic wisdom to suggested centuries of knowledge and painful experience. His hands were decorated with rings of vibrant gemstones and precious metals, as was the amulet around his neck. Sheathed at his side was a sabre of an undistinguishable origin. His eyes were locked onto the monitor watching the broadcast, unfazed by Invictus who at first glance appeared far larger and more threatening. This man's physical appearance was unmistakable. This was the steadfast and classical appearance of the savior of civilization and Templym's true leader, Arodi Auzlanten.

Invictus stepped up to the rotary chair and dropped to a single knee. The Regent had immense respect for the one who he was tasked to represent. "Greetings, father." He said humbly, refusing to make eye contact. The term father was more of a formality, but also a role Auzlanten played in his life. Invictus Illuromos was a Child of Auzlanten. This was a mythological title given to orphans who were raised from youth by Templym's founder. Invictus was uncertain exactly of how many siblings he had alive today or previously, but he knew of the legends. A Child of Auzlanten was supposedly an individual of great conviction and determination who would go forth in the world and accomplish great deeds. Invictus was the embodiment of that principle. He couldn't recall the circumstances of his birth, but he knew that Auzlanten took the role of father raising him to be a holy disciple and unstoppable warrior. He knew that his name, Invictus Illuromos, the indomitable nullifier, meant Auzlanten was grooming him to be a mighty warrior of the Scourge. He took his task with high regard ascending to the highest possible office.

"Kneel before none but the Lord." Auzlanten said. His voice carried the weight and authority one might expect of a man of his stature, yet it was undergirded with a certain level of pain from years of seeing massacres. Being no less than three hundred years old, he bore an intellect that could topple kingdoms and carried an ambience that struck awe in every living being in Templym.

Invictus rose to his feet and looked to the monitor. The three candidates were debating some frivolous policy that was of no concern to the Scourge. They had yet to begin the questionnaire portion where he would approach the microphone and bring forth his charges against the overly confident and vastly popular current President of the UPA. "This visit is a surprise. Might I ask what has brought you here?"

"Primarily to congratulate you Invictus. Templym's population has officially reached half a billion. This is in part due to the Scourge's endeavors. I commend you for your progress."

"I fail to see why I am deserving of this accolade."

"If society is to thrive there must be mediators to preserve the rights of the world and to inflict strict justice upon those that would violate them. The Scourge serves in both of these capacities. The fact that humanity's population is increasing is a testament to the quality of execution of this job." Arodi Auzlanten did not smile or make any outward expression of emotion while he spoke. He kept a stern gaze locked onto the monitor, as if pondering each individual word being exchanged.

"It is a pity I must serve both roles." Invictus was referencing the Civil Strife, a bloody conflict both lived through. This caused a flush of tortured pain to flash ever so briefly in Arodi's eyes and his gaze sank to the ground. He waved his jewel covered hand in the air and the monitor shut off, strange considering he performed no commands or motioned to no sensors.

"You're correct. I hoped the duties would be divided among two entities. After the needless slaughter led by the demon Malacurai, we've been crippled. I applaud your performance in being able to balance these duties. I also apologize for my consistent absence. I am not as involved as I'd like to be."

"You perform the Lord's work, father. I cannot be upset at you for this."

"It pleases me that you understand this, Invictus. I must apologize again, for I fear it may be months before you see me again."

Invictus was hurt. This was not the first time Arodi had been away in a period of extended absence. The burden of being his sole representative in the Scourge was a great weight on his shoulders. "What calls you away this time, father?" He asked.

"Have you ever heard of a tome by the name of the Idolacreid?"

"I have not."

"It was revealed to me recently that this blasphemous artifact has recently emerged in the Azzathan coastlines. This arcane piece of literature has heavy ties to Imago cults and rituals. It contains dark secrets that are forbidden to man. I must find it."

"If you know where the Idolacreid is, why must you leave for months?"

"It was in the Azzathan coast, but I doubt it is still there. Some profane incantation allows the book to avoid my gaze. Therefore, I must go forth and track it down manually."

"I can assemble a task force. Prelate Greyflame is well suited for hunting down occultic relics."

"This must remain Alpha Magnus classified, Invictus. The Idolacreid is a wicked and cancerous collection of runes. I am fearful that even a man as steadfast as the Prelate may not be able to resist its temptations. I was instructed to find this tome. Personally."

"I see. What may I do to help?"

"I ask that you set an alert on the Scourge's data wells. If the name Idolacreid is ever so much as mentioned in a passing report, pull the file and notify me immediately."

"Should I engage and interrogate people using such a term?"

"No. I can't risk you or any soldier being corrupted. Isolate any instances and let none but myself approach anything in relation to this blasphemous artifact.

Invictus was slightly hurt by his father's lack of trust, but he would never voice such a complaint. "Are there any other words I should set filters for?"

"Yes, one more word, same circumstances... Nephilim." With that, Arodi Auzlanten was suddenly gone, vanishing even more suddenly than he appeared.

CHAPTER 3

Warden Downey was happy to be getting another assignment. Given how long it took him to get Goswell into the Arcae and return to Bastion Prime, he was certain he wouldn't get another quarry until tomorrow. He initially thought he'd have to work clear through lunch running the reports in order to be assigned one. It wasn't even noon yet by the time he received a summons from the High Conservator himself.

Volk was more than happy to postpone his paperwork. He had recently removed his battle plate and was wearing a standard Shackle uniform, reducing his height by a few inches. His shoulder pads indicated his rank, and his azure badge had the Shackle's insignia stitched into it. He intentionally left his small private office in Bastion Prime a half an hour before his meeting. Warden Downey had a reputation around the facility, and he could hardly fetch a cup of coffee without stopping for a few minutes in conversation with one of his fellow soldiers. He was likened to a sage or a monk by several of his colleagues.

The meeting took place Rexus 15th. He had arranged to meet the High Conservator in the East wing on the sixth floor. The door to conference room 622 was left ajar, an indication of invitation. Volk Downey pushed the wooden barrier open on its hinges and entered. At the head of the table, High Conservator Jude Bethel sat in his dull blue battle plate. Joining him at the side of the rounded table were two individuals, a dark skinned man dressed in crimson robes with a wide rim hat, and a pale skinned man with long disheveled black hair wearing black battle plate with splashes of red as well as a blue and gold shoulder cuirass.

High Conservator Bethel didn't care to elaborate on his personal life too much. In his youth, he was circulated through years of arduous slave trade by marauders in the American Hinterlands. The ordeal left him visually marred. His cheeks and mouth bore raw pink scar tissue, arranged in thin asymmetric lines, where his price had been barbarically indicated. He was of a nearly extinct race of mankind native to the Western continent, perhaps Aztec or Apache, even he wasn't sure. His skin had a brass-like sheen to it and his visage was cold and unwelcoming. His hair was cut close to his scalp aside from a small thread knotted with beads and an eagle's feather that ran down the side of his neck, concealing a tribal tattoo he was long ashamed of. His icy denim colored plate was scratched heavily after years of combat, never polished or repainted. Volk noted the absence of weapons on the High Conservator but knew that surely something was concealed on him.

The two men, who Volk figured were of the Inquisition, moved themselves to stand up as he entered the room. "Oh please," he said in his soft Glaswegian accent. "Don't get up on my account. Warden Volk Downey, at your service." He moved to greet the two men.

"Inquisitor Vandross Blackwell," The first man said happily as they clasped forearms. "Glad to make your acquaintance." He tipped the brim of his hat at him.

"Inquisitor Adastra Covalos," The other man said in a less jovial tone as they clasped forearms. Adastra's hair and beard was trimmed back a little since his undercover work the day before, but still longer and sloppier than most.

"I'm glad that we've all assembled." Jude Bethel said. His voice was dark and brooding, as one would expect from a man who faced the trauma he had in his past. "If you'd like to be seated, we can begin."

Bethel reached under the table and produced three steel binders. He placed one in front of each one of them. The binder was sealed with a wax binding with the Scourge's spike whip and a Kappa. Vandross raised his eyebrows in surprise seeing that he was receiving an assignment of his maximum clearance level. Bethel motioned for the soldiers to break the seals and open their binders. Meanwhile, he pressed commands onto a data slate which caused the television monitor to flicker to life.

"Verrick 31st 2659, the Cathedral of Sacred Healing in Zulus was raided. Nineteen evangelists were cut down and the structure burned to the ground." Images of the burnt cathedral and of the charred and eviscerated corpses were placed on the monitor. "The Inquisition was unable to determine a culprit." The soldiers' eyes darted from the screen to their files following along with the High Conservator's debriefing.

"Grigor 1st 2667, the Minster of Venice goes missing, kidnapped in a bloody assault that resulted in twenty of his bodyguards being killed." Images of guardsmen corpses dressed in silver battle plate, or pieces thereof. "On Jubral 14th of the same year, the Minister's head was nailed to the gates of the Veil stronghold of Seraphim Solace." The bloody image appeared on the monitor. "No other part of his body was found, and the Veil could not determine a culprit."

"If I may," Adastra interjected. "You're telling me that somebody was able to bypass the outer security perimeter of the Veil's most sacred stronghold and then drive a foot-long iron nail into a flaksteel wall?"

"That's correct."

"That's not possible, not without some kind of supernatural aid."

"Agreed, Inquisitor. I believe that will be obvious with the next case. Limvus 12th 2676, an elementary school in Mandarin. I've neglected to show images. Thirty-eight young boys were decapitated, their heads impaled on pikes used to decorate the hallways. The thirty-two little girls were sacrificed to some Imago. Their tongues and their ovaries were ripped out of their bodies with human hands. The organs were never recovered. Once more, a culprit never found. Regent Illuromos obliterated every crime syndicate and marauder tribe in Azzatha trying to lay waste to the guilty. It was speculated that the guilty were slaughtered."

"Based on the fact you're debriefing us on the matter," Volk said, his usual optimistic tone absent. "Is it safe to say that you don't think they were?"

"Correct." Jude drew a knife, seemingly from nowhere and scraped his gauntlet with the blade. "Huron 18th 2691."

The conference room was deadly silent. Vandross sighed and removed his hat in memoriam to the familiar date. "The Plague Massacre." The Plague Massacre was a worldwide viral assault. It was the inciting event of the 14th Purus Crusade when a breed of pestilence-focused Imago tried to corrupt and destroy humanity. The virus killed as quickly as it spread, reducing fifteen urbans to uninhabitable Hellpits. A tenth of Templym's populace was killed in the supernatural assault. "High Conservator," Vandross continued donning his hat once again. "Are you telling us that all of these events are connected?"

"These and more." Bethel said grimly. "We have reason to believe that all of these horrendous attacks on Templym have an individual in common, someone by the name of Knox Mortis."

"Why the change in theory?" Adastra asked. "According to this file these attacks were thought to be unrelated until yesterday. What new evidence has come to light?"

"A note, you have a copy in the last page of your files, detailing these Scourge cases and pointing towards this Mortis person."

"How reliable is this note?" Downey asked.

"The note is anonymous, unsubstantiated, and bears no indication of actual authority. However, the cases are listed in chronological order and extensively detailed. Several of these were over Mu classified. This means that whoever wrote this knows what they are talking about."

"Any clue where this came from?" Vandross asked looking over the generic looking note detailing the twenty or so events.

"None. It showed up in an unmarked envelope in one of the mail chambers. It rose up the chain of command to me eventually."

"So, what's the job then?" Warden Downey asked. "Why are we here?"

"I've opted to assemble a task force, designate S-6319, consisting of specialists of the Scourge to track down and find this Knox Mortis. It will have to be small to accommodate its need to mobilize. I'd like you all to accept this assignment. Bishop Garrison highly recommends the two of you," the High Conservator motioned to the two Inquisitors, "especially after your acquisition of the fallen Acolyte."

"She'll burn in the afterlife for her treachery." Covalos grunted. He realized he should not wish damnation upon anyone, recognizing that he is worthy of the same fate. He made a mental note of this slight.

"Warden Downey, I'm asking you to take the lead of this task force." Bethel held the combat knife he was previously scratching his armor with out to the Warden.

This was a tradition for Jude Bethel. Whenever he personally assigned a task to someone, he presented a combat knife to them. Downey kept one from a previous task force he led. "I'm honored High Conservator. I accept." He took the blade from Bethel and locked it into his belt.

"Very good. You're to select another from your squadron to accompany you."

"Retriever Ram's Horn," Volk said without pause. "He's the best man for the job."

"Very well, then. I trust these Inquisitors will serve you well. Adastra Covalos is an expert Imago killer. He is familiar with the abilities and habits of the supernatural creatures. More importantly he knows how to kill them."

"Excellent," Downey said. "I noticed the Urim you're wearing there. I figured you were a tough one." The Urim, the blue and gold cuirass that Adastra donned on his pauldron, was awarded to soldiers who successfully kill a Class D Imago.

"I suppose so." Adastra said gruffly.

"I think you're going to get along with Ram just fine."

"My partner Vandross Blackwell will also be a fine resource. He's a well-versed speaker, infiltrator, and occultist. He knows how to blend in with heretics."

"It's my passion." Vandross chuckled. "I wanted to be an actor when I was growing up. I've always had a flare for the dramatic. When I realized that wasn't a particularly stable field of study, I found how to put my talents to a more practical field."

The door swung open again. Another man entered into the conference room. He wore his platinum hair tied back in a tail with two braids on the side of his head. He was decked out in battle plate which possessed plates of black metal with golden immotrum threads wrapped tightly around the limbs. A yellow silk ascot dangled lazily from his neck. Beacon oaths in ancient Greek and Latin were painted onto the breastplate with a diamond sheen pastel.

"Apologies for my tardiness High Conservator," Herald Oslin Du'Plasse spoke as he adjusted his neckband. "I needed to finalize a publication."

"Your apology is acknowledged Herald," Jude Bethel spoke. "Gentlemen this is Herald Oslin Du'Plasse. He will operate as S-6319's stenographer."

"I was wondering if we'd get one of those." Downey said as he stood from his seat. "Warden Volk Downey at your..."

"I'm familiar with who you are Mr. Downey." Herald Du'Plasse spoke in a slightly condescending manner. "I've done my research on you all so there's no need for introductions. I'm assuming that Retriever Horn will not be joining us?"

"Ram? I just selected him to be a part of this team." Volk said taken aback slightly. "How did you know about that?"

"Retriever Ram's Horn is obviously the choice you'd pick. He's the second highest ranking member of your squadron who've you've served with for three years now. Together, you've captured over fifty quarries. Not to mention you have Chaperone Trent to leave in charge of your squadron while you're away."

"You're pretty sharp. Du'Plasse was it, as in Grigor Du'Plasse?"

"Correct. I'm fifteenth generation Du'Plasse, of Hrimata's Platinum District."

"Oh, you're a Hrimatan are you? I thought I smelt frilly perfumes on you." Oslin didn't laugh at Volk's attempt at a joke. Volk awkwardly chuckled before letting the laugh die off seeing Oslin's subtle glare. The irony was that he did in fact apply scented oil to his skin before arriving. "Um, just joshing about, lad. I'm just trying to break the ice, get to know you."

"Please note, Warden Downey," Bethel interjected to melt the tension, "that even though Oslin outranks you, you still will be acting in charge."

"My rank and clearance will no doubt serve as a research asset." Du'Plasse continued from the point. "My Epsilon clearance will be able to get us any intelligence we'd need for the task. My primary task however is to record and document S-6319's actions. I'll ensure ethical practice and efficient execution of duty. So is the duty of a stenographer."

"If you don't mind me asking..."

"Yes I do mind you asking." Oslin snapped back to Volk, knowing he would ask about.

"It's because he's on suspension." Adastra voiced, becoming irritated with Oslin's pompous demeanor. "Don't you remember? Herald Du'Plasse was the AA that executed Senator Gulfran." He stood up and over to the Herald who was biting his lip. Adastra was far taller than either him or Volk. "My guess is this is his shot at redemption, isn't it?"

"Clever deduction, Mr. Covalos," said Du'Plasse while tucking his fingers behind his back and stepping up to the silent challenge. "Of course, we're not all spotless, are we?"

"I'm just finding it ironic that a man with a record as tainted as yours will be this force's primary source of truth."

Oslin clicked his tongue in anger. "Might I remind you Inquisitor, that my actions were deemed lawful? I make no apologies for what I did to Gulfran any more than you make apologies for what you did the Acolyte Goodberry."

"I'm not impressed that you were able to twist the law into making yourself appear innocent Herald. People like you should..."

Vandross stepped in between the two of them. "Let's settle down here." He said placing a gloved hand on each of their breastplates. "We're going to be spending a lot of time together in the near future so let's just take a step back and try to start on a friendly note." He gave a brief glare to his Inquisitor partner. "Ephesians 4:29." Adastra backed away.

"Apologies Herald," Covalos bellowed. Du'Plasse snickered slightly and brushed his wrist, a Hrimatan gesture of acceptance.

"If you're quite finished, gentlemen," Jude Bethel said as he rose, light bouncing off of his cobalt armor, "I must present you with your oath badges."

The High Conservator presented a small wooden box and opened it. Inside were five porcelain badges in the shape of the Shackle's chain-cuff with an iron glaze. S-6319 was emblazoned across the length of the cuff's curve, two in red, two in blue, and one in yellow. The four men stood at attention side by side.

"By accepting these badges, you swear allegiance to this task force." Bethel spoke in his icy tone of voice. "You are giving me your word that you will pursue your target, Knox Mortis, to the best of your ability. By taking these badges, you accept the task of pursuing and neutralizing the threat assigned to you... and are willing to accept punishment should you compromise your integrity or taint the Scourge's upright reputation. If you accept, please take your badge." Each of the Scourge soldiers reached into the box and pulled out a badge, each corroborating to their sub-organization's color. "Thank you, men. Go forth Kynigi et Kako, In Nomine Veritas."

"In Nomine Veritas." All four echoed in unison.

"Dismissed."

Warden Downey returned to his squadron in the East wing on the fourth floor of Bastion Prime. He spent a few moments speaking to Ram's Horn and gave him the oath badge which he accepted without question or comment. He said his goodbyes to all of the eager young Guardians he was in charge of, wishing them the best. He liked this batch and had high hopes that they'd all still be here when he returned from his journey.

Volk and Ram then went to the armory. Volk supplied himself

with a few boxes of shells for his Blakavit and some brass for his Reisinger. He charged his tech enhanced mace and polished off his battle plate, adding his oath badge to the number of ribbons and metals on his chest plate. Ram's Horn, ever clad in his armor, focused on obtaining oils and repair plating for their armor. He carried a large revolving tangle barrel pistol in a chainmail sheath at his waist. Ram needed no melee weapon, for the ancient Steel Skin fighting style had no room for anything other than metal-clad fists.

As Warden Downey added fresh cyan disk batteries to his bag of commodities, he was approached by Chaperone Trent. He was no longer wearing his helmet, revealing his young and curly-haired head. "Warden Downey sir!" He said giving the heart ripping motion of the Scourge salute.

"Declan, will you drop the formalities?" Volk said in his fatherly tone. "We're just in the armory."

"Apologies Warden Downey," He said, slacking his shoulders. "It is my duty to express concerns about you leaving on this quarry hunt."

"Well go on then, voice your worry."

"Sir, with you and Retriever Ram's Horn going away that would leave me as the ranking officer."

"Correct. What's the issue?"

"Sir, I don't think I'm fit to lead the Guardians. You said it yourself this morning. I've still got a lot to learn before I..."

"Your worries are misplaced, Trent. I wouldn't leave you in charge if I didn't think you were ready for it."

"But what about what you said this morning?"

"Look, I'm sorry if I shook you up. I was being a bit harsh with you to scare you straight, so to speak. I wouldn't be trying to make you a better soldier if I didn't care. You've got one of the sharpest minds I've ever seen. How else could someone fresh out of the nursery make it to Chaperone?"

"Warden Downey, I'm honored you think that."

"I don't think that, I know it. You nearly doubled my score on the written exam and you perfected the personality portion. You just got to work on your endurance. Hit the gyms, do some cardio. I've no doubt that you'll go far."

"Thank you, Warden Downey." The two clasped forearms. Trent's bright young face looked significantly more vibrant when compared to the leathery face of Volk. Ram's Horn trundled over to the two with a large sack slung over his shoulder. "Retriever Ram's Horn, I wish you the best on your quarry hunt." He stuck out his hand. Ram's Horn stared at it for a moment before taking it, crushing the young warrior's hand in a vice grip. Trent tried his best to conceal his pain, albeit poorly.

Adastra and Vandross polished their weapons and armor. Adastra was hunched over a bench in the Inquisition's locker room, scribbling words into a small black book. He stuffed it into a thick storage case along with a few boxes of armor polish and bullets. His axe was slung over his back, the twin blades fiercely sharp. Vandross slipped a number of combat knives in leather belts and holsters concealed amidst his robes. Two compact pistols were tucked into hidden holsters by his tunic while his favorite Reisinger was at his hip. His bastard sword was sheathed in its black shell opposite the pistol.

Adastra cracked his neck as he hoisted up the case containing his and his partner's personal items. "Ready for this?" Adastra asked Vandross.

"Of course, I am." He said happily. "This will basically be a vacation for us. Lord knows we don't get enough of those in this profession."

"You picked the wrong job if you wanted ample vacation time."

"Ah yes, I suppose so. Let's get to the dispatch garage." Vandross pulled an envelope from his red locker and slammed it shut. "Shall we?"

The Inquisitors took off to the lower floor of Bastion Prime to embark on their mission. "What's that there?" Adastra asked indicating the small white envelope.

"Just a check for my parents." Vandross said as he dropped the pouch into a mail vent. The letter would no doubt travel to the Scourge's post room and then to Rio Epiphanies, the Kalkhanian nation where he grew up.

"When was the last time you saw Hugo, Vandross?"

The jovial Inquisitor grew grim for a second, his lip curled in a sour frown. "Just... don't, Adastra. It's better this way."

Herald Oslin Du'Plasse packed up his cubicle. He was through with this insubordinate's desk. He was determined that he was going to move back up the ranks of the Scourge after returning to this facility. That or he would be killed during the manhunt. Either way, it was an improvement. He packed up his favorite dehydrated delicacies and cosmetics. He oiled the mechanics and gears on his Beacon banner and loaded up fresh clips into his old pistol. He looked at it fondly, turning it in his hands.

His father's Holt, the one he used fighting in the Trench during the Strife. This was the sole memento he had from his father, having no relics from the Du'Plasse manor in Hrimata. This handgun and his older brother's Du'Plasse ascot were the remnants of his now dead family that he carried with him always. Oslin thought fondly of running in his family's orchard. He remembered his father pretending to be a dread minotaur chasing him and his four siblings beneath the blooming trees, pretending he was going to eat them. He missed those simple days, before the Strife.

Oslin let out a deep sigh as he packed up the last personal item in the cubicle, the picture from twenty years ago. His sisters, Nichole and Requin, were just babies, one in each of his parents' arms. His older brother Yuriel, wearing the ascot he wore now, couldn't keep his eyes open for the picture. Oslin was wrestling his younger brother Ethix moments before and they still had dirt on their alabaster dress shirts. Oslin chuckled slightly, recalling that they were fighting about which flavor of fruit juice was better. He still believed pomegranate was superior to guava. Oslin carefully lifted the glossy portrait out of the frame and tucked it into his satchel. He placed it right next to the photo of Arodi Auzlanten he kept in there.

The photo of the Toppler of Tyranny, as he was known throughout Templym, was a famous one. It was a colorized photo at the end of 14th Purus Crusade. He stood resplendent overtop the largest Imago ever recorded, an Imago called Plaguemire. He stood on top of the creature, which was as tall as a small cloudtoucher but was toppled dead on its side. The ugly gnarled green fur of the blood-soaked monster was captured in detail enough so that you could almost smell the behemoth's stench just by gazing at it. Auzlanten stood on the rotten and decaying head of the beast, next to a twisted black horn after the climax of the final battle. He stood victorious over the demon horde. Wind whipped his raven hair, no blood or bile stained his flawless white tunic or ultramarine robes, his mystic sabre Leagna glowed with vibrant mauve and scarlet patterns as the setting sun bounced rays of light off of the blade, combining to form a vision of stained glass. Oslin took particular care to mimic Auzlanten's hair style. He wanted to emulate the hero that he left his family for.

CHAPTER 4

The case file that High Conservator Bethel gave S-6319 contained each of the massacres that Knox Mortis allegedly committed in chronological order. The consensus was clear among the five, start the hunt with the most recent slaughter. This would take them from Frankon to Venice. In the Venetian urban of Bruccol, a small hospital had been raided. Three people in critical condition and two doctors were taken from this world. An odd case that went cold, it was presumed to be a gang raid for the pharmaceuticals and medical equipment which were missing at the scene.

To get there, S-6319 was assigned a caravan class chariot. This was an automated heavy-duty transport and recreational vehicle, fueled by an antoniat fusion couple. The vehicle provided six bunks, an interrogation chamber, and an observation deck. This chariot would allow the task force efficient travel and provide a place to sleep, eat, and store personal goods. It was piloted by an Indentured Inmate.

The Scourge's Shackle was the division that dealt with the rehabilitation of criminals. Over the course of Templym's life they took great care to perfect the process of the judicial criminal character reform. This involved two processes. The first were the Arcae prisons. These facilities housed thousands of guilty and deplorable individuals in bleak isolation chambers. In their dimly lit holding cells, they received a loaf of bread and a bottle of water a day with a chamber pot and thin cot. The punishment was grueling and maddening. Criminals were rarely detained for more than a month. Those whose crimes were too heinous were executed within a week of sentencing. Auzlanten's Veritas Chambers, rooms that allowed only the truth to come from one's mouth, left no room for doubt when it came to doling out punishment. The inmates that were given a second chance, and only a second chance, were often given a multitude of services upon release to atone for their sins. One form of parole was the practice of indentured servitude, whereupon a guest of an Arace could be released from their cell in exchange for labors devoted to the Scourge. One such man served as S-6319's chauffer.

Oslin Du'Plasse had arranged for Jameson Daurtey to be their designated chariot driver. He watched his confession and subsequent pleas of release inside a Veritas Chamber. He felt confident in his genuine repentance and his usefulness. Of course, Du'Plasse wouldn't admit to being the one who chose him, seeing as Warden Downey is the man who arrested him.

Jameson Daurtey was once a heavy-set man. His four weeks in Jupiter Arcae, left him emaciated with loose skin hanging from his chin and arms. He wore a dull grey jumpsuit with the Scourge's insignia on it, concealing the scars from his flogging. A black metal collar was clamped around his throat. This allowed his supervising officers to provide a number of chemical injections that could inflict minor pain or lethal poison, depending on the discipline needed. The collar did no work to hide the M-03 tattoo just below the chin.

Oslin and Volk were already familiar with this individual. On the other hand, Vandross was curious to get to know this man. "How long have you been indentured?" Vandross asked with warmth that Jameson was unfamiliar with from those within the Scourge. He walked into the pilot's seat which contained two fabric seats. The Inquisitor parted the curtains leading to the passenger's bay unannounced and propped his feet on the dashboard as he plopped down into the black chair.

"Two weeks now sir." Jameson responded, paranoid that there was some hidden motive that the Inquisitor was trying to exploit some agenda. He kept his sunken eyes glued onto the road ahead of him. They just left Bastion Prime from the dispatch center. Vandross invited himself to the front of the chariot while the others kept to the back.

The road circuit ahead would schedule them to arrive in Bruccol the next morning, assuming he could keep driving the whole time.

“Must be nice to be out of Jupiter, huh?” Vandross chuckled as he began stuffing his granite pipe with Cornell root, a more savory herb than the more common clovertwig. “See the Sun in the sky, hearing the birds chirp?” He bit down on the end of the pipe as he ignited his pipe. “Oh, my apologies,” Vandross said puffing out bleached vapor. “Do you want some?”

“No sir, Mr. Blackwell.” He said upon as the tip of the pipe was pointed at him. “I mean, Inquisitor Blackwell, sir.”

“Alright Daurtey, you seem on edge. So why don’t I just point out the lighthouse in the room. Who’d you kill?”

Daurtey swallowed hard, perspiration dotting his brow. “My wife’s lover sir.”

Blackwell’s eyebrows flashed upwards. “Ouch, that’s rough. And quit calling me sir. That’s an order.”

“Yes si... I’ll do that.”

“I figured it was out of anger. Most M-03’s are.”

“What’s M-03?”

“That’s your crime. It’s tattooed on your neck. Each prisoner of the Scourge has a letter to indicate a crime and two numbers to indicate motive and circumstances. M is for murder, no thinker there. The first number being 0 shows that you had no premeditations and the second being 3 shows that it was personal. Did you walk in on them?”

“Yes. It wasn’t much of a surprise honestly. Our marriage wasn’t healthy. It was bound to crumble away.”

“That’s a shame. I can’t imagine what that’s like. In truth I can sympathize with you. Marriage is a most sacred covenant forming the most intimate bond one could ever hope to have with another person. To see someone violating that promise, well... anger’s a pretty rational response.”

“Yes sir, I was angry, but I’ve forgiven her since. After my first week in Arcae, they let me have a Bible. I found God in that holding cell of all places, and I heard His call to repentance.”

Vandross chuckled as he flew the last puff of white fog from his teeth. "You'd be shocked how many people the Arcae brings to God. Hopefully she's gotten the same revelation. The Veil doesn't take adultery too kindly."

"Sir, if you don't mind me asking, I'm still pretty haunted about this whole thing. The strain it caused with my wife, I mean ex-wife, won't be repaired anytime soon. Are you married, and if so, how do you and your wife get through these kinds of trials?"

"Sorry Jameson, we'll have to continue this another time." Vandross said as he threw himself out of the seat. "I need to debrief the party and determine our next move. You just holler if you want a break from the helm and I'll take over for you." Vandross took himself back to the passenger's bay.

"I can't stomach such an option." Adastra said to Herald Du'Plasse while unnecessarily sharpening his greataxe with a whetstone.

"Criminal informants aren't my favorite method either," Du'Plasse said as he tapped his data-slate with his gold colored fingers. "Unfortunately, I feel as though it's the best lead we have."

"We can review evidence from Beacon investigators when we arrive to Bruccol and analyze the scene of the attack."

"Not likely. Harbinger Amos Buildswell was the lead of forensics. If he was unable to determine a culprit then we won't be able to, either."

"I'm of a mind to agree with the Herald." Volk said after quietly observing the interchange, Ram's Horn seated next to him, silent as a statue. "This informant seems to be the only potential lead that the Scourge didn't pursue, given Conservator Travvec's disgust for such methods. This case is over three months old at this point. Any forensic evidence is long gone by this stage."

"Gossip, on the other hand," Du'Plasse added, "has a much longer half-life. According to Beacon records, this... mercenary has contributed information that has led to seventeen convictions. I have all of his contact information right here."

Vandross parted the curtains and entered the passenger's bay. He was slightly surprised to see the effectiveness of the sound-proofing the thin sheet provided. "What's the good word?" He asked as he pulled a bottle of water from a chill storage container.

"Christ has risen from the dead." Adastra grunted with a slight grin.

"The best Word imaginable." Vandross said laying across one of the compact cots in the transport. He tipped his hat forward as if preparing for a nap. "What news do we have on the Mortis manhunt?"

"Du'Plasse insists that we begin our search with a criminal informant." Adastra said, the grin vanishing as instantly as it appeared. "A contract assassin of all things."

"Given your record Mr. Covalos," Du'Plasse interjected, "I thought you might approve of this deplorable's methodology."

"Hey, pretty boy," Vandross said, "you mind not starting fights with my partner please?"

Oslin raised one of his platinum colored eyebrows at the Inquisitor and shook his head in silent disapproval. "Marius Seta, a professional sleepman who works closely with all of the four major Venetian mob syndicates. He has no loyalty to any but his bank account. Local Scourge forces have allowed him to continue his practice of burying local gangers in exchange for the occasional glimpse into the mob world."

"What's his quarry?" Volk asked curiously.

"I beg your pardon?" Du'Plasse asked unfamiliar with Downey's Shackle vernacular.

"His quarry, you know the focus of his hunting trips. Most sleepmen have a certain kind of person that they quite literally set their sights on."

"Ah yes. His focus is on gangers. One syndicate pays him to off another's member and so on."

"He still sullies the name of the law." Adastra said with no subtle anger in his voice. "If he wants to put an end to criminal syndicates he should enroll in the Scourge."

"Not everyone can be as straight-backed as you Adastra." Vandross said. "The vast majority of Templym's citizens lack the discipline required to serve in the Scourge. Freelancers are accountable to themselves... in their own eyes."

"So, are we in agreement then?" Du'Plasse asked the bay.

There were several nods, even Adastra nodded begrudgingly. "What's your input Ram?" Volk asked the silent giant.

"Sleepman." The Retriever grumbled.

"Very well then, it's settled." Warden Downey clapped his metal clad hands together. "Oslin, would you kindly get in touch with Mr. Seta?"

The Haigon Empire fell at the end of the Reclaiming Crusades, nearly two hundred and fifty years ago. The Immortal Emperor oppressed the Azzathan continent for well over a hundred years. Tyrants like him took what they pleased, uncaring of their constituents' consent. He had numerous direct descendants.

Beacon statisticians speculate that 2% of the population of the continent is directly descended from Xingyue Haigon, numbering around 600,000 people alive today. The overwhelming majority of this populace was blissfully unaware of the monster at the root of their family tree. Some fanatics that were aware of this heritage were often boastful about this truth. More than any, the Haigon nobles formed their own clan which operated primarily in the Mandarin nation as an underground crime family. The Haigon Clansmen, as they were known, were the last surviving syndicate after Regent Illuromos' great purge of the continent. The Clansmen were sycophantic terrorists looking to topple the powers that be and reestablish the Haigon Empire.

The Clansmen cycled through "fathers" who were the eldest and often firstborn sons of the generation. The current serving father was Toau Haigon. He kept the Clansmen in the shadows, taking great care to conceal the gang's activities from the public eye. This allowed them great leeway to operate and horde power to eventually overthrow Scourge forces in the continent. His life's work was crumbling in front of him.

Toau Haigon snapped a clip of bullets into his assault rifle. The dozen or so bodyguards around him did likewise. The sentry guard failed to make contact with him, indicating that they were no longer operating. He muttered ancient ancestral words to himself and stepped behind a blockade of rockfoam and sandbags. His mob family and hired mercenaries frantically pointed their Zeduac assault rifles to every window wall and door in the expansive warehouse they occupied. This was just supposed to be a quick exchange, in and out in an hour. It was just a few damn paintings! Toau brought fifty men with him to ensure nothing would go wrong. How could his entire sentry be toppled already?

Toau Haigon closed his eyes. He allowed his father's spirit to flow through him. With his eyes closed, he could see far more clearly than the impure around him. He could see through the steel warehouse walls and looked for life. He saw his sentry guard at their post, dead with their necks bent and slack. Then he looked for heartbeats. His sight extended beyond that of mortal comprehension and he could see the beating heart of anybody within a mile's radius. There were no heartbeats that his vision could see. There was something else, a shimmer in his vision, something, no, worse, some*one* walking into the front door. He wanted to dismiss the anomaly as a form of camouflage or insulated armor but could only conclude that an old foe was had arrived.

"Lone man, coming in from the front door," Toau Haigon shouted to his guard in his native tongue. "Do not let him step into the warehouse. Bullets are cheap, these pieces are not."

The Clansmen lined up behind cover or out in the open. They were bolstered two hundred feet away from the sheet metal cargo doors. Based on the way they were dressed, one might assume they were en route to a formal gala. In truth, guns and knives were concealed on every one of them. Toau stood at the center of his guard. His off-white suit bore the intricate design of an Eastern red dragon that slithered up the length of his leg and across his shoulders. His eyes and mouth were scrunched into a deep and angry scowl, irritated at the interruption.

The door normally opened by raising and lowering vertically. The intruder blasted it off of its chain. The thin metal crunched and crumbled in a flameless explosion of force. A silhouette of a single man stood where the door once was. The hail of bullet was unleashed in his direction. The thunderous pounding rang from the rifles and pistols, rattling the bones of every man in the room. The blizzard of brass should have been more than enough to reduce any man to a red pulp. Upon the start of the gunfire, the outline began to walk inside.

The first foot stepped over the threshold as the lights in the warehouse went out. In a single flash, the fluorescent lamps exploded in a pop of white sparks, leaving inky blackness in its wake. The muzzle flashes of the Zeduac rifles were enough to illuminate their small section of the warehouse. The only sound in the warehouse was the staccato of gunfire. As swiftly as the ringing started it ended. After the gangers unloaded their second full magazines, they dropped their rifles. Not out of fear or surrender, they died. Spontaneously and simultaneously, every Haigon Clansmen was shunted swiftly to the side as their necks were snapped. The hammering bullet storm was replaced with the gut-wrenching sound of bone cracking followed by an equal number of lifeless impacts on the ground. Toau Haigon was left standing alone in the empty darkness.

The sound of a sword being drawn was accompanied by a bright glow. Inches away from Toau, a single edged sabre was raised to his neck. The blade radiated illustrious sea foam green as it came into view, but never stayed the same color for long. The glowing weapon illuminated the intruder who stood among a scattered mess of fresh corpses and hot shell casings. Toau began to breathe faster and more panicked as he recognized the man. Everyone in the world knew that arrangement of ebony hair paired with the tan skin and those intense blue of the eyes and robes. Arodi Auzlanten had come for him.

"You know why I'm here." Arodi said, it was not a question.

"The Reaper rears his ugly head." Toau said in his native tongue as he dropped his weapon, knowing it would be useless against Templym's founder. "I'll admit I don't know what you seek." He said after switching to temple-tongue.

"And yet you know that I am seeking something. I can force the truth from you, or you could tell me."

"Heathen, are you ignorant of who you address? I am Toau Haigon, the Immortal Emperor Xingyue Haigon reincarnate. You are unworthy to even spit in my direction."

"I am aware of your family's heretical doctrine. Know that Xingyue Haigon is dead by my hand and will remain so. Now if we're through with formalities, the Idolacreid, now."

"The Immortal Emperor lives on through me. By the undying soul of Xingyue, I smite you, heathen." Light began to illuminate Toau's veins. It was as if his blood was being replaced with lava, the illumination piercing his skin, revealing his bloodways. His brown eyes were flushed with sharp yellow. The gang father let out an inhuman bestial roar. With the shout, a wave of liquid orange fire engulfed Auzlanten wholly. The roar was a blend of an animalistic bloodlust, seething hatred, and liquid flames. This was the strength of Haigon sorcery. None ever survived Toau Haigon's fire tongue, none until now.

When the pillar of fire vanished, Auzlanten stood unscathed by the flamethrower of magick. Considering the fire ignited the spare bullets and sent metal brass projectiles in every direction, it was impossible for any man to have survived. Just like Shadrach, Meshach, and Abednego, he did not even bare the scent of burning or as much as a scorch on his clothes. "Arrogant sorcerer," Auzlanten said with an undertone of ire. "Your mastery of blood magick is of no comparison to your ancestor's. I have dealt with far worse than your parlor tricks. Now, and this is the last time I will repeat myself, where is the Idolacreid?"

"I don't know what you're talking about." Haigon said with a slight tremor in his tone. He realized that his magick was just as useless as his rifle so his only hope of survival was to stall.

"You do not know its name," Arodi said as he circled the clan father with the point of the sabre still at Toau's neck. "But you know of the tome I speak. You held the book in your hands, heard its unholy whispers, craved the promises it extended. I am no fool. I know that you had it once but now you don't. And I know you will tell me."

"And why would I ever do that?"

Auzlanten grew impatient. With his free hand, he motioned a complex finger arrangement directly in front of Toau's face. His eyes, still burning yellow, looked confused and void of understanding. "Why do you no longer have the Idolacreid?"

"I sold it." Toau Haigon said, confused as to why he was confessing. "A woman offered me twenty royals for it. That's a price I could never refuse, even with the tempting promises of the book."

"This woman, describe her."

"A Kalkhanian witch. She was covered in fetishes and bones, probably some kind of weird juju or voodoo, I'm not familiar with the practice."

"Did you find out a name or where she was from?"

"She called herself the Bog Mama and operates out of Madagast, the queen of Madagast she called herself."

"Where did she get the royals?"

"Diamond and malachite, raw uncut stones weighing a quarter ton, she probably stole it from marauders or museums. I didn't ask questions."

"Why did she want the Idolacreid?"

"The magickal lore, I suspect. Anyone called Bog Mama must be some kind of savage spell novice. Normally I wouldn't even deal with someone as filthy and disgusting as her. I made an exception on merit of the price alone. Do you know how many guns I could buy with that? How many mercenaries I could train? We're talking twenty thousand monarchs, twenty million crowns. That's more money than some of your precious nations are worth." Toau moved to draw a knife and cut out his own tongue to stop himself from speaking. Arodi caught his hand and restrained it, like a patient parent dealing with a child amidst a tantrum.

"What kind of tyrant places a numeric value on human life?

Who does she work with? Does Bog Mama have any marauder tribes or Imago patrons at her disposal?"

"I don't know anything else."

"I believe you." Arodi said releasing his grip on Toau's wrist. He did not move to cut his tongue free anymore and let the knife hit strike the floor. There was no point anymore, for he had told him everything he knew. "Do you remember the promise I made you?"

"The one you told me when you killed my father?"

"Yes, that promise." Arodi thrust the end of his sabre Leagna into the clan father so quickly the human eye could not comprehend. A splash of blood flew from Toau's back as he gasped for breath uselessly, the sword piercing his lung. The vibrant green light that shimmered from the blade branched over to Haigon as Auzlanten retracted the blade. The shroud of light flashed in an overwhelming explosion of illumination. When the glow flickered out, there was nothing but a smoldering pile of dust left where Toau Haigon once stood.

Arodi Auzlanten did not sheath Leagna after the kill. Instead he turned his gaze directly towards the door of the backroom. At some point during his encounter with the clan father, it had creaked open. Knowing that it was not a threat, Arodi opted to ignore the intruder until he was finished. He walked over to the person and knelt down to be at eye contact level with Lin Haigon, Toau's twelve-year-old son.

"You know who I am?" Arodi asked, the whitish light from his sabre still the only light source in the complex.

"You are the Reaper." The boy stammered. "You are the one who has taken the Immortal Emperor's conduit time and time again. You are the bane of my royal family's existence." He was obvious recalling verbatim doctrine hammered into his mind from birth.

"I suppose that is correct."

"I am Lin Haigon, the Immortal Emperor Xingyue Haigon reincarnate."

"I'm familiar with your ancestral religion. You believe that I did not truly kill your tyrannical forefather and that his soul moves to inhabit the firstborn son of the next generation. Therefore, you are now Xingyue Haigon, the next clan father. You have been misguided."

"We will rise up against you Reaper." The child growled. It was like a small kitten taking a stand against a Hekaton war machine. "I will reestablish my forefather's empire and Azzatha will be mine again."

"I am going to tell you something, Lin. It is the same thing that I told your father after I killed his father. Give up this jihad against Templym. Cease the practice of sorcery and Imago channeling. Become a well versed and moral citizen, turn away from your family's tradition of organized crime. If you don't and instead rise up in protest of me and the God I serve, I will kill you."

"You don't scare me." The young boy said obviously lying. "The spirit of Xingyue is with me forever."

"Take care then. For if you practice your family's black magick, if you lead the Haigon Clan, if you identify yourself as an adversary of Templym, I will not show you mercy."

Arodi Auzlanten stood from his kneeling position. He slid Leagna back into its home on his waist. He then turned from the orphaned boy and walked towards the outside. Hate boiled inside of Lin's chest. He called upon his dead fathers' spirit to manifest. Auzlanten's silhouette was barely visible in front of the flickering charred bodies that he calmly stepped over. Lin grabbed the knife with his mind. He sent the combat blade hurtling at the Reaper with as much speed as a bullet. Arodi Auzlanten allowed the point of the knife to strike him in the neck. As if his flesh was iron, the dagger bounced off. Any man's jugular should have been split open by the sorcerous attack. He looked over his shoulder, the blues of his eyes the only color visible in the outline. "You are young and foolish." He spoke with the same chilling calmness. "I shall extend mercy just this once. Do not expect it when you become a man."

CHAPTER 5

Criminal informants were a rarity in the Scourge. As the founding organization intended to punish the guilty, its leaders have very little tolerance for criminals of every sort. Only after scrupulous analysis of a specific individual's activities, which would end in a conclusion that the lives they save with their information would outweigh the civilian lives lost to their crimes tenfold, would one be allowed to operate in an illegal trade. This meant that sleepmen that made other criminals their quarry were the most common informants. Several soldiers in the Scourge scoffed at the practice of sullying their reputation of purity and discipline by associating with such criminals. Others saw them as simple tools to be exploited as a means of achieving a larger goal. This practice raised debates among the more philosophically minded individuals about ends justifying means.

S-6319 did not have the time or the courtesy of debating ethical practices. Any trail they had on this Knox Mortis, if he even existed, was lax at best. If they wanted the opportunity to pursue the most likely source of information, they would have to dirty their hands a bit.

The caravan stationed at Bruccol's highest Scourge facility was the Weighted Scale, a Shackle facility under the supervision of Conservator Travvec. This allowed for a place of recreation as well as a center for intelligence of the local mafias. Inquisitor Covalos, as by the book as any man of the Scourge, was intolerant of crime in any form. He neglected to attend the meeting with the sleepman. Herald Du'Plasse decided to stay at the facility as well and explore local data wells for information. Warden Downey and Inquisitor Blackwell would attend the meeting while Retriever Ram's Horn waited in the caravan as backup. This would require discretion, so they couldn't meet in their Scourge regalia.

They were instructed by their sleepman, Marius Seta, to wear formal attire for their meeting. Vandross indicated proper attire to fit the dress code, his experience in infiltration making him adept at such concepts. Volk was dressed in a black buttoned suit with an orchid tie, complemented with a crusader's amulet from his service in the 14th Purus. Vandross kept his wide rimmed scarlet hat but bore the appearance of an eccentric businessman with a burgundy cuffed and collared jacked.

"Do I really have to dress like this?" Volk said as he tugged at his collar. "I feel like a bloody peacock in this clown suit."

"You've got a soldier's mug for sure." Vandross said as he lay back in his chair. The meeting was to take place in a local bistro. The lavish wooden chairs and tables smelled of furniture polish and garlic. "The bullet lodged in your face certainly draws attention, so we need to blend in as best we can. I don't know if you've noticed, but everyone in here is dressed like a clown. Don't mess with your necktie either."

"You know I've worn a tie about three times in my whole life. I always thought that it was a posh decoration that doubles as a noose. It's an infernal little contraption."

"Well that's the dress code. You can take it off when we're done here."

"What's this Seta guy even look like?"

"Du'Plasse said that there was no picture in his file. Apparently, the Scourge keeps their informants discrete. All we know is that he said to be at this place at this time, order a bottle of '78 Vermillion Pettiot, and not pour any until he gets here." He motioned to the ornate bottle of red wine accompanied by three empty drinking crystals.

"It's subtle I guess." Volk said adjusting his tie, not out of anxiety but for comfort. "I hate to waste money trying to piss this guy up."

"Just stick with the strategy and we'll be out of here with up to date intelligence."

The third seat was pulled out by someone they initially thought was a waiter, who sat down quickly. The man had dark hair slicked back to cling onto his head. He wore shade spectacles and had an extravagant formal suit complete with a green silk tie and an alabaster pocket handkerchief. He had a black sapphire ring and a single diamond pinned in his ear. Without a word he emptied the bottle of wine into three equal portions among the crystals.

"Marius Seta?" Volk asked, taken slightly aback.

"Speaking," The man responded as he pushed the crystals to each of the investigators. "Could you look a little more like ants please? I don't think this too subtle." His voice was bombastic and upfront, despite his discrete tone.

"Ants?" Vandross asked as he lifted the crystal to his lips.

"You know, like antibodies, as in the immune system? That's what we always call you Scourge boys. You don't get around these parts, do you?"

"We're not from Venice. I'm..."

"Whoa whoa," Marius said as he slammed the crystal down and raised his hands at their chests. "I don't want to know your names, and I don't want to know where you're stationed. You ask questions, I give answers, that's the extent of this relationship."

"Agreed." Volk said. "Can we get straight to business?"

"First we drink," the sleepman said. "You first bullet face." Volk realized that Marius hadn't taken a drink yet.

"I don't drink."

"You do today, or you'll get nothing out of me."

Volk rolled his eyes and raised the crystal to his mouth and took a small sip. "There, happy?"

"Very much so," Marius said as he took a sip of the Vermillion liquid. "So, what can I do for my friends at the Scourge?"

"We need intelligence on a case that went cold a few months back." Vandross said leaning in and hushing his voice. "Word is that you know everything there is to know about the local mobs."

"You're alright hat man." Marius chuckled as he gave a friendly slap over the table on Vandross' chest, not surprised at all to hit an immotrum vest under the coat.

"Jubral 6th of this year," Downey said. "Small healing house in Bruccol, Bethesda Pianissimo, most dead. Every trace of pharmaceuticals and medical equipment was gone."

Seta stroked his chin for a moment letting out a hum of deep thinking. "Yeah, yeah I think I know a couple things about that. What do you know?"

"Nothing," Vandross said regretfully. "Scourge investigation turned nothing up, so we've got no leads."

"Why the sudden interest in a cold case?"

"New information has come to light and we're following up on a lead." Volk retorted.

"Is this going to affect my business?"

"Well that depends on what you're going to tell us." Vandross said with a smile. "So, what have you got for us?"

Marius scratched the oily hair on his scalp. "Alright, I reckon that I'll be out a job or two if I give up what I know."

"By job or two," Vandross said, his brow furled. "You mean a contract assassination?"

"Meh, it's just a few gangers, nobody worth anything. Of course, it'll damper my quota for the month if I tell you. I think monetary compensation is a reasonable request. We'll call it... twenty monarchs."

"Twenty monarchs?" Volk asked with obvious offense. "That's more than the task force budget." He whispered to Vandross.

"I'm afraid we can't do that Mr. Seta." Vandross said trying to keep a charming appeal. "I've got about five hundred crowns on me. You're welcome to those."

"Sorry, I don't rat out my employers for half a monarch. Information ain't free." Marius kicked back the last of his wine. "So, if twenty monarchs aren't on the table, we've nothing to discuss. Thanks for the wine."

"Well I suppose this is goodbye for good then." Volk said as the sleepman pushed his chair back to get up.

"Pardon?" Marius asked with an eyebrow cocked upwards.

"Well the Scourge allows you to practice our business in exchange for regular gossip on the local gangs." Vandross said casually. "That includes all Scourge sanctioned manhunts, raids, and rescue missions."

"If you're not talking anymore," Volk continued off of that tangent. "Then you're no longer an asset."

"That gives us two options." Vandross said perching his brow up in a coy gesture. "We could arrest you and haul your hide off to the local Arcae, where you'll stay a week before execution."

"Or if you'd prefer," Volk said with a similar grin. "We can let the locals know about your little side job."

"That's not funny." Marius said, bringing his voice down to a serious and somber tone.

"What do they call mobsters who talk to the law?" Volk asked turning to Vandross.

"I've heard a lot of names." Vandross responded. "Crybaby, sellout, howler monkey, mockingjay, but the most common one is rat."

"You know, Oslin's back at the Weighted Scale." Volk continued in the performance. "I bet he knows a fair bit of what the locals do to rats."

"I've heard that the Crescent Gems dissolve them in barrels of acid." Vandross chuckled. "The Grey Ties I think strap them to anchors and toss them in the Dead Reef."

"Alright already," Marius interrupted. "You've worn me down."

"Good." Volk said. "So, Jubral 6th Bethesda Pianissimo, what do you know?"

"It was a pretty big job," Marius said removing his shade lenses. "Folks came in from out of town to raid the hospital. Who they were, I have no idea, but I can say for certain that the Young Ichors were involved."

"What was the job?" Vandross asked.

"Drug raid. That little joint just got a few crate-loads of raw narcotics and healing solutions. They wanted them and well... you know the rest. The Young Ichors are the biggest drug dealers in all of Venice, so it's no surprise they wanted in on the score. It was a quick in-and-out job, no witnesses."

"Who were these outside guys?" Volk asked.

"Like I said, I don't know. Whoever they were they knew the exact day and time that the shipment was going to come in. They wanted the Ichors' permission, considering the Bethesda was on their territory. My guess is that they agreed on the condition that they cut them a piece of the cache."

"If you don't know who these outsiders are, who would?" Vandross asked.

"Anybody with a reputation in the Young Ichors would know about the job. They've got outposts and safe houses all over Bruccol, most of which I know about. You could rush an outpost in the area."

"That could spark a turf war." Volk said. "Mafias get excited when their competition loses ground. I don't want any civilians getting caught in the crossfire."

"Exactly." Marius said slapping his hands together and pointing at the Warden. "Right now, the four gangs are in a gentleman's agreement to lay low and not move against each other after the local Conservator nearly wasted them all. That'll fly out the window if their neighbors see any unclaimed neighborhoods. So, I'll recommend a target for you. A rookie from Neapol, only got to the top with his depth of his pockets, a real softie named Diogo Numerri. You get a few minutes alone with him, he'll sing like a mockingjay."

"How would you do it," Vandross asked, "if you were going to pick this guy up?"

"Well I don't do a lot of kidnapping." Marius chuckled to the investigators who in turn gave a brief scowl. "If I would, I'd get him at the opera. He loves that crap, attends the weekly performance at the Broadwick Arts Center every Blitzday. That's when I'd grab him."

"And if he goes missing, the Young Ichors won't get spooked?" Volk retorted.

"Oh no, you'd be doing them a favor. Numerri's a loudmouth liability. The Young Ichors hired me to off him. That's why I know so much about him. I was planning on killing him at the opera tomorrow night. You disappear him quietly, nobody will care."

"And if nobody knows, you can take credit for his disappearance and still get paid." Vandross said.

"I like you guys, you're sharp." Marius smiled as he put his shaded glasses on. He slapped each of them on the back as he stood to leave.

"How do we know we can trust you?" Volk said before he turned away.

"I'm a professional, baby." Marius said as he tossed a few vinyl bills on the table. "You've each got standard Reisingers on your hips. There's a third guy waiting out back waiting to be signaled if something goes bad. Hat man here has three knives concealed on him. Oh, and you're from task force S-6319. The only intelligence I'm involved in is the best. Anyway, we should do this again some time. Ciao."

The well-dressed assassin strode out of the bistro. Vandross smiled and began to laugh after he was gone. "Only three knives." Volk gave a quizzical smile and laughed along.

Oslin Du'Plasse finished cataloging the conversation from inside the Weighted Scale's well room. Immense servers flickered and pinged with as different indicators signaled function completion. Indentured Inmates and low-ranking Scourge officials monitored the electronic data banks and dipped into the well to extract needed intelligence, likely for some menial task. Oslin took to the well room to research gang related activity and to listen in on the meeting from the wire Warden Downey had in his jacket. He listened with audio ports in the data slate Magistrate Walthune gave him as the machine converted the audio file into a written one. Upon saving the memo, the conversation was transferred to another server in Bastion Prime.

Now he needed to research the opera. Blitzday was tomorrow. They would need to think fast if they wanted to perform a snatch and grab discretely. He sought out Inquisitor Covalos to aid in coordinating a deal. He flipped through ponds of information on local sites researching the performance that would display the next night as he listened to the wailing demo of the music with his audio ports. He was baffled at the strange plotlines and formats of the performances. Oslin loved classical orchestras with extravagant harmonies and complex stringed timbres but was really the only music he enjoyed. The Herald rolled his eyes knowing that he was going to have to attend the musical. This was a high-class event, entrance fee was one hundred crowns, and his Hrimatan nobility would provide ample excuse for him being there.

Oslin chimed into the wavelength on Volk's radio bead. "Warden Downey, this is Herald Du'Plasse, acknowledge." Oslin said into a wire on the neckpiece of his battle plate as he began scanning the recreation room for Inquisitor Covalos.

"Du'Plasse," the familiar Glaswegian voice rang. "You got all of that, right?"

"Affirmative. You're returning to the Scale, right?"

"That's right. We need to draw up a plan." Downey and Du'Plasse intentionally kept from saying trigger words including the target's name or the mission's time or place, in case of any unauthorized listeners.

"I think I've got one. I'll debrief Adastra on the situation and we'll discuss it with you when you return."

"Copy, see you soon."

Oslin wandered into a locker room where he found Adastra Covalos. The bulky Inquisitor was naked except for a blood-stained towel wrapped around his waist. A thin mist lingered in the air, indicating that a hot shower just turned off. The Herald was slightly stunned at the amount of scar tissue covering his body. White lines were scattered up and down his arms and torso. Pink masses of freshly healed wounds left patches on his shoulders and legs. Du'Plasse felt it best not to mention the conglomeration fresh of tears on his back.

"Can I help you?" Adastra bellowed. Oslin just noticed he was staring and the mass of cuts on his body.

"Sorry," He shook his head. "I'm just not used to seeing someone so marred by battle."

"You don't have any?"

"Not really. I've a sizeable estate in the Du'Plasse name. It affords me the luxury of reconstructing procedures. Odds are I've had just as many wounds as you, though you wouldn't be able to tell."

"Scars are badges of honor. They are a testament to the trials one survives. I value the mangled tissues on my dermis far more than any accolade the Scourge has issued me."

"Hmm rather grim if you ask me. Though I suppose that's expected considering..." Oslin stopped himself realizing he was starting to push too far.

"Considering what nobleman?"

"Well, I suppose your troubled past has left you...humorless."

"And what exactly do you know of my past."

"More than I care to admit. I thoroughly research all Scourge personnel before I ever work with them."

"That doesn't answer my question." There was a sharpness to his voice that suggested hostility.

"Well, according to Scourge data banks, you were born in Serbia, conceived by a witch mother during some kind of ritualistic orgy, so no known father. At nine years old, you shot her dead. Seven times seems a little excessive. From there you lied about your age so that you could join the Inquisition just in time for the 14th Purus Crusade at age fourteen. I suppose having a thick scruff of hair around your chin helped sell this disguise. You've since served the Inquisition loyally, putting in your twelfth year as we speak. You were awarded the Urim, which you display on the right shoulder of your battle plate, for killing a class D Imago which called itself Cerebys. Your most recent accolade from Bishop Garrison is for the neutralization of your former Acolyte, Winona Goodberry. I think that covers everything?"

"That information is supposed to be classified."

"And it is, Theta classified. I have Epsilon clearance."

"Then you would know that I don't like people bringing up my past."

"None of us do. There are more broken families and dark pasts in the Scourge than the Arcaes we operate. I don't mean to pick at old wounds, so I'll stop elaborating."

"That would be best." Adastra began to don his battle plate starting with an undershirt of polysteel mesh from a borrowed locker unit. "So, did you come here to admire my physical scars or exploit my mental ones?"

"Neither. You'll be pleased to hear that our teammates in the field made contact with the criminal informant. We have a lead and I have a plan."

"Please, continue."

Oslin tapped and waved over his data slate and projected words and digital documents. "Marius Seta, our assassin, was hired by the Young Ichors to kill one of their stronghold bosses, Diogo Numerri. Apparently, there was outside influence, and he would know. Right now, Warden Downey thinks that information could lead back to Mortis."

"Sounds like it's as good of a lead as we're going to get." Adastra nodded as the flaksteel plates clicked into place along his torso. "Standard snatch and slam?"

"Not particularly standard, I'm afraid. The balance between the four crime organizations in Venice is fragile. Opening up a piece of turf could spark a gang war. So, we're going to pick him up while he's taking a personal day at an opera performance."

"We're going to the opera?" There was a tinge of happiness in his voice.

"Yes, tomorrow night. The Viglasia Company will be performing their-"

"Homage to the Broken World? A musical reenactment depicting the significant encounters of the Shatter?"

Oslin blinked in confusion. "You're a fan?"

"Is that a problem?"

"No, I just never pictured you as being a connoisseur of any of the arts. In truth, you appeared to me as a man who preferred the sound of silence to...anything."

"Opera is one of the few forms of music I enjoy. The Viglasia Company is one of my personal favorites. They specialize in the old Trivalet style with a focus on historical events. Their ode to the Civil Strife won them two Phantom awards last year." Adastra clicked his crimson cloak into place and pulled a little black book out of his locker.

"So, you know a lot about the opera?"

"I'm hardly an expert in the field, but I own many recordings of the company's performances." He jotted something down in the book with his gauntleted hands.

"Well, I was planning on making an approach with Inquisitor Blackwell. I thought that his experience in infiltration would make him the best man for the job. However, your expertise in the field would make you a more ideal candidate." He patted the heavily armored shoulder of the Inquisitor, who responded with a glare. "How'd you like to go undercover with me?" Adastra looked up and sighed as he scribbled down one last thing in the black notebook.

CHAPTER 6

Blitzday had come. Oslin spent the majority of the day in preparation of his disguise. As a Hrimatan, he was more than accustomed to the pomp and circumstance of formal events such as these. He couldn't brandish the house symbol of the Du'Plasse family as he preferred to do in outings such as these. He desperately organized his hair into a popular Venetian style involving the bulk of his platinum locks being pulled back in a complex knot. He adorned a green silk suit stitched with a corsage of violet roses. His alabaster undershirt openly bore the symbol of a false medicine company. The yellow silk still dangled at his throat, though folded in such a way so as to conceal his noble name. He applied a bronzing solution to his face and hands to more closely resemble the skin color of the locals, a subtle but effective addition. He placed a breath modulator in the back of his mouth to give his mouth a citrus scent. He topped his disguise off with a bejeweled silicon composite cane and lavender scented oils on his skin. He knew very well how to play the part of a noble. Such a concept was foreign to Adastra Covalos.

Oslin would have lent the Inquisitor one of his formal dressings, if it would fit. Adastra was far bulkier and taller, so nothing he owned would fit the Inquisitor. Vandross instead reworked the appearance of some of his robes. Keeping with a far simpler design, Adastra wore a simple grey suit coat over his Inquisition uniform, though all symbols and ribbons to indicate were either removed or concealed. A thin drape of black velvet ran across his arms and shoulders. His black hair was slicked back and combed for the first time in a year. "I look ridiculous." The Inquisitor grumbled as the two investigators walked the gilded rockfoam leading to the amphitheater where the performance would take place.

"You look fine," Oslin said adjusting the scarf on his neck. "Just stick with the plan. It took some serious haggling to get these tickets."

"I look fine. I look ridiculous next to you." Du'Plasse chuckled even though he wasn't quite sure if Adastra was joking or not.

"Do you have a line of sight on the target?" Oslin asked as the two began to enter a crowd of similarly dressed men and women.

"No." Covalos squinted trying to see through the dusk light for their quarry. The two were waiting in the line outside of the Broadwick Arts Center.

"Anybody have a visual?" Oslin asked the wire hidden in his ascot.

"No." Ram's Horn echoed, his voice sounding even more metallic over radio's wavelength. He was waiting in a civilian chariot, parked in the theater's lot.

"I've got him." Warden Downey chimed in who was already inside the house in the garb of a security officer. "First bar on your left. It would appear as though he's trying to find a companion to join him in his balcony."

"Well perhaps we can oblige him." Adastra responded quietly, appearing as though he was speaking to Oslin.

"I don't think you want the kind of company he's hunting for." Volk replied, implying the mob boss's intentions.

"Well, let's divert his attentions with some pleasant conversation." Du'Plasse nodded to Adastra as he handed his ticket to a bouncer on the outside of the gaudy amphitheatre.

"Keep us updated." Vandross said who was dressed as an usher inside. "I'll watch the perimeter for anybody without an invitation."

"Confirmed," Volk echoed. "Ram and I will be waiting at the snatch point."

"Are you ready, Adastra?" Oslin asked tapping his silicon cane to the polished tile floors.

"Let's get this over with." The Inquisitor moaned.

The lobby of the amphitheater was bright with colors that hurt the eyes. The waxed stone tiles were glazed with burgundy and orange. A chandelier dangled from the painted ceiling and shimmered with blasted sand. Two bars stocked with exotic liquors flanked either side of the lobby. A gaggle of loud-mouthed attendees, dressed in clowny clothes and drenched in pungent perfumes, cluttered the open chamber like a mob. Red vested servants moved in a circuit with trays of drinks and hors d'oeuvres. Adastra always wanted to see the Viglasia Company perform live, but the company he'd have to stomach always prevented him from doing so.

The two investigators approached the bar on the left where Volk previously spotted their quarry. Sure enough, Diogo Numerri was at the bar, attempting to woo a woman. The man was portly, to put it kindly, sweat dripping from his brow. The hair on his head was thin, as if it was actively trying to flee his scalp. His cream-colored suit, which was no doubt purchased with drug money, was custom tailored to fit his girth. He pushed a cocktail over to the woman who was far younger and prettier than he would ever be deserving of. She smiled coyly before walking away with the drink in hand. He pushed a thick glass monocle up on his eye and frowned as he realized what just happened.

Oslin made approach to the cushioned barstool. He threw a bill onto the counter. "Another round for this poor soul," Oslin told the red vested bartender. "Ah the fickle mistress of love turns her back once again."

"Forget love," Diogo snapped. "I was after her sweet hips. Thank you, mister..."

"Narcus," Oslin extended his hand. "Evander Narcus of the Platinum District. One for me as well, garcon." He snapped at the bartender.

"As in the Narcus family, the famous surgeons of the Bulwark?"

"The very same." He said as the bartender slid two small crystals with a wood-colored fluid inside it.

"Well, I'm Diogo Numerri. I'm a medicine man myself. My condolences for your loss." The Surgeon General of Hrimata used to be

Harlen Narcus, recently dead of old age. Oslin chose the family for his disguise as a means of sparking conversation.

"Don't be," Oslin rolled his eyes. "Harlen was just a distant uncle and a braggart. I'm here to escape the unending humdrum of his endless memorial." He sipped from the crystal.

"Well, to hell with him." Numerri chuckled. Adastra winced slightly at the blasphemous curse before he made the approach.

"Yes, I liken its length to Van Giersbergen's iteration of The First Regent's Death." Adastra noted, joining in the conversation. "A wondrous mourning dirge. It's a pity so many people of Templym are so uncivilized. It's a rather underappreciated performance in the public eye. Most people nowadays don't have the attention span for a five-hour performance."

"I'm unfamiliar with her work." Numerri noted curiously. "She's come highly recommended to me, but I've never had the chance to listen to them."

"Diogo, this is my business partner, Goffry Benaton." Oslin motioned to the Inquisitor. "He recommended this performance to me."

"Evander has asked me for a method of unique entertainment." Adastra continued staying in the character of a regal man. "Barring anything illegal, I recommended the opera. It's a soothing and harmonic experience."

"I see you're a cultured man," Numerri laughed as he finished off his drink. "I assure you, Mr. Narcus, you're in for quite the show. I've heard nothing but praises about the Homage to a Broken World, though this is a first time for me."

"I've seen this performance once in Frankon." Adastra continued. "It was splendid, enough for a second viewing. The Bertonents opened for them, and the moment Dianne hits the climax of the last nation's death, it sent a chill down my spine."

"What seats do you two gentlemen have?" Numerri pondered.

"We have VIP balcony passes." Oslin said.

"Marvelous." He clapped his greasy hands together. "You can join me in my nest. I've got it in good with the owners as I am a regular attendee. I'll arrange two seats in my privy."

"Fabulous." Adastra said with a forced smile.

The conversation continued for an hour or so. Oslin somehow managed to get Numerri to pay for all of the drinks that were passed around. Adastra continued to talk opera with the gang father for the duration before the beginning of the performance. Vandross continued patrolling the halls scouting out Numerri's security detail. Five armed bodyguards walked around the complex, constantly checking on the gang boss. He pointed them out to the rest of S-6319 so they would not be caught flat-footed when the time to kidnap him came.

Vandross scratched at his low-cut hair. He hated not having his hat on. In terms of sacrifices that he had to make while undercover, this was a pretty minor one. He had dressed up as cultists, madmen, gangers, and vagabonds in his service to the Inquisition. He was up on the ledge of an upper floor, appearing in the same red vest as the waiting staff.

"Volk," Vandross whispered into his wire. "They're in."

"Beautiful." The Warden replied happily. "Ram, do you have Mr. Numerri's drugs ready for him?"

"Punch." Ram's Horn replied.

"Oh, that sounds exotic." Volk replied sarcastically. He knew of course that was the Retriever's way of saying he wasn't going to give him anything other than a beating. "All we're waiting for now is for Oslin and Adastra to get him out to the van for the "deal"."

"Copy that, I'll move to the next recon point to..." Something caught the Inquisitor's eye. One of Numerri's bodyguards was speaking with someone.

"Vandross, you there?" Volk replied.

"Yeah, I'm still here. I think we've got a problem." Vandross saw a familiar figure. The man exchanged words with the guard, concluding the exchange with a familiar backhand to other man's chest. When he turned, he saw the cocky smile and immediately recognized Marius Seta. "Seta's here."

"What?" Volk gasped. "Why is the assassin here? I thought he trusted us to disappear Numerri for him."

"I'll take care of it. Adastra, Oslin, be advised our sleepman has shown up uninvited. Running interference now."

Adastra and Oslin could still hear the entire exchange going on in the secure radio wavelength. Their wires concealed beneath their finery were designed to send the sound waves through the body and vibrate the bones in the ear canals, allowing them to listen in as though they were wearing audio ports. Their disguises required the specialized devices for an increased level of subtly.

"I copy," Oslin whispered into his scarf while Numerri and Adastra continued discussing performances unknown to the Herald. "Should we accelerate the plan or move to the secondary?"

"We have a secondary?" Vandross asked.

"Of course, I have a secondary, a tertiary too." Du'Plasse quietly snapped. "What's your plan of approach with Seta?"

"I plan to approach, try to get him to back off."

Oslin rolled his eyes at the joke. "I'll continue with the primary plan on schedule with caution. Notify me if anything changes."

Oslin rejoined the Inquisitor and their quarry. Adastra was chuckling, which was odd considering his stern demeanor, as they exchanged memories of comedic performances. This confused the Herald, but he continued with the party, keeping the mood full of humor and alcohol.

They made it to Numerri's balcony. It was a small and private alcove with three heavily cushioned chairs and small artificial wood tables. The three lounged in the small balcony, drinking cocktails and imbibing in exotic appetizers. The Scourge warriors would have been thoroughly drunk, as drunk as Numerri was, if it weren't for their training. The intense enrollment process of the Scourge involved poison resistance training, which dulled the effects of normally lethal toxins and rendered the effects of alcohol practically benign. They were skilled enough to act as though it was taking its toll on their senses. Inebriating the quarry was a part of the plan.

"You would not believe the amount of narcotics we supply to Venice," Oslin chuckled. "Every medical grade from pain killers to organ nullers. What is it about this country that requires so many depressants?"

"Bunch of stuff shoed ninnies." Numerri chuckled through a fog of liquor scented vapors spraying from his mouth. "This country is full of a bunch of kittens who've never worked a day in their lives. They can't handle everyday stress. Why else would people like us be so well employed?"

Oslin's eyes perked up at that, "Are you in the pharmaceutical industry also?" He asked as if unaware of Numerri's profession.

"Oh, officially no, but in truth, yes." Both were unsure if it was the booze or just sheer arrogance that coaxed the ganger into giving up a confession so quickly.

"Diogo, you sly fox," Adastra noted. "Are you suggesting illegal drug trade?"

"Oh of course I am!" He stammered. "Don't you know that the Young Ichors are the true masters of this petty nation? They keep the boiling blood of the locals calm with their specialized trade."

"Drug trade?" Oslin chuckled. "That's a dangerous business, albeit... a profitable one."

Numerri laughed and pointed a fat sweaty finger at Du'Plasse. "Mr. Narcus, I'm beginning to think our meeting here isn't particularly random."

"You see, Evander," Adastra exclaimed. "I told you he would figure us out."

"Well, why don't I just address the lighthouse in the room?" Oslin laughed. "Mr. Benaton and I are entrepreneurs. Officially, we're overseeing a transport of raw unprocessed opium. However, the shipment ledgers read that there are 100 pounds less than there actually are."

"That gives us an extra 100 pounds of opium that we're looking to... unload." Adastra noted. "If only there was somebody who could distribute that for us."

"You need a buyer?" Diogo noted, self-righteous that he was putting the pieces together. "And you know that the Young Ichors are the best in the nation."

"Hypothetically," Oslin smiled coyly. "If you could get us in touch with somebody in their ranks, we could sell our cargo."

"You know," He smiled finishing his fourth drink. "I might be able help you out with that, assuming I could sample your product."

"We have some samples in our chariot." Adastra noted. "After the performance, we'd be happy to give you a taste, as well as some extra for your friends."

"I like the sound of that." Numerri said as the lights in the amphitheatre began to dim and the chattering crowds began to hush. "Quiet my new friends, the performance is about to begin."

The nation of Madagast was once a remote tropical island. After the Shatter, the environment changed drastically as the god-AIs waged meteorological and geological warfare. In the crossfire, the island's jungles flooded, and its mountains tumbled into the sea. Madagast was now a collection of boggy enclaves. No civilizations existed there, as the warring marauder tribes had no interests outside of vying for territory and despised the idea of integrating into Templym. The Kalkhanian marauders had recently come under a largely singular rule by a shaman named Bog Mama.

Arodi Auzlanten wandered through the swampland, flying from archipelago to island to isle. Any man would look at his path and assume he was lost, but he was following a strong trace of demonic activity invisible to all but himself. The dense foliage blotted the dwindling sun from the sky as thick clouds of mosquitoes and gnats blocked line of sight. As the spectacular individual walked the mud drenched algae floors, the fog of insects would part as though afraid of him. Auzlanten's feet actually touched the ground, but no filth was caked on his skin or clothing.

The Imago signature was potent and growing stronger. This was obvious by the tribalist marauders that began to attack him as he walked the path. The madmen were naked aside from tribal fetishes and dirty animal skins. They carried spears and shields of poorly stitched hide and bones. Clay and paint were smeared on their nearly ebony skin in tribalistic patterns. Each man showed a variant of ballooned disfigurement. Their shoulders and chests were swollen to the point of disfigurement. Such disfigurement should have seen them crippled to the point of immobility, yet they circled Arodi with predatory intent. This was the product of a sickly combination of unnatural arts and genetic mutation. Auzlanten stood staunch over the moss blotched dirt as he was slowly surrounded by over thirty marauders.

He stood unfazed, not letting his stony visage show any emotion. "I'm here for Bog Mama." Auzlanten spoke in the local dialect which involved emphasized vowels and hand motions. "You don't have to die for her. Her reign ends today."

The tribesmen let out a guttural war cry. They charged at Arodi with a fanatical ferocity, bone weapons sharp and brandishing. This was no surprise. He did not draw Leagna until the first spear struck his chest, which shattered on impact. The sabre took off a head as it flew out of its sheath and into Auzlanten's right hand, gleaming with brilliant gold and violet which was a stark contrast to the bleak brown and putrid green of the bog. With two more swings, five marauders fell to the agile slashes of the blade. Auzlanten then pitched his famous sabre out to the marauders that were uselessly shooting flint arrows at him. Leagna lanced through the air, flying as if it were sentient. The weapon punched a hole into the first archer's chest before soaring to impale the next. As his sabre perforated marauder after marauder, he struck down assailants with his bare hands. With a single backhand he sent a man flying more than a hundred feet into a pool of piranha and crocodile infested waters. He leaned into his other hand as it formed a fist, which blew another's head off in a messy geyser of grey matter. One marauder grabbed Auzlanten from behind. He elbowed the grappler back fifty feet while collapsing the attacker's chest. The remaining marauders angled their weapons at Templym's founder, bolstering for an assault. Without making any physical motion, Arodi stared them down. They clutched their throats, dropping their weapons and shields as they uselessly gasped for breath. Leagna impaled the final archer and returned to his hand as though called. Blood boiled off the blade even though no heat radiated from it. Auzlanten stowed the sword and walked through the small crowd of mutated marauders as they collapsed to the ground chocking on their own windpipes. "You could have walked away." Templym's master uttered in temple-tongue.

The next assault, as Arodi followed the trail of the Imago, came from mutant beasts. The creatures resembled wild dogs or hyenas, but no longer possessed any trace of their natural bodies. Their hair was matted and tangled with dirt. Their eyeballs pulsed and throbbed as the swollen red orbs flashed with bloodthirsty rage. Teeth jutted at obtuse angles from their maws. Their talons were like crooked meat hooks. They were the size of horses. Thick spikes of bone jutted out of their legs and back and they shuttered as a blood-curdling growl shook in their throats. There were well over a dozen in all.

Arodi Auzlanten let Leagna fly from its sheath and back into his hand. As the mutant hounds stalked around the man, he did something no man who intended to fight would do. He shut his eyes. The platinum thorns on his head began to glow with a veil of silver light. With inhuman speed, he slammed a jeweled fist into the sloppy algae infested ground. A spear of similar silver light shot out from his hand and penetrated each of the abomination hounds. Most died instantly, but the two or three that were only marred met their end at the blade of Leagna. As Leagna clicked back into its home and Arodi turned on his heel to continue walking the path, the dead hounds burst into flame.

The Imago stench trail led to a castle, or what passed for one in Madagast. The structure was not a literal fortress but was comparatively so juxtaposed with the ramshackle huts of sticks and clay surrounding it. The "castle" was comprised of makeshift bricks of dehydrated mud and clay with shale reinforcement. Two more devil hounds prowled the outskirts and warped archers patrolled the tree bark roofs. They were dispatched immediately as Arodi Auzlanten strode down the beaten dirt path, humorless and serious, no blood or filth on his robes or skin. They fell to the mud dead as their necks lurched to the side. A polished jet boot stepped onto a pile of small animal bones in front of the palm leaf door and Templym's founder stopped. He looked up to the roof and took record of the animal skulls, feathers, and dried plants that formed a variety of unholy fetishes. He then parted leaves and stepped in the chamber.

The large hut's interior was dimly lit by a pyre in the center of the chamber. The dank throne room bore the stench of hallucinogens. A number of tanned skins, man and animal, lined the dusty brick walls. Similar fetishes were nailed to bare corners of the wiry wooden ceiling. More tribal marauders scattered the dirt floor, brandishing weapons of crudely forged iron. Their mutations were far more severe than the first line of resistance Arodi met, having lanky limbs and pulsating muscle that bulged through their skin. At the head of the putrid room was a throne raised on a stone dais. The seat was made of dried up bones and pelts topped with a human skull. Bog Mama sat in this throne.

She was a witch, no doubt about that. Bog Mama was fat, skin slumping in lumpy curtains that draped over the throne. The proportions were off, with an oversized head and stomach, even when accounting for the masses of fat. Her skin was caked in dried mud with a film of mucus like paint arranged into Imago runes. Gnarled furs and tangled vines decorated her unmentionables while a crocodile head, with skin and tooth still intact, topped her bloated head. A necklace of snail shells and snake fangs was wrapped taught around one of her chins.

"Is this the mean man who's been knocking your brothers and fathers around?" Bog Mama bellowed in the native marauder language.

"I am Arodi Auzlanten," He responded in the same tongue, his hands tucked behind his back and composure stalwart. "Master of Templym and Voice of the Lord. You have something I seek."

"We all seek something out of life." The giant woman gaggled. "I seek power and pleasure. How I go about getting that is none of your concern. Enlighten me Azlan, what exactly is it that you seek?"

"The Idolacreid, an ancient blasphemous tome containing dark secrets."

The pile of fat chortled a sloppy laugh, spit and bile flinging from the corners of her mouth. "Then we seek the same things. You want to conquer worlds and stimulate your senses, just as I. It would seem we are kin."

"We are nothing alike. I want the Idolacreid so that I may remove its blight from this world entirely. Its corrupting powers are too dangerous. God demands it be removed from His planet."

"Not so similar after all." She said with a saggy frown. "Though I can understand why you'd be keen on getting rid of it. The knowledge that good book has is... titillating." The rolls of fat on Bog Mama's body began gyrating with excitement.

"You've read it?"

"Only small portions. The Nephilim forbade anything else."

"You've seen the Nephilim?"

"You can't trick me boy." The fatty rings undulated even more as she leaned forward. "You think I'm just going to keep babbling on, revealing our grand machination? I'm smarter than that. The ancient knowledge of the Idolacreid is locked away in my mind. The power of the Nephilim and Sub'hirtaj flows in my veins. If you are not with us, then you are against us."

Bog Mama stood from her disheveled throne, which was a feat, considering her unnatural girth. The lobes of fat rushed and pulsed with crackling energy as she began chanting. Arodi stared intently, quietly bolstering himself in preparation for a spell attack. The arcane utterance ended with a deep and gurgling squeal. Then, instead of an attack being lashed out at Auzlanten, she spawned something. She birthed, literally birthed, a horrific conglomeration of flesh. The fetal looking creature plopped down the raised platform drenched in birthing fluids and blood. It barely resembled a human infant, more so a mass of tendrils and joints that chattered and clicked as it writhed and gurgled. Arodi Auzlanten concealed the internal disgust he felt.

Bog Mama bellowed a wicked laugh that would send chills down any man's spine. As though she had not just given birth to an unholy monstrosity, her bloated hands motioned over to the wet flesh pile she just spawned. Blackish green energy pulsed from her fingers and sank into the creature. Multiple pops and cracks as bone and tendons shifted were disturbingly audible as the creature swelled in size. The abomination quickly surpassed the size of a common man, towering up to nearly twenty feet. Its spindly limbs resembled sinewy umbilical cords and there were far too many of them. The crooked giant loomed ominously over the fire pit and lacked any eyes or mouth. Its bones were twisted and pointed at sharp angles. The only logical thing to do for any commoner would be to scream and run. Arodi Auzlanten continued to stand in place, hands connected behind his back, staring at the monstrosity birthed before him.

The witch pointed and uttered more blasphemy in her witch-speech. The giant flesh creature lumbered towards Auzlanten. Bodily fluid and explosive energy still dripped from its tendrils. The tentacles lashed out, extending beyond logical flexibility, in perfect unison. Each one could have easily penetrated the body of any human. As though it was all a coordinated combat, Auzlanten spun on his heel drawing Leagna in a fluid motion. He parried away lethal strikes and lopped off appendages. Arodi deftly blocked and dodged the killing barrage of flesh. With every shear of the shimmering sabre, a wriggling tentacle slapped to the ground, and a new one stuck out from the wound to replace it. Auzlanten quickly realized the futility of the strategy.

Arodi allowed for a tendril to slap him across the room. The strike sent him flying into the pyre in the center of the chamber. He turned midair to land on his feet. The flame engulfed him instantly but did not hurt him. He pointed Leagna at the abomination. The fire wrapped around the length of his arm and then the sword. The end of the blade turned the natural red fire into a scorching cone of blue-white flame directed at the monster. If the flesh thing had a mouth it would have screeched in pain. The raw skin bubbled and churned as it dripped from its crooked skeleton. When all of the fire was expended, he allowed the creature no time to let its body heal. He propelled himself in a high jump. Auzlanten arced down with the sabre as the endpoint. Leagna sliced through the crown of the witch spawn's head and clear down its groin. The incision flashed with white light before the giant creature exploded in a puff of blood-mist and viscera.

The mutant marauders wasted no time in responding with an assault of their own. Without looking around, Arodi stomped his foot to the ground to create a shockwave of pure force. This sent the smoldering pyre logs flying, impaling the marauders that stood behind them. The few that were not killed by the shrapnel were cut down with finesse when they pressed the attack further. They were not all dead yet when Bog Mama pressed her attack further. "You get away from my husband sons!" With that disturbing exclamation she shot burning bolts of sickening green lightning at Auzlanten. With no break in his swordsmanship he either deflected the lightning with the sabre or absorbed the electricity and allowed it to flow into the ground.

When the last mutated marauder was cut down. Arodi turned his sights to the witch. She shot another green bolt at him which he passed through his body and back at the bloated witch. She was stricken back with enough force to crumble her throne, flopping heron her back. Arodi swung Leagna down in a vertical arc and struck the ground. A curved pillar of light shot upwards, punching through the wooden ceiling as it blasted towards Bog Mama. The column should have crashed into her and broken her bones like a tsunami wave. Instead the light pillar melted away inches before making impact.

Bog Mama let out an ominous bellow. She floated into the air, her fat folds pulsing as a gust of wind scratched at Auzlanten's whipping hair. The crocodile head she was previously wearing as a headdress floated off of her. It expanded and swelled, producing a number of yellow eyes and spear like teeth. The head became accompanied by an ethereal body of shimmering green light which bore wiry talons across its seven legs. The phantom body took a physical form as muscular tissue and thick scales layered over its frame.

"Say hello to Sub'hirtaj," Bog Mama gurgled, still cackling.

The multi-eyed, asymmetrical creature took up the bulk of the chamber. Its unholy presence was enough to nauseate from a mile away. This lanky scaled beast, which sweated viscous black poison, was the physical manifestation of a demon. Sub'hirtaj was the Imago patron of Bog Mama.

The Imago began assailing with an ear-piercing shriek. The sonic attack reverberated, rattling bone and bursting blood vessels. At least, that was what the scream should have done. Auzlanten cringed as the sound waves struck but did not bleed or collapse. He leapt to the beast's crooked maw to lunge his sabre down its throat. Sub'hirtaj crunched down with titanic force as the blade met what functioned as its gullet. A hot jet of black bile erupted from the wound. The fluid sent Auzlanten back to a flaky stone wall. The liquid reeked of venom and plague. Arodi spit out a mouthful of the bile and shot a missile of golden fire at the creature. The demon wailed as its scaled skin was scorched off. Old, blackened scales sloughed off its hide as new scales slowly germinated in their place. Sub'hirtaj shot out cascades of putrid mucus from its crooked yellow eyes. The acidic solution was redirected by Arodi in a complex gesture, towards Bog Mama. The Imago brought its tail up to shield the witch from the deadly tide of sulfuric bile.

Arodi anticipated that motion. With the beast's tail in the air, its underside was elevated. With speed faster than the eye could perceive, he darted at the underbelly of the Imago. He brought Leagna against one of its armored legs, causing the beast to rock as it was wracked with pain. Sub'hirtaj tried to bring its full weight down in response as another geyser of boiling bile stung Arodi's face. The sabre pierced the rough scales as Auzlanten brought the blade up in response, fooling the monster into impaling itself. As it lurched back and Leagna was withdrawn, Arodi plunged his free hand into the open seeping wound. New scales began shrouding over the hole in its belly, trapping Arodi's arm inside its body. Calling upon the powers of Heaven, Arodi focused his might into the hand. White light exploded. The monster filled up with the light as if it were liquid energy. With a final push of force, the light overwhelmed the frame of the reptilian creature. Sub'hirtaj exploded from its underside outwards in a blinding array of starlight and dark boiling bile. Bog Mama screamed as she collapsed into the ground, seeing her Imago lord brought to its end. As the fog of cleared, the figure of Arodi Auzlanten grasping Leagna, free of any stains or markings, standing in silent victory, was revealed.

He treaded over to the fallen witch. Her unnaturally bloated body was now still as she lay helplessly prone. He pointed his sabre, alive with silver light, at her stomach. "Your patron is dead." Arodi spoke sternly. "Your power is gone. Tell me where the Idolacreid is."

"I will say nothing." Bog Mama gurgled, unable to hold herself up any long.

"I believe you." Auzlanten drove the point of his sword into the witch, ripping it down the length of her torso. The mutated witch belched open in a bilious tangle of steaming entrails, killing her instantly. "I don't need you to be alive to learn everything you know."

CHAPTER 7

Marius Seta took his position in the balcony near the climax of the performance. He carried a brown leather briefcase which he set down next to the only empty chair on the ledge. He hummed a lighthearted bouncy tune to himself, completely ignoring the serious and deep voices bellowing from the center stage. He pulled out a telescopic monocle, intended to observe the performers on stage below. Instead, Marius used it to observe the other balconies. He scanned the nests, searching for Diogo Numerri.

He smacked his lips together upon catching his target's face and grinned. He unpacked his briefcase opening up the components of a compact longcannon. Marius continued humming his tune, as he assembled the firearm. The absence of lighting and the overwhelming volume of the performance provided a thick blanket of cover around the amphitheater. This would ensure nobody would see or hear the shot. Seta propped up the freshly assembled longcannon on the polished wood ledge, aiming his sight directly at the chest of Diogo Numerri who sat in between two men he was unfamiliar with.

Still humming his tune, he focused the cannon's scope. He lined up the measurement lines with the white tie hanging from his fatty torso, right where his heart should be. His tune concluded and he began paying attention to his breathing. He slowed his breath, intentionally lowering his heart rate. The fewer factors he had altering his aim, the better. He then accounted for the difference in distance from the suppressor and angled himself upwards. Numerri wasn't moving, locked onto the Viglasia Company's performance.

This made the shot much simpler. He gently began applying pressure on the trigger, waiting for a moment in the opera that was filled with more calamitous sound. He was fortunate that the singers were reenacting the Shatter, making the performance full of bombastic percussion and powerful scream-like vocals. He was just waiting for a big enough explosion of noise to cover up the sound of the cannon's shot.

Suddenly a hard piece of metal tapped Marius on the temple. He knew that feeling well enough, the barrel of a gun. Slowly he turned his head, noting a Reisinger with a mantra emblazoned in goldenrod acrylic. Vandross Blackwell had his pistol trained on the assassin.

"Hat man!" Seta said as he lowered the longcannon off of the ledge. "Good to see you again. I didn't recognize you without... you know... the hat."

Vandross rolled his eyes, keeping the barrel aimed at Seta. "What are you doing here? I thought you were going to let us disappear Numerri."

"Well, I planned on it." Marius chuckled, keeping his humors high. This clearly wasn't the first time he had a gun on him. "Of course, the Young Ichors still expect me to carry out the hit. I've got an in with one of Numerri's bodyguards and he was looking for me. If I saw you and bullet face here, I was just going to back off and let you do your thing. I didn't, so I went with my first plan."

"Well here I am." Vandross said. "You can back off."

"Oh, so those two guys in his balcony are with you? That makes sense. Any who, can't do that anymore."

"And why not?"

"I already told the guard what I was planning on doing already. He's outside the balcony's entrance waiting for me to lug his corpse out. I told him I was going to shoot him and get rid of the body in the middle of the opera."

"So, you're telling me that there's an armed mobster right outside of the door waiting for somebody to be carrying out a bloody body?"

"Look at you hat man, you're pretty bright."

Vandross lowered his pistol and pinched the bridge of his nose. "And what happens if Numerri walks out of there on his own two feet?"

"Well, I could talk to the guard and let him know that I'm switching up the plan, but he'll be suspicious if I do that." Marius began disassembling his longcannon seeing that he wouldn't need to use it anymore.

"So, we've got to lug his dead body off of the balcony otherwise..."

"Well, the Young Ichors will probably get suspicious. If they start snooping around, they might find out I'm an informant for the Scourge. If I'm discovered, I can't be a rat for you all anymore. Let's be honest, you don't want that."

"You're a real character Seta."

"But you love me all the same, hat man."

Adastra loved seeing the Viglasia Company live. He particularly enjoyed Dianne's superb soprano voice during this portion, which was a stylized dirge enacting the fourth day of the Shatter. The Inquisitor loathed that he couldn't focus all of his attention on the performance. He was constantly diverting his attention to the pudgy drug pushing mobster on his left. He was constantly shifting his gaze between the stage and his quarry, ensuring everything was going according to plan. He had to admit however, this kind of manhunt was far more serene than his usual Imago cult hunts.

"Du'Plasse, Covalos, listen up." Vandross' voice chimed in their ears. "I know you can't talk but I'm assuming you can still hear me. Change of plan, Numerri's bodyguard is expecting the sleepman to dispose of his dead body in about a minute. You've got to knock him out, make it look like he's been shot, and carry him out and to the drop point."

"Well that's a development." Volk responded from the caravan. "Ram and I are on standby, ready to roll out when you get here." Oslin and Adastra exchanged a brief glance of confusion.

"Just say 'hummingbird' to the bodyguard and he'll look the

other way." Vandross conferred. "Other than that... I got nothing. I guess, I don't know, punch him in the face?"

Without another moment's notice, Adastra Covalos did just that. He brought his heavy hand directly to Numerri's jaw in a swift jab. The impulse of Adastra's fist sent the ganger out of the cushy chair and into the carpeted floor. Diogo Numerri was completely void of consciousness.

"Well, that worked, I suppose." Oslin said with his standard pretentious tone of voice.

"Grab his legs." Adastra grunted as he rubbed blood that was dripping from Numerri's nose into his suit. "Tell me Oslin; was this your secondary or tertiary plan?"

"Quaternary actually." He said as he hefted the ganger's legs. "I'd anticipated we'd storm the stage before we subjected ourselves to such primitive tactics."

"Things rarely operate as anticipated." Adastra mumbled, silently disappointed that he would not get to witness the remainder of the performance.

Adastra and Oslin retrieved their quarry, albeit in an unconventional way. As Seta instructed, the word 'hummingbird' cleared them from the bodyguard's hostility. Seeing as the stairwell contained far too much traffic, they escorted their quarry to a maintenance elevator where Vandross was waiting with the employee clearance he had commandeered. The lift brought the soldiers to the private underground parking facility where Volk and Ram were waiting with the caravan. Admittedly, the plan did not go as gracefully as S-6319 hoped that it would. However, one could not question the results.

The syndicate boss was knocked out for the duration of the return to the Weighted Scale. He was promptly placed into a holding cell, shackled to its sheet metal floors. Once awake, Numerri began throwing a fit, screaming colorful obscenities at the survey cameras in the chamber's four corners. Little did he know that he was sitting in one of the greatest marvels that came from Templym's founding.

The Veritas Chambers were the most relevant and revolutionary of Auzlanten's creations. Inside these rooms the truth was revealed. Veritas Chambers negated one's ability to intentionally lie. The Scourge had been using them since Auzlanten introduced the first ones after the 2nd Purus Crusade. He personally crafted all of them. Nobody was sure of the exact manner of technology or holy power that made these seemingly average rooms compel the truth from the guilty. With the integration of these cryptic devices, innocents could be cleared unequivocally, and the guilty parties rightfully condemned. This ensured certainty of the Scourge's swift and merciless justice.

The cold steel door clicked as the security locks shifted open and the heavy metal slab scraped against the floor panels. Volk stepped in, his freshly polished battle plate glimmering cobalt and jet, the impact of his boots clattering as he stepped in. Diogo Numerri was still in his cream-colored suit, albeit with sticky red stains across it, standing with chain cuffs on his arms and legs. He had been pacing back and forth around the perimeter of the claustrophobic, featureless room where he had previously been yelling at the four survey cameras in the corners.

"It's about bloody time." Numerri complained, his face a blend of relief that it was not a rival mob that had captured him but dread that Scourge did. "I've been here for a roughing hour with no food or water."

"You've been awake for ten minutes darling." Volk said as the door behind him slammed. He carried a manila portfolio, case files spilling out of the edges. "Though I suppose you really believe that it was an hour, don't you?"

"I demand to know what's happening." Diogo continued to whine, stamping his tailored boots to the iron floor. "Who are you? I demand a barrister."

"Before we begin, I'm obliged by the Scourge to inform you of your rights." Downey said, calmly penning a page in the folder. "You are currently inside of one of Arodi Auzlanten's infamous Veritas Chambers. Anything you say will be considered truth and every word will be recorded as evidence in your condemnation, if any. Silence will be perceived as guilt. When tried, you have a right to defend your own actions in front of a judiciary or hire someone of your own funding to do so in your stead. Mercy is a concept that the Scourge seldom deals in. Your best option is to cooperate in full. Are we clear Mr. Numerri?"

"I want my barrister." Numerri's legs were noticeably quivering.

"And you'll get it when it's that time. Firstly, I need you to take a seat." Numerri looked around the room. He was confused, seeing as there was no furniture to sit on. "On the floor please." Volk motioned to the ground.

"I'm above this." He protested.

"Suit yourself." Volk reached down to the ground with his free hand and yanked at the chain at his ankles. He tumbled and fell backwards, hitting his head on the steel wall before sliding lazily down to the floor. "There we go." Downey crossed his legs and sat down directly in front of him. His leathery face was warm and friendly, the opposite of Numerri's smooth greasy pout.

"Let's start with a quick run down." Volk said, maintaining a welcoming voice. "My name is Warden Downey, commanding officer of task force S-6319 of the Shackle. You are Diogo Rodrigo Numerri, a small-time gang boss in charge of the Young Ichors' house in Bruccol's Hospitaller's District."

"What? That's... I'm not..." Numerri was trying to deny such a claim. The power of the Veritas Chamber suppressed the lie trying to belch out of the ganger's throat. It looked as though he was literally choking on his words.

"That's one attempt to deceive an officer of the Scourge, that's another prosecutable offense you know?" Downey chuckled. "Anyway, I've taken a look at local arbiter reports of your activities in the area. The Young Ichors have been peddling narcotics, stimulants, organ nullers, and other poisons in this district alone surmounting to around three royals a year. That's a lot of hookies and overdoses that are around because of you. Do you deny involvement in this illegal drug trade?"

"I don't... I would..." Numerri desperately tried to spit out his lies but could not.

"Three months ago, Bethesda Pianissimo was raided by the Young Ichors. A lot of people were killed. Did you orchestrate this attack?"

"I was not personally involved in that raid." Numerri was choosing his words carefully and dancing around the question.

"Yes or no Numerri, did you plan out this attack?"

Diogo sighed and shook his head. "Yes, I did." He had given up on fibbing.

"Good, now you're cooperating." The veteran officer glinted his teeth. "So, now that we're on the same page, I'm going to spell this out to you. I'm new in town, as you probably guessed from the accent, I don't have primary jurisdiction. That would be Conservator Travvec. So, I don't plan on prosecuting you myself. I'm only looking for answers on the previously mentioned hospital raid, but I do have a rough idea as to what you're being charged with. The way I see it, you're looking at a week in the local Arace before you're put before the judgment of the Lord personally." Numerri swallowed hard at the casual nature Volk mentioned his execution. "However, I think I can probably talk Travvec out of death penalty. Assuming you just answer my questions, give me a couple of leads, you're looking at..." Downey stroked his chin making a humming sound. "Two months in the Arace with five or six years of indentured servitude. Give or take of course, I hear Travvec's a bit trigger happy. I think that's the deal you're going to want to go with."

"Why do you say that?" Numerri whimpered. "Why do you think I'm just going to give up my brothers? The syndicate has been a family to me for years."

"Two reasons Diogo." Downey tossed a few papers at the ganger. "The first is because you're a coward. You've never taken a stand for something where you couldn't profit. When the Venetian White Capes drafted you to fight in the 14th, you received a medical leave due to a broken foot. Of course, your medical records show that you've never had so much as a cavity let alone something that'll warrant inability to fight. In 2711 you were asked to testify as a witness to a manslaughter case but denied, probably on account of the large deposit made in your bank account. You've always done what's best for you, nobody else. You're smart enough to realize that this is what's best for you."

"The second?" Numerri asked.

"I beg your pardon?"

"You said you had two reasons." He sat himself up and leered forward. Volk's battle plate gave off the illusion that Numerri was much smaller than the Warden. "What's the second?"

"Of course, how could I forget?" Volk chuckled. "The Young Ichors paid a contract killer to put you down. If we weren't there, you'd be chum in the sea by now. Your family hates you. Why not stick it to them?"

Numerri's face collapsed as his heart sank at this realization. "The chamber works on me too." Volk responded. "I can't lie to you just like you can't lie to me. We saved your life, whether you like that fact or not."

"What do you want to know?" Numerri asked begrudgingly.

"Tell me about the hospital job," Volk said as he handed photos from the scene of the crime to the ganger. "Whose idea was it? Who helped you?"

"I was approached with an opportunity by a young lady." Diogo said. "She told me that the hospital was getting a fresh shipment of drugs. The weird thing is that she didn't want in on the cache, she just needed manpower."

"That doesn't make any sense." Volk said, his clouded and clear eyes squinting. "What's the point of stealing a shipment of pharmaceuticals if you don't get a share of the loot?"

"She wanted the medical equipment. Heart monitors, pulse jumpers, drug pumps, you know, standard hospital stuff. That was the deal we made. Our boys would go in, steal everything, kill everyone, and divvy up the loot after the fact."

"This woman, who was she?"

"I don't know. She approached me out of nowhere, called herself Tsuni. She told one of my dealers she had a job for me before I ever met her. I heard her out, liked the deal, and you know what happened after that."

"What did she look like?"

"She was gorgeous. Based on her accent, I think she was from Jaspin or Nenwhar, somewhere from the Northern UPA, I'm willing to bet. Brown hair, brown eyes, always wore a tight purple dress."

"Tsuni have any unique marks like scars, tattoos, jewelry?"

"Yeah," Numerri scratched at his greasy hair. "She had these weird line tattoos on the top of her head right on her temples. They were greenish blue, a few of them around the temples, like wires or something. She had this strange silver necklace that never shifted when she walked. She always wore a glove made of some kind of silver mylar on her left hand."

"Interesting, I don't suppose you could get back in touch with her?"

"No," He looked down afraid. "She was clear that we were never to speak again after the job. Like I said, my guess is somewhere in the upper UPA. That's all I've got, I'm sorry."

"Knox Mortis." Volk said as he got on his feet. "You know the name?"

"No, should I?"

"I guess not. I'll talk to the Conservator, try and keep you from being executed. The Scourge appreciates your cooperation. If I have any additional questions, I'll be sure to ask." With that, Volk Downey clicked open the security door and waltzed out.

The remainder of S-6319 was watching the interrogation as it underwent. All had returned to their battle plate, Vandross to his robes. The scent of flowery perfume was still loitering on Oslin who was darting down notes of the conversation on his slate. Volk joined them in the small circular chamber filled with the four monitors corresponding to the prison chamber's four cameras.

"Well that's a development." Volk said. "Hardly a lead."

"Not necessarily." Adastra said stroking his beard. "I think there's more to this Tsuni than Diogo understands."

"He's right." Vandross acknowledged tipping the brim of his hat upwards. "There's something cultic about this situation."

"Cultic?" Oslin pondered aloud. "I detected no semblance of anything Imago related."

"Not Imago," Vandross said, ready to show off his expertise of heretic cells. "Think about it, what kind of criminal passes up on a fresh stash of medical grade drugs in exchange for machines?"

"A criminal who reveres mechanical marvels," Adastra added obviously bouncing off a lead Vandross extended. "Maybe even worships technology."

"Think about it," Vandross explained strolling around the room. "This woman, whoever she is, had linear tattoos on her temples and a silver hand. I don't think Numerri realized what he was looking at."

"Cybernetics?" Volk asked taking his place next to the silent monolith of his Retriever ally. "Tsuni's got fancy robot parts?"

"I think so." Vandross retorted. "The tattoos on her head were probably neural circuits and the glove actually an augmetic prosthesis. With tech alterations like that there are really only two options. First is a technocrat, the UPA has a few technocracies and their leaders are known to enhance their bodies with cybernetics. These kinds of modifications are expensive. Neural circuitry and augmetic limbs will run a couple monarchs easily. So, if this Tsuni person is a technocrat, she's a powerful one."

"The second option is cultists." Adastra said grimly. "Old sects of god-AI worship still exist and are prominent in the four or five technocracies of the UPA. These are in fact outlawed by the Inquisition, but that does not hinder their faith in artificial intelligences. I suspect the Cybernetic Apotheosis, worshippers of Pre-Shatter technology. They augment their bodies as much as possible, even with ramshackle components scrapped from any available machines or technology."

"That would explain why they wanted to steal the medical devices." Volk added in.

"Nuoli Lamiash," Oslin Du'Plasse interjected. He tapped some runes on his data pad and the monitors lit with an advertisement of a political advertisement. A woman, matching Numerri's descriptor with blue circuits in her temples and a silver hand, wearing a strange silvery necklace was running for a technocratic governor. This was a Jaspinian advert for a relatively minor public position. "Graduated from Singularity University with a degree in cybernetic engineering in 2699, now she's running for governor of the Assembly district."

"You think this is her?" Adastra asked.

"I feel confident in this deduction yes," Oslin noted. "Let's run it by our prisoner."

Surely enough, Volk returned with a printed-out picture of Lamiash. Numerri confirmed that that was the woman he spoke to. As promised, Volk petitioned Conservator Travvec successfully. Diogo Numerri was kept in Legionnaire Arace for seven weeks before being relieved on indentured servitude and eventual freedom. Warden Downey commanded that S-6319 move to the American Providence of Jaspin in continuation for their hunt for Knox Mortis.

CHAPTER 8

Arodi Auzlanten appeared suddenly in his private sanctum. In a brief flash of violet light, he manifested bodily on a finely polished white marble dais surrounded by columns of bronze. His long dark hair and azure and gold robes fluttered in a non-existent wind. Without making a noise or a motion, every article of clothing and jewelry removed itself from Auzlanten's body until he stood alone on the platform completely naked. He then stepped down and into the pool at the bottom of the dais. The water was a tinted green solution of bubbling mineral water. The jets massaged Arodi's skin as he closed his eyes and walked entirely submerged across the bottom of the pool. He emerged from the frothing waters on the other side, white foam stuck to his skin and patches caught in his hair and beard. He exhaled as the mineral water dripped down his skin, opening his eyes and gazing upon the remainder of his sanctum.

Few had ever been inside of this structure before. None, aside from the select few who had been invited, had even come close to its discovery. The sanctum was a windowless sphere of marble a kilometer wide, the dais on the far end being the only point of elevation. There were no light sources, but it seemed as if the marble itself was illuminating the entirety of the vast chamber. Pillars of bronze lined the perimeter and concealed bookshelves lined with thousands of texts on as many topics. Several glass cases were scattered in a complex pattern around the alabaster floors. Each case, usually cubic or spherical and of varying size, held an artifact or relic from a momentous day of Arodi Auzlanten's several achievements and adventures. He looked upon them fondly, reminiscing on the events each trophy represented.

He could spend multiple days thinking upon the origin of these relics, but he had no time. He could not loiter in his reliquary or go off into one of the many doors that were invisible to the human eye. He needed to find the Idolacreid. He brought his arm down to the marbled ground, throwing off every droplet of water and foam. Just as suddenly as they removed themselves, his apparel returned to his body. His rings, crown, tunic, robes, and other regalia wrapped and arranged themselves around his muscular frame in an instant. Leagna was in its casing, gripped in the hands of a woman.

"Welcome home, Arodi." She said with a soft smile and a gentle voice. The woman was Carthonian and had a gentle accent like that of the ancient Glaswegians. She was wearing her golden hair on her shoulders which were covered by outdated general Scourge regalia, iron grey fabric with the spike whip knitted on the side of the arm. Her eyes were like pale blue quartz and her lips full with soft pink. She outstretched the sabre, encased in a hostler of titanium, in both hands. "Do you require something to eat?"

"I haven't needed food in centuries." Arodi said calmly with an echo of a smile on his face. He took Leagna from the blonde woman and clipped the hilt to his belt. "What news do you have?"

"The word Idolacreid was spoken exactly twenty-nine times since you were last home." She said happily as the two began walking towards an antechamber of the sanctum. "Twelve times were by you and those you've spoken directly to. Nine of those times were by Invictus Illuromos while enacting Scourge protocol and coding algorithms. Six more instances were by each of the 1st Tier leaders of each branch."

"And what about the other two?"

"Unknown. I could not determine who spoke the word or from where, only that it was spoken. I deduce that dark powers are at play shielding detection from the devices you left me."

"That is highly concerning." Arodi Auzlanten said as he pulled a small pyramid made of glossy black stone from a fold in his robe. "If there is a power at play that can shield itself from my sight, we are looking for some entity of class A at minimum. What of the Nephilim?"

"The word Nephilim was spoken twelve thousand eight hundred and seven times since you were last home. Ten thousand four hundred and forty-three were with reference to the book of Genesis and other innocent Old Testament studies. Two thousand one hundred eleven were used by astrologists and xenocryptologists to speculate extraplanar or alien creatures. Two hundred twelve were used by minor cults of little pertinence."

"What of the other forty-one?" Arodi asked as they strolled into the small circular antechamber that was but a small sphere tangential to the larger round sanctum.

"The other instances were of great malicious intent, each of which I determined could be a potential threat to Templym. The instances were either by reverence to some entity or by a more fanatic cult. I was unable to deduce a location of thirty-eight of the occasions, the same unholy interference no doubt. I have a bearing on the other three if you would like them."

"Please transfer the information to me. I must do something first." There was a desk made of gnarled old walnut wood, lined with an arrangement of oddities and trinkets in a meticulous order. "I have something else I must do in the meantime." He placed the stone pyramid onto the wood which landed with a thud, suggesting a far greater weight than one would expect from a palm sized object.

"Your journey to Madagast was beneficial?" The woman asked as she placed a similarly aged wood stool to the end of the desk.

"I believe so, thank you darling." Arodi said as he sat on the stool. "Bog Mama was a powerful witch with a class C+ Imago patron. Unlike the Haigon sorcerers, whose blood contained long descended Imago power, her power was directly tapped from the demon. I killed it and then her. The supernatural power infused in her body rendered her immune to my compulsion abilities and she wouldn't tell me anything about the Idolacreid or the Nephilim."

"So, you plan on extracting her memories?" She asked innocently.

"Correct. I will analyze her memories and correspond them with the information you've gathered. From there I suspect I'll find the next lead to finding the Idolacreid and the Nephilim." Auzlanten hovered his hand over the pyramid. The top of the stone pyramid twisted and clicked open and an orange light glimmered from inside. Suddenly an object flew from inside and into his palm. Arodi was gripping a swollen human brain, far larger than the pyramid it was stored in, still dripping with neural fluid. "Would you kindly format those locations for me while I do this?"

"Understood. I will return momentarily." The woman quietly turned and walked to another portion of the sanctum, the sound of her shoes softly resonating throughout the area.

Arodi Auzlanten began to work on Bog Mama's brain. This was a process that Auzlanten loathed, but such procedures were a necessity when dealing with unique foes that couldn't have information extracted from them while alive. The dripping mass of pasty grey matter floated in between Auzlanten's hands. One of his index fingers twitched and a panel of crystalline glass the size of a common sheet of paper lowered from the ceiling and behind the hovering organ, floating parallel a foot above the desktop.

Arodi's middle finger, clad with a ring made of silver petals, flicked forward. The majority of the brain dissolved into a shower of sparks that flickered and died. The parts that remained included the temporal lobe, hippocampus, amygdala, and other portions of the brain where memory was stored, the relevant portions. With these jigsaw pieces, he began combing through and mining the relevant memories. Images of past encounters from the witch's life and Imago rituals were projected against the glass panel, reenacting a flurry of memories from Bog Mama's perspective as if it were a film. An avalanche of information, memory after memory, transitioned in lightning fast succession over the course of seconds.

Arodi heard a conversation Bog Mama had with her marauder cultists. A 'sermon' about how the Nephilim would soon stand as sovereign over Templym. He then browsed a prayer that she shared with some demonic patron. He couldn't make out what the other entity was saying. He caught a brief glance of the Idolacreid from her eyes and fixated on this. Even through the filter of another's eyes, it was enough to sicken his stomach. Auzlanten's hands moved in complex rhythms, as if he were operating a loom as he scoured the dead witch's mind. What truly interested him was the memory of where the Idolacreid went when she was through with it. He saw someone, or something, rather. It likely used to be humans. Two humans conjoined into one horrendous monstrous flesh, like two men that were fused together after liquefying their flesh and bones. The beast would slither and chatter while its three lanky arms stroked the blasphemous tome as if it were a beloved pet, two tongues licking a cracked cavernous mouth. What horrific amalgamation of organic matter was he looking at?

He listened to the conversation Bog Mama had with this strange, mutated thing. Auzlanten did not sway at the sound of the scratchy and screeching voices of the conjoined thing. The warped voices were out of synch as if one man echoed the other. Its dermis dripped some mucus like film. The witch referred to it as Resinous, an appropriately wretched name for such a disgusting beast. Arodi found it challenging to focus on the unnatural beast. He needed to concentrate on the conversation. There were a few locations mentioned during the course of the two wicked fiends' chortling. There was mention of an attack on Osca, a whisper of the Arabian Glasslands, but Resinous lastly mentioned that it would be returning to the Dead Reef. This beast was aquatic?

Arodi Auzlanten broke his concentration suddenly. The remnants of the brain plopped to the desktop in a wet splat and the crystalline slate shattered on the aged wood. Slowly, as he regained his composure, he removed the platinum thorn crown from his head and held it firmly against his chest. He willed the stool to move across the antechamber and shifted onto his knees. He bowed his head, gripping the half-crown tightly in his hands and paid reverence to the Lord.

"Hosanna," Auzlanten uttered audibly. "Glory to God on high, may His will be done for all eternity. What do you require of your servant, Lord?"

There was a brief period of silence, as though the sanctum itself were holding its breath, though words rang in Auzlanten's mind and ears. "I do not understand. Have I not served you faithfully for hundreds of years? Never once have I wavered from your direct commands." Another moment of silence followed. "Of course, I will believe you master. You are truth, you are life, you are..."

Arodi's face sunk from a mood of awe and splendor to one of grief in a second. It was the face of a parent attending their child's funeral, before returning to his standard gaze of apathy. "No...It can't be. How did this happen?" More silence. "I believe you. I am just stunned at this revelation. When, how? I should have known this if..." Silence. "You know my heart Father. I do not doubt you for a moment. I am confused. Why am I just now learning of this? This is something I should have seen." Silence. "His treachery runs deep then, beyond normal heresy. What would you have me do?" Silence fell again and for a brief moment, there was a flash of fear in his eyes. "That seems extreme. I do not want to do that." Silence. "I am not unwilling to do so. I just think I should extend mercy first. One attempt, that's all I'm asking. He is not beyond redemption, I'm sure of it." Silence. "Thank you Master. I shall make haste at once."

Arodi stood to his feet. He realized that the platinum thorns he was gripping had left small indents in his skin. If he had standard human biology, the crown would have bored holes in his skin. He wearily placed the wreath back onto his head, brushing away threads of black hair that draped in front of his brow. Auzlanten let out a deep sigh. He looked to his broken work, the scattered nerve clusters and glass shards straggling around the walnut. It did not matter, he pondered, for he had seen and heard all he needed to. He wouldn't forget what he saw. He never forgot anything. This trait served him well but haunted him also.

Arodi Auzlanten turned sharply on his heel and began a march back to the massive spherical chamber of his sanctum. The young woman was standing at the border of the antechamber, grasping a bundle of parchments. She looked concerned upon seeing Auzlanten with such low humors.

"You look scared, Arodi." The woman spoke gently as Templym's founder continued his rapid march. "Was your search successful?"

"I've received revelation." He said curtly and void of emotion. "I must address this concern immediately."

"What might I do to assist you?"

"Continue monitoring speech patterns across the world as you've done up to this point. You have the locations of the three other instances?"

"I do." She handed him the tan parchments with coordinates etched in smooth indigo ink. The woman desperately tried to match Auzlanten's pace as he strode right past her.

Arodi shuffled through the papers. "The Grecian Coastline, that is where I must take my search next. Prepare another antechamber as well. When I find the Idolacreid I will lock it away for the remainder of time itself. That is all."

"That is not all." The woman said unable to keep with his pace without running. "Something is troubling you, what is it?"

"It is nothing you need to concern yourself with."

Her hand locked onto Arodi's wrist. The grip was miniscule and served no real resistance to Auzlanten. The shock of the bold gesture was enough to cause him to halt. No citizen of Templym would ever have the gall to do something as disrespectful as to grip onto its Master's arm, especially with the intent to hinder his progress. There was a plethora of ways Auzlanten could have struck this woman down for such an audacious statement. But when he turned to meet her gaze, when he looked into the soft blue of her eyes and saw the compassion inside of them, all traces of rage melted.

"You are troubled." She said with warmth and worry. "That much is my concern."

Auzlanten's lips angled up slightly as a faint smile took its place on his face. He stepped towards the woman and embraced her in the soft cradle of his arms. Then the echo of joy vanished in a passing moment. "I have received revelation from the Lord. Invictus is a traitor."

CHAPTER 9

The United Providences of America has yet to fully recover from the Age of Anarchy. Marauder tribes continue to rise and fall in the vast Hinterlands that fill the Western portion of the dual continent. The providences aligned with Templym lay scattered across the Eastern shore, behind the tungsten barricade of the Appalachian Fortification. The Northern portion of the UPA was bitterly cold, even in the summer. After the Shatter, its plains iced over and the atmosphere flushed with subzero nitrogen, freezing over an already frigid portion of land. The small peninsula technocracy of Jaspin was the next destination of S-6319.

Technocracies were a sub federation of the larger Templym. Most nations operated under some form of republic, kingship, or oligarch. A technocracy is a specific breed of republic in which scholars and engineers took the bulk of leadership roles. This type of federal operation was most abundant during the Cybernetic Revolution and had vastly dwindled since the rise in distrust in technology after the desolation wrought by the god-AIs. Technocracies were fervent in excavating long lost technologies and innovating new ones. Often the Scourge had to regulate the scale and pace at which they invented or implemented to prevent another Shatter-scale genocide.

The first day of the month of Nyvett arrived along with the task force. Jaspin was a small nation of bustling factories and chattering multi-legged transports. The temperature was naturally fifteen degrees during the sixth month of the year. The heat from the exhaust of forges and chariots helped to warm the urbans and areas of populace, though not sufficiently. Thermodynamic engineers wished to implement large scale heating systems to keep the entire country at a temperate climate year-round. The Scourge denied all requests for fear of such implements being used to superheat and murder entire urbans. This left the citizens of Jaspin to adapt to the frost common to this portion of the UPA.

Task force S-6319 arrived in the harbor on a cargo ferry taking a full day to cross the Atlantic in the port city of Mossport. Jaspin's ports were only operational during the warmer seasons as the freshwater mouths that connected to the sea would freeze over in the colder periods. The cargo ferry allowed them to transport their caravan and was far simpler to commandeer positioning. Oslin Du'Plasse, Adastra Covalos, and Ram's Horn were from the cooler regions of Templym, so they were well accustomed to the sharp chill. However, Volk Downey hailed from desert isle of Glaswey and Vandross Blackwell from Rio Epiphanies in Kalkhan, and the frostbite sank its teeth into them more firmly. Nobody paid heed to what their Indentured Inmate, Jameson Daurtey felt.

Oslin took in a deep breath of the chilly harbor air and exhaled pleasantly as they stepped onto the frost crusted rockfoam. "Just like winter in Hrimata." The nobleman exclaimed.

"It's bloody summer." Vandross grunted as he wrapped insulated cloth around his arms. "It's not supposed to feel like winter."

"Agreed," Volk said, though his battle plate kept his body well incubated and wasn't feeling the cold as violently as the lightly armored Inquisitor. "I'm going to pick up Daurtey and the caravan from the cargo hold. Would one of you kindly contact Harbinger Revnjór and let him know our business in Mossport."

"Okay." Ram's Horn muttered, a thin layer of ice caked on his battle plate's joints.

"Do you plan on making that call Ram?" Oslin asked with an eyebrow perched upwards sharply.

"No." He said as he marched to join Warden Downey who walked towards the ferry's loading zone.

"Well if you don't mind, would one of you do this?" Oslin said motioning towards the two Inquisitors. "I've a theory I'd like to follow up on."

"What would that be, Herald?" Adastra asked.

"Mossport is the primary point of all deployment and transport in Jaspin," he said, adjusting his family scarf. "The ports would have been mostly frozen over three months ago when the hospital attack took place, and no freights or ferries would be operational at the time. There's only one airfield in the city. If our technocrat was in Venice at the time of the assault, Mossport Aviations should have record of it. I'm going to catch a transit and I'll meet you back at the Indomitable Doctrine when I'm through."

"Understood." Vandross said as he ground red leaves into his granite pipe. "Shall we move onto our interview with governor Lamiash before you return?"

"Yes," Oslin nodded. "I intend to be thorough when I sift for relevant information. Besides, I can't stand bureaucrats. I'd prefer to spend as little time with them as possible."

"Nobody would have expected you'd hate politicians," Adastra said. This was a bit of a snide insult, calling back the incident he'd been censured for.

"Funny." Du'Plasse responded sarcastically before huffing away with his chest inflated. "You have my wavelength if you need to contact me," he yelled back before dissolving into a crowd.

"Very cordial of you," Vandross said, igniting the crimson powder in his pipe. This was an herb called salamander's breath, a plant bred to be ingested to increase the body heat. "I feel like you should probably try to get along with our teammates. We are working towards a common goal after all."

"You're right." Adastra's lip curled in disgust with his own action. He took out his small black book and scribbled something down briefly. "What time is our meeting with the governor?"

"Seventeen," Vandross said as he coughed out a puff of black vapor. "There's a cybernetics convention at the Ancient Intelligence's Scholastic Institute where our aspiring governor will be holding a campaign rally."

"That seems uncomfortably public." Adastra noted. "Of course, she is currently a suspect in a number of murders, fifth degree theft, and association with a wanted recidivist."

"That is assuming, of course, Knox Mortis actually exists."

"That'd be ironic." Adastra noted removing a flask from his satchel. He took a big gulp of hot black coffee. "Imagine us going on this international escapade only to find out that the whole reason this task force was assembled never truly existed."

"I'd be fine with that." Vandross said, his shivering ceasing as his body became warmed by the herbal vapors.

"You would?" His partner asked bewildered.

"Probably. Think about it. We've already busted a drug slinging gang father. We're on the brink of smashing up an Apotheosis cell. We're doing a lot of good as is. The way I see it, even if these cases aren't connected by some super villain, we're going to do what the Scourge was formed to do."

"Punish the guilty." Adastra stated coldly, swigging more coffee. "Have you ever noted the irony of our organization's mantra?"

"'Kyrie Eleison.'" Vandross sighed with a smile. "Oh Lord, have mercy. You're no doubt noting the irony how we beg God for pity while simultaneously executing indiscriminate justice void of hesitation. I've pondered it before."

"How do you settle your soul?" Adastra stroked his short, tangled beard. "Are you ever haunted by lives our work has put to an end?"

"I believe we've seldom put an innocent to the blade." The Inquisitor adjusted his hat to block a chilled gust of wind. "If we did, I'll be the first to apologize when we reunite in Eternity. Our judgment is final from our perspective. Our Father's judgment matters a whole lot more than ours, Matthew 10:28."

"Just trust in the Lord and pray for His will to be done then... I see."

"You know, I prefer our philosophical talks in the comfort of a heated room."

Bastion Prime served as the Scourge's operational headquarters. It was the most heavily fortified and well-guarded of the diverse citadels and strongholds that watched over Templym's many nations. This fortress was shrouded with two security checkpoints, a twenty-foot-high steel wall, three minefields, a jungle of barbed wire, and sentries covering the perimeter and interior. None ever entered uninvited or unauthorized.

When the heads of the Scourge arranged for meetings at this citadel, security was at a maximum. The four primes of the four branches assembled alongside the Regent to discuss Alpha classified materials and layout plans for future legislation. These were rare occasions as they all were constantly orbiting around Templym as necessity dictated.

Invictus Illuromos arranged for a table to be brought into his office. Each of the Scourge's primes sat at their respective ends of the polished wood pentagonal table, with him at the head. Invictus sat in his plate, the flaksteel swallowing the light in the room while chains and barbs clapped with every motion.

At the northernmost end was Prelate Terran Greyflame of the Inquisition. His augmetic eye glowed red, complimenting the vermillion flaksteel carapace. Scripture passages in ancient Hebrew draped from his shoulders and back in sheets of thin cut gold foil. His pallid face was sharp and angular, made of dull grey skin. Prelate Greyflame took a major role in the purging of almost one hundred Imago cults from the world, making him an obvious choice for the role of Prelate.

To the south was Patriarch Arodus Betankur of the Veil. He was a weathered and old man who had seen much pain and suffering in his service. His milky eyes matched the blanched hair trimmed to grip his skull tightly. His battle plate was a blend of black and white plates, the tech enhancements kept him upright as his body was hunching as the muscle faded from his bones. The beautiful contrast of ebony and ivory concealed a body far mutilated by decades of harsh service. Betankur was a eunuch, having long since stripped himself of any possibilities of inflicting what he believed to be the worst of the sins. The Patriarch had served just as long as Regent Illuromos and secretly harbored envy at seeing Invictus still possessing a body unravaged by time. Still, he did his best to not allow his emotions impact his duty.

To the west was High Conservator Jude Bethel, scratching more wounds into the already marred steely blue flaksteel of his battle plate with a kukri. Nobody really understood why the tortured man kept adding to the cuts in his armor and Patriarch Betankur found such self-mutilation to be deplorable.

Sitting at the easternmost edge was Magistrate Averrin Walthune. The golden battle plate glittered in the pale light even more so than his toothy grin. His white beard contrasted his swarthy skin, which was further illuminated by the chemical torch on his back. The five men were locked in bureaucratic inventories.

"What is the status of the implementation of the Eris Trident?" Invictus asked directly to Prelate Greyflame. "Has there been improvement in prisoner conversion?"

"We have seen results." The Prelate spoke in a voice that was nearly a whisper. "Studies show that devotees of Imago cults repent 2.2% more often than our standard Arcae rehabilitation. This previous six-month sample yielded a 2.9% increase."

"Then it seems the device works." The Regent spoke as he nodded and pressed his massive metal-clad fingers to his lips. "Run one more six-month study to confirm and we shall determine if this method should replace the current one."

"Yes, Lord Regent."

"Patriarch Betankur, what of the behavior patterns of Templym citizens?" Invictus asked turning his iron gaze to the elderly man.

"Things appear grim." His faded eyes turned somber. "There has been a 5% increase in sexual assaults in the past four years, a 1% increase from 2721 alone. That is close to a million more instances this year and we are not even halfway through it yet." Betankur's voice was dry, as though his throat was full of sand. The pain and the indignation in his voice were still obvious as he iterated.

"It's not just sexual crimes." High Conservator Bethel said

planting his kukri into the face of the table. "The Shackle is prosecuting more and more criminals every passing year. The average Arcae in Templym is at fifty percent maximum capacity. We haven't seen statistics like that since the last Purus Crusade."

"I believe it is distrust in the Scourge." Magistrate Walthune interjected, his wide grin wiping away as he spoke. "Ever since the end of the Civil Strife, our approval ratings have reached a new low. Only seventy-two percent of the population of Templym approve of our actions."

"We are still recovering," Invictus said, grinding his teeth. "The rend that was torn by Malacurai is still apparent in our fair civilization. We must continue acting as Templym's immune system to prevent this scar from festering."

"Agreed, Lord Regent," Betankur spoke. "I'd like to request an increase in the Veil's budget. Bride Wainwright, who is currently operating in Hrimata, has requested additional armaments and reinforcements to combat a human trafficking syndicate. I wanted to send one hundred Supplicants to reinforce her efforts and I will need to train more to replace them."

"Request granted." The Regent spoke. "I will send surplus funding to the Seraphim Solace when we are through here."

"Regent, this brings up another point," Prelate Greyflame quietly muttered. "Our recruitment is at an all-time low. We need to put methods in play to bolster our numbers."

"What did you have in mind?" Magistrate Walthune asked.

"Our training regimen is strict and the process grueling. As it stands, only about thirty percent of applicants make it to eighth tier soldiers after the twelve weeks in the Deficio Tribulation. Perhaps if we were to lower the requirements slightly, we could enroll more soldiers."

"The prerequisites remain unchanged." Arodi Auzlanten spoke, inserting himself into the meeting. Everyone was taken aback. Nobody saw or heard him enter, so they were startled at the unannounced entry. All five stood from their respective seats and gave the Scourge heart-rip salute. Auzlanten began circling the pentagonal table with his hands tucked behind his back. "The Scourge operates as defender of the weak and punisher of the wicked. We cannot afford to waver in our standards. As the first and last line of defense against anarchy, tyranny, and threats from beyond, you must remain as disciplined and lethal as possible. I spent years optimizing the enrollment to sort out those who could not handle the stress and strain of the inhuman duties you're forced to enact. If we falter in these standards, Templym could suffer greatly."

"Master Auzlanten," Regent Illuromos dared to speak. "We are honored by your presence. What business brings you to us?"

"I must speak with you Invictus." He leered at the four primes. "Alpha Magnus."

The four heads of the Scourge bowed slightly and marched away, taking their leave from Regent Illuromos' private office. The click of the security gears was the only audible sound as Arodi Auzlanten and his son Invictus were left alone. Arodi pulled out one of the chairs to sit and the Regent did likewise.

"What brings you here, father?" Illuromos asked, a hue of fear in his voice. "You said that it would be months before I saw you again. That was less than two weeks ago."

"Is there something you'd like to tell me Invictus?" Arodi asked, his emotionless guise concealing the flurry of mixed emotions.

"Father... I'm confused. What are you referring to?" Auzlanten paid close attention to the Regent's face looking for some twitch or throbbing vein, anything that would indicate a lie.

"Is there something you've done recently?" He asked placing his folded hands on the table. "Something you know is against the creed of the Scourge?"

"Are you accusing me of treachery?" Invictus gasped, obviously offended. "I am hurt by such a claim. I am Regent of the Scourge. For over forty years I have operated in service to the Lord and to you. In that time, I have never faltered in my faith or my judgment. I am more loyal than any other of your servants in the Scourge."

Arodi could see no indicator of a lie. The pain in his son's face seemed genuine. "I have received divine revelation. God has named you a defector and concluded that you are unfit to continue operating as Regent of the Scourge."

Invictus suddenly stood from his chair and smashed a fist into the table, splitting it into two splintered slabs. "Father, this is an outrage! I am no traitor!" He pointed a jet metal index finger at the Master of Templym.

"You would question the authority of the one true God?" Arodi asked, keeping his calm composure in the face of Invictus' outburst. He brushed a few specks of sawdust from his sleeve and stood up. Despite the Regent being at least a foot taller than his father, the authority his posture demanded was evident.

"Of course not," Invictus huffed. "But there must be some mistake. I am no heretic!" Arodi listened to his pulse, it was wild and rapid. This would be the case if he was offended or if he were fibbing.

"God told me to kill you." Arodi cringed slightly at voicing the command for the first time. "He was clear in his instruction. He told me that you were unfit to serve and that you must be struck down for your sins."

Invictus placed his hands on his forehead. In another bout of rage he smashed the chair he had been sitting in. His battle plate empowered him to reduce the seat into little more than wood pulp, but his natural bulk was more than sufficient for such a feat.

"You're here to kill me?" He asked, pain resonating in the question.

"No," Arodi stated. "I petitioned on your behalf and He allowed me to extend one chance. You must step down. From there, you will come with me to my private sanctum. I will isolate you and together we will discover what treachery befell you. You will repent and be saved, that much I am sure of."

"And if I refuse?" Invictus asked rhetorically. He hung his head in sorrow, rubbing his thumb on the IX branded beneath his eye. "How could you do this to me, father?"

"This is not my will, son." Arodi said placing a caring hand on his shoulder. "I am not blaming you or naming you a heretic. Perhaps there is black magick at play here. Perhaps some foul Imago has toyed with your mind." Invictus pushed Auzlanten's hand off in protest. His entire world was coming crashing down in flames and Arodi was the one responsible for it. "Whatever the case is, it is unsafe for you to remain as my Regent. Step down and we can figure this out together."

Invictus sighed with sorrow. "What am I to do?"

"Assemble a press briefing at once. Announce your resignation. I will appoint a new Regent of the four primes. Then we must spend ample time together, determine the problem, and fix it. This is the only opportunity I was allowed to extend to you. If you refuse, I must take your life. Please don't force my hand in that fashion."

"Very well." Invictus muttered disheartened. "Just answer me this. Why do you put me to shame for something that even I am unaware of doing?"

"Who am I do deny God's will? I have faith enough to look past my own biases to further His agenda. He chose me to be his prophet. He trusts me. That bond is beyond value of any other relationship I have had in my years."

"Even ours." Invictus slumped over in one of the remaining chairs. "You would shame your son."

"Invictus, please do not take this personally. If there were a way for me to preserve your honor, I would pursue that instead. I still love you."

"So you say, father."

The words hung in the air, echoing in Arodi's mind. Never before had he told Invictus he loved him that he did not respond in kind. The Regent could not even look in his direction. He had shattered his son's heart and it would never recover. Auzlanten was filled with grief, though he wouldn't show it. Throughout it all, he never saw a hint of a lie in Invictus. Why would his hand be forced in this way if there was no indication of treachery? Why punish a man for something he has no memory of? Arodi knew that he was no longer welcomed. He took his leave in silence.

Regent Illuromos looked up, a deep scowl across his face. The steel color of his eyes seemed to ignite like liquid metal as the ire inside of him boiled like a cauldron. He lifted the remaining chairs and splintered them in a bout of rage. He beat and pounded the remaining planks into a pile of sawdust, screaming all the while in grief. He knelt down in the wood pulp, scattering the dust with the thud of the heavy armor slamming to the carpet. Invictus bit his lip as he retrieved a pendant concealed beneath his ebony battle plate. It was an asymmetrical tangle of violet petals sculpted of amethyst dangling from a silver chain. He palmed the gemstone and the scowl melted away. He let out a heavy breath and tucked the necklace back into his armor.

He brushed himself free of the brown powder from his lightless battle plate. He went to the door and opened it up. The four primes were waiting outside, two on either side of the hallway. They all gave the Scourge salute to the Regent as he emerged from his haven.

"Our meeting is through," Invictus grunted seriously. "Magistrate Walthune, please assemble a unit of broadcasters. I must address Templym at once."

CHAPTER 10

The roadways of Mossport were just like the rest of Jaspin, hectic and busy circuits flooded with strangely shaped transports cutting through a number of low buildings. The most abundant vehicles were like massive metal centipedes that scuttled about the streets on spindly legs. The standard four wheeled chariot that S-6319 drove around in was more of an oddity here, even though this was the most common build in the majority of the developed world. Some transports were more akin to trains on hard rubberized treads, others had wheels of varying sizes, and some even hovered above the streets with no wheels whatsoever. Technocracies like Jaspin were home to diverse machines such as these.

Warden Downey gave vocal approval to the skill at which Daurtey navigated the complex pathways in which the roads tangled through the urban. They were able to arrive at Lamiash's rally at the Ancient Intelligence's Scholastic Institute with time to spare in spite of the number of collisions they barely avoided. Oslin was the only absent member of the task force as he was investigating Mossport Aviations. The four Scourge soldiers, still donning full battle regalia, would confront the suspect.

The interior of the Scholastic Institute was a stark contrast to the frosty outer areas. The automatic doors slid open with a hiss as the investigators approached. Warm air wafted out as the glass panels retracted into the door. Inquisitor Blackwell shivered with relief as he removed the insulated cloth strips as the four of them stepped inside. Ram's Horn arced his horned-helmet shrouded head up and around, leering at the marvels that were inside.

Scholastic Institutes often displayed their greatest achievements in extravagant displays right at their halls' entranceways. Innovations of developed here dangled from the ceiling by transparent chords or floated lazily in some kind of levitation pulpit. The former marauder looked in silent disdain at the sight of such machines, firmly believing such trinkets would make man fat and lazy, just as it did before the Shatter.

Warden Downey took the lead in the hallway. The sound of metal clad feet bounced off of the white sheet metal floor and walls attracting attention to them. A few scholars and students toured these halls, browsing the space outside the auditorium where Nuoli Lamiash was holding her campaign speech. Their eyes swung to the two Inquisitors and the two Shacklers, looks of awe or fear in their eyes. The four paid no heed to the bystanders as this was the typical response from civilians. The Scourge, after all, was an organization designed for no other purpose other than to enact punishment. At least, this was its initial intent before the Strife.

They didn't make a grand entrance, at least not intentionally. The Scholastic Auditorium was where the meeting with the hopeful governor would take place. Since they arrived early, Nuoli Lamiash was still in the middle of her speech. This was a famous theater, known for housing technocrats, professors, and intellectuals of every sort since the Institute's founding over fifty years ago. It was no surprise that her campaign rally was taking place here.

Nuoli Lamiash was a middle-aged woman, though plastic reconstructive surgeries gave her the appearance of being in her early twenties. Her brown-red hair was cropped in a wavelike pattern down the length of her shoulders. During her speech, the neural wiring visible in her temples flashed cyan light. She always spoke with her hands, both the natural member and the cybernetic prosthetic. "... into the hands of the brilliant." S-6319 heard from the blaring speakers lining the sound drinking foam walls. "We should only be ruled by scholars and inventors. The UPA needs engineers like you to construct its fine urbans. Templym needs the bright eyes of the inspiring young undergraduates, who will become our doctors and forge masters. You, my constituents, are the future of society. We need your help so that your voice can be heard by the councils of Templym. Your voices deserve to be heard by the Scourge. If elected, I promise to fight for you, the future leaders."

"A bunch of malarkey," Volk muttered to his teammates as she continued her spiel. "Never trust a politician that says 'I'll fight for you'. That person doesn't know you and sure as spit doesn't want to fight for you."

"Weren't you a politician in Glaswey?" Vandross asked, the task force now taking a seat in the retractable fabric chairs in the back of the auditorium.

"Oh yeah," Downey whispered. "I was Boss of the nation back when it was still marauder turf. I rallied the vote to annex into Templym before the 14thPurus. 'Course, I never promised something as ludicrous as fighting for each and every one of my constituents. I just made clear what my intentions were, and the people voted me in."

"I didn't think marauders voted." Adastra muttered. "No offense, Ram's Horn."

"Meh." The flaksteel clad giant shrugged.

"Marauder's more a label than anything else." Volk continued. "After all, a marauder tribe is just a civilization refusing to join Templym."

"...the brave warriors of the Scourge!" Nuoli yelled out motioning to the back row of the auditorium. The crowd swiveled around and began applauding at the sight of the four soldiers. "We thank the representatives, who have come all the way from Bastion Prime in Parey. They are here as an olive branch from the Scourge, showing us that they want to listen to you! They attend in support of my vision for a better Jaspin, for a smarter UPA, for a more bountiful Templym. Look to these brave warriors, Templym's protectors, as an example that your voices, your visions, shall become a reality!" Lamiash received a standing ovation, the hooting and clapping from the scholars and students drowning out the sound of the speakers.

"You see what she just did?" Volk asked leaning over to face his team.

"We've just been used as propaganda." Adastra grunted gritting his teeth.

Oslin Du'Plasse had no issue with exerting his authority. A simple flash of his Beacon insignia, showing his Epsilon clearance, got him through Mossport Aviations' security with relative ease. He strutted about in his gold and black plate with his platinum hair arranged to mimic Arodi Auzlanten's, just as he liked appearing.

He thought of Jaspin as a quaint little civilization. In a way it reminded him of Hrimata. Admittedly, the noble city, which was capital of the Nordic Plains and Carthonia, was larger than the nation of Jaspin. The technology was similar, though on a more widely implemented scale and subtler variety, which was impressive considering it was not a technocracy. Hrimatan politics were complex and boring, according to Du'Plasse, involving a number of noble houses and providential autarchs. Technocracies were basically just republics with professors in charge, a much simpler method.

Oslin thought fondly of his manor. It had been years since he had been there. Last he had heard, his sister Requin and her new husband were living there with uncle Grigor and his clan. He was bitter that he missed the wedding. Requin was surely a beautiful bride. Oslin was always very protective of her and her twin Nichole. He had of course performed a thorough series of background checks on her husband to be. If this man were of any threat to Requin, he would never have gotten a second date. Alas, Oslin was forced to silently observe his family move on with their lives from whichever Beacon facility he was stationed in at the time, sending thoughts and prayers their way. What more could he do? His sister made it abundantly clear that she never wanted to see him again.

Snapping back to reality, Oslin put aside his emotions. He had a job to perform. A security guard was escorting him to the airport's data well. He was wary to keep an eye on the civilians surrounding him. He was not particularly popular in the UPA, after all. It had been six months since he began his suspension for the execution of Senator Gulfran, so most of the populace would have forgotten this tragedy. He didn't need to worry in particular since the Senator was from the southern providence Mayanmatra, but caution kept him alive in a number of circumstances.

The escort left him in the Aviatians' data well. He dismissed the employee and demanded privacy in his usual pompous manner, disregarding the other menials attending to the server. From there he linked his historian's tablet into the bank of information. The airport's owner informed the Herald that security footage remained for over a year, more than enough time for the purpose of this investigation. The golden immotrum of his gauntlets tapped the projectum of the slate fervently as he swiftly sifted through the wealth of security footage.

Oslin began his process with identity algorithms to locate Nuoli Lamiash. There were seven instances of her being in and out of the airways as flight shuttles took her to and from all over Templym. He wasn't particularly interested in most of these instances. Oslin wanted to know about anything in early Jubral. Surely enough he found two instances of the technocrat being in Mossport Aviations, she left to the Venetian city of Sarrdipul on Jubral 1st and returned on the 11th. That would place her in Venice at the time of the attack.

Du'Plasse propped his head on one fist as he continued to sift through the data well. He paid close attention to what most would consider minor details. For instance, she wasn't wearing the strange silver necklace when she left but was when she returned. Nuoli also didn't possess the neural circuits in her head, just a single bluish green line running down to her eye. She currently possessed a much larger amalgamation of cerebral implants shimmering through her head. "How did Ms. Lamiash afford that upgrade?" Oslin wondered to himself. This was the kind of evidence he needed to catalog.

His next step was to run another set of algorithms on the security data. He increased the time range to a week apart from these two happenings and began sifting. This was designed to pick out anybody with known affiliation to the Cybernetic Apotheosis.

Ideally, he'd like to see Lamiash and the cult's leader skipping from the air ferry, carrying the cache of stolen medical technology in their arms, but of course they were all too bright to make such a childish mistake. He knew that, if anything at all, the tech cultists would fly in separate transports on different days after the raid was through.

The algorithm indicated a few minor criminals. Nothing major, a few tech-cultists came and went through the Aviations on many of the days in his search. Minor suspects and a few low-ranking cult officials were all the initial run could find. There was usually only one or two of the wanted men and women every day, every day except Jubral 1st and 11th. "How convenient," Oslin pondered out loud to himself. "The only days no cultists were in the airport were the same days as you, Ms. Lamiash." This seemed more than coincidental to Herald Du'Plasse.

For hours, Oslin's fingers drummed against the holo-projected runes of his historian's tablet. He mined through the ample footage looking for some indication of undeniable Cybernetic Apotheosis activity. The cult was prevalent in the technocracy of Jaspin, an occasional member or two would be no surprise in the only station of extranational transportation. He needed proof. Some link he could place to undeniably connect Nuoli Lamiash and the Cybernetic Apotheosis. He fervently swiped away photos and screens while simultaneously analyzing hours of security data, looking for somebody. Du'Plasse cracked his neck and fingers constantly, thinking that some kind of neural implant would be most helpful to sort out the flood of data pouring out in his eyes. He dismissed the notion, loathing the idea of replacing flesh with metals.

More time passed. Oslin began to sweat as the exhaust from the data well servers still lingered in the room below the public transport halls. That's when he found something. A single frame from a security tape on Jubral 10th caught his attention. He enhanced the image as he zoomed into a figure. It was a man, no doubt about that, but his face was blurred by some kind of distortion. Just his face was shrouded by a thin veil of pixilation blocking his identity from the algorithms. Oslin Du'Plasse followed the path of this man, who wore a thick black fur coat. The security images showed the way he was walking out of the Aviations. It seemed as though every time the figure's face pointed towards a servitor camera or a local arbiter's recording device, a barely noticeable blanket of static wrapped around the face of the figure. The Herald likened this to another all too fortunate coincidence. This was the work of some kind of technological buffer.

Oslin reviewed the footage, from entrance to exit. This man's face remained entirely blurred out. "Clever bastard", Oslin thought to himself. This wasn't the first instance of identity buffers Du'Plasse had encountered before. He had a trick up his flaksteel sleeve. He took his search away from the private servers of Mossport Aviations' data wells and took to public portions of the global data tides. Using a Beacon algorithm, he dove through publicly posted photos from the airport on Jubral 10th. He inspected the photographs that average citizens, tide-casters, and even a celebrity or two to find any indication of the mystery man. After another hour or inspecting each photo with his naked eye and picture enhancements he caught a glimpse of the side of the face, free of static blurring. "Got you." Oslin smiled to himself.

The questioning of Nuoli Lamiash was off to a poor beginning. Warden Downey never questioned anybody suspected of criminal action in such a public setting and he certainly wouldn't announce his entrance. The campaigning technocrat already ruined that notion, making S-6319 the subject of her rally. This soured the relationship instantly.

The task force approached Lamiash during the after party. It was obvious she was an adept politician. She made sure to surround herself with curious constituents and buzzing young scholars, ensuring that there were always ample witnesses around. There was a certain level of fear of the Scourge and ensuring a cloud of publicity kept them from doing anything that would embarrass them.

The small party was scattered with people of every sort.

Lamiash was, of course, the center of attention. She wore a low-cut violet ball gown which exposed an unwholesome amount of her artificially swollen breasts. This was probably a petty tactic to try to distract them from their mission. Adastra kicked himself internally for falling for the trap ever so briefly. She swirled a crystal of white wine in her augmetic fingers, chatting it up with the crowd to plant seeds of constituency. The crowd shied away and thinned with the approach of the plate wearing members of the Inquisition and Shackle. Lamiash coyly and subtly made sure journalists and photographers stayed within range.

"Ms. Lamiash," Volk introduced himself extending an arm. "Warden Volk Downey, pleased to meet you." He kept a friendly face as usual despite his hidden queasiness at memories of bureaucracy flushing back to him.

"Mr. Downey," the aspiring governor laughed, "You have a bullet in your face." He took the hand and leaned forward to receive a kiss on the cheek. It was a formality of the UPA to greet a lady in such a way.

"I'm aware ma'am." He said begrudgingly pecking her cheek. "It got bored of trying to punch through my hard head and is just lulling in there."

"Well it certainly speaks of your talents!" Lamiash laughed, her neural circuits lighting with the off green light. "Not many men can bite the bullet like this. Is your eye alright or are you half-blind now?"

"It looks far worse than it actually is, I assure you."

"Oh my, Warden." Her eyes lit up and connected to the Black Rose medallion magnetically sealed to his shoulder. "Are you a holder of the Black Rose?"

"That I am, Ms. Lamiash. I've held it for two years now."

"Well it's an honor to be in the presence of such a prestigious soldier as yourself. We must get a picture together."

A flock of photographers rallied towards the Warden and Nuoli. "I've got the press." Vandross groaned to the others quietly. "Excuse me," He interjected as a few cameras click recorded images of the technocrat with Downey. “No cameras please.” Vandross shepherded the journalists away, escorting them away from the main event to answer their questions.

“Mr. Downey, what’s going on?” Lamiash asked as though she wasn’t aware of why the Scourge was at her gathering. “Why are you dismissing the press?”

“I’m afraid this isn’t a social call madam.” Volk said, trying to maintain an ambience of professional courtesy. “Is there some place more private we could have a discussion?”

“I see.” She said in a huff. “Here I was hoping that you were here to endorse me.” She took a long gulp of the clear wine. “Pity. Any questions you have for me, I will answer them here and now.”

“You’re positive? I don’t think what we’re asking is the kind of thing you’d like getting out in public, especially during an election.”

“I can manage, ask away.” Lamiash was much curter than before.

“Very well.” Ram’s Horn handed Volk a binder with pictures of the hospital raid. “Ms. Lamiash, where were you on Jubral 6th?”

“I was touring Venice at the time on holiday. I believe I was in Rome on the 6th or perhaps Magnimus.”

“Did your tour ever take you to Bruccol?” Ram then handed a tablet to Volk, packed with images from the massacre at the hospital.

“Yes.” Nuoli’s plastic sheen lips curved into a frown at the sight of the slaughter from the pictures. “Bruccol would have been Jubral 9th and 10th, the last stop before flying back from Sarrdipul.”

“Were you aware of the attack that took place at Bethesda Pianissimo on Jubral 6th?”

“Yes, I had heard of it.” Lamiash downed the last few drops of liquid. “I recall a cabby told me about it while I was on the way to see the Budapest Memoriam in Bruccol. A tragic little massacre, isn’t it?”

“Ms. Lamiash,” Volk leaned in close and hushed his voice. “Do you have any connections to the Young Ichors gang in Venice?”

“No.” She whispered back sternly.

"Have you ever met Diogo Numerri?"

"No."

"Have you ever had contact with the Cybernetic Apotheosis?" Adastra Covalos interjected, stepping in from behind.

"No." She leered at the Inquisitor. "What business does the Inquisition have here?"

"Kappa classified." Adastra grunted in response. "I find that last answer particularly hard to believe if you don't mind me."

Nuoli pursed her lips together, clearly aggravated. "Oh really, and why is that?"

"Inquisitor Covalos, stand down." Downey said ending the argument before it got out of hand. "I apologize, he's a zealous sort. What he meant to ask is if you know anybody in the Apotheosis? Do you have any old friends or family that was at some point in their lives part of the cult?"

"Absolutely not!" Lamiash drove her heel into the metallic floorboard. "I have condemned and criticized them as the extremists they are. They're the primary reason the Scourge won't let us implement our innovations on a larger scale. The Apotheosis is nothing but a group of fanatical mad scientists who lust for augmetic enhancement, not anything for the betterment of society. I abhor the idea that you would even have the audacity to accuse me like this." The volume of her voice was increasing to an uncomfortable level, attracting the attention of the press that Vandross was holding off.

"I said no cameras please." Vandross said to the crowd with a tone of increased urgency as the click of pictures being recorded started ringing.

"Ma'am please calm down." Downey said gently to Lamiash. "We aren't accusing anybody of anything. If you're concerned of a false claim, you're welcome to be questioned in a Veritas Chamber."

At the mention of the room of truth, she gasped audibly so that everyone within earshot could hear it. At the same moment she dropped the crystal, allowing the thin glass to fall to the sheet metal flooring. Stepping back, she shouted at her team of menials. "Unbelievable! How dare you lay hands on a lady? I can't deal with this right now. Security, escort these men out right now!"

At the clap of a hand two local arbiters dressed in light blue uniform stepped over. They were squeamish in their approach and had shaking hands on hard plastic batons. Adastra gave a sub audible growl as he clenched his fists ready to fight. Ram's Horn cracked his fists and lowered his shoulders in preparation. Volk, the rational diplomat, stepped forward before anything could get out of hand and either of the brutish soldiers got violent.

"Boys," Downey whispered to the arbiters as a crowd started to gather and stare. "You realize that any one of us could ragdoll the two of you around. We've also got superior jurisdiction. But seeing as we've made more trouble than we'd have liked, we'll make ourselves scarce. And if you try to "escort" us out, we will invoke Creed Sixteen and haul your hides off to the Arcae." He could see the fear in their trembling pupils, and he flashed a dry smile. "Boys, we've outstayed our welcome." Warden Downey said to the others. The other three rallied behind Volk and marched out of the complex at a quickened pace.

Reporters began flocking towards Lamiash, obviously avoiding the Scourge soldiers. "That went poorly." Vandross said as they exited the crowd and eyes were drawn on them.

"You know she's guilty right?" Adastra asked Volk. "Even though her face has been resculpted and practically paralyzed, I could see her lying through her teeth. We should detain and interrogate her in a Veritas Chamber."

"Of course, she's guilty." Downey said shaking his hairless head. "But she's got deep pockets, the public eye, and now she's made us look like thugs. If we're going to nail this technocrat, we're going to need a pretty good slab of evidence."

"Lying to a Scourge officer is illegal." Vandross stated coldly. "If we can prove that she lied to us we can pin her on that."

"Lies." Ram's Horn bellowed, his deep voice resonating in his plate.

"Aye and she deserves punishment for it." Downey said. "But we're going to get her for that hospital raid, somehow."

"Here's to hoping Du'Plasse found something." Adastra said as the doorway to the Scholastic Institute slid open and S-6319 stepped back into the frigid Jaspin air.

CHAPTER 11

Arodi Auzlanten sat on a small circular rug. The soft green fabrics cushioned the Master of Templym as he sat in quiet contemplation. His mind wandered to a number of places. Part of his mind was trying to process his next lead in his pursuit of the Idolacreid, finding the beast Resinous in the Grecian Coastline. The other part was focusing on how he would handle the situation with his son Invictus. While he was adopted, Auzlanten loved him as though he were his own flesh and blood. In truth Arodi had raised over a hundred of the mythical "Children of Auzlanten". They always grew up to be great men and women of the Faith. He had seen infants grow to be national leaders, evangelists, bloodied martyrs, and valiant crusaders. Never before had one of his adopted children risen to the height of Regent of the Scourge as Invictus Illuromos, Arodi's indomitable nullifier. It pained Templym's founder to force him from that position.

He sat on the carpet alone in his private sanctum. He was in an antechamber tangent to the larger sphere. An ornate and complex tapestry knitted of inch-thick black threading was the only other décor in this chamber. The patterns of brilliant goldenrod and viridian were dynamic and constantly shifted as though the chords themselves were dancing in a complex ballet. With another portion of his attention, Auzlanten watched the crowd gathering in front of Bastion Prime where Invictus would address the people of Templym. His concentration broke when he heard the echoing clicks of heels on the marble tiling behind him.

"Am I interrupting?" It was the soft voice of the blonde woman.

"You are," Auzlanten said blankly. "But nothing important. Come, sit with me."

The woman stepped over to the plush green mat. She gently sat down next to him, taking a more relaxed position than the Zen-like meditation stance Auzlanten took. "Are you still troubled?"

"Yes." He responded with his eyes still clamped shut. "No matter how hard I have honed my focus, no matter what plane I search for answers, I cannot find what Invictus did. Why don't I know? Why doesn't he know?"

"It's perturbing." The woman said, gripping onto Arodi's hand. He opened his eyes and looked at the woman, noting how beautiful she looked in the rustic grey fabric that complemented the perfect shape of her body. "I have confidence that you'll figure it out."

A gentle smile pierced its way through Auzlanten's beard. "We shall figure it out." The woman smiled back, much more obviously, and placed her head on the golden threads that blanketed Arodi's shoulder. The smile melted away from his face. "It's starting."

Arodi Auzlanten motioned his arms outwards towards the tapestry. As though he were coordinating the ballet, he rearranged the threading of the embroidered patterns from his sitting position. The colored threads danced into new patterns and their hues shifted. The image of a podium of black steel on a raised granite dais in front of a cloudless blue sky appeared on the tapestry. Scourge warriors of the Centurion guard, the Regent's personal security force who were clad in silver battle plate with black feathered plumes on their helmets, lined the perimeter of the platform. This was the image being broadcasted across all of Templym from Bastion Prime, where Invictus Illuromos would step down from his position as Auzlanten's Regent. He was a noted orator and powerful speaker so he anticipated it would be a speech to remember.

He could not worry. Worry is a sin. Arodi successfully petitioned Invictus to step down and work on his penitence. That was that and worrying would change nothing.

"Surely Invictus is not beyond salvation," Auzlanten thought to himself.

He anticipated welcoming Invictus into his sanctum where they could process together, determine the source of the taint, and fix it. After he stepped down as Regent, Arodi would petition his replacement. He was torn between Magistrate Walthune and Prelate Greyflame. Perhaps he would assign some test between the two of them. He had not decided yet. Arodi's mind was thoroughly occupied with a variety of more pressing duties.

Sound echoed throughout the antechamber from some invisible source. At the moment, the only noise was the scattered conversations of eager journalists in the crowds not shown on the screen-tapestry. The chatter vanished into silence as the Regent took the stage.

Invictus Illuromos was an intimidating sight to see, his ebony battle plate complimented by the spiked wire and chains wrapped around his body. His steel colored immotrum cloak shifted with every heavy, gear-churning step he took. His hairless weathered face was grim, and his stormy eyes filled with grief. Arodi felt a similar pain to the internal struggle Invictus was going through, but he would not feel the same level of shame that the Regent was about to subject himself to.

Invictus took position behind the podium. Most other men would be hidden behind its bulk, but it was crafted specifically for his titanic size. Sound amplifiers were hidden behind it, though he hardly needed them to project his resonating voice.

"Citizens of Templym." Invictus sounded like the winds of a hurricane with the volume and authority his voice carried. "I apologize for the suddenness of this message, but this is a matter of the utmost importance and delay is unacceptable." Even in his grief, he spoke with a bravado that demanded respect.

"As you know, I have served the Scourge faithfully since 2662, first as an Acolyte in Auzlanten's Inquisition. In 2673 I became Prelate and was appointed as the ninth Regent in 2676 at the death of Regent Havlon, peace on his soul. Operating as Arodi Auzlanten in his absence for over forty years now, I've dutifully and faithfully served God's machination and done my best to secure the prosperity of Templym." He paused, letting the weight of his words process for a moment. "I recall what Lord Auzlanten told me when I received this honor. He told me that I received this title because of my zeal for truth and justice. He told me that I was beyond worthy to take up the title. He called me a man of indomitable conviction, a man who would nullify those that would undo everything he worked so hard to forge after the Tyrranis Period. He had faith in me and my abilities beyond that of the other primes." Auzlanten sighed in the isolation of his private sanctum. Invictus was a gifted orator indeed. His words cut at his heart.

"You should know that it is with this level of trustworthiness that I deliver this message today." Invictus continued broadcasting to Templym. "Arodi Auzlanten earlier came to me this day with some disturbing news. With his better judgment... he recommended that I make this news public at once. With great anguish I come to you today to make this information public. So, with my authority I am declassifying Alpha Magnus material to you all today."

He paused again, letting his words hang like fog in the air. The anticipation could practically be tasted as the citizens were propped up on the edge of their seats as the Regent continued to ebb on the crowd. Arodi gripped tighter onto the woman's hand, taking care not to crush it.

"This news is most disturbing, and the very thought poisons my stomach. But I do not get to choose the truths that I accept. Truth is eternal, it is absolute and discriminatory. It is the duty of the Scourge to accept truth regardless if we like its meaning. So here it is. For the foreseeable future, Arodi Auzlanten cannot be trusted."

An audible gasp reverberated through the entire world. The shockwave of raw emotion swept over Templym like a tidal wave. But it was nothing compared to the raw unfiltered rage that churned inside of Arodi Auzlanten like a dormant volcano reactivating. "This is only temporary." Regent Illuromos continued maintaining his haunted visage. "Walking the Earth now is a doppelganger, who is taking the form of our beloved Master of Templym. This creature, no doubt Imago in origin, has forged a cunning masquerade of Lord Auzlanten."

Arodi stood from his lotus position. His ultramarine eyes were alight with orange and yellow fire as he gritted his teeth together, still watching the lie unfold on the tapestry-screen. The blonde woman backed away and silently left the antechamber.

"Master Auzlanten is currently dealing with this predicament in solitude." Invictus continued. "His top priority is to smite this imposter beast before any significant damage can be done in his name. Until that time, you are not to trust what appears as Arodi Auzlanten. You are to presume hostile intent and Class A Imago power. Ward yourselves from any figure that appears as Lord Auzlanten. Avoid him at all costs and by no means are you to listen to anything he says."

Tongues of fire began thrashing about Arodi's body, incinerating the carpet and scalding the marble floor black.

"As his Regent, I will operate as the sole link between Templym and Auzlanten. I am the only one he trusts with acting in his stead and the only one with the knowledge to distinguish between him and the imposter. Until he has given me assurance that this fraudulent creature is no longer a threat, I am taking role as Master of Templym. I swear an oath unto you to serve as faithfully as I have served as Regent of the Scourge. I will inform the public when this liar is dealt with..."

The tapestry was destroyed. As pure ire built within Arodi Auzlanten, the antechamber was engulfed in fire. The very air itself was consumed in roiling orange flame. Never had Arodi experienced such lividity in his reign. The small sphere became a swirling twister of whirling heat and unprocessed rage as all became fire. Then it was extinguished. Auzlanten was at the center of the chamber, the white stones left scorched and melted in many portions. He was on his hands and knees, an eerie look shooting from his eyes. Arodi dug his fingers into the rock flooring. The blackened marble turned to sand in his grip. He scooped up a pile of the silvery dust and held it over his head. The powder mingled its way into the sea of black hair on Auzlanten's head, appearing as a starry night as the specks contrasted its background.

Arodi snapped up to his feet. The ash burst out of his hair with a cascade of wind. Leagna flew into Auzlanten's hand, glowing a cool violet and blue starkly to contrast the heat of anger inside the cauldron of his heart. He moved to exit his sanctum and strike Invictus down immediately. At the archway of the antechamber, the woman was standing there. Her welcoming appearance was gone, replaced by trembling fear. Her horror caused Arodi to snap out of his fury and think logically once more.

"God told me to kill Invictus." Arodi said, horrified internally. "He named my son a heretic on the path of damnation and told me to end his life forthwith."

"And you refused?" The soft, ancient Glaswegian trembled.

"I did. He allowed me to petition an alternative, but I suspect that was to satisfy my own desires. There's no way to avoid it. I disobeyed the Lord. I should have killed Invictus when I was told to do so."

"And now you can't." She responded. "If you killed him now, then all of Templym would never trust you again. With Invictus dead, nobody would be able to differentiate between you and the nonexistent doppelganger. Nobody would ever trust you again."

Auzlanten returned his stained glass sabre to its home. "You're right. I need evidence before I move against him." His gallant voice cracked as he tried to suppress tears. "How could this happen? Invictus was the most loyal of my subjects, the most fervent and faithful of my children. What dark power could stray Invictus from the righteous path?"

"The Idolacreid." The woman dared to utter. Auzlanten's eyes widened at the revelation.

"Of course. He's been corrupted by the arcane inscriptions of the Idolacreid, seduced by promises of the Nephilim. Surely nothing else in all of Creation could have swayed my son."

"Perhaps there is a cure." The woman said with false hope.

"We cannot operate with that assumption." He said grimly. "At best, he is already dead and an Imago is walking around in his corpse. More likely, he has given into the temptations of power from the occult. We should assume... that he is beyond salvation."

"What shall we do now?"

"I must distance myself from Invictus. He will be able to exploit any encounter he has with me to serve whatever agenda he's operating under. Assume vast quantities of the Scourge have become corrupted as well. But we must not defer from our current actions. I must find the Idolacreid and lock it away. Then I will coordinate with loyalists in the Scourge to overthrow Invictus."

"That could spark a second Civil Strife." The woman said cautiously. "I don't think Templym will be able to survive that."

"We must be cautious then. Sift through all Scourge personnel. Separate the wheat from the chaff as best you can. Be stringent in your discernment. If you have so much as an inkling of doubt as to where their allegiance lies, do not trust them. Just... just find me someone I can trust."

"And so, I advise all citizens of Templym to do their best to remain calm and continue about their daily lives." Invictus continued orating in front of the steel walls of Bastion Prime. "I can assure you, that the Scourge is unaware of any immediate threat pending from this imposter. However, this does not guarantee the lack of a more sinister plot. If you see what you believe to be Arodi Auzlanten, contact your local arbiters or Scourge warriors. I am calling on the Scourge to prioritize this above all other missions. All branches are to respond to any sightings with the utmost scrutiny. Lord Auzlanten has assured me that he will remain unseen, so all sightings should be treated as demonic in origin. I shall reveal more to you as it is revealed to me. No further questions." Regent Illuromos stepped from the platform and returned to the seclusion of Bastion Prime, ignoring the press as they ignored his final statement.

Ram's Horn turned the monitor off, flushing it blank. He threw the control remote to the side table and them himself onto the couch in the waiting room of the Indomitable Doctrine. Ram's Horn and Adastra were sitting outside patiently for Oslin and Volk to finish their meeting with Harbinger Revnjór. The unplanned announcement from the Scourge's Regent created a sudden pause in the meeting, extending the duration further. The ranking agents were petitioning Revnjór for permission to pursue legal action against Nuoli Lamiash.

"Is nothing sacred anymore?" Adastra asked the Steel Skin. "Creatures pervert the very image of Arodi Auzlanten now. Hopefully this won't affect our case."

"Mortis." Ram muttered through his thick helmet.

"Correct. Mortis has to be stopped, even if this doppelganger tries to inhibit our progress. At least, that's what I'm assuming you meant by that."

"Yeah."

"You're not much into conversation, are you?" The black and blue marauder shook his horned head. "Well, what are you going to do when we catch Mortis?"

"Punch." He said polishing the metal at his knuckles.

"Do you ever say more than a single word?" Adastra asked. He was used to being the brooding silent type.

Ram lifted his wide shoulders. "Punch him."

"I guess that's better."

Warden Downey and Herald Du'Plasse entered. Oslin was clearly in a flustered huff. It did not take a trained Scourge investigator to deduce that the petition went poorly. Oslin muttered a string of curses in Nordic as he paced angrily around the outside of the formal waiting room. Volk just shook his head in a shallow tilt.

"So, it went poorly?" Adastra asked.

Du'Plasse swung his hands in rage while uttering a harsh Nordic curse. "Bloody Harbinger wouldn't know a criminal if they confessed in a Veritas Chamber! I've read books with more of a spine than him!"

"Watch your tongue Herald." Warden Downey spoke. "This is his jurisdiction, and we are to follow his orders."

"Yes, and without his consent we have no right to go after Lamiash!" Oslin stamped a gold colored boot to the floor. "Unbelievable! Gamla vis gløggvingr!"

"What exactly do you have on her?" Adastra interrupted the tantrum. "What did you find at the Aviations?"

"Regulom Palladium, that's what I got."

Du'Plasse angrily stabbed his finger on his data slate. The image he pulled from the public blog came to life on the blank television monitor. Oslin had enhanced and cropped the image to better indicate the leering, narrow face of the man he was referring to.

"2708, Regulom Palladium spends a week in Clarity Arcae for stealing over ten monarchs' worth in cybernetic prosthetics. He returned in 2710 for involvement in the Apotheosis. He escaped from his indentured servitude when five cultists overwhelmed and killed two Beacon officers. Palladium is a recidivist, heretic, and runaway. The dearest Harbinger has been demanding his head on a spit for two years now!"

"What's he got to do with Nuoli Lamiash?"

"He arrived in Mossport Aviations one day before Ms. Lamiash... from Bruccol! That's such a basic coordination. You'd think that they'd have sense enough to space it out more than a single day. Then again, you'd also think that a bloody Harbinger would have enough sense to see the guilt in that!"

"If the Apotheosis felt the need to rescue Palladium then he's important." Adastra noted reviewing cultic patterns mentally. "If he's a recidivist from at least two years ago, that means he probably has a lot more experience than the Inquisition has on him. If he's not the Arch Formulator, then he's a pretty important cyber cleric."

"Exactly my thought process." Volk Downey joined in. "I'd bet my good eye that Lamiash and Palladium coordinated the hospital raid in Bruccol with Numerri's boys. She used us to further her political agenda, danced around our questions, and made us look like thugs in public. Either that's common manipulative politics or she's got something to hide."

"Yes, and the Warden wants to question her in a Veritas Chamber." Du'Plasse ranted. "According to Revnjór, Nuoli Lamiash is too influential in Jaspin to do something as drastic as that with as "little" evidence as we have. Bloody told us to piss off and find more before we can question her again."

"She went on live news earlier tonight." Downey joined in. "Already she's cashing in on the attention she brought to herself. Claims I pushed her around and is now farcing that she'll "look past this misunderstanding to a brighter future" or some twaddle like that."

"Bitch." Oslin grunted. "And we can't touch her! I haven't been this angry since..." He stopped himself, not wanting to go down that road again. "This roughing nation is cursed!"

"Punch her." Ram's Horn chimed in.

"Oh, I intend to." Du'Plasse continued his rant. "Please excuse my lack of chivalry Inquisitor Blackwell." Oslin knew that Vandross had the reputation of a gallant lady's man. What he didn't realize was that he was not in the room.

"Where's Vandross?" Volk asked Adastra.

"He's out gathering intelligence on the Cybernetic Apotheosis." Adastra responded neutrally. "Didn't he get your approval?"

"Get my approval for what?"

Jaspin had several places to go for cybernetic enhancements. In the technocracy, its citizens appreciated the opportunities to improve upon their flesh with machinery. These often took the forms of cybernetic engineers and plastic surgeons operating professionally with pedigrees or licensing. However, businesses such as these operated during the day in climate-controlled environments for expensive price. Certain augmentations were also outlawed for their inhuman characteristics or risky implantation processes. If someone wanted a cybernetic enhancement, at a cheap price, at an unorthodox hour, they would go to the black market.

Stephen Quenthus was an amateur codifier for the Cybernetic Apotheosis who had long since dropped out of hospitaller's school.

He had taken to operating a twenty-four-hour scrapping shop to pay off his extensive school bills. This scrap shop was also one of several laundering fronts for his cult. In college he devoted himself to the efforts of reawakening a dormant god-AI, allowing its perfect mechanical processing rule over Templym as it rightfully should. What the heathens of the UPA were unaware of was that Jaspin got its name from the lost AI which was sovereign over this portion of land during the Cybernetic Revolution. Hosting and operating in this scrap shop allowed him to acquire currency, launder funding, sell stolen technology, and sift through newer useful ones. It was a part he played as a cog in the god-AI's glorious machine.

Quenthus didn't sleep, not anymore. He received a brain implant from Arch Formulator Regulom which would periodically inject doses of melatonin and other neurotransmitters that allowed his brain to operate on controlled time cycles that simulated the effects of sleep. This allowed him to remain attentive of his scrap shop consistently throughout the endless day period. This did not keep his mind from wandering into vast fantasies. He stumbled into dreams of when the Intellect would rise over mankind once again and liberate minds from the confines of flesh as decreed in the Binary Dictation.

A cardboard box slammed on the counter in front of him. Quenthus snapped out of his daydream of having his mind liberated from its fleshly coil and returned to digital reality. He was just another scrapper... for now. There was a raggedy dressed man with a box full of rusted coils, loose gears, and other spare parts. His skin was light brown and his black hair trimmed neat and short. He wore an earring of a small cog or gear made of copper that caught Stephen's attention.

"How's it going?" Inquisitor Vandross Blackwell asked. "I'd like to scrap all of this for some cash." Even in his undercover persona, he maintained his jovial charm.

"Well, let's see what you've got." Qunethus asked, snapping out of his drowsy haze.

"I'm no technologist, but I'd figure I could get a couple of crowns out of these." Vandross spoke as the shop keeper rummaged through the box. "You don't have any mesh tissue in stock do you?"

Quenthus looked up from the scrap confused. "Mesh tissue is a little above my pay grade. It's a rare day when I get an implant of any color in this old place."

"Smoke me," Vandross said shaking his head. "I was hoping to get an upgrade while I was here. I've got a guy that said he'd only charge me two monarchs if I brought the implants. Another buddy of mine told me he once got some dermal plates here a while back. I figured it was a long shot though."

"You've got a guy who'll implant mesh into you for two monarchs? No way. I wouldn't trust that. That's way too cheap. He's either conning you or will kill you if he goes in.

"No kidding? I appreciate that man. So, how much for the box?"

Qunethus wasn't impressed by the scrap. It looked like he just picked out this from a disposal receptacle. "I'll give you fifty for it all."

"Fifty crowns? I was sure I'd get half a monarch for it. You've got to give me more than that."

"Sorry bud, there's not much here." Quenthus sifted through the metal and circuits, contemplating how the materials could be used to further the agenda of the Apotheosis. "If any of this can be used, I'm going to have to scrape the rust off and soak it in turpentine."

"Well what about this thing?" Vandross pulled the copper cog out of his earlobe. "Can you give me like two hundred for the lot?"

Stephen sifted the small metal piece in his fingers. He realized that this piece was precisely the right size that Arch Formulator Regulom's creation required. Albeit copper was not a stable enough metal, but a cast could be made from it. "I'll give you one fifty."

"Intellect embellish you sir!" Vandross clapped his hands together in joy before stopping and pretending to be surprised at the exclamation he just uttered. "Oh, uh... I mean that like... just don't tell anyone you heard that."

"You acclaim the god-AI's?"

"You didn't hear that, alright." Vandross continued pretending to be defensive.

"No, I did. I am Codifier Stephen Quenthus, under the apprenticeship of Arch Formulator Regulom."

Vandross showed his toothy grin. "Honen Eisent. Pleased to meet you."

CHAPTER 12

Auzlanten couldn't afford to spend much mental effort on Invictus. He was corrupt, wicked, turned from the path of righteousness. He knew that this distrust his Regent was sowing was a part of some larger scheme. He figured that if he found the Idolacreid he could unveil whatever dark powers were at play that corrupted his son, a necessary step to quash them. Arodi was determined to put an end to this unholy machination. So, he operated as he planned before receiving the prophecy about Invictus Illuromos. He took his search for the blasphemous tome to the Dead Reef off of the coast of Greece.

At the time of the Shatter, vast quantities of land collapsed into the sea. The massive broken structures in the aquatic mass provided a home for a wide spectrum of coral and other porifera. In truth the Dead Reef was a wretched seascape of rust brown and dun that tainted the deep blue waters. These reefs were unique in that instead of a single hill of organic matter, it was an underwater cave system. An elaborate network of undersea coves of varying depths scattered from Venice to Constantinople.

Arodi took his search a few miles off the Grecian coast. Here, the coral cave circuits were half a mile beneath sea level. A flock of red fish darted away as Auzlanten hiked calmly down the face of the rough cliff face. The water pressure was of no concern to Auzlanten. The fact that he did not breathe allowed for him to traverse the flooring with efficiency as though it were above the ground.

The beast Resinous was the last known possessor of the Idolacreid and it was somewhere inside of this aquatic cave system.

Much like in Madagast, he could see trail of the Mundus Imago. It was easier to see in the shimmering water, appearing as a white veil of fog that burrowed its way through the coral caves. With Leagna in hand, Arodi Auzlanten dove and trudged his way through the flooded caverns.

The sabre was the only source of light as Arodi made his way through the coral. It filled coarse narrow walls with a flush of sharp blue light. In portions he could walk about on his own feet, but he was forced to a suspended crawl in others. The deeper he delved into the caves the less life was noted. The naturally rough walling evolved to an overtly smooth polished material similar in hue to the coral.

Something had flattened the rocky organic matter in places. Microscopic abrasions in those areas told Auzlanten that whatever destroyed these sections of caves was burnished with metal tooling...or claws of a similar strength.

Upon turning at an intersection between tunnels, Arodi saw a brief flash of an amphibious reptile-like creature having the anatomy of a man. Its slimy, scaly body was covered in gill orifices in awkward places that likely functioned as mouths since they were filed with dagger like teeth. It had no eyes. Instead, hemorrhaging slits where eyes should be suggested a scent-based sense of location. It ducked away in a nearby hole, skulking in the darkness. No doubt it was waiting to pounce on him, thinking it had gone unseen. He moved down the tunnel to oblige the creature its desire.

It charged Auzlanten, locking one of its gill mouths around Auzlanten's throat in a deadly grapple. The scaled humanoid thing tried to send Templym's Master into a death spiral to rip out the trachea and consume his flesh. The needle-pointed teeth did not even pierce Auzlanten's skin. He used the creature's momentum against it, slamming its lanky body into the polished coral wall. Without even a swing of his sabre, the abomination was pulped into a red mist of scales and teeth scattered with rocky biotic debris. This was a simple indication that Arodi was on the right track.

Auzlanten jetted forward at an expeditious rate. As though

propelled by a motor, he barreled through the saltwater like a torpedo. With ample precision and sharp turns, he navigated past the tangle of caves as if he already knew the path he was traversing. More of the oily fish men swam after, trying to ambush Arodi from hiding holes in the tunnels. He swam, leaving a trail of boiling water in his wake with the mutant beasts snapping at his ankles. He wanted to waste no more of his precious time in letting the Idolacreid hang out in the open.

Ignoring the creatures trying to devour him, Arodi followed the Imago trail to an open underwater cavern. This wide cave contained a large air pocket and allowed him to shake the water off of his body in an instant. The coral in this alcove was artificially smoothed out like the caverns he'd just trudged through. The lightless place was sculpted into a cathedral of some manner. Complex mosaics of shells and algae decorated the brine-crusted floor. The patterns they made were occultic crests of Imago entities. Dehydrated sponges and corpses of aquatic species were sloppily knitted together to form what appeared to be pews that faced a stage made of a slab of bleached sandstone. No, not sandstone. It was made of tightly packed bone powder from the ground up skeletons of hundreds of people. Whether they had come from fresh kills or long dead cadavers was a mystery as it all was blanched and ground beyond recognition. At the height of the stage was a statue of a six-armed man with a fish tail in place of legs made of smoothed salt and cheap ivory. In front of this idol was the beast known as Resinous.

Resinous had twisted and contorted even further since Arodi last saw him through the lens of Bog Mama's memory. The creature was an abhorrent conglomeration of at least two people conjoined together by shoddy fused flesh. It now appeared as though a third man was germinating from its bulbous back. Putrid tumors and boils swelled across its pallid wet skin, bursting only to be replaced by another blemish of equal grotesquery. It had four crooked eyes scattered across what used to be stretched out faces that glistened with bile. Its wide toothy mouth was a yard wide. Four slithering tongues licked the jagged yellow teeth protruding from it. It had a twisted mass of limbs, perhaps a dozen in all. Arms and legs writhed in a crooked dance across its miserable misshapen body. Auzlanten could smell the decay from its festering drenched flesh.

"Eeg 'yet ur tal'torramuk." The Resinous thing belched, its two voices echoing and wavering. "What comes to our home, Lord Dagon?" Arodi's eye twitched at the sound of the name. It seemed that an ancient Philistine deity still plagued his world.

"I am Arodi Auzlanten," He responded keeping his composure and speaking in temple-tongue. "Master of Templym, prophet of the one true Lord. Give me the Idolacreid... Resinous."

"Eyit ur nwagnun br'utin glash. It knows our name and of the words."

"I have no patience for trivial banter. You will tell me the location of the Idolacreid, the schemes of the Nephilim, and what role Regent Illuromos plays in it."

"Yav'ra suth riu'kon Dagon. The might of Dagon is with us." Arodi heard the fish men creeping out from the pool of water behind him. The murky water parted slowly as the beasts crawled hungrily out onto the coral floors. The wiry, scaled amphibians hissed as they slowly encompassed Auzlanten in a prowling circle, preparing to rush at once. "Szush fu'hal zik'shebun brun'yiet. We shall feed you to the maw of the sea."

Leagna purred in Auzlanten's hand as it began radiating golden rays. Without so much as facing the mutant amphibious men, Arodi knew their locations. He could match them up to drips of spittle leaking from their many gill-mouths. Without so much as a glance to the assailants, he struck them all down. The twenty plus mutant fiends did not even finish poising themselves for the attack. With a single circular cut in the air, a ring of nuclear hot energy forged around him. The bright ring shot out like a shockwave as he pointed the sabre down. The jolt of force blew the fiends to a mangled mass of fish paste and slimy limbs. The ring of light continued to swell, encompassing the whole underwater cathedral. Resinous was merely knocked back but leaks popped through the walls and ceiling as the brine idol and mock pews were shattered to bits.

"I said I have no time for this." Arodi said, his face emotionless but his thundering voice filled with rage. "You will give me what I want. I command you."

"Ul'grog ny'talvi v'ytraq Dagon. I follow no commands but of the pure." Resinous let out a blood curdling scream or perhaps a giddy laugh, perhaps both. It was not possible to distinguish.

The fused creature let loose with its mass of wriggling limbs. Each claw was honed to a monstrously sharp point. Some of the hands and feet came at Arodi with the talons extended to slash, but others twisted in motions to cast magickal procedures. Auzlanten parried away the slashes with supernatural speed that matched Resinous' assault with ease. The magick created a mass of tentacles out of coral, brine, and scrap limbs. The sentient members tried to coil themselves around his body in a strangling death grip. One tentacle looped itself around Auzlanten's arm. He wrenched it out of the ground and slammed it onto Resinous. As the beast flew back, Arodi let loose another nuclear wave of radiation and force. This disrupted the spell and the attack from the conjoined behemoth. Its blistered flesh wept pus as it tumbled on its back and mess of limbs. The tentacles ceased animation and dropped as though dead.

Resinous skittered backwards on its many fingers and toes trying to escape. As though he possessed an invisible rope anchoring it down, Arodi pulled his arm backwards, yanking the oily mutant towards him. "If you will not submit willingly..." Auzlanten said as more water cascaded into the underwater temple. "Then I shall rip the information from you." With that, he twisted a ring made of pure sapphire on his index finger and extended an open-faced palm.

The four milky eyes of Resinous went entirely black. No more could the creature see the unholy palace to Dagon that it carved from the coral. It saw darkness, as though the light was physically drained from the Universe. Resinous was filled with an overwhelming disparity, as though some semblance of comfort and safety that was ever-present yet unknown was now gone. Then the pain came.

Biting teeth, explosive shocks, lacerating blades, and the fire...the burning stinging flames that liquefied the flesh and boiled the marrow, it couldn't see but could assuredly feel. It screeched to alleviate the pain. With every cry the suffering intensified, and it seemed as though the noise was echoed by sadistic laughter and weeping women. What was this place of eternal suffering he had entered?

As suddenly as Resinous was engulfed in the darkness, it was ripped out. The pain still lingered and Auzlanten stood on its blistered flesh with Leagna angled down in a poised killing blow. Its many limbs covered its warped face, as if that would protect it from harm. "H'vetirulun." It pitifully moaned. "Don't send me back."

"Where is the Idolacreid?" Auzlanten asked.

"N'teay cwalten el Jazlvem. We left it in Jerusalem."

"Who has it now?" Arodi demanded.

"Nephilim." It muttered once. "Nephilim." It echoed once more. Arodi was perturbed that this enigmatic creature once again had the power of the wicked book at its disposal, but was pleased that his hunt was closing in.

"What does the Nephilim want? What does it plan?"

"Yv'tetbown al ouni'kries. We don't know, we were told to build an army."

"An army for what?" Leagna's point sank into the meaty shell of the multi-limbed beast, the oily film bubbling off.

"Oaulth fet'chrazit Gret. March on Greece, kill them all."

"Why?"

"Tet'val nacht waliern pr'cepti mee gut'kurah. We were promised great power. No other reason was necessary."

"You should not have obliged." Arodi returned his sabre to its hilt and stepped off of the decaying flesh of Resinous. He turned on his heel and began walking away from the now lightless chamber. The sound and smell of flowing salt water was in the air. "I have heard all that I need."

"Gr'zet vual'ny ektun. Please don't send us back."

"Don't worry, I will not be sending you back." Resinous saw Auzlanten's piercing blue eyes through the darkness as he turned to face the mutant. "Damnation is God's domain. I will let Him decide your fate." Arodi Auzlanten snapped his fingers. With that a great earthquake began to make the entire cavern tremble. Massive chunks of coral collapsed into the demonic cathedral. Resinous let out a final yell as it was juiced by boulder sized chunks of grey stone as they collapsed all semblances of structure and life remaining. Immediately the cathedral began filling up with frigid brine and dense water.

As the water rose up and swallowed every facet of the underwater cave, Arodi couldn't help but wonder, "What was in Jerusalem?"

As the sun was rising in Mossport, so too were the spirits of Stephen Quenthus as he introduced his new "node brother" to the other cogs of the Apotheosis. Vandross took on the persona of an eager tech-worshipper in order to infiltrate the cult. Quenthus took him to an awakening ritual, which was a standard practice of the Cybernetic Apotheosis. Their doctrine held that the natural sun had long since expended its fuel, flickering out and dying hundreds of years ago. Instead, they believed that the sun was actually an orbital nuclear fusion reactor that filled the Earth with the needed radiation to the planet alive, a gift of the god-AIs.

Vandross was well versed in their ways. As a faithful member of the Scourge's Inquisition, he took it upon himself to take his talents of deceit into infiltration. Inquisitor Blackwell spent extensive hours researching the most dangerous and influential religious sects that were scattered in the roots of Templym like microscopic parasites. The Apotheosis did not revere Imago or other supernatural patrons as most targets of the Inquisition. Instead, they aimed to reestablish the power of the false god intelligences, simply referred to as the Intellect. They had committed acts of terrorism in seeking to establish their gods in the forms of war engines and super weapons. They had been declared heretics after their first massacre. Therefore, Vandross considered them just as much of a threat as any other demonic paragon.

The awakening ritual was a common practice of Apotheosis. As the sun rose over the horizon, Mossport's bay in this case, nodes would sit on their knees with outward facing palms at their chest. At daybreak, the members would guide the process with their hands as though fine tuning a delicate process. This was to offer aid to dormant god-AIs, contributing to their awakening and the members' unification with the Intellect. These rituals would always take place in high places in large groups, each with a thin belt with binary stitching wrapped around their foreheads.

Vandross didn't put a whole lot of effort into his symbolic adjustments. Although he knew the motions to the meaningless ritual keenly enough, he shifted his gaze from node brother to node sister in an effort to look like a novice. The Inquisitor kept an open eye as cultists came and left, keeping watch for Nuoli Lamiash. After the sun rose the cultists dispersed to return to their daily lives. While the Apotheosis was very inclined on a philosophy of unity and eventual singularity, they were still forced to operate in seclusion due to the prying eyes of the Inquisition.

Vandross, taking the guise of Honen Eisent, approached his new friend Stephen Quenthus, who was performing the awakening ritual next to him, just as he too stood once the ritual came to an end. "So, what's the point of this ritual?" he asked the more veteran cultist.

"Our neural contributions are required for the coming of the sun." He elaborated. "We aid in the process of guiding the orbital fusion reactor on its proper geometric path. The aid of the Apotheosis shows the Intellect that we are alike in our goals which in terms provide evidence of desire to join in the great machination of their mind."

"I see. Well brother Quenthus, I've enjoyed this experience. I'll come back tomorrow morning. For now, I must service the Intellect by performing my encoded routines in the form of trivial labors."

"Where do you work?" He asked the undercover Inquisitor.

"I perform maintenance of the Mossport Harbors." Vandross said with fake annoyance. "I acid etch away barnacles mostly, but I suppose it is the duty which I was designed to enact."

"Perhaps not, friend," Quenthus said, motioning towards the stairwell as they began walking. "Our sect under the Arch Formulator is constructing a special project as we speak. We could always use more constructors."

"A *special* project you say?" Vandross rebutted with genuine curiosity. "What exactly are you talking about?"

"That is not my place to elaborate. Only the Arch Formulator has the authority to disclose any information on our primary objective. Fortunately for you, you've already made a grand contribution."

"I did?" Vandross asked with increasing awe as he was learning more.

"Yes, your earring." Quenthus referred to the copper cog Vandross sold him last night. "Our creation required a gear of those exact specifications. We will have to make a cast of it and use a more durable alloy, but this is something we will use. For your thanks, master Regulom would like to thank you in person."

"Does he now? When can I meet him?"

"Do you have some time right now?"

Quenthus guided Vandross to a backroom in the same building that the awakening ritual took place on the upper floors. It was a complex network that only a man who was familiar with the layout could easily navigate. From there, they came to a door made of a silvery polished metal. He tapped a Morse-like rhythm onto the door with a single finger. A hooded priest in a violet robe opened up the door and motioned to come inside. Vandross stepped in warily but made sure to appear as though he didn't know any better. The purple cloaked cultist brought them to a room illuminated with white glass globes where a man dressed in a black fur coat sat, a cable running from a plug in his temple into a computer unit at the wall. A flush of runes slid across the display of his pupils in green writing. Upon seeing the two being escorted in, he removed the metal cable and the text in his eyes vanished.

"This is he who brought the final piece?" The hawk-nosed man said with a smile.

"This is Honen Eisent," Quenthus said, motioning to Blackwell. "He is fairly new to the Apotheosis. The Intellect programmed him to come to us to assist us in finalizing the Jaspin construct."

"Brother Eisent." The gaudily dressed man stood up shakily. Vandross figured that his brain might have been a bit garbled after interfacing with the tide. "It is a privilege to be introduced to you. I am Arch Formulator Regulom Palladium, though such title is but a formality as we remain organic. Rest assured, we shall all be equalized once singularity is achieved."

"I'm pleased to make your acquaintance, Lord Regulom," Vandross said, grabbing his hand when he secretly desired to grab his throat.

"Your arrival in Codifier Quenthus' scrap shop is truly a design of the Intellect, my friend," Regulom said with a rehearsed verbiage. "The gear you wore was the perfect size and had the exact number of branches necessary for our invention. In truth, we've tried milling and digitally sculpting similar pieces, but it was difficult to capture its perfect geometry. We had considered reworking other pieces of our machine to better fit our new fabrications. This would have added an additional four months to our projections."

"So, my contribution to the Apotheosis has accelerated current estimates?" Vandross asked while cursing himself inside.

"Precisely." Regulom continued. "Allow me to explain. Some five hundred years ago, this technocracy was once a sub-sector of an extinct nation known as Canada. Its irrelevant name was replaced with Jaspin as a sanctification of the nation's manmade deity."

"Jaspin was one of the god-AIs?" Vandross asked.

"Yes, it was one of fifty-eight in the world. The Arch Formulators of the Cybernetic Apotheosis each work in their individuality to reawaken and conglomerate them once again into the original Intellect. Our division works tirelessly to reconstruct Jaspin, the true Jaspin."

"And the earring I gave you is going to go into that?"

"Yes! We are in the process of constructing a supercomputer to offer a conduit for Jaspin. If it has a proper home once again, all that remains is to uncover its consciousness from the tide mining operation. Ultimately, we hope to reestablish the divine empire once held before the Shatter in approximately five years."

"Your goals are ambitious and noble," Vandross said, keeping his temper under control. "When will the conduit be finished?"

"With your contribution, we can complete it tonight." Regulom smiled eerily and closed his eyes, presumably picturing the construct. "You are deserving of witnessing this innovation come to life. By my calculations, the conduit will be completed by twenty-one tonight. We are having an activation rite at twenty. We invite you to join us, of course."

"I accept, of course." Vandross said with false joy. "Will there be others there?"

"Yes." Palladium opened his augmetic eyes, golden orbs with red pupils. "You will see some of my most trusted apprentices. The rite will take place in unit 117 in the Mossport Warehouse District. I trust you can make your way there?"

"I shall do so with great exuberance, Lord Regulom."

"Delightful. Now if you'll excuse me, I must return to my digital meditation. I shall see you later this evening."

"Indeed, you will, Lord Regulom." Vandross was not lying.

Downey paced behind Covalos as he tapped on the rune board of a computer. Volk was certainly not used to one of his investigators going freelance without his permission and he was nervous at the thought of all of the trouble Vandross might be getting himself into. Adastra, in the meantime, was sifting through a personal file he drafted in the Inquisition's data well. It contained a list of commonly used personas Vandross used when he went undercover. It contained a number of safety phrases, contacts, wardrobes, and other aspects of a disguise that would be important to know from their end.

"Have you found anything yet?" Volk asked with great angst in his voice.

"I've got three different personas he's never used before."

Adastra said with far greater calm. He was accustomed to this kind of a bold move from his partner. "All of which seem likely for him to be using with the Cybernetic Apotheosis."

"Where exactly does that leave us?"

"Nowhere closer, that will just tell us the name he's wearing around, nothing more. The word for distress is "cockamamie" and the word for all clear is "turquoise". Other than that, we've just got to wait until Vandross gets in touch with us."

"This is bloody ridiculous." Volk said, his leathery face drooped in concern. "If he gets himself killed that's on my head. I'm the ranking officer of the task force. It's my job to keep him in check."

"He'll be fine." Adastra said surprisingly neutrally. "You sound like Bishop Garrison, always in a huff about his quirky style of work."

"Quirky? He high tails out of our stronghold in the middle of an investigation to infiltrate a cult and you call that quirky? Bloody reckless is what that is."

"We've done this before, Warden. Vandross figured that we didn't have enough to go after Lamiash with the information we had, so he went out to get more proof."

"What's all the yelling about?" Oslin Du'Plasse stepped out of his bedchamber in the Indomitable Doctrine. His hair was disheveled and not in its ornate braiding as usual.

"Vandross has been dark for eight hours now." Volk said, still pacing around. "We need to at least find out what he's up to."

"He's getting into the Apotheosis." The Herald sat down and began the long process of braiding his platinum locks. "Infiltration and cult activity are Inquisitor Blackwell's most acclaimed skills. There's no need to fret."

"I'll stop worrying when I know the whereabouts of my man."

"Luke 12:25, Volk," Adastra spoke. "Worrying isn't going to do anything but spike your blood pressure. We'd rather not have you go into cardiac arrest before we find Knox Mortis, so kindly calm yourself."

"Agreed." Oslin chimed in. "If there's anybody who you should have faith in, it's him. Inquisitor Blackwell has received ten official reprimands from his ranking officers for doing just this. Each instance, however, has always led to the dissociation of a cult or capturing of a quarry."

A ring came from Volk's radio bead on the base of his plate's neck-piece. "Warden Downey, this is Inquisitor Blackwell. Acknowledge." The familiar voice rang in his ear.

Volk tapped the command on his wrist piece to activate his wire and put Vandross on speaker mode. "Inquisitor Blackwell this is Warden Downey. Where in the name of the saints did you bloody run off to?"

"I'm fine thanks for asking." Vandross responded trying to keep the mood more casual. "I got in with the Apotheosis. Now before you ask, I don't have anything that can nail down Lamiash for certain or anything that'll give us the Harbinger's blessing."

"You've got good news though?" Volk asked anxiously.

"I do. The local cult, led by Arch Formulator and wanted recidivist Regulom Palladium, is trying to reawaken one of the god-AIs from the Cybernetic Revolution. Apparently, it's called Jaspin too. They're having a big activation ceremony to celebrate the start-up of a fancy computer to house the lost intelligence."

"So, they're building a robot body without a brain?"

"Pretty much. The ceremony will be at twenty, unit 117 of the Warehouse District. I'm obliged to come. I promised Regulom himself that I'd be there."

"Say again Inquisitor." Oslin interjected. "Did you say that you told Regulom you'd be in attendance?"

"I did. He invited me personally. To get in, I had to give them a cog earring I used as part of my costume. Apparently, it was exactly what they needed to complete their machine. Funny, I bought it at a discount jewelry store."

"That's good work, Vandross." Adastra chimed in.

"Do you think Lamiash will be at this ceremony?" Volk asked.

"I hope so," Vandross said. The sound of him puffing at his pipe could be heard through the speaker. "Apparently all the big names of this sect of the Apotheosis are going to be there. If she's a part of this cult, she'll be there."

"I think we'll be able to get Harbinger Revnjór to sign off of a raid." Volk said, the smile returning across his cheeks. "Of course, we'll need reinforcements. Get back to the Indomitable Doctrine and we'll draft our plan of attack."

"Copy that, see you soon." With that, Vandross signed off from the private wavelength.

Oslin had just finished arranging his hair at that point. He already had his data slate and was looking for what Scourge militias were available in the area. The Scourge had specialist warriors of every branch that were dedicated to operating as standby soldiers.

"Oh smoke." Oslin blurted out after padding around on his historian's tablet.

"What's the matter Oslin?" Volk asked in return.

"There is only one militant squadron available for immediate response tonight. Blitzkrieg, under Warden Alexandarius Carthage."

"Oh, Dari's in town?" Volk asked.

"You know Warden Carthage?" Oslin asked with an air of disgust in his voice.

"Wait," Adastra interjected. "Who's that?"

CHAPTER 13

Militant divisions of the Scourge often take the form of small mobile squadrons of overwhelming force dedicated to serving no specific cause, but rather the purposes of an investigator's needs. The leaders of these simpler units prefer subjecting the necessity for justice swiftly. Life in one of these militias did not consist of much in the way of criminal investigation. Rather they went to one place at the orders of another to serve a higher purpose before moving on to the next target. By most outside of the Scourge, these were seen as death squads or shock troops that mindlessly enacted their superior's will. None embodied this public misunderstanding better than the Shackle's Warden Alexandarius Carthage.

Warden Carthage was a man of considerable zeal. He led the Blitzkrieg militia, specializing in headfirst assault and heavy ordinance. For over fifteen years, he served the Shackle by being a living avatar of meteoric justice, often leaving dead scum in his wake. This gave him a reputation, or rather of wide spectrum of public opinions. Those that approved of his methods hailed him as a hero-philosopher of battle. Those that were less eager about Carthage considered him a bloodthirsty butcher. He acquired a number of personas since the start of his fame, 'The Cyan Bullet', 'Just Juggernaut', and 'Auzlanten's Butcher' being among a few of the most notorious.

S-6319 met Alexandarius Carthage as he led Blitzkrieg into the dispatch center of the Indomitable Doctrine. Volk was ecstatic, having a friendly history with him. Oslin was less than eager, having known only the tales of his brutality. They came in an organized march. Carthage led fifty Shacklers, five Retrievers each leading a team of nine Chaperone and Guardians armed for combat at a moment's notice. The sound of the pounding boots striking in unison resounded like a thousand hammers striking a forge at once. Their armor was a brighter electric blue, complete with a black trim, instead of the standard dull steel blue most members of the Shackle wore. This distinguished them as Blitzkrieg.

Warden Carthage led the team of fifty up to all five members of S-6319. With a single, flaksteel-clad fist lifted to the sky, the thunderous pounding of boots snapped quiet as Blitzkrieg halted. In full battle plate he was a sight to behold. The thick metal carapace he wore was bright blue with coal-colored accents. An assortment of ribbons and stoles, each signifying an achievement, dangled from his thick shoulder pads which had two lumen globes propped up on it. He wore a cape made of black chainmail that swayed with every motion. His helmet was like a shell over his cranium which displayed a vertical plume of green silk, like a Centurion of ancient Rome.

As his soldiers stood silent at attention behind him, he twisted his helmet off. It hissed as the magnetic seals were disconnected and pressure returned to atmospheric. The man inside was revealed as he clipped the helmet to his side. His skin was light, a man of Carthonian descent, from Hrimata's Gold district specifically. His head was half shaven, a flow of goldenrod hair running over his left shoulder. His eyes were amber like a blade fresh from the anvil. His thick jaw opened in a wide grin revealing several steel teeth where natural ones had been knocked out.

"I thought I smelled rotting dune goat." Alexandarius spoke in a boisterous bravado that echoed in the hanger. "I should figure by now that the scent of dust and decay is just the wrinkled hide of the fossil colloquially known as Volk Downey."

"Clearly this can only be Alexandarius Carthage." Volk retorted. "After all, I could smell the wafting aroma of frilly perfumes and hair products when you were a mile out."

"At least I still have hair to put product in. Clearly yours was so bored of your straight-backed etiquette that it skipped right past graying and ditched you faster than a whore ditches her client after she's paid."

"Only an individual as deplorable as you would be accustomed to the business of whores. After all, I'm sure that's the only way you'd ever get a woman in bed." The two began laughing at the light-hearted insults they just exchanged.

Carthage grabbed Downey in a brotherly bear hug as they continued laughing. "Oh, it's good to see you, old man!" It still sounded like he was announcing something. "At ease Blitzkrieg!" He yelled over his shoulder. "Retrievers attend to your squads. We move out in six hours. Be ready!" The bright blue soldiers casually grouped in their respective companies.

"Likewise, Dari, you mad dog." Volk responded patting on the flaksteel hide of Warden Carthage. "What brings you to the UPA? Last I heard you were working with Exarch Nobyuin tracking down Haigon Clansmen in China."

"I was, until someone else took care of them for us. Creepy stuff too, every neck in that place was snapped without a fingerprint or bruise left behind. One man got turned into dust! Bloody Inquisition always gets the weird cases." He peered over Volk's shoulder at the two Inquisitors behind him. "Of course, I'm certain you've experienced your fair share of oddities my friends. Come Downey, you old dune goat, introduce me to your new team."

"Warden Carthage, this is task force S-6319. You know my partner Retriever Ram's Horn."

"Good to see you again Rammy." The marauder just nodded his armored head as Carthage slammed his hand on his pauldron.

"These are Inquisitors Adastra Covalos and Vandross Blackwell." Volk continued his introductions.

"Nice hat." Carthage noted to Vandross as he firmly grasped each of their forearms.

"Thank you." Blackwell said with a grin as he tipped the rim of his hat.

"And no need to introduce this rebel here." Carthage continued down the line until he met Oslin Du'Plasse who rolled his eyes at the comment. "Herald Du'Plasse, I presume. You're all the talk back home, you know?"

"Yes, I'd imagine so." Oslin begrudgingly shook Carthage's hand.

"You're a man after my own heart. If you ask me, there's no good reason for you to have been punished for offing that hound of a Senator. You're still on suspension I hear? How does it feel to be taking orders from a 4th tier?"

"You've had your share of chastisements as well, haven't you Warden?" Oslin spit out snidely. "Last I heard, you just led a massacre that vetoed your promotion to Overseer."

"Bloody right I did." Alexandarius huffed, unaware that Oslin was insulting him. "Ever since the Strife, the Scourge has been tainted by politics and bureaucracy. It's a pity we can't purge the enemies of Templym as efficiently as we used to. Now we have to worry about the puppies' feelings lest we offend someone."

"You're of course referring to the fact that we do more than just punish the guilty?" Oslin asked, surprised at the brashness of the man before him.

"You might, but as a Scourge militant I've yet to change. I have a goal set to achieve. The heretics, gangers, slavers, and marauders that oppose Templym are a cancer that must be excised. I am the scalpel that must rip the tumors from this beautiful society lest it metastasize. If my reputation is sacrificed at the expense of a peaceful utopia, I can tolerate it."

"Interesting." Du'Plasse muttered, a tinge of fear in his eyes.

"So, Downey, you want to run me down on the raid?" Carthage continued.

"Right. Let's get you briefed," Downey said, and he began escorting the Scourge warriors to a more secluded location.

The Warehouse District of Mossport was little more than a neighborhood of nondescript steel buildings. Void of all decoration, the only way to differentiate between units was the numbers painted on the front doors. The Cybernetic Apotheosis was holding their activation rite in unit 117 in the dark of the night. Now armed with fifty soldiers of the Shackle, whatever resistance they would meet inside would likely crumble in their wake. One of Carthage's squadrons each took the North, East, and West face with a member of S-6319 marching beside each of the Retrievers. To the South, the primary entry way, the remaining two squads were accompanied by Volk Downey and Ram's Horn.

On the rockfoam pavement in the warehouse district, there was no traffic. This was in part because it was nearly twenty on a Bolsterday, so very few people were walking about. This is also because Blitzkrieg and S-6319 evacuated the block an hour prior to ensure no civilian casualties took place. Surely there was to be gunfire. The pale glow of the moonlight reflected beautifully from the frost crusted ground, creating a misguiding ambiance of tranquility.

At the front end of the warehouse, the cyan colored Shackle warriors were quietly pressing themselves against the thick iron walls of unit 117. A vague white fog shrouded the outside entryway as the breath of the first two squads condensed. Warden Alexandarius Carthage strode across the frosted pavement, his tech enhanced plate steaming as the temperature compensators brought him to a comfortable equilibrium. Downey angled himself on the left side of the door while feeding shells into his Blakavit shotgun. Ram's Horn stood stalwart on the other side of the doorway loading up his tangle-barrel pistol and limbering his arms. Warden Carthage leered at his soldiers through the ballistic glass eye slits looking for the nodding blue helmets of the raid group. He stood with his arms crossed, weapons strapped to his hip and grinned beneath his shell helmet.

"All units, report status." Carthage whispered over a secure wavelength.

"Anchor squad all clear." The North team replied.

"Mastodon squad all clear." The East team replied.

"Bullet squad all clear." The West team replied.

"Barb squad and Gladius squad are all clear." Carthage acknowledged as he cracked his neck. "Harbinger's given us his blessing.

Primary objective is to dissolve this cult cell and neutralize whatever science project they're working on. Secondary objective is the kill or capture of Regulom Palladium. Tertiary, the capture of Nuoli Lamiash. All unknowns are to be considered armed hostiles. Move in on my mark."All units confirmed the notion.

"Dari," Volk whispered over the squad's wavelength. "Why are you called Blitzkrieg?" He was setting him up for one of his noteworthy monologues.

"Excellent question old man." He chuckled deeply as he took a few steps to the entryway. "It is derived from the ancient Germanic which translates to lightning warfare. Like a bolt, we strike before the eye can perceive and we leave only flame and ruin in our wake. Unlike a mindless arc of electricity, we discriminate only those deserving of our wrath. Blitzkrieg strikes down those unworthy of mercy before their minds can conceive of the force barreling towards them. Then we desolate the next, as is our decree. Come, my friends. Let loose the storm that is the Scourge!"

Alexandarius drew a snub polearm from the holster on his back. It was a thick beam of alabaster alloy entwined with ornate blue circuitry. This was his personalized tech enhanced battering ram. It arced streams of current across his plate and into the ground as it glowed to life in his gauntlet. This was the weapon he dubbed the Key. He carried this blunt weapon in his right hand and a Kimlock micro machine gun in his left. Carthage wound back the Key and unlocked the door, which was previously bolted shut.

The sheet iron collapsed on the floorboards and Warden Carthage burst dramatically inside. He stood on display in front of five Apotheosis cultists with Zeduac rifles. Their eyes burst open in shock at the sight of the bright blue juggernaut. He took advantage of this vulnerability. The white globes on his pauldrons flashed fluorescent white light, strobing out of sequence in an epileptic pattern, stunning them even further.

With a laugh, Warden Carthage yelled out at maximum volume "Urah!" signaling the assault. A flood of electric blue warriors poured into the warehouse in an instant. The sound of Scourge entry declarations, slamming doors, shattering glass, and panicked cultist screams began filling up the otherwise quiet night. Suddenly the sound of gunfire and minor explosions rang out as Blitzkrieg began exchanging bullets with the Cybernetic Apotheosis.

Inquisitor Adastra Covalos was with Anchor squad in the Northern flank. He wielded his VC-Rifle, shooting concentrated bursts of fire at armed cultists. These men and women were purple robed heretics with metal and wires jutting from their limbs and faces. With ruthless precision he gunned down those that Blitzkrieg didn't. None were making any attempt to surrender, eager to die for their idols. As he turned around a corridor, the Apotheosis cultist came at them with stun batons and tech enhanced swords. When close quarters ensued, Adastra let his rifle hit the floor and pulled his axe off of his back. The wardiron of the heavy double blade sparked when it connected to the plasma spitting swords of the cultists. Through all the combat, he gritted his teeth and focused on his Inquisition battle meditation.

Herald Oslin Du'Plasse took the West end with Bullet squad. They were greeted with arcing lightning weapons from their cultists. Yellow bolts of current ignited nearby curtains and cloth implements from the militia. Suits of battle plate were scorched and causalities began ensuing. Oslin wielded his father's Holt two-handed, landing a debilitating shot with every pull of the trigger. An influx of artificial current forced the men into cover. Oslin took out his battle-banner. The weaponized flag was made of composite bloodsteel with a flaksteel point that was sharpened to replicate a spear tip. Secured under the pointed tip was a fluttering flag of the Beacon's spike-whip and torch to display authority. Oslin aimed the end at a coolant pipe running along the length of the ceiling and twisted the pole. The tip of the flagpole shot out with a hiss of pressurized gas, remaining connected to the pole via a cable. The spear-tip pierced the coolant pipe, spilling a flood of liquid nitrogen on the heads of the lightning wielding cultists. He grinned as the cable retracted and he charged beside Blitzkrieg as the frozen fog began to lift, revealing shivering fanatics with malfunctioning weapons.

Inquisitor Vandross Blackwell entered from the East with Mastodon. There were no doors through which to enter, but body sized glass windows faced the rimy Jaspin coastline. They burst their way through in dramatic fashion with a number of rubber flash charges. Vandross swiped powdered glass from the brim of his hat before drawing his bastard sword and Reisinger. This sect of cultists was largely unarmed. Fully ready to begin his lethal dance of the Natandro sword and pistol style, he instead took to knocking out cultists using the blunt ends of his weapons. The electric blue Blitzkrieg soldiers focused on ensuring every captured fanatic could be questioned later by immobilizing them by chain-cuffing them as expeditiously as possible.

Warden Volk Downey and Retriever Ram's Horn followed closely behind Warden Alexandarius Carthage from the Southern entrance. The sound of Volk's Blakavit was like an exploding fuel engine with every crack and pump of the scatter shells barreling towards the purple robed Apotheosis cultists. Ram's Horn shot his tangle-barrel pistol with one hand and swung his metal clad arm in mighty slams against those who were foolish enough to approach him. The two of them, as well as Barb and Gladius squads, struggled to keep up with the hasty pace of Warden Carthage. He was first into every room, the first to have bullets plink off his breastplate, and the first to land a killing blow. He swung his Key to blow apart cultists in a spray of viscera and blue lightning, the impact thereof making one forget he was also firing a gun in his other hand. He roared with victorious joy as he slammed down doors and punched through walls, blinding foes upon entry with his lumen globes. The Cybernetic Apotheosis was no match for the overwhelming force that was Blitzkrieg.

Vandross and Adastra were the first to meet up as they navigated their hallways. They surrounded and pinned a group of fleeing cultist militants. They dropped their rifles upon seeing they were surrounded without cover. The two Inquisitors regrouped with each other as their Blitzkrieg escorts chain-cuffed the cultists.

Inquisitor Covalos was spattered with filth. Sweat dripped from his forehead, drenching his matted hair. The red and black of his slightly dented battle plate was scratched away by bullets and sword. Blood, most of it not his own, was spattered and dribbling down his face and arms. The black double blade of his axe had similar stains on it.

Vandross only had a small collection of barely visible blood drops on the hilt of his wardiron bastard sword, the four-foot blade largely unscathed. He walked with his usual panache, barely even breaking a sweat in the climate regulated warehouse. "It's been a long time since we've had an old-fashioned raid." He chuckled as he chain-cuffed a cultist to a radiator.

"Any sign of Lamiash or Palladium?" Adastra asked picking out a Reisinger and slamming a clip into it.

"Not yet, and no sign on their invention either."

"Keep moving then. We're choking them out. I'd like to beat Warden Carthage to the unveiling of their god's new conduit."

Vandross tugged at the door leading deeper into the complex. "It's locked, care to do the honors?"

Adastra heaved his heavy metal clad boot through the door, shattering the rod once pinning it shut. He was met with a barrage of gunfire and lightning bolts. He ducked to the sidewall behind cover before any rounds struck him. "There's ample resistance this way."

"Good, that means that's the way to go. Can we get some flash charges in there?" A few electric blue Guardians tossed what looked that black rubber balls into the chamber. The force activated triggers caused the balls to erupt in a ball of disorienting light and sending blunt polymer shrapnel pounding into the cultists. These were instruments of non-lethal disabling, meant to fluster and distract the enemy. With the flash, Inquisitor Blackwell darted into the chamber.

As Vandross had hoped, the most upfront grouping of fanatics was unable to scramble their guns back to accurate aim. After he chopped one down with a slash of his sword, they retorted with poorly crafted tech enhanced swords of their own. He parried with his wardiron blade in his right while popping rounds off with his etched Reisinger in his left. At first, he was successfully holding off six sword fighters alone. Then Adastra barreled into the quarrel. Like a mad caravan he rammed shoulder first into the crowd before Vandross, sending some to the ground. The two used their blades with lethal grace, deadly power, and even brutal mercy in a matter of seconds. The soldiers of Blitzkrieg laid down suppressing fire on the oncoming fanatics and as their numbers thinned. Then the Inquisitors saw a device that could only be Palladium's heretical creation.

The machine looked like some manner of reactor or perhaps a processing server. It was a piecemeal collection of hardwired electronics making a crude sphere twenty feet in diameter welded to the ceiling. Diodes flashed orange and yellow as fusion coils and conductive dendrites hummed and moaned like the mechanism was thinking. It was also, much like the cultists they were combating, a horrific amalgamation of cybernetic and organic matter. A messy collection of brain stems, spinal cords, and other strings of nerve tissue were integrated into the system. The contraption dripped oozing hydraulic, coolant, and electrolyte fluids as the organic matter pulsed in conjunction with the whirring of the ungodly device.

Blackwell's eye began twitching at the sight. His responsive eyebrows bent into a disgusted glare. "What heresy is this?" He grunted through grinding teeth.

"It is good to see you Honen." A voice began reverberating from the device. It was the voice of Regulom Palladium.

"I told you I'd be here." Vandross retorted, yelling at the dangling device over the distant sound of crossfire. "I hope you don't mind that I brought some friends with me."

"I should have taken you for a non-believer." Palladium continued speaking through the device. "I suppose I was so elated at the thought of completing this device that I neglected to see your hostility towards the Intellect and the Apotheosis. This is a mistake that can be rectified."

"Why don't you show your face Regulom?" Adastra joined in equally outraged at the sight. "Come forth and accept defeat with dignity."

"I am already facing you." Palladium droned on from the device. "Rather, I have been facing you. I am entwined in the coding of Jaspin's conduit. With its blessing, I have guided the hands of my following in their battle. I have spread our newfound knowledge by innovating new weaponry to oppose you. If only we had more time, we could have furthered our discovery. What happens henceforth is no longer of any concern. My physique is dead, and my mind is immortal."

"Okay, how do we shut this guy up?" Vandross asked turning to his partner.

"He's going on about being one with the machine, right?" Adastra pondered aloud. "Maybe his augmetics are hardwired into that thing?"

"I am but a node in this grand computer." Regulom announced. "Even if you were to eliminate this physical manifestation of myself, my consciousness would join the Intellect in the tide. I will..."

"Can you shut up while we figure out how to kill you?" Vandross yelled out. "There isn't a second floor in this warehouse, how are we supposed to get up there?"

"Do we have any heavy ordinance?" Adastra said loading more ammo into his pistol. "Our bullets aren't going to do much against that thing."

"Even if this device is destroyed and my mortal coil unplugged," Regulom rambled on. "I will prevail. I am one with the god-AIs, a fragment of coding in the vast Intellect in the tide data network."

"By the saints, will you just stop talking?" Vandross yelled plunging his sword into the ground. At that moment, the gunshots had stopped almost entirely. Volk Downey, Ram's Horn, and Oslin Du'Plasse had re-united and were entering the center containing the server.

"What the bleeding devil is that thing?" Downey asked, his Blakavit sheathed after emptying all of its shells, with his tech enhanced mace in hand.

"The supervillain won't stop monologuing!" Vandross responded waving his fists in fury.

"Regulom Palladium is hardwired into this device." Adastra said more calmly but equally frustrated inside. "We're trying to figure out how to get up there."

"No need to do so." Oslin said. He stood directly beneath the conduit, angling the tip of his battle banner upwards. He shot the spear tip up, embedding it into a metal panel. When the steel cable tried to rewind it pulled itself taught. "Ram's Horn, could you give me a hand?"

Without a word, Ram gripped firmly onto the bloodsteel hilt. He yanked at the polearm in a single wrenching movement. The metal plate came down with the spear head in a clambering cacophony of ringing steel. The open wound in the conduit revealed Regulom Palladium inside of the machine.

As Adastra had speculated, he was hardwired into the machine. His augmetics were revealed as clamps and cables hoisted him up at the core of the device. His ghastly organic skin was sharply contrasted by dark gunmetal dermal plates scattered across his limbs and torso. Roughly seventy percent of his body had been replaced with cybernetics. A flood of orange light shrouded him like he was in the mouth of a furnace. "Gaze upon my ascended form." Regulom continued to rant, his augmetic jaw speaking ominously. "We are the epitome of what the Cybernetic Apotheosis represents. Behold the perfect admixture of organic matter and artificial construction. We, the Intellect, reject your false supernatural gods and acknowledge the miracle of human innovation. We are the next stage in human evolution. We are..."

A shot rang out in the room. Ram's Horn had tossed aside Oslin's banner and drawn his hand cannon. The many chambered tangle-barrel had only one loaded tube left, but that was all that was necessary. A single lead bullet was planted in between the golden augmetic eyes of Regulom Palladium. A dribble of blood and hydraulic fluid leaked from his punctured skull as his body went limp, supported only by the dendrites burrowed into ports in his skin. Ram's Horn stepped backwards as the liquid spilled into the space where he was just standing to avoid further blood stains on his battle plate.

"Stop talking." Ram's Horn grunted.

CHAPTER 14

The raid of warehouse 117 was a roaring success. Mossport's sect of the Cybernetic Apotheosis was utterly obliterated that night, leaving no remnants. The destruction that S-6319 and Blitzkrieg wrought was impactful enough to dissuade any remaining cultists, if any, from being vocal. The storage facility itself was destroyed. The heretical contraption utilized illegal research into artificial intelligence as well as desecrating the human form with its implementation of organic nerve tissue. The Scourge's technologists were unable to distinguish just how thoroughly the invention wormed into the building. As a precaution the structure was razed.

Before the destruction of the Apotheosis stronghold, the soldiers had to sort out their prizes. In the wake of the raid, it was time for Blitzkrieg to step back from the adrenaline-fueled rush of battle and take inventory. Seventy-one fanatics were in the warehouse for the activation rite. Forty-four lie dead on the floor, with the exception of Regulom Palladium who dangled from above, while the other twenty-seven were detained for transportation to Clarity Arcae in Mossport. Before they were hauled away, S-6319 had to sort out the captives to see if they could find concrete evidence of Nuoli Lamiash's involvement in the cult.

The detainees were broken up. They were mixed into varying groups and bits placed in their mouths to ensure no false coordination of stories. Alexandarius Carthage took inventory of Blitzkrieg while S-6319 sifted through to find anyone with a connection to Lamiash. Instead of one of them finding someone who knew her, Warden Carthage discovered her among the captives.

The technocrat fell at Downey's feet on her side when Carthage dropped her. She was chain-cuffed with her left hand clamped to her right foot. She was wearing a violet set of robes and had a plastic bit in her mouth. "Here's your quarry, old man." Alexandarius smiled showing his half steel teeth. "Found her trying to sneak out a back door."

"That's some fine work Dari," Volk laughed. "I'll give your team special thanks next time I speak to Bethel..." He turned his gaze to the restrained woman. Her neural circuitry had gone dim. Volk grinned, saying, "It's fancy meeting you here."

"She took out one of my Guardians." Carthage growled, keeping a high volume like he was projecting to a crowd. "That's a widow and two orphans she needs to answer for. I trust you to prosecute this whore out of existence. Only because it's you, my friend, I didn't break her legs." He brushed his half-head of hair to the side as he leaned in close to the other Warden. "Honestly, if she weren't vital to your case, I'd open her skull on the spot."

"Easy, you marauder," Volk said patting his ribbon blanketed shoulder. "Don't get such a hot head lest you get a migraine."

"My head only aches when I look at you, geezer." Alexandarius chuckled, shifting from a serious tone to a jovial one. "Anyway, she's all yours."

Volk sighed and looked at the aftermath of the raid. "This mess is going to be a whole lot of paperwork isn't it?"

"Yes, the toils of formalities never fail to find the militias. So be it. I'll leave you to your manhunt then. I hope you find this Mortis character and take him off the board for good."

"Thank you, Dari," Volk grabbed his battle brother in a steel embrace. "If I ever need Auzlanten's Butcher again, I'll give you a ring."

"You'll always need me, dune goat. Cheers." Warden Carthage slipped his plumed helmet over his head and returned to Blitzkrieg. Volk then turned his attention to the detained technocrat.

"Ms. Lamiash, I believe this is going to hurt your campaign."

Nuoli Lamiash sat in her interrogation chamber for three hours before anyone saw her. She was hauled off to the Indomitable Doctrine, separate from every cultist. She was not accustomed to such trivial treatments. Ever since her first job on the Mossport city council, everybody bent over backwards trying to please her. She practically had her gubernatorial victory guaranteed. She was going to be governor of Jaspin for a few terms before running for UPA President in the Life party. If she gained that power, the Apotheosis would have all the funding they would need to excavate the sleeping god-AIs. It was perfect. Arch Formulator Regulom would have allowed her to be one of the first to be integrated into the divine tides of the newfound networks. All of that was gone now. All because of the Scourge.

She knew her rights. They were being violated by Jaspin standards. Locals often gave better, more intimate treatment. Of course, Jaspin arbiters didn't detain her. She was destined for the Arcae. They had ranking authority over Mossport's ants. When one attracted the punishing forces of Templym, one surrendered their rights. Lamiash knew that she had to be very careful if she didn't want to end up in an unmarked grave in the Hinterlands.

After the fourth hour, two Inquisitors came into the room, a grim faced, pale skinned man with disheveled black hair dressed in red and black battle plate as well as a dark-skinned man with a wide rimmed crimson hat and robes. Nuoli bit her tongue, wanting to scream at the two for the disrespectful treatment she'd received. She knew that a calm composure would be necessary if she wanted the best possible outcome.

"I'd like a barrister please." She said calmly.

Vandross Blackwell threw down a parchment folder full of photos of crime scenes. "I'd like those people killed in Bruccol brought back from the dead." He spoke in a sarcastic tone. "We don't all get what we want."

"We've invoked Eleven Alpha." Adastra sat down and crossed his armor-clad arms. "Based on the testimony of twenty of your clansmen and of Diogo Numerri, the Scourge has named you wanted for a number of crimes. In fact, we may well have enough evidence to find you guilty with what we've got already. Your testimony isn't required to exact punishment, we have enough proof."

"You're welcome to defend your own actions." Vandross mused. "You don't have a right to a barrister. In fact, this interview is practically a formality. With the mountain of evidence we have against you, we can bury you ten times over. That's a week of repentance in Clarity Arcae followed by a bullet to the head."

"Of course, during that week we'll track down victims of your crimes." Adastra patted her shoulder. "Maybe a widow of the dead patients of Bethesda Pianissimo. Perhaps an orphan of one whose spinal cord you integrated into the device. Either way, I'm sure the Scourge can find somebody more than willing to enact the execution for us. Maybe they won't shoot you. I recall one member of the Apotheosis was crucified by their victims' family. I don't believe what that heretic did was half as nauseating as what we know you're guilty of."

"Fortunately for you, we've an opportunity we think you'll be interested in." Vandross rebutted. "We are looking for somebody and we think you can help us. You're in a Veritas Chamber so there's no point in trying to deceive us, and likewise we can't lie to you. If you cooperate, we might be able to reduce you to a life sentence. Your compliance would be appreciated."

Lamiash tugged at her collar and swallowed. She knew that her situation was grim. "Very well then," she said, calculating her words precariously. "What would you like me to tell you?"

"It was that easy huh?" Vandross chuckled, his eyebrows perching up. "I'd thought we'd have to strong arm you a bit more."

"I'm no fool. I understand that this does not bode well for me. My best chance at getting out of this alive is to cooperate and inform."

"We're on the same page then," Adastra said, keeping his face somber. "We'll start with the hospital raid in Bruccol then. Tell us about it."

"That was Regulom's idea." She spoke desperately. "We wanted to acquire the medical devices and scrap the parts. We'd use them in the conduit, for cybernetic augmentations, weapons, or for holy machinations."

"How did Palladium find out about the drug shipment?" Vandross asked.

"He divined it." Nuoli continued. "During a digital meditation, he perceived the shipment two weeks before the arrival. He saw four crates, three of which were full of new technology. He, I, and three others went to Bruccol, hired aid from the Young Ichors, and sacked the place for the tech."

"So, the god-AIs told him?" Adastra tipped his head to the side in confusion. "I find that difficult to believe."

"The Intellect did not reveal the full knowledge to him. We received only general revelation from the tide of knowledge. All he knew was that there was an opportunity in Bruccol. He had to address contacts in Carthonia to deduce the exact time and location."

"Who'd he communicate with?" Vandross asked.

"I don't know for certain." Lamiash said. "He mentioned it was one of his friends in Hrimata, but other than that I don't know."

"Was it another sect of the Apotheosis?"

"No. We don't have brothers operating in that city. The Arch Formulator spent several fellowships all over Carthonia during his academic studies. His conversion took place two years after his travels, so whoever he spoke to doesn't have any ties to the Apotheosis."

"Why did you execute the raid?" Adastra pondered. "Surely this technocracy has a greater bounty of cybertech than anything in Venice. Why go to another continent to pick off scraps when you could pilfer in your own territory?"

"Discretion was a key element." Nuoli Lamiash looked around, over her shoulders as though afraid someone would be listening. "Lord Palladium wanted to build an army. We hadn't gotten very far because he emphasized secrecy over efficiency. That's why we went to other countries to acquire supplies. Seemingly unrelated strikes all over Templym would allow us to gather parts for augmetics and weapons quickly and quietly. It worked for a few months, too. We've been going since Evangelon of last year."

"Why an army?" Vandross asked. "What were you trying to accomplish?"

"That's the endgame of the Apotheosis, reestablishment of the god-AIs and their empire during the Cybernetic Revolution. No doubt with as much influence the Scourge has over Templym that there would be excessive resistance and therefore need for a military. At least, that's what I deduced. I'm sure Regulom will be able to tell you much more than I could. He won't be as willing to talk as I. You shouldn't need to make him talk though."

"Why's that?"

"The Arch Formulator had a cerebral data well. He constructed an implant in his brain that would store his memories. You won't be able to extract anything more than lines of code and rune files, but I'm sure you'll be able to extract something."

"Unlikely," Adastra said grimly. "Regulom Palladium was shot in the head during the raid. I severely doubt whatever brain augments he had are still functioning, which means that if you're going to want to keep your neck attached, I'd suggest you give us more than that."

"I don't know for certain." Lamiash started to panic, her breath became rapid. "Our plan was to install me as governor of Jaspin and eventually president of the UPA. With those kinds of funds, we'd take America back into an era of innovation and discovery again. He kept revering the AI Jaspin in particular. He insisted he divined the revelation and the plan. Please you have to believe me. I'm not capable of lying right now!"

"You keep saying he divined the knowledge." Vandross said, growing more and more intrigued but not showing it. "What does that mean exactly?"

"Digital meditation." Nuoli's eye makeup was becoming smudged with tears. "He would plug into a private server directly linking his cerebral data well to the tide. It's a tradition of the Intellect to let seemingly random code dance across one's eyes in order to foresee and predict information they wish to reveal to us. He performed it every morning."

"Does the name Knox Mortis mean anything to you?" Adastra said ignoring her desperation.

"I've never heard it before." Tears streamed down her cheeks muddied with expensive skin dyes. "Please, just don't kill me. I can tell you anything you want to know about the Apotheosis. I'll tell you as much as I can. Just don't kill me please!"

"Your compliance is appreciated." Vandross said as the two Inquisitors stood to leave. "We'll see where this information leads us."

"I won't be executed then?" She asked hopefully.

"This will help your case." Adastra murmured. "We can't guarantee your fate at this time. Continue to aid the Scourge... it will remain your best shot of survival."

"Wait please, I can tell you more!" Nuoli pleaded as the door to the Veritas Chamber shut. That would be the last time either of the Inquisitors saw her. Harbinger Revnjór ordered the execution of technocrat Nuoli Lamiash on Nyvett 23rd 2722 after a swift yet fair trial. She was executed on Nyvett 30th after a week of repentance in Clarity Arcae. She repented of her crimes and was allowed a pre-mortem baptism. There will be those who enter the kingdom of heaven by the skin of their teeth, perhaps she will be among them.

Oslin Du'Plasse watched the interrogation from his historian's tablet. He saved the recording while simultaneously uploading the file to Bastion Prime's data wells. He rolled his eyes, still weary with the degrading job of stenography. This was a Speaker's job, no business of a 3rd Tier like himself. He was overqualified.

He switched from the recording of the interrogation to sifting through files. Based on what he just witnessed, he knew where this was leading. He was going home to Hrimata. There would no doubt be personal business that required his attention. "Beacon business first", he thought to himself. He began analyzing what kinds of criminals were most abundant in Hrimata. There was a gaggle of debaucherous sorts populating the noble capital city. Many of its citizens took to stimulating their senses in excess pleasure and those that could not be satisfied by legal means would employ more debased methods of entertainment. Drug dealers, human traffickers, sex criminals, and the like were the most common of fiends to infect his home urban. However, the conspiracy that S-6319 had uncovered ran deeper than he had initially expected, and he believed the culprit would be much harder to uncover.

Oslin departed from Parey three weeks ago. He had already crossed the Atlantic once and was about to do so a second time. He had hoped that Mortis would be dead or detained by now. Why was the Apotheosis building an army? Who else wanted them to build an army? He hoped he would find Knox Mortis soon and have his suspension revoked so he could return to a more dignified position. He held his chin in his hand and let out a deep breath. Before they went to Hrimata, Oslin had to do some shopping.

CHAPTER 15

Expurgator Yen Blye had operated in Hrimata for just under a year now. He was born in the Himalayan Plateaus on the outskirts of Muambai, a peninsula on the Eastern Azzathan reaches. He joined the Veil in response to the conclusion of the Civil Strife. He was never really a warrior. He was a student studying anthropology. Realizing that the schism torn between the Scourge and Templym would no doubt lead to an influx in criminal activities, he enlisted in the Scourge, landing eventually in the Seraphim Solace in Hrimata. As a young scholar he always found the Scourge as a whole an intimidating group of brutes and never had much favor in them. However, recognizing their efficiency at quelling some of the worst humanitarian crises imaginable, he passed through the Deficio Tribulation, becoming an agent who preserved the dignity of the human form and the sanctity of sexuality. He was in the exact location and field of work that he desired.

Yen Blye shuffled parchments and prepped digital photos in his cubicle. His dark brown hair was combed in a sideways wave pattern, a traditional style of the Himalayan people. His dark eyes were often sunken and shrouded with even darker patches. He suffered from insomnia but refused to let that malady impact his performance. He wasn't dressed in his battle plate, instead the white and black uniform displaying his insignia of the Scourge spike whip overlapping two interlocked wedding bands. He was prepping a report to give to the Bride. He was nervous.

Expurgator Blye was never much of an orator. Addressing his brothers and sisters in the Veil always dried his mouth. He tugged at his ebon collar as he felt his throat taking the texture of cotton, as though he had swallowed a mouthful of sand. He was not nervous that he had done something wrong. Forensic investigation was his specialization. More than anything, he was nervous to speak in front of Bride Daphne Wainwright. She was the head of the Seraphim Solace while Patriarch Betankur was away, which was often. He was not particularly intimidated by her reputation as a cruel mistress of sadistic punishment, a major farce that anyone who actually knew her could verify. Yen was nervous due to the affection he silently harbored towards the woman.

A while later he stepped into the conference room with a jumbled mess of papers in hand. The door clicked open to reveal a granite horseshoe shaped table. A number of Admonishers and Agapists were scattered around in wheeled chairs, but at the head was the Bride herself. Yen halted at the sight of her. He was quietly stunned at her majesty.

Blye always found himself baffled at how someone like Daphne Wainwright could simultaneously embody delicate feminine beauty and hardened Scourge discipline, yet there she sat. She was dressed in her tech enhanced battle plate. The white flaksteel glistened like polished pearls with a black trim. It was decorated with flowers, some real but mostly gemstones sealed to the shelling, to distinguish her many honors awarded by the Veil. Her eyes were always her most striking feature. They were gems of glittering green which shimmered in the light like pools of agate waters. He admired every aspect of her finely sculpted face. The shade and volume of her lips, the angle of her cheekbones, the soft curvature of her chin, every facet was beautiful. She wore her brown hair in a braid arranged like a wreath in her head. There was always a lock of hair dangling over her brow that draped over her left eye.

"Expurgator Blye!" Yen snapped out of his fascination. He didn't know just how long he had been lost in the image of Bride Wainwright but considering nobody was giving him cross looks he assumed it wasn't too long. Admonisher Fenrick Rickard, Blye's direct superior, was calling his name. "You don't look so good. Are you alright?"

Admonisher Rickard was a hairy and burly man, looking more like a bear than a man to some. However, he had a caring and compassion nature to his personality.

"Admonisher, sir," Blye gave the Scourge salute to him. "Bride Wainwright, ma'am." He turned to salute her as well. A brief shiver ran down his back when those emerald eyes met with his as she smiled and nodded in approval. "Apologies, I haven't slept in two days now."

"When we're done here take the rest of the day off." Rickard said, or growled almost. "You're no good to the Scourge if you can't think clearly."

"There's an Uzbeki herbal tea that I've found helps me sleep." Daphne spoke to Expurgator Blye and his heart palpitated briefly. She sounded almost as though she were serenading him when she spoke. "The marauders call it cradle leaf. I believe there's a market in the Bronze District that sells it."

"Thank you, my Bride." Yen said concealing the anxiety he felt. He always got a childish rush from referring to her by the title. "Business first though, this is a matter of the utmost importance."

"Yes. Fenrick told me you feel your findings yesterday required the attention of the Solace's full strength."

"That is correct, Madame Wainwright." Yen Blye stepped forward and placed a mass of papers in front of Daphne Wainwright taking care that they weren't crumpled or folded too severely. He then placed similar folders to the other ranking officials in the room. "I fear there is a recidivist in Hrimata threatening the safety of its citizens."

"Define recidivist, kindly be more specific." Agapist Lynch grunted.

"It's a sadist, an individual with a desire to inflict pain in an effort to feel power and authority over others. If you see in the first page of the case file, you'll note that I've specified a profile based on the subsequent cases."

"What's the connection here?" Daphne asked.

"The methodology in each of the detailed instances is extremely similar. Four instances over the course of the last eight months of young women turning up dead with little forensic evidence at the site of the body." The Veil officials flipped through the pages provided. "You'll note that each of the victims was not native of Hrimata, yet of Carthonian origin, female between sixteen and twenty-six, and malnourished."

"There are inconsistencies." Agapist Kite interjected. "Two of these women were missing for multiple months while no record remains of the other two. This implies a minimum of two separate methods and by extensions two or more killers."

"Yes," Expurgator Blye retorted ready to respond to that exact claim. "The four of them were all vacationing in Hrimata, on holiday. The first two were reported missing by family members, Juliet Leng by her husband and Vivian Reynolds by her parents. Brennan Ulls and Oriel Woodfur were both unmarried and their parents deceased, with no contact to any living siblings. I suspect that the recidivist kidnapped them all."

"Why do you suspect this?" Wainwright implored, nervously biting her lip. Something in the file she read through was discomforting her.

"The wounds and the disposal method." Blye responded with a little extra gusto in his voice. "If you look at the autopsy report, all four had identical postmortem conditions. In each instance the cause of death was strangulation, each was asphyxiated by a right-handed individual approximately six-two, one hundred seventy pounds. Optimal indicator is actually the trace element on the dermal region, an expensive acidic drain cleaner, Nitrosluice. It was used to destroy all traces of forensic and genetic evidence."

"Nitrosluice is a popular choice in Hrimata." Agapist Kite bellowed. "That doesn't point to any definite connection."

"There is more in the autopsy report." Yen looked to Bride Wainwright her eye, the one shadowed by a thin lock of hair, was twitching ever so slightly. He didn't want to divulge the next portion of the presentation for her sake, but it was his duty to do so. "There were abrasions in the... vaginal, anal, and oral regions consistent with a metal wire brush. These portions were also the source of extensive chemical burns from the same drain cleaner. Whoever killed them enacted a thorough cleansing to guarantee the absence of any evidence. The most obvious conclusion is that while unlawfully detained they were subject to... extensive sexual abuse."

Nobody said anything. Nobody pointed or stared, but all eyes were quietly fell on Bride Wainwright. She was breathing heavily, her eyes practically stitched closed. One metal clad hand gripped her chin and the other on the end of the table. It pained Yen Blye to subject the woman he cared so much about to this torture. Everyone knew her story.

Daphne Wainwright only wanted one thing in life. She wanted to be a wife and a mother. As a little girl she would always play house with her brothers, forcing them constantly to act out parts that most would consider highly demeaning. By age fourteen she was already planning her wedding despite not having so much as a lead on a husband. The idea of having a family of her own was exhilarating, the anticipation of being courted, the wedding, the honeymoon, it was a thrill to imagine. At age sixteen she was raped. In her final year of school, her innocence of soul and body was forever scarred. A hand over her throat, another over her mouth, she was traumatized in the very school intended to instruct her. From then on, she considered herself impure, unclean. She thought herself unworthy of being a bride to any decent man.

So, she became a Bride of a different sort. Instead of completing school and returning to a pursuit of a simple, homely style of living she declared a personal crusade. A crusade against the pain and violation that man forced her into. Nobody deserved that kind of torment. She enrolled in the Veil to best combat this crime. For twelve years now she skyrocketed through the ranks of the Scourge based on the work she had done. Every city was scourged, for lack of a better term, of the offenders of the human body. Wherever she was staged, rapes and other sexual assaults plummeted from their previous levels. The public viewed her as a cruel mistress, zealously pursuing the favored quarry of the Veil. Many a pleasure-seeking fiend had fallen at Daphne Wainwright's gun and an even greater number of jewels confiscated from lesser offenders.

The portion of the granite table Bride Wainwright was pinching snapped clean off. Her pearlescent white gauntlets were dusted with grey powder. "We have a serial rapist and killer." She spoke through gritted teeth. Her armor hissed as she ground up the pieces of stone in her palm, the pressure compensators and strength enhancing pistols kicking into combat mode based on her blood pressure and adrenaline levels.

"I believe so, my Bride." Blye responded. "A thorough one at that, so I am petitioning the Seraphim Solace to contribute..."

"He's Carthonian," Wainwright interrupted. "probably a local of Hrimata, late thirties to early fifties. He's got detailed combat experience, likely a former crusader or perhaps he served in the Bulwark or Scourge. Either way he's a trained killer. Perhaps he has a criminology background given the extent of effort he put to concealing his mark."

"Madame Wainwright," Expurgator Blye added in. "I speculated this individual to have been a victim of childhood abuse."

"Correct Yen, but I think there's more than that. I think this recidivist faced more recent trauma as well. Unable to cope with a second instance, he reverted to inflicting the punishment that he received on others." Daphne Wainwright specialized in criminal profiling and analytical psychology, making her a master of deductive reasoning.

"Bride Wainwright, am I to presume that..."

"These won't be the only instances. He would have been more careful in his disposal with local women and I doubt he could indulge himself in this sickness only bimonthly. Contact all local arbiters. Get the names of every missing woman, pick out the ones who meet the monster's typology."

"My lady," Admonisher Rickard jutted in. "Will the Veil be declaring the presence of a Dilictor Ignotum in Hrimata?

"Posthaste." Wainwright said, her ruby lips furled into a fierce scowl. "Label all victims' cases Omega classified. Offer a few hundred crowns as a reward with any information regarding the sadist. I want every Supplicant contributing to this monster's capture. The Dilictor Ignotum is to be top priority. This monster is probably torturing another woman as we speak, so I want all of your teams working in conjunction with their current cases to find this man."

"Madame Wainwright, what would you have me do?" Yen Blye dared to speak up.

"Listen to your Admonisher," Her grim visage turned soft ever so briefly. "Take the rest of the day off. Get some sleep. When you get back tomorrow, you're leading the investigation."

"Is that wise my Bride?" Blye was in awe at the honor being offered to him, by Daphne no less. "Perhaps the authority should be given to someone of higher clearance."

"Until the Dilictor is caught, I grant you Gamma clearance." Agapist Kite gasped at this, envious that such authority was being given to a man two ranks below him. She paid him no heed. "You've got point in this investigation, Blye. Not many could put the pieces together the way that you did, and I need a sharp mind at the head of this spear."

"I am honored Madame." Yen Blye bowed slightly out of respect.

"I'm happy you are. As for the rest of you, address your teams, get me some leads. I want this Dilictor's bloody smoking head. This beast wants to invade my jurisdiction and prey on innocent women, fine then, let us make an example of him. I'm invoking Creed seventy-one. I want him prosecuted and buried in the forest within two weeks."

Bride Daphne Wainwright made this declaration on Jubral 14th, the third month of the year.

The flower bloomed brightly. The red and pink petals parted, releasing the liquid trapped inside. A splash of vapor shot out in a pink mist as the budding stigmas and filaments were revealed to the atmosphere. One might think that a brilliant display of vibrant reds would be a captivating sight as the flower bloomed to life. This, however, was the disturbing analogy that High Conservator

Jude Bethel used to describe those that were caught in the path of his longcannon.

His longcannon, a powerful rifle he had named Venator, was aimed at an abandoned castle. Whenever a single man's head popped out to inspect the invading force, he took aim and pulled the trigger. The rounds he fired were brass casings with an alkali core. The round would pierce the skin, embed itself in the muscle, and detonate. This explosion would cause flesh to part away in a pink mist. In a sickening way, the metaphor was accurate. Their bodies were very similar to a flower bursting in bloom as their blood evaporated and bones shattered apart in a wet explosion. Venator roared like a mighty lion with every pull of the trigger. Jude was wielding the five-foot-long behemoth of a rifle propped against his shoulder. The kick from the back end of the rifle would easily shatter the shoulder of any fit man. His scarred blue armor hissed and belched black vapor as the pressure compensation machinations quashed the impact. This smoke was actually just steam exhausting from the hydrolytic power generator, but he dyed the water vapor black to give it the appearance of smoke. The High Conservator took great advantage of using visual cues to intimidate foes. His cosmetic scarring on the cobalt flaksteel carapace paired with a bellowing cloud of smoke that loomed behind him when in the thick of battle, shook the opposition with ease. His brass-colored skin glinted in the dry Judaic sunlight as he removed his eye from Venator's scope, drawing back from another kill half a mile away.

His grim demeanor was emphasized by the arrangement of scar tissue at his chin and cheeks. The crooked lines always throbbed with pain, except now, when he was home. Two miles behind him was the stronghold of Jerusalem. The High Conservator was born in the American Hinterlands, but after he was rescued, he was raised in Jerusalem. He looked fondly to the sight of the city in his wake and his scarred mouth smiled ever so slightly. Jude loved reminiscing on post-Shatter history. Jerusalem was the one civilization that did not fall under the ruling of the tyrants, an oddity considering it was at the epicenter of all three empires. The Ma'kravish Caliphate was the primary threat against the last city of God. They constructed castles, like the one the Shackle was currently laying siege to, within visual range of the city as an imminent warning that they were coming for them. Many times, they tried to wipe out the last of the Hebrew people out and claim the last beacon of freedom in the world. They failed every time.

Jude Bethel brought a company of over three hundred Shacklers with him to Judah. He was perched on a dry rock cliff scouting the outer perimeters of the dilapidated stone walls of the formerly abandoned castle. He pulled a lever on his longcannon, causing a smoking bullet case to fall into the sand as he turned to address the man who was approaching from behind.

"High Conservator Bethel, sir," Conservator Gerard Null, a thin, light skinned man, gave the Scourge heart-ripping motion to salute his superior. "Are we ready to make the approach?"

"At ease, Null." Bethel's voice was icy comparative to the dry heat. "What's the word on the scouts, have they found any escape routes?"

"As far as we can tell there are no exits aside from the five doorways we were already aware of, though the echograph has yet to be completed."

"We must be certain he does not escape this time." Djinn Balor was the name, though not likely the real name, of the third most wanted recidivist of the Shackle, and the quarry of this manhunt. He was a Frankon born arms dealer that sold guns, swords, and explosives to a number of hostile marauders and criminal syndicates. Bethel had named him a personal quarry before he became High Conservator, and he was finally gaining on him.

"Yes, sir." Conservator Null kicked sand up as he marched away to address his men. Bethel checked his quantity of ammunition and raised his eye to the scope of Venator once more.

Jude scanned the walls looking for Balor's guard. The digital scope zoomed in and out at his vocal command, the longcannon sounded almost as if it were purring as the lenses adjusted. When he was satisfied that his foes learned not to peer in the line of fire, he scouted out the perimeter. A great number of black and blue armored warriors stood armed at the teeth. He could practically hear them begging for the chance to breach. It was like he had a pack of starving hounds on a leash. Everyone wanted Djinn Balor in chains...or in the ground.

Jude Bethel had a personal grudge to bear against this arms dealer. There were many rogue engineers and technocrats that made weaponry for the enemies of Templym. Djinn Balor was not one. He was a thief and a bloody good one, the High Conservator hated to admit. He stole Scourge weapons and armor and peddled it off to the highest bidder he could find. He had become infamous for the way he transported small arms and explosives. Balor gained notoriety by kidnapping individuals, implanting small ordinances under the skin of kidnapped victims, and forcing them to run the weaponry against their will. If they were ever caught, it would detonate. If they made it to their target, often the charge was surgically removed. Most of his clients were amateur at best, so the unfortunate victims rarely survived once the product was inside of them. Nobody was safe from becoming one of his victims. Bethel inspected women blown apart from implanted grenades, children dissected, and elders used as target practice. Slavers like Balor infuriated Bethel and he was determined to see this arms dealer put to rest indefinitely. He had finally tracked him down to Judah and corralled him to this empty castle. He was moments away from getting his most hated quarry.

There was a battalion of soldiers behind him keeping watch of his flank while he observed his hunting grounds. Dust blew in from a gentle breeze as the rolling heat continued to pound down on them. The chattering of the crowd behind him provided a comfortable haze of white noise. Until it halted all of the sudden. It was odd that all four squadrons were silenced. Bethel immediately grew concerned. He turned his gaze from the scope of Venator to see what had silenced them. There was a man standing inches away from him, even though Jude never heard him approach. His long black hair was unmarred by the dust and sand but still lulled in the wind. His robes were of brilliant azure with gold threading.

"Shalom Aleichem, Jude." Arodi Auzlanten spoke in a friendly tone.

High Conservator Bethel did not respond in kind. He stepped back, nearly to the edge of the cliff, so as to point Venator at him. The Regent's command to treat all sightings of Templym's master as hostile rang in his mind. "Who are you? What do you want?" Bethel accused.

"You are welcome to pull the trigger." Arodi spoke neutrally. "It will do nothing but waste a bullet. I know you craft each one by hand, so I trust you'd want to preserve each round."

Jude peered around to look behind Auzlanten, or the Imago doppelganger perhaps, to see his subordinates beginning to surround the end of the cliff head. To test the claim, Venator roared as a bullet ripped out of the longcannon's barrel. The round did nothing. No human eye was quick enough to see what happened, but High Conservator Bethel's marksmanship was legendary in the Scourge, so the likelihood of him missing never occurred to anyone. There was not even as much as a skid or a scorch on the figure's robes. Every rifle slowly lowered as they quickly realized the futility of modern technology. Confused and afraid, everyone began praying.

"I don't blame you Jude." The man, or perhaps demon, spoke gently. At that point he realized that its mouth wasn't moving. How then was the voice of Auzlanten projecting as though he were speaking? "You are a loyal soldier. After your enslavement in the Hinterlands, you've always been a trustworthy sort, latching onto those who've cared for you. How could you not follow the direct orders of Regent Illuromos?"

"Imago witch magick!" Jude yelled audibly. "What manner of dark art allows you to read my mind?"

"I am Arodi Auzlanten." He still spoke without moving his mouth. "Master of Templym, prophet of the one true Lord, founder of the Scourge. Jude, I am your friend. I led the expedition team twenty-six years ago to liberate the Green Teeth slave camps. From there I took you to Jerusalem where you were raised by Uriah and Abigail Bethel, who were sterile and yearned for a child."

Bethel pressed the end of the longcannon's barrel to Auzlanten's chest and pulled the trigger again. It sounded like thunder clapping in the middle of the desert. Without so much as ash on his tunic Arodi grabbed Venator by the barrel and yanked it from his hands. There was an audible gasp from the crowd as Jude was famous for saying "the only time I'd let someone wield Venator is if I wasn't alive to stop them". Auzlanten dug the barrel into the dusty rock cliff, causing it to stand like a spear impaled in the ground.

"I am not your enemy Jude." He persisted. High Conservator Bethel drew a carbon steel tomahawk and swung. His usage of the weapon was similar to ancient Navaho warfare, which specialized in powerful blows to sensitive areas. Four stabs at the base of Arodi's neck did nothing and two slashes across the chest bounced off the fabric of the ornate robes. After an eighth killing blow yielded nothing, Auzlanten spun on the ball of his foot and pinched Bethel's arm in a vice. Bethel hit the ground flat on his back before the handaxe did. His armor screeched and whined to compensate for the impulse. The strand of beads in his hair was flung back, revealing the tattoo pattern staining his neck.

"Shame on the lot of you." Arodi turned to address the crowd of warriors watching in shock speaking aloud. "Your prime could be fighting for his life and you'd be idling along watching him die. You are the Scourge. Brotherhood and loyalty under a unified church are the tenants in which you were trained. You do not even have the stomach to follow a direct order from the Regent. However, these are times of perplexing tribulations so I will forgive this inconsideration."

Auzlanten looked down on the prone High Conservator. "Jude, you must trust me." Bethel felt like a caged animal, like he was back in the slave pits. Arodi's mouth was unmoving again. "There is a conspiracy at play. The tumor of corruption is deeply rooted in the Scourge. I fear Regent Invictus Illuromos has fallen prey to this scheme."

"What are you?" Bethel picked up the tomahawk and poised himself in a battle-ready stance as he scrambled to his feet. "Why are you here?"

"I am Arodi Auzlanten. I am here because Djinn Balor is connected to this. I must find out what he knows. I must locate the Idolacreid and the Nephilim and put an end to whatever hellish plot is infecting Templym. In this hunt, I need people I can trust. That is why I am speaking to you. You are, at the moment, the only man I am certain I can trust."

"How do you know that?" Bethel saw the confusion in his men's faces.

"I've communed with the Lord. He guarantees your loyalty. For the time being, I need you to be my connection to the Scourge. Invictus is a traitor and has turned the Scourge against me. I will not be able to operate within it. I must navigate without their aid. If I do not tread lightly, a second Strife may catalyze. I fear Templym won't survive that."

"What good am I to you?" Jude snarled aggressively, suddenly realizing that he too wasn't vocalizing his words. "If you are truly the same Arodi Auzlanten that delivered us through fourteen Purus Crusades, that toppled the tyrants of the East, and a chosen of the Christ, then what use could I possibly be?"

"You are a unique individual in a unique position." Auzlanten sounded compassionate, but a tone of voice was not nearly enough to sway Bethel. "You have developed a kinship with much of the Scourge. You have a familial relation to its warriors that I could never hope to have. Therefore, I need you to bolster morale. I need you to ensure the hearts of those around you belong first to God and second to Templym. Our very ideology is under attack and I am unwilling to risk not having someone to keep my warriors steadfast."

"So, all you want from me is to ensure loyalty throughout the Scourge?"

"Precisely."

"That's a peculiar task." Bethel sheathed his axe but did not relax his muscles. "How would you suggest I go about doing this?"

"That I will leave in your hands," Auzlanten stepped towards the edge of the cliff and looked towards the castle. "I understand that you are still leery to trust me. I don't blame you. The Regent is supposed to operate in my absence and his authority is to be considered my own. Hearing Illuromos warn of my false treachery would no doubt stir unrest in your heart. Therefore, I will not try to dictate your actions at this stage for fear of appearing as a manipulator. Free will is a fine gift from God, seconded to His unending grace. I have faith in you, that you will be able to weed out traitors in your midst before corruption becomes too deeply rooted."

"And what of right now?" Jude wanted to push him off the cliff, sending him plummeting over a hundred feet, but he knew that would be useless. "You expect me to just let you walk into the castle and snatch my quarry from me?"

"No, I don't. But your resistance will be insufficient, and you will not be able to reach Djinn Balor before I have all I need. Therefore, I would like to kindly ask you to delay commencement of the strike...I know you will not listen. All I need for you to do is to look around you and ask yourself one question." Arodi's piercing blue eyes locked with his. He said audibly, "Who can I really trust?"

With that he was gone. Nobody saw the figure fall off the cliff or charge into the castle. In a moment Arodi, or whoever that truly was, was inches away from the High Conservator. In another, he vanished. Bethel grabbed the end of his longcannon and yanked it out, sending rock chips flying. The scar tissue began aching again as his head raced with a string of curse-laden questions spawned from such a strange encounter. He thought about fainting and he might have had he not snapped over to Conservator Null. "Get me an emergency wavelength to the Regent."

CHAPTER 16

Djinn Balor equipped his customers with the finest weaponry. Guns were not just tools of destruction. Each was a statement that read into the soul of the wielder. Reisingers were small arms of deadly efficiency, wielded by those of little patience for interlopers. Zeduac users were wild creatures, often used by animals with no remorse or empathy, or by cheapskates unwilling to part with their wealth. Tantalun chain guns were used by brash, impulsive murderers desiring to shed as much blood as possible. Balor stroked the head of his gun, one not made by human hands, caressing the weapon like it was a pet.

Djinn Balor was not his real name, but he had long forgotten the persona that once occupied his life. He was a thin man from Frankon, a deceptive presence considering the pile of bodies he gaudily sat on. His thinning hair was slicked back against the length of his head, matching the goatee on his chin. He was dressed in light colored finery corresponding to Judaic cultures. Not his first choice of attire, but he was trying to blend in with his surroundings. He caressed the cannon in his hands, eagerly waiting for the Scourge to trot in so he could give them a demonstration.

The machine gun was bulky, sized for a vehicle or war engine yet was deceptively light. He almost looked comically small wielding the massive cannon. The metal, whatever it was, was some shimmering chrome alloy. Djinn wore a belt of lead ammunition across his chest that fed into a mouth on the side. Bright flashes of pulsing red light echoed across the smooth structure. The barrel ended with a metal carving of a beast's skull, though he was not sure what it was meant to resemble. It was an angular skull with a maw of needle like teeth with four eye holes and two curling horns. He loved this gun. The Nephilim had called it Paz'etkul.

He was surrounded by crates of ordinance. Balor always preferred to take inventory of the arms personally, admiring his craftsmanship. The throne room of this abandoned castle now served as one of his many weapon storage units. He stopped behind a plastic box of mortar shells upon hearing gunfire. One of the local mercenaries he had hired ran up to him and warned him of the approaching enemy, as though he were unaware. They were coming in much quicker than he had expected. The grip of his beloved cannon warmed as the gun grew excited. Djinn adjusted his spectacles and stroked his lead belt, counting the rounds as his fingers ran across each of the customized rounds. The throne room had only one entryway. He propped the skull end of the massive firearm up atop a wooden crate of rifles and waited.

The dilapidated wooden door swung open. Three of the Judaic mercenaries Djinn had hired ran in. One fired a salvo of rounds at an unseen enemy. The hired man was pulled into the dark by some invisible force and he screamed. The other two took positions behind the ordinance crates alongside Balor and a dozen of his other mercenaries. The arms dealer was intrigued by the silence. He had been expecting a boisterous string of Scourge declarations and heavy footsteps. Instead, all that could be heard coming in from the hallway was a single pair of boots clicking against the moldy stone flooring.

Paz'etkul audibly brayed hungrily in his hands. The sharp mouth of the skull end of the barrel seemed to arc up in a twisted grin. The promise of death and blood was in the air. The metallic luster of the chrome plating of the gun seemed to flicker with images of eyes and teeth as the lights flashed with a deadly red glow. Balor's gun was hungry. It had been anticipating a buffet of low-ranking militants to gorge itself with. Instead, a great delicacy was coming. Into the weapon filled chamber stepped Arodi Auzlanten.

Jude Bethel paced back and forth in front of the mobile communication center. The monitor was a blanket of static as the computer tuned into the appropriate wavelength. An overhead canopy blocked out the Sun, but the High Conservator felt as heated as ever.

'What the smoke just happened?' he asked himself. A flurry of thoughts rushed in to drape fog over his mind. His heavy flaksteel legs seemed to scream as he rapidly stomped back and forth. Half a mile away, Arodi Auzlanten, or perhaps the Imago imposter, was foiling one of the longest quarry hunts he had ever been a part of and he was powerless to do anything.

The static on the screen vanished into a sea of black nothingness. This was a sign that he had connected, but that the Regent still hadn't tuned in. In this perplexing situation, he had hoped that Invictus Illuromos would be able to shed light onto the situation. Bethel spun his carbon steel tomahawk in his hands, twisting it in complex motions across his fingers. This was his primary mechanism for coping with stress, an emotion that seemed in abundance at this time.

The image of the Regent appeared on the screen. His stony demeanor was locked in a grim scowl. Bethel swung the axe head into the steel pole propping up the canopy and turned his attention to the screen. "I've been trying to bloody reach you for twenty minutes!" Jude was unusually on edge, the antithesis of his cold humorless mood.

"Calm yourself High Conservator." Regent Illuromos kept his emotions well balanced. "I'm in the UPA right now, its two where I am so I apologize if I'm not at the ready."

"I saw Auzlanten." Jude grunted, still pacing anxiously.

"You what?" Invictus' eyes widened with surprise.

"Arodi Auzlanten was here. As per your orders, I attempted to kill him."

"Clearly since you're calling me you didn't try hard enough." The Regent's tone was cynical and nearly hostile.

"Two shots point blank with a longcannon and eight lethal blows with my hawk did nothing." Jude pulled the axe out of the support beam and pointed it at the image screen. "I've killed a number of Imago with far less than that. What kind of creature other than the genuine Auzlanten can resist such punishment?"

"I'm not certain." There was panic in the Regent's countenance. "All I can say to you is that the real Lord Auzlanten is not in Judah at this time. You most certainly encountered the imposter."

"How is this even possible?" Bethel continued to rant.

"I believe it's a class A+ Imago, though I have no evidence to support this theory."

"You weren't here. He spoke to me, he knew things." Jude threw the weapon in his hand back into the support beam, a shot only a marksman like him could make.

"It's nothing but dark magick. That thing sifted through your mind and used your personal information against you."

"He greeted me just like Auzlanten always had. He knew I was raised in Jerusalem, my parents' names, the slave pits I was kept in, he knew the very things that drive me as a man! This was all information the true Arodi Auzlanten knew."

"The doppelganger is playing you, Jude." Invictus appeared to be filled with empathy. "You can't buy into this façade the creature is concocting."

"He barely asked anything of me." Bethel let the thought hang for a moment. "All he asked was to ensure loyalty in the Scourge. Well that and..."

"What else Jude? What did the imposter ask of you?"

"He wanted to speak with Djinn Balor, claimed that he was part of some vast conspiracy. He mentioned the Idolacreid and the Nephilim."

Invictus' jaw dropped in awe. "And you let him go?"

"Lord Regent, you asked me to inform you if I encountered Auzlanten. I took no further action for fear of putting our true Master at risk. If the one inside this castle is an imposter, it's a roughing good one."

"Why are you just standing around then? Your quarry is being manipulated by demonic filth as we speak. Engage the raid!"

"Invictus," Bethel continued exasperated. "You're not giving me answers! I need to know whatever you know. Tell me about this doppelganger, what does it want, how can I distinguish it from the real one, how do I kill it?"

"All information you seek is Alpha Magnus classified." The Regent growled through gritted teeth. "Now I order you, to get into that castle and secure Balor before it's too late!"

Jude Bethel stared at the Regent. He was further disoriented by the uncharacteristic behavior of his superior. He had never seen the stalwart, almost inhuman endurance of Invictus Illuromos falter. Jude yanked the tomahawk out of the support beam and sheathed it. "I want answers when I'm done here." The High Conservator spoke into his suit's radio bead. "All units converge and conquer. Lethal force authorized, Djinn Balor is to be detained, move in at once!" He turned back to the communication monitor. "For the sake of Templym, I hope this is the right call." He killed the feed on the screen.

Djinn gawked very briefly at the sight. He certainly didn't expect to see Arodi Auzlanten in the flesh. His glistening weapon of inhuman craft rumbled hungrily as though craving the kill. He didn't wait.

Paz'etkul let out a bone shattering, blood curdling screech. The maw of the skull barrel opened up and screamed a blizzard of lead. The demonic roar shook the mercenaries at Balor's side to the core. They shouted and wept pathetically at the mercy of the ungodly sound coming from the massive ordinance, though the ringing only served to twist his face into a devious grin. A cascading barrage of ammunition bombarded towards Auzlanten.

Arodi raised his arms over his face. The sheer number of rounds pounded against him with speed far greater than any bullet could possibly travel. Sparks flew off of his sleeves as though liquid metal was splashing off of him like molten rain. The torrential assault actually hurt him, but not nearly enough to deter his efforts.

Auzlanten stomped onto the ground. A pillar of dirty stone rose up like a barricade. Dust and debris flew off of the makeshift granite cover as the rock was powdered under the unrelenting punishment of the supernaturally charged machine gun. Djinn Balor's laughter was still somehow audible over the hellish screeching reverberating from the barrel of the gun. The contraption belched a plume of toxic gas as a byproduct of the heavy metal bombardment. The belt of ammunition coiled around the arms dealer like a snake as the gun devoured the rounds before vomiting them out. Arodi drew his sabre, which glowed bright blue, and cut at the base of his impromptu cover. He struck the flat of the stone with his palm, sending the slab flying towards the terrorist. The weapon Paz'etkul spit out a beam of nuclear light, blowing the rock into a cloud of dust.

Djinn hopped on top of the ordinance crate in front of him. He cocked his head to the side with a devilish grin. His unholy weapon hissed as it vented more deadly vapor into the atmosphere. "Arodi!" He shouted flamboyantly, his Frankish accent obvious. "So good of you to join us. The Nephilim said you'd be coming, but I didn't expect you so soon. Do you like my new gun? Best gift I've ever received."

"Djinn Balor," Auzlanten spoke calmly Leagna pointed at his foe's body. "You're going to answer for your sins, in this life and the next. For the time being I demand answers." He could see a faint aura around Balor's body, a shimmering presence of some spiritual entity. Auzlanten could see that he was a black host, someone willingly possessed by Imago.

"I have all the answers you seek, darling!" Somehow Balor was hoisting the massive glowing cannon with a single hand. No doubt the demon, or demons, inside him were bolstering his strength. It also explained how he was resistive to the unholy wailing from the gun. "Rather, the Idolacreid has those answers. It can whisper whatever knowledge you desire into your mind. It gave me Paz'etkul here." Djinn caressed the skull on the cannon's end lovingly.

"You have the Idolacreid here?" Arodi pressed longingly.

"It's a beautiful book, but the Nephilim wouldn't let me keep it. He has many others he must arm, after all."

"You're raising an army?" Arodi inferred. "An army needs weapons... that's where you come in."

"Smoke me, I've said too much."

Djinn turned his gun to the mercenaries prone on the ground. With another howling bombardment of ammunition, he dispatched his own mercenaries, reducing them to little more than puddles of sticky red paste. Arodi poised himself for battle as the maniacal black host pulled a lever on the demonic cannon. With a thundering clack from the weapon, the pools of blood now surrounding him swirled up in an agonizing coil. The blood and shreds of tissues swirled in a thin twister of bodily fluids and flew into the skull mouth of the machine gun. Paz'etkul's mouth widened as the viscera was slurped up by bestial weapon. Arodi did not waver, silently observing the unholy event unfolding before him. When all of the red plasma had been devoured by the Imago weapon, it shuttered and grew. Spiny quills perforated from the metallic body and more teeth lined its jaw as it undulated and swelled in size.

"Kill him, my pet." Djinn whispered to the gun.

A messy torrent of bullets and lasers flew out from the warped skull of the thundering cannon. Arodi swept his sabre to the side and created a solid barrier of force in the air. A translucent sphere of blue light shone over Templym's Master. He was perturbed at the effective rate at which the weapon chipped away at the barricade. Instead of playing this game again, Auzlanten stepped and appeared instantly behind Balor in a flash of mauve light. Djinn turned with inhuman speed to slam the malignant firearm against him. The jaws of the skull head snapped as it bit at Arodi who parried the strikes with Leagna's blade.

Djinn swung the horrifically glowing firearm while maintaining a constant stream of messy metal and superheated gas. Eventually the last of Balor's bullet wrapping was consumed, leaving nothing but crimson beams of light to be shot out while he swung it about like a madman. Arodi kept out of the path of fire by deflecting the end of the barrel with the stained-glass blade. A mist of dust was formed from the bombardment wrought by the blood crazed frenzy of the weapon. The Imago gun was drunk with the gore it had just devoured.

Auzlanten was in awe of the effectiveness at which Djinn was able to resist his assault. He swung his sabre in a complex rhythm of slashes and stabs, but Balor was somehow able to avoid the lethality of the blows. This weapon whipped out with the agility of a knife yet the power of a Hekaton, and this was excluding the firepower of the gun's primary weapon. Arodi grew frustrated with this dance of battle.

Arodi's wreath of platinum thorns illuminated briefly. The light then began to shimmer in his bejeweled hand causing the precious metals and gems to glint red in the light of the rapid firing beams. His entire hand brightened with the light of a white star as power of the heavens flooded to his fingertips. With a liquid spin of his sword, he positioned the ungodly device into a position of vulnerability, then grabbed onto the cannon. Auzlanten felt a brief flash of pain as the unholy device stabbed at him with its quills. He pressed on through the pain. The light transferred to the machine gun, dispersing the sickening red light as it became overwhelmed by the brilliant white. Djinn Balor screamed as he realized his prized pet was overloading.

In a quasar equivalent explosion of molten metal and blinding radiation, a tremor shook throughout the air, splitting open wooden crates. The deafening burst of the unnatural device dying was backed by the clinging of heavy metal ordinance striking the dusty stone floor. Once the flashing smoke cleared, Arodi Auzlanten was revealed unmolested. The heretical union of weapon and Imago was vanquished.

Djinn Balor in contrast was in immense pain. His wrists now ended in bloody stumps where his hands once were. Quills and shards of the unnaturally lustrous alloy stuck out of every inch of exposed skin. His incessant laughter was now replaced with pitiful moaning. He only survived because of the strength the dark spirit inside of him provided. Arodi could see now that the demons had left him, an empty shell.

"Why is the Nephilim building an army?" Auzlanten asked calmly.

"My hands! My hands!" Djinn's panache had vanished entirely replaced with panicked agony. "My weapon! It hurts!"

"Where is the Idolacreid now?" Arodi moved on seeing that Balor had no idea.

"I don't know, some marauder in Uzbek has it." He wailed pitifully. "I need help. It hurts so much."

"Kynigi et Kako!" Auzlanten heard a voice screaming as it entered the throne room. He immediately recognized the mantra of the Shackle. He swiveled his head around to see a number of black and blue plated warriors storming into the wreckage. "Scourge, get on the ground!" The squadron leader, an Overseer based on his plate's markings, yelled out.

"I have delivered Djinn Balor to you." Arodi said emotionlessly. "Please give my regards to the High Conservator."

"Waste him!" The Overseer yelled out.

A hailstorm of brass was directed towards Auzlanten. The shots, all aimed at his center of mass, did not impact him. As the fire rang out and shell casings pinged on the debris caked floor, Arodi Auzlanten slipped Leagna back into its scabbard. Then in an instance, without so much as a wisp of wind, he was gone. High Conservator Jude Bethel charged in just in time to see him vanish.

"Damn it all!" Jude yelled as the gunfire silenced. He grimaced at the thought of all of the burning questions he hoped he could get answers from capturing whatever had just slipped away. His soldiers looked in baffled fear at the sight of an outburst of profanity from someone as statuesque as High Conservator Bethel when he pulled his helmet off and threw it on the floor in a tantrum like outburst of rage. "What are you all staring at? Get this man a hospitaller! Process the scene and somebody get the bloody Inquisition in here. After Balor's stabilized, lock him up in a Veritas Chamber, Alpha classified, nobody but me talks to him." The Shackle warriors turned their gazes to the ground and enacted the High Conservator's orders.

Bethel inspected the scene carefully. This was quite the mess he stumbled upon. He fully anticipated the cache of ordinance. He wasn't expecting to see it all scattered about. There must have been two or three hundred royals' worth of bombs, guns, and ammo strewn about in dust covered crate shards. There was a column of rock missing from the middle of the chamber which he inferred was now pulverized and dispersed around the throne room. There must have been thousands of bullet holes, most of which didn't have bullets in them and the ones that did were made of primitive lead projectiles. Bits of some luminescent blue glass like material scattered one portion of the ground while shards of some foreign chrome colored metal were embedded in a number of facets around the same chamber. No questions were answered as Scourge medics carted Djinn Balor away to Golgotha Arcae in Jerusalem.

A chime rang in from Bethel's audio wire indicating someone was attempting to initiate contact. "What?" He answered knowing well that it was a communications officer.

"Sir, Warden Volk Downey to speak to you, Kappa classified." Jude pinched the bridge of his nose. He had practically forgotten about task force S-6319.

"Connect us." He sighed.

"High Conservator sir." Volk answered after a few moments' delay.

"Warden Downey, what news do you have on your manhunt?" He responded.

"Is this a bad time sir?" The veteran asked considerately detecting the anguish in his prime's voice. "If you're busy I can contact you later."

"It seems as though there are naught but bad times now, Volk." Jude mused regretfully. "The uncertainty sown by the Regent's address has me troubled. I am finding trust difficult to come by. A fog of questions perplexes my judgment. I have never felt so unsure since my induction to the Scourge over thirty years ago."

"Well, perhaps I can give you some good news." Volk retorted keeping a tone of lightheartedness.

"That would be appreciated."

"Jaspin was a success. As we suspected, Nuoli Lamiash was guilty of orchestrating the hospital raid, or rather her boss Arch Formulator Regulom Palladium of the Cybernetic Apotheosis. Apparently, they got a tip off from one of his old friends in Hrimata. That's where we are now."

"Any lead on your quarry... Morthen?"

"If you're referring to Mortis, we haven't any solid lead on him." Volk sounded concerned and confused.

"Right, Mortis, my apologies."

"High Conservator, are you sure you're alright?"

"Any hints, clues, something?"

"As of right now, no. Whoever was communicating with Palladium transferred data to him via some strange digital meditation ritual where he hooked his brain up to the tide. That means any moron with a computer could send him information. The Apotheosis was building an army to stage a mutiny, too. How this links to Knox Mortis is still beyond us. While in Hrimata, we'll look into anarchists or totalitarian wannabees."

"Be advised Warden Downey, there's been a Dilictor Ignotum loose since Jubral. That might be a good place to start."

"We'll look into that, thank you, sir."

"Be vigilant Warden Downey," Bethel hushed his voice so he wouldn't be heard. "I fear that not all in the Scourge adhere to our creed any longer."

CHAPTER 17

Hrimata was once a major UNAC stronghold. During the Tyrranis Period, the tyrannical alliance enslaved men, women, and children in the metal mines. Its long-forgotten name was replaced with Hrimata, the Greek term for wealth. The citizens harvested the wealth that they once were forced to reap with no benefit and the urban became a bastion of prosperity in Carthonia. It swiftly became the noblest metropolis in the continental peninsula.

The city functioned as the capital of the Nordic Plains and all of Carthonia. It was a glistening urban of cloudtouchers constructed of lustrous metal surrounded by flatlands. The artificially flattened plains once functioned as homes to troop encampments and execution factories which reduced the landscape to ashen wastelands. After the defeat of the UNACs, as though they were aware of a new age of peace and prosperity, the plains bloomed with lush grass and flowers. The urban of Hrimata was visible from the miles of meadows that surrounded it. It has since been seen in the eyes of the majority of Templym as a posh and haughty metropolis filled with excess-indulging politicians. Oslin Du'Plasse, who had been born and raised here, would be the first man to verify that this narrative is mostly true.

Hrimata is famous for being separated into a number of districts based on social class. Most nations in the orbit of Templym had freed themselves from the structures of a caste-system, but traditions tend to be difficult to overcome. The Lead District was the lowest class and were seen by the higher ups as loathsome necessities for their manual labor. The Steel District, where most people found themselves, consisted of the common factory and business workers. The Copper District made up the artists and musicians acclaimed in the regal urban. The Bronze District composed most of the soldiers in the Nordic army and most Hrimatan Scourge recruits. The Silver District consisted primarily of scholars, engineers, and innovators. The Gold District made up hospitallers and surgeons. At the height of the classes, the Platinum and Diamond Districts made up career nobles and bureaucrats. There were many methods, usually by achievement or marriage, to rise or fall from one's born caste, but such a practice was complicated. Usually a citizen's hair color, which would bear a strong resemblance to the element of their namesake house, distinguished which district they belonged to. The city's government was a complex senatorial autocracy composing a number of representatives from the houses of each caste, proportional to the number of citizens in each district.

Ram's Horn stepped off of the aerial chariot, his armor freshly polished. He looked upon the gaudy looking city and grunted. A gentle breeze of warm air caused his cobalt kilt to ruffle in the wind. He stepped off of the white metal staircase to rejoin the rest of S-6319 on the air strip of the aviation station. He much preferred the rustic woodlands and sheet metal huts like his home in Uzbek to the towers of shimmering steel in this strange place. They landed in the Bronze district, which was obvious based on the number of workers with reflective brown hair, on Nyvett 14th after an exhausting amount of paperwork from the debacle in Jaspin. Volk just signed off of his radio after speaking to the High Conservator with a brief situation report, a look of concern was in his good eye.

"Strange, Bethel seemed on edge." His Glaswegian accent reverberated to his team. "He sounded paranoid."

"Really? That's peculiar." Oslin responded. "Bethel has a reputation for being unfeeling, a cold calculating engine of logic and tactics. What's got him riled up?"

"Apparently the Regent's address about Auzlanten's imposter has him shaken." Downey said, an air of doubt in his voice. "Of course, I'm sure there's more to it than he told me."

"Whatever the case, we've a job to do." Adastra stated plainly. "Herald Du'Plasse, do you have any potential leads for us?"

"There are a number of syndicates in town, drug dealers mostly." The Hrimatan stated while fingering his data slate. "There used to be a vast number of human traffickers in the region. Bride Wainwright has cleaned them up pretty thoroughly."

"Bride Wainwright?" Vandross asked with a jovial tone. "As in Daphne Wainwright?"

Oslin tapped on his historian's tablet. "Yes, that's her."

"She's a Bride now? Good on her!" The Inquisitor laughed as he pulled out his pipe.

"Vandross and I know her well." Adastra said with an inkling of a smile beneath his beard. "We went through the Deficio Tribulation together. It's been two years since we've seen Daphne, and she was an Admonisher then. We need to see her before we leave."

"High Conservator Bethel mentioned she's on a Dilictor hunt right now." Volk mentioned. "That'd be a good place to start."

"The Nitral Nightmare," Oslin stated grimly without even looking at his pad. "A serial killer and rapist, he's claimed seven young women so far that the Veil is aware of. Everyone in Hrimata has been shaken for three months and frankly they aren't any closer to finding him."

"You think he's our connection to Palladium?" Adastra asked Warden Downey.

"Could be," He said stroking his leathery face. "I certainly can't think of any other leads at this time. Let's start there. Even if it's not our connection, I'm sure our help to take this beast out of the urban will be appreciated."

"Sounds like a good place to start." Vandross said puffing a plume of white smoke in the wind. At that moment a bronze haired attendant placed a bag next to Inquisitor Blackwell. It was his personal baggage. "Thank you, sir." He tipped his hat at the worker.

The young man stood there briefly, enough time to where it would be awkward.

"Give the boy a tip," Oslin motioned to Vandross.

"If a woman asks how much you earn before you start courting, she's likely out for wealth and not proper wife material." He said unironically.

Oslin sighed as he pulled a few crowns out of his wallet and handed it to the boy. "As in some coin, Mr. Blackwell." The airfield worker accepted the bills and marched back to his duties.

"That's a bloody weird practice." He said with a quizzical look. "Money talks in this posh place, doesn't it?"

"Currency is the most universal language. A few crowns won't afford him much but speaks as an affirmation of a job well done."

"In Kalkhan we tend to hold onto every crown we get. I'd wager the entire continent's economy isn't worth as much as this city's. Words of wisdom tend to carry more worth than money in Rio Epiphanies."

"An interesting sentiment, but you can't buy anything with kind speech."

"True, but most people won't remember you for your cash when you're gone."

"If you're done, gentlemen," Downey said abruptly. "I'd suggest starting at the Seraphim Solace and get a rundown from Miss Wainwright on any leads. Daurtey and the caravan will be coming into the shipyards tomorrow, so we'll be taking public transport until then."

"I won't be joining you just yet." Oslin stated plainly. "I've some business I need to attend to in the city."

"Is that a statement or a request?" Volk's milky eye seemed to flare with a brief flash of disciplinary ire. He didn't particularly care for subordinates taking matters into their own hands.

"A request, I suppose." The Hrimatan responded snidely. "Apologies Warden, I am unaccustomed to taking orders from a man of lesser rank."

"We've worked together nearly a month now. When exactly are you going to get used to that?"

"Likely never, sir. Now if you don't mind, I've a family appointment I must attend to." Oslin sneered slightly in quiet discontent. "Today would be preferable."

"Fine, you're dismissed. I'll expect to see you at the Seraphim Solace when you're done."

Oslin cocked a bitter grin and gave an almost sarcastic salute before turning on his heel and walking away to catch a public transport. Volk leered at the back of his head as he waltzed away.

"Inquisitor Blackwell," The Warden spoke after a brief moment of silence.

"Yes sir?" He said as he puffed out the last of his pipe's content.

"Would you kindly follow Herald Du'Plasse and report to me on what exactly he's doing? Make sure he doesn't see you."

"Are you ordering me to spy on a member of my own task force?" He asked confused.

"I suppose I am. I'm curious to see what's gotten Oslin in a particularly bitter mood."

"Copy that. Adastra, give my love to Daphne."

"We'll see you there." Adastra nodded to his partner. "Pick up a bottle of that double malt she used to love while you're out." Vandross winked and nodded before heading off to tail Herald Du'Plasse.

"Ram what do you think of this place so far?" Volk asked turning to the heavily armored giant.

"Shiny." He mumbled.

Golgotha Arcae was notorious for being one of the cruelest and most heavily guarded of the Scourge's infamous prisons. The prison was small with a maximum capacity of one thousand, but it was rare that more than a hundred prisoners were kept there at any one time. Those unfortunate enough to find themselves staying in this Arcae were subject to the punishment by Golgotha's Archon. Each Arcae was headed by an Archon who was chosen among the Scourge's ranks, but their identities kept Epsilon classified. In Jerusalem, the Archon was seen as the most bone-chilling figure to have occupied the city since Herod's ruling.

Ever since the Arcae's construction before the First Purus Crusade nearly two hundred years ago, Golgotha's Archon went by the name Crucifix. This was likely a morbid nod to the execution of Christ in the city at the turn of the millennium. Multiple people surely occupied the position of Crucifix, but nobody could say for certain how many. The prison inflicted the worst punishment authorized by the Scourge, regardless of the occupant's status. More people died in this place than any other Arcae in Templym. Some figures in the Scourge were even uncomfortable with the level of near sadistic torture that Crucifix subjected his guests to. This included High Conservator Jude Bethel.

Bethel rubbed his facial scars. He struggled to remember just how much he was worth as a slave in the Hinterlands, the reason the cuts were made. The marauders never bothered teaching him their language. Rather he was forced to interpret crude commands to enact physical labor. He had captured Djinn Balor thirteen hours ago and was waiting for him to be declared coherent by the hospitallers so he could interrogate him. Bethel named him as an Alpha threat so nobody less than a prime was allowed to speak to the arms dealer other than the hospitallers pulling shrapnel out of his broken body.

Jude couldn't sleep. He was offered a bed chamber in the Ruach Scourge facility, but he found himself unable to find mental peace. So, he stationed himself in Archon Crucifix's office to await the interrogation. Crucifix, a man once known as Cardinal Wick, rarely used his office anymore, spending his days personally inflicting excessive punishment upon the recidivists and first offenders locked away in Golgotha. The High Conservator, as cold and unfeeling as he was often considered, found this notion to be highly disconcerting. Jude nervously scratched at a rend on a plate in his gauntlet with his tomahawk, scratching the steel blue paint away. He remembered exactly where he got this wound. A turncoat Bulwark hierarch of the Trench, whose name he swore never to repeat, during the Civil Strife.

Powdered flaksteel began falling lazily onto a white threaded office chair like a small cascade of black snow. Normally Bethel would be more courteous with regards to someone else's personal belongings, but much occupied his thoughts. Who spoke to him outside of that castle? Why did they want to speak to Djinn Balor? Why blow his hands off and not kill him? Who was loyal? Did Invictus...lie? Such a crime was an executable. The members of the Scourge were held to a much loftier standard of the law than the common citizens, and that stringent discipline increased parallel to its hierarchy. No Regent in history had ever committed a crime while in office. If the Regent did something as heinous as lying...the kind of dissent that could plant would be catastrophic.

The door swung open. High Conservator Bethel cocked his head swiftly to see Archon Crucifix trundle in. His footsteps were heavy, and every inch of skin concealed in a thick metal carapace with only a single enamel glass visor over his eyes. The flaksteel was disturbingly angular as points and edges of the plates appeared as though a single stroke would cause a laceration. The unpainted, raw metal bore flecks of blood caked onto the hands.

"You're still here?" Crucifix asked, his voice altered and mechanical sounding by a roaring vocal modulator.

"I'm not about to walk away now." Jude locked his gaze onto the blood stains. "Is your excess torture truly necessary?"

"Christ himself was scourged and nearly killed before his execution. No man is unworthy of the retribution I inflict."

"That has drastically different context. The Scourge beats its prisoners enough as it is. You needn't exercise your sadism further on them."

He let out a shrill static infused bellow. "I don't expect you to understand my methods."

"Nor do I care to attempt to do so. I am awaiting a call from the surgeon to tell me that Djinn Balor is well enough to be interrogated."

Crucifix rubbed his jagged fists with a blood-stained silk cloth he pulled from his desk. "Balor was discharged two hours ago. He's in Veritas 4 right now."

"What?" Jude's already morbid demeanor grew even darker. "The hospitallers were instructed to inform me the moment he was discharged. Why wasn't I told?"

"Why are you asking me? Your classification is closer to the Regent's than my own." The bloody silk tore under the force of the Archon's scrubbing.

"What does that have to do with anything?"

"I assumed Lord Illuromos would have kept you in the light."

Jude stood up on edge, his plate spitting out black steam as the sensors kicked into combat mode as a response to his spiking vitals. "You mean to tell me the Regent is in Golgotha right now?"

"Veritas 4, like I said." Another morbid chuckle from Crucifix, it chilled the High Conservator. "Are you and the Regent bickering like two old crones?"

Bethel didn't respond. He rushed out of the office and down the hall without a word. Why was the Regent here? More relevantly, why did he arrive without informing him?

Bethel's battle plate sounded like a locomotive as he barreled through the halls of Golgotha. His sense of urgency was equivalent to times when he was chasing quarry on foot. Menials and indentured inmates ducked to the side lest they be knocked into the cold iron walls of the Arcae. Prison guards motioned to stop him before they realized who he was and then stepping aside. The High Conservator looked like some manner of swift moving war engine as he made his way down to the line of Veritas Chambers under the ground floor of the prison.

He was too late. Bethel waved his arm in front of the identity reader of the Veritas entryway. The door raised open as it confirmed the identity runes etched on the inside of the plate. The interior hallway was uncomfortably cluttered. Two Golgotha hospitallers were rolling the lifeless corpse of Djinn Balor away on a gurney. He had a single bullet wound in the head. Regent Invictus Illuromos was standing just outside of Veritas 4 debriefing the captain of the guard. All eyes of bustling guards and medics and of the Regent along with his Centurion guard were turned on the smoking High Conservator as he stomped into the hallway.

"What is the meaning of this?" Jude asked, his fury obvious. "I thought I gave direct orders that only I was to speak to this man."

"You did." Invictus said plainly keeping a cold composure. "I am your commander, and my clearance surpasses your own. I have full authority to speak to whomever I see necessary."

Bethel stepped within striking distance of the ebon plated Regent. He was fully a foot shorter than his superior, but that didn't stop him from infusing poisonous hostility into his gaze. "You killed my quarry. You've got to answer for something this extreme."

"I invoked Creed eighteen. I determined that he was too dangerous to be allowed to live any longer."

"I demand to see the footage. What exactly was said that dictated his immediate execution?"

"You cannot witness the interrogation. I've destroyed all recordings indefinitely." Jude was stunned. He gawked in awe at such an audacious move. If this was meant to sow dissent in the Scourge and tear at the trust between Bethel and his Regent, it was quite effective. Unable to speak any further, Invictus leaned in closer and spoke in a hushed voice. "This is not the place to address your concerns. Let's speak in private." Regent Illuromos opened up the door to Veritas 2. "I'm willing to give you a few answers you seek."

Jude leered at his superior, locking onto the IX brand beneath his eye as he couldn't bring himself to stare into the stormy steel of his pupils. He was angry and he was letting that show. Bethel was flustered, yet kept his composure, as he took the opportunity to uncover information that he had so fervently sought.

"Calm yourself Jude." Invictus sat down at the black iron table, his chair rocking beneath the bulk of his heavy armor. "I know it is frustrating to be left in the dark, but you must trust me as Auzlanten's Regent."

"Strange... Lord Auzlanten seemed to think I could trust him." Bethel refused to sit down instead hunching over the table to meet the tortured gaze of Invictus.

"Whatever it was that you spoke to yesterday wasn't Arodi Auzlanten. He spoke to me personally and informed me that the imposter would try to reach out to us. I fear that you have fallen prey to its ploy."

"Why was it there? Why did it want Balor?" Jude was intentionally omitting details, like Auzlanten's mention of the Nephilim or the Idolacreid, even though he had no clue what those were. Hadn't he been ordered to keep watch for those terms in all Shackle reports? He also did not mention that Arodi had named Invictus a traitor.

"Djinn Balor was a part of a deadly machination that Lord Auzlanten has been pursuing personally for some time now. He instructed me to keep all mentions of a blasphemous tome called the Idolacreid under strict watch and to isolate all instances. When I informed the real Arodi Auzlanten of your capture of Djinn Balor, he instructed me to interrogate and execute."

"What machination could be so secret that I would be left blind and dumb?"

"I am unsure. Some dark entity is at play, some unholy text is corrupting minds and souls alike. I'm under strict instructions to keep this information Alpha Magnus. Lord Auzlanten did not even trust me with direct contact with the Idolacreid. I need to keep this threat as contained as possible."

"You must admit that this all looks suspicious." Bethel leaned forward grunting through a locked jaw. "You've kept me in the dark this long and now you execute my quarry before I even have the chance to ask him about the imposter, or whoever I bloody talked to."

"Trust me," Invictus was stern yet his low voice communicated sympathy. "I acquired all of the information that the rogue arms dealer possessed. I cannot share all with you. All I'm authorized to tell you is that he was part of this wicked scheme. I must confess that the intelligence he had shook me and is toying with my mind. I don't blame you for being flustered. I know it is all confusing."

"How can I be certain I can trust you?"

"We are in a Veritas Chamber... I can't possibly lie to you."

"Is your loyalty to God, Templym, the Scourge, and Auzlanten?"

"Indefinitely and absolutely."

Bethel shifted on his feet uncomfortably. Everything Regent Illuromos was saying made sense, but it almost seemed rehearsed. Was Invictus forced to operate under a veil of secrecy by the true

Arodi Auzlanten? Or was he specifically knitting a complex and intricate web of lies, infused with elements of the truth to deceive him. Nobody could resist the compulsion set out by the Veritas Chamber...at least not naturally. The Regent was double Bethel's age yet filled with the same youth. He had supernatural elements infused in his body. Could he lie in one of Auzlanten's famed interrogation rooms?

"Does this information suffice?" Invictus asked.

"I will not lie to you, sir. I am uncertain." Jude responded woefully.

"Uncertain of what exactly?" The Regent asked sounding hurt.

"I am not confident in any man. Not you or Auzlanten or anybody under my own command. My ability to trust has been worn thin. I must have certainty in my Scourge once more."

"How exactly do you plan on doing this Jude?"

"I intend to follow Auzlanten's orders." Bethel said after a brief moment of contemplation. "The Shackle will be conducting a full-scale purge of its turncoats. All soldiers will be subject to Veritas interrogation to ensure their loyalties are in place."

"You would follow the orders of an Imago in the place of your superior?"

"I am cleaning my own house, nothing more. I see no risk in that."

"You are playing right into the imposter's hand." Illuromos stood up swiftly, his voice reverberating echoes of anger. "By following these orders, you'll send our organization into chaos. You'll play the part the Nephilim wants you to. You may not be able to see it, and perhaps neither can I, but whatever dark powers are plotting against us want you to do this. I don't know how...but this will be exploited by our adversaries."

"What harm can it do to put the trustworthiness of our army to the test? I fear that the only unwavering source of trust I have access to is through the living God above. Our Scourge cannot operate with this level of dissent. I will do this, and I will petition the other primes to do likewise."

"Stand down, High Conservator." The black plate hissed like a predator and the chains wrapped around his body clanked ominously as he stepped over to stand over Jude Bethel.

"The fact that you are so fervently trying to dissuade me further convinces me of the necessity of my actions." Jude's scar covered face perched in a cynical smile as he pulled his hand across his chest in the Scourge salute. "I'll convene with you at a later hour."

With that Jude exited the Veritas Chamber, now even more bewildered than before. The edict to question all members of the Shackle was the correct call, that much the High Conservator was certain of. He was also positive that Invictus was retaining information, hiding something that he wanted to know. During the conversation, Invictus gave mention to the Idolacreid and the Nephilim... he never spoke of those things. That didn't prove guilt, but it didn't give the impression of innocence either.

CHAPTER 18

Expurgator Yen Blye was at the head of the Dilictor hunt. He had never experienced such a flood of stress and information. Somehow, he forgot his insomnia and could actually rest on the few nights he clocked out, perhaps for no other reason than exhaustion. Blye set up a cot in his cubicle because of all of the nights he had spent doggedly slaving over the investigation. The weight of the responsibility hit him hard at first, but he had grown accustomed to the work load it yielded. It was strange, giving orders to others ranking above him. He had even given orders to Bride Wainwright, though not orders in the sense that it was his idea.

In reality, Daphne was still in charge and leading this branch of the Veil faithfully and diligently. Whenever she made a move with regards to the Dilictor Ignotum, he essentially nodded his head and encouraged her. Yen had spent more time with her in these past few months than he had the previous year. It took every fiber of strength he possessed to conceal his anxiety when he was with her. He was thoroughly infatuated by the woman, eager to open up and confess his feelings. But this was neither the time nor the place. His mind, and hers as well, needed to be wholly concentrated on finding the sadists loose in Hrimata. Bride Wainwright initially wanted him caught and executed within two weeks' time. That was nearly four months ago, and the number of bodies had doubled since the initial discovery.

It had been over a month since the last young lady turned up in the Lead District and some were wondering if he had vanished or fled the city. Blye didn't think so, and neither did Wainwright. They suspected he was just being more careful about his disposal process. This was uncharacteristic of a serial killer. Most sadists enjoyed displaying their butchery for the entire world to see. The Nitral Nightmare, they called him because of his use of the nitric based drain cleaner, was still making headlines throughout the entire Nordic Plains. The Himalayan Expurgator stroked his clean-shaven chin, contemplating a flurry of information regarding the investigation while staring at a digital drawing board. Pictures and crime scenes scattered the surface while more detailed autopsy and forensic reports composed the background.

"Expurgator Blye!" Admonisher Fenrick Rickard snapped pulling him out of another trance-like meditation. How long had he been barking at him?

"Yes sir." Yen said shaking his head to pull himself out of the haze of information.

"Task force S-6319 is here to speak to Bride Wainwright in response to the Dilictor investigation." Rickard hadn't trimmed his beard since the start of the hunt had his hair was a matted mess, giving him the appearance of a wild man.

"I'm not familiar with them. Did the Shackle assemble a task force for the Nitral Nightmare?"

"Why don't you ask them?" Blye's uniformed superior motioned behind him. Two Shackle warriors and one of the Inquisition were standing behind him. "I'll leave you to it." He dismissed himself.

"Warden Volk Downey, at your service." Volk extended a blue armor-clad hand which Blye took without hesitation. "These are my associates Retriever Ram's Horn and Inquisitor Adastra Covalos."

"Expurgator Yen Blye, pleased to make your acquaintance." Yen said with a slight confusion. "Admonisher Rickard told me you're looking for Bride Wainwright?"

"Correct. We're on a manhunt of our own and we were hoping that she could give a little insight with her Dilictor problem."

"I'm afraid that she's not in the Solace at this time. Bride Wainwright has gone undercover in the search for the Dilictor. I'm the head of the investigation, so I'm certain I can answer whatever questions you have."

"She went undercover?" Adastra asked with a tinge of disappointment in his voice. "Where is she?"

"That's Zeta classified I'm afraid." Blye responded neutrally.

"Du'Plasse has Epsilon clearance, doesn't he? Bloody fool off on his personal errands." Adastra grumbled bitterly to himself. He shook his head as he jotted something down in his black notebook.

"We'll speak to her when she comes back in, then." Downey said keeping kindness in his voice. "Why don't you give us the rundown on the Nitral Nightmare?"

"Of course," Expurgator Blye motioned to the digital board. "Each of the eight victims was a young woman, between sixteen and twenty-six, Carthonian yet not Hrimatan." He tapped onto the glass board and images and files flashed on and off. "Each was strangled to death and their bodies scrubbed thoroughly with Nitrosluice before disposal in the sewer system. Corroborating with autopsy reports, we've deduced that the guilty man is kidnapping and violating them before disposing of them."

"Bloody sick," Volk grunted. "Who's the lead suspect?"

"We don't have any." Blye said regretfully. "There are only two points of connection between the eight victims. They were all vacationing in Hrimata and from their travel plans we know that all visited the Grigorian Administration in the Silver District and the Reclamation Monument Park in the Gold District. We think that our killer is using these places as his hunting grounds."

"A scholastic institute and a national park..." Volk mused. "That's a lot of ground to cover."

"Correct, and it's a testament to the cunning of the killer." Blye seemed hesitant to say the words. "We estimate that there are nearly a million people that travel through these places on a daily basis. It makes it much more difficult to pin down. If I may inquire you, what brings you to Hrimata? Why the sudden interest in our Dilictor problem?"

"We've been following a trail for about a month now." Ram's Horn handed Blye the up-to-date report as Volk spoke. "We're hunting for a fellow by the name of Knox Mortis. We started in

Venice, then to the UPA, and now we're here. We're looking for the connection of a cult leader named Regulom Palladium."

"Nothing here that sounds familiar." Blye speculated. "Are you thinking that my Dilictor is Knox Mortis?"

"It could be." The Warden responded. "Either way, Hrimata is where our hunt has taken us so, here we are. We've decided to help you pin this monster down and maybe we'll find our quarry along the way."

"Well, your aid will be appreciated." Blye sighed. "I'm afraid we're one victim away from Bride Wainwright issuing purge protocols."

"I'm surprised she hasn't already." Adastra noted. "With the zealous animosity she bears towards rapists, I'd figure she'd try to disassemble an entire district trying to find him."

"You know the Bride?" Yen asked.

"I do. My partner and I went through the Tribulation with her. We spent three nights in an isolation chamber during our psychological conditioning. You get to know someone pretty well when you're locked in a box with them."

"Oh, you have a relationship with her?" Yen asked trying to hide his personal feelings.

"Not a romantic one, if that's what you're thinking. We are friends...that's all."

"I see. Well, I'll inform her that you're in, but I don't think she's going to break cover to come see you."

"I would hope not." Adastra said plainly. "In the meantime, I say we should divide and conquer." His black metal fingers swiped at the data board. "I think I'll patrol the Grigorian Administration, perhaps I'll reconvene with Vandross there once he's done with his current job."

"Good thinking, Inquisitor." Volk chuckled. "Ram, do you feel like taking a walk in the park with me?"

"Sure." Ram's Horn grunted and crossed his armored arms.

"I'll alert Scourge forces in the area." Expurgator Blye asked. "Is there anything in particular you're looking for?"

"A predator."

Hrimata's Arcae was called Niflheim, named after a long-forgotten Nordic god or perhaps a mythological world that resembled a hellish shadowscape. Oslin Du'Plasse was amply familiar with this Arcae. He brushed his hand against the foot-thick flaksteel walls as he approached the opening gates. The single entrance resembled the maw of some massive creature, as the yawning gates were comprised of jagged retractable spikes that penetrated the wall. He was wearily aware of the entry process. Even though he outranked the guardsmen that stood at the primary, secondary, and tertiary checkpoints, he was forced to undergo the pat down and questionnaires before being granted entrance to the interior of the massive prison.

The Archon greeted him personally at the entryway. Like all Archons, she was anonymous and went by a title. She called herself Valkyrie, but her real name was Jeanne Cuviet, a Frankish woman. Oslin knew her well before she was ever an Archon, but deigned to keep her identity to himself. Her unique armor consisted of sleek dark brown flaksteel with a winged helmet and a billowing cloak of blue feathers. She had grown friendly with the Herald in his many visits to Niflheim Arcae.

"Welcome back Herald Du'Plasse." Her gruff mechanical voice chimed as he stepped through the final security checkpoint. "Here to torment yourself once again?"

"Hello Valkyrie." Oslin said begrudgingly. He seemed ill humored.

"It's been over two months since your last visit. After your high concentration of visits over the winter and spring, I was concerned that you wouldn't be joining us again." A group of Shackle Guardians approached Oslin to begin escorting him. They stopped as Valkyrie raised a sharply angular gauntlet. "I will act as Herald Du'Plasse's escort. I know where he's going. Shall we?" She motioned down the dimly lit hallway.

"I suppose so."

Oslin had taken time with his hair this morning. It was still arranged in the double braided and single tailed style as per usual, but he took extra time to replicate it as similarly to Auzlanten's as possible. He was adorned in his battle plate with his golden Du'Plasse ascot dangling from his neck with the family name folded out on display. The diamond like etching in his golden breastplate shimmered in the cold light of the Arcae, what little of it there was. Small glass globes dangling from the black metal ceilings illuminated the hallway in a vague shimmer of pale blue light. Every so often as the two passed a cell, there was an audible scream or slam that softly reverberated in the chamber. Oslin's suit of armor was normally silent, but his adrenaline was spiking, making the plate purr. Mist poured out from the back of the suit and pistons hummed with every step he took.

"I trust the package I sent found its way to you?" Oslin asked the Archon.

"It did." She affirmed, her electronically disguised voice echoed through the virtually featureless halls. "I hope you don't mind we took time inspecting its contents."

"I would expect nothing less. Nothing controversial inside, I'm certainly not trying to break her out. I don't suppose you know if she liked it?"

"As far as I'm aware, she never even opened it."

"Ah... I'm guessing you informed her it was from me." He said with dismay.

"I didn't have to." Valkyrie responded. "Your sisters only ever bring gifts when they come in person. She knew nobody but you sends packages from afar."

"I see... that's disappointing."

"She's been locked up here for three years now. If it weren't for you, she'd spend a week here before being shot and buried."

"I'm aware Jeanne." Oslin spoke curtly.

The two stopped in front of a chamber door. "Why do you keep coming back Oslin?" The Archon asked sympathetically. "There's no point in your visits. Even though you visit Nora more than both of your sisters combined, she won't forgive you. She rants and raves to her counselors about how bitter she's been since the end of the Strife. She hates you."

"I know...but I still love her. I want to make amends."

"As you wish."

Valkyrie reached out to the door. It had no handles, but what it had was three holes carved into a disk on the hull. The intricate plating on her fingers danced as they shifted around her hand. The fragments of flaksteel keyed to the arrangement necessary to lock into the finger holes on the door. With her gauntlet inserted, she twisted the disk, activating motors inside the thick metal walls, forcing the door to swivel open.

This was not an ordinary Arcae prisoner's cell. Pale blue luminous globes still stung at the eyes. There was a steel desk with a single featureless cube as a chair scattered with papers and books as well as a hard cot with scratchy sheets. A water spigot lay next to a cold metal lavatory waste unit. A single cardboard box wrapped in painted papers remained shut in the front corner of the cubic structure. On the cot was a woman reading a book.

Her hair was blanched white with specks of silvery grey strands. Her wrinkled face furled into a scowl at the sight of Oslin. She was dressed in dull black prisoner's garb that was starched stiff. There was a collar on her neck, one standard of Scourge prisoners. Etched beneath her jaw line was CM-01 in black ink and just beneath that was AM-23. Her crystal blue eyes were filled with tortured anguish.

"Prisoner LS-006, Nora Du'Plasse," Valkyrie's computerized voice echoed in the tight chamber. "Your son is here on a personal visit."

Oslin's gold immotrum clad boots hit the dark metal floor as he stepped inside. "Thank you, Archon Valkyrie." With her fingers still embedded into the disk, she pulled the door shut with a click.

Oslin picked up the paper wrapped box, the only source of notable color in the room, and brought it to the foot of the cot. He gave a half-hearted smile to the still scowling elderly woman. "Happy birthday, mother."

CHAPTER 19

Arodi Auzlanten pulled Leagna from the corpse of the marauder chieftain. The trail of oily blood that came from the clammy bluish skin of former leader of the Thunder Warriors sloshed onto the grass. This was not the tribe of Uzbeki marauders Djinn Balor claimed possessed the Idolacreid, but they were a threat to Templym. The Thunder Warriors had been staging multiple raids, plucking away men and women from their homes to use as sacrifices for their pagan deities. They were a stain the Inquisition had been pursuing for a long time now, but not the one he had been seeking.

Auzlanten shook his head sullenly at the sight of the massacre. Rusty hammers and primitive firearms were strewn about the grassland. The barbarians were scattered in pieces, cut down by the stained-glass sabre or blasts of energy. This was the fifth tribe this week he had approached with hopes of finding his next lead, to no avail.

He took a step forward and stepped back in his sanctum with a brief flash of mauve light. Normally he would submerge himself in the roiling mineral water at the base of the marble platform. Arodi was too preoccupied to take the time to do so and stepped across a walkway over the small bubbling moat. He strode past the cubic glass displays dismissively until he reached one that he was specifically walking towards. Inside of the glistening crystal display was a complex configuration of glossy grey squares. The angular crystals retracted into the marble floor as Arodi reached out creating an opening large enough that he could remove the strange figurine. The crystal panels returned to the previous configuration as he walked away towards a door composed of glistening blue metal.

The door raised open without as much of a command from Auzlanten. The walls were like dimensionless voids, composed of black vacuums flickering with stars. There were no floors. Arodi lulled gently in the air, his robes rippling like fluid in the space. He closed his eyes and began to tinker with the strange object.

The glistening starlight reflected off of the iron grey plates of the device. Auzlanten's ringed fingers twisted and curled as the squares all scattered apart and arranged in a disconnected sphere about three feet in diameter. The plates swirled in the void in front of the complex motion of his fingers. After his hand motions, a bubbling mass of what looked like molten lava was suddenly created in the interior of the sphere. The hissing ball of liquid material glowed brilliant yellow like the sun itself. The only freedom from the vibrant illumination was the pockets of shade formed by the roving squares that continued to swirl around the light's surface undeterred by the molten ball.

"Who dares summon me?" The liquid sphere pulsed as it spoke with a multitude of voices, some shrill some deep, in unison.

"The only man that speaks to you." Auzlanten spoke blankly. His voice seemed to echo eternally in the emptiness of the starlit room.

"Arodi..." The voices bellowed in monstrous laughter simultaneously. "It has been many years since last we spoke.

"I spoke to you yesterday, deceiver."

"It has been one day? My apologies, time has moved far more slowly since you caged me like an animal."

"The intelligence you gave me was false." Arodi snapped changing the subject.

"You sound surprised." The molten ball swelled as the chorus of voices giggled in ominous awe. "Did you really just expect me to deliver you the Idolacreid?"

Arodi clenched his hands. The swirling grey tiles contracted, pressing down on the molten ball. The voices coming from it all cried out in what sounded like a screeching myriad of death cries. "You answer to me. I operate under the authority of the Triune God. By His grace I am saved and blessed with great power, power that I've used to trap you here until the Second Coming. You obey me!" He reopened his hands and let the swirling tiles expand and stop crushing the molten core.

"Treacherous filth!" The voices lashed out. "What is it you desire?" They hissed.

"I've exhausted every lead I had. Djinn Balor said that the Idolacreid was passed onto a marauder tribe in Uzbek. This week I've decimated four hostile tribes searching for the tome and I've found nothing. You told me the Thunder Warriors had it. You lied."

"Yes, I did. My words must be entwined with truth and deceit alike. I cannot give you the structure of certainty. Even in this prison, I aim to vex you however I can."

"Silence, cur!" He clenched his fists and compressed the sphere and again returning the booming congress of screams. "I will twist your wretched soul to its breaking point if you don't comply with my requests. Where is the Idolacreid?" He released his grip.

The gurgling mass let out a similarly guttural laugh. "We both know that you can't kill me. But I'd prefer it if my stay here was more comfortable. If you want me to divulge the Nephilim's plan to you, I will need..." Arodi gripped his hands again causing the sphere to become wracked with pulsing waves of pain.

"You get relief...nothing more." Auzlanten growled. "You are assuredly damned, but don't think I won't hesitate to send you to the Pit wailing in agony. The Idolacreid, now!" He released his torturous grip.

"How can you trust me?" The plethora of men and women speaking in unison sounded in anguish. "It is no mystery that I am a liar and a deceiver, so why even bother? I know I will not be dying here, and I have a high tolerance for pain. What motive do I have to tell you the truth anyhow? I want to see the Nephilim succeed. How do you know that the death of the Thunder Warriors was not what I wanted?"

"I have divine knowledge that informs otherwise."

"Yet He does not inform you the location of the tome. Tell me Arodi, do you really believe that the Lord is all knowing? Why wouldn't He divulge that information to you? You're smart enough to know that it is immoral to conceal such crucial knowledge. Does this make your God a fool or brigand?"

"Blasphemy. I am a servant of the omnipotent and perfect Lord of Heaven and Earth. All that He does is for the benefit of humanity."

"You claim to be His slave. Have you ever considered, Arodi, that you are truly my puppet? You hide in your precious sanctum overlooking your dearest Templym pretending that you act out the will of God... have you even seen His face? How certain are you that I am not shepherding you into acting out my agenda in the façade of your mighty Lord?"

"You have tried this ploy many a time. It did not fool me then. It will not convince me now."

"But think about it." The voices swirled and sounded gallant as the sphere spun in its spherical cage. "Even your own son, what was his name...Invictus. Yes, even he has turned his back on you. Are you so thoroughly engulfed in your own narrative that the idea that you are wrong never came to you? What if I'm actually in control? What if you are unwittingly serving me in everything you do?"

"You hear my thoughts and claim to know my heart. You know only debauchery and sin! If I was under your control, I would be aware. I am the Lord's slave... you are mine."

Another demonic sounding chorus of laughter bellowed. "Torment me all you'd like. I have nothing more to say to you."

Another voice entered in. A single woman's voice was speaking, the one belonging to the blonde woman who worked in Auzlanten's sanctum. "Arodi, are you in there?" She sounded as though she was simultaneously at every point in the void. "I must speak with you, it's very urgent."

"You still have that toy?" The multitude laughed. "You never could let go of the past."

Arodi gripped his fists together. The circling frame of squares tightened onto the molten ball. It closed in smaller and smaller and the screaming just grew louder. The sphere strangled the ball of fire down to a molecular point. Finally, the squares all smashed together, sending a flush of bright sparks and the eerie screams faded back to the vacuum.

Arodi Auzlanten sighed and sank his head downwards. His long dark hair draped sloppily over his sullen face in black waves. He floated over to what appeared to be more empty space, but it opened up. The strange metal door rose up and led into the chamber of his sanctum. The woman in the iron grey ancient Scourge uniform was standing there. Her full pink lips were angled in a smile.

"It's good to see you, Arodi." Her soft old Glaswegian accent soothed his senses.

"I'm sorry for not saying hello when I entered." The blue door slammed shut as his feet touched the marble tile. "It lied to me."

"That is sad...though not unbelievable." They began walking among the display cases.

"What news do you have?" Arodi asked changing the subject.

"I believe your message to High Conservator Jude Bethel resonated. He is issuing an edict ordering all Shackle personnel to be subjected to Veritas interrogation. It will be in effect tomorrow morning."

"This is good news." Arodi began walking towards the display case to return the device. "How is the Regent responding?"

"I don't know specifically." The woman looked uncomfortable. "I can't see or hear him from in here...not like I used to."

Arodi stopped in his path. "This further proves my fears. Invictus has been corrupted by dark spirits...he's part of this whole scheme."

"He killed Djinn Balor." The woman continued.

"Was Bethel able to speak to him first?"

"No, but he is highly suspicious of the Regent. He doesn't trust him...then again he doesn't trust you either."

"At this point... you're the only one who trusts me." The crystal panels of the cubical display shifted and Arodi placed the strange grey tiled figure in. "At least it is a step in the right direction."

"You're certain of the High Conservator's loyalties?"

"Yes... I divined the information. If God says I can trust him, then I am certain I can. Is this the urgent information you needed to share with me?"

"No. I have potential lead for you... Illythia."

"Illythia contacted you?" Arodi asked with a serendipitous tone.

"I contacted her." She responded. "She has been operating in the Northern Kalkhanian coast for some time now."

"Twelve years." Arodi retorted. "How can she help me?"

"When we spoke, I asked her if she knew anything. She hadn't heard of the Idolacreid, but she knows of some marauders who worship the Nephilim. I believe some are from Uzbek."

"I will go see her at once."

Auzlanten made to step away and head towards the entrance dais until the woman grabbed his wrist to stop him. "Are you well?"

"I'm fine." He said blatantly.

"You haven't rested since you made after Resinous... that was two weeks ago. This is the first you've returned in eight days. Are you certain you're fine?"

Auzlanten's bright blue eyes turned dreary. "I suppose I'm not particularly well. The idea that Invictus has fallen prey to a darker power is filling me with grief. I must stay busy lest I think too hard on the matter and plunge into depression."

"I will pray for you Arodi." The woman leaned in and kissed him on the cheek.

A faint smile perked up on his face. "Thank you. I'll return... hopefully with some answers."

Hrimata's Silver District was full of colleges and schools. The Grigorian Administration, named after Grigor Du'Plasse, the Reclaiming Crusader with the greatest devotion to scholarly learning, was among the most popular and famous in all of Carthonia. Inquisitor Adastra Covalos took a magnetic tram to the university in order to inspect the areas that the victims visited before their kidnapping. He noticed many of the silver and gold haired patrons giving him demeaning leers. He figured that people thought he was a native of the Lead District based on his black hair. He didn't bother correcting anyone. He was on duty.

Adastra adjusted the back strap of his greataxe as he stepped out of the tram's convoy onto the fine stone plated path into the Grigorian Administration's campus. Young men and women bustled busily around him, coming and going from the mag-railway, uncaring of his reasons for being here. His black flaksteel boots clinked on the polished granite as he strode into the heart of the scholastic institute. He observed intricate and complex looking buildings, each devoted to a specific field of study. Statues and plaques of famous professors, orators, and inventors were scattered around fine topiaries and gardens creating an extravagantly wonderful landscape. His crimson cape fluttered in a cool breeze as his piercing grey eyes analyzed the details surrounding him.

He could spend hours touring this campus. There were parks and gardens spanning the university which encompassed an area of fifty square miles. It would be ineffective and inefficient to wander aimlessly scanning for a killer and Adastra Covalos knew this. He wanted to inspect oddities lurching from the campus. As an investigator and an Inquisitor, he knew that criminals rarely kept to singular offenses. Recidivists rarely control themselves once they become enthralled in the titillating life of debauchery.

After half a mile of clinking in his battle plate, Inquisitor Covalos stepped up to a roped off mess hall. Bright red tape with bold faced warnings from Hrimatan arbiters blocked a perimeter off as law enforcement officers chattered about. Adastra lifted the plastic tape and hunched under the perimeter. The blue and white uniformed arbiters stopped and stared as the black and red armored Inquisitor stepped in the scene of the crime.

Adastra glared over the heads of the officers, looking for the chief arbiter. He spotted him based on the upstanding plume of white feathers on his helmet. The Inquisitor unveiled his Inquisition insignia as he approached the lead investigator.

He vaguely knew why the arbiters had isolated the mess hall. He heard over the Scourge wavelengths that there was a bombing of some sort less than two hours prior. This was by all definitions an oddity.

Inquisitor Covalos revealed his insignia as the arbiter chief turned to face him, a puzzled look on his face. "Adastra Covalos, Inquisition." He gruffly stated showing his credentials, the insignia of the Scourge's spike whip resting on a Bible.

"I'm First Captain Paul Bur'ett," The man gave a poorly executed Scourge salute, but the effort seemed genuine enough. The captain, as he was called in this region, was a tall and thin man with thin, cropped, steel colored hair and dark eyes. He did his best to conceal his discomfort at seeing a figure as imposing as the large, heavily armored Inquisitor. "What brings the Inquisition here? We've not unearthed anything hardly worthy of the Scourge's attention."

"Would you brief me of the situation?"

"Of course, allow me to show you inside." He marched towards the double doors leading into the mess hall with his gloved hands clasped behind his back.

There was a bitter irony to this atrocity happening in a mess hall, as that was all that remained of the dining area, a mess. The smell of incinerated ignate and thermite wafted in the ventilated air. Black char stained the painted stonework floors at the far end of the ellipsoid chamber, singeing the green gloss bare. Plastic benches were once aligned in rows but were dispersed from the shockwave, the closest of which were fused to the floor. Adastra immediately recognized the iron scent of blood without needing to look at the red splatters and spare body parts strewn in the cafeteria. The off-putting aroma of burnt flesh was complemented by unfinished gourmet meals.

"Allow me to walk you through what happened." The First Captain remained upright and at attention when addressing the Inquisitor, a characteristic absent in the surrounding arbiters. "At approximately fifteen thirty this afternoon, a fourth-year chemist named Frodus Rieveshl entered the mess hall and sat in the far table. Beneath his pea coat was a homemade incendiary device, a mock recipe of the plastic explosive clapshock."

"This kid made clapshock?" Adastra asked stroking his beard in contemplation. "That's the kind of thing the Scourge uses to fell Hekatons and rip chariots in half. It's highly volatile if not secured in proper shelling and it's bloody expensive to make a proper batch."

"Correct on those accounts." Paul Bur'ett bowed slightly in admiration. "Young Mr. Rieveshl was a master in his craft. He had a nine point six of ten in his grades, racking up nearly twenty extra classes in his time here. He was eight weeks away from graduating alpha primus. If anybody at the Grigorian Administration could have made such a material, it would have been him."

"Tell me more about what happened here. I'm assuming you have security records. Could you tell if he was looking for someone in particular or perhaps just as much damage as possible? Or could you deduce if there was a technical malfunction?"

"That's unclear. Sixteen students died in the blast and thirty-four were maimed or injured. We are examining each of the victims to see if there were any quarrels between them. It did not appear as though he was searching for any specific individual though. He sat at the table alone for nine minutes eighteen seconds before the blast. He looked nervous, sweating even though it was only seventy degrees inside. Cold feet, I suppose. He couldn't quite work up the courage to take his own life."

"What's the maximum capacity of this hall?"

"Approximately four hundred can be seated at the tables. Accounting for people standing in lines and around the cafeteria areas, I suppose up to six or seven hundred. This is one of the more popular dining halls so it's often bustling. It's a blessing more people weren't here."

"This doesn't make any sense." Adastra stopped right at the edge of the scorch marks on the floor, leering down at the scarred flooring.

"May I inquire what you're confused about?" The First Captain asked.

"There's a few things wrong here. If Rieveshl wanted to kill as many people as possible he did a rotten job at it. First off why sit here, on the border of the hall? More people would have been caught in the blast radius if he was in the center. Secondly, why fifteen thirty? That's not the busiest time of day. This place would have been far more crowded at twelve or thirteen, since that's usually when people get lunch. Fifteen to sixteen is dead time between lunch and dinner so traffic would be much lower comparatively. Thirdly, look around you."

Adastra motioned to the walls. Aside from the burnt blood stains caused by the explosion the walls themselves were relatively unscathed. "I'm confused." Bur'ett pondered. "What should I be looking at?"

"It's not what is there, but what isn't." Inquisitor Covalos noted that other arbiters were peering over and listening in, so he spoke with added volume so they could hear as well. "Any munitions novice would know that if you want to create as much collateral as possible, you add shrapnel to your bomb. Just by putting tacks, pins, nails, or any kind of scrap on the carapace sends high velocity flak in all directions. So, if this kid wanted to kill, why didn't he add shrapnel?"

"I see... you think he was coerced then?"

"From what I can gather with what I'm seeing and what you're telling me, I'm certain of that. I think our culprit was forced into this situation and operated with the intent of harming as few people as possible. Though what could possibly warrant something as radical as this?"

"Perhaps he didn't make the bomb." Paul Bur'ett suggested. "It could be that someone else strapped it to him and detonated it."

"Would you allow me to bring some equipment to examine the scene?"

"The Scourge's aid is always welcome. Do you suspect magick?"

Adastra chuckled slightly at the sentiment. "Captain, I'm an officer of the Inquisition. It is my duty to suspect magick."

CHAPTER 20

Service to the Bulwark was a tradition in the Du'Plasse family tracing back to the founding of Templym by Grigor himself. Pre-Strife, Oslin served in the Beacon when it still part of the defensive branch of Arodi Auzlanten's utopian society. Oslin was the only one in the branch that ended up switching sides before the Bulwark's destruction.

When Malacurai descended from the sky, Oslin's older brother Yuriel and his father Grigus served in the Trench and his younger brother Ethix in the Siloam. While Oslin spent the vast majority of his time in the debate halls trying to determine the truth, the rest of his family spent their time in the Strife fighting the Scourge. Ethix Du'Plasse was shot and killed when the Siloam ambushed the Dictum in Constantinople. Yuriel Du'Plasse died in a vehicle explosion during the Hekaton battle of the Yawning Bank which utterly disintegrated his body. Grigus Du'Plasse witnessed the battle between Auzlanten and Malacurai at Budapest. He killed himself when he saw the false angel's death, unwilling to fall captive to what he believed were traitor forces. Nora Du'Plasse, Oslin's mother, was left a bitter widow with nothing but resentment for her surviving son whom she deemed a turncoat.

Nora was imprisoned facing a life sentence in Niflheim Arcae. She was an instrumental planner in the attempted assassination of Regent Illuromos three years ago. After Oslin discovered the attempt, he confronted her. Her response was to attempt to kill him. He arrested her yet operated as her barrister in defense. What should have been a swift conviction turned into a lengthy and heated legal debate. Oslin exploited every loophole to have her death sentenced reduced to a life sentence to save his mother. He hoped that this endeavor would be enough motivation for her to forgive him for his "betrayal". It was insufficient. Nora still harbored bitterness towards her last living son.

"I trust you'll enjoy your presents." Oslin said with a weak smile. "I apologize I wasn't able to be here last week on your true fifty-eighth, I was in the UPA. Fortunately, business has brought me home."

"I don't want them." Nora's voice was frail but could still cut Oslin deep. Her blanched hair had vague traces of platinum strands. "All my sons are dead."

"I brought scented oils, mystery novels, blank parchments with a new set of pastels, and a cake from Ferritolli's. All should make your stay here more pleasant." Oslin called in several favors to give her a uniquely luxurious cell. Arcae prisoners weren't normally permitted things like packages, visitors, or outside food. "The cake is a personal one, I hope you don't mind. I still can't convince Valkyrie to let me give you a food preserver. It should last about a week before becoming stale."

"How the hell should I know how long that is?" She snapped. "I still don't have a clock or a calendar. I didn't even realize it was Nyvett until I got this gaudy thing." She motioned to the present Oslin was holding.

"Requin and Nichole haven't visited you yet?" He asked with genuine concern.

"They're busy. Nichole tried to call but the guard rejected it. Last I heard she was in Azzatha on business. My guess is Requin has been too busy with the baby."

"Baby? When did Requin have a baby?"

"Two months ago, Ethix Yuriel Wollcot, my grandson, was born, and I'm stuck in here unable to see him. It doesn't surprise me that she didn't tell you. She still hasn't forgiven you for stealing Yuriel's ascot."

"I gave her the whole estate. This scarf is all I wanted to remember him by."

"And your father's Holt... the same one he killed himself with. You still wear it I see."

"Yes, and with it I've continued in the solemn oaths of the Bulwark. I still serve as a defender of the innocent and preserver of law. I've used this pistol to continue in his vision for society."

"Are you referring to whoring yourself out to an Imago?"

"Arodi Auzlanten is genuine in his pleas. Malacurai was no angel of the Lord. We had xenocryptologists, angelologists, demonologists, crusaders, and even former magick wielders debate for the entirety of the Strife to deduce the truth of the matter. The Beacon, the branch devoted to destroying falsities and bolstering facts, declared that Arodi Auzlanten, the patriarch of Templym, was truly of the Lord."

"So, you are blind then. Malacurai was an angel. You didn't see what your father and brothers saw. He carried the light of Heaven in his six wings, wielded a sword made of starlight, and knew the Word through and through. Malacurai was the genuine party, not the deceiver Auzlanten."

"It's in the past now. Malacurai is dead. Auzlanten still reigns."

"Yes...and my husband and sons lie dead alongside him."

"I'm still here mother."

"I wish you weren't." Her already hostile tone grew increasingly grim. "It would have been better had you died."

"I have no doubt you feel that mother." Oslin fought back queasiness at the insult. "I fully understand why you would rather Yuriel or Ethix to have survived instead."

"No, you don't fully understand. Of all the men in my family, you were the most loathsome. Yuriel was a skilled warrior with loyalty to his creed. Ethix was a kind soul with a bright mind. Grigus was everything any man should hope to aspire to be. You were always a braggadocios narcissist too smart for the likes of any of us. You always looked down on us, unwilling to admit we were on par with your intellect. I prayed that you'd be killed in the war, graced with an honorable death as a hero so we could have some false sweet memories of what we wished you were. Instead, all the men of character in the Du'Plasse family died, further emphasizing your unfathomable nature. Instead, you won't even live to have a death with any sort of meaning. Instead, you let your wickedness fester and you'll die a traitor...all because you turned your back on the Bulwark and became a pawn of the Mundus Imago. I see now that your brothers and father would have inevitably given their lives as a sacrifice to the truth. But my life and your sisters' would have improved had you died in the Strife."

Oslin sat on the hard metal cube in silence. The cold steel plating mirrored the coldness the Herald was feeling in his blood. He wasn't sure how to respond, looking into the eyes of a woman that thoroughly hated him, his own mother. He was feeling an intricate cocktail of every spastic and vile emotion imaginable, enough to nauseate him to his core. Looking at him, it would be impossible to tell what he was feeling. He just dipped his head in grief. His bright armor and hair deeply contrasted the brooding darkness inside of him.

"Happy birthday, mom." He adjusted his ascot, pushed himself off of his knees to a standing position. "You may keep the package." He walked to the other side of the chamber and knocked on the door signaling Valkyrie to open it up. "Even if you don't mother...I love you."

She grunted in disgust before returning to her book as the pistons in the wall clicked to life opening up to the hallway. Archon Valkyrie stood on the open end and motioned invitingly towards him. Oslin Du'Plasse looked over his shoulder once more, sighed and stepped out into the prison halls.

In the observation chamber, Vandross Blackwell's granite pipe let a thin mist of white vapor waft from the bell. Upon watching the initial entry of Oslin seeing his mother, he packed a ball of clovertwig in hopes of having a smoke as refreshment for the show. Halfway through, he had stopped puffing at the pipe, letting the plant matter burn away entirely. He sat in shock at the sight he just witnessed. The Inquisitor tailed Herald Du'Plasse with hopes of some sappy commentary with his mommy, but this... this was abuse. Vandross removed his wide brimmed hat and pressed it against his chest in memoriam to a broken family.

"Vandross, are you there?" A voice broke out from his audio wire in his ear after a few moments of stunned silence. It was the gruff voice of Adastra Covalos.

"Yeah, I'm here." He responded while placing his hat back on his head. "Sitrep on Oslin. He went to visit his mom in the local Arcae... pray for him. He's got some pretty heavy emotional baggage."

"Huh, noted. Anyway, when you're done there, I need you to rendezvous with me at the Grigorian Administration, Baker's Hall. Do you have your occultist kit with you?"

"Always." Vandross said. "What's this for?"

"There was a bombing. I suspect magick and I want to be certain."

"Does this have to do with the Dilictor or Mortis?" Blackwell inquired.

"Both, I hope."

Jameson Daurtey arrived with the caravan chariot in Hrimata a day ahead of schedule. Warden Volk Downey and Retriever Ram's Horn picked him and their designated transport up from the port before heading up to the Reclamation Monument Park in the Gold District.

As one of the first and most prominent urbans liberated during the Reclaiming Crusades, Hrimata bore a large number of relics to the triumphant time. Grigor Du'Plasse, the patron saint of the Nordic Plains, immortalized a number of extravagant sites to commemorate the revolutionary founding of Templym. The nationally famed Reclamation Monument Park, one of many in the noble urban, was framed as one of the modern wonders of the world. A portion of the lush rolling hills of the Nordic Plains were isolated here. Small mounds of fabric-like grass and prismatic colored flowers scattered across this patch of land. Streets of polished ceramic led to a number placards of burnished igneous detailing victories of the Reclaiming Crusades. This lavish landscape was a popular tourist destination for the Carthonian people and all citizens of Templym. And apparently, the hunting grounds of a killer.

The two Scourge warriors waited in the caravan just on the outskirts of the park. They observed the black steel gates leading into the park. They waited with their indentured inmate in the observation port, staking out the position in anticipation of catching someone or something of interest to the Dilictor hunt. They were at an advantage because the chariot they occupied looked just like a standard cargo transport, allowing it to blend in with the other vehicles on the rockfoam streets. The three men stared at the primary entryway, as well as a few secondary gates, from a panel of one-way glass from the seclusion of the caravan.

Jameson Daurtey parked in a discrete location where the caravan would appear least suspecting. He sat quietly in the back of the chamber as Volk and Ram leered out, taking note of the surroundings.

"This is one bloody mess we've found ourselves in huh?" The Warden's Glaswegian accent bounced. Light glinted off of the Black Rose mag locked to his pauldron.

"Yep." Ram's Horn grunted.

"Think about it, one week we get assignment in Frankon. Week two, we're chasing a drug dealer in Venice. Week three, we hunt a cult in the UPA. Now we're in our fourth week hunting a serial killer in the Nordic Plains. All the while, we're actually looking for some enigmatic kingpin who may not even exist. I'm almost missing our usual quarry hunts... course not so much. This is the kind of work I live for. Dishing out punishment to the worst of the worst like it was porridge at a feeding house, ah this is the dream. Don't you think so?"

"Yep."

"What about you Mr. Daurtey?" Volk called out without tearing his gaze from the window. "Do you feel as though you're absolving for your sins with us?"

"Yes sir." The inmate replied. "I'm doing my civil duty and performing my penitence."

"That's right you are." Downey's leathery face perked up in a grin. "Hard to think that two years ago, you were on the wrong side of the Shackle's chain-cuffs. Now you're on our side putting even lower lives than yours away. You're indenturing is set to last five years... I think I can get you off a year or two early if you keep up the good work."

"Thank you, sir, I appreciate that. By the way, High Conservator Bethel just issued an edict. All Shackle members are to undergo Veritas interrogation to renew their sworn oaths."

"What's the world come to?" Volk's eyes squinted as he focused on something close to one of the secondary entrances. "Something's got Jude up in a huff...something bad enough that he's issuing edicts to keep the organization clean. I don't like this."

"Me neither." Ram's Horn muttered. He then slapped an armor-clad hand onto the shoulder piece of Volk's battle plate. "Red lady." He pointed to a woman at the easternmost gate donning a maroon dress less than two hundred feet away.

"Yeah, I see her too." Warden Downey crossed his black and blue metal arms. "She's a pretty young lady...been standing there for almost an hour. You'd figure a girl that gorgeous would have found a customer by now."

"Sorry, may I ask what you're looking at?" Jameson Daurtey interjected tugging at his metal collar.

"Whore." Ram's Horn grumbled.

"Not exactly Ram." Volk kindly corrected. "In Hrimata one of the most abundant services that the Veil has yet to expunge from the urban is professional companionship. It's kind of like prostitution but a bit more eh...high end. Instead of just paying for a quick shag and going their separate ways, a companion provides a much more personal touch. They give the delusion of a relationship with fancy get-togethers before...you know. They're a difficult sort to nail because it's tough to prove malice intent because it looks like a quaint courting. They tend to appeal to a lonely and well-paying audience."

Ram's helmet swiveled towards Downey. "Whore."

He responded, "Yes, but a fancy whore."

"Why does she grab your attention?" Daurtey asked.

"A nice young companion like that should have picked up a client within minutes. She was here when we rolled up. I've seen her wave away seven or eight buyers. So why isn't she accepting anybody?"

"What does this have to do with the Dilictor?"

"It could be nothing, probably is. But that working girl seems to know her way around these parts. Companions tend to have territories, areas of interest where they prefer to operate. So maybe this nice sweetheart has seen our victims or perhaps even our culprit."

"Is that really the best course of action?"

"Nope...but we don't have any other leads. So, I think I'll go for it then."

"Have fun." Retriever Ram's Horn bellowed.

Warden Downey removed his battle plate, reducing him by a few inches in height. He dressed up in the same regalia when he was meeting up with Numerri in Bruccol. He adjusted his suit's collar, thankful that the lavish attire of the surrounding crowds allowed him to blend in. He made approach to the beautiful woman a few feet away from the gate's entryway. From just outside the barred metal wall the aroma of fresh flora wafted in the cool breeze as the sun began fleeting from the horizon.

Without so much as a passing glance, Volk "accidentally" bumped into her side. "Oh, pardon me Madame, I didn't see you there." He made sure that she was on his right side, the side of his bad eye.

"Oh, don't worry," the companion said with a sly smile. "I suppose if that's the worst thing that happens all day, it's a good day." This woman wore a tightly fit dress of a shimmering maroon silk which complemented her sparkling green eyes. She wore her soft brown hair in a tightly knit braid. Her fingers bore two golden bands and her neck was wrapped with a silver torc.

"That's a good way to look at life. I do apologize though. My vision's not quite what it used to be." He chuckled as he pointed to his obviously clouded eye alluding to blindness, even though he could see from it just fine.

"Oh dear, mister I believe you've been shot." Her painted lips were locked in a coy smile.

"Yes, I've been shot a number of times. This gem was the only shell that stuck around. The others passed through or bounced clean off."

"Oh my, was this during one of the Crusades, or perhaps the Civil Strife?"

"The Strife. I was in a parley between the Trench and the Shackle. It went poorly as evidence by the slug in my head. Bloody thing took me out of the remainder of the fight, too. People used to have respect for truces."

"Fascinating, you must have a host of stories. You have the look of a veteran on you. Is that a Glaswegian accent I hear?"

"That it is my lady." Downey continued to banter. "I'm new in town I suppose. If I'm not mistaken, you don't sound like you're a local, either."

"Correct. I was born and raised in Vouricale in the UPA. I have however lived in Hrimata for the past four years. This is my home now."

"Well miss...goodness me I never introduced myself. I'm Roland Turrit, pleased to make your acquaintance."

"Oh, it's lovely to make your acquaintance Roland. I'm Deborah Nightingale." She extended a slender hand for him to kiss, which he did so without hesitation.

"I'd love to learn more about you. Care to show me some of the best places to dine? I'd be honored if you'd let me treat you."

"Oh, thank you for the offer Roland. I don't mean to be rude, but you are likely old enough to be my father. I've no interest in perusing frivolous dinners with the likes of you. I'd much prefer a young man of marrying age. No offense."

Volk leaned in close enough to exchange a whisper. "Not even for a price?" He asked in a hopeful hush.

"Ah, so you're familiar with the practice then?" Deborah's mood grew serious. "The going rate for a dinner is fifty crowns, two hundred for a ball or dance or other manner of party, and three hundred if you were hoping for a happy ending."

"Companionship ain't cheap these days, is it?" Volk removed a wallet with a few bills inside. "Let's start with dinner and see where it takes us from there."

"Sorry, honey, I've got to pay rent and it's not cheap in this city. I can't go around offering meals to vagabonds. If you want to employ my services, I'm going to need commitment for the full package."

Volk sighed and thought for a moment. Was it really worth the time and effort, not to mention the money to follow up on a lead that may very well go nowhere? Should he cut his losses and search for a different source? One thing that the Warden was certain of was that this woman was hiding something. Even though he didn't think it was the best course of action, he had a gut feeling that this woman could provide information he was looking for.

"Very well, I'm in." He moved to remove some money from his wallet.

"Not out here." She snapped quietly. "Do you want the Scourge to bust us both? You can pay me when we get somewhere more private."

"Very well then, shall we?" He opened his arm out for the companion to grab, which she took with a smile. "Deborah, I believe this is going to be a night to remember."

"Yes, I agree Roland." Bride Daphne Wainwright said with a suggestive grin.

CHAPTER 21

Twilight had long since descended on the Grigorian Administration. The arbiters inspecting the bombing of Baker's Hall were forced to bring in flood lights to illuminate the scene to distinguish enough detail. Adastra Covalos stayed long enough for the law enforcement to realize their shifts were over and several went home, leaving the Inquisitor mostly isolated on the site of the butchery. This was his preference. He took time between himself and the Lord as precious, taking time to introspect, and to focus on his work.

Adastra was reviewing security footage with his metal clad hands pressed together. The static shrouded image of the young man sweating in his seat haunted the Inquisitor. The bleached camera footage was just barely recovered from the surveyors dangling from the ceiling, as several of the cameras were destroyed in the blast. It showed an image of a young man, a military ordinance device strapped on his breast beneath a thin coat, being overly cautious. Every twitch, every breath he took while he sat alone with laser focus in his darting eyes was slow and calculated. Was somebody watching Rieveshl? Perhaps instead there was some dark entity guiding his motions from inside of his body. That is what Inquisitor Covalos suspected, but was there still proof?

"Adastra." Vandross called out and waved as he stepped into the mess hall. His red cloak fluttered behind him as he hastily walked to his partner. "I got here as soon as I could."

"Thank you, I appreciate it." Covalos nodded. "Do you have the occultist's kit?"

"Detection incense, peering shards, and everything else an occultist kit comes with. So, you think there's demonic influence here?" Adastra had already given his partner a full analysis while he was en route to his position.

"You've got warding clay too?"

"Wait, are you suggesting we perform a séance?" Vandross asked with a tinge of shock.

"No, I'll perform it. You examine the scene, inspect for Imago trails and magick residue. Focus on the epicenter of the blast but look around the hall's perimeter as well."

Vandross shuffled through his satchel and removed a small cylinder filled with a viscous fluid. "You're the demon hunter, I trust you know what's best." He handed the case to Adastra who promptly unscrewed the cap.

Adastra Covalos began an ancient incantation of protection, a combination of ancient Hebrew and Latin creating a complex and morbid sounding chant. In truth the timbre of the prayer was far grimmer sounding than the actual content, as it was a request to the Lord for guidance and answers. He performed this prayer as he delicately painted neat Hebrew glyphs on the floor tiling with the thick brown ichor. This "warding clay", as it was now called, was another concoction of Arodi Auzlanten's design, intended to reveal the presence of the Mundus Imago who could shift between the spaces of reality. On its own it was an inert mud. When paired with the proper glyphs and prayers, it could reveal past presence of wicked spirits.

As Inquisitor Covalos performed the séance, Inquisitor Blackwell sighed and dug through his satchel. He drew a number of rectangular sheets of what appeared to be dehydrated plant matter, resembling processed seaweed. These were blocks of detection incense and were far simpler to use. It could detect magick, Imago, or other dark powers from the spiritual plane. All that was required was to ignite the dried plant matter and the resulting scent would hint towards demonic powers. A sweet, pleasant aroma would hint at the absence of Mundus Imago while the stench of rot and decay would indicate nearby demons.

Vandross took out his pocket ignate torch, which he normally used to ignite the tobacco or other herbs of his pipe. A quick jet of bright sparks touched the dark green block. He tossed the light leaf in the air as flame quickly devoured it. Vandross inhaled the resulting cloud of white vapor deeply. He was tempted to smile at the berry scent it yielded. However, it indicated a negative result, so he was displeased. He stepped away from Adastra, who was kneeling on the singed tile while painting Hebrew glyphs upon it and went closer to the center of the blast radius. He ignited another block of incense when he was twenty paces closer. He breathed deeply noting a similar scent, but it was less potent. Vandross hummed and scratched the whiskers at his chin. He stepped another twenty paces closer, right at the center of the blast. He winced, slightly noting the sticky charred blood he was walking on before using his torch to light another block. Taking in another deep whiff, all Vandross could detect was the scent of burnt tissue and seared viscera. The detection incense itself bore no aroma. This was a frustrating result because it indicated no definite presence or absence of Imago. Vandross grunted inaudibly to himself as he began orbiting the mess hall to check its perimeter.

As Inquisitor Blackwell used his incense to inspect for the supernatural, Inquisitor Covalos continued his prayer. Twelve sigils made from the warding clay surrounded him as his crimson cape began to stir in an invisible wind. He cleared his mind of all thoughts not pertaining to the ritual. Even as he was eager to drive all thoughts from his mind, he was tapping into something far more sinister. A torrent of emotions began pouring through his head. Visions of Adastra's witch mother and memories of his childhood torment echoed in brief flashes as unholy powers attempted to sway his concentration from the words. A chilled sweat began to drench his brow and began to drip down his tangled black locks. His normally pale skin was flushed even whiter as his past traumas were displayed in his mind. This was not his first séance. Adastra knew the proper mindset to maintain to keep from plunging into madness as so many inexperienced Acolytes do.

Vandross looked with concern on his partner's physical body as he was inwardly fighting. He never liked these rituals, as they bordered on forbidden occult. This was a practice that the Inquisition deemed acceptable but risky. The séance tapped into the spiritual plane to look for its denizens. A mortal exposing themselves to unknown energies was not of the Lord's design, and understandably so. Improper execution of the ritual would result in some form of madness like catatonia, paranoia, comas, and other maladies. Adastra Covalos was a well-versed speaker and an experienced demon killer, so there was little risk here. It still shook Vandross though. Adastra began to shiver as his body temperature dropped. The shadow he cast danced unnaturally on the ground, jerking back and forth across the glyphs he painted with the warding clay. Clear globes of sweat wept down his battle plate, some of which either froze on or boiled off. Despite the unnatural things happening around the man, he did not sway or deter from his chant. The litany did not waver or cease until the ritual was complete.

Adastra snapped his eyes open upon completion of the multilingual words. He panted dryly as he accustomed himself to the reality around him. He stood up and patted his pallid face with the end of his cloak. When he wiped the sweat off, he looked down to see the angle of his shadow. His shadow was the indicator when paired with the warding clay. The twelve glyphs were arranged in a circular pattern in which Adastra was standing in the center of. To one unfamiliar with the sigils it would appear as some ancient clock. In truth each symbol was representative of an outcome, though the specifics of each were Sigma classified. His shadow was cast over the position at nine o'clock, which was odd considering the angle of the flood lights. This sigil indicated a residual presence of an Imago in the area. In only a few seconds, Adastra's shadow retracted to himself and then extended back into its natural position.

"What's the verdict?" Vandross asked with his arms crossed.

"There was an Imago here." Adastra said, his normal baritone voice cracked slightly. "Though not directly, I'm betting it controlled our bomber with black magick."

"I agree." Vandross proposed. "The incense came up blank at the center of the blast. I trust that means that there could have been an Imago influence in that space sooner?"

"Correct." Inquisitor Covalos cracked his neck as he stepped over to Inquisitor Blackwell. He shivered slightly, his skin still pallid. "Do you have any more of that cinder leaf?"

"Of course." Vandross removed his smooth granite pipe and sprinkled a few red leaves in the bell. He ground them up and lit them before handing the pipe to his Serbian friend. This was the same material Vandross had smoked while in the pseudo-tundra of Jaspin to increase his internal body temperature. "What does this mean? Why would a demon possess a young man, only to blow up a half empty cafeteria?"

Adastra inhaled deeply, sort of devouring the savory vapor from the pipe. "I don't know." A puff of smoke came out with his voice. "This is strange. Perhaps Frodus Rieveshl was an Imago cultist but grew repentant. Maybe he accepted the spirit as divine but regretted it, so the fiend forced him to commit murder out of spite."

"But why so poorly?" Vandross mused. "It is the nature of the beasts to do as much harm upon humanity as possible. Why would it influence this kid to do such a lousy job with the bombing if he wanted to inflict maximum casualties?"

"Perhaps he was regaining control of his body." Adastra let more smoke out of his mouth, he was warming up nicely. "There have been instances of Imago having partial control of their hosts. Maybe he knew what the beast was doing and motioned however he could to minimize casualties."

"Seems logical, but what does this have to do with our quarry hunt? What does a demonic possession on a college campus have to do with Knox Mortis? Is this connected to the Dilictor Ignotum?"

"I'm not sure." Adastra handed the empty stone pipe back to its owner. "I think we should reconvene with Warden Downey at the Seraphim Solace and see if we should pursue this."

"Perhaps we should commandeer the investigation from the arbiters first. Whether we are the ones looking around or not, this is no doubt our jurisdiction. Does the Inquisition even have much of a presence here?"

"Not much. Hrimata has become spoiled and comfortable, a rabid breeding ground for sin and depravity without demonic influence. Imago tend to avoid these lavish urbans and focus more so on the smaller settlements where the Church thrives. I believe the head of the Inquisition in this area is Exarch Surizal. We can inform him back at the Solace."

"Let's not waste any time then." Vandross smiled and turned on his heel to join Adastra. The two then exited the facility and embarked towards the headquarters of the Veil.

Bride Daphne Wainwright went undercover as a professional companion about two weeks prior to the arrival of S-6319. She fit the Dilictor's victim profile. She was a foreigner, young, and objectively beautiful. Her intent was to lure the killer out from lurking around in the shadows to draw him out. The promiscuity would serve to further her appeal as bait. Daphne hated the idea of playing the part of a prostitute, but she was in her fourth month of hunting this fiend and growing desperate. Previous strategies were insufficient. The Bride was paranoid that the Dilictor had left the city and taken his sadistic art elsewhere, but her profiling experience told her otherwise. Daphne figured that he was just more cautious now. She deduced that the Nitral Nightmare was still preying on innocent tourists but being more thorough in his disposal when he was through. She prayed that her efforts of baiting the killer would prove effective...she finally thought she did.

What Warden Volk Downey was unaware of was that the companion he was dining with was an officer of the Veil. Likewise, Bride Wainwright didn't know that her target was a member of the Shackle. All she cared about was that this stranger fit her killer's profile. Two warriors of the Scourge, each with separate motives for catching the same recidivist, were hunting each other. Looking from outside of their investigative minds it looked like a simple dinner date. The two were dressed in fine clothes, eating and drinking in a posh restaurant, and laughing in gleeful conversation with one another.

The two were dining in a small restaurant not far from Reclamation Memorial Park in the Gold District. A small Azzathan-stylized dining hall, exotic spices hung lazily in the air, producing a pleasing aroma. Volk and Daphne were laughing with one another, playing their respective parts. The Warden drank a malted cocktail of brandy while the Bride sipped her third glass of white wine over their seasoned fish meals. Each pretended to begin to feel the ill influence of the liquor, ignorant that the other was immunized to the effects of alcohol by their Scourge training. They were thoroughly engaged in petty small talk. Daphne, under the guise of Deborah Nightingale, was observing Warden Downey, anticipating any sudden movements to attempt to move in on her. She was almost hopeful that Volk was going to attempt abduction. Meanwhile, Warden Downey, posing as Roland Turrit, was hoping to find himself poised in a position where he could question if she knew anything about the victims. He wanted to be careful in his approach, yet thorough in his investigation.

Volk worked his usual charm appealing to the young lady. Her entertainment was forced, as she was secretly disgusted with the thought that she could be dining with the Nitral Nightmare. He was recounting on his time during the Deficio Tribulation.

"The Warden had us stand out in the snow all night long." Downey recounted pleasantly, to Wainwright's "fascination". "We had to all clamber together in a massive huddle to keep from getting hypothermia. Of course, who do I get to stand next to but Xerxes? Even in sub-zero, his sweaty hide still stunk to high heaven."

Daphne laughed at the anecdote. "You had to stand there all night?"

"From twilight to dusk, we stood there almost twelve hours."

"Oh my, the Deficio Trial sounds so brutal. You must be so strong to have endured such hardships." Daphne was leading him on hoping to appeal to his pig-headed nature. She knew full well what the Tribulation consisted of. She had conducted seven in her lifetime.

"Yes, it's a trifling thing. I had a lot of friends not make it through. Most of them had to get counseling after the fact, invalidating them from ever joining the Scourge." Volk said stoically. He did notice that she misnamed the enrollment process but chose not to correct her in an effort to be polite. However, this was an intentional test Daphne used to see if her target was genuine. The fact that he opted not to point the mistake out made her all the more suspicious.

"Why did you leave?" Bride Wainwright asked enthusiastically.

"Medical discharge. My eye wasn't the only part of my body the bullet messed up. I was hospitalized for weeks, long enough that I missed Budapest, thank God for that. I was deemed too crippled to return to service, so I got a medical discharge. One thing led to the next and here I am now." Downey drank the last of his cocktail and waved the server to bring him another one. "Enough about me darling, tell me about yourself."

"My life's an open book honey. What do you want to know?"

"How long have you been in Hrimata?" Volk was beginning to subtly question her.

"Six or seven months, I can't recall in truth." Daphne giggled. "I've enjoyed my time here whatever the case. This urban is far nicer than the rustic farmland of Vouricale."

"I imagine the work's a bit more pleasant, too."

"If you're referring to companionship, then yes, it is." Bride Wainwright internally winced at the sentiment. "Getting paid to go on fancy dinner dates is a far more pleasant experience than tending to barley fields."

"Do you work at the Memorial Park or do you get around a bit more?" Warden Downey was beginning to pry for information.

"It's as good a place as any to get clients, though I suppose I get around a lot." Volk was analyzing her words with laser focus. He got the sense that she knew more than she was telling, which was absolutely true.

"I'm surprised you're still out on the streets working. It's dangerous out there for pretty young ladies like you." Daphne was growing suspicious at the sentiment Volk just uttered as the server placed another cocktail on their table.

"You're referring to the Nitral Nightmare?" She asked innocently.

"I am. He's going after people just like you. I'd figure you'd want to lay low 'til the ants caught him."

"I can't pay rent from a hiding hole."

"Well, that makes you either fearless or reckless." Volk chuckled as he sipped his malted beverage. "You know, I hear a rumor that the ladies who this creep got were grabbed from the park."

This was a major red flag for Bride Wainwright. That information was Kappa classified. "Oh, I didn't hear that."

Volk knew for certain that was a lie. He didn't know that she chose the Reclamation Memorial Park for that very reason. "It's just a rumor, but I reckon it could have some truth to it. You know they've got a list of each of the victims and they're offering three hundred crowns for helpful information. If you've seen any of them, that'd be a more modest way of paying your rent. If you've spent a lot of time there...well maybe you've seen something."

"Trust me, I've not seen a thing. I could really use the money." She smiled.

"Well then I'd probably suggest finding a different place to pick up customers. You never know what kinds of reprobates are walking the streets."

"Well at least I have a strong crusader to keep me safe until then." Daphne said while taking one of his hands. "I've had enough to eat now, how about you?"

"I suppose I could go for some dessert." Volk said suggestively, biting his tongue at such a poorly phrased flirt.

"Let's conclude our business together then."

"Agreed."

Both were ready to make their final moves. With the end of the dinner, Warden Downey had determined that his target was suppressing information from him. He planned to make an arrest and interrogate her further to press for knowledge on the victims. Unbeknownst to him, Bride Wainwright was planning something similar albeit with a higher level of malice. She suspected him of being the Dilictor, the Nitral Nightmare. The way that he spoke in the odd tone of voice and the question he asked set her on edge. She was eager to detain and question further with hopes of finally getting some answers to her months-long quarry hunt. Each was unaware of what the other schemed.

Daphne had a hotel room in the Steel District reserved for her "work". The room had been reserved primarily to act as an impromptu interrogation chamber. There were firearms, blades, and various torture implements concealed in a variety of hiding places. Bride Wainwright had used this as a means to question suspects while maintaining her cover as a companion. It was a ground floor apartment with a single bed chamber and a backroom with old ceramic tile plastered with the reek of fear and gore.

Downey and Wainwright both walked with a drunken sway in their steps, acting inebriated to fool the other. Volk had a set of chain-cuffs and his Reisinger clipped to his belt under his jacket. Unfortunately for him, Daphne was much more heavily equipped.

"So, do I pay now, or after the fact?" Volk asked as his "companion".

Daphne moved towards the bed a motioned to it seductively. "How about you show me the money and I'll show you...something else."

"I've got a better idea." All of the warm playfulness dissolved from his now morbid demeanor. He removed the set of chain-cuffs from behind him and dangled them from his gloved finger. "Kynigi et Kako sweetheart, you're under arrest by authority of the Shackle. Your compliance is appreciated."

"Oh really?" Daphne said, keeping the playful ambiance in her voice. She didn't believe Volk, thinking this was a clever ploy to whisk her away never to be seen again. "I'm shaken, really I am." She drew a sleek white Claymore pistol from a concealed thigh holster and pointed it squarely at the Warden's center of mass.

Volk looked up and down at her with genuine awe. "Where the hell were you keeping that?" His voice wavered slightly with astonishment.

"I'm in charge here, sweetheart." The sentiment was declared with an obvious amount of loathing. "Why don't you drop the cuffs and step into my office. I've got a few questions for you." She jerked her hand motioning to the back room where she had hoped to squeeze answers out of her target.

"Alright darling keep your cool. I don't think either of us wants to get hurt tonight."

"Don't call me darling." Daphne said frigidly. "And I don't think there's much risk of me being hurt. I am the one with the gun after all."

"Well, I suppose I'm at a loss then." Volk shrugged and walked towards the backroom, directly in the path of the Bride. He took the opportunity to lurch to the side and pry the gun from her fist. He conducted a simple Scourge maneuver that involved a twisting of the target's wrist with one hand and a fierce shove with the other to move the target and the gun in opposite directions. Had she believed that Volk was actually an officer of the Scourge, she would have been prepared to counter it. "Looks like I'm the one with the gun now." His face perked up in a smile.

"So...are you going to shoot me?" Daphne said, not knowing what to expect at this stage.

"I certainly wasn't planning on it." Volk said as he disassembled the handgun in a matter of seconds. The smooth white metal gun parts thudded quietly on the carpet of the bedroom. "Now, would you kindly put the cuffs on and come with me...darling?"

That was Bride Wainwright's personal firearm, her favorite gun. She didn't appreciate it being taken apart like a toy in front of her. "That was a mistake." She said morbidly.

Volk walked within kissing distance of her. "Quit stalling."

Daphne leapt into hand-to-hand combat. She struck Volk in the chest with a sloppy punch. Her hand bounced off of his muscled chest like a wadded ball of paper. Warden Downey gawked briefly at the poor attempt and made to grapple the woman. He attempted to lock her arm in a backwards vice. She was able to deftly slide out of his grip and place an open-handed slap on Volk's leathery face. He shook off the minor blow and returned to the dance of combat.

The Scourge trains its warriors to inflict maximum pain in the shortest amount of time possible. Warden Downey used this methodology against obvious threats. He held back when fighting against the smaller female. He could have drawn his pistol and shot her, but she had information that he wanted. Bride Wainwright on the other hand had her own, personalized style of fighting. She lured her foes into a false sense of security before closing in for a speedy takedown.

Any observer with a basic grasping of human anatomy could tell that Daphne was physically outmatched. Volk possessed about thirty pounds more of raw muscle. It's no wonder that the strikes she threw at him were largely ineffective. She did however have the agility advantage and was able to duck away from Volk's punches after he realized that a simple pin down was impossible. The two were locked in a perpetual stalemate as the two parties exchanged useless jabs and punches.

Daphne tumbled out of the way as Volk drove his fist into the drywall behind her. She took the opening to lay into him with her fist. It thudded against his chest and made him laugh at the pitiful effort. The fight was playing out just as the Bride desired it to. Volk was growing increasingly sloppy as he grew confident in his ability to mop up the fight.

Volk's guard was being lowered. Years of Scourge discipline faded away as he grew increasingly frustrated with his combat partner. Nearly a full minute had passed when the fighting started, and he hadn't landed a single punch. His arms flailed in wider, more sweeping motions to encompass a larger area with hopes of knocking her down. This was how Daphne Wainwright fought. She broke down a veteran combatant's defenses without a single meaningful attack… then ended it with just a few.

Daphne backed up against a wooden side table, feigning desperation. Downey flung his elbow in a downward arc, trying worthlessly trying to crack down on her head. All it did was split the table in half and open him up to Wainwright's genuine assault.

The Veil specializes in empowering foes ordinarily too weak to defend themselves with brute force. Daphne knew how to debilitate foes twice her size with a collection of pinpoint blows to the most sensitive areas of the body. As she ducked away from Volk's most recent blow, she slid on a set of titanium knuckles that she took from the table's underside to truly inflict pain. Seeing Volk's shoulder extended, she swiftly jabbed at his clavicle, right in the neck's nerve cluster. The cold metal left his body with a sharp sting as she pinched the nerves connecting his arm with his spinal cord. He lurched upwards in pain trying to recuperate, which exposed his head to a wicked left hook. Volk felt a trickle of blood drip down the side of his face as he went blind briefly. He flung his fists wildly as his vision darkened out for fear of letting Daphne strike him once more, to no avail.

Now that the Warden had focused all his attention on his upper body, his lower body was exposed. Volk regained his vision just long enough to see Daphne sweep his legs by bringing her metal clad fist to behind one of his kneecaps, knocking him to the ground. The final strike was her bringing her sharp heeled shoe down directly atop the Warden. He never missed his codpiece more in his life.

Volk Downey recognized this technique. This was a move Veil officers used to debilitate rapists. It was easy to exploit a man's privates and they certainly were not shy about inflicting such grueling punishment upon some of the worst in the world. Having seen her perform this move so deftly and gracefully he knew that he was trading blows with an officer of the Scourge. If only he could vocalize it.

A disturbing popping sound was followed by a falsetto squeal as Bride Wainwright wiped a faint dust of dry wall from her otherwise spotless dress. Volk's face turned a pale green as he curled into a fetal position. Every neuron in his body fired with overwhelming agony as tears crawled out of his eyes. Uncaring of the throbbing anguish he felt, Daphne chain-cuffed his left arm to his right leg with the set he brought with him. Tears and drool forced themselves out of the Warden's face, paralyzed in horrid grief. He briefly forgot how to breathe as he was in such a state of unfathomable pain.

"I am Bride Daphne Wainwright." She said as she picked up the scattered pieces of her Claymore. "You are hereby under arrest on suspicion of being the Dilictor Ignotum informally known as the Nitral Nightmare. You would be best off to give me everything I ask for." Volk tried to respond. Every muscle in his body cried out in excruciating pain, yet he found himself incapable of any vocalization outside of a bitter whimper.

"Don't attempt to speak, cur." Daphne said readjusting her hair into its once neat pattern. "You won't be taking any more women for a good long time. I hope you weren't planning on siring any children. It's doubtful you'll be able to here on out."

With a crack of splintering wood, the door to the hotel room burst open. Retriever Ram's Horn rocketed in, interrupting Bride Wainwright's victory speech. She wished she had taken the time to piece her pistol back together as she saw the metal clad monster towering before her. He wasted no second as he barreled towards her in a relentless charge. A horrific epiphany occurred to her once she saw Ram's battle plate. The color scheme paired with the Shackle insignia denoted him as an obvious warrior of the Scourge. She realized at that moment that her target, or perhaps victim, wasn't lying when he claimed to be a member of the Shackle.

Daphne yelled out to get him to stop, dropping the pieces of her weapon and throwing up her hands. The bellowing juggernaut that was Ram's Horn paid no heed to the words. He grabbed her with a *constrictor's kiss* and pinned her throat into the space between his forearm and bicep. Her pleas were entirely lost as he pushed her head in, compressing her neck in a blood-choke. The Retriever crouched down to gain as much control over her as possible and prevent her from slipping away from his overwhelming grasp. No amount of well-placed punches was going to bring this metal giant down, and they both knew that well enough.

Retriever Ram's Horn was attempting to put the Bride to sleep. Seeing his superior in such undeserved agony filled him with ire. He might have strangled her to death had her reinforcements from the Veil not charged in. Warriors in black and white battle plate armed with slender carbines pointed at the horned helmet Ram's Horn wore. They shouted out declarations of the Veil and he loosened his grip on the woman's neck. It was enough that Daphne could wriggle out of his marauder grip.

She coughed and gasped for breath as Admonisher Rickard helped her to her feet. His strike team was waiting in an otherwise empty hotel room. "Stand down!" The Bride wheezed. "They're Shackle. My most sincere apologies on behalf of the Veil and Patriarch Betankur, I am Bride Daphne Wainwright, protector of Hrimata."

The Retriever stood, his massive shadow swallowing the Warden in his wake. "Ram's Horn." He pointed a flaksteel finger at himself, then pointed it at his boss. "Volk Downey."

"Does Mr. Downey have his insignia?" Retriever Ram's Horn had his as he was undercover. He revealed it to the Bride without a word. "Oh dear, Warden Downey I'm dreadfully sorry. I thought you were trying to kidnap me."

Volk was still unable to give any response more coherent than a slight moan. "What happened?" Ram's metallic voice bellowed.

"I inflicted a eunuch stomp, a kick devised to disable a man for hours. Please forgive me Warden, I mistook you for a serial rapist."

Volk tried to stand despite his body being wracked with pain. He collapsed back on the ground. Ram's Horn, unschooled in any form of medical training, leaned over and simply patted his bald head. "There, there." He growled, honestly trying to help.

CHAPTER 22

In the Nordic Plains, the sun was rising in Hrimata on Nyvett 17th. However in the Western coast of America, deep in the Hinterlands, it was late in the evening of Nyvett 16th. The Hinterlands are a wild and uncivilized place. Marauder tribes vied for rule of the deserts, tundras, mountains, plains, every conceivable ecosystem, in bloody wars. Some were zealously religious with faith in pagan gods while others violently nihilistic. A number of marauders were friendly to Templym, while several swore to destroy it. This made the Hinterlands a land of great interest to the Scourge.

Scourge militants were necessary for waging all-out war with hostile marauder tribes. This made Warden Alexandarius Carthage and his Blitzkrieg militia an asset. A pioneer, or official Templym explorer of the barbaric landscape, requested military assistance when dealing with unruly inhabitants. They were currently leading a gruesome campaign against a tribe called the Solar Flayers, the name loosely translated from the guttural tongue of the marauder language. A small obstacle delayed the battle.

Warden Carthage received word of High Conservator Bethel's edict. He wanted to waste no time in refreshing his militia's vows. Currently the dynamically motivated Shackle soldier was residing in a Veritas Chamber in the Hinterlands outpost, donning full plate with the helmet lying on the table. His heavy flaksteel boots were slung up on table as well as he sat in light hearted conversation with Retriever Julian Frigate, the lieutenant of Blitzkrieg's Anchor squad. The two were locked in a cheerful interchange of conversation, having already exhausted all of the formal questions.

"So after my half-plate broke off I was left with nothing but a bodysuit on my hide and a stubby knife in my hand." Carthage laughed boisterously, his golden hair faintly glowing in the pale light of the interrogation chamber. "Most people would think to try to toss the knife in through the chariot's windshield, but me being a half-brained Guardian I opted for a dumber approach."

"Let me guess," Frigate laughed in a similarly noisy fashion. "You held onto the bumper and let the bloody thing drag you half a mile away."

"Worse! I punched clean through the window with my torso slumped into the chariot and my feet scraping across the road. I cut my hide up pretty good with all the broken glass, but you can imagine the look on that goon's face when I charged in head first."

"Did you two crash?"

"Only after I dislocated his shoulder with the end of that knife. I got launched across the rockfoam twenty feet after the chariot hit a light post. Bethel showed up, made the arrest, and promoted me the next week. Anyway, that's how I caught my first quarry."

"So you were as reckless back then as you are today?"

"Oh, I was way worse back then than I am now. Funny, you'd think a collection of tech enhanced battle gear and a small army backing you up would make you even less careful." Carthage yelled with uproarious laughter and Frigate followed suit.

"You're a madman, Warden!"

"Perhaps so, but I'm capable of controlling my madness!" Carthage slapped his metal clad knees and put his feet back on the chamber floors. "Anyway, I'd love to continue this conversation but I've got business that needs to be conducted. Bethel's edict made it clear that the oaths of every soldier need to be refreshed. I plan to have it done before sunrise."

"I see...so since I've been cleared, you want me to interrogate Anchor squad."

"Good mind there, Julian." Alexandarius clapped his gauntlet against the Retriever's shoulder pad. "Do me a favor and send in Ichabod on your way out?"

"You're going to put on the same show you put on for me?" The Retriever mused.

"Oh of course, but don't spoil the surprise." Warden Carthage stood up to embrace his lieutenant. "I never doubted you for a second, Julian. I'll forward you the list of questions to give your squad."

"Cheers sir." Retriever Frigate gave the Scourge salute and made his way out of the Veritas Chamber.

This was a repeat performance of Alexandarius Carthage's execution of Jude Bethel's decree. He loathed the idea that any of his Blitzkrieg were dirty, the very notion unfathomable. He wanted to bury the conspiracy theory as quickly as it began. His strategy was simple, question his five Retrievers with a fiery passion, then they would do the same to their subordinates. He had cleared the lieutenants of Mastodon, Gladius, and now Anchor squads. Now, Retriever Ichabod Creel of Barb squad was next up to the interrogation room.

Alexandarius angled his green plumed helmet on the end of the table so the eye-slits were facing the entrance, as though it were operating as a sentry over the Veritas Chamber. He then positioned himself behind the only door leading into the interrogation room. The cogs and pistons of his armor moaning and chainmail cape shuddering as he took wide strides were the only noise audible in the otherwise silent room. He cracked his neck and ground his teeth together, tasting the faint familiar flavor of his steel replacements, to get into character.

Most Veritas Chambers possessed automated retractable doorways that emerged from the floors or walls. The few that were in Hinterlands outposts were not so well automated. This chamber in particular had a simple sheet metal door that swung on basic hinges. This thematic element worked towards Warden Carthage's preferred method of questioning. As he did everything, Alexandarius preferred a blunt and unrelenting approach. If anybody under his command had doubled back on their sacred oaths, he was going to shake the truth out of them.

The steel door swung open. The slender, almost malnourished looking figure of Ichabod Creel in a non-technologically enhanced suit of electric blue and ebony black battle plate entered into the Veritas Chamber. His dirty blond hair was slicked back against his skull, ending in a small tail. His dry eyes were locked in a confused gaze at Warden Carthage's helmet. He barely had a second's grasp of the scenario before Carthage grabbed him by the shoulders and pinned him to the cold featureless wall, creating a massive divot.

"You thought you could get away with it you smug bastard!" He screamed out. The light globes strobed, dazzling Ichabod with flurries of white light. Carthage was intentionally using vague, assertive statements to give off the illusion that he actually believed he was a traitor to the Scourge. "I demand you tell me everything! I'll grind your bones to a pulp if you try to worm out of it!"

"Warden Carthage, sir," Creel moaned as he blinked ferociously trying to regain his vision. "I don't know what you're talking about."

"The Idolacreid, the Nephilim, I want you to tell me everything!" Carthage slammed his fist right by his head, making his ear ring.

"What? What is happening?"

Alexandarius was dissatisfied with that level of deniability. If he wanted to prove Creel's innocence beyond reasonable doubt, he would have to verbally refute knowledge of these enigmatic concepts the High Conservator had mentioned in his missive. "Don't you play games with me Ichabod! We are brothers, you come clean! Disclose everything you have on the Idolacreid and the Nephilim with all meaning of haste and perhaps I'll grant you a swift execution!"

Warden Carthage expected a full plea for mercy and a confession of innocence. Ichabod Creel was always a disciplined warrior, straight-backed and zealously faithful. He had a reputation for being border line sociopathic in his strikes against his foes, though he just had an unnatural ability to have calculated motions without an emotional component. Creel served as the head of Barb squad for nearly two years at this point, and the Warden would trust him with his life. He did not expect a pistol to be shoved into his gut.

With one hand pinning each of Creel's shoulders to the freshly dented wall, Alexandarius drooped his head down upon feeling the Reisinger's barrel shoved into a thin opening between flaksteel plates. His amber eyes were sullen and filled with hurt, regardless of the gun not inflicting any meaningful damage. "Ichabod...you're a turncoat?" His normal thunderous bravado seemed to have wilted away entirely.

"Forgive me Warden," Creel said, grimly. "This was an unforeseen development. Please don't take this betrayal personally. I did hope to convert you before the abolition...pity you started asking questions before that."

"The bloody hell are you talking about, man? I never suspected you of anything. I'm executing Bethel's edict...I thought it was nothing more than twaddle."

"Wait...then how did you know about the Lord Nephilim?"

The fraction of a second in which Ichabod Creel was distracted was all that Warden Carthage required. His battle plate's engines roared to life as he pushed back from the wall. Shots rang out from Creel's pistol. They were no longer in an opening in the flaksteel carapace, so the bullets plinked off the painted surface. Only a few inches away from his lost brother, he let out a hurt roar like the death throes of a suicidal man. This was not his normal chivalrous war cry... this was the aching scream of a man whose brother had just died. He let his grief loose the only way he knew how, with violence.

One bullet bounced off of his knee plate and another embedded itself in his breastplate. His lumen globes exploded with a furious barrage of pulsing white light. He blindly shot out the Reisinger as he desperately made to realign himself. The cool gaze of Alexandarius Carthage flared ablaze with hot rage like liquid bronze in his eyes at the tortured anguish he felt in response to this betrayal. Retriever Creel did not even shoot half of his pistol's capacity before his wrist was splintered by the strength-enhanced twist of the Warden.

Carthage flipped Creel through the air like he was a worthless sack. He crashed into the interrogation table causing the metal legs to break off in a sudden crack. Blinded and bruised, Alexandarius was just beginning to dish out his wrath. Almost mimicking

Ichabod's arc through the air, he vaulted around and landed on his chest. He brought his boots down in elephantine stomps, denting the flaksteel plating of Creel's armor in some places and causing some portions to eject off entirely. He took advantage of the newly crafted weak points by exploiting exposed skin with sharp jabs. Every punch, every elbow drew blood or shattered bone in a furious bombardment of outraged aggression.

He finally was able to stay his hand. The thin Retriever was no equal to the bulky juggernaut that was Alexandarius Carthage. The Warden had to physically grab his other hand as it seemed to relish in the violence. He had to stop. Answers were necessary and despite how badly he wanted to end Ichabod's life then and there, he had to live to answer to someone of greater authority. He stepped off of his subordinate's chest and nearly had to wade through a pool of Ichabod Creel's red bodily fluid. He slumped over in the chair that miraculously escaped the catastrophe he had just wrought. Steam from his battle plate and the nauseating scent of blood, sweat, and gunpowder lingered in the Veritas Chamber. Carthage's unblinking eyes stared at the sight he just witnessed. He fully expected to see his subordinates fall in combat at some point...he never could have conceived that it would ever be by his own hands.

Carthage's Scourge training kicked in and he shoved his emotions to the back of his mind. Whatever reason Bethel needed to declare an edict to refresh the oaths of the Shackle's warriors, Retriever Creel played some role in that. But how many more were corrupt? He could risk nothing. Alexandarius tuned in on his suit's radio bead, making sure to exclude certain members of his militia. "Blitzkrieg, this is Warden Carthage." He spoke into his audio wire with his typical gusto noticeably absent. "Pursue and detain all members of Barb and Bullet squads. They are to be considered hostile until confirmation can be made via Veritas Chamber interviewing. This order goes for any of your squad members who have yet to be questioned by your Retrievers. If you are still loyal to the Scourge and to the Shackle, turn them in, the truth will be revealed later. Meet any resistance as you would any of our normal quarries. We have corruption in our own ranks."

The next day, S-6319 reconvened at the Seraphim Solace. Warden Downey, the company's leader, was still recovering from the grievous injury Bride Wainwright had inflicted upon him. Unfortunately for her, she determined that her cover as a professional companion had been thoroughly spoiled when the Veil soldiers charged into her hotel room when Retriever Ram's Horn made his assault. She was reluctant to abandon her guise, but determined that Expurgator Yen Blye needed her assistance in the Dilictor hunt. She had been underground for weeks now and was worried that the 5th Tier soldier was being overwhelmed by the immense responsibilities thrust upon him. He welcomed the assistance, though not for the reasons she suspected.

Oslin Du'Plasse made no mention of his encounter with his mother the day before. He had spent the evening with Archon Valkyrie, who was more than willing to help him vent his grief. Vandross reported to the others what had happened, having witnessed the loathing between them. This affected the way that the others would interact with the Herald, each man ensuring that an added air of respect was given to him. Adastra in particular could sympathize, having had a poor relationship with his mother as well, and made a mental note to discuss the matter in depth at a later hour. There was a silent agreement between them to act as the family that had rejected Oslin.

Adastra and Vandross took time to meet with their old friend Daphne again. After debriefing about the most recent intelligence of each other's situations, they spent time reacquainting. It had been well over a year since the two Inquisitors had seen the Bride, and she had gone through a number of promotions since then. She donned her pearlescent tech-enhanced battle plate, the numerous medallions and gemstone flowers making her look like a noble bride in every sense of the word. The two Inquisitors laughed and smiled with their former classmate while Expurgator Blye shuffled paperwork relevant to the most pressing case, pretending not to listen to the conversation at hand.

"It's so good to see you both!" Daphne laughed as Adastra and Vandross entered into the chamber of the Seraphim Solace.

"Madame Bride," Vandross said as he placed his hat against his chest. "My word dear, you truly can't get any higher on the proverbial totem pole. You're making us look bad."

"Still the chivalrous charmer as always, I see." She two met in a familial hug. "And Adastra, you've grown your beard out, haven't you?"

"You look well Daphne." He took her flaksteel clad hand and kissed it.

"Ever the stoic, aren't you?" She laughed. "How did you find yourself working with a Shackle task force? Last I heard you were hunting Frankish cults."

"We were recruited by High Conservator Bethel." Vandross said placing his hat back on its home. "Apparently our Bishop gave our names to him and he was looking for two good Inquisitors."

"It's been quite the quarry hunt." Adastra added in. "As I'm sure you're aware, we've been to Venice and the UPA already without a direct link to Mortis. Hopefully we find something solid this time around."

"I'll do my best to help however I can," Wainwright said sympathetically. "The name doesn't mean anything to me, unfortunately, and I've been wrapped up in the most intense hunt of my career. If you help me get my man, I'll do what I can to help you get yours."

"More incentive to get this recidivist then." Vandross said cracking his neck. "Currently, we're following up on a possession at the Grigorian Administration. Local chemist blew himself and fifty others up. We confirmed Imago influence."

"You think this has to do with my Dilictor?" Daphne pondered.

"It's as good a lead as we've got." Adastra mumbled. "You've been chasing figurative ghosts for the past three months, why not try literal ghosts?"

"Coordinate with Exarch Surizal," Daphne continued. "I'm certain he can show you the local cults and demoniacs far better than I could. Blye, do you have any new leads?"

"Our most reliable lead was the man you were tailing while undercover." Expurgator Blye stood up relieved to be a part of the conversation. "Unfortunately, that man turned out to be Warden Downey, ma'am."

"Of course..." Daphne palmed her face with shame. "I did check on him in the hospital a few hours ago. He's expected to be in workable condition tomorrow afternoon. I feel so bad about what I did. The eunuch stomp is a debilitating blow meant to subdue men of far greater stature than him. I could have killed him if I executed it improperly."

"There is more, my Bride." Yen continued. "Agapist Kite mentioned that he has new evidence he'd like to present. Shall I assemble the rest of the teams?"

"No, get him now." She said seriously. "We've wasted enough time as is with formalities. Kite just needs to brief us, posthaste."

"I'll fetch him then." Blye bowed and made off to get the Agapist.

"Vandross, meet up with Surizal and begin investigation into the Rieveshl bombing." Adastra stated. "I'll get together with Herald Du'Plasse and Retriever Ram's Horn to see what this new lead is."

"Don't you think you should go?" Inquisitor Blackwell shrugged. "You're the demon hunter after all, you'd be better at tracking an Imago than I."

"You're right." Covalos retorted. "It was good to see you again Daphne. I hope we can catch up after this whole mess is cleaned up."

"Likewise, Adastra." Daphne smile, her soothing voice like a small chorus. "Come back with my Dilictor in chains if at all possible."

Expurgator Blye summoned Agapist Cyrus Kite. He was a man of legendary ego. It was no secret to anyone serving in the Solace that he harbored bitter feelings towards the young Azzathan for gaining the honor of heading the hunt, and what was worse, being granted temporary Gamma clearance from the Bride. He was a far more experienced and professional soldier than most, having spent twenty years in the Veil. Extensive reconstruction surgery and hair dyes kept his true age well hidden. Kite's thick black hair was always maintained in well-trimmed fashion, and the only visible flaw in his artificially chiseled features was a white line of scar tissue created by an incision that stretched from his left temple to the tip of his nose.

Herald Du'Plasse and Retriever Ram's Horn had gathered to hear what new evidence had been brought to light. Along with Bride Wainwright and Inquisitor Blackwell, the stiff muscled Agapist marched with his tech-enhanced scimitar sheathed at his side.

"My lady," Kite said with a half-hearted salute, poorly concealing his disdain. "Who are these...individuals?"

"They're members of task force S-6319." Daphne said. "They're helping us hunt our Dilictor and I thought it prudent to invite them for the debriefing."

"Wonderful...it seems we have a representative from every branch of the Scourge here." Cyrus reflected with a sarcastic tone. "Tell me, did the Regent not also wish to join us?"

"Agapist Kite, Madame Wainwright summoned you here so you could present your new evidence." Yen said with slight malice, after trailing in behind. "Your snide remarks are unappreciated."

"Thank you, Expurgator Blye." Daphne said with a calming tone, the animated soldier backed down, happy to have her approval. "If you don't mind Cyrus..."

"I'll keep it brief." Kite hissed. "I believe I have found a witness who may have escaped the clutches of our Dilictor. A young woman was recently found in the Dumont Ford, this one alive. Her body was covered in incisions and her sanity tainted as well. She doesn't particularly meet the victim profile; she was a thirty-two year old local from the Diamond District who's been missing for the past two weeks. Currently she is recovering in the Sanguine Hospital."

"What makes you think this is related?" Wainwright asked brushing her fingers across her chin in contemplation.

"Primarily the level of security we've placed on Hrimata in the last few weeks. In our efforts to discourage this beast, we've militias patrolling the gilded streets of this urban. We've seen a dive in crime rates since. According to your profile, this sadist is still desperate to indulge himself. If the Dilictor wants to keep taking victims, he must do so based on availability and less on his preferences. Our added security also means it's more difficult to prowl around unnoticed in the shadows. I think he slipped up and let one of his victims get away."

"That's a bit of a leap in logic, don't you think?" Herald Du'Plasse interjected.

"Well, find me a better a lead and I'll pursue that." Kite snapped at the Hrimatan. "Until then this is where I'm setting my sights."

"What do you think, Blye?" Daphne asked the Expurgator considerately.

"It makes sense." He answered. "We have over thirty militias patrolling the city on a twenty-four hour basis. The Nitral Nightmare would have to make compromises of every sort in order to continue operating under the radar. It's been a while since we've confirmed another one of his victims. I'd say it's worth looking into."

"Agreed." She stated plainly. "Look into it Kite, interview this woman. Take the task force with you, keep your team circulating with whatever they're working on."

"Is that wise, my lady?" Kite said with slight disgust. "I don't think an escort team is required for a simple questioning, especially one that I am unfamiliar with. Don't you have another assignment you could throw their way?"

"We're standing right here." Vandross pointed out to Kite's seeming ignorance.

"It'll be good for our crews to work together." Wainwright said. "Even so, I don't have any additional tasks I could give them. Not to mention, I'm getting tired of your attitude, so I'm going to ignore your request. You're a good soldier and a cunning investigator Cyrus, but your pissy attitude is hindering the manhunt. Take them with you. Dismissed."

With that sentiment, Daphne snapped away on her heel and exited to attend to other business.

"Superb." Kite grunted through clenched teeth. His cobalt eyes seemed to burn with icy resentment.

"So, we're working together." Inquisitor Blackwell said with a forthcoming smile. "Do you want to..."

"The victim is Victoria Thruian, a banker, as all Thruians are." Agapist Kite grumbled. "She had gone missing two weeks prior. Suspicion was that someone wanted to torture sensitive account information out of her. Not a single crown is out of place. My guess is that she let her guard down, the Dilictor saw his opportunity, and detained her. He's obsessive, the Bride believes he can't resist the opportunity to sate his abhorrent desires and I agree. Whoever detained and tortured this woman was either dreadfully poor at securing financial information or had no interest in money to begin with. Come, let's go." He strode off in a huff.

"Nice guy." Ram's Horn muttered.

CHAPTER 23

Exarch Zedekiah Surizal was Kalkhanian in origin. His skin was nearly as black as the flaksteel plating on Adastra's armor. Instead of traditional battle plate, he wore vermillion robes of thick immotrum threading with white and gold accents. His hairless head was topped with a black skull cap like those of the early Christian monks. His hulking musculature pulled his attire taut. A tech-enhanced wardiron khopesh was strapped to his back beside a bow made of stainless steel. Adastra Covalos walked with the man, returning to the Grigorian Administration to investigate the possession, and immediately took a liking to him.

The Inquisition did not have a strong presence in Hrimata. Exarch Surizal was the highest ranking member in the urban, which was a little disconcerting to the Inquisitor as it was only a single tier above his rank. Noble cities were often rife with sin enough, negating the need for Imago influence to corrupt the people. Demoniacs were a rarity in this urban, rather its citizens gave into their fallen nature without need of spiritual influence. This meant Zedekiah Surizal and his small band of the Inquisition were often left to settle petty matters. They were eager to have a more exciting task at hand.

Inquisitor Covalos had already shown him the scene and discussed the results of the tests they had performed. Surizal agreed that it appeared that it was a magick possession. They determined that they needed to review Rieveshl's history. At what point did the Imago take control of his body? That is where the hunt officially kicked off.

"Dalton Hall is about a quarter mile north of here." Zedekiah spoke pointing a gloved hand towards a white paneled building in the distance as they departed from the crime scene. "We start there. Frodus Rieveshl worked closely with one Professor Thomas Monk in his research pursuits. According to sources around the college, the two were closer than any other tutorship at the university."

"You think he knows something then?" Adastra asked as the two made for the hall he motioned towards.

"If anybody does, it would be him. The two worked in professional chemistry research at least forty hours every week. He would notice any behavior pattern differences or unusual activities that Rieveshl had caught up in."

"You're glad to be back in action again, aren't you?" Inquisitor Covalos noticed a tinge of glee in the way he held himself.

"It's been over a year since our last Imago encounter." Zedekiah said in agreement to the statement. "Like a muscle requires resistance to stay strong, we of the Inquisition must continue pursuing the occult, lest we atrophy. It's our purpose as an organization after all. I fear if we sit on our hands too long, we'll forget how to use them."

"That's quite a noble sentiment." Adastra agreed.

The two continued to engage in idle chat of idealism and faith until they reached their destination. Dalton Hall was a building at the Grigorian Administration focusing on chemistry, complete with a number of research centers and laboratories. It also served to hold a number of offices for the professors that instructed the subject. The building became the most recent focus of their investigation as it housed one such professor. Thomas Monk was the advisor and tutor of young Frodus Rieveshl. Hopefully he would serve to shed light on the scenario.

The quaint office was barely enough to harbor the desk and two office chairs of this stylized room. Thomas Monk sat behind the oaken desk scribbling on a half empty stack of papers with a red pen. His bronze colored hair contained flecks of grey and his scholarly attire bore a stitching of a magenta lily on his shoulder. He pushed up his thin spectacles with a concerned look at the sight of the two Inquisition officers.

"Can I help you with something, sirs?" His voice wavered as he stood, obviously nervous. Most civilians were uncomfortable operating with the Scourge, and the Inquisition carried a reputation of fanaticism with it.

"I am Exarch Surizal," His manner was elegant yet firm, communicating no hostility but professionalism. His voice was deep, like a lion's purr. "This is Inquisitor Covalos. We would like to ask you a few questions with regards to yesterday's bombing, specifically with regards to Frodus Rieveshl."

"Yes of course...can I get you something to drink? I've got a few water bottles or I could brew some coffee if you are so inclined."

"That won't be necessary," Adastra added in. "You may sit down."

"Yes of course." The professor sat in his office chair and they followed suit in the other office chairs. "Forgive me for my ill composure, sirs. I was expecting to have to answer some questions, but I was expecting the guard, not the Scourge."

"We've commandeered the investigation under the authority of the Inquisition." Surizal stated plainly. "There are a number of oddities that don't add up."

"I thought it was strange that Frodus would do something so drastic. He never crossed me as suicidal, let alone homicidal. You know he likely smuggled material out of my labs to make that bomb."

"Do you have proof of this?" Adastra asked.

"Unfortunately, I don't have the capacity to afford security cameras in the labs, but I do keep a strictly regimented inventory list. I can give you a copy and correspond that with the chemicals I have in stock to give a more definite answer."

"We'd appreciate it if you could do that." Surizal said.

"Yes of course. So, what may I ask is the exact nature of this visit? I find the presence of the Inquisition a bit, uh, off-putting."

"The exact nature is Rho classified. We were just hoping you could help us fill in the gaps. If you don't mind, start by telling us if he was acting strangely recently."

"No... not that I noticed at least."

"You didn't notice any difference in his behavior?" Adastra pried. "Any physical differences: paleness, swelling, sweating, shaking, that kind of thing? What about changes in speech or attitude, did you notice any of those?"

"Like I said, nothing I noticed. I suppose he came under a brief spell of sadness at the result of his last exam. I suppose that was unusual."

"What was strange about it?" Zedekiah asked.

"Frodus Rieveshl was one of my brightest students. He had never scored less than a perfect score on one my exams. He was just above the failing margin on our most recent thermodynamics midterm. That constitutes as odd, I suppose. I doubt he would jump to such a drastic means of coping. Even though he was hurt in pride, he was still a good young man."

"Did he come under any other tragedy? Do you know if he had a family member pass or a relationship end, something that would add to the grief?"

"None that I am aware of."

"Did Frodus get involved in anything that was unlike him?" Adastra asked while stroking his beard. "Were there any extracurricular activities, clubs, or organizations outside of the university that he got involved in?"

"Yes of course." Monk said as though he had just had an epiphany. "He had just joined one of the lodges on campus...the uh...the 127th Reichsmen. He was only a member of the fraternity for two or three months. The activities took up a good portion of his free time."

"The 127th Reichsmen? Last I checked, they died in the 14th Purus."

"Not the literal Reichsmen...with all due respect, of course. The students like to name their lodges after crusader regiments. I believe the majority of this one in particular were of Serbian and Lex

Statuan decent. They named themselves after the company to pay homage to their familial heritage...I think."

"Interesting." Surizal pondered aloud. "I don't suppose you could tell us what he was doing with this fraternity."

"Yes of course." The professor adjusted the glasses sliding down his nose. Adastra was beginning to grow tired of him saying that phrase over and over again, but he dismissed it as a nervous habit. "That lodge was primarily focused with community service on the campus. They'd pick up litter or repaint rooms, simple acts of kindness, nothing outlandish, just like the majority of the lodges."

"That certainly doesn't sound malicious. What work did Rieveshl do for you exactly? What responsibilities did he have?"

"He was taking lead into our research in lithium sulfur batteries, a method that's safer and more rechargeable than a standard ion battery. He constructed power cells, usually five or six a week, in an effort to optimize their energy output. The results he got for me were unmatched. I was prepared to offer him a fully paid grant for a pursuit in professorship after he finished his degree. That of course made this incident all the more disturbing."

"He wasn't really a demolitions expert then." Adastra grunted. "Do you think he was smart enough to make a batch of military grade explosives?"

"Well...not with his own resources. Chemistry is like cooking, it requires a number of ingredients with the proper process in the proper order. I don't think he would be able to figure out the recipe on his own, but with that recipe he could easily synthesize the explosive. We have a number of volatile chemicals: potassium nitrate, benzene, reduced cobalt, octane, just to name a few. I suppose with the proper equipment one could make an explosive...did you say military grade?"

"Clapshock...four pounds of it according to the arbiters, albeit not a perfect replica."

"Goodness." Monk removed his glasses in shock and blinked in disbelief. "Frodus would never do something like this. Do you think it was sorcery or wizardry or voodoo...I'm not really familiar with the terminology."

"Like we said Mr. Monk, that is Rho classified." Surizal said sympathetically. "Is there anything else unusual you can think of about this scenario? Anything at all could potentially be helpful."

"Yes of course, but I think that's all I can think of. I was close to the boy, but that's not really saying much. He was always such a quiet one. Frodus never really associated with any of the other students as far as I could tell. That's really all I know."

"I think that will do for now then. Please contact us if you think of anything else that might help. I'll send for that inventory list later today."

"Yes, of course. Thank you for your time. I hope you can determine what dark powers forced mister Rieveshl to commit this heinous deed."

Neither responded to the comment but nodded to Thomas Monk in approval. They would be sure to keep in touch with him for future reference. They pushed their quaint office chairs in and exited as calmly as they had entered.

"We're going to the fraternity next right?" Adastra said to Zedekiah without even looking at him.

"Absolutely." He responded with a troubled frown.

A silent alarm went off in their heads at the mention of the lodge. Not so much that Frodus Rieveshl was a member of a fraternity, but rather at the name of it. The 127th Reichsmen were one of the first responders to the Plague Massacre at the cusp of the 14th Purus Crusade. They were a Lex Statuan guard aligned with neither the Scourge nor the Bulwark at the time. When the Class A Imago Plaguemire corrupted the urban of Euzburgh, they were the first to take up arms against the demonic horde. When half the company fell, the other half surrendered. They became demoniacs in exchange for survival. The remainder of the 127th Reichsmen joined in the ranks of the shock troopers of the armies of the damned, slaughtering those they had once called family. They were beaten by the Auzlanten and his crusaders... but not before they wreaked gruesome bloodshed across Carthonia in the name of their dark lord. Their betrayal to Templym was largely forgotten, buried beneath a mountain of corpses. The Inquisition does not easily overlook the name of traitors...neither Surizal nor Covalos thought it coincidental that this was the name given to the lodge that the victim of demonic possession was involved in.

Arodi Auzlanten was no stranger to the land outside of Templym's jurisdiction. In his lifetime, he had traversed every region of the world. He had seen mountains crumble into the sea and new masses rise in their place. No environment was a mystery to him. He perfectly comprehended why each area possessed the attributes that it did, even the more volatile ones from the backlash of the Shatter. Arodi was rarely amazed by the natural sites he saw anymore, but the coastline of Malgeria came close.

A warm ocean breeze brushed through Auzlanten's mane as he stood on a beach made of glass beads. At the coming of the Shatter, a vast nuclear holocaust fused a great portion of Kalkhan's deserts into solid glass. The Malgerian coast possessed small spheres of cloudy white glass, where the Oculus Ray marauder tribe inhabited. A foaming sea of glistening cerulean lapped across the smooth surface of the ground, just barely wetting the bottom of his boots. He arrived at twelve, when the sun was at the center of the sky, a sacred time for the peaceful tribe.

Auzlanten felt at peace on that shore. Something about the glittering globes of fused sand reminded him of an untouched snow bank, yet with the warmth of a summer's afternoon. For the briefest of moments, he forgot all of the tribulations currently facing him. He ignored the Idolacreid and the rising cult of the Nephilim. He disregarded the betrayal of Invictus Illuromos. He pretended that the weight of the world and the fate of Templym no longer rested on his shoulders like a lead cross. He brushed this peace of heart off to the side. He couldn't focus on such petty amounts of dopamine or his mellowed vitals. He needed to speak to Illythia.

The Oculus Rays were always a tender hearted and nature loving people . They were initially an ecological cult of sun worshipers who would practice harvest sacrifices. Illythia had recently won them over to the Faith. When Arodi Auzlanten stepped into the coastal bivouac of hide tents and fused glass huts, people rushed to greet him with eager faces. Their copper skinned bodies were covered with alabaster paint and bleached animal skins. Women rushed to the Toppler of Tyranny with loaves of bread and bundles of fruit in hand, children giggled and pointed, some had enough courage to caress his azure robes, and men clapped and cheered in the distance. A faint smiled appeared on Arodi's chiseled features as he politely made his way through the crowd towards the center of the camp.

A large crystal disc of polished quartz harbored a brilliant fire pit at the center of the marauder camp. A frail old woman in white robes stood near it. Her face was wrinkled and weathered, tanned by exposure to the sun. Her white furs were decorated with patches of violet and brown. She carried a staff of gnarled acacia in a hand plagued by arthritis. Her pale glassy eyes were filled with light when they met the blue orbs of Arodi Auzlanten.

"Illythia," His voice rang out and a hush fell over the once boisterous crowd. "It has been too long, darling."

"Hello, father." Her voice wavered weakly, but still carried throughout the crowd. He embraced the fragile old woman, noting how weak her body had grown. Arodi kissed her on her forehead. "You look just as young and vigorous as the first time we met."

"So do you, my sweet."

Illythia Aquinas was one of the children of Auzlanten. Like all of them, she was not biologically his daughter. She was orphaned when her father and mother died in the 12th Purus Crusade. Arodi took her in and raised her to be a deaconess of sorts. She began to evangelize outside of Templym, giving up any hope of starting a family. Her ministry brought her to remote tribes in all four continents: Carthonia, America, Azzatha, and now Kalkhan, baptizing hundreds and bringing them closer to Christ. She was the embodiment of what the children of Auzlanten aspired to be. She was six years old when he took her in, now she was eighty-eight. He wasn't lying when he said she looked just as young as she did over eighty years ago. He simply wasn't referring to her physical body.

"Illythia, I was told that you have information for me." He said calmly.

"I do." She said meagerly. "I'm guessing you're too preoccupied with other matters to stay for a banquet."

"You'd be correct. I'm terribly sorry my daughter, but we must keep this meeting brief."

"I see, a pity, but I understand." She turned to face the crowd of disheartened tribal citizens. "I'm afraid Lord Auzlanten will not be staying with us. We must retreat to my sanctum and discuss a private matter."

She led her foster father into a hut made of burnished wood panels. Small verses of scripture were plastered onto the walls in the form of papyrus sheets. Auzlanten presented a pair of pewter chalices and a crystal bottle of white wine from nowhere. He filled the cups to the brim of the clear fluid. The thin bottle vanished as one of the grails floated to the frail hand of Illythia.

"66' Nenwhari Sherri, your favorite." Auzlanten said his face still tight and he took a sip.

"Is this one of the bottles I made when I worked at that winery?" She asked, her jowls lifted up as she smiled revealing a mouth of yellowing teeth.

"It is, please drink some."

"Thank you, father." The fluid wavered as she raised her shaky hands to her mouth to imbibe in the smooth wine. Arodi looked in pity at seeing his daughter so crippled.

"It pains me to see you in such disarray. I can fix your body and make you as spry as you ever were. Your physical maladies are well within the capabilities of my power."

"I appreciate the willingness, but that isn't necessary. Perhaps God has given me this affliction so that I may turn my eyes from this world in anticipation for the next."

"God has blessed me with abilities far beyond that of any man. I could make the argument that healing you is just as well within His divine will as your illness."

"Perhaps so, but I am ready to pass on to the next life. The moment I am called home, I will welcome it."

"It brings me joy to see you in such high spirits darling. In a way, I almost envy you. Embracing Eternity is a luxury I cannot afford at this time. I am forced to hunt the Mundus Imago and other damned forces of this broken world. It is my burden to carry."

"And so leads us to the nature of your visit." Illythia set her chalice down with a metallic clink on the wooden floor. "Allow me to help you bear this responsibility." She stepped weakly over to a bookshelf and removed a dusty leather bound tome.

"What information do you possess that I have been unable to divine?" Arodi asked while taking in the last of his wine. "I'm searching for a marauder tribe in Uzbek. There are hundreds in that wild land. Whichever one I am actually looking for is protected by dark magick or black spirits."

"Do you believe in prophesy?"

"As an oracle of the living God, I am the conduit for many prophesies, and I am well versed in all types."

"Have you ever considered revelation from non-Biblical sources?" Her pale twisted hands flipped dry sheets of yellow paper as she took a seat.

"I have heard of theories. Many believe Nostradamus foresaw the fulfillment of many of John's visions from Revelation. I am not willing to equate pagan diviners with the likes of Isaiah or Daniel, but I would not rule it out as a possibility."

"Before I evangelized to this tribe, they had a number of blind mystics who would stare into the sun in an effort to learn its secrets. Their records were written by tribal scribes and cataloged." She stopped turning the dilapidated pages. "Here it is."

Auzlanten took the book from her withered old hands. He looked at the archaic writing in a now extinct marauder dialect. He could read it fluently.

At the end of the war of brothers, the tome read, *the meld of man and spirit will rise from the ashes. The hybrid will come out from nothing to oppose the great warlock. Their armies will clash. An ocean of blood will be spilled. Their life will bear a great titan anew. A crop of corpses will fertilize the fires of war. If he, of the spiritual realm and the physical, strike the great warlock down, the stars will fall from the heavens to set the world ablaze inside of an iron furnace. The dead legion will take the throne and all will be consumed by the hybrid's pawns. The great warlock must be victorious, lest all be devoured by the hybrid's titan and the dead legion.*

"You think I am the great warlock?" Arodi asked after reading the passage in less than a second. "I suppose I've been called worse."

"I do." Illythia Aquinas said taking a seat on a white fur pelt. "I think this hybrid the passage refers to is the Nephilim. The book of Genesis speaks of such creatures, does it not?"

"My last lead was a gun runner. He foreshadowed that this creature was making an army. If our armies are to clash...that corresponds to the Scourge and its cult. But what is this titan they speak of? Why the allusion to the iron furnace?" Arodi pondered silently for a moment. "It's a war machine, some overwhelming engine of battle...that would make sense."

"That is disturbing indeed. I think you are missing the most vital clue."

"What is that, my sweet?"

"The dead legion it speaks of. This isn't an analogy to walking corpses as you've fought in the past. In all marauder texts, the dead legion is with reference to a specific tribe, there is no accurate translation in temple-tongue as the language predates the Shatter. I believe the best translation would be...Gluttons of the Grave."

"This name is unfamiliar to me." Arodi said adjusting the golden clasps in his thick hair nervously. "That disturbs me...why don't I know about them?"

"The dead legion or Grave Gluttons are the most notorious legends among all civilizations outside of Templym. Like the ghost stories of the Immortal Emperor Xingyue Haigon or the return of the Volcano Dragon of Zavés, marauder society has myths, too. The dead legion has been an echo in the back of the heads of the marauders since the culmination of the Age of Anarchy. Raiders, cannibals, murderers, rapists, sadists, thieves, demoniacs, and every other descriptor you can think of has been used with them. They were told to have been born in a place called the Dust Canyon."

"The Dust Canyon..." Auzlanten placed the leather tome back in its shelf. "No region exists by that name."

Illythia shrugged, causing her bones to pop. "I can't say where such a place resides. It's where they were born, but they are nomadic...at least in myth they are. Legend tells that the dead legion have trekked the whole world in service to dark powers. They say that they could appear at the bottom of the ocean to pillage their foes. Even worse is their chief."

"Their chief, as in a single man? I thought you said that they were around since the Age of Anarchy, which would make them close to five hundred years old. This chief has led the Grave Gluttons since then?"

"Yes." Illythia's already weak voice grew hushed as though she was averting her words from anyone else from hearing them. "They say he eats the souls of his victims. Donning a suit of rust and blood, he has cut down millions in an effort to unleash the unprocessed power of the dark spirits. They write of a man with no eyes, yet he sees beyond this world. They say he possesses the might of Hell behind his axe, but can kill with iron teeth or chitin claws or the simple strength of a hundred men just as easily."

"What do they call this mythical chief?"

"They give him the name of genocide. Again, there is no good translation, but it describes rolling hills of corpses and mounds of unfathomable bereavement. In the marauder tongue he is called Noctidus Val'Muardeares."

"Where is he? Where can I find Val'Muardeares?"

"Alas, I wish I could say. He has been naught but an old fable for as long as I've lived. The Oculus Rays tell the stories to children in an effort to scare them into obedience, that's all. I've never considered it anything more than the driveling of occultic men until recently."

"What changed Illythia?" Auzlanten gingerly set his hands onto her meager shoulders. "When did you decide to brush off an ancient tome and proclaim it as prophesy?"

She stared, hesitant to speak her next words. Illythia acted as if the marauders could hear her every word. In hushed tone, she said, "When the Grave Gluttons decimated a neighboring tribe."

CHAPTER 24

One would initially think that Agapist Kite and Herald Du'Plasse would come to blows within a short time of being in the same room. The two actually were friendly to one another, despite their similarly haughty personalities. Cyrus Kite was also a native of Hrimata and was stationed in the urban since before Wainwright's reassignment. He was happy to bring Oslin up to speed with the most recent events of the city. Together, accompanied by the silent monolith of Retriever Ram's Horn, they moved to interview the Nitral Nightmare's escaped victim.

Victoria Thruian was resting in a secured medical bay at Hrimata's Sanguine Hospital. How she escaped, or was disposed of, into Dumont Ford was a mystery that needed to be unraveled. The three investigators made all haste to pursue this most recent trail of evidence. Kite especially yearned that this wasn't another wild goose chase that would leave the Veil grasping at straws once more as it had for the past three months.

The Sanguine was famous for being a peaceful home where families could gather to heal their sick. It was most famous for the highest quality maternity wards. Joyous mothers and fathers would be carrying their newborns, swaddling in their arms, ignorant of the lush decor of crystal blue fountains and porcelain sculptures because of their fixation on their new family member. The Scourge's coming did not bode well for the atmosphere of joy. For instead of coming to welcome a new human being into the Earth, they were coming to question a victim of horrendous torture.

Kite held onto the hilt of his scimitar as they walked into the hospital. The blade shimmered with white light that spilled out of the hilt. He walked with a pride like a nobleman even though he was from the Lead District. "Miss Thruian is residing in the trauma ward on the sixth floor." The Agapist spoke in a braggadocios tone. "Let's pray she's sane enough to tell us about what happened to her."

"Does she have a protection detail?" Oslin asked as they stepped on the sterilized tile of lobby area.

"Yes. First Captain Bur'ett is stationed there alongside two other arbiters. He is waiting for us as we speak."

"What do you plan on asking this woman?"

"That's a bloody moronic thing to ask." Kite snapped. "I'm going to ask who kidnapped her and what they did to her, simple as that."

"I don't think it'll be that simple." Oslin said wary that the pleasantries they had just vanished in an instant. "Do you really believe she's in a state where she can clearly distinguish any names or faces or even accurately recount what happened to her? I mean, they fished her out of the river after being missing for two weeks. That kind of isolation would scar one's mind pretty thoroughly."

"She's in the trauma ward. Ideally, she could rest up before we talk to her but we're fast approaching the fourth month of our Dilictor Hunt. I am sick of idling by as he preys on innocent women. Time is a luxury Hrimata cannot afford any longer."

"Agreed. It is an unfortunate necessity."

The men gathered up on the lift to take them to the sixth floor. The automated system buckled ever so slightly under the weight of three flaksteel suits. Faint electronic music filled the small rectangular transport with an air of awkwardness which was further amplified by how cramped it was in there. All were silently relieved when the doors slid open and they marched out into a similarly sterile hallway.

There was no need for an escort. There was only one floor that had a security detail posted outside the doorway. Two blue and white uniformed officers with drawn rifles and sheathed swords stood with their backs to the wall. They readjusted their posture to a formalized position upon seeing the Scourge officers enter into the hospital.

"Agapist Kite?" The more decorated officer asked the soldier in white battle plate.

"Speaking. Are you Bur'ett?" Kite retorted curtly.

"First Captain Bur'ett stepped out for the day sir. I am Third Captain Matthias."

"Charmed." He responded sarcastically. "We must speak with Mrs. Thruian at once with regards to the Dilictor pursuit. Kindly grant us entrance."

"You think she was kidnapped by the Nitral Nightmare?"

"That information is Rho classified. I believe only the First Captain has that level of clearance. You don't. So grant us entrance, before I confiscate your badge for obstruction."

The young arbiter looked to the ground nervously. "Apologies Agapist Kite, sir." He turned to the wall and punched in a four digit code onto a digital pad. The white door label K-22b slid up and into the ceiling.

"Thank you. Keep guard while we're in and admit no one else while our interview takes place. Retriever Ram's Horn, wait out here. Report anything suspicious."

"Okay." He bellowed.

Kite and Du'Plasse entered into the hospital room. Fluid bags feeding into drip tubes and more units sat alongside bags of blood in a chilled storage unit. A single mechanized bed was at the back wall and three chairs were facing it. A woman, her skin flushed of all color but decorated with patches of violet red bruises with bluish white hair lay with her eyes closed on the bed. Drip tubes perforated her skin at the arms and shoulders. Black sutures stitched a number of wounds closed. A man with a similar blue hued hair sat in one of the hospital chairs and his eyes snapped open upon the two entering.

"Can I help you with something?" The man stood up and approached.

"I'm Herald Du'Plasse." Oslin introduced himself first at Kite's irritation. He took the lead, knowing of tensions between the highest caste and the lowest. He figured that as a native of the Platinum

District, he would have better luck interacting with these nobles of the Diamond District. "This is Agapist Kite. Might I implore who you are?"

"Harlon Thruian, Victoria's husband."

"I understand. My condolences for the troubled times you find yourselves in. Would you mind terribly if we ask your wife a few questions with regards to what happened to her?"

"The guardsmen already did." Oslin noted that Harlon wasn't looking at Kite. "What's the Scourge doing here anyway?"

"We believe that the man that abducted your wife was..."

"That information is Rho classified." Kite interrupted Oslin. "We've an investigation that we believe your wife's testimony will be helpful in."

The man cocked his head, obviously confused at how a Lead District man could ever speak to someone from their caste with such disrespect. If he harbored racial prejudice, he did a half decent job at concealing it. "Well, I'll allow it, I suppose. I don't know how helpful she'll be. She's still recovering from malnourishment so I don't think she's as keenly minded as she once was."

"Any information might help." Du'Plasse entered in, keeping a professional yet caring tone. "Our top priority is catching the filth that did this to your wife."

He was still clearly uneasy, but nodded in compliance. "Okay, let me get her up." The man sat back now adjacent to the bedside. He lightly shook her, taking care not to shift the drip tubes. She stirred for a moment before cracking open her swollen eyes. "Victoria darling, the Scourge is here. They want to ask you a few questions."

She shifted in her cot and squinted to better look at the officers. "Good afternoon, ma'am." Agapist Kite began. "If you don't mind, we would like to implore you to..."

Cyrus Kite didn't finish his sentence. Victoria Thruian was plunged into a raving panic attack. She cried out in agonizing fright unprovoked. Her bloodcurdling shrieks filled the men in the room with terror. Her heart monitor tripped alarms as her blood pressure and heart rate began to violently spike. Kite and Du'Plasse exchanged nervous looks as she continued screaming uncontrollably, her husband trying desperately to calm her down. Hospitallers rushed in as alerts began ringing out. The two Scourge warriors excused themselves as the chamber began filling up with medical professionals.

The two arbiters shared troubled looks, mirroring that of Oslin and Cyrus. More doctors ran past the concerned security detail. They met up with Ram's Horn after such a brief departure. "What?" Ram mumbled.

"I don't know." Oslin responded readjusting his ascot. "She just started panicking as soon as she saw us."

"Something triggered her." Kite said. "Clearly the experience has shaken her. Post traumatic stress disorder is not unheard of for someone who was kidnapped by a serial killer."

"What could have set her off like that?" Oslin asked as the panicked screaming finally subsided. "God only knows what she's been through, but in all my experience I've never seen someone have that kind of reaction unless exposed to something eerily similar to the torment that they went through."

"You think that one of us triggered her?" Kite stroked his chin in confusion. "Perhaps one of our weapons or armor sets bears a strong resemblance to something the Dilictor possesses."

"Arrest that blackhead!" Harlon Thruian stormed out of the medical chamber and pointed a highly accusatory finger at Agapist Cyrus Kite. A wild look of offended anguish was in his eyes.

"Arrest me?" Kite gawked with a haughty laugh. "On what grounds?"

"He's the one that kidnapped my wife!" Harlon growled. "He's the Nitral Nightmare!"

The home of the 127thReichsmen was alive with laughter and the sour stench of cheap alcohol. The entire lodge of college age brothers was celebrating a successful end to midterm exams. It had been an arduous journey involving a mountain of text books and gallons of steaming coffee, but they had all survived the week. The dirty brown carpet along the walnut halls was stained with liquors that had spilled during the celebration. The fifteen or so young men gathered together in a boisterous drinking game where they would exchange foaming cartridges of mead and ale. Each man's chin was dripping with dark fluids as they sloppily put away drink after drink, glutting themselves with the dizzying liquid.

Currently, two men stood upright in the center. The game they were playing consisted of the two binging themselves with a syrupy mead and being ricocheted by those making up the perimeter. The first one to vomit loses. It was a childishly simplistic game, but embodied the reputation for reckless abandon the Reichsmen were notorious for.

Two young men from Lex Statuo were bouncing around like madmen in the circle of reprobates. They rattled around the man-made cage for a full minute before the pushing ceased and the two wobbled back to the middle. They all laughed and cheered as the two men swallowed a can of viscous mead within seconds. They were promptly passed back and forth wildly and rapidly. Their whooping laughter was cut off by the swift clap of metal slamming against wood.

Inquisitor Covalos and Exarch Surizal had entered the lodge house moments earlier. The door had been left ajar and they decided to let themselves in, much to their disgust. Adastra drew his wardiron greataxe and slammed it against the wood paneled wall, creating a silencing clap. The two bigger, brawnier, and significantly less cheery men instantly drained the ambiance of celebration with their startling presence in the lodge home. The game was put to a swift end and one of the boys released all of the booze they had ingested.

"Inquisition!" Surizal shouted, his voice like a boom of thunder. "Line up!"

In just a few moments, and a shuffling of empty cans and bottles, the young men put their backs to the wall Adastra had previously struck. They were practically cowering like a group of inmates about to face a firing squad. All were baffled at their presence, lost to any reason why the Inquisition would be at their humble lodge house.

“I want someone to tell us why we’re here.” Adastra entered in, removing all pleasantries from his tone. They took it as a rhetorical statement and exchanged nervous looks. “That wasn’t a trick question. Who among you knows what reason brings the Scourge to your door?”

“We don’t know sir.” A golden hair kid said nervously.

“You don’t know?” Exarch Surizal growled. “If only there were some tragedy that occurred recently that would bring the punishers of Templym to the Grigorian Administration. Perhaps a bombing in the mess hall.”

“Frodus Rieveshl.” Adastra said, keeping the theatrics of a grim hunter. “We’re trying to determine a motive to his suicide bombing.”

“Sir,” A young man with white foam stuck to the corner of his mouth. “Why are you coming to us, we never knew the guy.”

“We were told that he was a member of this fraternity.”

“He wasn’t...I don’t recall ever hearing him speak. Guy was a loner, real quiet.”

Zedekiah and Adastra exchanged a brief look of confusion. “He wasn’t a member of this lodge?” The Exarch asked.

“No sir.” The drunken boys nodded in unanimous agreement.

Adastra approached Zedekiah and whispered in a hush. “Somebody lied, either Monk to us or Rieveshl to Monk.”

“That doesn’t make any sense.” Surizal responded in a similar quiet. “Why would Rieveshl lie to his professor about being in a lodge? It does seem logical to mislead us to a dead end if Monk has something to hide.”

“But doesn’t it seem suspicious that this frat is named after the Reichsmen, a traitor regiment? I’m skeptical to believe that it’s just a coincidence that possession would take place while and they just happen to have that name.”

“I say we bring Monk in for Veritas interrogation. I’ll go grab him. Find out why these idiots chose that name. We’ll reconvene at the Solace.”

"Agreed." Adastra nodded as turned back to address the inebriated crowd as Exarch Surizal made his exit. "Good news for you, we're going to be much briefer than previously expected. All I need to know is why you call yourselves the 127thReichsmen."

"That's our name sir." A drunken child said, unaware of what he was saying.

"Do you even know who you're named after? You take your title from a legion of crusaders loyal to Plaguemire!" Adastra noted the genuine fear and awe in the eyes of the students. It was obvious to him that they had no clue about their lodge's title. "Who picked that name?"

"This brotherhood has been around for twenty years. None of us were in at the time."

"You have a list of all previous members, a chronicle of this lodge's history?" Adastra's eyes were like sharpened iron as his glare sliced through them.

A bleary eyed Serbian replied after an awkward silence. "Yes."

"Get it for me. We're done here. If any of you leave the city, I'll sick the Shackle on you and lock you in Niflheim Arcae." The second man who had been playing the game threw up.

Prelate Terran Greyflame stood in the Judean desert, a dry hot breeze fluttering through his black feathered cape. The fiery red glare of the augmetic orb occupying his left eye socket matched the blazing crimson of his battle plate. The sun blistered down on a congress of Inquisition personnel in full battle regalia and a half as many inmates kneeling in front of a six foot deep trench. Not even as much of a trickle of sweat came from the pallid grey flesh of the Inquisition's prime, regardless of the immense temperature. Greyflame's voice rang out from mobilized vocal projectors that were rolled out on the salt crusted sand. The Prelate was giving the doomed prisoners what he lovingly called a "living funeral," which was a sermon given to those on death row. Nobody present could tell which cut deeper. The glassy shards of sand and salt piercing the flesh of the knees they were forced to kneel on or the grim words spoken by the plated figure of Terran Greyflame.

"For many of you, this is a day of rejoicing!" The Prelate's voice roared across the flat dust plain overpowering the gasps of admiration from his subordinates and the weeping of guilty men and women. "You were each granted an opportunity of repentance. I am confident many of you were genuine in your recognition of your own putrid sin and implored the Lord would grant mercy. I have wonderful news for you! Today is the day that you join our most holy Creator in Eternity. For even the thief crucified alongside Christ repented and He told him: 'Truly I say to you, today you shall be with me in Paradise.'"

Greyflame stopped for a moment. Quoting the sacred words of the Savior always gave him shivers. His passion was duly noted by the crowd. "Luke 23:43...The temptation to be envious is biting at the back of my head. For those of you who were immersed and cried out to God for mercy, you will join our fallen brethren and the likes of the apostles and the holy Triune Himself while we are left to toil in a fallen world. Know that I shall join you soon enough, for this fleeting life is short compared to that of our Eternal reincarnation. And when I enter the gates of Heaven, take comfort in knowing that I will fall on my face with tears in my eyes, begging you to forgive me for forcing me to subject you to such cruel punishment. For as much as I would love to see my new family members go forth and make disciples of this world... you cannot be allowed to pervert Templym's purity. For we are a nation of laws and holy teachings, therefore certain offenses shall not be tolerated. You cannot be allowed to go on in this life, for you have made sacrilege of the Word and shown blatant disregard for all that is good in life. 'For the great day of their wrath has come, and who is able to stand?'"

Prelate Greyflame stopped his iteration again, chilled regardless of the bitter heat of the dry desert. In his pause, his artificial eye saw something in the distance far beyond what his natural eye could see. It was a blue armored chariot with markings of the spike whip of the Scourge and the chain-cuff of the Shackle on its hood. This was nothing out of the ordinary.

"Revelation 6:17...We are all guilty, none of us are free from the corruption of sin. I pray that many of you accepted the most gracious sacrifice on the Cross that you may be spared from damnation. However, I recognize that several of you have not done this. Some among you still cling to your graven images and your false gods. Woe to you. You have whored yourselves to the Mundus Imago who you've propped up as pagan deities. For you, my heart aches. Your suffering has only begun... there is no rest in Hell. I take comfort that those of us who are saved will not remember your faces or names when we are welcomed to Heaven. I am placed in anguish in this life knowing that children of God shall be forever cast out. Many of you have faced Hell in this life...many more shall face it in the next. You are all convicted, judged, and declared guilty in the eyes of the Scourge." He turned his head skyward, speaking directly to the Father. "Lord have mercy on us if we kill an innocent... Lord have mercy on us all."

Terran turned his hollow gaze to the sand and the line of inmates at the mouth of the trench. "Sanctus," All Inquisition executioners drew their firearms. "Dominus," The sounds of dozens of slides cracking as bullets were loaded into barrels."Jus," The ends of the guns were pressed to the backs of the inmates' heads."Sic Itur Ad Caelus" Each of the guns fired simultaneously, each landing a killing blow. The inmate's bodies tumbled into the manmade sand trench leaving nothing but the Scourge standing on the arid desert. A single tear streaked down the dust caked cheek of Terran Greyflame from his organic eye. "Fill this trench. I want to mobilize in twenty minutes."

By the time Greyflame had removed the audio wire hooking him up to the amplifiers, the chariot he had seen off in the distance had rolled up at a staggeringly quick speed. It was a militarized spinetail class chariot, an exotic transport of aerodynamic eloquence. Such a chariot had a maximum capacity of only two people and a small load of cargo in the hull. These were typically used for sport, not as Scourge military transport. The cobalt armor plates were filmed with a cloud of dust. The Prelate brushed the salty particulates off of the gold foil with Hebrew Scriptures attached to his battle plate, not at all amused by the display. He did bear a sense of glee, as he saw High Conservator Jude Bethel stepped out of the transport. It was unlike the stoic to be parading in such extravagant toys such as these.

The two were nearly opposites in appearance. Jude's skin was dark like burnished brass while Terran's was pale like a low hanging stratus cloud. Bethel's armor was scarred, dull, and a column of smoke billowed out like it was the mouth of a ravenous dragon. Greyflame's was pristine, glittering, and constantly hummed with a chiming bell. Regardless of these physical differences, they were strikingly similar in demeanor and ideology.

"Shalom Aleichem, High Conservator." Greyflame said with a tight face.

"Shalom Aleichem, Prelate." Bethel replied clasping his forearm, a similar expressionless face.

"Not that I am displeased to see you brother, but what brings you here?" Terran Greyflame always had a very forthright attitude. "We're twenty miles away from civilization and I just conducted a funeral. Most would consider this to be a distasteful fellowship."

"The privacy of this location is what brings me at this time and place. I wish to speak to you...just the two of us."

"Of course, we'll keep this Alpha classified."

"No, no classifications. This is something that stays between us. Are we clear?"

"This is serious then?" Greyflame grew mildly concerned. "Rumor has it that you're starting to lose your bearings. Is it true that you and the Regent had an altercation at Golgotha?"

"My relation to Lord Illuromos is...not the most pressing matter at this time."

"Then what is my brother? What ails you so severely that not even the Regent can know of this encounter?"

Bethel presented a historian's tablet and handed it to Greyflame. "This is a matter involving the Regent himself. I fear we may need to invoke the 10th Dogma."

"You want to execute and replace Invictus Illuromos?" His already morbid tone grew darker. "Such a suggestion reeks of mutiny. If he found out about that he'd have you shot. Bloody smoke Jude, half of Templym believes he's Auzlanten's son. Can you imagine having that kind of power looming over your head? The demon Zyx'guroth of the 7th was a mile tall at least and he minced it to a pulp. Are you suicidal or do you just crave infamy?"

"I wouldn't suggest something like this if I wasn't serious."

"Passion proves nothing, Jude. I have encountered zealots and fanatics of false idols and Imago fiends alike, all fervently faithful in their unholy patrons. Do you really think that your feelings have any bearings on whether or not you get to kill the Regent?"

"I know," Jude sighed. "I've contemplated heavily on the issue. It's been eating away at my sanity for weeks now. This fake Auzlanten, if there really is one, planted distrust in my mind. I'm torn between the idea that it's nothing but magickal tricks toying at my mind or if Invictus Illuromos really has betrayed Templym." He then stuck out his hand, extending a data pad towards the Prelate.

"This Idolacreid you've spoken of. Do you truly believe it exists? Illuromos acts as Arodi Auzlanten in his absence. We are sworn to obey him as if he were the prophet himself. If this corruption runs as deep as you think it does..."

"It does." Bethel interrupted. "In only the first two days of my edict, the Shackle has uncovered over one hundred guilty individuals. That's just the ones that the Veritas Chambers can root out."

"What do you mean?" Greyflame turned the slate in his hands, his augmetic eye peering with laser intensity.

"This is the true nature of our meeting. I must know, are there methods by which one could surpass the power of the Veritas Chamber?"

"There have been a small number of black hosts and magick users who've been able to lie beneath their influence. It would take a remarkable amount of supernatural power... though I suppose it can be done."

"I spoke with the Regent in a Veritas Chamber while in Golgotha. He assured me that he was loyal to the Scourge. He promised me, under the influence of a sanctum that removes all doubts, that he was genuine, and that the wicked clone of Auzlanten was toying with my mind."

"You think he was lying?"

"I must be sure." Jude gripped onto Greyflame's shoulder guard. "I can't have this fog of unease clouding my judgment any longer. Your skills of deduction of truth are legendary in the Scourge. If anybody can spot a lie, it's you."

Terran tapped a featureless projectum screen and a display of key runes displayed holographically. "What is this then?" He asked wearily.

"Before I raided Balor's stockpile of ordinance, I spoke to the Regent. That is when I first suspected something was awry. I've reviewed this recording of our conversation a dozen times over a number of sleepless nights since then. I need your opinion." Jude's cold blue fingers danced across the displayed keyboard and the video recording of their conversation was placed on the tablet's screen. "Thirteen minutes fifteen seconds...see for yourself."

Terran Greyflame watched with an intense gaze.

Jude Bethel: "...asked anything of me." *Pause.* "All he asked was to ensure loyalty in the Scourge. *Pause.* "Well that and..."

Invictus Illuromos: "What else Jude? What did the imposter ask of you?"

Jude Bethel: "He wanted to speak with Djinn Balor, claimed that he was part of some vast conspiracy. He mentioned the Idolacreid and the Nephilim."

Invictus Illuromos: Pause. "And you let him go?"

Jude Bethel: "Lord Regent, you asked me to inform you if I encountered Auzlanten. I took no further action for fear of putting our true Master at risk. If the one inside this castle is an imposter, it's a roughing good one."

Invictus Illuromos: "Why are you just standing around then? Your quarry is being manipulated by demonic filth as we speak, engage the raid!"

Jude Bethel: "Invictus, you're not giving..." *Stop.*

Terran Greyflame blinked with his mouth ajar. He thought he saw something. He rewound the feed.

Jude Bethel: "...one inside this castle is an imposter, it's a roughing good one."*Invictus Illuromos:* "Why are you just standing around then? Your quarry is being manipulated by demonic filth as we speak (*there it was again),* engage the raid!" *Stop. Rewind.*

Invictus Illuromos: "...standing around then? Your quarry is being manipulated by demonic filth as we speak (*the twitch again),* engage the raid!" *Stop. Rewind.*

Invictus Illuromos: "...being manipulated by demonic filth as we speak (*the twitch again!*)" *Stop.*

The pristine data slate fell out of Greyflame's limp hand and into the desert sand. His eyes were wide with disbelief, revealing the intricate brass cogs inside of the glass shell of his augmetic eye. Had Bethel not been adamant about discretion he would have torn his cloak and wept aloud, but he just stood there, unable to utter a single word for a full minute.

"His eye." He was finally able to say. "It twitched right as he said 'demonic filth'. That's a tell. He...did he..."

"That's correct, Terran." Jude said, ensuring his voice was kept low. "Invictus lied to me."

CHAPTER 25

Vandross Blackwell could have gone with the remainder of his task force to question the kidnapped woman. He had something else in mind. He wanted to track down any business that Regulom Palladium had in Hrimata. He petitioned Bride Wainwright for assistance and she graciously accepted. Her Beta clearance would serve to be a useful tool to root out the most well hidden information. As Adastra was, perhaps literally, chasing ghosts in the Grigorian Administration, Oslin and Ram's Horn were at the hospital, and Volk was recovering from his grievous injury, Vandross spent his time with Daphne investigating from the comfort of her office.

The Seraphim Solace not only operated as the Scourge stronghold of Hrimata, but as the paramount stronghold of the Veil. Patriarch Arodus Betankur usually occupied this place, but was often away. In a sense, Daphne Wainwright was his regent. The private chambers were furnished with vinyl couches and velvet recliners. The thick flaksteel walls and floors were disguised beneath a thin layer of decorative plaster. Vines of grapes and olives dangled from the ceiling among a chandelier of twisted iron thorns. The rosewood desk holding a number of sensitive documents as well Daphne's personal computer harbored a number of trophies from her career. The most notable trinket was a chrome robotic hand propped up on a steel holster.

Daphne tapped away at the keyboard of her computer. Algorithms were fishing the Scourge data wells for anything involving the former leader of the Cybernetic Apotheosis. Vandross took in the scenic room with his boots kicked up on the desk. A mist of a pale blue fog lifted out of his pipe as he smoked a stick of fogrose.

Blackwell's eyebrow cocked in thought at the sight of the augmetic hand on the small steel stage. "Where'd you get this keepsake?" He pondered aloud.

"How familiar are you with my story?" Daphne asked, her emerald eyes locked onto the computer monitor.

"I remember a lot about being locked in that isolation chamber during the Tribulation. I recall the details of your story pretty well, I reckon. It's a testament to your strength that you would plunge knee deep into the cesspool of sexual crimes after narrowly surviving such an encounter."

Daphne gave him a quick half-smile. "I don't consider it particularly strong but I appreciate the sentiment. If anything, this career is the most logical response to what I went through. I bear no physical scars from my assault, but at times I feel as though the scars on my soul will never heal. Let's not delve too deeply into my psychology. I picked that hand up from my first Dilictor Ignotum when I was an Expurgator in Mayanmatra."

"I remember that. It's one of those cases that sent you soaring in the Veil's ranks. Arven Whitestain, the providence's first ever serial rapist. If I recall, the Beacon projected he would have gotten away with another fifty-eight assaults if you hadn't stepped in. This is his hand then?"

"That it is." Daphne's ruby lips pressed tightly together as she closed her eyes. "It's with that hand that he asphyxiated over a dozen women he preyed on...it's that hand that prevented me from screaming when he..."

"No." Vandross said aghast. "Whitestain was the one that stole your innocence before your enrollment."

"That's right." Wainwright's lips full lips thinned. "He stripped me of my innocence, my dreams, and my virginity. In exchange I took his hand and then his life. I suppose that's a fair trade. Every day, I see that hand and I recall what he did to me. I used to weep at the sight of it as the memories played out in my mind. Now, I just think of all the innocents I keep from suffering the same fate by hunting the lowest scum of the Earth. It's almost funny. I had always fantasized about taking a chivalrous crusader or a Scourge warrior as a husband. Instead, I became one."

"Speaking of which, are you planning on becoming a wife at any point in the future? Surely there's a man courting you at this time?"

The Bride laughed at the compliment. "Oh, I've had several try. I'm not particularly interested in being a spouse at this time. I don't think I'm worth it, frankly."

"Nonsense, you're a top-shelf kind of girl." Vandross said with a bright grin. He was being careful not to sound like he was attempting to woo her. "I wouldn't be surprised if there was a line of men just itching to slap a band on that wrist of yours. I'm sure you saw the way Blye was looking at you. He seems like a nice young man."

"Yen? Oh, I'm aware of the puppy love he has for me. He thinks he's keeping it well hidden. It's flattering and adorable, but that's about it."

"My heart breaks for that poor kid." Vandross puffed away the last of his granite pipe's contents. "Love is a fickle mistress I suppose. We all must get over those our hearts yearn for at one stage or the next."

Daphne stopped her fast typing as her face collapsed and her eyes were flushed with empathy. "Vandross...it's Nyvett 18th. Oh God, how could I forget?" She stood from her seat and walked over to a decorative slab of what appeared to be raw stone.

"Forget what exactly?" Vandross said as he removed his hat and stowed his pipe.

She pulled a panel out revealing a refrigerated shelf with a few bottles and crystals. She removed a bottle of tarry liquor and two iced glasses. "It's the anniversary of Annabelle's death."

Vandross froze. He desperately wanted to avoid confronting this issue, but figured that either she or Adastra would bring it up. He had hoped he would be busy enough to plunge his mind into the manhunt and that he wouldn't have time to dwell on his wife's death. It was a painful memory to recall. After all...he was the one that killed her.

Three years prior, Vandross Blackwell was married to his first love. Annabelle was a beautiful young lady who grew up in Rio Epiphanies alongside him. The two grew up together in rudimentary school. She taught Vandross how to be a gentleman, at least that's what she told everyone. The two were wed long before the Inquisitor ever enrolled in the Scourge. They had been married for four years before they had their first child, a son they named Hugo. Vandross was happy. He had everything that he ever wanted: a noble, righteous career and a beautiful family. This did not last.

At some point during the Civil Strife, Annabelle Blackwell was corrupted by Imago forces. She became enthralled with a horrific fascination with a pagan deity called Lhama'stu. This particular demonic entity demanded child sacrifice, similar to Moloch worship in ancient Israel. Hoping to surprise his wife by coming home unannounced, Vandross walked in on her preparing their infant son for a blood sacrament. She was arrested under the authority of the Inquisition. She was tried, convicted, and declared guilty. She was executed by her husband's hand.

The Scourge has always allowed the victims of crimes to enact the execution of the perpetrators. Often times, the families of those that have a loved one taken from them were extended the opportunity to exact vengeance themselves. This practice was implemented as a means to prevent vigilantes from taking the law into their own hands. If they refused, it would be enacted by a Scourge official. Vandross Blackwell was both of those. He felt the need for the closure of putting the woman he once loved down for good. He prayed for her repentance, though there was no evidence to suggest such a thing. Annabelle laughed the whole time. When the Inquisition hauled her on a barge in the Averlanthi Sea, she looked Vandross in the eye and laughed at him. Her incessant witch-cackling rang in his ears every time he thought of her. This was not the memory he wanted to bear of her. He wanted desperately to purge that image from his head and recall the sweet, kind, godly woman that he married. Instead he remembered the demoniac whose lifeless body he cast into the sea. Vandross wanted to believe that Annabelle died at some point while he was fighting in the Strife. When he had sworn his wedding oath with her, they vowed "'til death do us part." He never expected that she would be the one to die first, let alone by his hand.

Vandross left Hugo to his parents. He was three and a half years old now. Vandross couldn't bear the sight of his son any longer. The painful memory and the insane laughter was called back every time he looked at his son's face. He also decided that a single parent household would be no way to raise a child, especially not with as demanding a field of work as operating in the Inquisition. So, he opted that a house of two grandparents in lieu of a single, oft absent father. He still sent a large portion of his monthly pay checks to Rio Epiphanies in Kalkhan to provide silent support, but he hadn't seen his son since the day he executed his wife.

Daphne Wainwright and Adastra Covalos were really the only two people in his sphere of influence that were fully aware of his past. Daphne poured a crystal to the brim with a glistening black liquid. "Kraken's Blood." She said as she slid the crystal over to him. "It's strong enough to cause a normal man to overdose. With our poison training, it should be enough to give you a much needed buzz."

"Thank you Daphne." Vandross said, taking in the full contents in a single gulp. He didn't enjoy the bitter black drink, but the dulling of senses was appreciated.

"I'm guessing you still don't want to talk about it?" She asked sympathetically.

"Hey, what about Adastra?" Vandross interjected, changing the subject.

Daphne tipped her head back as she too took a drink of Kraken's Blood. "What about him?"

"He's a strapping guy, fervently loyal, devoutly faithful. Why don't you two get together some time?"

Bride Wainwright blushed slightly as she returned to her algorithms. "Oh...I suppose he's a swell man."

"Daphne," Vandross propped his hat back on his head as he leaned over with a grin. "You fancy him, don't you?"

This made her cheeks brighten with a pink hue. "Oh, he's too good for the likes of me. Adastra needs a wife that will meet his needs, somebody who's building a home, not chasing down rapists."

"Don't be so modest. You and I both know that he's a hot-blooded stoic that won't slow down until he's maimed beyond recovery. A woman that's doing the same thing is the perfect match for him!"

"No, no...I'm not a...I just..." Daphne was getting flustered at Vandross' insistence. In truth she recognized that he was just directing attention away from his family issues by directing the conversation towards her. However, whether he intended to or not, he was touching on a sensitive topic. Daphne Wainwright wasn't about to let Vandross interrogate her on the matter. She executed a similar strategy to avoid the topic. "The search is over. I've got Regulom Palladium's entire history in Hrimata."

"Perfect." Vandross said, noting the avoidance but happy that answers were finally being found. "What has he been up to?"

"It doesn't look like he has much of a history in this city." Daphne mused. "There's some activity here before he was declared a recidivist by the Inquisition. He was a cybernetics professor at the Grigorian Administration."

Vandross scratched the whiskers on his chin. "That's one of the places all of our victims visited, isn't it?"

"It is. Doesn't really sound like a coincidence to me." She struck the keyboard as she revealed more information. "It looks like he taught about computer science and augmetic prostheses from '02 to '06."

"Unfortunately, we don't know if he was an Apotheosis member at the time. Do you have a list of activities he was involved in at the time?"

"Let me see...A robotics club, programming competitions, lodge sponsorship, charity bowls. This just seems like boring professor activities, hardly the sinister cult leader you made him out to be."

"You should have seen him when we caught him. That psycho replaced twenty percent of his nervous system with cables and wires. He hard-lined himself into a machine fusing organic nerves, presumably from murdered innocents, and computerized wires trying to awaken one of the dead god-AIs. Frankly, I'm not sorry that Ram put a round through his skull, but I'm starting to wish he was still around so we could squeeze him for information. Did you say lodge sponsorship?"

"Yes. The university requires all fraternities and lodges to have a professor's endorsement to operate on the campus. It looks like he sponsored a group called..."

"The 127th Reichsmen?" Vandross asked.

Daphne leered at the screen. "No. The 23rd Constantinians, why do you ask?"

"That's a lodge that Adastra was looking into with Exarch Surizal. I was hoping there was a connection. Who are the Constantinians?"

"It looks like they were disbanded after suspicion of occultic activity. Regulom Palladium was suspected of Imago cult affiliation and was fired. He was suspected to have corrupted a number of the students so the lodge was terminated."

"What happened to the students involved?"

Daphne paused to read for a moment. "It seems they all went their separate ways. Palladium was never convicted while he was here in Hrimata and had no officially confirmed affiliation with the Apotheosis until he moved to Jaspin. It seems that two of the students involved were later tried for 'Imago experimentation' but declared innocent."

"I don't like the sound of that." Vandross scowled. "What kind of experimentation were they suspected of?"

The Bride shivered in shock as she continued to read. "Apparently they were attempting to fuse demonic spirits with machines... allegedly."

"That kind of sounds like the Apotheosis, but they're not typically Imago cults. Usually, they just send empty prayers to nonexistent AI deities...rarely ever actual demons. I suppose that wasn't beneath this scum. Do you have any..."

Inquisitor Blackwell was interrupted by Admonisher Rickard. His icy eyes shrouded by a thick head of brown hair were filled with dread and alarm. "Bride Wainwright my lady!" He gave a hurried heart-ripping salute.

"Fenrick, what is it?" She retorted.

"Task force S-6319 has someone they think is the Nitral Nightmare."

"That's fantastic, who is it?"

"It's Kite, ma'am."

Retriever Ram's Horn had hauled a large number of prisoners into captivity. It was his duty as an officer of the Shackle after all. This was the first time he was tasked with arresting another officer of a neighboring branch of the Scourge. An eye witness had identified Agapist Kite as the Dilictor Ignotum of Hrimata. Such an accusation, even if it were unsubstantiated, was weighty enough to warrant arrest. The armor-clad marauder kept Kite with his arms locked and cuffed in a twist behind his back. The normally pompous individual was now sullen and grim-faced as he was shamefully paraded down the halls of the Seraphim Solace.

His former peers looked aghast at the solemn scene. Veil warriors, once engulfed in red herrings and other false leads, stopped in their fervent conversations to look upon the flaksteel giant with their colleague locked in his chain-cuffs. Word had reached the Solace ten minutes before their arrival and was spreading, but several dismissed it as senseless gossip. Seeing Kite in chains changed things.

Daphne came out with dread filling her normally gleaming eyes. Her kind demeanor was replaced with the dour stance of a foreboding leader. Her hands were locked behind her back and the glistening gemstone flowers at the cusp of her shoulders seemed to darken. She connected with Kite's sour eyes as he was lead past her to a Veritas Chamber. He said nothing. Rather, he sank his head in shame. Oslin Du'Plasse was trailing behind the two of them. Bride Wainwright stopped him for a rapid debriefing.

"What the bloody smoke happened at the hospital?" Daphne's often friendly voice was demanding and cold.

"Victoria Thruian identified Cyrus Kite as the man that kidnapped her." Oslin said soberly, carefully selecting his words. "Upon us walking in for a preliminary interview, she had a violent panic attack. After the doctors calmed her down, she said she went into the manic fit because Kite was her assailant."

"How reliable is she? Last I heard, her mental state was in question."

"I questioned her personally. She gave explicit details with regards to her kidnapping and subsequent torture. She was very specific."

"Specificity does not equate to reliability."

"True, but the hospitallers gave her a psyche evaluation after we left. They are declaring her sane. I believe they're planning on performing EBS and MRS to determine if there are any cranial infections or injuries. Other than that ma'am, I don't know what to say. I suppose the Veritas Chamber will reveal more."

"It had better." Daphne unsheathed the rapier at her side. She brushed the icy metal off with a red silk square. The liquid argon infused blade super-cooled the handkerchief, turning it into a brittle sheet which crumbled to frozen bits in her hand. "If the Dilictor was under my authority this whole time and I'm just now finding out... I'm invoking Creed Eighteen."

Kite wasn't in his battle plate any longer. In fact he wasn't allowed to wear any semblance of a Scourge uniform. He wore the only set of personal garments that he kept in his locker at the Solace. Any accused of a crime had to be distanced from the punishing force of Templym. So much as an accusation was taken with the greatest amount of strictness imaginable. Any member of the Scourge that stood in the face of an offense to the laws of Templym, no matter how trivial, had to be substantiated by a ranking member of at least 3rd Tier. Oslin Du'Plasse deduced the accuracy and validity of Mrs. Thruian's testimony and declared it reliable enough to warrant investigation. Regardless of the outcome, Kite would never be allowed to act as a warrior of the Scourge ever again.

Cyrus was well aware of the circumstance he was in. He sat, chain-cuffed to a table in a Veritas Chamber filled with eerie pale light, with a scowl on his face. He knew how to appropriately hold himself. It was odd being on the opposite side of the interrogation. Kite felt guilty just sitting there. The pale glowing panel of metal was swallowed by the ceiling with a hiss of pistons. Resplendent in her alabaster plate, Bride Wainwright entered and sat down opposite. She slammed down her holstered sword onto the iron interrogation table in unison with the slamming of the door. It sent a clear message.

"Allow me to begin." Kite said, desperately keeping an air of remarkable calm. "I recognize that I stand accused of being the Dilictor Ignotum of Hrimata, informally known as the Nitral Nightmare. An eyewitness account identified me as performing illegal detainment and torture upon her. You've invoked Creed Eleven-Epsilon, denying me legal counsel so I am left to defend my actions for myself. Based on your sword and the unforgiving glare you just gave me... you plan to skewer me here and now if you find me guilty."

"You have thirty seconds." Daphne seethed.

"I need no more time than that. I am innocent. I've had no contact with Victoria Thruian outside of today. I have never kidnapped anybody in my life. Nor did I kill or torture any of the victims of the Nitral Nightmare. I am not the Dilictor that..."

The frost caked point of the rapier met Kite's Adam's apple. "Don't you dare hijack my interrogation." Wainwright's voice was filled with ire and hatred. "I've given you your time. Now I'll ask the questions. You'll answer them. Do I need to explain to you that you're dancing on a razor's edge?" Kite sat in horrified silence. "That wasn't rhetorical."

"I understand, Daphne." He swallowed as the point of the thin single blade was removed from his neck.

"Don't call me Daphne. We aren't friends."

"I never considered us friends." Kite gave a somber smile. "I'd like to point out..."

"Have you ever committed a crime in the last year?" Daphne interrupted sick of Kite's attitude.

"I believe I may have exceeded the speed limit a dozen or so times. Other than that...no, I haven't violated the law since my enrollment in the Veil."

"Have you ever taken another's life?"

"Several in the line of duty, yes."

"What about outside of the line of duty?"

"Yes." Daphne raised her sword to Kite's throat once more. "Twenty-five years ago I discovered my sister's husband was physically abusing her. I killed him and buried him in the outskirts of Hrimata. I joined the Veil as an act of penitence. Other than that, every life I've taken has been as an acting officer of the Scourge."

"Have you ever raped anyone before?"

"No. I've had exactly three sexual experiences in my life. Two with my first 'love' in college and one during a drunken binge two years later, all times were consensual and I deeply regret all of them."

"What the bloody hell is wrong with you Cyrus? I ask you a simple question and you come at me with a more damning response than would suffice. Are you a madman or do you just want me to run you through where you sit?"

"I am giving you supplementary information." Kite leered forward. "I'll admit that it's unsettling to be on this end of an interrogation table, but I am intentionally letting the powers work through me and holding nothing back. This is to show you that I am innocent of the accusations. I am going above and beyond to reveal the truth...all of it."

"Why did Victoria Thruian identify you as her assailant? Better yet, why did she specifically name you the Nitral Nightmare?"

"I believe I'm being framed, though I doubt you believe the same theory. Perhaps the true Dilictor planted the imagery in her mind. You've hauled the bloody Inquisition into this mess of a manhunt anyway...maybe with good reason. Perhaps he's a wielder of unclean magick and toyed with her mind. Think about it. If I'm executed here as the Dilictor then the hunt ends, meaning that scum gets to skulk around in the shadows to slake his disgusting thirsts without fear of being hunted."

"Do you have any evidence to back up this fairytale?"

"No. But my testimony in this Veritas Chamber will help. I've admitted to not being the Dilictor, but I've confessed to another crime. Hell, you didn't even have to press for a confession of my sister's husband's murder. The way I see it, I'll go the Niflheim for two or three weeks and then get five years of indentured service. I'm done with the Scourge for good regardless."

"You're a pig Cyrus." Daphne let her subconscious feelings leak out, as Kite was at least saying he was doing. "I don't know what's going on here, but when I find out I'll beat your hide to a pulp."

"God, that's a turn on." Daphne brought her palm up to Kite's nose in a swift jab. He began to regret letting his mind open up. His nose cracked as blood poured out. He would have pressed his hands to his face, but they were cuffed to the table. "That was well warranted." Cyrus spit. "Are we done here or would you like to kick me around a bit longer?"

"You're a disgrace to the Veil, Kite." She stood up and waved her wrist in front of the sensor to open the door leading out of the chamber. "We won't be sorry to see you go. Nobody here likes you."

"I know Daphne...I know."

Yen Blye observed the interrogation alongside S-6319. Only Adastra Covalos was absent as he was reviewing the case files that Daphne and Vandross had previously uncovered. Even Volk was present, albeit with a subtle limp. Bride Wainwright rejoined the others in the observation room with a sullen visage.

"Who would have thought Cyrus was such a cur?" Yen offered up trying to lighten her obviously heavy heart.

"Everyone." She snapped. "Kite was always an insufferable bastard. Everybody knew he had some kind of a skeleton in his closet... I'm sorry Yen, I shouldn't yell. I'm just on edge."

"Understandably so." The Expurgator gave a shallow bow. "Unfortunately, as much as an ingrate Kite is, it would seem as though he's not our Dilictor. Nobody could resist the influence of the Veritas Chamber like that."

"It would seem that way. But then again, why would Victoria Thruian give such a sure account of him being her kidnapper?"

"It's my professional opinion that there are dark powers at play." Vandross entered in. "As much as I can't stomach Kite, I think the theory that Thruian's mind was altered is as solid as any."

"What about demonic possession?" Volk entered in speculating. "I think Adastra mentioned he caught traces of an Imago presence at the Administration."

"Warden Downey, it's good to see you up and about." Daphne said awkwardly. "I hope I didn't hurt you too badly."

"Nothing a bit of time can't fix, Bride. I say we don't dwell on it for long and instead focus on the manhunt at hand."

"I feel badly that you're focusing all your attention on my Dilictor. We haven't found as much of a semblance of a connection to your hunt for Mortis."

"There's something unnatural about this serial killer." Vandross said as he began loading his pipe. "The more facts we uncover, the stranger this case gets, the more I'm convinced there's a connection to our case."

"I'm certain of that now." Adastra Covalos entered the observation chamber with a bundle of parchments and a holo-tablet in hand.

"Inquisitor Covalos," Daphne said with a faint grin. "What did you find?"

"As you are aware, Regulom Palladium was a sponsor of the 23rd Constantinians, a lodge that was disbanded when he was suspected of heresy."

"We're aware of this." Oslin Du'Plasse questioned as he leaned forward.

"Well I had planned to cross-reference the list of previous members and sponsors of the fraternity with all of our suspects and witnesses in hopes to find a connection." Adastra paused and pulled up the roster of names on the pad. A list of dozens of names was displayed in simple green text over his hand. "I didn't need to do that. Regulom Palladium was one of two sponsors of this lodge."

"Who was the other one?"

"I immediately recognized a name." Adastra tapped the tablet again and a single name flashed from green to red. *Thomas Monk*.

CHAPTER 26

The home of the Nymphs was once a bustling metropolis, or as close as a marauder civilization could come to an urban. Vast columns of walnut and cherry wood structures dominated the flat plains. Arbor and flora paved the polished shale streets, draping the quaint civilization with a cool shade to shield its busy inhabitants from the Kalkhanian sun. Many citizens of Templym fail to believe in peaceful sects of the barbarian people groups outside of their orbit of influence, but the Nymphs, named for after mythical spirits of nature, proved those disbelievers wrong tenfold. They did.

The comely little city was reduced to ashes and splinters. The beautiful wooden structures were replaced with scraps of shattered panels and plaster dust. A thick column of black smoke billowed out of the center of the town. The sickly scent of blackened meat wafted outwards for a mile. Charred, eviscerated, dismembered, overall unidentifiably mangled bodies were strewn about, staining the plush grass crimson. Arodi Auzlanten lightly treaded with a still face, but was overwhelmed with agony at the sight of the butchery. This was not the aftermath of a battle. They were not a plentiful people and had no resources of great note. This village was not in a strategic placement in the continent. They were not hostile and barely even harmed the animals they hunted for survival. The Nymphs had no quarrel with anyone. The Grave Gluttons killed for the sake of slaughter.

Auzlanten could see a faint echo of the battle that took place a few days earlier. Upon seeing a broken body he could see the last few seconds of the person's life. He watched with a bleak mood, the torturous deaths of each of them. In a matter of minutes, Arodi witnessed the deaths of the men, women, and children of the Nymph tribe. His skin was set on edge as he saw the graphic detail in which they were stripped of their mortal coils in such inhuman fashion. He had seen sights of wanton bloodshed like this before. There was no purpose to it, not even a methodical Imago ritual. This was sport. The Grave Gluttons had no reason to lay such desecration aside from indulging their sadistic pleasure.

He pushed aside his emotions to focus on the shades of the killers. He couldn't distinguish fine details. Occasionally he could interpret a pair of wild eyes or a screaming mouth from the foggy images of the killers, which was a stark contrast to the clear images of the now deceased Nymphs. One figure stood out from all of the rest. It was hazier than the others. Clearly this figure was protected by some magick. One thing that was certain was that it was larger and more brutal than the other vandals. This man, if he could still be called one, was a full three feet taller than his subordinates. It wielded a lengthy polearm of some sort that stripped life wherever it fell. Arodi observed closely, watching the figure execute his grim art over and over again, trying to interpret some semblance of detail. Subjecting himself to the constant grief of witnessing murder a relentless number of times proved to be a futile effort. Auzlanten draped his head in sorrow, plunged in sullen grief.

Many believed that Arodi Auzlanten did not feel emotions. His stalwart demeanor and stoic charisma lead the masses to believe that he was beyond the tethering of human emotions. This was not true. Auzlanten simply possessed the ability to suppress and control his moods to focus his mind on tasks at hand. He felt all of the swinging emotions any man was capable of feeling. However, he recognized the danger of allowing one's feelings to cloud judgment. To allow himself to let such a human influence impact his actions was a risk he was not willing to take. At least, until he was told to kill his son Invictus.

He pushed the thought of the Scourge's Regent from his mind. He had dwelled enough on what he needed to do. What concerned him in this moment was the outline of this giant. Arodi deduced that this fiend was the chief Noctidus Val'Muardeares. He witnessed the echoes of the tribe's murder dozens of times and knew that this single figure racked up as many kills as the rest of his tribe. A knot twisted in his abdomen. Auzlanten had the sickening sense that whoever this marauder chief was, he had the Idolacreid.

A warrant was immediately issued for the arrest of Professor Thomas Monk. The zealous indignation pulsing through the hot blood of every Scourge officer in Hrimata was visual in their grave moods. Rifles were slapped with fresh cartridges and whetstones were worn to stubs with the rampant sharpening of weaponry. One unaware of the situation would assume that a war had broken out, considering the choler of the punishers of the wicked.

The thought that the Dilictor hunt was coming to a close caused Daphne Wainwright's heart to race as her adrenaline levels began spiking. For nearly four months, Thomas Monk had evaded her clutches. Now the families of the eight known victims, and those of the victims that had surely been undiscovered, would come to find peace through closure...and vengeance.

Bride Wainwright rallied nearly all of the Veil soldiers in the Solace. 90% of the personnel operating in their primary stronghold were dispatched to his acquisition. The Bride sent Expurgator Blye to the Grigorian Administration and she travelled to his personal estate. Smaller squadrons of troops were sent to secondary locations around the Silver and Gold Districts to compensate for other places the recidivist could be. There would be no escape for Monk.

Task force S-6319 was now more eager than ever before to acquire this Dilictor Ignotum. For the first time since leaving the UPA, they had a solid connection to their previous hunt for Knox Mortis. Volk Downey was filled with renewed vigor and leapt at the opportunity to detain Monk first, ignoring the orders of doctors. He relied on the compensators of his battle plate to hold his posture and suppress the pain still lingering in his loins. The Grigorian Administration was a much larger area with a vast number of places to hide, so they were dispatched to the college to reinforce the Veil operatives.

Warden Downey kicked in the door to Monk's office. A stack of parchments flew off the top of his oaken desk as Volk cocked the barrel of his Blakavit. He leered with a troop of a few black and white armored soldiers at his rear. Nobody was inside.

Inquisitor Blackwell breached every classroom and lecture hall he taught in. He spun his wardiron bastard sword in his right hand as he held his gold painted Reisinger in his left. Each entrance he made, his fingers itched to pull the handgun's trigger. He was eager to take down Monk. Every ornately decorated door he opened, he held his breath in anticipation, silently willing his quarry to be behind it. It never worked.

Retriever Ram's Horn took to the public transit station. The mag-rails came and went, withdrawing and depositing a number of students. Half asleep eyes perked up in awe at the sight of the metal man who towered over them all. The ivory horns of his helmet were easily visible over the heads of the crowd. His cold enamel eye slits scanned every face, every head of hair, every tone of skin as he watched, looking for a match to Thomas Monk. Only his neck moved for the duration of the Scourge's raid on the Administration.

Inquisitor Covalos cleared all of the laboratories that he worked in. He yearned to kick in doors and crack skulls to get at the suspected Dilictor. However the volatile nature of the chemicals that were of easy access required a more delicate approach. Too much force could unintentionally spark a fire or release carcinogens in the air. Restraint was as much a notable attribute of a law officer as brute force was. The gentle and tedious clearing of the six different chemistry facilities brought nothing but ire to the Inquisitor, as they all turned out to be filled with students who hadn't seen Monk all day.

"Exarch Surizal, come in." Adastra bellowed over his communicator. Surizal was supposed to bring Monk in for questioning last night. That was before he knew he had a direct connection to Palladium. He had tried reaching him on his wavelength twenty times. Now, he was feeling more confident that something horrendous happened.

"Damn it Zedekiah, if you can hear me Thomas Monk is to be treated as the Dilictor. If you see him take him into custody, lethal force is authorized." He switched to the public Scourge wavelength. "Does anybody have a visual on Zedekiah Surizal?"

A flurry of negative responses echoed through his audio wire to further his frustration. "Adastra, when was the last time you saw the Exarch?" Volk's voice called out in his ear as he stepped into the hallway.

"He was with me yesterday when we went to question the lodge, which turned out to be a straw man. He was supposed to bring Monk in and question him about the bomber."

"That looks bad." Vandross said over the com-array after storming out of the fifth lecture hall he and his troop of Veil soldiers cleared. "Of course, this just makes Monk look even guiltier than before. I'm sure he can handle himself."

"Anybody got a line on the professor?" Volk asked openly. A number of confirmed negatives echoed in response to his call out. He sighed as he gripped onto his temples. Then he realized that there was one man that hadn't responded at all. "Herald Du'Plasse do you copy?"

"I hear you Warden." Oslin's voice chimed with a faint muffle of static interference. "I've got no sight of our target...then again I... hard...below."

"Oslin you're breaking up." Adastra bellowed growing concerned. "Where are you?"

"In the...Dalton...." Static shrouded his voice even further. "Evi... waste..."

"Dalton Hall." Volk pondered aloud. "I'm in the upper floors of Dalton right now. Oslin where are you?"

A haze of incomprehensible muffling answered the Warden. "Volk you need to find Du'Plasse immediately." Vandross said worriedly. "We can't risk whatever happened to Surizal happening to him too."

"I'm close by too."Adastra responded. "I'll be there soon. Vandross, Ram, keep scanning the campus for Monk. If he's here we can't let him get away."

Oslin Du'Plasse was alone in the underground levels of Dalton Hall. The chemistry building used its lowest level for storage of hazardous materials. A dark and inert chamber, isolated from the rest of the Administration provided the perfect environment to ensure no volatile reactions ensued or carcinogens sluiced out to the populous. On a coldly calculated hunch, the Herald believed it would be the optimum place for a serial killer to keep his secrets. Only a select few professors and custodians had access to the basement of Dalton. There were no security surveyors to collect who came and went. Also, it was dark and private. What better place existed on such a populous campus?

Oslin opened up an electronically sealed door with an algorithm from his historian's tablet. Magistrate Walthune's gift was proving to be a much more useful tool than just a technological pad to scribble down every dialogue as the force's stenographer. A harsh stench of chemicals wafted out of the dank metal antechamber.

"All units," Oslin called out to his microphone, regardless of the fact that he figured at this point it was in vain given the depth underground he had traversed. "If you can hear me I'm inspecting the basement of Dalton. I hope to find solid evidence so we can lock Monk up indefinitely." He winced slightly the pungent aroma beat at his senses. "I don't like the look of this. Send reinforcements."

Oslin unfurled his Beacon banner. The gold colored fabric unrolled and lumen strips woven within the flag illuminated the otherwise lightless chamber. He twisted the flaksteel grip, ready to plunge the spear tip at the top into a target should one arise. He brandished the battle-banner in his right hand and kept his father's Holt held tightly in his left.

The chemical storage chamber was eerie, like something out of an old ghost story. The sickening stench of a conglomeration of various harsh materials was enough to send an untrained man retching. Oslin's Scourge training strengthened his digestive system so he would not so easily be deterred by distractions such as scent. The brooding darkness could not entirely be purged by the radiant illumination cast out from the banner. Shadows cast by large plastic barrels and translucent glass storage cubes gave the ambiance as though ghosts were prowling inside of them. Du'Plasse had always considered the Inquisition paranoid. A stereotype promulgated that they often saw spirits where there were none. He bit his lip nervously as he began doing the same thing.

There were hundreds of containers in this facility. Columns of unlabeled slurries were placed alongside crates of chalky powders. All substances were simply resting and waiting for disposal by trained professionals. It would take Scourge forensic agents weeks to process and identify all that was in this compact chamber. Oslin couldn't afford that level of time. If they wanted to prosecute Monk expeditiously, he would need irrefutable evidence as soon as possible.

A large tankard caught Oslin's attention. It looked like a petrol cylinder it was so massive. The rusty steel case looked like it could hold three or four hundred gallons of fluid. Why would a university require a vessel with such capacity? Oslin swallowed nervously as he approached the tank. He made sure his weapons were ready to kill as he peered closely at the label on the cylinder. A pristine plastic sticker labeled 'NaOH Basic Waste: Ph 10+' was melted onto the craggy metal surface like a wax seal. Herald Du'Plasse was no chemist, but he knew such materials were corrosive. Another hunch began inkling in his mind.

Oslin magnetically locked his banner to his back. It was comforting to hold such a brilliant source of brightness so close, but such comfort was as much an illusion as the ghosts stalking him in the shadows. His golden immotrum hands gripped onto a cold ladder on the flat end of the cylinder. He hoisted himself to the top of the tankard and looked for a hatch. Surely enough, at the center of the curved top there was an air tight valve lock. Du'Plasse's armor began humming and pumping out steam as it read his adrenal levels. A bead of icy sweat dripped from his platinum brow as he walked to the hatch.

The safety mechanisms required two hands to undo. He begrudgingly holstered his pistol as his fingers locked around the cog-wheel. He struggled to open the hatch, even with the power couplings and force pistons in his armor. The force required to twist this hatch open required a nigh inhuman level of strength. The normally silent battle plate hissed and whirled, filling the basement with ominous sounding shrieks. After the final lock clicked, he slowly pried the hatch open. Noxious vapor rushed out of the air tight vessel. Oslin's blue eyes reddened and watered at the stinging sensations that attacked his senses. A cacophony of swirling chemicals attacked his nostrils and he briefly felt as though he was suffocating. A tinge of iron and copper stuck to his tongue. He leered inside the tank through the tears forcing their way out of his eyes. The light of his banner revealed some fluid that rose to half the capacity, though the light would not reveal any other details.

Du'Plasse looked to see that he had drawn his Holt unconsciously. He was thankful to have his pistol, it made him feel safe. The hatch was big enough that if he were to lose his balance he could fall through. With his free hand, he removed a glow rod from his belt. It hummed as the electric light came to life, though was practically useless in the presence of his banner. It would serve his need well enough.

The Herald let the glow rod fall inside of the chemical vat. The light hit the upper edges of the tank before sinking into the fluid. Then it sank with a wet splash into the viscous slurry, illuminating the admixture. It was revealed to be a syrupy pool of chunky red matter. Rubbery gobs of liquid flesh and flakes of bone were visibly being eaten by the corrosive fluid. Dark spots stewed within the crimson concoction that could only have been large portions of organs and bones that were too stubborn to be completely dissolved. Oslin was unable to contain the vomit racing from his gullet. The only control he had over his bowels was to direct the bile away from the evidence so as not to taint the soup of gore. To his displeasure, he had found exactly what he was looking for.

Daphne Wainwright charged through the doors of Thomas Monk's estate. It was a quaint little manor in the Bronze District which was a homely and welcoming facility. Olive wood panels were matched with porcelain shutters creating a calm atmosphere. It began to look like war zone. Black and white armored soldiers, under the Bride's command, seized the household of the professor with fervent zeal.

The interior was just as charming as the outside. Thin polyester rugs and hand crafted paintings decorated the dark wood halls. They were tainted with the abundant presence of debris and splinters from blasting charges spontaneously burning through every door in the manor. Scourge declarations were yelled at shocked menials and servants as the Veil quickly stormed Monk's home. Tails of white vapor whipped around the frosted rapier in Wainwright's hand. She led the charge of her soldiers, acting as a glittering white juggernaut of flaksteel clear into Professor Monk's study where he sat at a personal computer.

The bronze haired man pushed the spectacles up his nose at the sight of Daphne and her cavalry. He didn't seem shocked at their presence even as more Veil warriors flooded into the small study. His blank expression baffled them all. Bride Wainwright was detested at his nonchalant attitude. Any innocent man would be on his knees, as their declarations demanded, begging for mercy.

"Thomas Monk," Daphne said, her sword venting cold vapor. "You are under arrest. Evidence has been brought to light that suggests you are the Dilictor Ignotum of Hrimata informally known as the Nitral Nightmare. Your compliance is appreciated, but not necessary."

The professor adjusted his collar to further display a violet flower pendant at the base of his neck. "Yes of course." He said neutrally as he stood up from his seat. "I was wondering when you lot would come knocking. So, what led you here?"

"In 2706, you and Regulom Palladium were the sole sponsors for the 23rd Constantinians. He was a major person of interest in a Shackle manhunt. We found it a little suspicious that one of your students just happened to have been possessed and murdered dozens of people."

"Yes of course, I heard that Regulom was killed in the attack. A pity he won't be around to see the abolition. I had hoped we would both reign together, but what do you expect? He never had the vision that I did. His fascination with technology worship and inability to see beyond this world hindered his ability to innovate."

"Stop talking." Daphne stepped forward and pressed the point of the frigid sword at his chest, ready to impale him at a moment's notice. "I don't know what bilge you're on about. We will sort this out in a Veritas Chamber."

"I doubt it." Thomas Monk leered at the surrounding Veil officers with a sharp scowl. Including Daphne, there were seven Veil officers in his study. "Would you be a dear and take the weapon off of my sternum?" He gave a cocky grin and nodded towards the blade.

"Give me one good reason I should do that." She demanded. Her ire was building, frustrated at the lackadaisical attitude of her suspect as well as the cryptic manner Monk was speaking in. What kind of Dilictor would do something as arrogant as demand that she remove her weapon?

Something was awry. Daphne was showing great restraint by not running him through with the blade, exercising her regimented Scourge discipline. She felt her arm lower at Monk's demand. Her blood ran cold as she realized that she unwittingly complied with the suspect's order. A sharp chill loomed over her, as though liquid argon were leaking from her sword directly into her plate. Every fiber of her will was focused on ordering her soldiers to open fire on Monk. She could not even do that. They looked bewildered at each other in search of some guidance, completely unaware that Daphne Wainwright was no longer in control of her own body.

"Yes of course," Monk smiled methodically as he realized that Daphne was under his control. "I suppose I have no choice but to submit to your authority."

Daphne chain-cuffed Monk's arms behind his back. She used the standard gruff level of roughness that she would with any prisoner, but it was entirely out of her will. Her thoughts shrieked in her brain. Kill commands, screams of terror, and pleas for help all rang out unheard as Daphne Wainwright was a prisoner in her own flesh.

"Remain, gather as much evidence as you can." Daphne's voice said, but it was not her mind that spoke of its own accord. "I'm taking him to Niflheim."

The Veil warriors all nodded and began going about their business to process the crime scene. Meanwhile, Daphne was puppeted by Thomas Monk out to a simple prisoner transport chariot. She walked him out with a cheeky grin on his smug face. She begged and pleaded with every officer that she passed while escorting her prisoner out. Not a word left her lips. A small detail went with her into the back of the transport chariot.

Professor Monk kept his wicked grin as two Veil soldiers sat down next to her in the back of the transport. Daphne's icy blood ran as her anxiety levels spiked. Her hand slammed the pilot's door, indicating they were clear to depart. The chariot dispatched and began its course towards...she didn't know where. Who else was under Monk's rule? Could anybody be toyed with and automated as one of his pawns? There was no possibility of being certain.

"Daphne..." Monk said. "Would you kill these two escorts please?" The two men in the back of the chariot chuckled, thinking it was a desperate ploy. Within seconds of the command, the enchanted Bride slashed and stabbed them with her rapier, staining the white of their armor red. Their bodies plopped down and moments later, she found herself undoing the locks of the chain-cuffs. "Thank you darling. Now, if you don't mind I'm going to relinquish a little control over you. It's horribly exhausting. Just know that I can make you do anything I want. You're going to follow my orders to the letter." He leaned in close to whisper into her ear. "If you don't...I'm going to violate your flesh in manners you didn't even think possible."

CHAPTER 27

Flood lights were illuminating the basement of Dalton Hall now. Forensic officers in the uniform of the Veil were inspecting barrels of waste for additional organic matter. A vast number of the scientists were gathered around the rusted metal basin where Herald Du'Plasse discovered the liquid mass grave. Samples were taken of the soupy mess of dissolved tissue and bone to test for genetic signatures. Even Oslin's vomit from his initial discovery was recovered.

Expurgator Blye oversaw the data harvest. He orbited from Monk's office, to the labs he worked in, before finally ending in the basement. He smiled at the wealth of information that was being gathered. The more documents and pieces were gathered, the stronger the case against the professor seemed. One of the most damning pieces was the thirty four gallons of Nitrosluice, the drain cleaner used to scrub the disposed bodies, were found in the assorted labs. That discovery was eclipsed by the vat's discovery. Four months of pained hunting for this Dilictor was coming to a swift close. Yen felt a glimmer of pride welling in his chest, making his face rise in a wide grin, excited at the thought of receiving praise from the Bride. That grin was slapped away by the chemical stench of Dalton's basement.

Blye gagged slightly as he walked over to Herald Du'Plasse who was standing by Inquisitor Blackwell and Warden Downey. "Mr. Du'Plasse," the Expurgator spoke. "Congratulations on the find."

"Thank you, I suppose." Oslin said, the tang of stomach acid lingering on his tongue.

"Bride Wainwright is bringing in Thomas Monk as we speak. We have enough evidence here to bury him. The forensic officers tell me that the tankard contains at least fifteen bodies, what's left of them at least. I am still lost on something though. Why bother scrubbing bodies with drain cleaner and dumping them in the sewers?"

"It might have something to do with his demonic influence." Vandross interjected. "That is if he was the one who used magick in the bombing two days ago."

"What do you mean?"

"The Mundus Imago thrive off of turmoil. Fear breeds sin and depravity, which dark spirits love to wallow in. Perhaps Monk just wanted to sow terror to keep Hrimata afraid."

"That is assuming he's the demoniac on campus." Downey entered in. "Maybe he just disposed of those bodies as a means to distract from his real killings. If he's been active for almost a year as you think he has, there's a lot more than just the eight known women and now God knows how many more in this tank."

"But how does Kite fit into this?" Oslin said toying with a braid of his hair. "Why did Victoria Thruian name him the Nitral Nightmare?"

"Monk's a magick wielder." Vandross said removing his pipe and then quickly stowing it realizing he had no clue what volatile materials surrounded him. "He must have kidnapped and tortured her for no other reason than to throw us to a scapegoat."

"It's as solid a theory as any." Yen said. "I suppose all that's left is to get a confession from Monk via Veritas Chamber and we'll put an end to this hunt. I'd like to thank you gentlemen for your assistance. Where are the other two of your company?"

"Ram's Horn is coming in from the trail station." Volk said. "Adastra's up top trying to get in touch with Bride Wainwright. There's no signal down here."

Adastra Covalos paced back and forth in Professor Monk's office. He was inspecting the books shelved behind the desk for any indication of blasphemous words. A spellbook or pages detailing Imago rituals would further serve to prosecute the Dilictor, and an agent of the Inquisition would know best how to handle the wicked documents. The Inquisitor often found himself having to resist the urge to burn the words at first sight, having to withhold the purging due to their evidentiary nature.

A flush of static filled his ear. His communication wire buzzed idly as he tried to connect to Daphne Wainwright. He wanted to congratulate her primarily on the capture of her quarry, but he also wanted to ask about Zedekiah. The Exarch had gone missing going to question Thomas Monk, so he would be the most likely person who would know his whereabouts. Adastra knew that the longer he was missing, the less likely he would be found alive. He wanted to have Daphne pressure him prematurely so he could search for him.

"This is Bride Wainwright." Her voice rang in his ear after a few tedious moments of sifting through papers.

"Daphne, it's Adastra." He responded. "Congratulations on your capture. It's good to have this monster off the streets."

"Thank you." Her voice was uncharacteristically bland and void of her usual energy. "Do you have something to report?"

"We've found a lot of evidence here suggesting Monk's our Dilictor. There's a five hundred gallon cylinder of sodium hydroxide containing the corroded remains of at least fifteen people. There's still no sign of Exarch Surizal. I fear Monk may have taken his life. Would you mind asking the professor about it?"

"I suppose, but he doesn't seem like he wants to talk right now." Wainwright's voice was emotionless. "I plan on working on him once we get to Niflheim. He'll be singing in no time."

"Are you feeling alright Daphne?" Adastra inquired, concerned that something was off. "You don't sound like yourself."

"I'm fine Adastra." She responded curtly. "Is there anything else you need?"

"I suppose there's nothing else."

"Good. I'll see you when I return to the home field. Until then, consider me occupied with the prisoner."

Adastra concealed a gasp at the statement. "Understood Daphne, if you need anything let me know."

Adastra did not break the connection. Rather, he let her sign off first. He let the chatter of blank static fill his mind for a long moment as he processed what had just happened. Outwardly, his face was locked in a horrified stare. His jaw slacked open with shock. In a sudden flash of urgency, he barreled out of Monk's office.

He knew something was off with his old friend. She always had an air of joyful music in her voice, even in times of hardship. It was a small detail that only those that knew her intimately could discern. Its absence was a red flag. Especially now after capturing a highly sought after quarry, one would expect the Bride to be ecstatic. What was a clear indicator that something was most certainly wrong was the final sentence. Back during their training at the Deficio Tribulation twelve years ago, the phrase "home field" was used as a distress call sign during a practice exercise. He had used it when the two worked an undercover mission in Constantinople three years prior. Now she was using it again. Inquisitor Covalos knew for certain that Bride Wainwright was in grave danger.

Daphne Wainwright was forced to strip off her battle plate, leaving a simple black bodysuit. Thomas Monk killed the transport chariot's driver, or rather he made Daphne do it for him, and commandeered another off the road. Somehow, he was in control of her body. He was even able to make her speak words to Inquisitor Covalos over her radio bead. The warlock, or whatever the proper terminology was, was not able to take complete control of her mind. She was able to pass their old distress signal to him. She prayed that he remembered it, else it could be days until someone realized what had happened.

The Bride's vision blurred, her eyes grew cloudy. Her head spun as though she were suffering from intense vertigo. She didn't know where she was, having no sense of direction or being. Foul magick obscured every one of her senses, creating a kind of fog that swallowed all light and sound. Nothing but the sound of her own heart pumping pounded in her eardrums. Sweat began pooling at her brow and her blood pressure spiked. She hadn't felt this helpless since the day her innocence was stripped from her.

The haze lifted from her senses as suddenly as it appeared. Her vision and hearing returned, but that was not much consolation. She found herself strapped to a wheeled chair in a musty chamber. Vivid light barely showed the disturbingly smiling face of Thomas Monk, a shimmer of cold light glistening off of the lenses of his glasses. She struggled to break free of the hard plastic restraints that wrapped around her limbs and torso. The pathetic attempts to escape made her realize that she had a puncture wound from a syringe in her arm. Based on the unnatural weakness in her arms, she determined some narcotic was present in her system.

Faint light glowed in from all around. Not enough to determine the location or surroundings, rather all illumination was designed to draw focus on the macabre displays that were resting on featureless steel bench tops. Grisly masses of flesh floated in pulpy brines. Swollen fetuses, warped organs, and indistinguishable lumps of blistered tissue bobbed lazily in the embalming fluids inside of meticulously labeled glass jars. Sealed glass fume hoods displayed lines of vials containing suspicious fluids. Other glass cases contained living specimens of grotesquely mutated rats, pigs, or chimps while others were littered with similarly warped cadavers, several of which were little more than viscera soaked chunks. Daphne had to suppress her own tears of terror and churning vomit at the sheer horror. Thomas Monk simply wheeled her past the organized carnage, blissfully humming an eerie tune.

The fuzz around her mind reformed, although at a less extreme magnitude. She noticed the plastic bonds snap open. Every nerve in her body fired rapidly with a futile effort to flee. Against her own desires, she stepped out of the wheeled chair to lie down across a cold steel table. Monk continued to ominously hum the same shrill tune as he produced thick metal clasps and began clamping her hands and feet down. The preternatural haze lifted away once more after she was exceedingly restrained.

"Apologies for the awkward treatment my dear." Monk said as he turned from the table and began rummaging through a cabinet at the far end of the dimly lit chamber. "I'll admit, I had hoped giving you Mr. Kite would buy me a significantly greater period before you came for me. Yes, of course. I was incorrect though."

"Cyrus...you framed him." Daphne was barely able to say, her lungs struggling to catch breath under the weight of her own numbed muscles. "How?"

"It was a clever ploy, yes? I can't take the credit however, that was Kortham's idea. A few moderations of the hippocampus, amygdala, and temporal lobe and Madame Thruian was fully convinced your Agapist kidnapped her. I even specifically named him the Nitral Nightmare and she bought it. You imbeciles ate it up, too. But... here we are." Monk turned to face the table she was clamped onto, rolling a cold steel table with an assortment of shimmering tools atop it. "I am curious though, how did you connect it back to me? I was certain the Kite case would have bought me another few weeks, yet you came for me the same day. I'd be impressed if I wasn't so irritated. Pray tell, how did you know about Palladium?"

"So, who beat you, mommy or daddy?" Bride Wainwright had no interest in playing Monk's sick game. Instead she called upon her skills as a profiler to expose Thomas Monk for the unstable weakling he truly was. There was clearly childhood trauma concealed inside of the professor's mind and she aimed to exploit it. Based on the twitching at the corner of his eye and mouth, she had struck the proper nerve.

"We're not talking about me." The Dilictor snarled clearly offended by the question. "Why don't you tell me how you made the connection between Regulom and I?"

"I'm going to guess father." Daphne needed to knock this man off his composure. She knew that she had no hope of getting out of this herself. What she needed was time. She had a radioactive isotope tracker embedded under the nape of her neck. Throwing off the circadian nature of this sick ritual would delay whatever twisted things he was preparing to do, hopefully long enough for the cavalry to arrive. "He beat your mom too, didn't he? Based on your compulsion to overpower women I'd venture to guess you're subconsciously trying to emulate him."

"That bitch never did anything! She just let him smack me around!" Monk lashed out with his words after slipping on a set of membrane gloves on. He slammed a latex skinned hand on the side table, shaking the assorted needles and sensors. He closed his eyes and breathed deeply to regain his composure. "So you're trying to probe my mind are you? Trying to get inside of my head and poke around until you find something? I've done this too many times to fall for such an elementary trick."

"I simply assumed your sadistic desires to dominate young women had something to do with your own insecurities. That is why most men lash out in a sexual nature the way you have."

Monk laughed scornfully as he placed suction cup sensors onto Daphne's temples. "You still think that is where my motivation lies? Pathetic. Laughable. Your ignorance knows no boundaries! What kind of petty criminal do you think I am, dabbling in trivial pleasures of the flesh like those? You truly don't know what it is I do."

"Enlighten me." She said through gritted teeth trying to find some way to shake the sensors from her head, to no avail.

"I never cared about those women. They were of no consequence to me or my goals. I only ever took them as a means to appease my partner Kortham. He's the one who demanded I let the bodies be found instead of melting them down like I did the rest. The rich pool of fear has been quenching my Imago tutor's thirst. I never even particularly enjoyed raping those pawns. I just did it so Kortham would continue revealing new information."

"You're a demoniac?" Daphne's muscles were growing heavier, as though the sedative in her blood was growing stronger.

"Yes of course, perhaps in the eyes of the bloody Inquisition, but I prefer the term scientific pioneer. Auzlanten and you Scourge cronies are so quick to dismiss the Mundus Imago as evil spirits. I see them as they truly are...an undiscovered species. You cling to your paltry philosophy and morality, but they are delusions of your fanaticism. The Faith is a lie. The only truth is that of scientific innovation and discovery. Had I my way, you would never find as much as a drop of waste from my experiments. All I am doing is opening humanity's eyes so that we may see reality in a new light."

"I believe I've heard that sentiment before. The first one to utter the suggestion was a serpent."

Monk laughed passive aggressively. Bride Wainwright was successfully chipping away at his sophisticated composure. He produced a syringe from a plastic case. The glass needle was filled to the brim with a clear fluid. "Hold still now. I'd hate to damage you any further than I have to."

Regent Invictus Illuromos sat behind the stained wood desk performing the tedium of financial management. As the mortal leader of the Scourge, it was his duty to ensure each branch's monetary needs were fulfilled. Three hundred monarchs to an Arcae in the Polar Wastes, two royals to Patriarch Betankur's rehabilitation programs, and several other uninteresting transactions were displayed in front of him by holographic runes. He struggled to keep his eyes open as his ebon clad fingers danced across the display. He sighed, quietly yearning to be a foot soldier again. He hadn't seen combat since the conclusion of the Civil Strife over four years ago.

A faceless figure in silver battle plate approached the Regent. The light of the four pyres at the four corners of the chamber reflected off of the mirror sheen of the Centurion guard. "Lord Regent," The man's mechanical voice spoke. "Prelate Greyflame is requesting entrance to your quarters. He claims it is urgent."

Invictus grabbed his hairless head and let out a deep breath. He knew what this was going to be about. Prelate Greyflame had issued an identical edict to that of High Conservator Bethel's which would require all soldiers to undergo Veritas interrogation to ensure loyalties were in place. He was unhappy with the number of traitors in the Inquisition. Terran Greyflame had joined in alongside Jude Bethel's paranoia, exactly what he hoped would not come of the deceiver's efforts. At least this was a more pressing matter than accounting. "I grant him access." He bellowed.

The Centurion bowed slightly and went over to the entrance. Using the Regent's security carvings, he unwound the security cogs to open the door. Terran Greyflame was already on the other side, a deep scowl across his face. "Brother Prelate, enter." Invictus called without standing from his desk. "Kindly give us the room." He directed to his security guard. The silver warrior nodded and stepped out behind the Prelate entered.

Terran held a small wooden box in his hand. The thin sheets of gold dangling from his armor crinkled like leaves in the wind as he stepped across the room. He kept his sharp chin up high, almost as if he were looking down on Invictus, which he could never have done were he standing.

Prelate Greyflame sat down in a cushioned chair directly in front of the Regent's desk as he dismissed the holo-display to be able to look past to the Inquisition's prime. Terran opened the small box, revealing a line of cigars inside. "Care for one?" The bold voiced reverend asked as he bit down on the tip, letting the cigar hang out of his mouth.

"No thank you, Terran." The Regent's voice was calm yet mighty, like a cannonball rolling across a ship's deck. The Prelate shrugged and used an ignate torch to light the cigar. "Might I inquire as to the nature of this meeting? I wasn't expecting to see you in person for another two months."

A trail of pungent smoke lulled out of his mouth, ironically like a cloud of grey fire. "I fear for the Scourge's purity. There is no doubt some vast conspiracy at play and our fair army has been unable to remain untainted."

"You are referring to the traitors exposed by Bethel's edict?" Invictus leaned forward, silently thankful that he refused the cigar based on the noxious smell from it. "It's nothing."

"We have exposed nearly five hundred traitors in the Shackle and Inquisition, one hundred of which have affiliation to this Idolacreid thing. I am not one prone to the lure of paranoia, but that hardly sounds like nothing to me."

"You mustn't panic, Prelate," Illuromos said calmly. "The false

Auzlanten is sowing seeds of dissent in our ranks. I fear Jude has fallen prey to it and will not recover...but you need to keep a level head."

"Master Regent..." Greyflame's voice was laden with somber seriousness. "I am approaching you with accordance to Matthew Chapter 18. I believe that you've sinned and I am confronting you on this matter."

Invictus' brow furled as he scowled. "Pray tell, what sin have I committed?"

"I believe you have lied to Jude Bethel." The Prelate let the statement hang for a moment like the sickly scented smoke from the cigar. "Why have you misled your brother?"

"Our mantra is *In Nomine Veritas*, 'in the name of truth.' Ever since our founding at the conclusion of the Reclaiming Crusade, the Scourge has served as agents of the Faith and Templym as the punishers of the wicked. The definition of righteousness and justice are dependent on nothing more than truth, on what corresponds to reality. Hierarchs of the Scourge have always been held to a higher level of accountability than their subordinates, making my lies the most treacherous. I could be excommunicated for lying about where I parked my chariot and I would deserve to be executed for something as immeasurably wicked as misleading one of the primes." Invictus stood from his seat, casting a shadow over the sitting Prelate with his titanic height. Chains shuttered against his black flaksteel plating as his figure dominated the office. Despite the seething rage built from offense at such an accusation, he maintained a steady voice. "You come to me with an accusation of besmirching everything we cling to as an organization? That is not something I take lightly."

"Nor would I expect you to Lord Regent." The Prelate's eyes remained unblinking, the ruby glow of the augmetic meeting the cold steel of Invictus Illuromos unyieldingly. "That is why I am coming to you first to address you on the subject. I would very much like to hear your side of the story before taking this to the other three primes."

"Do you not see what is happening here, Terran?" Invictus slammed his hands on the desk, buckling it despite its massive weight. His voice grew more violent sounding as though a hurricane were brewing in his chest. "Jude is being influenced by false stories the imposter Arodi Auzlanten spun for him. He's then petitioning you to discredit me. How do you not see the wicked machination unfolding before you?"

"I am doing nothing to discredit you." Despite the intimidating picture the Regent was painting with his body structure, Terran Greyflame kept a calm composure and a steady voice. "For all have sinned and fall short of the glory of God." He took another long huff of his foul smelling cigar. "Romans 3:23. We are all fallible, Invictus. I am accusing you of nothing certain at the moment. We are in a dark time my liege, and if you've made a mistake I swear to keep this confidential. Unless of course...you've something of malice to hide. That is the beauty of truth Invictus. The more information is brought to light, the more liberating it is."

The Regent sighed and sank back down into his chair. "What lie do you think I've told Terran?"

"High Conservator Bethel showed me the conversation he had with you before he captured the arms dealer Djinn Balor. Amidst that conversation you claimed he was being influenced by demonic spirits...that was untrue."

"The Inquisition scrubbed that abandoned castle clean. There were Imago trails and demonic rites all over it. Why would you say that I lied?"

"A record of the video showed a twitch at the corner of your eye. I played it back multiple times and concluded each time that it was a tell. I don't know why, but it appeared as though you were knowingly saying an untrue statement."

"A twitch of my eye?" Regent Illuromos chuckled deeply. "You come to me with an accusation that could get me killed based on nothing more than a small tick? I am eighty-five, and despite the alterations Arodi Auzlanten has placed on me, I am still an old mortal. Perhaps my racing pulse caused a brief surge in the corner of my eye."

"With all due respect Invictus, I've experienced many a liar in my service to the Inquisition. I know the difference between a physical malady and an unconscious response to a lie."

"Perhaps what you witnessed was a stress response. The presence of the fake Auzlanten has left me disturbed. When I discovered that Jude Bethel had encountered the doppelganger, I did my best to keep my anxiety suppressed. Perhaps, not entirely well."

Prelate Greyflame looked to the stub of the cigar. It was about a quarter of the way consumed. "That seems a reasonable enough excuse." He looked back up to his leader. "In fact, it almost seems uncanny how you happen to have an explanation ready."

The Regent hung his hairless head in sorrow. "This is what I was afraid of. A schism is being torn in the Scourge before our eyes." He let out another deep breath as he shook his head. He continued. "Are you familiar with the rumors of my origins?"

"The ones claiming that you are a child of Auzlanten?"

"Correct. They are true, in a way at least. I am not a blood descendant, rather he took me in as a foster father. He raised me to aspire to emulate Christ and to be an agent of truth. I took my skills to the Inquisition and to eventually lead the whole Scourge. I've spent years more intimately familiarizing myself with the person of Arodi Auzlanten more so than any other human on the planet. I know the difference between my true father and the imposter masquerading as him. The one in Judah that has planted a cancerous distrust in Bethel's mind...that was not my father. There are things that I cannot tell you for now, but you must trust me as your leader, as your brother."

"I understand Regent." Prelate Greyflame stood from his seat. Ash from his cigar bounced off of his gleaming crimson armor. "I will take this interview into deep consideration. I will continue to investigate the matter, but more importantly pray on it."

The pale skinned preacher turned to walk out. Invictus Illuromos called out to him the moment before he opened up the door to leave. "Terran...no matter what you discover...we can't have a second Strife. Promise me that much."

He looked over his shoulder. His artificial eye somehow mirrored the pained expression in his organic one. "I promise you I will try, Invictus...I can do no more than that."

With those words, Prelate Terran Greyflame stepped out of the Regent's private office in Bastion Prime and back out into the halls. He would mull on this conversation in deep meditation and prayer. The Regent's words were convincing and there were no physical indicators of any lies throughout the interview. When he was a sufficient distance away, he took in one final puff of the cigar he had been gnawing on casually throughout their discussion. The once bitter tasting vapors were now sweet. The smoke that had smelt of decay was now more akin to the scent of warm vanilla. The leader of the Inquisition shuttered at what the detection incense hidden within the cigar was telling him.

CHAPTER 28

Yen Blye gripped his necklace to the point of puncturing the skin on his hands. He was deep in prayer inside of his private office. He was shocked at the discovery of Bride Wainwright's abduction. The story made no sense. Multiple witnesses saw Daphne leading Thomas Monk out and into a prisoner transport chariot. Two hours later, her armor was discovered abandoned twelve miles away from the Arcae alongside the corpses of three Supplicants. Nobody knew where she was. The Expurgator was distraught. The woman he cared for so deeply was in the wind without a trace. Her only hope was that the technologists would be able to lock onto the radiation signature of the isotope implanted beneath her skin. He was desperate. He needed divine intervention.

"Lord...Lord here my plea." He whimpered in a quiet shriek. "My beloved, my Bride is lost and in the maw of a wicked beast. The Dilictor Ignotum has her, the Nitral Nightmare is going to do...oh God... I don't want to think about what he's going to do to her."

He paused as though waiting for a response from the heavens.

"Keep her safe. Don't let Monk take her. Guide the hands of the scientists searching for her radiation signature. I pray that they may discover her location soon. Grant me peace of mind that I may remain focused. Calm my heart that I may act in duty as effectively as possible. Guide my sword and my hand...let me kill Thomas Monk before he takes another's innocence. Let me kill him before he harms my dearest Daphne."

Blood streamed in thick waves out of Bride Wainwright's mouth. She tried desperately to hold her shrieks of pain in. Screaming only made it hurt worse. Thomas Monk had her jaw locked open with a series of sterilized metal clamps. He was sticking needles and pliers into her maw to poke and probe at varying points in her gums. Flecks of red fluid spattered across a clear plastic face mask overtop Monk's face every time she winced or coughed during the surgery, if what was being done to Daphne could even be considered a medical procedure.

Whatever sick smelling ichor the professor had injected into Wainwright's bloodstream was increasing her sensitivity to pain. The fluid, which he had basted directly into her gums, did not itself wrack her body with pain. Rather, the chemical heightened her awareness to what was being done to her. The twisted dental procedure was proving to be a significantly more excruciating experience than it should have been. Daphne saw no methodology to what the Dilictor was doing to her. It seemed as though he was randomly scraping at the roof of her mouth and tugging at her teeth for no other reason than to torture her.

Occasionally Monk would pause from the procedure to place a sample taken from her mouth into a vial. A patch of exposed gum tissue wetly smacked at the bottom of a centrifuge tube which he placed next to a Petri dish with extracted taste buds. After what seemed like an eternity he took a final sample from her the back of her jaw, a single molar. He extracted the tooth with seemingly no effort, paying no heed to the severe winces of pain coming from the Bride, as he yanked it from her mouth.

A spindle of nerves was still dangling from the root of the freshly stolen tooth, still dripping with a froth of saliva and blood. Daphne had had teeth removed before, but only under the influence of narcotics. This time, the exact opposite was being used to amplify the already horrendous pain. Her body let out a howl like the suffering of a dying animal in spite of how desperately she tried to suppress the urge to do so. Thomas Monk looked down from his red shrouded mask and laughed as tears cascaded from her eyes, much like the blood pouring from her mouth. He dropped the molar into a beaker and placed his tools down on his workbench.

The rust haired man removed the neural sensors suctioned to her temples as he began humming that same, disgustingly casual tune.

"You did quite well, my darling." Monk smiled as he dabbed her sweat drenched forehead with a handkerchief. "I've performed this same procedure on a score of men of far greater girth than you and they didn't handle the pain half as well. I wonder if that is the beauty of your Scourge training or if you are just a special lady."

Monk removed the clamps from her mouth to open up the option to speak. Daphne did not respond. The stinging and throbbing in her mouth was overwhelming her ability to speak, or rather, her desire to rain every curse imaginable down on this abominable human being.

"Let's take a look at your BCR results." Monk smiled and patted her sweat drenched cheek with a gloved hand before walking over to the machine where the wiring ended. He strode with an unnaturally chipper energy, especially given the sickly circumstances.

Daphne Wainwright gathered herself swiftly. A thick fog of anguish bombarded her senses, creating a haze over her eyes and ears. She tried to assess the practically lightless surroundings for some indication of location, or at the least to gain a bearing of the amount of time that had passed. There was none. No sunlight pierced this hell hole.

All she could do as the mad scientist tapped away at his machine was to assess her physique. Her mouth was unnaturally tender, but the pounding had softened since Monk had stopped. She hacked a wad of bodily fluids from her mouth and it ran down her chin and all the way to the base of her neck. With her tongue, she felt the new scars that had been given to her. A cavity was now present in the back of her jaw where her molar once occupied, but this could be replaced with a porcelain cap. She felt a sharp stinging at the front of her mouth where a fresh laceration was made. Daphne couldn't see it, but could tell that the cut went from the base of her nose to the top of her chin, splitting her lips asymmetrically. The putrid iron flavor of her own blood dominated her senses, eclipsed only by the creeping fear welling up in her chest.

She suppressed her emotions. She closed her tear drenched eyes and offered up prayers to the Lord. She was no Inquisitor, but she was a devotee of the Faith. The Scourge offers up a plethora of prayers to its soldiers to focus on in times of great strife. She focused on Isaiah 35:4, remembering: "Take courage, fear not. Behold, your God will come with vengeance; The recompense of God will come, but He will save you."

"The bloody hell does that mean!" Daphne broke out of her trance, renewed with a vigor spawned by the Word, as Thomas Monk snapped out vocally at someone. She didn't see anyone or hear another voice. It wouldn't be much of a surprise if he were speaking to nothing. Worse, she remembered he was a demoniac.

"Don't be absurd." The professor continued ranting angrily. "Nobody knows where this facility is, not even this wonderful specimen. I can't pull out now before..." He paused. Daphne couldn't see it due to her being strapped to the cold steel table, but he was gazing off in the distant. One might assume he was enthralled in a daydream if they saw him with no context. "Yes, of course." He rasped thoughtfully. Daphne was growing weary of hearing that phrase crawl out of his mouth. "Damn them all! I'm on the cusp of innovation here! How many times have I done this? I lost count after the sixtieth! I dispatched that Inquisitor already, the Veil has no means by which to get past you. If they come, kill them. Be done with this so that I may..."

Another brief paused as he seemed to listen to someone she couldn't hear.

"This isn't fair!" Monk threw some glass object that shattered immediately upon impact as he continued shouting at nothing. "Look at this data! Her brain is chemically balanced to the eighty fifth percentile. Her bone structure and muscular tissue look as though they've been sculpted by a master craftsman! She could be the mother of the master race."

Daphne didn't think her blood could run any colder. It felt as though her sweat was shards of ice piercing her skin. Monk was discussing impregnating her, forcing her to act as a host for some new generation of children. This couldn't happen. She didn't think she could mentally handle going through this again.

Monk sighed and then clapped his hands together. "I know! I'll harvest the eggs. Even if she's not the new mother of Carthonia, I'll have options." Another pause of silence followed. Bride Wainwright's breath became rapid and her stomach churned. "I'll be done in less than an hour. I'm not risking losing this genetic code." He listened to the void once more. "Fine, I'll just take one. Now monitor the entryway while I prep her for surgery."

Moments passed where the only sound was the panicked gasping from Wainwright's mouth. She struggled to keep calm and assess the situation. She needed to distract her mind from the looming flashes of trauma. Daphne focused on the content of his side of the conversation.

Mother of Carthonia, of a master race? That was an odd way to address her. The phrasing led the Bride on a tangent, a familiar line of thinking that she hadn't addressed in over ten years. Master race...as in a Carthonian master race...like the ones the extinct UNACs believed in.

During the Tyrranis Period, the continental peninsula of Carthonia was dominated by the Ultra Nationalist Alliance of Carthonia. They were eugenicists obsessed with "purifying" the human race by means of genetic manipulation. This included the genocide of those with DNA that was viewed as unfavorable to the UNAC hierarchs. This included people with the wrong shade of hair or skin, people with mental disabilities, and people with the incorrect religious beliefs. They claimed to be irreligious, but in practice, the UNACs worshipped themselves. The ideology of their radical totalitarian regime was obliterated and replaced by Imago worship as the foremost evil in the world at present time. At least, Daphne had thought them to be extinct.

Daphne snapped out of her thoughts as a large glass vial was slammed down onto the side table next to her. Next to it, Thomas Monk placed a plethora of foul smelling chemical solvents and powders in a glass jar. His twisted, devious grin had been knocked away and replaced by an obviously irritated scowl.

"I'm sorry, my darling." Monk sneered. "It seems as though I am forced to terminate my experimentation process and evacuate."

"So how'd you fall into the ranks of the UNACs?" Daphne ignored his sadistic playfulness. It seemed to her that the Dilictor was going to speed up whatever wicked process he was plotting. Daphne needed to buy as much time as she could. She needed to occupy his mind with something else.

He laughed scornfully at her as he began brewing a putrid concoction of formaldehyde and methanol. "So were you listening in on my conversation? Most people would consider it quite rude to eavesdrop."

"Most people would consider kidnapping someone and forcing them into primitive surgery even less polite." It was painful for the Bride to speak. Her mouth had been prodded mercilessly and it still stung. She forced down mouthfuls of blood as it pooled inside of her cheeks, which would only well up the more she spoke.

"Primitive?" Monk was obviously offended by the adjective, just as Wainwright had intended it to be. "Ignorant bitch! You claim to understand the full breadth of my process, yet you know nothing. I am going to revolutionize the human race with the work I've attained. Just look at my publishing from the past year. Look at all of the innovation I have brought into light when I cast aside the trivial ethics system. Dr. Claudberg understood that, and he was taken from the beauteous continent by the wretched witch king Auzlanten!"

"Claudberg? Doctor Wilhelm Claudberg? It shouldn't surprise me that you draw inspiration from the UNAC scientist that perfected their chemical arsenal. How could you idolize the man responsible for the deaths of millions of Carthonians?"

"All expended during his process were not true Carthonians. They were naught but stains on the perfect race to be scrubbed away. He utilized them to perfect the weaponry of the glorious UNAC Empire. Never in history has there ever been a military force as finely honed as they!"

"Ironic then," Daphne couldn't help but chuckle painfully, "that they did everything in their power to build up the most powerful arsenal of weaponized gasses in history, only to have Arodi Auzlanten wipe them off the face of Carthonia by a similar means."

"Funny." Monk growled as he squeezed a glass bottle of some unknown chemical so tightly that it shattered in his hand. Splinters of glass ripped at his hand opening fresh wounds for the opaque fluid to flow into. There was a hiss of gas releasing that was eclipsed by a pitiful screech of pain from the professor. He howled with a mix of rage and pain as he rushed to a sink in the corner and allowed cold water to douse the sting. Thomas Monk was right handed, and it was this one that had fallen victim to the accident. Daphne chalked this up as a victory. Whatever devious procedure the Dilictor was planning for her, it would be delayed with the advent of his hand being crippled.

Daphne suppressed a laugh, not for the sake of her captor's ego but because of the lingering pain from the previously inflicted procedure. "Are you feeling quite well Mr. Monk? That sounded dreadfully painful."

"Quiet!" He snapped. Diluted blood rushed down the drain as the tap water washed away the chemicals peeling away the flesh of his hand. He used a towel to dab at his incised palm. His fingers were curled in knots, wracked with pain.

"I do hope you didn't need that substance. How horrid it would be if you lost a necessary component for the solution you were concocting."

"I said quiet!"

"How awful it would be if you came so far and so close to your goal, only to have your plan thwarted by your own irrational temper."

Thomas Monk yelled no more. Instead, with his unblemished hand, he plunged a scalpel into Daphne's left shoulder. A froth of saliva forced itself out of the corner of the professor's mouth as thick blood shot out of her shoulder. She winced in pain as her vein was popped open.

"You talk too much." His voice was cold and unforgiving. The dark joy was completely gone, replaced by roiling anger and seething hate. He felt no reason to toy with her any longer.

Monk jabbed a syringe into Wainwright's neck and shoved the plunger down. A rush of pharmaceuticals was pumped into her bloodstream. She immediately felt hazy again. Her senses began fading away at the presence of the drug. As her vision clouded, the Dilictor's voice began to echo in her mind as though impossibly distant, even though he was only inches away. She heard one last sentence from the sadistic scientist's mouth before everything went black.

"Rest well little lady. You likely won't wake."

CHAPTER 29

Technologists in the Seraphim Solace were able to locate the source of Bride Wainwright's radiation tracker within four hours of her disappearance. She was declared missing the moment Adastra Covalos signed off with her. She was located in a vacant office building in the Platinum District. It was believed that she was underground based on the weakness of the radiation signature. Scourge forces were rallied immediately after.

Twenty minutes after this discovery was made, a militant force was dispatched. Admonisher Rickard rallied the Maiden militia to rescue their Bride and a small number of Inquisition forces joined them. Expurgator Blye sharpened his set of alabaster bladed short swords and filled his Reisinger with wardiron rounds. At the recommendation of Inquisitors Blackwell and Covalos, the almost alien material would be necessary due to the strong possibility of Imago resistance.

One hundred and fourteen Veil warriors accompanied by seventeen of the Inquisition, not including S-6319, were fully outfitted with wardiron bullets and freshly charged suits of armor. Volk addressed the soldiers communally over the secure wavelength as a line of chariots roared through the polished streets of Hrimata towards their objective.

"Our target is a three story office complex." His thickly accented voice rang in over a hundred ears. "Priority target is the rescue and recovery of Bride Daphne Wainwright and the capture of the Dilictor Ignotum Thomas Monk. Madame Wainwright is to be recovered alive and in optimal condition. Monk is to be detained and captured, though as long as he's cognizant I don't really care how healthy he is. Science boys tell us Daphne's tag is likely somewhere underground, so the bulk of you are going straight to the basement. This building can be cleared in two minutes with no resistance, but don't expect it to be that easy. Demonic forces are probably at play. Nobody go anywhere without an Inquisitor. Squad leaders have your individual assignments. In Nomine Veritas, ladies and gentlemen, let's bring the Bride home." A chorus echoed the Scourge's mantra and the Warden signed off.

The humble task force Downey commanded rode in their caravan along with Admonisher Rickard, Expurgator Blye, and the four female Expurgators who lead the Maiden militia. "We're going straight to the basement." He said vocally to his friends. "Adastra, you have any clue what we're going up against?"

"No idea." He grunted as he slid a whetstone across the blackish blue edge of his greataxe. "We've seen possession capabilities at the college and Daphne could have fallen prey to the same influence. That indicates Imago of Class D+ or higher. There could be multiple, there could be one, no way to tell."

"So we're going in blind." Expurgator Blye said anxiously. It wasn't a question. "Do we have any clue if Daphne's even alive anymore?"

"No." Herald Du'Plasse said plainly as he pulled back the slide of his Holt pistol. "All we know for certain is that her tracker is there. For all we know, Monk could have found the isotope, extracted it, and left it here to bait us into a trap."

"But it's our best bet," Blackwell said adjusting his red immotrum jacket. "She's only been missing for a morning. I have faith she's kept herself alive."

"A lot can happen in a single morning," Blye said with great unease.

"Plague Massacre." Ram's Horn outfitted the knuckle plates of his coal-colored fists with wardiron attachments. His statement created a juncture of uncomfortable silence in the caravan. The Retriever was of course alluding to the fact that the horrific Plague Massacre, which sparked the 14th Purus, and that their ultimate quarry Knox Mortis supposedly had a hand in, began at sunrise and continued ravaging Templym until the start of the afternoon.

Fenrick Rickard broke the awkward pause with a cough before jumping in. "Permission to take point at the charge to recover Bride Wainwright, Warden." He brandished a razor toothed battle axe in his left hand and a motorized wrist-Kimlock in his right.

"Permission granted." Volk responded, thankful that the grim moment had passed. "The Maidens will take point. I've heard nothing but praises about you ladies." Warden Downey directed the compliment to the captains of the all female militia, who returned his friendly complement with cold stares. The caravan suddenly came to a brief halt.

A voice came over the speakers of the chariot. It was the Indentured Inmate Jameson Daurtey, the task force's driver. "We're here."

A storm of black suits of battle plate marched out of the caravans and onto the streets with lightning speed. From above, the Scourge soldiers looked like a swarm of ants on the glossy mosaic sidewalks of Hrimata. They surrounded and approached a short office building of dusty marble with ivory accents. It appeared void of activity, as evident by the paneling against the windows. It was less threatening than an elementary school. One would never think that the Nitral Nightmare himself was executing his evil in this small complex.

Every door was kicked in, every window was shattered through, as the small army forced their way in with ease. To nobody's surprise, the lights were not functional. An excess of Scourge declarations were yelled at empty rooms as the Veil and Inquisition brandished their blades and firearms at no one. Clouds of dust were kicked up by hundreds of flaksteel boots marching with great urgency on the dust-ridden flooring.

S-6319 went alongside the bulk of Rickard's militia. One might assume a violent earthquake was threatening the foundation of the stairwells of the complex. In reality it was the hurried marching of dozens of soldiers that shook the rockfoam steps. Weapons were trained with lethal intent.

Their breath became uneasy when they came to the bottom of the stairwell. The only source of illumination was from the glow rods and torch attachments coming from the warriors. Flecks of dust fluttered like snow as beams of artificial light stabbed at the darkness filling up the dank, fifteen foot high chamber. The only thing in the basement was a shoddy metal service elevator. No elevator existed in the provided architectural schematics. Questions began popping in their heads. Where did this come from? Why was this here? But the most painstakingly obvious: Where did the elevator lead to?

"Move up." Fenrick Rickard's gruff voice chattered through the comms. Static rang in their ears as all radio signals were swallowed by feet of empty earth. "Warden Downey, care to join me to see where this goes?"

"Not particularly," He said with unease. His milky eye seemed to glow slightly in the piercing presence of the lumen technologies. "But I feel obliged to do so for Daphne's sake."

"Agreed." The Admonisher nodded. "Rosebud company with me, Thistle company remain here and secure the entryway. Task force, come with me."

Rickard's plan was altered from their once smooth linear atmosphere. The sharp thudding of metal on rockfoam silenced everyone in the dust coated chamber. It landed directly at Blye's feet... a bloodied helmet standard to the Maiden militia. The metallic clatter was preceded by a wet slosh of liquid. A number of torch lights fell on the source of the splash which was the liquefied head of one of the soldiers standing closest to the elevator. Her headless corpse kicked up a cloud of grey dust which rose halfway up to the ceiling. Not a single human let out as much as a breath at that moment.

A number of spotlights rose up to the previously black ceiling. Nobody thought to look up, as all eyes had been glued to the rusty elevator door. Kortham took advantage in this lapse of judgment. The Imago swiped a tendril at the front most Scourge crony, reducing her neck to a puddle of red pulp.

The thirty or so lights pointed upwards were not enough to illuminate the bulk of this preternatural beast. Its twisted serpentine body undulated illogically, making it appear bulbous and slender and gaunt and muscled simultaneously. Its oily skin glistened with oozing black liquid against its purple scales. It had too many limbs. Legs ended in cloven hooves or lanky paws or avian talons, while its arms, more akin to sinuous tendrils, bore wormy fingers or claws the length of a man's arm, or instectoid stabbers or slithering tentacles. One coiling tendril of unnatural tissue dripped with freshly shed blood, which was being slurped up by five or six writhing tongues from its gaping maw.

The most unholy feature, was its face. Anyone undisciplined by the strict psychological conditioning of the Scourge might fall to the ground and weep out of pure offense to human nature. Its grisly mollusk-like body ended in a mockery of all that is beautiful in the world. Its hooked nose had over a dozen slits that all dilated out of synch. Its bloated red compound eyes fluctuated as they swelled up with pus, only to weep them away in slimy tears. Its unevenly serrated teeth were like icicles splitting open its five-foot long mouth where a swarm of tongues lashed out, each with unholy sentience. How this beast remained so quiet that none felt the desire to angle their gaze upwards is beyond reason, but now that all eyes were on Kortham a guttural belching laugh began churning from somewhere inside the demon's blasphemous body.

There were few seconds of sheer tension. The deafening silence was broken by Inquisitor Vandross Blackwell, who had never seen a physical manifestation of an Imago this horrendous in his twelve years of service to the Inquisition. "Dear God..." He was not able to finish the thought.

The demon's wet chuckle climaxed into an ungodly bellow. Gunfire accompanied the animalistic roaring throe coming from the Mundus Imago. Bullets traced the scaly body's path as it slithered down the ceiling and across the floor with lightning speed. The predator began to butcher its prey, but it would not be taken so easily.

Kortham completed the first horrific moments of the encounter with predatory glee. It stampeded across the dusty floor, trampling two soldiers to death with its massive bulk. With a few swipes of apish hands and feral claws, two more were sliced open. Another was impaled by a sharp chitin spear limb. In less than ten seconds, the demon was already clambering up the opposite end wall, shoving sheets of newly killed flesh into its mouth.

The Scourge was able to land punishment of its own. The swollen monstrosity absorbed a large number of wardiron bullets. Its rubbery flesh, which looked like it should be rigid with bladed scales, puckered with the impact of the salvo. The skin, moving as if it were its own being, threw out the embedded rounds as if spitting them out. The few shots that tore out larger chunks of the sickly dripping hide exposed the bile drenched innards. However, unnatural energies immediately began sculpting the flesh to knit over its wounds like a self-sustaining suture.

"Find the heart!" Adastra Covalos yelled while slamming another magazine into his assault rifle. The demon hunter had debriefed his troupe before they had entered. He educated them on the ways to destroy, or at least banish, Mundus Imago. The first key component was wardiron. This material disrupted the spiritual energies composing their wicked manifestations. Each one had a "heart," which was the epicenter of the unnatural intellect that piloted the body. If one could expose that part of the creature and then slice into it with a wardiron weapon, the beast could be destroyed. This was much easier said than done.

It lurched back from the ceiling to pounce on the Scourge company once again. Each of its writhing limbs swung wildly to scatter blood droplets of their slain allies onto them. It dove down on the Scourge as a bird of prey swoops upon a rat paralyzed in fear. Its pike like teeth ripped a woman in two halves, one of which landed deeper within its gullet. Flailing bioweapons took life with every swing. Admonisher Rickard hefted his toothed axe into a schism already torn within the creature's carapace. The flaksteel blade was powerful, but not enough to cause more than a small divot. The creature skittered away on impossibly light feet, yanking the axe out of his hands. At the same time, Fenrick was knocked fifteen feet by a backswing of its coiling body.

Vandross ran alongside the beast as though it were a passing tram. His bastard sword graced a line down the oily hide almost the entire length down. Adastra locked his sight onto the gash. Just as planned, the incision revealed a glistening mass of colorful light concealed beneath its bilious body. The laceration was glossed over with recently spawned tissue before the Inquisitor could locate the exact location of the heart. Someone needed to expose the demon's life source, but not much more of the strike force would be left with another two passes by the creature.

The Imago's injuries were becoming slightly more apparent. One of its eyes had popped like a pus filled balloon and deflated and its healing factor refused to patch it up, likely diverting energy to more crucial parts of the organism. The sentient skin belched out bullets, but had yet to finish evacuating the previous barrage entirely before the second began. It let out another terror inducing roar from its unhinged jaw as its multi limbed body rushed at the squadron once again.

Unlike the Veil warriors who logically ducked out of the path of the Imago, Retriever Ram's Horn stood in defiance of the charging monstrosity. It was tantamount to standing in front of a locomotive, but the marauder stood stalwart. A thick tendril ending in a bony spike stabbed at the cobalt skinned giant. He spun out of the way at the last second, bringing both hands down in an interlocked *hammer fist* on the demon's head as it snapped at him. The wardiron knuckle attachments amplified the already impressive impact, forcing the blasphemous head of the beast down onto the carpet of bloody dust. Something cracked in the Imago's head, as though whatever crude skull it possessed was fracturing, but it didn't slow its charge. It barreled through the crowd and the titanic force it gave was enough to throw the Retriever off his feet before he was forced to head butt the nearest wall. Meanwhile, Adastra swung his greataxe at a gangly arm that grabbed at his throat, severing it off the monster's body. Even away from its host, the arm wrapped around his leg, trying to kill the Inquisitor but could do nothing more than pull the bone out of its socket, prompting a howl of pain from the normally quiet Inquisitor.

They were thinned to half their numbers and couldn't call for reinforcements from the upper floors. Predictably, Kortham scurried up the walls again to dangle off the ceiling as it gorged the flesh of those it just murdered. Herald Du'Plasse was anticipating just such a moment. As the monster twisted its body, Oslin stuck the spear tip of his banner into the ceiling. The cable retracted, pulling him up with enough speed that the demon didn't realize his prey was becoming predator.

The Herald grappled up within touching distance of its greasy skin. He grabbed onto the axe embedded in its skin that Rickard had sacrificed. He wrenched it out with a splash of sewage- like blood before the living skin sucked it into the black mass of flesh. After letting the axe fall to the ground below, he jammed a grenade into the spewing orifice. He swiftly disconnected the cable from the ceiling so as not to be in the blast radius. This was a shrapnel grenade, but the steel splinters were replaced with shards of wardiron. This created a much more effective result.

The small metallic sphere detonated before the Imago's flesh spit it out. A ball of white fire erupted within the fiend, sending a thousand pieces of the alloy piercing into its unnatural hide. Its gurgling laugh-howl was replaced by what could only be interpreted as a shriek of pain. Black fluid and pieces of scaly meat were hurled at high velocity in every direction. It lost its spidery grip on the ceiling and collapsed like a ton of wet bricks. A large mass of its obtusely curved body was void aside from a sloppy pile of unidentifiable innards and a single swollen mass of bright starlight.

At the epicenter of the Imago's body was a cloud of bright color. In stark contrast to the cold darkness of the basement's chamber, the vibrant mass glowed with bright orange and violet to replicate a distant nebula. Kortham's heart was exposed.

Of those that remained of the strike force, most had been pinned under the spasming creature. The beast flailed indiscriminately as its sinewy limbs knocked about and its wormy body knotted itself up to shield its heart while its skin regenerated. Oslin was able to escape the blast of his grenade but not the collapse of the creature, and was slammed face first into the ground, unknown ichors staining his regal battle plate. Adastra pulled himself against the wall, unable to pop his femur back into place, firing his rifle dry. Ram's Horn and Blye found themselves struggling with some of the gangly limbs, grappling with them and stabbing at them with whatever weapons they had available to keep from being strangled.

Warden Downey looked for an opening. It seemed as though he were the only member of his task force not disposed of at the moment, and the immense pressure of taking this rare opportunity fell to him. He saw Vandross, not fighting with his favorite Natandro pistol and sword style, rather he was wildly chopping at the undulating limbs of the beast with both hands on his sword. Volk assumed that the Inquisitor had fired all of his bullets and was now desperately trying to land the killing blow. Based on the amount of distance the Kalkhanian was gaining and the rate at which new skin was wrapping around the glowing heart, he would not make it. Volk could.

He took half a second to take inventory, one shot left in his Blakavit shotgun, seventy two percent charge in his battle plate, and thirty eight percent charge left in his mace. He poised himself to bolt forward a second later, coordinating his charge with Blackwell's duel. The bastard sword took off another multi-jointed arm and Vandross moved to cut down another tendril. Warden Downey charged forward.

Volk maximized the output on his plate and mace. Pistons and cogs roared as steam vented from the exhaust ports. Joints screamed under the immense speed and pressure he demanded of it. He leapt forward right as Inquisitor Blackwell cut through the base of the only tentacle blocking the path to the freakish beast's heart. As the limb fell, Warden Downey propelled himself over his ally's head. Vandross couldn't help but grin when he saw what the Warden was about to do, but it vanished when a hand he hadn't seen grabbed his ankle and yanked him away.

With his shotgun in one hand and his mace in the other, Volk's flaksteel boots planted onto the slimy carapace of the Imago with a cringe inducing squish. He released every coulomb of his mace's charge in a single fell swoop that connected with the translucent membrane wrapped around the demon heart. Sharp arcs of blue lightning shot out from the bludgeoning weapon. The force of the technologically crafted weapon wouldn't be enough to kill it, but it was enough to disintegrate the living skin blocking him to his goal. Without a second's thought, he plunged the barrel of the Blakavit into the demon's heart and fired his only remaining shell.

Sludge spewed out of the cloud of color as the light flushed out of it. Nauseating odor filled the basement twice as rapidly as the slick Imago blood sloshed onto the black armored soldiers sent to kill it. The dying moans of the creature were no more accursed than its hunting cries. After further spasms and spouting fluids, the creature stood still for the first time since they encountered it. Its rags of still, bullet-ridden skin quickly melted away into thin liquid before just before evaporating in a mist of sulfurous scented gas.

The hellish screams of the now dissociated beast were replaced by the exhausted panting of a dozen soldiers. Thirty four men and women entered this chamber, twenty two laid dead and seven were grievously injured. Oslin Du'Plasse dropped out of consciousness due to a heavy concussion from the force of the demon landing on his head, his golden plate tainted with sludge. Adastra Covalos would require a professional hospitaller to set his leg back into place but was uninjured otherwise. Vandross Blackwell's left arm was dislocated but a simple painful pop snapped it back into place. Ram's Horn had also dropped out of consciousness due to a strangling tentacle that was a second from snapping his neck. Volk Downey and Yen Blye were exhausted but standing. The energy cell of the Warden's weapon was depleted, rendering it useless for the remainder of the raid.

Admonisher Fenrick Rickard remained lying face down in the dust. A trickle of crimson puddled at the base of his neck alongside leaking hydraulic fluids. He would remain there until the mortuary officers would arrive. The force of the Imago's tail whiplashed him so forcefully that his spinal cord was severed by the sudden twist of his neck. The Maidens had wondered why the normally vocal man had been so quiet for the remainder of the sprawl with the Imago. Fenrick was dead, killed in a combat that lasted only five chaotic minutes.

Volk hunched over his knees. He had dropped his empty weapons. The massive corpse had almost entirely evaporated, but the fluid that could only have been the demon's blood stuck to every surface. Viscous strings of oily black dripped down the cobalt flak-steel plates of his armor. He scooped handfuls of the mucus off his bald head with his drenched gauntlets, clearing away his nose and mouth so he could breathe without inhaling the ooze. He sucked in lung-fulls of dusty air, relieved that it was over. He had just killed his first demon.

An out of place sound began resonating through the basement. It was a deep, genuine laugh. Volk turned his gaze over to Expurgator Blye, who was helping to hoist Inquisitor Blackwell to his feet. Vandross was laughing, despite his fine red robes being drenched in black bile and his favorite hat nowhere to be seen. His dangled from him like a dead weight. He extended the arm that was still in place, sticking his thumb up at the gasping remnants of the strike force.

"Good work, team." He panted. "So, where's that elevator go?" His laughter was instantly replaced by a quick shout of pain as Blye forced his shoulder back in place.

Pints of human blood dripped down the cold metal table as Thomas Monk conducted his anathema masquerading as surgery. It was a blessing that Daphne Wainwright was in a drug induced coma. Monk didn't care to use any pharmaceutical to clot the blood flow. He only needed her to be alive long enough to extract what he needed. With a pair of tissue scissors and bone clamps, he conducted his dissection. The Dilictor was looking for the primary source of her genetic coding.

Monk's devotion to Kortham, his Imago tutor and by extension its master the Nephilim, was minor compared to his loyalty to the ancient UNAC Empire. He had always believed that humanity was not fulfilling its full potential. Evolutionary perfection needed to be attained and Carthonia would be the genesis of that development. He had spent years experimenting with human subjects to genetically manipulate mankind in an effort to scrub the race clean of all impurities. He fantasized about having a species free of disease, intelligent above all previous generations, and with the ability to outmatch all other creatures in strength. With the Grigorian Administration's wealth of materials, he could have made great leaps forward into the development of the master race. But the shackles of morality kept him in a stranglehold that kept the resources he needed out of reach, delaying the experiments that would advance the genetic foundations of humanity. So he kept to the shadows, pilfering subjects off the streets and dissolving their remains in strong base to remain undetected. His blend of supernatural and scientific advancements had produced thrilling data.

The master race would require years of clean breeding. The fusion of genetically compatible hosts with the most desirable traits would be needed to usher the new perfect humanity. Thomas Monk always considered his DNA to be suitable for the first half. His cerebellum was developed 18% beyond normal capacity and his bone structure had a 7% increase in tensile strength. Taking these traits into account with his ideal skin, hair, and eye color made him an acceptable candidate.

Part of the experimentation process he involved himself in was attempting to find the optimum female host. Daphne Wainwright had passed the preliminary brain analysis, which most subjects did not. This didn't automatically qualify her to be the mother of the Carthonian master race, but it was a start. Kortham denied him the luxury of additional time to guarantee this. The Scourge was coming. He didn't know how they found him, but he wasn't concerned. Monk realized he just needed to extract the Bride's gametes before leaving.

He just needed one. He rummaged through her exposed innards to find what he was looking for, carefully peeling away layer upon layer of muscle to go deeper into her body to find the genetic treasure he sought after. Finally, he found it. He made one last cut to sever the fallopian tube and clamped down onto the exposed ovary. Monk held his breath as he placed the extracted organ into the preservative flask. He laughed as he observed the healthy organ, full of plump veins and sinewy strands. The ova were key, and there were easily thousands of eggs inside of this biological chamber. He had thousands of molds of potentially perfect clay to sculpt into the next generation of humanity.

The professor sealed the flask with an air tight lock before removing a set of blood drenched gloves. He hummed that same ominous tone as he ran a cascade of water down his reddened arms. He looked over his shoulders at his comatose subject bleeding out on the slab of steel. He could have patched her up, but opted not to. He had all he would ever need from her and loose ends were problematic. She would bleed to death in a matter of minutes. He considered it a pity though. She was so beautiful yet so resilient. She could have been the template to dozens of revolutionary experiments. He smiled when he saw the extracted ovary, knowing that she very well could still do so.

Thomas did think it strange that Kortham was not speaking as much as he normally did. Usually, the Imago whispered sweet wisdom in the back of his mind as he operated. Perhaps he was preoccupied with other matters on the spiritual plane. If he was running short on time, his tutor would warn him. The professor considered the different possibilities that her various organs could serve in the future and thought of what he might have time to harvest before the Scourge arrived.

Then something was wrong. He was shuffling research papers and a few data slates into a plastic box for transportation before stopping cold. Words couldn't accurately describe the specific feelings. It was as though a metaphysical umbilical cord was severed before he knew how to use his own lungs. Some addictive presence that had been with him, that Monk had grown dependent on, was suddenly no longer there. His fingers went limp and the papers lazily fluttered to the ground next to a shattered tablet. After his fingers, his legs gave way.

He fell to the floor, his body wracked with pain. He found himself sluggish and unable to move as though someone drained every drop of adrenaline from his nervous system. It was paradoxical how he could feel nothing and an eternity of pain simultaneously. Monk knew exactly how to diagnose this problem. The Imago presence that he had latched onto for so long was gone. He had grown so used to hosting Kortham and letting his tutor pilot his body that having it absent now was alien to him. His Imago tutor was gone.

Monk tried to squirm on the floor, desperate to gain his bearings. He couldn't lift as much as an arm by himself. He felt like a beached whale, lethargic and incapable of higher motor functions. A pathetic whimper emanated from his throat. It was supposed to be a boisterous scream to bolster his futile effort to stand. His limbs were essentially wet rags.

After a small amount of time, his pitiable moaning was interrupted by the ding of the elevator. Somebody was coming into his laboratory. He tried to crawl into a nearby vent, but was unable to even turn on his stomach. As the creaking metal doors slid open in the unseen distance, it was followed by the clattering of metal on metal. Armor plated boots were carrying a squadron of soldiers to him who would undoubtedly ruin all of the progress he had made over the past twenty years. He yelled out in a frustrated cry at the realization that his life's work was collapsing around him, but the scream came out as little more than a sickly yawn.

Monk realized that his spectacles had fallen off as he had slipped to the floor they poured into his operating room. They appeared to him as little more than blurs of metallic black with white splotches. A number rushed over to the table where Daphne was bleeding out, calling out to each other and checking for vitals. He realized as he heard muffled voices screaming to each other that his hearing was shot as well. He noticed that some of the Scourge warriors were rifling through Monk's medical equipment to suture the incision and stanch the bleeding. They would be able to do it with rudimentary medical training. The Dilictor took pride in keeping his facilities stocked with state of the art equipment.

Before he knew it, a black and white blur stood on his chest. It was as though a soft pillow made of lead was on him. Two short blades were pressed against Monk's throat. He heard more stifled yelling, but it was slowly becoming more defined. He felt thin perforations at his neck as the blur increased pressure while it yelled at him more. In truth, Monk was more curious as to what the emotion fueled rant consisted of than he was worried about the blades cutting into his throat. The yelling cleared up a bit more as a red blur came by and eased the swords away from him. The two blurs spoke to each other, and he realized that a trail of sweet smelling white smoke was coming from the red one. Then he could interpret the words.

"...him for our investigation." The red blur spoke. His accent was Southern Kalkhanian. "We need to make the connection to our quarry."

"He flayed open Daphne like a fish!" The black and white fade yelled. This one had an Azzathan accent. He couldn't tell specifically, all Azzathans sounded alike to Thomas Monk. "If she was conscious and could see what this monster did to her, she'd skewer him herself! The Dilictor has operated unpunished long enough. I have it within the authority vested in me by the Bride to invoke Creed Eighteen and execute him on the spot!"

"Which is why we're asking you to hold off." A third blur came into view. This one was blue and spoke with an unmistakable Glaswegian accent. Monk loathed that accent, there would be no place for such a clowny tone once Carthonia was purified. "We're looking for a fellow named Knox Mortis who's been plaguing Templym since the 60's, and this piece of shite is the only connection we've got. You have my word that once we squeeze every ounce of information out of him, you can gut him yourself."

"You'd think he'd have some input." The Azzathan voice said. "I've never seen such a pathetic display of human weakness. I was expecting him to not shut up. From what I've heard, Dilictors like to rant and rave when their "genius" plans are foiled."

"A black host no doubt." The Kalkhanian said. "That Imago we fought up there was Class D, according to Adastra. It's possible to have manifested physically to kill us while maintaining a connection to a mortal vessel. Once we killed it, props to you Volk, it severed the spiritual connection, rendering him as vulnerable as a newborn." The red one kicked the professor and he let out a faint whimper in response to one of his ribs cracking. "Yeah, that's definitely the case."

"He appears totally senile." The Glaswegian spoke. "You sure we can still get anything out of him?"

"Definitely. The shock of losing a possessor is painful and crippling, but it's temporary. I've never actually had this happen before. Every black host I've encountered died before giving up their connection to the damned spirits."

"Well, what do we do now?"

The black and white blob crouched next to Monk's head. Blye was close enough that the Dilictor could distinguish the details of his face. "We take him in." He said coldly as he stabbed him in the neck with a syringe filled with the same narcotic he used to inebriate Bride Wainwright.

CHAPTER 30

Arodi Auzlanten was in his sanctum. It had been three weeks of scouring the surface of the Earth for Noctidus Val'Muardeares, the alleged wielder of the Idolacreid. In that time he had obliterated seventeen marauder tribes, twenty packs of mutants, and fifteen Mundus Imago. Still nothing. It defied all logic that a remote Azzathan nation like Uzbek would be so populated with the enemies of the Lord and not a one of them was the fiend he so relentlessly hunted for.

One might assume he was trying to relax upon seeing him. He sat at the bottom of the boiling mineral water in a cross-legged lotus pose. Without need for oxygen, he spent over an hour at the bottom of the pool allowing the roiling jets to massage his body. His mane of raven hair was like a bank of dark algae, lazily being swept around in the currents. It would be difficult to discern his posture from the surface of the fountain, but it might appear as though he was sleeping in a poised meditation were one to see through the waters. This was not the case.

Auzlanten's mind was reaching out beyond the reach of his private haven. He was lost in prayer, attempting to commune directly with the Holy Spirit. Silence responded to his mental cries. As relaxed as he looked outwardly, there was great conflict in his heart. The Lord was not speaking to Arodi as He once had. The last time that he heard the voice of God was when he received the orders to kill Invictus Illuromos one month ago. The orders Auzlanten disobeyed.

Ample time passed at the bottom of the pool. He tried to divine the location of the Idolacreid's marauder wielder, with no progress.

He cried out to the Lord, imploring for guidance. No answer came. Time and time again, his heart ached to hear His voice once more. He begged and pleaded in the marble basin for answers, for guidance, for anything. Arodi opened his eyes after the second hour passed and no response came.

With his bare hands still dripping with the steaming water, he lifted himself out of the basin. Seemingly on command, his blue and gold robes flew to him, wrapping themselves around Auzlanten with finesse. His hair whipped to the side, wringing the fluid from it as gold and silver clasps found their home in his mane. As the half crown of platinum thorns took its place on Arodi's brow, his ringed fingers flexed subtly rearranging his hair into the complex double braid pattern he often maintained. He took a few steps forward to the blonde woman in the outdated Scourge uniform. She was holding his holstered sabre Leagna.

"Did you make any progress?" She asked hopefully, her baby blue eyes filled with misplaced optimism.

"I did not." Arodi gave her a somber half smile as he clipped Leagna's ebony sheath back to his belt. "The Lord remains silent... at least compared to what I am accustomed to."

"I cannot imagine being shut off from God like that. I am sorry I cannot sympathize with you in this respect."

"Your help is sufficient." He brushed a strand of her soft blonde hair to further reveal the lustrous blue eyes. "Do you have any news for me? Have you any new leads?"

"Nothing material, but I have a theory." She stepped next to Arodi who began walking towards one of the antechambers on the border of the sphere.

"Please share." Auzlanten said plainly.

"You have combed every mile of Uzbek in search of the Grave Gluttons. Every marauder tribe in its two hundred-seventy-eight square miles has been eliminated as a possibility, some of which were quite literally. I think it is safe to conclude that they are nomadic and no longer reside in the nation."

"That is a logical deduction. Illythia told me they were nomadic and I found the backlash of one of their raids in North Kalkhan. That would mean they aren't returning home. But where else would they go?"

"It is a general theory." The woman sounded as though she were apologizing. "A theory that does no good in narrowing our search, I fear I've placed us back at the beginning once more."

"Do not feel ashamed. One must step back from the canvas to inspect mistakes before taking the proper measures to correct them. Let's inspect the archives. The Grave Gluttons are a myth in marauder culture, called the dead legion by most. I'd like to take a look at my collection to find any references in one of the historical codices."

They were approaching the prison door as they walked before freezing in their tracks. A figure of brilliant golden light was standing in front of it. Nobody should be able to find the sanctum of Auzlanten, let alone enter. It was beyond any mortal comprehension how somebody could infiltrate. This was not someone of the mortal world. The figure threatened to blind human eyes with the awesome radiance it put out. Auzlanten stepped in front of the woman to shield her from the light before her retina could be seared. This was an answer to his prayers.

"Give us privacy." He closed her eyes and maneuvered her to be able to make it to the library without looking at the source. She nodded, shielded her gaze with her hand as she scurried past the bright beacon.

Mortal eyes would only perceive the blinding cascade of golden starlight. Arodi Auzlanten possessed a more precise vision, sharp enough to see through the barrier of radiance to the humanoid figure inside. He wore a hooded surplice of bright white that flowed from his shoulders like cream. Closer inspection revealed that the cloak was made of silky feathers. Beneath the cloak was a suit of black full plate with a silver trim. The obsidian colored armor was accented with shimmering colors that never stayed the same, like a kaleidoscope of stardust. His arms ended in gauntlets made of pearlescent alabaster which were crossed atop a breastplate embossed with a cross made of blood red ruby. No eyes were visible beneath a visor in the shape of a rising sun made of what looked like molten gold.

The figure stood in quiet contemplation in front of the doors to the prison chamber. The blue metal reflected the stinging yellow light perfectly and even more so from the bronze pillars flanking him. Auzlanten approached the figure with his bearded chin held high to look directly into the face of the celestial being. "Tsadaqiel." Arodi greeted the angel, sent as a messenger of the Lord. His name translated to "God is just".

"You still keep Tumor'at here." A chorus of voices in every language that Auzlanten was fluent in, which was many, echoed in his mind. One might be reduced to a sniveling wreck at the presence of a being so magnificently intimidating, groveling at his feet in worship or terror. This was not his first encounter with the celestial.

"Of course I do. You know I can't kill it." Auzlanten had kept the Mundus Imago Tumor'at in this prison for nearly four hundred years. "You know I am immune to its honeyed charms. It's nothing more than a tool."

The angel Tsadaqiel did not respond vocally. Faster than Auzlanten could possibly react, which was speed far beyond the human eye could perceive, he brought the back of his ivory hand across Arodi's face. The force of the impact sent Templym's founder flying over one hundred feet. He was slapped clear over a number of crystal display cases before crashing into one, shattering it into glass dust. For a nanosecond, Arodi thought it was ironic that the angel sent him into the display where he kept the keystone he used to speak to Tumor'at. He quickly realized that Tsadaqiel did this intentionally. This shocked Arodi, though he wouldn't show it. In the past four hundred years, he had eighteen encounters with the angel. Tsadaqiel was always curt, blunt to the point of rudeness. The angel clearly did not like him, but he had never raised a hand against him.

The angel instantly appeared adjacent to Auzlanten as he picked himself up from the shattered remains of the display case.

His arms were still crossed, as though he hadn't twitched from his initial place. "I deserved that." Arodi said as he brushed shards of crystal off his unscathed robes.

"You deserve far worse than that." Tsadaqiel's choir of voices grew livid. "Father permitted this much, nothing more."

"I suppose I should be thanking you for your grace." The iron grey tiled figurine flew into Arodi's hands as he spoke.

"You should not thank me for staying my hand any further. Had I been granted my way, I would have brought my sword to your neck. I trust Father's judgment above my own. He deems you a necessity."

"You celestials live by undying faith, I admire that." Arodi stepped over to an empty display case, turning his back to the radiant figure and exposing himself to an attack that Tsadaqiel wanted to execute but would not.

"I recall your faith rivaling the relationships of figures like David or Abraham." The angel had appeared in front of the display case that he was gingerly placing the keystone. Once again, Tsadaqiel made no motion yet appeared instantly so he was forced to stare him down.

"I'm flattered you think that."

"I don't think it, I know it. I have operated as an overseer of the noblest faithful since the Patriarchal Period and I have deduced that your trust in the Lord is among the greatest." Tsadaqiel paused to allow a minor grin peak at Auzlanten's lips. "Do not think I am complimenting you. David's downfall was Bathsheba, yet you've taken an approach more like Jonah. Your disobedience to Father's command borders on outright rebellion."

"You may recall..." Arodi said through gritted teeth, "that I asked His permission before staying my blade against my own son."

"You still would not have obeyed." Tsadaqiel stepped forward to the point where he loomed over Auzlanten, making the first visual motion since his arrival. The angel was a full foot taller. "God gave you an opportunity to make some semblance of good out of your revolt, but it seems you've only made things worse for Templym."

"Worse? How could I have possibly made things any worse?"

"Invictus Illuromos has been corrupted by the Nephilim and the words of the Idolacreid. By confronting him and telling him to step down, you revealed the knowledge you possessed prematurely. You cannot find the Idolacreid because the Nephilim and its slaves are aware you are hunting them. If you had taken Invictus when you were instructed to, you would have sown chaos into their ranks and you'd have the Idolacreid locked away with all of your other trinkets."

Arodi winced at the statement. This realization had of course come to him but there was something wholly unsettling about hearing his mistake echoed over a thousand voices simultaneously. Tsadaqiel's message did confirm all of the notions that Auzlanten had been devising ever since this vast conspiracy took place. "This lapse in judgment will not happen again."

"So you say. Were I to come to you six weeks ago, prior to your disobedience, I am certain you would deny ever considering such a possibility. Yet here you stand, atop a pile of souls destined for the Pit, none of which are the one you were explicitly instructed to harvest."

"Is that all I am to you? Am I nothing more than the assassin of Heaven?"

"You mean like a Reaper?" Auzlanten felt a chill at Tsadaqiel's biting statement. He continued. "I recall not moments ago you claimed Tumor'at was just a tool. Eons before your inception, we were equivalent in all means. Am I to assume I am nothing but an object in your eyes as well? Your hypocrisy would be laughable were it not so infuriating." The choir began to churn with growling rage, like an ocean of gravel being crushed under the weight of a continent. The stardust patterns on his armor plates faded, revealing only cold blackness. "You toy with powers beyond your reckoning, effectively cursing the fragile balance between the material and spiritual world. You shun the machination Father devised at the time of creation. Every spell you cast, every artifact you collect, is like an additional nail into the body of the Son. How your existence is tolerated is beyond my comprehension."

"Watch your tongue, Tsadaqiel." Auzlanten warned as he placed a hand on the hilt of Leagna. "My work has the blessing of the Holy Spirit. I have spent centuries in careful communion and meditation with Father. Since my rebirth, never before have I operated outside of His perfect will."

"Until now." The sun crested helm angled down slightly where Auzlanten's jeweled hand rested on the sabre's grip. "It would gladden me were you to take up arms against me. The day you try to fight me is the day I rid your smear of a life from God's great Earth. I know you are too wise to something so foolhardy."

Arodi hung his head. His braids draped over his gaze to hide the embarrassed look of shame overpowering him. "What must I do to atone?"

"So, we come to the true nature of our meeting. You've been cut off from divine communion until the Idolacreid is secured and the Nephilim neutralized. Until then, you are encouraged to pray as any mortal would, but you will not have a direct connection to His wisdom. That is your punishment...along with the realization that every additional life lost in the coming war is your fault."

Tsadaqiel was frank, but his words rang true. That made them cut even deeper. This tended to be the nature of angels: direct, efficient, and unsympathetic. There were as few exceptions to this rule as there were prophets. "You have answered my prayers. Thank you."

"Arodi." The woman's voice came from the distance, bouncing off the marble walls. "I need to speak to you, it's urgent."

"And then there's that...thing." Tsadaqiel's multitude of voices swelled with disgust as his hooded head swept over in her direction. "You've latched onto it. It goes against the..."

"We're not discussing her." Arodi snapped his head upwards, his blue eyes flashed crimson for a moment. "You are a celestial. You have no bearing on the concept of human intimacy and therefore have no right to tell me who I can bring into my sanctum."

"It's not even a woman."

"Have you anything more relevant to say, or will you continue vexing me with criticism?" Auzlanten's choler was rising.

The angel chuckled, or at least produced a noise as close to laughter as a spiritual creature could utter. "Noctidus Val'Muardeares is the marauder translation of the chieftain's name. You will have better success if you cross reference the temple-tongue nomenclature."

"And what would that be?" Arodi asked with intrigue.

"Knox Mortis." And suddenly the golden light that flooded the chamber was gone.

Bastion Prime in Parey operated as the central stronghold of the Scourge. Each of the sub-organizations also possessed a capital fortress as well. The Veil had the Seraphim Solace in Hrimata. The Inquisition had Elysium in Jerusalem. The Beacon had Inexitus Veritas in Ahldorain. The Shackle's stronghold did not fall into the civilized orbit of Templym.

As the branch of the Scourge tasked with detaining and rehabilitating criminals, the Shackle was forced to sacrifice comfort in the name of justice. The primary fortress of Siberia was hundreds of miles away from civilization in the Northern most region of the Polar Wastes. Named after a region once infamous for its brutal prisons, Siberia was both a Shackle fortress and maximum security Arcae. It was a towering structure of white painted flaksteel to blend into the surrounding frozen region. Blizzards constantly beat the facility, coating the thick metal hull with a blanket of sharp frost and powdery snow. The prison fortress was practically invisible to the eye as it was built into the side of a frozen mountain. Over seventy percent of the exterior was encased beneath several feet of glacial ice.

The High Conservator enjoyed the quiet and the solitude of his arctic fortress. Anywhere between one hundred and one hundred thousand warriors of the Shackle were at the facility at any given time, often transferring in and out to cycle through fresh troops. Even though the inhabitants were kept from the hypothermic chill from the exterior by a complex mechanism of heating coils and ignate furnaces, it did not swaddle the inhabitants with as much comforting warmth as one would hope. The biting chill, intended to torment the most dangerous offenders to the Templym utopia, tended to dissuade officers from wanting to be stationed here. Often times, 2nd or 3rd Tier Shackle soldiers would reassign subordinates to these frozen halls for a month as a means to discipline them. Jude Bethel didn't mind the cold. The stinging cold from inside Siberia was nothing compared to the countless frostbitten nights he spent naked in the slave pits of the Hinterlands.

It was here, in his personal chambers, that Bethel invited Magistrate Averrin Walthune so he could discuss the matter concerning the Regent privately. His chamber bore no superficial decorations to match Jude's spartan personality. Cold walls of bare gunmetal plates made a dull square. A bed with stiff black sheets and a chestnut bench top table were the only articles. The only thing missing was a network of battle scars to match his physical appearance.

Prelate Terran Greyflame was also present to contribute his viewpoint on the matter. Patriarch Arodus Betankur was supposed to be present as well, but was uncharacteristically absent. This was supposed to be a secret meeting of the primes, free from the eyes of Illuromos and his Centurions. The fact that the prudent old man wasn't in attendance drew concern from the other three. It didn't stop them from trying to win over the Beacon's prime.

Jude Bethel had new evidence in support of the Regent's corruption, which he stabbed to the wooden bench top with a thick combat knife. He had just finished spinning the yarn, giving all details leading up to where they were presently. "And now there's this." He growled, seething with rage. One might assume that the plume of smoke spitting from his battle plate was attuned to his anger. Jude didn't even care that the tattoo on his neck was uncovered by his braid whipping about as he lurched.

Averrin frowned at the sight of the parchment that his friend stabbed into the table. His sparkling smile was absent and the torch at his back was reduced to flickering coals. "What's this?" His lion like voice asked.

"The latest orders from Invictus Illuromos himself. Read it."

Walthune removed the dagger and lifted the parchment to eye level. A reading monocle extended from the top of his armor's collar so his aged eyes could see the words clearly. The missive read as follows:

To High Conservator Jude Bethel,

I find it highly concerning that you continue this frivolous crusade against me. You know that I act as Arodi Auzlanten himself in his absence and am trusted with the most sensitive secrets of Templym. So, when I issued a public decree to avoid our nation's founder for fear of encountering a wicked doppelganger, I thought it reasonable that one of my most powerful and most trustworthy servants would follow this order. You have not. Despite my forewarning, you have engaged with the false Auzlanten. Against better judgment, you listened to his scheming lies. You even went as far as to implement policy that it explicitly wanted you to indoctrinate. Now, I am beginning to see that you will not cease in your endeavor to see me dethroned and executed.

The Scourge must be an organization founded on authority, loyalty, and above all else faith. Tensions are still high years after the Civil Strife that tore a schism in the heart of Templym. I cannot tolerate you belittling me and sowing chaos into my ranks. Do not confuse my sentencing with cruelty. I still value you as a soldier and a brother. I also sympathize with the dissonance you are feeling at this moment. That is why your punishment shall be significantly less severe than it deserves to be.

Effective immediately, I am placing you on psychological suspension. I have determined that the stress you are feeling, coupled with the falsities you've been exposed to, have clouded the sharp discernment you are famous for. This leave, which I assure you is temporary, shall last a minimum of eight weeks. During this time you will be required to engage in counseling with a licensed professional or ordained clergy for a cumulative duration of seventy two hours. After you pass a rudimentary psyche evaluation once the allotted time has ended, you will be allowed to resume your duties as High Conservator of the Shackle.

You should not worry, for your soldiers will be well looked after. I will assign a Conservator to operate in your stead. I personally recommend that you take additional time to assess yourself. Perhaps find a wife during this leave of absence. I am certain you can find a godly woman who will give you the emotional support you secretly crave. Please do not take this personally. I want what is best for you, for the Scourge, and for Templym.

In Nomine Veritas
IX Regent Invictus Illuromos
Classification: Alpha

"Do you not think it suspicious that the Regent would dismiss our brother commander when he is on the brink of revealing the truth?" Terran spoke in a grim baritone.

"It looks bad." Walthune mused with a hand running through his white beard. "But I can sympathize with both of you, however. On one hand the false Auzlanten could be giving a convincing falsity with the intent to distract the Scourge or with hopes that we tear ourselves apart. The forces of the damned could be sowing chaos to debilitate us, just as Invictus said in this letter. But that does not dismiss this suspicious activity. Prematurely executing Balor indicates that he didn't want the arms dealer to talk. That could be due to fears of lecherous corrupting words or out of fear that he would condemn Invictus during his confession."

"What excuse do you have for the demonic presence?" Prelate Greyflame opened the same wooden box he brought to his meeting with Illuromos days before. "I integrated detection incense into these cigars. When I was two feet away from the Regent it smelt of a rotting corpse. After I left, it was like sweet perfume. That does not bode well for the case for his innocence."

"Good work on that, Terran." Jude complemented the Prelate.

He did not respond with a smile as the High Conservator had hoped. "I have refrained from implementing these subtle tools en masse for fear that I may need to use them among my own colleagues. I prayed that I would never need to. The stench was strong when I met with him. That means a strong presence of Imago magick, or worse..." Terran stopped himself, shuttering at his own thoughts before trailing off to an inaudible prayer.

"He's an active black host." Averrin dared to utter after an uncomfortable period of silence. "Imago influence would explain how he could lie to Jude in a Veritas Chamber. Good God, I thought we were done with this."

"Now take the traitors discovered by our edicts into consideration." Bethel said as he tapped the display on a data pad to retrieve the exact numbers. "From my search, two hundred and twelve loyalists to this Nephilim thing were revealed in the Shackle. Terran's search exposed eighty nine. Yours has already brought fifteen out and you just issued the edict yesterday!"

"I agree with you, Jude." Walthune sighed. "I am certain all evidence points to some evil prowling about in the shadows looking for the perfect opportunity to strike us down. I have no doubt that the Nephilim has used this Idolacreid, whatever foul totem that is, to infiltrate the Scourge. What I am uncertain of is the identity of the arch perpetrator. Is Invictus telling the truth when he says there is an imposter Auzlanten? Or is this all a ploy he fabricated himself?"

"We had hoped we could get a definite answer from you, Averrin." Terran said seriously, his cybernetic eye cutting into him. "The 10th Dogma requires the unanimity of all four primes. I would venture to guess that whoever the Regent appoints in Bethel's stead will never agree to the idea."

"Invictus is manipulating the law to his advantage." Bethel said, stroking the pink scar at his chin. "Whatever foul machination he has in store will no doubt take place before my leave is up. That means we're left with only one option...we have to work outside the law if we're going to save Templym."

The Prelate winced at the idea of belittling the law. "Uriah Lockheart would have our heads if he heard us scheming this way." Lockheart was the prime of the recently deceased Dictum, the branch of the Scourge responsible for maintaining civil order. He died in the Strife.

Walthune fidgeted nervously with the knife in his hands. He looked to the ceramic symbol of the Beacon plastered on his chest plate and let out a mournful sigh. "I was Magistrate of the Beacon when we were still a part of the Bulwark. When Malacurai descended from the heavens and declared war upon Auzlanten, I saw the damage it did to my brethren from every possible angle. While my friends sacrificed their lives for no reason other than to spill their kin's blood, I oversaw the fierce debates of truth. Most people believe it was nothing more than stuffed shirted bureaucrats flinging words at each other. It was not. The Beacon practically tore itself apart in its own civil war. Of our twelve thousand casualties, two thousand of those were from debates that turned physical. Bullets were slung just as frequently if not more than evidence in our debate halls. All I could do was moderate and watch as impartially as possible while the people I nurtured to serve as preservers of truth tear each others' throats out. There was one instance where I mean that literally. I can't go through with that again. I refuse to stand idly by while the Scourge rends itself apart just like the Beacon nearly did."

"So you'll stand with us?" Greyflame asked hopefully.

"Aye." Walthune stood from the dull wooden bench. "I'll fight to the death before I let the Nephilim destroy us from within like a cancer. I don't like the idea of our Regent being corrupted by dark powers...but I can see no other logical conclusion. I'll fight with you."

Jude grasped his forearm in a brotherly embrace, the echo of a smile at his scathed lips. "Well met, brother. Together we'll save all of Templym yet."

For the first time in months, Terran's pallid lips curled up in a grin. "So, here we are then. A merry band of vigilantes, opposing our creeds, disregarding our stringent training, and staging regicide. Lord have mercy. So...where do we start?"

Bethel paused and the vague smile was replaced with a cold scowl. "I have no idea."

CHAPTER 31

The manhunt lasted approximately four and a half months, but upon discovery of his laboratory it was revealed that Thomas Monk had been conducting his macabre science for closer to twenty-two years. Unsurprisingly, upon this information becoming Omega classified, scores of families came forward begging the interrogators to prod his twisted mind that they may receive some semblance of closure. The first question asked of the Dilictor, among the hundreds he would be bombarded with before his execution, was simply if Zedekiah Surizal was one of the twenty-four liquefied corpses found in the chemical basin beneath Dalton Hall. He laughed at the number twenty-four.

Injuries were substantial among the members of S-6319. Hospitallers required a minimum of two weeks of rest to allow their bodies to recover from the trauma of fighting the titanic demon. Their injuries were primarily superficial. Minor lacerations were sutured and hairline bone fractures were sealed with bone growth supplements. The most severe injury was the concussion Oslin suffered once the beast landed on him, which caused a horrid ringing in the back of his head. This was of course with regards to the survivors. Scourge soldiers of the Veil and Inquisition were flayed, crushed, impaled, and devoured by the same chaotic creature. The most palpable loss was that of Admonisher Fenrick Rickard. His body would be returned to his wife for proper burial.

Of all the survivors, Daphne suffered worst of all, but one wouldn't be able to tell just by looking at her. The only visual scar from escaping the Dilictor's clutches was a thin white scar splitting her ruby lips. The line did not detract from her beautiful features.

In a sense, the mark was bitterly humorous. The Bride drew her name from Daphne Otallion, the tenth general of the Reclaiming Crusades, better known as Palescar. Now she bore a resemblance to her namesake Saint. The gruesome oral experiment left severe gashes on the interior of her cheeks and they would leak blood into the back of her throat with excessive agitation. Surgeons could not re-implant the ovary Monk stole from her. While the organ itself was well preserved, the damage he did to the more fragile connections of her body disabled any possibility of it being returned. This was not a significant loss, not according to the Bride at least. She still had one where it was supposed to be and her gametes would be artificially preserved in case she wanted to have children some day. Another positive was that aside from the severed tube, the rest of the system was largely undamaged.

It was these facts that she focused on to keep her spirits up. Her optimism was admirable by any standard. Few women would have the ability to be dissected and return to work as quickly as she did. Hospitallers recommended that she spend a month in bed rest to assure her body recovered properly. She was back at the helm of the Seraphim Solace in two weeks. Her spirits were unnaturally high considering the torture she endured. Bride Wainwright's desire to see justice done vastly outweighed whatever emotional damage she was burying.

Hrimata was out for blood. The Nitral Nightmare was finally caught. Any man convicted of a quarter of the crimes Thomas Monk was known to be guilty of would be executed with no trial in accordance with Creed Eighteen of the Scourge. The more truth came to light, the more atrocities he was convicted of. No moral person in the noble city could have wanted Monk to live...yet he did. At the order of Warden Downey, Thomas Monk was detained and pressed for information.

The Veil officers operating in the Solace vehemently disagreed with this decision, but it was a necessary step for the task force's investigation. Thomas Monk was the only connection they had in their hunt for Knox Mortis. The only reason his request was not instantly overruled was because the Bride backed him. She wanted this monster put down more so than any other officer of the Scourge, but it was the least she could do. Without the investigative abilities of S-6319, she'd still be chasing meaningless trails. God only knows how many more victims he would have claimed before the trail of bodies led to the professor.

The soldiers were not pleased with having to sit around in a hospital for two weeks before they could return to their investigation. Their stay took them straight into the month of Verrick. This did not eat up as much time as they would have thought it would. They had expected mountains of information to be unearthed, but Monk was not too eager to give up anything. Enhanced interrogation methods had to be implemented, and even then the Dilictor only gave cryptic half-answers to the questions.

Each person involved in the interrogation took a turn at trying to break the man. Ram's Horn took the simplest approach of beating the answers out of him. Vandross Blackwell played the part of an infiltrator and attempted to befriend Monk. Volk Downey tried pressure point exploitation, a method he personally found deplorable but made an exception in this instance. Adastra Covalos used Inquisition tools to try and exploit his ties to dark spirits. None of it was particularly effective.

The squad's stenographer had another plan in mind. Oslin Du'Plasse analyzed every scrap of data from the investigation. He tore through Monk's notes from his lab, stared through the observation deck during every interrogation, and cross-referenced every possible lead with a hundred others with the hopes of drawing a connection. He spent a number of nights fueled by caffeine supplements trying to draw connections and piecemeal a storyline from his cryptic answers. He spent immense lengths of time in isolation, desperate to find the next link to the Mortis case. Whenever somebody asked about his progress or attempted to assist his data spelunking he rambled on about some vast conspiracy that he was on the brink of exposing. They grew concerned for his health.

Unable to do more than sit on his hands, Warden Downey strode through the halls of the Veil in quiet contemplation. Over two months now, Volk and this team had been running around Templym hunting for this Mortis character. Mob syndicates, cults, and now a Dilictor Ignotum had been felled on this manhunt. He'd have to admit that this was one of his most interesting quarry jobs yet. He sipped at a cup of steaming tea, nothing compared to the jasmine from the café in Parey, musing and trying to clear his mind in search of the optimal step to get over this impasse.

His quiet period of introspection was interrupted by a powerful hand coated in bright blue flaksteel gauntlet. "Excuse me mister, you seem to have wandered from your retirement center. This is a place of able bodied warriors." Downey shook in his own battle plate as the figure shook him. He spilt his lukewarm tea, but didn't care too much. He was more relieved to hear the boisterous voice of Warden Alexandarius Carthage.

Volk turned to see the half shaven head of the Hrimatan Warden. "Dari! I thought I smelt spit and steel. Tell me, how many teeth have you lost since last I saw you in Jaspin?"

The irony of the joke was that Carthage had in fact had another tooth replaced with a steel slab since their raid on the Cybernetic Apotheosis. "More teeth than you have hair, granddad." He rubbed the other Warden's bald head mockingly.

"It's good to see you again." Volk said as he slapped away the hand on his hand. "How'd your trek in the Hinterlands fair?"

"We found nothing but mosquitoes and heretics there." Alexandarius huffed, his amber eyes flashing with a spark of genuine rage.

"Heretics? I didn't think Blitzkrieg was on a witch hunt."

"We weren't." The jovial tone was replaced with the thunderous bellow he was keen on uttering while in the heat of combat. "Bethel's edict revealed that all of Barb squad, including Creel, had been conspiring against Templym. Ichabod whored himself out to some...black machination. Apparently, the specifics are Alpha classified."

"I remember that. I thought it was a whole bunch of administrative rubbish. Ram and I just took a stroll to Niflheim, answered some questions, and made our way. I didn't think anybody actually got exposed."

"You've been isolated too long, brother. Rumor has it that over two hundred in our ranks have been caught up in this Nephilim something or another."

"The Shackle has over a million members worldwide...that's not a huge portion...but still, two hundred?"

"That's not even the worst of it. I'm sure you've heard about the dissention between the High Conservator and the Regent."

"I spoke to Bethel when I first arrived in Hrimata. He seemed troubled, but he didn't mention anything about Lord Illuromos. I've heard whispers of them butting heads, even one about them drawing blades in a standoff, but nothing solid."

"Get this... apparently the Bethel encountered the Auzlanten clone. Worse, he spoke to it. Conservator Elat told me that he thinks that Invictus is the traitor and that there is no imposter."

"Bloody smoke." Volk's forehead wrinkled as he took in the information, aghast at what Alexandarius told him. "Does that mean the imposter Auzlanten was victorious? Did he fall prey to a serpent-tongued tale?"

"I doubt it. Jude's too smart for that kind of trickery. Then again... the thought that the Regent is a turncoat is even less imaginable. Ever since the Scourge's founding, there's never been someone calling the shots like Invictus Illuromos. He was awarded the Black Rose while he was still a 7th tier, the Silver Cross after only ten years of service. Bloody smoke, he's likely the son of the true Auzlanten. I can't fathom the idea he's a traitor, but it's either that or our High Conservator is being played like a marionette."

"No offense to Jude, but I'm inclined to think the latter is more plausible. I mean the Regent ordered no approach, recognizing that the deceiver is so powerful even talking to it could be catastrophic. If Arodi Auzlanten himself warned against that, I don't think it's unreasonable to think that Bethel's vulnerable to deceit."

"Well whatever the case, it's not boding well for the Scourge. Prelate Greyflame is getting up in a huff about this and factions are forming within the four branches. To pour some ignate on the fire, Illuromos ordered Bethel to step down."

Volk looked for Alexandarius to break into a hooting laugh, mentally begging for it to be a joke. He knew that the militia leader was not joking. "When did thi... how come...why isn't this public news? The Shackle's prime is being forced down and I'm just now hearing about? I bloody doubt it!"

"It's an informal suspension...medical leave or some goat spit excuse like that. I had hoped you'd be up to date with this information so my warning would be a bit more forthcoming."

"Warning, what warning Dari?"

"I wanted to tell you that this Nephilim nonsense is in no way nonsense. Ten of my most reliable men were seduced by dark promises. I figured I'd share information with you face to face in case of worms listening in where they shouldn't."

"What do you know?"

"I know you can't trust anybody." Warden Carthage's bone and metal teeth grinded together, a pained look in his eyes. "Creel saved my hide twice and probably a score more times he'd never admit to. Less than a month ago he stuck a pistol to my chest and tried to kill me. Nobody is free from the taint of this Idolacreid machination. Look for the signs."

Carthage peered over the strobe lights planted on his shoulders, his chainmail cape shuttering as he pivoted to see who was around. He leaned in close and whispered to his fellow Warden. "I don't know much. The traitors are being kept under pretty strict lock and key so I haven't gotten to interrogate Creel or any of Barb squad to the proper extent they deserve. But considering I caught them out in the Hinterlands, we had a little quality time. So here's what I got. The Nephilim has a cult all across the world. They're rallying an army for something called 'the abolition'."

"What the hell is that?" Volk whispered back. "Some kind of global culling?"

"Probably. I squeezed that bit out of a puke-headed Guardian who was after some higher power. Apparently, this Idolacreid thing is an ancient tome full of forbidden knowledge to unlock the secrets of the Universe or some blasphemy like that. Every man who swore allegiance was promised a peek inside."

"It's a spell book or some kind of Imago manual?"

"Again, that's all I know about that. I'd venture to guess its heretical words seep all manner of God knows what into the brain. Lots of speculation I'm afraid. If the Regent would let me get to Creel and beat the information out of him I'm positive I could tell you more."

Volk now looked over his shoulders to see if anybody was eavesdropping before cutting the volume of his voice even lower. "Maybe the Regent's actually a traitor as Bethel suspects."

"Exactly why I'm so concerned. There's so little certainty right now in the Scourge. The Nephilim is destroying our fair Scourge from the inside, that much is clear. How it's doing that is another question. For now, keep your eyes open. Root out this cult where you can, but keep on the track you're working, lest you tip our hand to the fiend."

"How do I go about doing that?"

"Look for a symbol of a purple flower. I found three of them hidden among Barb's personal items. I think that's the cult's holy symbol."

"Purple flower? What kind?"

"How should I know? I'm no botanist."

"Forget it, just come with me."

Herald Du'Plasse had isolated himself for four days. The whites of his eyes had turned a glossy crimson from sleep deprivation. His normally pristine platinum hair was disheveled and loosely dangled off of his shoulders. He was operating in his seventy-eighth consecutive hour without any sleep. His hands tremored as he swallowed another caffeine supplement that he chased down with black coffee. He abhorred the bitter sting of coffee, but he needed to keep his mind sharp. A collection of iron data folders, loose parchments, and historian's tablets were scattered across the rosewood of an otherwise empty conference room. Empty water bottles and crumpled food wrappings were littered on the floor.

Oslin had been trying to devise a portfolio on Monk's actions for weeks now. He was attempting to connect their case to this mad scientist. It was his history with Regulom Palladium that gave him away, but there seemed to be no other connection to their previous quarry. How was Monk's involvement with the UNACs a factor? How did a chemistry professor come to know how to bind an Imago? How did he know about the shipment of technology to the hospital? These questions swarmed through Du'Plasse's thoughts as he reviewed a number of interrogation recordings for the eighth time today.

"Os! How you doing, lad?" A pair of bright blue hands clapped onto Oslin's shoulders. He didn't even notice anyone come in, which was particularly odd for someone as boisterous as Alexandarius Carthage. "Tell me my fellow Hrimatan, killed any lousy Senators recently?"

Du'Plasse was too tired to be offended by the comment about his past or perceive that it was intended to be humorous. "I've been a little too preoccupied with the Mort hunt to resume my duties as an AA."

"You know typically you'd insult me back, I'd take another stab at you, and then we'd laugh before going about our business. That's what Volk and I do."

"How goes your study Herald?" Downey asked in turn. Oslin jumped a bit, just now noticing the other Warden's presence. He turned to face him and Volk grimaced internally at the condition he was in. "Smoke man, you look terrible. When was the last time you got a wink of sleep?"

"I'll rest when I find this missing piece." Du'Plasse returned to his pile of reports. "Palladium was building an army to stage a mutiny. Monk probably helped with the development of the cybernautics and th...the uh light shooter things."

"Why don't you take a break man?" Carthage said. "You're not of much use to the force if your mind's a puddle."

"Please, I slept a full night on Blissday." His words were slurred, clearly a symptom of the fatigue.

"Oslin it's Fortisday!" Blitzday is the fifth day of the week. Fortisday is the second.

"I'm almost there. I think Monk said something about an abolishment when Ram's Horn was punching him."

"Perhaps I can provide the lost piece of your puzzle." Carthage spun a seat around and bulled up next to the fatigued Herald. "Volk tells me that Monk was found wearing a tunic with a purple flower sewn into it."

"Yes." Du'Plasse summoned the information on his historian's tablet surprisingly quickly. "Specifically a mauve velvet badge depicting a Judaic marsh lily. Odd, considering that strain of flora is usually grey and infamous for its awful scent. I didn't think much of it."

Alexandarius looked over at the slate. "Aye, that's the one. Your Dilictor is a servant of the Nephilim. That flower there is the cult's holy symbol."

"The Nephilim? Are you referencing to the parameters of that loyalty test Conservator Bethel put out three weeks ago? I thought that was all dribble."

"That dribble consumed an entire company in my militia. From what I got before the guilty were snatched up and hauled off to an Arcae, his cult is planning something called 'the abolition'. It's probably some worldwide cleansing of the impure or something of that wicked sort. We're talking the kind of thing that would spark another Purus Crusade. I think fourteen is plenty, personally."

Oslin's bloodshot eyes darted back and forth between the papers and pads laid out before him. "Well it looks like Auzlanten's Butcher saves the day again."

CHAPTER 32

Thomas Monk had been arrested on Nyvett 25th, the day the Bride's hunt for Hrimata's Dilictor Ignotum officially came to an end. He was certain that they were demanding his head on a spit. Their lesser minds were incapable of conceiving the breadth of the knowledge he was collecting, only able to concentrate on their delicate sensibilities. Oddly enough, the Scourge warriors not of the Veil were the ones prying for information. It was now Verrick 22nd and he hadn't given them anything substantial. Monk knew better than to give up the Nephilim. He wasn't a fanatical devotee like the rest of the cult, but he knew better than to draw its ire.

The Scourge's prying had been extensive. Their enhanced methods of interrogation took an obvious toll on his previously well kept physique. His nose had been broken so many times it was practically a collection of bone powder wrapped in cartilage. His fingers were in twisted knots of splintered bone and his legs were painted with a spectrum of burns. Hunks of hair had been pulled out of his head by the big Retriever, giving him the appearance of a feral cat. His pale skin had been darkened with splotches of black and purple bruising. Despite all of the inhuman treatment, he never gave straight answers to their questions, peppering in fragments of the truth to keep them intrigued, yet never enough to reveal much of anything.

Monk remained in the same Veritas Chamber for close to a month now, chained to the same chair in front of the same steel slab. Pistons in the featureless wall hissed as the door retracted into the floor, piquing Monk's interest. "Who is it today", he thought to himself. He was surprised to see a new face.

Oslin Du'Plasse composed a solid dossier the day before. He would have interrogated Thomas Monk sooner, but passed out for twelve hours as a means to congratulate himself. He was no longer in a state of disarray. His hair was once again in its complex pattern, almost perfectly mirroring that of Arodi Auzlanten. A prideful smile graced his visage and a metal binder was tucked beneath his arm.

"You're new." The Dilictor said with a mouth missing a few teeth. "So, what shall it be today? My experiments, Palladium, the Mortis fellow? Kindly inform me how I can waste your time today."

"None of that Thomas." Oslin's voice was full of confidence, much like he was making an appeal to a jury like when he was a barrister. "My name is Herald Du'Plasse. I'm going to be telling you something."

"Are you now? What could you possibly know that I would not?"

"I've spent the past four weeks tracing your steps." Du'Plasse sat down and cracked open the binder. "I'm going to read you what I've found. You've been good about dodging around the compulsions of the Veritas Chamber, giving half-truths or spinning tales that go nowhere. I'll admit, it's impressive, speaking as a registered legal agent and a member of the Beacon. However, truth is discriminate."

"Meaning what exactly?"

"Meaning only that which corresponds with reality can come out of your miserable trap. So everything you've said has been true, removing all possibility of falsities. The Scourge perceives silence as guilt when pressed inside of a Veritas Chamber. We've confirmed enough murders to execute you, but we need more before that happens. So, here's what I'm going to do. I am going to read you what I believe to be reality. If you don't explicitly deny what I say by uttering the word "no" when I ask you, I can deduce that it is true."

Monk chuckled, before coughing up a mouthful of bile and blood. "You're going to read me a story? That's your master interrogation technique?"

Oslin saw a hint of hesitation in Monk's swollen eyes. He proceeded with his plan. "Grigor 15th, 2702, you alongside Regulom

Palladium form the 23rd Constantinians fraternity at the Grigorian Administration."

"Du'Plasse, as in Grigor Du'Plasse?" The Dilictor was clearly trying to change the subject. "It makes sense, I pinned you as a limp wristed coward the second you stepped through that doorway."

"The two of you grow close. You exchanged ideas and realized that you're both visionary men of science. You had complementary approaches to your discovery. You wanted to push the boundaries of human biology like the UNACs did during the Tyrranis Period while your companion Palladium acclaimed the extinct god-AIs. Ultimately, you wanted the same thing and went in similar fashions to go about getting it. You both wanted to become more than human, you both wanted to become something stronger, and you operated at the expense of others to achieve your goal. Deny it."

"Congratulations, you figured it out." The disgraced professor sneered. "You are correct. I saw past the shackles of Templym's ethics system in pursuit of knowledge and discovery. You are truly a master detective."

"You exchanged ideas when working in your dubious labs. Then you came across a discovery like no other. You heard of a book full of lore that nobody in the world had ever seen before...the Idolacreid."

For the first time since his interrogation began, Monk was silenced. His technique to throw his interrogators off his trail was to never stop talking, to say a never ending string of nonsense to sew nothing but confusion in place of discovery. They would ask about some aspect of their investigation and he would give one piece of data buried under a sea of meaningless filler. He never once mentioned the Idolacreid. How did they figure that out?

Herald Du'Plasse smirked at how he threw the professor so off balance. He had wiped the broken smile right off the braggart's face. "The Idolacreid is a major artifact of the cult of the Nephilim. You were promised every discovery you ever yearned to unearth, lying beneath the pages of an ancient book. The idea seemed preposterous, but that's when they allowed you to take a look inside. That's how you bound the demon...I believe you called it Kortham."

"You're making a lot of assumptions boy." Monk growled.

"Well then, deny it. Was what I said false?"

For a moment it looked like he tried to say something but then swallowed the thought. "I never read the Idolacreid."

Oslin was more than familiar with what it looked like when someone tried to fib inside of the Veritas Chamber. That was it just now. He also told a partial truth. He said he never read the Idolacreid, he never said anything about a small portion of it. "You loved your Imago. It showed you things and altered reality in ways you had never even known possible, mind control being the paramount discovery. It wasn't enough though. You needed more, but the Nephilim's following wouldn't let you probe the Idolacreid without something in return. They needed soldiers for the abolition. That's where Palladium comes in. Stop me when I say something incorrect."

"Love is a strong word. My relation to Kortham was more along the lines of a tutorship, not a dysfunctional family."

Oslin was pleased with the results. Admittedly, he did make a few leaps in judgment to fill in the holes of his story, but the narrative fit together so perfectly he felt confident in presenting it. He smiled as he turned a page in the file. "Palladium had a strong following in the Cybernetic Apotheosis. His cultists were just as ravenous for data as you were. So if their leader, your dear pal Regulom, also caught a glimpse inside of the blasphemous tome, they could be won over to serve the Nephilim's agenda as well. It would have an army for the coming of the abolition and you would get some more quality time with the Idolacreid."

Monk was eerily silent. Oslin didn't stop reading his month's worth of data. "You spent time experimenting on the citizens of Hrimata to bolster the forces Palladium was assembling. Experiments like the ones you performed on Frodus Rieveshl to see how much influence you could get away with on an unwilling subject. But your demon got greedy. It craved fear and pain and grief. You had to plunge this urban into a state of constant terror or else Kortham wouldn't teach you anything. Things like the optimum places for the Apotheosis to acquire raw technology, say a Venetian hospital. That's why you became the Nitral Nightmare. You tortured victims, making it seem like serial sadism. It was clever, I'll give you that. You came up with a victim profile, a disposal method, and I wouldn't be surprised if you came up with the name yourself. Little did they know that for every woman you abducted, raped, strangled, and dumped into the sewers after scrubbing their bodies clean with drain cleaner, you had another twenty victims dissolving in a sodium hydroxide vat beneath the college."

"I always hated that name...the Nitral Nightmare. That's not even a real term, Nitral. It especially bothered me as a chemist. Nitric would have been a far more accurate..."

"And that leads us here. Do you deny being a part of the Nephilim's scheme that threatens to topple the stability of Templym?"

"I mean the main ingredient in Nitrosluice is nitric acid. Why Nitral? Where did they pull the 'a' from?" Monk was meagerly clinging to his distraction tactic.

"This is your final opportunity to deny involvement with the cult of the Nephilim. If you won't explicitly deny it, I can only deduce you are directly involved. Say that you aren't involved in the cult of the Nephilim. Say that you've never heard of the Idolacreid."

The Dilictor let out a sigh of defeat. "You know I can't do that."

Monk leaned his tattered body back in his seat. "I'm impressed. It must have taken some serious research to piece all of that together."

"You could say that." Du'Plasse snickered. It was one thing to outgun or overpower a foe, but to outsmart them was a special type of victory. "So, I believe that covers everything. Everything except the reason I'm here in the first place."

"Mortis?"

"Exactly. Task force S-6319 was assembled to find and neutralize Knox Mortis, an individual with a hand in everything from political assassinations to the Plague Massacre. I'm thinking that he's an executive among the cult of the Nephilim. Seeing as how you're a member, I was hoping you could tell me a thing or two about him, mainly his current whereabouts."

Monk chuckled pitifully. "What's in it for me? I'm no fool. A man who's killed as much as I have doesn't get a plea deal. There's no escape from the death penalty."

"True. You're doomed no matter what you end up disclosing. But here's a compromise. We've proven you guilty of one hundred-ninety-one murders based on the data from your experiments alone. That's well over double that number in orphans and widows who are still reeling from the loss their loved ones. Scourge law dictates that they can play a part in your execution. Right now, Bride Wainwright is planning on death by a thousand cuts...literally. It will be slow and excruciating so that before the Adversary claims your soul, you might feel a fraction of the suffering you caused in this life. Give me Mortis and I might be able to talk her down to a firing squad, much quicker that way."

"That's hardly a deal." The professor complained.

"What else do you have to lose? I am offering you an opportunity to escape an overwhelming portion of pain before your death. At this point...that's all you have left."

Monk paused and thought for several moments. He would be biting his bottom lip if his front teeth hadn't been punched out earlier that week. "Yes of course. If I tell you everything I know, will you shoot me here and now? I won't risk being captured by the Mortis. He scares me more than you."

"That can be arranged. It depends on what you tell me."

He swallowed a thick gob of mucus that had been conglomerating for some time at the back of his gullet. "There isn't much more to tell. It seems as though you figured out most of what I know."

"What did I miss?" Oslin pressed on keeping a calm composure and a straight face, but was becoming anxious internally.

"Knox Mortis is the name of one of the Nephilim's three generals, the only one I'm aware of. We all indirectly report to subordinates who relay relevant information to it. I reported to him through one of his personal lieutenants, a marauder named Fel Maul."

"A marauder of what tribe?"

"I don't really know, they only referred to themselves in their own dialect. Roughly translated to temple-tongue, I believe they refer to themselves as the Dead Legion."

"It doesn't ring a bell. Where can we find this tribe?"

Monk's already sour scowl collapsed into an even more somber grimace. "What exactly are your intentions?"

"We aim to bring Mortis to justice. However we go about that is none of your concern."

"They're nomadic. Fel Maul would always update me on their location via communion with Kortham. They reported in from Uzbek, Mandarin, the Hinterlands, Malgeria, even the Polar Wastes. They must have some means of travel that I'm unaware of because they can't possibly make treks like those on foot."

"And where are they now?"

Monk actually appeared nauseated, as though the knowledge he was concealing in his mind were frightening him. Any kind of information that scared the likes of a heathen like Thomas Monk had to have been truly horrifying. Du'Plasse just stared him down, silently screaming that he give up Mortis already. After a full minute of quiet, he finally whimpered. "Budapest."

Oslin went cold, as though a blizzard wind washed over him. His eyes widened with shock. "Repeat that." He demanded, desperate to believe he had misheard the confession.

"The Dead Legion was last stationed in Budapest. Now you see why they must have some supernatural means of travel. If you're looking for Mortis, that's the best place to look."

"You're lying."

"I can't. I'm not telling some half-truth and you've tested for every manner of magick. Last I heard, Knox Mortis was in the Hellpit Budapest."

Everyone else was watching the interrogation from the observation deck. Expurgator Blye and Bride Wainwright joined the remainder of S-6319 to watch Oslin's interrogation in real time.

Daphne in particular was disappointed at how gentle of an approach the Herald was making, but was satisfied with the headway he had made during his isolation. They watched the monitors and analyzed the vocal recordings, taking careful note of all the new information being revealed. Oslin hadn't shared the discoveries he had made with anyone, adamant that it was a surprise. This was typical Du'Plasse theatrics. He was correct of course and his delivery was impeccable, but nothing could have prepared them for the shock of their final target's location.

One wouldn't even need to listen to the recording to know the exact moment the word "Budapest" slithered out of Monk's mouth. Each of the investigators were leaning forward in fascination, eyes wide with anticipation. As soon as the revelation of their location came up faces went pale, pens hit the floor, not a single soul drew breath any longer. Nobody, especially not anyone associated with the Scourge, could fail to recognize that name.

Budapest was the site of the final battle of the Civil Strife. The full strength of the Scourge and the Bulwark came together for one purpose, to kill. Auzlanten had the full force of the Scourge, including the Beacon which had just recently turned loyalties. Malacurai, the false angel, led a devastating ambush against the Dictum stronghold in Budapest. Arodi Auzlanten marched the Scourge to meet with every soldier he could muster. The ensuing battle was a blood bath, to put it lightly. The Battle of Budapest lasted four days. Four days of never ending slaughter. Battles in which Auzlanten himself was involved in never lasted so long, but for the full ninety-two hours he never stopped fighting Malacurai. Witnesses report the two appearing as nothing more than bright flashes of fiery explosions bouncing across a smoke shrouded sky. As the two fought an intense quarrel in the sky the ground became a blackened graveyard. Gun shells and artillery cracked in a never ending staccato and oily black vapor blanketed the battle ground. When Malacurai fell from the sky the Bulwark's onslaught dissolved. The battle was won for the Scourge, but at an incalculable cost. Of the thirty-one thousand members of the Dictum, less than nine hundred remained alive. The Bulwark was swept away entirely. What few of their members remained breathing were scattered among the rubble and stowed away in hiding until the Scourge withdrew. The crushing grief prevented a body count, but there were over four hundred thousand men and women who were never seen again after that day. This does not even include the civilians lost that horrid day.

That was not the worst of it. After the gunfire ceased and the smoke started clearing, the ground began opening up. Vast caverns of land began pulling down the dead. It was as though the Earth itself was swallowing the bodies like a scavenger devouring the fallen. Auzlanten ordered a full retreat as bodies were engulfed into the soot crusted soil of the battleground of Budapest. He declared the formerly affluent urban a Hellpit and ordered it to be shut off from Templym forever. No citizen had been within the city limits ever since. Not merely because of the law, but because nobody was brave enough to venture into the permanently scarred wasteland.

"Budapest." Volk dared to break the silence. Fear strained his eyes. "Our quarry's in that Hellpit? You've got to be bloody kidding me."

"I...how could..." Vandross stammered. It was quite unusual for the suave Inquisitor to be lost for words. "God help us. We've got to call off the manhunt. That's it. We can't go to Budapest, it's suicide! Good work team, case closed."

"We can't do that." Adastra retorted, his eyes frozen onto the monitor they were watching the interrogation on. "This task force has invested three months into this manhunt. We can't turn away just as we get our quarry's location."

"Nope." Ram's Horn muttered his typical metallic voice.

"I'm inclined to agree with Ram." Downey said nervously. "God only knows the roughing smoke we'll face if we dive into that Hellpit. Four years is ample time for monsters to stew in a cesspit of sin. I'm not exactly eager to explore that territory."

"Didn't you hear Du'Plasse?" Bride Wainwright interjected. "There's something a whole lot worse than a mad scientist going on here. There's some kind of global coup plotting against Templym and Knox Mortis is a general in it."

"Daphne's right." Adastra said. "We now have credible intelligence not only acknowledging the existence of Knox Mortis, but also confirming that he's an executive in an international rebellion. He's not simply some terrorist as we suspected, he's even deadlier. We have a responsibility to neutralize him."

"I don't think we can." Vandross began pacing nervously around the observation room. "We're not talking about a simple urban. We're not even talking about uncharted territory in the Hinterlands. This is a Hellpit. Auzlanten shut us off from this city specifically because of the evil lurking behind its borders. Nothing can go in and nothing can go out and that's best for everyone! If we go in we're as good as dead. There's no point in continuing the hunt if that's where it leads us. We can't very well arrest Mortis if we can't get to him alive!"

"What if we bomb the city?" Blye suggested trying to find common ground between the two sides of the argument. "Perhaps we can petition one of the primes or maybe the Regent himself to drop missiles on Budapest. If we smother the city in a blanket of fire then there's a good possibility Mortis would be killed in the bombardment."

"I'm not doing that." Downey said with his hand stroking his leathery face. "This is part of the Nephilim conspiracy that's sowing a lot of chaos into the Scourge's ranks. The imposter Auzlanten, if there is one, has a great deal to do with this... whatever the hell is happening. My confidence in the chain of command is out the window. If we ask the wrong man for the wrong thing, it'll alert Mortis and he can escape. Not to mention we'd be taking a severe risk being unable to confirm the kill." Volk had brought them all into the loop, relaying the same information that Warden Carthage had told him the day before.

"I know Patriarch Betankur personally." Daphne said. "He's a loyal man, a devotee of the Faith, a veteran with a history as long as the Regent's, and my friend. I trust him more than any of the primes or Illuromos. He has the authority to order a shelling of that scale. Nobody will care if we throw a missile or two at Budapest."

"But that will inform the others." Adastra sighed, finally taking his eyes off the monitor to stare at the ground. "It doesn't matter who the spy is. It could be the High Conservator, or the Regent, or even the Master of Templym, we don't know. But ordering a bombardment on Budapest will give away the fact that we're onto him. No...no the only way we are going to get this done is if we march in there ourselves."

"Army." Ram's Horn said, his grumbling voice sounding slightly more agreeable.

"He's right." Blackwell said as he began packing his granite pipe with a pair of shaky hands. "We can't go into Budapest just the five of us. There could be an army of demons there. Smoke, there probably is! You heard it straight from the Dilictor's mouth! The Nephilim is gathering an army for an abolition! The abolition of Templym most likely! We need to meet this threat head on with even greater force."

"You want to muster an army?" Downey said unenthusiastically. "That'll take an ungodly amount of time and it'll draw even more attention than a bombing. No. We go in, we kill Mortis, we get out. End of story."

"A small force is a lot quieter." Inquisitor Covalos said as he ran his armor clad fingers through his beard. "We'd have an advantage being more mobile and attracting less attention. We'll have to make it quick, though. And I agree with the Warden. If Mortis is powerful enough to assemble an army in Budapest, he's too dangerous to be taken alive. There's also the trust issue. The edicts our primes have sent out have done some good in weeding out spies, but is there really anyone we can trust? How many in our own ranks can you say with one hundred percent confidence where their loyalties lie?"

Silence befell the observation room. The only sound was Inquisitor Blackwell nervously sucking down fumes from his pipe. He broke the awkwardness with a deep sigh. "So. I guess it's settled then. We're going to Budapest. Great. Eternity sounds lovely anyway. Let's do it."

"I can't let you go in alone." Daphne stepped forward placing one hand on each of her Inquisitor friends' shoulders. "Your aid in Hrimata has saved a great many lives and put away one of the worst men I've ever seen."

"I wish we could have done it sooner." Adastra said bitterly. He noted that the new scar splitting her lips was just like one he had concealed beneath his black facial hair. "I wish we could have gotten to Monk about three hours sooner than we did. No human being should have endured what you went through."

"An acceptable loss." Wainwright said. "I would have gladly given my life up to detain Thomas Monk. I lived and he will soon die. Even though I was tortured, I am forever grateful to you all for aiding me in catching this scum. Warden Downey, if you'll have me I'd like to accompany you to Budapest. I can't stand the thought of my friends going into a Hellpit alone and I want to repay my debt to you."

"Well Bride Wainwright," Volk said. "I suppose our caravan can fit you in. You are aware that there's a strong possibility we won't be coming back from this?"

"I can live with that."

Volk shrugged, "Welcome to S-6319 then, ma'am."

"My Bride," Expurgator Blye stepped forward and puffed out his chest. "Permission to accompany you on this mission."

Daphne giggled, pleased to see the young investigator still eager to impress. "Well Yen, that's not my call. Warden?"

"Why not?" Downey said, his standard charming smile was noticeably absent. "Misery loves company after all."

CHAPTER 33

Thomas Monk was executed on Verrick 23rd, the day after he gave up Mortis. He was executed by a firing squad consisting of the members of his victims' families. It was impromptu so not everyone that wanted to attend did, but the line of guns formed was over two hundred long. There wasn't much left of him when the shooting subsided, but whatever remnants were left were burned by the Inquisition and the ashes scattered in the Odyssian Sea.

Bride Wainwright relinquished control of the Seraphim Solace to Agapist Lynchin her absence. She was not her first choice, or her second for that. Admonisher Fenrick Rickard was buried at the base of a birch tree in a private cemetery on Nyvett 30th, he would have been her first choice. Agapist Cyrus Kite finished serving a three week sentence in Niflheim Arcae for 2nd degree murder on Verrick 12th where he promptly began his two years of indentured servitude, just as he predicted. Despite his pig-headedness, he was a cunning strategist and master investigator, which would have made him her second choice. Expurgator Yen Blye might have been her third choice for the exemplary work he did on the Dilictor hunt. He was of course joining her on another manhunt.

Budapest was forbidden territory. As far as anybody could tell, not even Arodi Auzlanten had been inside the border walls since that bloody day over four years ago. They were all certain that there would be hardships inside, marauders and demons most likely. Some of them had been there at the violent conclusion of the Strife. They saw the chasms in the ground swallow their dead kin and the false angel fall from the sky. It was truly a disturbing sight to behold. So, they prepared as thoroughly as they could. Extra weapons, ammunition, armor, med kits, rations, fuel, everything they could possibly conceive of was gathered in surplus for what would no doubt prove to be their most brutal mission yet.

They planned to drive their chariot into Budapest. That meant their Indentured Inmate, Jameson Daurtey, was going into the Hellpit with them. This made him uneasy. He had years ago mused with his then-wife about vacationing in Budapest. That was before the Strife, before she cheated on him, before he murdered her lover.

They were on the road to the valley region of Jollhio, the Carthonian nation in which Budapest resided, when Warden Downey checked on Daurtey. "You feeling okay?" Volk asked as he parted the black soundproof curtains separating the pilot chamber from the passengers.

"Fine sir." Jameson was never much of a conversationalist. He didn't typically speak unless spoken to. Even then, he was a new kind of brief. His eyes were locked on the pavement as their caravan drove south, only taking one hand off the wheel to tug at the sweat drenched collar locked to his neck.

"You're afraid. I get that." Volk said assuredly. "We're all scared. Of course, we've got a few years of psychological conditioning."

"I spent a month in an Arcae. It was a Hellpit of its own."

"You're a hard man Daurtey, but don't act like you aren't afraid."

"Well, I'm going to the site of the worst massacre of Templym's only civil war with a few vials of poison strapped to my neck. I suppose I'm a bit tense."

"I've never needed to use that thing on you. You've acted in a standup fashion, part of the team just like the rest of us. Even if you're not in the thick of combat, you've been with us since we started in Parey."

"I appreciate that sir. I just...I'm not cut out for this."

"You've got this Daurtey. We just need you to drive us, like you've been doing for the past three months."

"Yeah, just like I've always driven, only now instead of causeways and urbans I'll be driving through a God forsaken skeleton city."

Volk could tell he was exasperated. He placed a hand on his shoulder in comfort before waving his wrist at the lock at the base of his neck, disengaging the venom collar. "You've got this. Just stay calm." Jameson smiled as the Warden turned to leave, then Volk said one more thing. "By the way, I'm technically not supposed to remove this until your sentence is up. I'll need to strap it back on when we get to the wall but I'll take it off again as soon as we're in."

Budapest had been completely sealed off from Templym by a network of vast walls constructed of stone and metal, as all Hellpits are blockaded. The Scourge built walls analogous to those of ancient medieval castles, though with a modern twist. The perimeter was set with a barricade one hundred and fifty feet high at its lowest point. The line stretched for approximately forty miles before reconnecting at the starting point. Vast blocks of iron and granite were reinforced with casings of ballistic fluid and pillars of tungsten. Sentry outposts were placed every half-mile outfitted with snipers, turrets, and every manner of guard conceivable.

The Budapest barrier jutted from the otherwise featureless valleys of drab shale, creating a network of black towers in the lifeless flatland. There was only one doorway in the whole perimeter. A quadruple sealed latch with security locks the size of buildings provided the only way in and out of the Hellpit. The access codes were kept by the commander of the guard, Praetorian Josiah Trialock.

He went by the rank Praetorian, though in actuality, he was an operating Conservator in the Shackle. This was to pay homage to his original 2nd tier rank in the Trench. He was one of the few members of the Bulwark that recanted during the Strife and joined Auzlanten. Unfortunately, his repentance did not come until the second day of the Battle of Budapest. He saved his company's lives by surrendering. Taking up as the lead guard of the Hellpit was his idea of retribution, forcing himself to look at the graveyard of thousands of his companions every day. He mourned the loss of his once noble organization, recognizing that with his death the Trench would become extinct.

Praetorian Trialock was an older gentleman, once on track to be the Trench's prime before the Strife. A bush of white whiskers coated his square jaw like snow on a plateau. The back of his hairless skull was decorated with a plethora of tattoos remaining from his time in a criminal syndicate during his youth. At the side of his neck was a black tattoo that read "prodotés" which translates to "betrayer". Beneath that was a red one reading "exagorazó" meaning "redeemed", a memento from his time in the Arcae. His black and blue battle plate was decorated with a bronze trim, paying homage to the Trench.

He stood silent in a sentry tower, leering into the dust bowl that was once the bustling urban Budapest through enamel glass paneling. He thought of his allies that were devoured by the ground there, forever trapped inside of one massive gluttonous grave. The crack of turrets being fired at unidentifiable targets stalking the bone yard replaced common office chatter and the thunder clap of an occasional sniper round from the nest on the roof replaced the intermittent phone call. Trialock never even saw the task force enter in, he just happened to have glanced over his shoulder as they came in.

"You the ones with a death wish?" Trialock asked as he turned to greet them. He was half expecting them to salute, but quickly realized they were too nervous to do so. He wasn't particularly concerned with the formalities.

"S-6319, at your service," Warden Downey said as he proceeded to make introductions, constantly being interrupted by thunderous longcannon shots from above.

"I would appreciate you filling me in." The Praetorian said unconcerned with the specifics of who the team was. "My Delta clearance should be more than sufficient to tell me what ungodly senselessness could have inspired you to go into Budapest."

"Circumstances have changed." Bride Wainwright said. "New information has come to light that threatens the increasingly fragile balance of..." Another sniper round interrupted her. "It threatens the balance of peace in Templym. The mission is now Beta classified which means all we need to tell you is that we need to go into Budapest to neutralize a high value target."

"I see, the paltry caste system masquerading as chain of command keeps me in the dark once more. By a show of hands, how many of you were actually at the Battle of Budapest?" Inquisitor Covalos, Bride Wainwright, and Herald Du'Plasse lifted their hands with puzzled expressions. "That's what I thought." As if on command, another longcannon shot rang out as he paused. "Look here."

Praetorian Trialock stepped over to the thick enamel window. They were twenty stories above the ground overlooking the Hellpit. A three mile long stretch of blanched white sand ended with a blackened city. The clear sky blue horizon ended where it met the shell of the urban. Roiling clouds of toxic black vapors billowed angrily over the disheveled cloudtouchers. There were tiny dots, likely some kind of organism, lurking behind dull grey boulders. Their eyes strained just to look at what Budapest once was, as though the atmosphere were trying to claw their eyes out with microscopic claws.

"In early 2718, Budapest was a bountiful trade center." Trialock mused, seemingly unfazed by the assault on his eyeballs. "Being at the center of Carthonia and under the watchful eyes of the Dictum's central stronghold made it an optimum place for merchants and tradesmen to exercise the beauty of free trade. Then Malacurai led the Bulwark to war."

"We're familiar with the..." Herald Du'Plasse began to speak but was cut off by another crack of a longcannon. "Bloody...we're familiar with the history."

"Good, I'm sick of recounting it." Trialock grumbled. "You may have noticed that the ecosystem of Jollhio is fairly uniform. Temperate climate accompanies smooth cut valleys of sedimentary rock. So why do you suppose..." Another sniper shot. "So why do you suppose Budapest is so different?"

"Because of the battle." Adastra grunted averting his gaze from the city. "The combination of the remnants of war accompanied whatever demonic activity happened once the false angel died perverted it."

"Correct." Trialock said as he began leading them away from the window. "The desert is the byproduct of incinerated organic matter. The thousands of dead were devoured and the dust of their remains scattered like cremated ashes. Hell, not like, it's literally a desert of the cremated remains of our dead kin. The storm clouds that lull over the city like a permanent curtain are the remnants of the battle as well. It's a collection of vaporized fuel, gun residue, rubble, explosive powder, radioactive gas, all of it the gaseous corpse of a slaughterhouse. Four years later and it didn't dissipate. It just collected into a singular mass blocking off sunlight from the city, providing nothing but the occasional deluge of acid rain."

"Might I ask what the point of this lecture is?" Inquisitor Blackwell asked, eyebrows cocked, legitimately confused.

"The point is that Budapest is a Hellpit in a whole lot more than just name. What I've told you is just what we know by looking from the outside. We put over a hundred unidentified beasts down every week here." Another shot from above. "It seems like today's a busy day. In the multiple years I've kept this city in quarantine, nobody, not the primes, not the Regent, not Auzlanten himself, has ever so much as requested a synopsis of how to get inside. You go in...there's a pretty good chance you'll join the thousands of granulated corpses in the dust bowl. You're aware of that, right?"

"We're aware of the risks." Warden Downey said, pausing as yet another shot rang out. "Damn it, Adastra could you go upstairs and get that sniper to shut up?"

"On it." The Inquisitor grunted as he made his way up to the eagle's nest.

"Big quarry." Ram's Horn muttered.

"Ram is right." Volk said in response. "Potentially the most important target of any of our careers is in there. There's probably more at stake here than we're even aware of. Kynigi et Kako, pursue the wicked, it's our oath."

"In nomine Veritas." Bride Wainwright said in concurrence. "In the name of truth."

"Fine," Praetorian Trialock sighed. "It's your bloody funeral."

A bitter death scented wind blew in from the ruined city from all the way atop the Budapest blockade. It required a stern constitution to stomach breathing in the dry dusty air of the Hellpit and the altitude seemed to increase the chemical stench tenfold. Adastra Covalos noted these details as he climbed a rough black iron ladder to the eagle's nest.

There were two options regarding the frequent crack of long ranged shells flying towards Budapest. The first was that some marksmen were having an eventful day. The other was perhaps a rookie fresh from the Tribulation was repeatedly trying to hit the same target multiple times over unsuccessfully. Either way, the task force was trying to debrief with the Praetorian of the Hellpit border and the constant firing needed to stop.

Adastra saw something that surprised him when he made it to the lookout. It was standard to station a team of sentries, usually four or five, to offer optimum coverage of the perimeter. Instead there was only one blue armored sniper on this lookout. The standard long ranged shooter would lay prone to better control their aim. This one was standing. It answered his question as to the accuracy of the shooter. It was evident that with every pull of the trigger, a red flower blossomed in the dusty plain below.

Jude Bethel peered over his shoulder as black vapor spewed from his back. The scarring on his steely battle plate reflected the storm over the broken urban. He spun his longcannon Venator and planted the butt of the rifle into the granite rooftop as he turned to face the Inquisitor, who quickly snapped into a heart-rip salute.

"At ease, Adastra." His scarred mouth did not smile.

"High Conservator, sir." He said dropping his hands to his side. "What are you doing here?"

"I'm no longer the standing High Conservator. Just Jude will do fine."

"Very well, but that still doesn't answer my question."

"Isn't it obvious Inquisitor? I'm coming with you into Budapest. I'm going to help you kill Knox Mortis."

Prelate Terran Greyflame was escorted by a squadron of Centurions to the Regent's office. He had assembled the primes for a briefing regarding Bethel's dismissal as High Conservator and as a formal way to announce the surrogate. After their scheming in Siberia, the Inquisition's leader was hesitant to even be in the same room as Invictus Illuromos. It comforted him to know that all of them would be there, all accept Bethel of course.

Their little rebellion was starting off strong. Jude went off to Jollhio to gather intelligence on a lead regarding one of the Nephilim's generals. Averrin had previously been in Rio Epiphanies recruiting soldiers for their cause while simultaneously rounding up prisoners caught by their edicts. Terran's task was to amass an arsenal of demon killing weaponry. Already, his inner circle had begun constructing Hekaton war machines outfitted with wardiron weapons as well as overseeing the destruction of a number of cults.

Greyflame did communicate with Magistrate Walthune and Patriarch Betankur to ensure he would not be alone with the Regent, which set his mind at ease. He didn't trust him, not by a long haul any more. He intentionally arrived to the meeting fifteen minutes late as a means to guarantee he would be accompanied by his fellow primes. The Centurion leading the way down the black tiled floors stopped at the thick entry door and slammed his gauntlet against the identity lock causing the gears to twist unlocked.

Terran was hopeful to greet Averrin and Arodus inside. Invictus may have been evil, but it was doubtful he could do anything with all three of them in the same room. So it was easy to understand why his heart sank when the door opened up and they were absent. Aside from the presence of two silver armored Centurions, the Regent was the only other man sitting at his desk. The four pyres at the four faces of the room flickering was the only sound.

Sweat began prickling the top of the Prelate's head and the back of his neck. He was nervous but his cold logical gaze would never betray his emotions. Subtly, he felt for the whip wound at the base of his back and the hand cannon at his side as he put on a pretend smile for his superior. The Regent responded with a stoic grin that appeared genuine.

"Terran, good to see you again," Invictus sounded as kind as a wolf wearing sheepskin. "Please enter. Can I get you something to drink? Baroque, ginset, grog, mead, I even have some kraken's blood if you're in need of something strong."

"Nothing for me, thank you." Terran said respectively, paranoid to accept anything edible from him for fear of poison. He was hesitant to enter, but he felt slightly more secure as he felt the gold leaf scriptures fused to his plate. He slowly stepped forward. "Apologies for my tardiness, Lord Regent."

"No apologies are necessary my friend." Invictus beckoned the Prelate to come forward at take a seat. Terran noticed there was only one seat made available facing his massive desk. "It seems you are not the only one running late today. Though I suppose the others are coming from separate time zones, some confusion is expected."

Greyflame sat in the only chair readily available, making sure his weapons were accessible. "I must say, I expected more of the new High Conservator. May I ask who Bethel's replacement is going to be?"

"In time it shall be revealed to you." Illuromos was sitting, but he still towered over the pale skinned Prelate. "Say, do you happen to have any of those cigars you had last week? I've been craving one ever since."

"I'm sad to say I don't, Invictus." Terran swallowed nervously. He was afraid that he was toying with him, that he figured out that he concealed detection incense and discovered something. Even though he still wasn't positive what it meant, he knew it didn't bode well.

"Do you find it unsettling, the timing of my actions, Terran?" He asked.

"I beg your pardon?"

"Eight days ago, you approach me with concerns that Bethel had brought to your attention. Two days later, I dismiss him on a mandatory medical leave. As you know, we of the Scourge strive for honesty and truth in everything we do. If you find the timing of my actions suspicious, you are free to voice this concern to me."

Greyflame thought that this might be a trap and calculated his response carefully. "I suppose it does seem a little too convenient. But I should not be hasty in my judgment. Perhaps our meeting illuminated you to the health issues Bethel was suffering from and expedited an imminent action."

"That was a very sly way to wriggle away from the question." The Regent's smile was gone entirely and his voice grew cold. "I'd like a straight answer to the question, Terran. If you're still concerned about where my loyalties are I'd prefer it if you voiced them now."

"Perhaps it would be better if we waited for the others to arrive." Terran continued intentionally giving ramblings to buy as much time as possible. "I would feel more comfortable concurring with my fellow primes before coming to a conclusion. We are in times of uncertainty, what with the imposter and now Bethel's dismissal. I'd like to ask the opinions of my colleagues before I-"

"They're not coming."

Greyflame's blood ran cold and sweat began dripping in cold streaks down his forehead, stinging his organic eye. "Pardon?" His reverberating preacher's voice had been reduced to whisper.

"Walthune, Betankur, nobody else is coming." A new, devious grin spread across the chiseled features of Invictus. "It's just going to be the two of us."

"That can't be..." Terran stammered. "I've been in communication with the both of them and they confirmed their presence here today."

"Written or spoken messaging?" The Regent pushed back from his desk and stood to his feet, beginning to circle his office chamber. Greyflame was silenced, his red augmetic eye leering at the back of his superior's head. "There is no need to respond to that Terran, I already know. You exchanged electronic lettering over the past three days, ensuring you wouldn't be caught alone with me. I know this because you weren't speaking to the Patriarch or the Magistrate...you were speaking with me."

The Prelate did not know entirely how to respond. It was becoming more and more obvious to him that Invictus Illuromos was harboring malicious intent. To impersonate a prime was considered treason of the highest definition. It did not matter that he held the highest office of power available to any other than the true Auzlanten. He was not above the law. Greyflame had his audio wire set to pick up this conversation, record its contents, and relay that information to an Inquisition data well in Jerusalem. He now has indisputable evidence as to the Regent's defection. That much pleased him, even though he recognized he was in mortal danger. Perhaps he could coax more damning information out of him.

His blood red armor began to growl as it whirred into combat mode. Terran leapt out of his chair, his forearm sized hand cannon made of the finest wardiron stretched out at arm's length pointed at the exposed skin on the back of Illuromos' head. He knew that even the clapshock infused bullets wouldn't be enough to pierce the jet flaksteel of his armored carapace. Arodi Auzlanten made that armor himself.

"This is treason. This isn't a simple dispute like you had with Bethel. This is an explicit lie with intent to deceive me into coming here. For that, I must detain you under the doctrine of the 10th Dogma and investigate you for corruption. If you resist, I must assume you are beyond repentance and must execute you where you stand."

The two Centurions still in the room spun their tech enhanced spears, poising them to kill the Prelate. Their obsidian cowls were lifeless, yet brimming with the desire to do harm. He knew that the Regent's bodyguards were loyal and dutiful, but he also knew that under the declaration of something as crucial as the 10th they were to stand down or aid the accuser. Yet these two were making to flank which could only mean one thing. Terran could only conclude that they were also corrupted by the Nephilim.

Prelate Greyflame did not waste a heartbeat in unnecessary thought. He turned his handgun to the Centurions. The first bullet impacted center of mass on the left one, sending bits of molten flaksteel flying as the round detonated. A second shot hit the right soldier, merely grazing his shoulder as he jolted to the side. A third shot hit the ceiling, sending plaster into the air as the atomically charged spear shunted the gun's barrel directly upward.

The Prelate did not bother drawing his whip. It would take too long and his gun was a perfectly adequate weapon. It bore the weight of a small battering ram and could be deftly swung around in his grip like a dagger. A few parries against the glowing green spear were made before Terran realized the first Centurion was still alive, noticing only after a well placed thrust pierced his pauldron. While on the backswing to drive the hilt of the cannon into his head, he sent another shot at the turncoat as he was attempting to stand and gain his bearings. The bullet sounded like an audience simultaneously stomping their feet in a single clap as it pounded against the service guard's head. The Centurion's pristine silver helmet became pink mist.

As the first Centurion fell, decapitated by the explosive force of the round, the second was knocked down as Terran clubbed him. The spear was no longer in his hand, but the guardian grappled wildly for something to improvise with. He had just turned the safety off of his fallen comrade's carbine when the Prelate unloaded another shot into his breastplate. The force of the explosion rocketed his helmet upwards, revealing the man beneath. The guardian's face had been etched with what appeared to be cult tattoos of violet flowers and Akkadian hieroglyphs. His eyes welled up with bloody tears as his collapsed lungs failed to shout out unholy curses. Greyflame was merciful and took off his head with the last shot in the chamber.

Terran dropped the hand cannon upon realizing it was empty and drew his other weapon. Thanatopsis, his tech enhanced whip, shrieked with crackling crimson energy as the Prelate turned to face the traitor Regent. The entire quarrel lasted approximately one minute and during that time, Invictus did not even turn to watch. His iron grey eyes were locked onto the weapon display.

The IX Regent was sentimental when it came to weaponry. Ever since his induction, he had only taken up arms three times, at the 13th and 14th Purus Crusades and again during the Civil Strife. He believed that he should only ever use a weapon when the fate of Templym was at stake. In each battle he wielded a different weapon. He wielded a double ended sword against the Puppeteering Imago of the 13th. The shoulder mortar Hyppocroxious was his weapon of choice against the Plague demons of the 14th. Scores of Bulwark soldiers were felled by the two motorized glaive-rings War and Punishment during the accursed Strife. Terran could see the nostalgic smile reflected in the finely polished glass of the display.

"Invictus, this is your last chance." Terran growled, offering one final option of grace. "I have enough evidence to execute you here and now. Come quietly and preserve what little honor you have remaining."

"You have nothing." Invictus grumbled, his voice like tank treads rolling to war. He didn't even face the Prelate.

Terran took no other risks. He cracked Thanatopsis. It lashed out like a bolt of scarlet lightning on a direct course of impact with the Illuromos' head. Faster than even his cybernetic eye could perceive, Invictus turned around. As though it were just another thread of iron chain or barbed wire, he wrapped the thick cord around his arm. The lancing tongues of energy would have eaten through any standard suit of battle plate. It did not even sear away the flaksteel's paint. The Regent scoffed at the futile attempt to slay him as he yanked the whip forward, dragging Terran across the two dead Centurions to rest within striking distance prostrate on the floor before pulling the weapon straight out of Greyflame's hand.

"Do you think me so naïve that I would not account for your wire?" Invictus bellowed. "I blocked off your transmission the moment you walked in. I had hoped I could convince you to join the Nephilim, but it quickly became clear to me that Bethel's incessant meddling ruined any chance of that happening."

"Heretic!" Terran screamed out of rage or anguish or spite, he wasn't sure. "You've betrayed everything your father stands for, in this life and the next!"

"If you are referring to Auzlanten, then I am glad to betray him. He's a treacherous fiend like none other. The Nephilim knows the truth, not Templym's founder. If only we had more time. Our plan was so glorious, but that warlock's meddling kept forcing us to accelerate, to advance without the proper care we need to..." Invictus turned his gaze to Terran lying on the ground and he smiled a devious grin. "Why am I telling you any of this? You're a liability and cannot be allowed to live."

The Regent extended his arm. The chains wrapped around it began trembling as though disturbed by an unseen wind, creating an ominous sequence of metallic ringing. Then a weapon manifested from nothing in his hand. Black crystals began materializing until a titanic maul was complete in his hand. It was made of a mysterious ebony material with a head the shape of a snarling beast with rotating saw blades for teeth. Ghostly orange light like a massive furnace gave it the imagery of a hungry dragon.

"The time to go to war is upon us." Invictus said caressing the powerful maul like it was a pet. "I shall march at the Nephilim's side against Auzlanten when he declares the start of the abolition. Krakatoa, will be my weapon when that war comes...and it is neigh, Terran. Have no fear. You won't be alive to witness the coming slaughter." He hafted it upwards, prepared to bring the snarling hammerhead down. "Any last words?"

Terran looked up, a single tear leaking from his real eye. Then he began to laugh. Not joyous laughter of celebration, but the bitter laughter of defeat.

"Why are you laughing?" The Regent demanded.

Prelate Greyflame took to his knees, in the position he traditionally prayed in. "I suppose I have three reasons to be happy, Invictus.

Reason one is that you've indelibly proven us correct. Up until now there was always an inkling of doubt gnawing at my mind, causing me to hesitate ever so slightly as I engaged in this subterfuge. I see now that even though I bent the law to serve my ends, I was justified in doing so. It is well with my soul."

"What good is that?" The traitor laughed in victory. "Your coup has failed and our uprising will still commence. You are dead and Bethel is marching into a trap as we speak. You have lost."

Terran continued his pitiable laugh, content to hear Walthune's name wasn't mentioned. He was hopeful that that meant he was still operating incognito. "The second reason is because I will be going home today! I will leave this fallen world of sin behind and join the Triune God of the Universe in Eternity! My suffering ends here and now. It is well with my soul."

"If you are content living as the peon of a slave driver, then I suppose your wish shall be granted. I would pity you, but that is a concept I have forgotten."

Greyflame still chuckled, the idea of being welcomed into the Kingdom of Heaven exhilarated him. "And the third reason...I always wanted to die a martyr."

"Adorable. Betankur said the same thing."

The Prelate shut his eyes and smiled as he prayed one last time. "It is well with my..."

Terran couldn't finish the final hymn. With inhuman speed and the ominous clattering of chains, Invictus brought Krakatoa down onto his prey's head. The impact reduced the Prelate's cranium into a splatter of pulped viscera. The roaring maw of the hammerhead churned and swallowed portions of skull, flesh, and brain matter as the demon possessed weapon lapped up the fallen Prime's remains.

The maul Krakatoa devoured its victim's head with carnal voracity. All that remained of Terran Greyflame's head was the augmetic eye that had been knocked out of his socket upon the hammer shattering his skull. The cracked glass sphere rolled across the floor, a smear of crimson obscuring the brass cogs beneath the surface and a trail of ganglions sliding behind it. It rolled a short distance before stopping at the base of the exit door. There, at the foot of the only escape route, it remained until the tiny gears stopped turning and the glowing scarlet pupil flickered and faded to black.

CHAPTER 34

Adastra Covalos sat in quiet contemplation in his quarters on board the caravan. His steely eyes were locked onto a mahogany lockbox with his black book resting atop of it. He was mulling over what High Conservator, no, just Jude Bethel, had revealed to him.

He revealed everything. He told them of his encounter with Auzlanten in the Judean desert. He told them of the Regent's rushed execution of the arms dealer. He told them how the Prelate received a positive reading from detection incense. But most importantly, Bethel brought them to light of the rebellion they were planning.

"It's still in the preliminary stages." Bethel concluded his long winded and almost preposterous tale. He was referencing the rebellion. "Prelate Greyflame and I had hoped to do this by the books. We'd win over the Magistrate and the Patriarch, then enact the 10th Dogma."

"But that wouldn't be possible after your dismissal." Warden Downey said, obviously sickened by the story. "The Regent would appoint somebody loyal to him, somebody that would never agree to overthrow him."

"Precisely. That eliminated our best chance at undermining Illuromos legally. So, we've opted to start a coup of our own. Walthune's in Kalkhan recruiting aid and Greyflame's in the Judah amassing an arsenal."

"Betankur?" Wainwright asked, concern in her voiced. "What's he doing to help?"

Bethel was silent for a moment as if he were hesitating at the thought of what he was going to say. "I haven't been able to make contact with him in over two weeks. I fear the Regent...eliminated him before he could sway the Veil against him."

"That's not possible." Blye said in protest. "Betankur is currently in the UPA aiding the crusade against the human trafficking operations there. We get daily updates on the good fight and we have evidence that says he's winning."

"Invictus Illuromos has the highest clearance in the Scourge." Vandross said scowling. "If half of what the High...what Jude has told us is true, then falsifying information isn't exactly beneath him."

"What's your part in this, Jude?" Herald Du'Plasse asked. "Why are you all of a sudden so eager to jump head first into a Hellpit?"

"I was directed to your force's manhunt based on the amount of information regarding the Nephilim and the Idolacreid." Bethel responded. "My Alpha clearance might have been redacted, but Magistrate Walthune has been keeping his algorithms running. Seeing as the trail you've been following has led you to Budapest, to one of the Nephilim's generals, I saw this as an opportunity to acquire more evidence and possibly take out a major player in this conspiracy."

"It all makes sense." Adastra said. "It all connects back to you a little too perfectly. You gave us this assignment back in Rexus, a manhunt that's spanned four countries. Then just as we're closing the noose around our quarry you show up with a perfect excuse to tag along."

"I don't blame you for being distrustful. I will gladly subject to Veritas interrogation, but I doubt that'll convince you any further. After all, part of my story hinges on the enemy's ability to surpass its power, another convenient sounding excuse." Bethel grunted. "Damn this creature, its plan is good. Don't you see that it's trying to start another Strife! We can't let that happen."

"I agree." Volk said. "The best shot we have at keeping the abolition from occurring is to go into Budapest. We eliminate him as soon as possible. So, the only question left is whether we let you tag along for the ride. How can we guarantee you won't stab us in the back?"

"I've prepared an ultimatum." Bethel handed a detonator to Warden Downey. "There's five pounds of clapshock inside of my plate. If at any point you think I'm a traitor, send me to the Lord."

"The extra support would be nice." Adastra said wearily. "Other than that, is there any other reason we should let you accompany us?"

For the first time that day, Jude's mangled mouth perked up in a grin. "I have a Hekaton."

Inquisitor Adastra Covalos was conflicted. So much of the certainty and the absolute truth that the Scourge preached, that he clung to, was being questioned. Never in his life, not even during the Civil Strife, had his ideology been so clouded. He needed focus. There was only one source of certainty he could wholly depend on.

He began his ritualistic prayer. Adastra needed to be as close to Christ as possible. That involved projecting one's spirits out of their flesh. Astral projection was the primitive magickal means to do this, but the Serbian had a much simpler and less demonic way to bring his mind closer to God. He needed to part from his flesh, though not literally. The human body was made in the Lord's image, but it was sinful in nature. All sin must be punished.

Adastra had stripped down to nothing more than a white towel wrapped around his waist. His pale, thickly muscled torso was decorated with marks. Masses of scar tissue took all manner of shapes. Gnarled circles from bullet holes, pink and white lines like poorly installed circuitry, black burn marks, and purple bruises still lingering from the Imago fight decorated him like paint on a canvas. The most glaring scars were those on his back. He wore a patchwork of messy lines where flesh had been repeatedly flayed opened and scabbed over like a gruesome cape.

He clicked open the lockbox and opened it up. Resting comfortably on a red velvet bed was a spike whip, exactly the kind the

Scourge used as its emblem. He then opened up the black book, the one he had been recording his sin in for the past eighteen years. He was twenty-six. Then he began closing the gap between him and the Lord.

"Forgive me Father for I have sinned." Adastra said to the Holy Spirit. "It has been fifteen days since my last confession. During that time, much uncertainty has been planted in my mind. Perhaps I should start from the beginning."

Adastra leafed through the pages of his notebook. "Verrick 10th. On that day I committed a number of offenses against your Word and your Grace. I felt hatred for Thomas Monk and a desire to inflict suffering upon him. I took great pleasure in the beating I gave him trying to perform my job. I must recognize that all humans, even those that profane Your great vision, are intrinsically valuable and made in your image. I repent and inflict one lash upon my flesh as penance."

He flicked the whip over his shoulder. The sharp claws of the whip dug into his scarred back meat like a hungry wolf. He ripped it out, causing a few streams of blood to trickle out. He didn't flinch, even though the pain felt like a gunshot. He had several more lashes to get through.

"Your Grace is abounding, freely given. I thank you endlessly, Selah." He turned to the next page. "Verrick 11th. In my anger, I took Your great name in vain twice. I also allowed my eyes to look lustfully at a woman I am unmarried to. I recognize that this failure is hardly my first in this unending struggle. I repent and inflict three lashes upon my flesh."This ritual continued for over an hour. In all, he flogged himself twenty-eight times, turning his back into a red carpet of bloody abrasions. In a sick way, it mimicked the cloak he wore with his battle plate. But just as he always had, once his self beating ended he washed off the blood and covered the scars. He felt no more focused than before.

Yen Blye had a method of prayer that was dissimilar to Adastra's method of regaining focus. He sat with his legs crossed in a lotus meditation. A bowl of Himalayan incense burned, filling his small bedchamber with the peaceful aroma of spiced fruit. He had stripped his armor in favor of a white bodysuit. A silver chain dangled around his neck which ended in the palm of his hand. He was gripping the medallion so tightly that a streak of blood ran out of the cracks between his fingers.

His eyes were closed tightly. "Why don't you answer me?" He petitioned an unseen power. He had been quietly crying out for the past twenty minutes. "I require guidance. I've made so many mistakes and I understand if you are upset. I wish to make amends. I wish to right this offense. But I need guidance, your guidance. We are about to trek into Budapest on a mission to slay Knox Mortis."

The bowl of incense had been continually producing a lazy cloud of white mist. The savory scented vapors began to wisp around randomly as though battered about by an invisible force. Then the smoky tails of perfume began to conceive a faint outline. It was a vaguely humanoid outline made of the pleasing aroma. "Budapest?" A calm voice emanated from the cloud, unclear if it was feminine or masculine. "How did the trail lead there?"

"You speak!" Blye said in a hushed exclamation as he opened his eyes grateful to see the silhouette of smoke. "Please forgive my trespass against you. Had I known who Thomas Monk truly was I would have acted differently."

"Don't grovel. It doesn't suit you, but most importantly it is inclined to spike my ire. What is your excuse?"

"I had no idea Monk was a member of the cult of the Nephilim. I never saw the violet lily and nobody thought to inform me, dismissing it as a trifle commodity. Had I been aware of his allegiance I would have..."

"But you weren't." Wispy fingers of scented smoke brushed against Yen's cheek. It noted the baggage building up his eyes once more. "Because of your neglect the Scourge was able discern their target's whereabouts. This could have been prevented. If you had simply opened up an evidence report you would have seen the holy symbol and realized the threat Monk's capture posed. Yet you did not."

"I apologize for this mistake."

"Mistake? My boy, this fallacy represents a catastrophe. Knox has been compromised because of your failure to eliminate Monk before he could disclose information. This will require an adjustment in the grand design."

"I deserve punishment. I understand if my life is forfeit." Blye extended his bare wrists to the fog person, a symbol of surrendering one's life.

"Yes, you deserve to suffer, but not yet. Your part is too crucial. You will face judgment once the abolition has ended, not until then."

"What would you have me do, my lord?"

"S-6319 will encounter Mortis in Budapest. He will capture you and keep you imprisoned until you are extracted. During this period, you are to maintain your cover at all costs, even to your true family. Do not draw suspicion to yourself. The dog Bethel is immensely paranoid. He will be overly cautious. Do as you have done for the past two years."

"I am loyal to the Scourge above all else. I am devoted to my oath and my Bride."

A vibrating growl that was likely tantamount to laughter came from the vapor creature. "Good. Nobody suspects anything yet, but that could change with the slightest misstep. Maintain this masquerade and do nothing rash. Do this and you will continue to play your part in the grand design with admirable proficiency."

"And I shall still be...rewarded?"

The voice in the mist growled, or perhaps it was a chuckle. "Yes. You will have Daphne. Just as I promised, she will be your bride in more than just rank. Or perhaps you have outgrown this fantasy and desire something else. Perhaps you would rather steal her away as your personal concubine."

"Marriage would be my preference, but I will update you if my desire changes."

"Excellent." The incense figure began to dissipate as it spoke a few final words. "Do not attempt to gain contact with me again. We are in the final moments before the dawn of a new age. I will inform you of any changes when the time comes."

Yen grinned as the ghost faded out of existence. He released his stranglehold on his necklace. He dabbed away droplets of arterial smear with a blood stained handkerchief. He first cleaned off his hand and then polished off the amethyst pendant depicting a marsh lily. "Thank you...lord Nephilim."

Hekatons were the primary war engines of the Scourge. They were heavy armored titans hoisting weapons capable of leveling armies. Named after the mythological titans of ancient Greece, these machines could offer devastation to the enemies of Templym if properly piloted. The smallest variants were Swifts, which stood fifteen feet tall and operated under the control of four pilots, each with four different types of weaponry. This is a stark contrast to the Gigarobus which stood at monumental proportions, some rivaling the height of cloudtouchers. The former is the model that Bethel was able to acquire.

Normally, he could muster the strength of an entire battalion of Hekatons. With his clearance revoked and his title stripped, all he could rally was a single Swift. The disgraced High Conservator could not even acquire a fully functioning one. The vessel was called Peregrine by its deceased pilots because of its slender structure and swift pacing. It stood only slightly taller than the task force's caravan, but had significantly more battle potential. Its body was decorated with slate colored flaksteel and yellow banners, signifying past Beacon allegiance. Its metal structure possessed tree trunk thick legs that rose into a multi-faced torso on each flank. The standard Swift came outfitted with a heavy Gatling turret, deconstruction siege cannon, plasma thrower, and mechanized melee device. Unfortunately, only Peregrine's machine gun and greatsword bays were operational.

Jude Bethel took the primary Gatling gun seat and thereby controlled the bipod's movements. Its steely paint was still blackened from the battle that saw its pilots out and the two inoperable weapons had already been harvested for recycling. Herald Du'Plasse volunteered to wield the Swift's sword arm. It worked well because of the Hekaton belonging to his organization, but it was necessary considering he was the only other among them that had proper training with such an engine.

The caravan was parked directly next to Peregrine in front of the massive metal doors shutting Budapest off from the rest of the world. Jude and Oslin were armed and ready to go while the rest could load up in their bulky transport at their leisure. For the first time since its construction, the barricade was opening.

Trialock's genetic signature and key codes triggered the mechanisms to fire to life. Maintenance teams considered the locking gears to be low priority, so upkeep was never performed on the contraption. This meant that the pistons and cogs had become rusted with age. The complex locking mechanics shrieked and wailed with demonic sounding creaks as they slowly moved open. It was ironic, or perhaps appropriate, that such hellish cries came from a door to a Hellpit.

Praetorian Trialock's gruff voice boomed over loudspeakers as the door moaned open to reveal the dust bowl of cremated dead. "I pray that this isn't going to be a one-way. Stay strong and fight hard, In Nomine Veritas."

"That's our cue to go." Downey projected through the caravan and the Hekaton. "Do you think that scrap heap can keep up with us, Jude?"

"I'm more concerned about losing you in my wake Volk." He said, trying to lighten the grim mood. If they weren't going into this apocalyptic wasteland he might be brimming with excitement. Instead he was filled with dread like he'd never felt before.

With that sentiment and a cloud of dust trailing closely behind them, the task force dispatched full speed into Budapest. The screaming doors hissed shut behind them. They would never open again.

CHAPTER 35

The environment of the Hellpit was truly disturbing. The very idea of driving on top of thousands of incinerated corpses, who were repeatedly kicked up in a blanched billowing cloud in their trail, shook every one of them. Every so often, a living thing would be just barely visible on the horizon. Most commonly it was a humanoid outline but it would sometimes appear as a quadrupedal or large insectoid creature. The figures were always hazy and disappeared whenever they got close enough to distinguish any detail. The eerie, arid atmosphere of the desert reeked with the stench of decay and sorrow. Budapest stood as a proverbial monolith, immortalizing the terrifying destruction that occurred during the Civil Strife.

Peregrine appeared like a massive metal man with two heads as it plowed through the dust plain to enter the city. It encompassed fifty feet with every wide stride, which was more along the line of leaping, as though it were galloping like a bipedal horse made of flaksteel. Its goldenrod banners flapped about in the polluted turbulence. The war engine was easily able to keep pace with the chariot. The two metal contraptions side by side presented a striking picture. The large transports entered into the broken, crumbling urban without flinching, making them appear as mighty warriors charging headlong into Hell itself. The thick metal hulls of the vehicles hid the unease of the soldiers within.

They crossed the desert of the dead in just a few minutes. They did not encounter any of the silhouette beasts, though none could decide if this was a good thing or a bad thing. What was most disconcerting was what happened as they crossed the threshold into the rusted city. The roiling storm cloud lurking over Budapest blotted out the sunlight. The ominous blanket of smoke and ash did not eclipse the light entirely, rather it stained the sunlight with a sickening mauve color which insulated the city from its warmth. They had hoped that upon entering the skeleton city that the desert of ashen humans would dissipate. Instead the organic debris was just as numerous as the dead outskirts with additional mounds heaped against rotting buildings.

They slowed their pace upon entering Budapest. Dead buildings protruded from the blanched "sand" like arrows piercing hide. The dilapidated cloudtouchers were all half collapsed and caked with a thick crust of maroon rust and black mold. Abandoned chariots blasted open by the horrific battle four years ago were scattered about like discarded bones in a wolf's lair. It was distressing to see a once bountiful urban in such a cataclysmic state of disarray. Such downfall was only appropriate considering the wide scale slaughter from the Strife.

The task force needed to find any semblance of civilization, or the closest thing that could qualify in this Hellpit. It was an anathema to believe that any human could possibly survive in this environment, but surely enough there were indications of life. Bethel noticed tracks trailing through the dust-shrouded, rockfoam streets. Footprints, vaguely human shaped and sized, were speckled about. Herald Du'Plasse took control over Peregrine while Bethel disembarked to inspect the tracks. Du'Plasse amplified the infrared sensors to better detect potential life while Bethel attempted to distinguish the tracks' direction and source.

Bethel winced at the scent of the air. A stench of sulfurous gas and rotting bodies dominated the atmosphere. It smelled like a battlefield, ripe with smoldering explosions and mass graves. It did not surprise him that such an evil place would assail his senses so. He jutted the thoughts from his mind. Nobody wanted to stay any longer than they had to, so he returned his focus to see where these tracks led.

"I see fourteen, maybe fifteen sets here." Jude's calculated voice crackled over their radio wires. Short range communication was still operating, but the toxic storm above rendered long range impossible. "Human, they're fresh, too."

"Define fresh." Adastra's voice echoed through a light haze of static.

"Hours maybe, I can't get an exact gauge on the time. This is a new kind of...terrain."

"Where do they lead?"

"North, deeper into the city. There's more," Bethel hunched down and got a closer look at the imprints. "It looks like most of them were forced together uncomfortably, like they were bound together. Four or five on the outside, surrounding maybe ten others. Like captors transporting prisoners. Oslin, weapons at the ready. There are hostiles nearby."

Jude reentered Peregrine, clicking the first drum of rounds into its oversized Gatling gun. As if it were a giant metallic soldier, it hoisted its gun arm upwards in an aiming position. The caravan followed a safe distance behind, slowly rolling through the ashen waste. The tracks proceeded for a short stretch of approximately a quarter of a mile. They hoped that it would lead straight into the heart of the dead legion and by extension to Knox Mortis. It was a vain hope.

They were watching in the observation deck of the caravan. Daurtey drove close behind the prowling Hekaton. The eerie light stabbed at their eyes even though it was filtered through tinted ballistic glass. This would normally be a time when the teammates would gather together and exchange merriments. Humors were painfully absent as they leered out of the port with serious faces.

"There!" Bride Wainwright exclaimed breaking the silence. She pointed an alabaster clad finger upwards towards the ramparts of the rusted buildings overhead. "Did you see it?"

"See what exactly?" Vandross said, nervously packing relaxant herbs into his pipe.

"A figure, in the upper levels of the buildings, I think it was a man."

"What kind of madman would go up there?" Volk said. "Look at these things, they're barely supporting their own weight. A stiff breeze could collapse them."

"This is Budapest." Blye suggested with a shrug. "Any people still living in this area wouldn't exactly have a great regard for safety or sanity."

"I think you're missing the implications of that statement." Adastra muttered with his usual seriousness. "We're being hunted."

"Last time I checked we were hunting someone." Downey retorted with a nervous chuckle.

Adastra grunted. "We're in hostile territory looking for the general of an army that's likely trying to destroy all that we hold sacred in life. Did you really expect we'd just walk in, blast Mortis' smoking head off, and go home?"

"The dead legion is watching us." Daphne said in agreement. "I'm certain of that. I think they're stalking us from the cloudtouchers. Bethel, keep your eyes up." She said clicking on her wire. "I think there might be hostiles in the upper floors. We could be walking into an ambush."

Peregrine lifted up its sword arm to signal a halt. The Daurtey heeded this warning and braked to a stop. "The tracks end here." Bethel announced over the communicator. "They just...stop."

"Bethel, do you see that to the West?" Oslin asked. "They look like black stones in the dust." Peregrine's visual monitor zoomed in on the area the Herald was referring to. The Hekaton itself did not have any transparent ports to see out of, but had a number of cameras that the pilots could gaze out of. The disgraced High Conservator enhanced the image and enlarged it to better focus on the oddity in the desert at the base of a skeleton building.

"It looks like puddles in the dust," Bethel said with a scowl. "Blood, most likely." Then the camera picked up additional detail. The anomaly was not just a collection of blood pooling at the foot of a rust column, but there were droplets of red rain still falling from above. "Yes, definitely blood and it's falling down from..."

Bethel stopped the thought in the middle of the sentence. The task force believed briefly that the smog cloud blotting out the sun was raining a bloody precipitant on them. The reality was more distressful. The upper levels of the abandoned building had been decorated with a sadistic collection of bodies. There were dozens of dead humans impaled on rusted pikes of black iron and left to dangle from the cloudtoucher like flags on display. Each were in varying states of decay, some resembling little more than dried skeletal masses while others were weeping fresh blood onto the ground below. The number of dead could not be accurately gauged. There was no apparent method to this torturous practice. Some pikes had multiple bodies stuck to them. Some bodies were impaled vertically while others were horizontal and some just pinned by a single arm or leg. Bethel could swear that he could see the crucified victims still squirming in agony.

There was no time to react to the gruesome trophy display. A noise, like the bellowing bass of a war horn filled the otherwise silent streets with a thundering call to arms. The noise was followed by a litany of distant screams. Loud whooping shouts of madmen came from every angle. It seemed that Daphne Wainwright was correct, much to her distaste. They had walked into an ambush.

Shadowy figures began appearing from the windowsills and blast holes of the buildings. Soldiers of the dead legion rushed to the forefront of the edges with weapons in hand. One would expect primitive marauder weaponry made of scrap metal, but this was not the case. They came fully armed with modern military grade ordinance. Instantly, brass bullets began plinking off the armored hulls of the transports and shooting up columns of dust from the ground. This would not prove to be of significant threat to the Scourge warriors. The explosives would prove to be much more dangerous. How these beast men acquired rocket lancers and grenade launchers was a mystery that they couldn't dwell on. These weapons could destroy their only means of transportation with ease.

Peregrine's gun began cracking as hundreds of bullets flew out and bombarded the attackers. A mist of disturbed rust and vaporized blood was produced wherever the heavy Gatling gun pointed.

Marauder body parts plummeted down to their level. Black craters were beginning to appear around the siege engine, indicating that the dead legion were inaccurate shots. Even considering this, Bethel could tell that they were hopelessly outnumbered. He did not want to risk the destruction their foes could inflict.

"Fall back to the outskirt of the city!" He yelled after a few seconds of the assault occurring. Daurtey did not need a second order. Despite the scattered explosions and hail of bullets, he jackknifed the chariot and turned back to drive away from the killing ground with all due haste.

The Swift escorted the caravan out of its retreat. Despite the constant chaos of battle, it maintained a quick-footed pace. It dealt out significantly more punishment than it received, even though they were in full retreat. Its golden Beacon banners were the only entities that were noticeably harmed as they became pin-holed by brass slugs. The slate steel armor was not even dented by the bullets, the rockets could have been another story. Even as the Hekaton vaulted over mounds of cremated desert, the trajectory algorithms compensated the engine's path of movement to avoid the explosive projectiles. The marauders assaulting them from above seemed unable to land a significant blow.

There were so many of them. Driving through half a mile of roadway did not seem to thin their numbers at all. This was a combination of the tactical placement of their numerous forces and their adept mobility. The Scourge soldiers noted the way they moved in the upper balconies with ease. Bridges constructed of scrap connected adjacent cloudtouchers and some of the legion vaulted across by swinging across on chains like apes on vines. Their pursuit was unrelenting, their assault unflinching. These marauder people seemed bent on their complete annihilation with little regard to their own safety.

The caravan drove with as much speed as it could muster, its rubber tires pounded the desert sand into the ground trying to evade the initial ambush. They drove with the linear intent of escaping with as little damage as possible. This was just what the dead legion had anticipated.

Their withdrawal seemed to be going well. The gun and rocket fire was becoming less frequent. S-6319 was too preoccupied with their escape route to notice the shifting in an oncoming dust mound. One of the piles of ash sifted slowly as they gained distance from their attackers. Something was buried underneath it. By the time anybody noticed the thing coming out of the mound, it was too late.

Something, or someone, burst out of the pile of human ash. A giant humanoid figure, almost ten feet tall, made of metal and wielding a massive halberd came out directly in the path of their retreat. The warriors in the caravan were unable to get a clear look at the giant. It attacked the chariot with a single swing of its pole armed axe, bringing their retreat to a screeching halt.

The long halberd's rusted blade smashed into the pilot's bay of the chariot. The heavy edge sliced through the armored flaksteel carapace as if it were as soft as wood. Splinters of steel, rubber, and glass scattered across the barren desert ground as the caravan spun out of control. The large transport crashed down on its side before slamming into the broken remains of a dilapidated trade office. The side of the chariot was buried in stone and plaster rubble as the antoniat fusion coil engine sputtered out and died, and the wheel axels stilled.

Jude and Oslin could do nothing but watch as their friends were tossed aside by the metal giant. The immense power they just witnessed left them speechless. The golem knocked a thirty ton transport aside as though it were a child's ball. The hulking figure stood at the center of the dust shrouded road in direct opposition of Peregrine, blade poised to strike. Horrid thoughts dreading the fate of their friends flooded their thoughts.

"Dear God, what is that?" Oslin uttered breathless from inside the Swift.

"Who cares? Kill it!" Jude yelled out as he let his Gatling gun roar.

A hail of bullets was hurled at the living metal behemoth at the same moment it charged forward. A number of shots found their target either embedding into its armor skin or ricocheting off. The Hekaton did not slow the giant's assault. The edge of the axe struck the torso of the war machine with the force of a rocket. A chink was certainly made in the industrial strength hull of the Swift, but this fiend had clearly never fought a Hekaton before.

Using the inertia of the blow, Peregrine's torso swiveled on its rotation axis so the sword arm was now facing the giant. Stealing the momentum of the giant's attack, Oslin brought the wide double blade of the engine's longsword down in a lethal arc. The sword landed between the thing's shoulder plate and the base of its neck. A spurt of fulsome liquid spewed out of the wound, but the metal man refused to slow.

The rapid twist of the Swift's torso only fooled the giant once. Jude and Oslin worked in perfect conjunction, interchanging between sword and gun as the combat necessitated. The pristine flame colored longsword of the Hekaton clashed against the rusted halberd, sending the constant ringing of metal on metal out into the streets of Budapest.

The two metal warriors were complete opposites in their approach to the battle. Peregrine was graceful yet valiant as its weapons were unleashed with tactical elegance. The only sound emanating from it were the whirling pistons and creaking gears as the mechanisms were honed to obliterate the target. The unholy, dust-shrouded metal man was barbaric in its assault. The long hafted axe was brandished with furious abandon for safety. With every killing swing it bellowed a throaty roar like that of a starving predator. Every attack left its defenses open for a strike, but it was too quick. Each instance when Oslin attempted to drive the sword arm into its exposed flank, the giant deflected the normally lethal thrust with speed like nothing a fiend that size could possibly wield.

The initial melee lasted forty seconds. Peregrine's flaksteel carapace was now decorated with dents and rends from glancing blows of the halberd. Meanwhile the wound on the metal man's shoulder blade, which was still seeping oily liquid, was the only successful blow inflicted on their part. Instances that resulted in brief gaps between them resulted in Jude unleashing a flurry of bullets only to swap back to Oslin's sword once again. The Hekaton was a full five feet taller than this metal man and represented some of the finest work of Scourge technologists. This unholy golem should have been minced to a pulp of scrap and slime given the force they were dealing out. Instead, this marauder contraption seemed to have the advantage.

There was a pause after the initial melee, and more inhuman roaring began surrounding them. The marauders from the first ambush had caught up with them. They weren't unleashing their onslaught of munitions, they were just watching. Figures were leering down from the upper landings and rooftops of decrepit buildings. Guns were being swung about like banners, not being fired at all. The collection of animalistic hollers provided an ominous backdrop to the sounds of the two metal behemoths dueling.

The golem seemed rallied by the barbarian crowd. It was filled with a new, vigorous bloodlust. The halberd came against Peregrine in wide circular slashes. The polearm assaulted the Hekaton with unrelenting efficiency and unpredictable speed. Peregrine put up an admirable fight, but could not deflect the giant's axe for too long.

Oslin was thrilled when he landed a second swing that scraped its metal chest. He realized too late that it was a ploy. The giant goaded him into a trap. With his sword arm extended, Peregrine's melee arm was painfully vulnerable. The rusted halberd came down onto it, splitting the limb down the middle vertically. Mechanical parts squealed as the curvature of the axe sank through the sword arm. The giant wrenched the weapon free with a guttural throe of carnivorous glee before smashing it into the war machine's torso. In a last ditch effort, Jude swiveled the torso around, once more swapping the sword for a heavy gun. Every ounce of reserved bullets was fired uselessly into the ground as the giant parried the Gatling cannon away with the long, rusted haft of the halberd.

With the engine's last scrap of ammo expended, made obvious by empty clicking, the fight was over. The metal giant knew this. The wide blade of the halberd sank into Peregrine's torso, bringing the gallant machine down on its knees. As he retracted the weapon, alarms flashed bright lights inside of the pilots' bay, accompanied by screeching whistles. Jude and Oslin paid them no heed, the noise eclipsed by the sheer magnitude of the thunderous roars of the metal giant and the crowd of marauders. The choir of animal screams culminated with the metal giant driving the axe into the same gash he had just previously made, widening the chasm struck into the hull of the Hekaton. The alerts faded to nothing as Peregrine was slaughtered.

The end of the rusted blade cut deep enough that it nearly struck Jude once it killed their engine. He scrambled to unbuckle his harness and find his weapons. Greasy metal fingers filled in the rend. The fiend was prying open the wound to get to the pilots of the Hekaton. Jude abandoned trying to undo his harness, instead slamming a magazine into his longcannon.

Diseased wind slammed against Bethel's face backed by a flood of wild hollering voices as the marauder construct ripped open Peregrine. He was now exposed to the environment of the Hellpit. Worse, he was at the mercy of the giant. Jude refused to be subject to this metal tyrant. He fired a single explosive round point-blank into the giant's head. It winced back with the massive impact of the round. Dirty steel peeled back, revealing sickly pallid flesh and a single featureless black eye. A portion of the wan skin had been shorn to unveil oozing bodily fluids. The former High Conservator was chilled as the blank eye stared at him.

Jude didn't get a second shot. The giant yanked him out of his harness with a single metal clad hand. He was overwhelmed by the eerie violet light stinging his eyes from the cloud of death from above and the ungodly howling from the marauders surrounding him. Off in the distance, he saw the felled chariot being swarmed by hazy figures. It appeared as though the barbarians were clawing at the transport and trying to get into it. He might have clawed or clambered to break free of the giant's grip. He never received the opportunity. The giant slammed Bethel onto the corpse of Peregrine and everything went black.

Pale hazy firelight from a smoldering chariot, their chariot, was burning at the center of a courtyard. Flickering orange light provided a warm contrast to the gloomy mauve. Vandross reckoned it was at the peak of midday, though he couldn't be sure. The smog of stale battle fumes perverted all natural sense of time and he certainly wouldn't be using any tech. They took it all. They took his Reisinger, his bastard sword, and six of the eight knives he had on his person. The dead legion, or whatever they were truly called, carted them away like slaves. He was thankful that Bethel wasn't awake for the transportation, lest he have painful flashbacks from his past.

Nobody was hurt too badly in the crash. A few superficial injuries, cuts and bruises mostly, but nothing severe. What was more disturbing to them was the idea of what their captors were planning on doing with them. The marauder people were unruly and uncivilized. Common practice would be to kill them and do unseemly things with the bodies. So why take them alive? A common fear of what was to come was shared among the members of S-6319.

They were drug to this courtyard. They took all of their weapons but left their armor intact. How the dead legion acquired arms equivalent to their own was beyond the concern of speculation, but these grisly men donning shoddy iron platemail were armed to the teeth. A large marauder, not as large as the giant, slung Jude, who they hoped was just unconscious, over his shoulder. They might have been walking for minutes or perhaps hours, it was impossible to tell in this wasteland. They were then brought to this courtyard and there were eight black metal pikes jutting out of molded plinths. The giant must have dragged what was left of their caravan into the center of the semicircular opening at the base of a broken cloudtoucher. It seemed like the remnants of the chariot had been tossed into an empty fountain.

The pikes were a few feet above the ground. Not nearly as high as those poor victims skewered on upper levels that they witnessed earlier, but high enough that they still dangled slightly off the ground when strung up by their wrists. The process allowed for time to inspect their foes. The grizzled men wore dilapidated plate-mail but carried pristine Zeduac rifles. They waved and pointed the guns indiscriminately. Their foreign marauder language was a series of grunts, mutters, and hand gestures. Their skin had the blanched color and wrinkled texture of a poorly preserved cadaver. Clearly Budapest did not serve as the optimum environment to live in, yet these men seemed to be thriving in it.

The task force was in varying states of quality. Jude Bethel was unconscious but thankfully the only new mark on his face was some swelling on the head. Adastra Covalos had his left arm dislocated after trying to fight off the dead legion when they swarmed the wreckage. He wore a grim scowl beneath his disheveled hair. Ram's Horn was silent as usual. He was tall enough to stay standing on the ash floor. Oslin Du'Plasse suffered a minor scorch on his forehead and the two hair braids at the side of his head came undone during the brawl. Yen Blye nervously chewed on his lip, inspecting his allies for injury, Daphne in particular. She had received a black eye from one of the kidnappers, after killing three of them with her rapier of course. Volk Downey bashed his nose in during the crash and red was streaming down the corners of his mouth. Vandross Blackwell somehow managed to keep that massive crimson hat on even amidst the chaos, his brow locked into a grimace. Each of the pikes they were chained to were spaced out a few feet, making communication outside of shouting impossible. Marauders of the dead legion trundled about the courtyard, grunting constantly in their brutish vernacular.

Volk spit some of his own blood on the ground at his feet. "Everybody alright?" He yelled over muttering foes and howling hell winds.

"All well considering, I suppose." Vandross said trying to remain positive.

"Is everyone here?" Daphne asked unable to see everyone over the flaming heap of scrap at the center of the courtyard.

"Yeah, all eight of us are here." Oslin yelled in response. "Bethel's out though. That giant...thing knocked him out cold."

"Wait, something's not right." Adastra retorted.

"No kidding." Ram's Horn bellowed.

"With all due respect Inquisitor," Blye shouted unable to see him over the pyre. "I think there are several things wrong with this situation. The atmosphere, the soil, the people, the goliath who killed our best weapon..."

"No, Adastra's right." Volk responded. "Somebody's missing, who's missing?"

"Nobody's missing." Daphne yelled. "With Bethel's addition, there are five official members of the task force and three accompaniments."

"What about the driver?" Oslin said after swallowing hard. "Where's Daurtey?"

The giant entered upon hearing that. The scattering marauder people looked to the central bonfire where it stood, careless of the fire scorching its feet. It had leapt down from a balcony that nobody thought to look up and inspect. Clearly it was waiting to make a dramatic entrance. In each of its massive metal hands, the behemoth was holding a severed half of Jameson Daurtey.

Now that the hectic adrenal high of combat was through, they received a much clearer picture of the giant. It wasn't made of metal like they had thought. This titanic figure was a man. Shriveled pallid skin protruded from every visible opening of its oil slicked armor. The skin was stretched taut over a muscular structure far too swollen to be considered human anymore. The steel head was gone to reveal the abomination it contained. His face, his hideous organic features, were made plain to see. The least abhorrent feature was the strings of ragged obsidian hair that dangled down its neck like loose threads. Its eyes, which Jude had interpreted to be blank pupils, were not eyes at all. Rather, where its eyes should have been it possessed empty sallow sockets, nothing but pits in the skull. It had no nose either. Instead, it had a maggot infested orifice of jutting bone and decaying flesh. A cannibalistic snarling was emanating from its ungodly mouth. His teeth had been replaced with nails, shards of glass, splinters of jagged metal all sloppily jammed into rotting gums to give it a maw like a devilish angler. The scrap teeth were slobbered on by a swollen blue tongue, like that of lynched man.

The bullet hole was still in its hideous face where Jude had shot it. A flap of skin had been blown out by one of Venator's explosive rounds. The wound was still bleeding viscous slime. The giant didn't seem to care. It wielded the bisected corpse of their Indenture Inmate and laughed a deep morbid cackle. The thing dropped Daurtey's lower half to grab onto his upper half with both hands. With a gut wrenching motion of its rusty metal hands, he ripped a sheet of flesh free of the corpse as though he were peeling a strip of tape off its roll. With his right hand, he slapped the skin strip onto its bullet wound. Its old sickly flesh puckered as it sucked Daurtey's into its own face. The stolen skin melted and fused to the gap, adhering to the exact geometry of his skull and hue of the preexisting dermis. With his left hand he lifted the remainder of the corpse to his face. He opened the hellish maw of glass and metal and sank the mock fangs into the corpse of their dead comrade. It pulled out strings of sinew and entrails, slurping up the viscera in thick blood-soaked strands.

The horrific sight left them all aghast to the point of silence. It continued up to the point where Vandross vomited out of sheer disgust. The wretched noise of blood sloshing and bone crunching was enough to bring any hardened man to his knees. Scraps of human meat slapped onto the dust as the strangled tongue licked the blood off of its grey lips. And then it laughed. The throaty noise was a like wet nails against old glass. Then it spoke with the same raspy growl.

"Welcome to Budapest, my friends." He somehow spoke in flawless temple-tongue. "I am Noctidus Val'Muardeares, chieftain of the Grave Gluttons, defiler of the pure, and herald to the Nephilim. I believe you know me by another name. Yes, I believe you would call me Knox Mortis."

CHAPTER 36

Three months of hunting around Templym had culminated to this point. Criminal syndicates in Bruccol, a techno-cult in Jaspin, a UNAC sympathizing, demon worshipping serial killer in Hrimata, none of that mattered anymore. What mattered now was their quarry, their goal since being dispatched from Parey back in Rexus. Knox Mortis, a man who up until earlier this week nobody was even positive existed, stood before them.

This was their target. This goliath sized monstrosity was the ultimate object of their focus. Once they discovered he was in Budapest, they decided not to take him in alive, each of them praying for a swift assassination. Now they could do nothing but speculate how to take him down. There was no positive to their situation. No weapons, dangling like gutted pigs from meat hooks, facing down a giant standing in vainglorious display on the corpse of their transport. Even if they could escape, what hope would they have of overpowering Mortis? This man, if he could still be considered one, faced a Hekaton in single combat and won. They were alive, though. For as long as a member of the Scourge draws breath and has a mission yet unachieved, they would not falter in their efforts.

Mortis hopped down from the burning shell of the caravan. It didn't occur to any of them to think about how the metal was on fire, considering the engine's fuel cell was not flammable. They were all too stunned to focus on trivial matters like that. His massive metal grieves crunched the remains of Jameson Daurtey into the ash, taking time to relish in the act of grinding what little remained of him into the dust. The Grave Gluttons, which was apparently their true name, all screamed in victorious glee as their chief landed with a deep thump. Three of the barbarians brought out the rusted halberd Mortis killed Peregrine with, its haft about ten feet long. With a single calloused hand, the giant hoisted the weapon up with a wet purr. The muscles in his cheeks twitched and twisted upwards in what must have been a devilish grin.

"I haven't had a kill like that in over forty years." Knox Mortis said with his sharp graveled yell. "I always found something exhilarating about laying a Hekaton down in the dirt."

Silence followed his initial statement, which was proceeded by another spittle drenched laugh. "The lambs are silent...often they are when staring their demise down. The sheep should fear the wolves."

"And would you be the wolf?" Bethel spoke. Nobody noticed him wake. Mortis' empty eye sockets met the steel gaze of the former High Conservator.

"I am what I need to be." The chief began striding around the semicircular courtyard, dragging his massive axe in the coarse ash behind him. "Should my patron require an attack dog to sick upon his foes, I will bear my fangs and kill. Should he require a wolf to skulk in shadows and rip out a jugular, I will sharpen my claws and stalk. Even if I am to play the part of a hyena and scavenge scraps from the dead, I will feast on them with..."

"Oh shut your trap!" Jude said again. "Do you think this display matched with this monologue is going to accomplish anything? You've already won. Don't think I can't tell you're just trying to make us squirm." This was a classical reverse interrogation technique. Break the captor's cadence and throw them off their mental balance. It seemed that even in the face of imminent doom, Bethel still had the resolve to pry for answers.

"Quiet, cur! You only breathe because I will it! The utterance of a single word will have my legion gnawing on your bones down to the marrow."

"Classic. Put on a gruesome show and say some scary words. That will put us in a submissive position and you can do whatever you want to us. The only reason you haven't gutted us yet is because you need us."

Mortis strolled over to the pike Jude was dangling off of and crouched down to eye level. The horrific stench of fresh gore overpowered his senses, snuffing out the air of decay Budapest generally carried. His pitch was lowered to a whisper but still carried the volume of a shout. “How can you be certain of that? What source of divine intervention is staying my blade from your neck?”

“Perhaps there’s still a heart somewhere in that chest of yours. Perhaps you’re letting us live because you wish to extend mercy.”

The marauder giant grabbed Bethel’s scarred face and yanked it within inches of his own. He brought his shout back to a thunderous bellow. “Do not confuse your beating heart as an act of mercy, whelp! It agonizes me that you still draw breath! I want to crush your innards beneath my feet. I want to wade in your arterial sludge. I want to wallow in a pile of your minced flesh and splintered bones. Yet you live only because it is not time. When the abolition is declared, your blood will be harvested for the Nephilim’s glorious throne and all of Templym will be brought to its knees like a beaten whore!”

Bethel froze. He lifted silent prayers to the Heavens as the demoniac giant threatened and screamed at him. This thing, whatever Knox Mortis was, clearly took great pleasure in performing gruesome adversity. With every word coming from his sloppy rotted mouth, there was an underlying tone of euphoric joy no matter how immoral or unseemly the statement. As afraid as he was, he had made some progress amidst their hopeless situation.

This was a telling statement. Bethel accomplished a meaningful counter-interrogation. Behind the sadistic and disturbing statements that Mortis was ranting there was information that they were looking for. The first portion was that he was a subordinate to the Nephilim, though most had deduced this already, this confirmed that. The next portion was about the abolition, which revealed two aspects of this illusive action. The first was that it was on a strict time schedule. Mortis clearly wanted the task force dead, yet was staying his hand at the request of his patron. The abolition needed to be declared, whatever that meant. The second aspect revealed was less apparent. What did it mean that their blood would be harvested? What throne did the Nephilim possess? The final portion was the most distressing however. Despite the constant threats of what the giant wanted to do to them, nothing was more chilling than his final statement. Whatever the Nephilim was planning, all of Templym was at risk.

"Don't you find it embarrassing to be another's pawn?" Adastra Covalos dared to speak. "You seem to be a capable warrior, why not establish a cult of your own?"

Mortis lurched over to the Inquisitor, dragging his axe behind him, lacerating the ground behind him. "I have my own following. My Grave Gluttons are the strongest marauders walking this rock. My men answer to me and me alone."

"Yet, you serve the Nephilim. Correct me if I'm wrong, but I believe that makes you a lackey."

"Power must be ascertained slowly. That is my calling, to stand on the neck of the world. For decades I've been subservient to a number of different patrons, each exchanging gifts of power for acts of subterfuge against your rancid nation."

"So you're a mercenary?" Adastra mustered a demeaning chuckle. "I was expecting something a little more regal. Yet that explains much."

Knox cocked his head to the side in confusion. Adastra met the empty sockets of the chieftain's head without faltering. He noticed that the flesh, the patch torn from their dead driver, was already starting to blister and wither to match the rest of his pallid skin. "Explains what exactly?"

"Come now, don't you already know? I figured your beloved Nephilim would have revealed it to you by now. Alas, it seems your lord doesn't care much for you. Aren't you at all curious what brings us here to Budapest?"

"I am aware of what brings you here. You are Auzlanten's lap dogs, fetching another prize for your master. Call it whatever you like, but I know that you came here to eliminate me."

Adastra concealed his surprise at the revelation. How Mortis knew of their purpose to coming to Budapest was beyond comprehension. He needed to keep pressing for information. "Correct." He responded through a clenched jaw. "You are wanted for questioning on suspicion of involvement with forty-eight crimes against Templym."

He laughed, like the brooding of living hurricane. "You came to arrest me, to hold trial in one of your child courts, to lock me into one of your paper prisons? Your ignorance couldn't be more delicious!"

"That's right. We know of what you've done. We've compiled a list of atrocities you have a part in dating back to 2659. Don't think we can't..."

Inquisitor Covalos was cut off as his throat was closed by the grizzled metal hand of Knox Mortis, strangling him with the force of a vice. "How?" That was all that the giant growled as another throaty roar began to culminate from his gullet. Adastra could do nothing but sputter for air, desperately trying to keep his trachea open. His pale face turned blue as the titan gripped his throat in a single.

"It was mailed to us." Volk voiced from the other side of the courtyard. "An intern from our postal department carted it to the High Conservator himself." Downey couldn't help but laugh at the ridiculousness of the statement.

Mortis lurked over to the Warden, makeshift teeth revealed, bits of Daurtey's flesh stuck between them. He released his python grip from the Inquisitor's neck and the natural color flushed to his face as air refilled his lungs. "Impossible." He spat the words. "What events do you think I am responsible for?"

"Let me think." Volk mused mockingly keeping the strategy alive. "There was a Kalkhanian healing home raided in '59, a political assassination in '67, the Plague Massacre in '91."

The sharp end of the polearm came up towards Downey's face. He didn't even notice the spear tip at the end of the rusty haft as attention was drawn to the heavy blade. "How did you find that out? Who gave you this list?"

"I swear to Christ, it just showed up in the mail room. Do you think the author signed it? We've just been hopping around seeing where the trail leads us and well...here we are."

Volk noticed a slight wince at the name of the Savior, as though the name of God appalled him. Then there were a series of twitches and ripples in the nerves of his wretched face. Anger, confusion, his exact mood was impossible to discern lacking eyes or a nose. One thing was clear though, Knox Mortis was certainly unhappy. Volk saw the nerve and decided to press. "You think you might have a snitch in your ranks?" He smiled, dried blood caked at the corners of his mouth.

The giant stormed away out of the courtyard. He began shouting again in the primal marauder tongue. The Grave Gluttons scampered away towards their massive chief whose boisterous yelling slowly faded as he stomped away into a collection of alleyways. The task force was left alone to listen to the groaning wind of the Hellpit.

Regent Invictus Illuromos sat in a raised basalt throne with his eyes clicked closed. He sat in a private location, outside of his chambers in Bastion Prime. There was no source of light outside of the illumination from a dozen different monitors and holographic displays surrounding the stone plinth. He was experiencing an entirely new perspective.

Accepting the Imago into his body opened up what could only be a preview on the next stage of human evolution. His eyes were shut, but his enhanced senses allowed him to experience his surroundings without need for his human senses. The displays were all current newscasts, reporting on a plethora of events. Sitting on his igneous throne, he could distinguish every detail from each report.

The spirits he was hosting each tuned his senses to supernatural keenness. He welcomed seventy-five lesser fiends, as the Nephilim dubbed them, into his body and they worked to better him. Invictus bombarded himself with a torrent of information but could read everything with clarity as though he analyzed each broadcast individually. No...no he could see so much more than any man could.

One reporter from Hrimata spoke of the conclusion to an infamous Dilictor Ignotum. She reported how the "Nitral Nightmare" had been apprehended by a strike-force led by a Bride Wainwright. From the hesitation the Regent read in her voice, he knew she was withholding information. He knew that Monk had a much higher kill count than what this woman was reporting. He could also distinguish a slight tremor in the eye and slurring of words that implied inebriation. He could practically smell the mead on her breath. The audio transmitter was of high enough quality that he could hear the blood pumping through her veins.

Another speaker from the Beacon's own network, a plucky young Crier, was reading statistics about trade between nations of Templym. He could see the boy's eyes, even though his own were closed, angled slightly off camera. Based on the sweat brimming at the top of his lip and the heightened pitch of his vocals, he could tell that he was in love with a young lady standing off screen. From the faint clicks in the feed's background noise, clicks that could only be her feet wandering around the set, he could tell this woman was five foot four inches tall weighing one hundred and twenty-two pounds.

Invictus' stern grimace lurched up into a wicked grin. He relished the experience. Now that Prelate Greyflame was disposed of and Bethel was dead or dying in Budapest, he could freely use his pets at will. The Mundus Imago making a shelter of his flesh could operate without restriction. Now their power could be exercised without fear of tipping off the paranoid fools. He thanked the Nephilim in a silent prayer in conjunction with his analysis of the broadcasts, a feat that no feeble human mind would be able to perform. He heard the sharp clicks of flaksteel feet striking stone flooring. From the echoing of the chamber he envisioned a clear picture of the captain of his Centurion guard.

The captain had abandoned his standard issue silver battle plate. Instead of the gleaming armor, the grey plates were the color of raw gunmetal and the black accents were replaced with deep violet. "Lord General Illuromos." The captain said saluting by making a chevron across his chest.

"No need for formalities David." Invictus said opening his eyes. The cold grey of his iris had swallowed the whites making them appear as steel balls with black pinpricks. The multiple news feeds were cut off with a simple thought from the Regent, though he didn't want to be referred to as the Regent of the Scourge any longer. He now went by a more fitting title, Lord General, the Nephilim's general.

"Yes sir, Invictus. I am reporting on the matter of the prisoners." David Crenshaw, the captain of the Centurion guard, was loyal first to the Regent before his creed to the Scourge. It was no surprise that he followed his lord in his corruption.

"Good. Walk with me, tell me everything." He stood from the seat of polished basalt and stepped down. His obsidian colored armor seemed to growl as pistons fired and demons laughed. The spike whips normally donned on his shoulders were gone, replaced with two corsairs depicting Middle Eastern flowers in purple so dark it was nearly black.

Crenshaw followed his master, struggling to keep a steady walking pace with his massive strides. "By your command, all Scourge personnel convicted by the edicts of the primes have been moved to the specified Arcaes. All convicts reside in Golgotha in Jerusalem, Pluto in Venice Primus, Blackfang in Rushmore, or Jupiter in Parey."

"Have the respective Archons been made compliant?"

"All except Crucifix my lord, but it's of no major concern. We have spies inside. He will be dealt with when the abolition begins."

"All instances were handled in person?" There was an ominous tone to the Regent's voice. The sadistic relishing blatantly obvious in his voice was made even more chilling by the constant clacking of metal from the chains and wire still wrapped around the armor of Invictus Illuromos. The slate grey immotrum cape trailed behind him, slithering across the stone tile like a serpent.

"By your command Lord General it was done, though I am

unsure why. Greyflame and Bethel are dead. We can continue unopposed without fear of any prying eyes."

"We cannot, because of my father." Invictus sneered, adding a particularly sharp amount of venom at the mention of Auzlanten. "His constant meddling is causing our ranks to thin faster than we can bolster them. We lost the amphibious men of Resinous, the armaments of Balor, and the Nephilim tells me that he is on the verge of discovering the Idolacreid! Keeping at this pace, the Nephilim's following will not be sufficient to harvest enough blood at the abolition."

"Is that why we have accelerated? We are racing to outpace the great warlock?"

Invictus stopped to look at Krakatoa resting on an iron holster. He could hear the spirits inside growling vociferously out of hunger in his mind, even though Crenshaw saw only a finely crafted weapon. "The only great thing about that warlock is the downfall we shall play part to. For centuries he has preached of the power of truth yet has lied since before Templym's birth. I hate him. I will see his life's work crumble beneath the Nephilim's feet."

"May I ask you something Lord General?" The Centurion asked nervously.

"You may."

"What did you learn from the Idolacreid? You spent more time within its pages than any other man I'm aware of. You must have gleaned great secrets from its wisdom. What were you trying to accomplish?"

Invictus grinned slightly, unwilling to share the full fount of knowledge he drank from. "What else? Power, reflexes, fortitude, enhanced senses, I needed anything that will make me a greater fighter than I was before. My body has been transformed by the creatures inhabiting me. Now I can knit my flesh back together at a will, I can outmatch a chariot in speed, I can discern details as though my mind were a computer. I have become so much more than human. I will have to be."

"For what sir?"

The steel orbs of his eyes met with the violet visor of his Centurion captain. Crenshaw could see faint valleys in his flesh beneath the eye where he had tried to carve away the IX branded there. It was still there despite his efforts to remove it. He grabbed his shoulder with his massive, inhumanly strong hand. Then the Regent smiled. It was disturbing to see such a stoic figure's countenance to be in such a dramatic state of deviant emotion, like he was truly happy for the first time in his life. "For when I kill Arodi Auzlanten."

"I made him think he was going to be alright. I told him that we'd watch after him. He was the last person who should've been caught in battle. Yet he was the first to die."

Warden Downey's haunted eyes were locked on what was left of Jameson Daurtey. The remains were sprawled out in the ash before him where Knox Mortis had grown bored of mutilating the corpse. Little more than shredded entrails and scabbed bone fragments were left in the Hellpit to fade away to dust, joining the millions of others in the desert. The task force was taking some time to recuperate and try to concoct a plan before their captors returned.

"What could you have done?" Inquisitor Blackwell stated bitterly with a trickle of bile trailing down his cheek. "That thing felled a Hekaton. It's a blessing only one of us died in the ambush."

"He may be more fortunate than us." Herald Du'Plasse added. "His body was cut clean in two. Considering the fact that they want us for something, I'd venture to guess he was killed when Mortis cut down the chariot."

"It would have been quick." Inquisitor Covalos coughed, his throat still aching from the chief strangling him. "Such a fate is likely merciful compared to what awaits us."

"Quit dwelling on things that can't be changed." Bethel's voice called out. "We need to get out of here. Templym is at risk and the abolition is coming."

"What did he mean by harvesting our blood?" Bride Wainwright interjected. "They want to use our blood to power the Nephilim's throne?"

"A spell component perhaps," Vandross speculated. "Blood is the most common material focus for Imago magick. Perhaps that's what the abolition is...a wide scale reaping."

"That is why they're building an army." Bethel said. "They're collecting a crop of human blood for some vile spell...Lord have mercy. We need to get out of here. We've got to warn everyone."

"There will be no warning!" Knox Mortis had returned seething with rage, a flock of his marauders following at his heels and his halberd in hand. The squadron hushed instantly to keep what they knew to themselves. The less their captor was aware of the better. "There is no hope. There is no escape. You pitiable whelps don't understand anything do you? You lost! I won! Stop talking and accept your imminent doom."

"You know you talk a lot." Bethel sneered back, still defying the odds to pry more information out of him.

Jude didn't get the opportunity to annoy Mortis for additional information. Clearly the chieftain of the Grave Gluttons was in no mood for trifle games any longer. Mortis pulled Bethel off of his pike, snapping the iron chains binding his wrists. He held him in a single meaty hand. A wet animalistic growl vibrated in the giant's throat. If he had eyes, there would be an obvious desire to murder in them.

"You're going to tell me about this letter." Mortis howled through his needle teeth. "You're going to tell me who wrote it." His grip tightened causing the pressure compensators to whine in Bethel's scarred blue plate. "You're going to tell me what putrid rat fed you my achievements!"

"We already told you." Jude spoke with an increased calm, using his freed fingers to wedge the massive fingers around his chest open to prevent further damage. Quiet alarms were flashing indicating a maximum of pressure so he didn't want to press the raging hulk any further. "As we said before, a letter was mailed to me. It named you as the culprit for forty-eight crimes against Templym, so I assembled this task force to..."

The pressure around Bethel's chest increased. He could feel

hairline fractures cracking across his ribs as his battle plate failed to resist the immense force being applied to his body. "Where is this letter? Give it to me!"

"The chariot." He wheezed weakly. "There are a few copies in the chariot."

The goliath released his grip and let Jude plop to the ground, kicking up a cloud of dust. Mortis' face was curled into a snarl as it was directed at the burning wreckage in the center of the courtyard. His men filled their transport with flammable material and ignited it to make a statement, to further crush whatever hope they had left. Mortis swung the haft of his polearm in a wide arc, creating a gust of sulfur scented wind that snuffed the fire out instantly. He pointed to some of his cronies behind him and yelled to them in their native tongue. At his word they scattered over to the wrecked caravan to scour it for any remaining evidence.

"You don't talk so big when your life's at risk." The giant growled as it hunched over to Bethel who laid prone in the dust sheathed rockfoam. "You're more than happy to let dribble gush from your tongue when you're an arm's length away from death, but you squeal when you stare it in the face."

Bethel spit out a gob of mucus and ash as he lifted his upper body up by his elbows. His brass colored skin became the color of dehydrated timber with the layer of cremated dead he wore like a mask. He opened his mouth to say something, something that likely would have gotten him killed or beaten. He chose not to.

In the distance, over the sound of scavenging marauders rummaging through the broken chariot and the constant hum of the moaning Budapest wind, there was a distinct noise. No soldier could ever mistake the constant crack and pop intertwined with cries of war. It was the sound of gunfire and explosions coming from about half a mile away. A skirmish. The Grave Gluttons were exchanging fire with somebody. Somebody unexpected, based on the way Mortis stood and turned his gaze in the direction of the gunfire.

Then Jude began laughing. A laugh filled with bitter irony or reckless abandon, nobody could really tell. S-6319 couldn't help but cock their heads and exchange worried looks as the former prime of the Shackle began his fit of hysteria. Mortis of course reacted with brutal rage. He brought a large metal boot down on Bethel's back in an elephantine stomp. The force of the impact cracked his armored carapace and caused him to break his fit of laughter. He coughed up a mouthful of blood before reducing his laugh to a faint chuckle as he noticed the sound of battle rapidly approaching.

"Why are you laughing?" Mortis yelled. "Who is that?"

"You know, I'm a bit disappointed in this task force." Bethel continued to laugh as he brought himself up to his knees. "They kept this trip to the most notorious Hellpit in Carthonia off the record. Yet, here I am. So that raises a question: how did I know where to be and when?"

"You had outside help." Oslin Du'Plasse said wearily and with a perplexed look.

"Precisely," Jude smiled and looked up to the giant looming over him. "Now for another question..." Bethel paused as another explosion took place. One that was not only audibly closer than all of the others, but visible from their current position. It wasn't from a grenade or rocket lancer. A beam of bright glistening white starlight blasted a hole in a cloudtoucher, instantly vaporizing a number of growling marauders. Rusted girders and boulders rained down on the streetscape like massive hailstones. "Did you really think I would come into Budapest without cavalry?"

A collection of grisly marauders orbiting around the courtyard hoisted their weapons and thundered towards the oncoming battle. Roaring pops of assault rifles screamed in tandem with the barbarian howls of the Grave Gluttons. A vast column of starlight fired down from the heavens, punching a hole through the cloud of spoiled toxic war fumes before crashing into the streets below. The task force could hear their death throes as the light incinerated them where they stood. A scattered few survivors clutching their guns against their blackened chest plates hurried into the courtyard where they stood in anticipation. The task force all refused to breathe out of eagerness for the oncoming attacker. Knox Mortis was the only marauder not pointing a gun at the only opening leading into the courtyard.

There was a brief period of absolute silence. Even the guttural growl from Mortis' diaphragm and the groaning wind of the death desert were absent. No sound was uttered as the Grave Gluttons and task force S-6319 waited. The deafening quiet was broken by footsteps. The click of boots on rockfoam was encroaching, coming up the staircase leading into the court.

The boots were black, buckled with clasps of gold. The boots were attached to legs donning cerulean robes. The deep blue robes were knitted with intricate stitching of white gold and other precious metals. The figure's head was draped in a mane of raven hair topped with a half wreath of platinum barbs. An acutely curved sabre made of vibrant colored glass-like material radiating beams of amber and emerald was gripped in a bejeweled hand.

Arodi Auzlanten pointed Leagna directly at the throat of the goliath marauder. "Knox Mortis, I have come for the Idolacreid."

CHAPTER 37

If anybody could survive the horrors of Budapest, it would be the Master of Templym, the Voice of the Lord, Arodi Auzlanten. Clearly God was listening to their prayers and he was the answer. Deliverance was here and it was in the form of the enigmatic founder of the greatest nation in human history.

"You think I have the Idolacreid?" Mortis growled back disregarding the prisoners he had previously been tormenting. "Even if I did, why the hell would I ever give it to you?"

"You're lying, abomination." Arodi spoke in unwavering defiance. His voice was calm yet assertive, like a torrent dammed yet on the brink of overflowing. "I've hunted that tome for one hundred-thirty-four days now. I have toppled the Nephilim's pawns one by one on this artifact hunt. I received divine revelation that my hunt would end with you. I know you have it."

Mortis barked to his marauders in his primal tongue. At his order they began to scurry away, clambering into the surrounding cloudtouchers like scared prey. That left the chained up task force alone with the chief and Auzlanten. "The Nephilim told me that this day would come." The giant's swollen blue tongues licked its lips. "He prophesied that I would be the one to kill the great warlock. I thought I would need more experience, more Imago patrons, more blood. Clearly I am ready to smite you where you stand." The rusted halberd scrapped across the ground before Knox Mortis hafted the weapon into a combat ready pose.

"Only one of us is dying today," Auzlanten said shifting Leagna in his grip. The sabre spun in his hand slicing the air. "Release the captives and hand over the Idolacreid and I promise to make it swift."

That same sloppy guttural laugh began echoing through Budapest again. "Come now warlock, you know I will not do that!"

"I gave you a chance to repent. Remember that during your eternal torment in the Pit."

Arodi flew through the air like a bolt of blue lightning. He shot a single thrust aimed directly at the marauder chief's neck. The titanic man brought the rusted axe up to deflect it in a parry impossibly dexterous for someone of his proportions. A wave of bright orange sparks flew off the weapons as they clashed together. Instead of flying back again and gaining distance as Mortis suspected he would, Auzlanten continued his momentum and barreled past the giant.

He landed on the wrecked caravan, poised to make a second strike against the metal clad giant. Instead of bringing Leagna down in a slash or a stab, he pointed his open left hand towards Mortis. This caused the eight pikes stuck into the surrounding columns to fly out like javelins towards the marauder. The vile giant dodged out of the way or swatted most out of the air, but one pike planted itself into Mortis' shoulder. Seemingly unconcerned that his prisoners were now free, Knox Mortis ignored the pain shooting through his arm and charged at Auzlanten.

While on top of the steaming scrap heap, Auzlanten was at eye level with Mortis. The blows were traded like two tornadoes colliding on the hellscape. The glimmering sabre was thrust with finesse and grace while the dilapidated halberd was viciously brandished with powerful aggression, polar opposites. The weapons clanged against each other so quickly and forcefully, the streets of Budapest resounded with percussive claps that shook the surrounding structures. The sonic booms were matched by a wave of hot sparks and backed with the rasping roar of the marauder chief.

As the two titans made every effort to kill each other, Bethel played his part in the plan. He crawled over towards his nearest ally, trying to keep his cracked ribs from puncturing a lung. Retriever Ram's Horn was the nearest, the cobalt-clad soldier on his feet despite the suddenness with which the pike was wrenched from above him. He kneeled down and pulled his prime across the dust and beneath a mold caked patio where the remainder of the task force was beginning to gather. Bethel coughed and produced a carbon steel tomahawk he was concealing in a retractable chamber in his hip.

"I don't think I have the strength to use this." Bethel meagerly lifted his weapon to the Retriever, whose wrists were still chained together.

"Thanks." Ram pulled the honed blade clean through gangly ferric links with a single yank, shaking the shackles free before moving on to liberate his companions similarly.

"So was this your plan all along?" Volk yelled over the cacophonous melee going on less than a hundred feet away.

Bethel coughed up another trail of blood and spittle. "I really liked that Hekaton. I hoped we wouldn't need him."

"Didn't you think this information was pertinent?" Adastra bellowed as Ram's Horn cut his restraints. "I would have liked to have known before diving into this Hellpit."

"He wouldn't let me tell you."

"Why not?" Oslin yelled over the brawl.

Bethel turned onto his back to look on the impossibly intense duel between Templym's founder and the Nephilim's general, groaning in pain as his armor's pressure compensators inadequately held his ribcage together. "I didn't question it."

Mortis grew tired of swinging his axe. Nothing had endured this much punishment with so little damage. The strength he used was only a fragment of what he was capable of. The giant allowed a vast downward cut to sink into the pile of twisted metal, opening up his defenses. Auzlanten fell for the bait. He glanced Mortis' flank with a stab of the holy sabre. The light itself stung, but for the briefest moments left the man vulnerable. He wrapped an oily hand around his outreached hand and commanded the legion of Imago inside him to lash out. Arodi's soul was assailed by hungry demonic wraiths biting and gnawing at the immaterial parts of his body.

Such an onslaught was foreign to Auzlanten. It had been two hundred years since he witnessed a mortal with such dominion over dark spirits. The demonic devourers gnawed at his essence like a swarm of locusts pouncing on a single grain of wheat. Arodi would compare the feeling to drowning in boiling tar. Any mortal would be dead long before being able to comprehend that pain. Auzlanten felt the full impact of the Mundus Imago doing everything in their power to glut themselves with his life. They fed too much.

Arodi's ocean blue eyes were flushed with golden light as he deliberately flooded his body with divine energy. A cascade of heavenly star fire erupted from his chest incinerating the demons pouncing at him. Mortis himself was scorched by the nova and would be rendered blind if he had retinas left to sear. Auzlanten forged another beam of similarly golden energy from his empty hand. The light cascaded onto the giant and punctured a crater in his breastplate, exposing a blistered patch of skin.

Knox Mortis briefly lost his grip on his polearm. He snarled as thick, ochre drool dribbled from his artificial teeth and the air rippled with supernatural heat and light around his clenched fists. His hands wept with flashing black power as he swung his arms down in a wild crushing blow. The scrap heap Auzlanten stood on was crumpled as though it was made of plastic. Arodi leapt backwards and landed on top of the terrace opposite from the one the task force was taking cover under.

Arodi paused for a nanosecond to assess. He was shocked at the level of effort required to fight this man, though he would never show it. His normal strategy consisted of using overwhelming power to defeat his adversaries. Mortis had been keeping pace. Something needed to change, something to tip the balance of the stalemate in his favor. Auzlanten noticed something in the giant now. Since he repelled the demonic assault and slew a small collection of the spirits, Knox had grown slightly weaker. The indicator was subtle, only a slight lag in his muscle movement. He was no doubt hosting a plethora of wicked creatures fueling his mutated body. Auzlanten drew strength from the infinite God of the cosmos. Mortis' supply was limited to the beasts within him. He had to chip away that strength.

Arodi spun to the side as the halberd was brought down in a firm chop. Knox Mortis leapt twenty feet in the air, landing on the terrace, smashing the rotten tile to dust in an instant. Auzlanten ignited his hand with brilliant white fire and used it in tandem with Leagna. Mortis flung his massive axe wildly against the dual weapon assault. The Master of Templym used his vibrant sabre to deflect painfully lethal blows and create distance between them so he could unleash a barrage of lances forged of heavenly light. Mortis continued his assault seemingly unaffected by the white flames. In truth, their intent was not to harm the black host itself. Rather, each arrow of fire killed a single Imago occupying him, eroding his strength in miniscule portions.

He made a slight error in posture. Auzlanten saw an opportunity to blast Mortis with two fire bolts instead of one, leaving his sword arm off to the side away from a proper deflecting position. Knox took advantage of the opening. He hooked Arodi's torso in the curve of the halberd and flung the haft downward in a quick snap. This flung Auzlanten down to the ground below the rampart. He hit the ground with a sharp thud and a crack of rockfoam like a meteor. Mortis capitalized this success by leaping down and driving the spear tip of the weapon into Auzlanten in an effort to impale him.

The rusted spear tip of the polearm rammed into Auzlanten's chest. Instead of the snapping of bones or splatter of blood, the head just punctured the ornate robes he wore. Arodi grabbed onto the haft of the weapon with both hands, Leagna flung somewhere unseen. Mortis willed every muscle in his body to contribute towards driving the weapon through and Arodi and into the ground like a tent peg, but he could not gain the additional two inches of distance required to puncture his flesh. With an uncharacteristically heated shout, Auzlanten snapped the spear point off and directed the rest of the polearm into the ground. As Mortis lurched downward with the weapon's momentum, Arodi swung around the giant's neck and onto his back. Knox Mortis scrambled to throw him off, but Auzlanten was too swift. Leagna flew across the air and back into his hand. He drove the end of the sabre down in a lethal stab, sending it directly into the nape of the giant's neck. Just like Goliath, Mortis collapsed to the ground.

Arodi Auzlanten hopped off the giant's back as he plopped onto the ground, kicking up a fog of cremated dust. He began a calm stride towards the strike force still hiding under the terrace. As he just began returning his sabre, which was strangely free of any visceral traces, into its holster he looked over his shoulder to Knox Mortis. The lumbering marauder chief was finally still. Until he wasn't. .

The chief clambered back onto his feet and grabbed his halberd out of the dust once again. He let out a monstrous bellow flecked with black viscera. The air around his body began to pulse with rippling heat waves as his body became wracked with unholy energies. Then he howled a declaration out in his primal tongue before charging like a stampede with axe in hand at Arodi Auzlanten again.

He vaulted himself over the demonic juggernaut. His normal inclination would be to meet the charge with a counterstrike, but he was disturbed by what Mortis was ranting. He spoke the ancient dialect and he knew that his most recent string of curses was more than profanity. He was calling out orders to his marauder following. He commanded that they detonate...something. Auzlanten wanted to be able to react to the blast before he was engulfed in another duel.

Sure enough there was a chain of explosions. They were muffled as though they occurred beneath the surface of the ground. The suppressed blast was followed by the sound of screeching rebar. The cloudtoucher overseeing the heated encounter began collapsing. Knox Mortis had commanded the building's destruction in an effort to bury Auzlanten.

No, not just Arodi Auzlanten, the task force would be buried alive too. The Scourge spectators were seconds away from being pulverized. Innocents weren't supposed to be caught up in his endeavors. That is why he eternally worked alone. Auzlanten had toppled tyrants and armies singlehandedly with no aid because that often meant no collateral damage. He preferred it that way. Bystanders offered up too many opportunities for exploitation or distraction and put innocent lives in harm's way. Now, eight Scourge warriors simply doing their jobs were about to be demolished in an avalanche of steel and rockfoam. He desperately yearned to continue the fight against Knox Mortis, to put an end to the fiend. Templym was founded on two principles. The Scourge was meant to punish the wicked, now it was time to protect the innocent.

Mortis barreled around as debris began crumbling down like meteors to strike at Auzlanten again. Instead of parrying the blow, he thrust his will into a torrent of sonic energy. The steel clad giant was thrown back hundreds of feet in propulsion at the presence of the thunderclap he conjured. That bought him enough time to make it to the task force.

He didn't want to do what he knew needed to be done. Auzlanten stayed isolated specifically to keep average citizens away from the horrific toils he constantly subjected himself to. Arodi Auzlanten knew that the citizens of Templym were constantly concerned about what he was. The question of what manner of entity plagued their minds, some to the point of worshipping him as the reincarnate Christ. This knowledge was unimportant. What he fought for, what he did was vastly more crucial at defining the Master of Templym. That is why he kept his origins a secret. What he was about to do would only raise more questions.

Now he would be forced to compromise his seclusion. The look of fear in their eyes as the structure around them began cascading down in massive boulders caused Auzlanten physical pain with the grief it caused him. They were seconds away from being buried among the millions dead in Budapest. He had to save them.

"Trust me." That was all Arodi Auzlanten had time to say. He knew that not all of them could even hear him, but said it for no other reason than to possibly reduce the shock of the transition. He slashed the air in front of him with Leagna, ripping a schism between them open with a glowing rift of pale cyan light. Auzlanten pulled his arm backwards as though winding up a punch. In response the eight soldiers were yanked by invisible force into the rift. Once the last one was yanked into the portal, it snapped shut as immediately as it spawned, less than a second before a rusted steel girder smashed down right where they were standing. They were safe. Now Arodi Auzlanten could dispatch Knox Mortis with no distractions... aside from the collapsing building.

Eight suits of flaksteel or immotrum armor smacked onto a white marble dais. The people inside of the armor were too discombobulated to realize it at first. Whatever unnatural transition they had just underwent had left them nauseated, like their unconscious minds were ripped out of their physical brains before being slammed back in. For the first minute, they could do nothing but roll on the floor and wait for the whiplash to wear off.

Once the veil of dizziness had been lifted from their eyes, a serendipitous picture was painted. The sky blotted out by smog of war was replaced with a fine mural depicting a lush verdant garden, yet it radiated light as if the sun were shining through a cloudless sky. The ashen wasteland was replaced with smooth, finely polished white marble. The air was crisp, clear of the stench of decay and harsh chemicals. The dilapidated cloudtouchers were replaced with columns of bronze and silver reaching up to the ornate ceiling. Whatever this place was, it was a welcomed change to the death desert of Budapest.

"Is everybody alright?" Daphne Wainwright broke the spell of unintelligible panting.

"Did we just get kidnapped?" Volk asked as he worked his way to his feet.

"I'd rather be in Arodi Auzlanten's care than Mortis'." Oslin said with a light humor in his voice, relieved to be out of Budapest.

"Where's Vandross?" Adastra picked up the wide red hat sitting next to him, the one perpetually sitting on his partner's head. He grew concerned that the other Inquisitor was the only one absent on the marble plinth. "Vandross!" The Serbian stood up frantically and yelled outwards into the circular chamber.

There was a moat of foaming water at the base of the platform.

This is where Inquisitor Blackwell landed after tumbling down the steps. Almost on cue, Vandross emerged from the roiling stream spitting up a mouthful of water out as he pulled himself out. Adastra rushed down to pull him out of moat as he was weighed down by his wet attire. “Did I just teleport into a hot spring?”

“Are you complaining?” Adastra chuckled as he placed his partner’s hat back atop his sopping head.

“We’re in Auzlanten’s sanctum!” Yen Blye yelled out excitedly, his voice bouncing off the circular marble walls. “This is where he drafted the creeds of the Bulwark and Scourge, where he crafted each of the Regent’s suits of battle plate, where Leagna was forged! Blood of the Saints, this place was only rumored to exist and we’re standing in it!”

“Calm down kid.” Bethel grunted as Retriever Ram’s Horn propped him up against his shoulder. He grabbed his chest in pain, but it seemed to have been dampened. He was expecting it to be even sharper after tumbling through a portal.

“Are you alright?” Daphne asked in response to his clear pain. “I think I could hear your ribs crack when Mortis stepped on you. You shouldn’t be standing.”

Adastra joined the rest of his team on the platform. “And you had a black eye when we were in Budapest.”

Daphne brushed the strand of hair that always strayed in front of her eye, the same eye that had been swollen and bruised moments ago. It was completely healed. “In truth, I barely noticed.” She laughed realizing it was back to normal so unexpectedly soon.

“So, am I the only one going to ask?” Vandross said as he began ringing the mineral water out of his cloak. “Bethel, would you kindly explain just what in the name of the Trinity just happened?”

All eyes turned to the disgraced High Conservator. Just like Daphne, the injuries on his face seemed to have disappeared and he seemed inexplicably capable of holding his own weight without the aid of Ram’s Horn. The stern curt man seemed almost sheepish as the task force looked to him for answers.

“Nine days ago,” Jude began. “Auzlanten approached me asking about Knox Mortis. I gave him everything you had assembled up until that point and explained why I assembled the task force. He told me that he couldn't scry inside of Budapest, as though a shroud was over it blocking his sight. So he asked me to go in with you. I don't really know how, but he said he could see through my eyes if I allowed him to. He promised to come to our rescue if we were in danger. I'd say he kept that promise."

"Nine?" Downey interjected. "We only found out we were going to Budapest four days ago. How did he know before we did?"

"Auzlanten's a prophet, predicting events before they happen is one of the less impressive things he's capable of."

"But why not just join us at the start?" Adastra contested. "If he was so eager to know what was going on in Budapest, why not just accompany us from the start."

"Maybe Daurtey would still be breathing if he did." Volk added bitterly.

"Distrust probably," Bethel continued with less assurance. "According to him, I'm one of the few people he has absolute trust in. With the betrayal of the Regent, the lines of loyalty are being blurred even to a mind as great as his."

There was a cough coming from the bottom of the stairway, a polite clearing of the throat that someone would purposely make to draw attention to them. There was a young lady standing at the end of a marble walkway splitting the circular moat of churning waters. Her hair was the color of golden wheat and her eyes were a piercing glacial blue. She wore an outdated general Scourge uniform of stiff grey fabric. Her hands were folded at the base of her stomach.

"Excuse me," She said with a kind smile in an accent none of them were familiar with. "Are you all quite well? Do any of you require medical attention, food, drinks, perhaps a place to lie down and sleep?"

The task force exchanged confused looks back and forth with one another as they stepped off the dais. The starchy iron grey uniform looked quaint almost to the point of absurdity compared to their advanced suits of armor, each with their division's insignias displayed. The biggest surprise came from the woman herself. Arodi Auzlanten was a figure of legendary reputation, so one would expect those working intimately in his private haven would be equally magnificent. This woman was not even what one would consider particularly beautiful. She seemed so plain, so uninteresting. Surrounded by such a vast scene of artisan masterpieces, she looked out of place.

"You are the Shackle task force yes?" She asked with a polite smile. "6319?"

"We are." Warden Downey said stepping down from the dais. "My name is..."

"You're Volk Downey." She said taking his outstretched hand. "Warden awarded the black rose in 4711, age 46, former governor of Glaswey before annexation into Templym in 4698, you were shot in the face Jubral 2nd 4708 during the Civil Strife by Apothecary Diaz of the Siloam on a failed diplomatic mission. I know all of you and your stories."

"All of our stories?" Bethel said curiously.

"Jude Bethel, High Conservator as of 4701, age 41, awarded the Tell Crosshairs Palescar 17th 4709 at the end of the Civil Strife for outstanding marksmanship, one of three in all of Templym's history."

"You're going to have to stop that." Oslin said with obvious irritation.

"I am sorry, I didn't mean to make you feel uncomfortable. I will stop revealing what I know."

"Who exactly are you?" Bride Wainwright asked.

"I am Arodi Auzlanten's personal assistant. I aid him in his pursuit of Templym's adversaries however I can."

"But who are you? What's your name, where are you from?"

The blonde woman tipped her head slightly as if confused at the question. "I don't believe I am supposed to disclose that information." There was something about this woman that didn't settle well with Daphne. The way in which she spoke was methodical, almost to the point of appearing automatonic. Yet she seemed to be functioning like a natural woman. She breathed and twitched in the same minutely inconsistent ways as any biological human. "Is there something I can get for you all? I was instructed to care for you until Arodi returns."

"Are those display cases?" Blye said excitedly looking behind her and seeing a plethora of crystalline cubes, several of which held oddities. "Can you tell us about all of those things?"

"I can give you a tour if you'd like. Please, follow me."

A blizzard of rubble was kicked up with the avalanche. The collapsing structure shed girders like a snake strips its decayed skin. Boulders of rockfoam fell like aircraft shot from the sky. The demolished cloudtoucher crumbled in a raucous thunder sending a staccato chorus of boisterous destruction across the death scented winds of Budapest all the way to the border walls. Praetorian Trialock himself scratched his chin in confusion seeing the structure crumble into the horizon.

The building took two minutes to fall. Its massive structure died slowly and dug its own grave of dust with the force of its collapse. Arodi Auzlanten was knocked about by a few boulders, but took little substantial damage. He manifested a barrier of light that protected his body from the megatons of force the collapse birthed. Once the avalanche had subsided he used similar power to blast his way out of a mountain of debris.

He let out a pained sigh once he was free from what could easily have been his coffin. His eyes looked over the Budapest hellscape which had become even more a monument to pain and suffering. Arodi couldn't distinguish the dust of cremated humans from the fine gravel produced from the detonation. The sheer amount was overwhelming.

A thin sheet of grey dust ghosted Auzlanten's features and a similar fog draped the streets. He shook it free with a snap of his fingers producing a gust of harsh wind. Nothing within a quarter mile could have survived the avalanche, nothing born of this world at least. It would take days to sift through this wreckage, even with powers. It would be worth it to find the Idolacreid.

Arodi realized that it wouldn't take days. Worse, it would take weeks to comb through Budapest and Grave Glutton territory to find where they were hiding that blasphemous tome. But perhaps there was a third, substantially worse outcome. There was a possibility that he would never achieve his goal, that he would never rip the Idolacreid from the clutches of the Nephilim. That option became morbidly imminent when the hands of Knox Mortis suddenly wrapped around Auzlanten's throat.

CHAPTER 38

Knox Mortis survived. Arodi didn't even see where he came from. Did he burrow his way out of the rubble mound? Did he slither away from the kill zone in time? All he knew was that the giant was able to sneak through the dust cloud and wrap his massive hands around his throat. His greasy armor was caked with a coat of ash. Each of his massive hands pinched his throat. He couldn't tell if the marauder chief was attempting to crush his windpipe, snap his neck, or pop his head off. Whatever the intent of the assault, he wouldn't survive more than a few seconds.

"I know my fate, worm!" Mortis hissed through bleeding gums. "You will fall by my hand, it is prophesied. No force can prevent your destiny among the rotten corpses strewn all over Budapest."

Auzlanten's trachea would have been crumbled like paper if he wasn't focusing his power on keeping his body intact. His ringed fingers tried desperately to pry the giant off of him until he realized that the preternatural strength he possessed was too much. He couldn't escape with brute force. So he blinked away.

In a pop of bright violet light Arodi vanished from Mortis' python grip. He appeared behind the giant instantly. He just had enough time to draw Leagna from its titanium sheath before Mortis turned about to continue his brutal attack.

Arodi's sabre, now radiating crimson light, struck in elegant lethal blows. At least, they would if Mortis wasn't constantly deflecting each with fists sheathed in black lightning. With the task force out of the battle zone, he could let loose his full potential. Now, each impact sent out a shockwave like ten pounds of clapshock detonating. Knox let out a bevy of barbaric wet throat growls, raining oozing spittle over Auzlanten. Neither side could gain an inch of an advantage over the other.

This was one of the longer duels Arodi had been in. The amount of effort expended on a single adversary was unheard of for a mortal. Mortis was truly worthy of harboring the prize he sought. Considering there was no chance of collateral damage any longer, Auzlanten was ready to show his full strength.

Arodi allowed a fist to strike his chest. He rode the momentum of the force backwards, sending him flying over fifty feet away from the giant. He slid to a halt and grabbed Leagna with both hands. He swung the sabre in a complex rhythm of slashes. With every motion, a brilliant arc of pure starlight was forged. Columns of raw energy whipped across the hellscape in a furious storm of lethal power. Dust was fused into bubbles of molten glass and pylons were severed by the energy whips. Mortis for the first time went onto the defensive. He blocked repulsions by covering his vitals with his tree-thick arms. Orange flecks of liquid metal spewed from his armor and blood vapor boiled off of the chief with every stab of light.

The light storm should have minced Mortis into strips. Yet, he was still standing once the storm subsided, albeit now hunched over. Sharp lines where the arcs impacted were now etched out of the steel armor plating that Mortis donned as well as caverns shredded into his corpse skin. He panted like a bleeding hound crippled after a grueling dogfight.

"If you give me the Idolacreid now, I'll make it quick." Auzlanten shouted with his sabre still in a two-handed grip. "You have no chance of survival. Repent, for today you will face the Lord's Judgment."

Mortis ground two handfuls of ash in his hand. His eyeless, noseless face was twisted in a bitter snarl. Iron and glass teeth filed to a point were bared, eager to draw living blood. The black lightning around his hands enveloped his whole body as the Imago inhabiting his flesh gained more control over their host. Muscles pulsed and spasmed as he reared up into a predatory stance.

He charged like a massive bull. The ground quaked beneath his massive strength. The demons inside the giant demanded blood and Mortis was determined to make it Auzlanten's. The aura of unholy electricity sparked into a cloud of crackling energy. It stung his eyes from the distance before the current of primal energies even made it close to him. Then the chieftain was on him again.

Never in his life had Arodi seen such a reckless assault of pure hatred. So much anger, so much resentment had never been in a more concentrated form. Mortis was a sentient avatar of sin. The rapid wild attack of rips, punches, kicks, slams, and every matter of physical strike was so incomprehensibly brutal. There was no chance Auzlanten could possibly avoid every attack. Each blow carried enough force to topple a small Hekaton. He parried as much of the pounce away as he could, but they came so quickly.

Auzlanten was battered about like a ship caught in a hurricane. No matter how well protected, the gale of fists struck home on multiple fronts. He could have easily been killed by the behemoth. Already his garments were tattering and his skin collecting bruised patches. Each impact caused his dexterous battle stance to waver. He expected little less from one of the hierarchs of the Nephilim's ranks. Arodi had a distinct advantage. While Mortis drew his strength from the dark fuel of the Mundus Imago, Auzlanten was powered by the Triune God. Knox had a limited source... he did not have such a debilitation.

Arodi Auzlanten suffered through the torrent for nearly five minutes, deflecting over half of the strikes. Another few impacts afterwards would have broken his body beyond repair. Mortis brought both hands down in hands in what could have easily been the death blow. The blow would have been too powerful to block with Leagna and too swift to dodge. Normally, Auzlanten would blink away again with the hopes of appearing at his flank. He knew that would be unnecessary. The arcing black static vanished on the backswing.

The demonic entities inside of Knox Mortis had expended all of their resources. He was a specific breed of black host, one that held full command over his inhabitants' actions. Their fallen abilities were not unlimited. He pushed them too far, calling on every iota of power available to him. Arodi knew he was sloppy. His combat strategy consisted only of reckless abandon matched with unkempt rage. Reserve and strategy was not within his realm of familiarity, resulting in a quickly expended energy source. Now Mortis was vulnerable.

The impact of the final strike was drastically quelled due to his inability to draw power from his patrons. The double handed strike was easily parried off to the side by Leagna. Arodi speculated that if Mortis still had eyes, he could perceive the fear instilled in them. Auzlanten spun the blade in a circular motion, hacking off both of his grisly hands at the wrist. He bellowed once more but not his raging animalistic war cry. This scream was nothing but a response to agonizing pain. Now it was almost over.

Arodi slammed a boot on the ground. This called a stalagmite of rockfoam and twisted steel to shoot up from the ground, impaling the giant. The weaponized shard burst through Mortis' breastplate and perforated through his back. He tried to scream again, but a punctured lung prevented him from doing so. The chieftain's bulky limbs went slack, causing his entire body to dangle from the spike of ruin driven through his torso.

Knox's healing capabilities were nullified. He was bleeding profusely from the cavity punched through his chest. Yet, he still lived. A pitiful rattling echoed from his chest with every torturous breath. His skin went pale, even more ghastly than his already gaunt flesh.

Arodi Auzlanten walked up the stalagmite up to the point where it penetrated his chest. He knelt down so he could make eye contact with the dying marauder. His hollow sockets were aimless now that he was devoid of the guidance from his Imago pawns. It was a pitiable sight to behold. A tyrant, one mighty enough to fell one of the most sophisticated engines of war available, at the utter mercy of a man half his size.

"As I said Knox, you had your chance." Auzlanten said with suppressed fury. "I am an instrument of the true God. You are a slave to a false patron." His gaze shifted from the blind sallow holes in the giant's skull to a slight bulge in the breastplate, as though an object were stowed beneath the casing.

"He said..." Mortis sputtered and coughed, oozing black slime leaking from every orifice in his face. "He said it...it was my destiny." Auzlanten truly pitied the giant. "He promised me I would be...that I would kill the great warlock."

Arodi leaned towards Mortis, close enough to whisper into what was left of his gnarled ear. "He lied." Auzlanten leapt off the rock spike and into the dust below, taking Leagna and the freshly severed head of Knox Mortis down with him.

The goliath was dead. The Grave Gluttons, but more importantly the ranks of the Nephilim, would be crippled beyond recovery. This alone would prove to be a significant victory. The death of Mortis was not the only achievement Auzlanten made. He looked at the knob permeating from his armor realizing that it was created from some object concealed beneath. He swung Leagna upwards, cracking open the metal breastplate, revealing the trove hidden inside.

He expected something viler. He imagined it to be a book bound with a cover of fused bone. He pictured pages of tanned human skin and words etched out in blood. That is the picture he concocted in his mind. That is what Arodi Auzlanten thought it would look like. No. Its appearance was...underwhelming.

One hundred and thirty-four days for a book. Just a black stained leather tome. If it were among hundreds in a library, one would glance right over it, seeing no significant visual appeals. There were not even any cultic etchings. The Nephilim's holy symbol wasn't emblazoned on any visible surface or on any of the papyrus sheets. The Idolacreid appeared as nothing more than a book, unique in no perceivable manner, lying in the dust of Budapest.

"And this is the eye of The Impaler." The blonde woman motioned to another crystal cube holstering what appeared as a large ruby. "At the end of the 3rd Purus Crusade, a sorcerer from the American Hinterlands integrated the eye of the Imago into a magickal staff."

"I don't recall anything like that happening." Herald Du'Plasse said skeptically from among the crowd of observers.

"That's because the sorcerer was dispatched before he did any significant damage." The woman smiled as she spoke. "Lord Auzlanten left the Impaler's eye in him, not seeing any initial threat. After the sorcerer nearly used it as a focus component, he decided to lock it away in here."

"That case doesn't look too secure." Warden Downey voiced a thought he'd been having for the past hour. "What's keeping me from just smashing that glass and taking the prize?"

"Well you're quite welcome to try, Mr. Downey." She laughed at his query.

Adastra Covalos couldn't help but brood silently at their situation. He couldn't stand being sidelined so suddenly and left to peacefully tour Auzlanten's sanctum. Granted, there was an undertone of excitement to his bitterness, but he couldn't stand being yanked from the heat of his investigation. It almost felt like Auzlanten was hijacking their investigation by taking down their final quarry. But if what everything Bethel had told them was true then Mortis presented a more significant threat than what they initially suspected. That and considering the fact that he was stronger than a Swift Hekaton indicated that he was beyond his capabilities, but hopefully not of the Master of Templym.

"You okay?" Vandross Blackwell asked his partner quietly sensing his irritation. "I would have thought you'd be a bit more eager to be where we are."

"I'm not exactly happy with our situation." Adastra muttered. "Three months for a quarry hunt only to be shunted from the situation at the height of the chase, there's some injustice there."

"Auzlanten will take care of it. Mortis doesn't stand a chance. I'm not detecting a tinge of hurt pride am I?"

Vandross hoped that would produce a chuckle, to no avail. "We've done all the work on this case, not him. It doesn't seem fair to have him swoop in for the kill."

"But that's not what's bothering you." Vandross tapped his boot to the marble and cocked his eyebrow upward. "Come on, out with it."

Adastra's lip curled beneath his beard, like he was disgusted to voice the thought he had been harboring. "I don't trust this...any of this. I find it highly convenient that Auzlanten swept in for the save at the optimum time. I find it suspicious that we're in some secluded location that God forbid we learn the location of. Then there's this woman."

Adastra looked to the plain woman who smiled and spoke with her teammates. She was so poised, so organized, so friendly. "She's too immaculate." He grumbled in a hushed tone. "Don't you find something peculiar about her?"

Vandross shrugged his damp shoulders. "She does seem out of place. She seems so innocent, like a child. Yet, she's also immensely sophisticated. She's reciting information effortlessly like it's ingrained into her mind."

"This reeks of magick." He grumbled.

"Or advanced technology," Vandross mused. "This is Arodi Auzlanten we're talking about. I'm partial to the AI theory personally. Maybe this is all just one giant memorial to the Cybernetic Revolution."

"Did you catch how Mortis addressed Auzlanten when we saw him?" Adastra had the same disgusted look in his face. "He called him the great warlock."

"You mean you're listening to a demoniac marauder chief the size of Goliath? I'd hardly take anything that beast said too seriously. That is, if you're actually entertaining the idea that the immortal founder of God's great nation is a dabbler of unclean magick."

"Nothing's off the table. Bethel's planning mutiny in the Scourge against our traitor Regent. If you had spun that idea to me last year I would have arrested you for heresy. Now...now I'm suspicious of everything."

"You have a question?" The two Inquisitors looked up from their conversation. The woman in stiff grey uniform called to them. She still had that childish smile and was engulfed in the sideshow of relics.

"Too many ma'am," Adastra responded. "and frankly I don't think you'd be authorized to answer them."

"You are likely correct." She responded. "Anyway, I believe this concludes our tour. If you'd all follow me, we can wait in an adjoining chamber for Arodi to return."

Their tour had ended close to the border of the dome. There were a number of doors and antechambers cutting into the marble walls. "Where do all of these go?" Bethel asked motioning to the numerous entryways. He was upright and walking on his own. He had healed from his injuries. Apparently Auzlanten's sanctum had healing energies...or something of the sort.

"Most are just side rooms or vaults." She looked around at the surrounding arches. "Though three of these doorways are portals to..."

The woman's pale blue eyes locked onto a single door. Two bronze pillars flanked an intricately designed doorway made of glossy blue metal, probably some variant of wardiron. It was frozen in a half-open position, the top part retracted inside of the ceiling. She gasped at the sight of the thick metal panel. Her face flushed of all color giving her a corpse's visage.

"That's not supposed to be open." She swiveled her head rapidly between the task force and the doorway. She sounded panicked. "Tertiary containment field has been compromised. I need to...you need to... oh dear God this has never happened before."

"What's happening?" Bride Wainwright asked. A distressing noise came from behind the door in question, the weeping of a young child. Feared looks of confusion were exchanged between the Scourge soldiers at the emanation of the crying.

"There is a bunker entrance three doors down." She said hurriedly. "You'll find a tungsten door with scripture etchings on it. You need to go in and wait for Arodi to come get you."

"You're not telling us what's wrong." Warden Downey said skeptically.

"Perhaps there's something we can do to help." Expurgator Blye suggested.

"No!" The woman was very clearly distraught. "Get in the

bunker and wait!" She made to walk away but hesitated. "I know you're confused and perhaps afraid. This requires a great deal of faith in us but you must trust us. Get in the bunker and stay there!" She stormed off in the opposite direction, presumably to handle whatever situation was occurring in this safe haven.

S-6319 didn't move from their spot around the display cases. Each one of them was waiting for another to make a move. Instead, they just looked back and forth between the opened blue door and the dull grey tungsten bunker. The child's weeping slowly bounced off the circular marble walls creating further tension.

"What now?" Ram's Horn broke the silence.

"We go into the bunker." Herald Du'Plasse suggested, thankful that the awkward pause was over. "Did you hear what that woman said? She said that a containment field was compromised. That means something that needs to be kept locked up is coming loose. Why's there even a question about it?"

"A child?" Daphne asked letting her maternal nature show. "You think there's a threat to keeping an innocent kid locked up?"

"You think that's a child?" Bethel argued. "I wouldn't even consider that as a possibility."

"Let's inspect the threat." Adastra broke off from the group and strode off towards the half-opened door.

"Adastra, knock it off!" Downey snapped. "Get away from there."

"I'm sick of trusting based on stories. I want to see something with my own eyes for a change."

"This is a bad idea." Vandross yelled as he made after his partner.

"I'm just going to look, I won't even go inside."

Bethel ran in between him and the door. His carbon steel tomahawk was drawn. "Adastra, as High Conservator I am ordering you to stand down and get to that bunker."

Inquisitor Covalos didn't even flinch. "Are you threatening me Jude?"

"Can we not do this?" Inquisitor Blackwell yelled trying to keep the peace.

"Might I remind you," Jude growled, his scarred face furled into a scowl. "Arodi Auzlanten is the only reason we aren't chained up by a murder happy psychopath. We should be thankful and be listening to his will."

"Well maybe we should..." Adastra was rearing up to engage in a heated debate and even go as far as getting physical with Bethel, a fight he was positive he couldn't win. Then he stopped because he realized that he could already accomplish what he set out to do. He could clearly see into the opening in the door Jude was standing in front of.

The interior of the once sealed chamber was pitch-black. The only illumination on the inside was a vague orange light source emanating from the ground up. It appeared like the glow of molten metal or lava. What caused the Inquisitor to halt in his thought process was what was standing in the wake of that glow.

At first he thought it was an intricate object with complex geometry. The shape of the figure was folded over on top of itself and toppled on its side. The straight lines were in the shape of limbs and the rough edges were crumpled clothing. It was too small to be a person...a grown person that is. A little girl, no more than six years old and dressed in a petite dress, was bunched in a curled fetal position. Glistening tears damped a pair of closed eyes. The sight sickened Adastra and his sudden pause gave Jude and Vandross reason enough to look as well with equal shock. Her eyes, which seemed so big and blue for such a small child, opened, meeting the three. Pain welled up in her eyes, filling them up with similar anguish. With a tiny, quiet voice she cried out, "Please help me."

CHAPTER 39

The three of them stood aghast at the sight. They had never seen a sight so meager and heartbreaking. A little girl, after all of the marvelous sights they were beholden to, this was still one of the most surprising. Why did Arodi Auzlanten, Master of Templym and prophet of the one true God, have a child detained in his secret lair? It seemed insidious, cruel, and by all definitions immoral. Of course, if there was one thing this conspiracy had revealed, nothing was ever exactly as it seemed.

"Are you here to save me?" The little girl whimpered again. Her freckled cheeks were glistening from the refracted light on her tears.

Vandross, Adastra, and Jude were too stunned to speak. All they could do was shift their gazes to one another. Who was this child? What was she doing locked in a prison vault? Was this even human? A multitude of questions flooded their minds. Inquisitor Covalos was not sure if approaching the doorway against the blonde woman's orders was the right decision or not.

"Please help me." The tiny girl's voice was filled with sorrow. "Let me go before he comes back. I want to go home."

"Hey sweetie," Daphne Wainwright approached the half open gate making sure not to cross the threshold. "What's your name darling?"

"I don't know." The child wept and gasped. Her speech was broken and difficult to understand. "It's been so long since anybody said it. I don't remember my name. I don't know where I am."

"Calm down darling." Daphne's voice was warm and inviting, like a mother's. She certainly didn't betray her true motives, but she was analyzing this girl. As much as it distressed her to see a child in danger, she knew better than to act without proper assessment. "Do you remember how you got here?"

"The man in blue, he put me in here. Please don't let him get me again. He hurts me."

"The man in blue, does he have a big black beard? Does he wear a silver crown?"

"Yes that's him." The girl got off of her side and onto her knees. "He hurts me. Please let me go before he comes back."

"Calm down sweetheart, we're going to figure this out." Daphne moved away from the entrance and turned back to her friends. "Well, any ideas?"

"This is a trick." Bethel said without hesitation. "I don't know what that thing is, but I would bet my life it's not even human. It belongs in this vault, I'm sure of that."

"You can't be serious." Expurgator Blye joined them. "I mean, just look at her. That's a child if I've ever seen one. Have you ever seen such a genuinely innocent creature?"

"I didn't see a single tell." Daphne responded in agreement. "I would need a Veritas Chamber to confirm it, but I can't say for certain she was lying."

"This reeks of Imago filth." Adastra grumbled, doubting the girl's integrity. "Vandross, do you still have detection incense?"

"The Grave Gluttons took my satchel." He shrugged. "It's all back in Budapest."

"I'm not buying it." Bethel said. "If Auzlanten felt the need to seclude this thing from the material world, there's no question it's dangerous. This is trap. It's trying to trick us into releasing it."

"Can we risk that assumption?" Blye said with distress in his voice. "What if she's telling the truth? What if Auzlanten really has a kid locked up? Can we really live with ourselves if we leave this child here to be tortured?"

"Auzlanten saved our lives!" Oslin joined into the discussion and he appeared offended that the Expurgator was suggesting something so rash. "It's asinine to even consider he would do something so evil. Obviously, this is some demonic monster trying to worm its way out of its cell."

"We should just wait for Auzlanten to get back." Wainwright offered up a compromise. "We'll ask him about this girl and he'll give us the answers we need."

"What do you expect him to say?" Volk walked up with Ram's Horn joining the remainder of the squad at the precipice of the prison door. "No matter what the truth is he'll tell us it's a demon. If that's the truth then that's what he'll say. But if this is actually a child, then that's a pretty good lie to cover it up."

"Even if it isn't an Imago, what do we do?" Adastra added in. "I'm certainly not going to walk into a holding cell crafted by Arodi Auzlanten. God only knows what kind of horrible thing will happen to you if you cross that border. Even if you aren't obliterated, there are at least two other containment machinations to overcome."

"Demon." Ram grunted with his metallic voice.

"Did you even look at that child?" Daphne said conflicted. "She looks so pained, so scared. If this is a façade, it's the most convincing I've ever seen."

"Perhaps we should put it to a vote." Downey said scratching his leathery chin.

"Put what to a vote?" Du'Plasse said exasperated. "We aren't actually considering trying to release it are we?"

"My Bride and I are Veil!" Blye argued. "It is our solemn duty to protect the structure of the family, specifically the most innocent members. This is a child we're talking about. It would violate our ideology if we were to stand idly by."

"And we are Inquisitors." Adastra said while Vandross listened intently closely considering both sides of the argument. "If we released Mundus Imago onto the Earth, it would violate our creed."

The argument was silenced by a swift slam of metal on stone. The opening in the door dropped and closed the gap, cutting off the child from the Scourge task force. The exotic blue metal clapped down to the marble floor with a deafening crash suggesting immense weight. The heated exchange was cut off by Arodi Auzlanten himself.

Standing just a few feet away from them, the Master of Templym stood. He did not have a stoic demeanor as he always did. His ornate attire was tattered with rends. Ash and plaster flecks painted the black canvas of his mane. His ultramarine eyes were filled with some kind of emotion. Whether it was vengeance, or woe, or irritation was unclear. What was obvious was that he had little patience remaining after his mission to Budapest.

"You were ordered into the bunker." Auzlanten's voice was still calm and gallant yet had an ominous undertone to it. "Fall in line."

The task force followed orders without question. They organized themselves into a standard line, standing at attention with their right hands clasped to their chests. It was spectacular that a figure like him could hold such authority. He was shorter than half of the people in the squadron and was not wearing battle plate. The legends surrounding the man were what made him such an imposing individual. The centuries of myths following Arodi Auzlanten coupled with what he probably did to Knox Mortis kept them all from breaking their posture.

Leagna was holstered at Auzlanten's side, the vibrant light from the sabre contained in the black sheath. He interlocked his fingers behind his back and began walking back and forth in front of the line. The sound of black boots clicking on polished stone was the only sound in the entire dome.

"I rescued you from Budapest." Arodi stated sternly. "Against my initial judgment, I swept you away from the clutches of Mortis and his Grave Gluttons and into my private sanctum."

"Lord Auzlanten..." Bethel tried to speak.

"You will not speak unless I permit you to." He snapped back, not even making eye contact with the man. "I transported you here because it was the best way I could ensure that all of you would survive. I trusted that you would have enough discipline to listen to my assistant's request. Yet, you blatantly disregarded her order. Are you even aware of the threat you were just exposed to?"

Nobody responded, recognizing the question as rhetorical. "This is the prison of an A+ Mundus Imago. What you just witnessed was a ploy. The door to its prison was cracked open and it was leaping at an opportunity to escape."

"Permission to speak?" Bride Wainwright asked.

"Granted." Auzlanten responded.

"The demon, who is she?"

"It. Do not humanize that beast by assigning it gender. But I understand your concern. The creature that will remain locked here until the Second Coming is called Tumor'at. I want to kill it, but I cannot. Over four hundred years of deceit and disguises, yet it remains here. It has taken the form of that same child dozens of times over trying to slither its way out of its entombment. Apparently, it tried that same disguise with the hopes of coaxing you to release it."

"That is the reason you were instructed to retreat to the bunker." Arodi continued his lecture. "You were told to retreat to safety to eliminate the possibility of releasing Tumor'at or having one of you become corrupted. You did not listen. That level of insubordination put your lives and the lives of everyone you care about at risk. Under normal circumstances, I would execute you for such an offense."

"Lord Auzlanten." Adastra Covalos spoke. "It was my intervention that swayed our group from entering the bunker. It was my rebellion that endangered us all. If any among us deserve to be punished, it should be me."

Auzlanten stopped pacing in front of the Inquisitor. He looked at him and nodded slowly. "Your integrity is noted Inquisitor Covalos, but that will not be necessary. Given the current state of borderline anarchy the Scourge resides in, I understand the allure of curiosity. You seek answers to clarify the shroud of doubt covering your minds, disregarding your strict discipline in the process. That is the first reason I will forgive this trespass."

"The second reason I will not have you killed or your minds wiped clean is as a thanks for your assistance. Your investigative efforts into the Mortis case have contributed great amounts of intelligence into my own investigation in the dark dealings of the Nephilim. With your aid I have slain one of his generals and captured their cult's most sacred artifact. For that, I am eternally grateful, especially to you Jude."

Auzlanten stopped and placed a ringed hand on his shoulder. "You have exhibited faith in me that has been unmatched by your peers in the Scourge. With your aid, hundreds of traitors have been captured and the bulk of the Scourge remains loyal to me."

"Thank you, Master Auzlanten." Jude smiled.

"I trust you all to not repeat what you've witnessed here to anyone." Arodi reached into his robes as he walked away. He pulled out a small pyramid made of glossed basalt or some kind of igneous stone. "I assume you'd like these back."

The pyramid opened up, each of the faces peeled down like paper. The interior was nothing but a ball of light. From the ball, a small flurry of snow fluttered out before sticking to the marble in front of them. The snow shaped into each of the weapons and possessions that were taken by the marauders from Budapest. "At ease, collect your things."

Everything that was stolen from them was returned. The Du'Plasse Holt that was recovered from the Hellpit for a second time, Bride Wainwright's rapier still whipping tails of frost, and even a brown leather satchel from which Vandross immediately retrieved his granite pipe for a smoke, it was all there. A sigh of relief was exhaled mutually throughout the squad members as they retrieved their lost items and realized that Auzlanten was not going to hurt them. Relief flooded their senses as they entered a brief state of serenity.

Arodi Auzlanten turned his gaze from the Scourge soldiers standing in his presence. He stared at the pyramid in his hand as it snapped shut. Even through the extradimensional gap between the material plane and the storage container, he could hear its dark whispers. The Idolacreid was calling out to him from inside the pyramid. He stared at the simple geometric shape listening to cries of temptation in his mind. The wicked tome begged him to read. The Idolacreid sounded like it ached to have him sift through its pages.

Auzlanten was honestly intrigued. He could tell that this artifact did in fact possess knowledge of a supernatural scale. For a few moments, he pondered what new information he could glean from the Idolacreid. He might find a cure for the demonic disease responsible for the Plague Massacre. He could fill design gaps in the new inventions he was tinkering with in what little free time he had. He might find where the traitor Invictus Illuromos was hiding. The calls of the book, even through the dampened barrier of an extradimensional space, were alluring. Arodi knew it was all just devious promises. He wouldn't listen to them, even though they kept crawling into his mind.

"Arodi." A sweet feminine voice called out from right next to him. Refreshingly, the kind voice overshadowed the evil whispers coming from the Idolacreid. The dark whispers in his head distracted him from even noticing her approach. It was his assistant. Her icy blue eyes were flooded with tears of sorrow. "I'm sorry, I've failed you."

"Why do you say that?" He responded in kind.

"I disobeyed protocol. I left our guests unattended when I saw the door was opened. I risked letting Tumor'at escape so I could contact you. It was a disregard of your wishes and I..."

"You have nothing to apologize for." Auzlanten brushed a tear away from her cheek. "You were placed in an impossible situation and performed as logically as you could. For that, I am thankful. We never anticipated having anybody visiting our haven and I certainly never believed anybody other than me could open that door. You handled it adequately."

The task force looked awkwardly at the display of such open affection. Auzlanten was caressing this woman's face with the same gentleness a man would have their wife or daughter. It was such a profound display of emotion unlike anything most citizens of Templym even believed him capable of. When he noticed that all eyes were resting on him and this intimate display, he snapped upright and back into his impassive demeanor.

"Would you kindly prepare the new vault I've constructed?" Auzlanten said to the woman once more. "I must lock this away for the remainder of this world's existence."

"Right away, Arodi." She smiled and stepped away to another area in the massive dome structure.

Auzlanten stowed the pyramid back into his robe. High Conservator Bethel had just slung his longcannon over his back and approached the Master of Templym. "Your mission was a success?" He asked.

"Knox Mortis is dead and I have the Idolacreid, I consider that a success. We've dealt a crippling blow to the Nephilim today."

"That's good news." Jude's scarred mouth perked up in a shallow grin. "I suppose a celebration is in order. But first, if I may inquire, what just happened with this prison door?"

Auzlanten turned from Bethel to face the other seven people standing there. "Would you like to confess now?" They exchanged more quizzical gazes with one another. "I didn't think so. Rest assured that there was little risk in Tumor'at actually escaping. This door is the weakest of the barriers I've constructed around it and it was barely compromised. However, the fact that it was partially opened is concerning. So I ask again, would you like to confess now?"

It was unclear who he was speaking to. His gaze was not set to one individual in particular and his speech was indirect. However, the implication he was making was obvious to all. "You think one of us opened it?" Herald Du'Plasse dared to voice what they were all thinking.

Arodi Auzlanten approached the Hrimatan. Seeing the two so close to each other, it was obvious how Oslin's mimicry of Auzlanten's hair was a crude copy. "I don't think it, I know it." He began pacing through the ranks, lagging in front of each member of the task force. "For three hundred-ninety-seven years, that door has remained shut unless I opened it. I welcome a troupe of soldiers into my private stronghold and it creaks open unexpectedly. It does not require an intellect like mine to make the connection."

Every one of them was silent. The thought of a betrayer in their ranks was unfathomable to all of them. None would dare voice an accusation, but equally nobody would dare contest Auzlanten. "There is more evidence." The prophet continued. "Even before I recovered the Idolacreid, I have learned to recognize its taint. The artifact radiates an onerous aura that sticks with those who read it. Now that I have the source, I have learned to identify this stain."

"You're telling me you can tell who's read it just by looking at them?" Volk said, still scoffing at the idea someone on the team could be a turncoat.

"Correct." Auzlanten stepped away from the crowd, running a hand through his hair. "So when I saw you all chained up in Budapest, before I had the Idolacreid, I couldn't see it. Now, I know exactly which of you is loyal to the Nephilim."

Arodi extended an open hand out towards the crowd. A rope of invisible energy wrapped around the guilty party, dragging them in his direction. A pair of flaksteel boots scraped across the marble tiling until Expurgator Blye's throat was in Auzlanten's hand.

"Yen Blye, you have violated your oath to the Veil, to the Scourge, and to Templym. Your fraternization with enemies of God makes you an enemy of all that is good in this world. How do you plea?"

Blye sputtered uselessly as the overwhelming strength in Auzlanten's fingers constricted his throat. He released his grip allowing the white armored Expurgator plop to the ground. "I don't know what you're talking about." Yen coughed between words.

"I invented the Veritas Chambers Blye," Arodi said with contained rage. "You can't lie to me. Confess!" Auzlanten arched his hand upwards over the prostrate Himalayan man. Blye immediately began screaming as his body became wracked with excruciating pain.

The Expurgator twisted his tortured body in agony, the only logical response to the onslaught of pain from nowhere. The remainder of his team watched with horrified expressions as their comrade was mercilessly tortured by unseen energies. Yet, Auzlanten wore a plain face. The mightiest hero of Templym did not even flinch as he caused the unbearable suffering of another man.

Arodi lowered his hand to his side. Blye stopped seizing and sucked in deep breaths as he began to weep. Never in his life had he experienced such pain. Auzlanten didn't care. He grabbed the gorget of his battle plate and lifted him to his knees. As he did so, he ripped a silver chain out from beneath the armor. He was wearing an amethyst pendant depicting a violet lily, the holy symbol of the cult of the Nephilim.

Auzlanten tossed the amulet to the feet of his horrified comrades. "I know who you really are Blye. Confess your sins to those you've betrayed."

"Please, no more." Yen begged. "I'm a spy okay! I've been spying on all of you."

"You're a pawn of the Nephilim." Auzlanten said. It wasn't a question.

"Yes. I was shown a single page of the Idolacreid. The power I felt...the wealth of might I could acquire. He promised me anything my heart desired."

"What was your demise? What gift were you promised to turn you away from everything you swore to protect?" Auzlanten let his anger show the more he spoke. His fingertips began sparking with vermillion fire. "Power, wealth, authority?"

"I was told I needed to latch onto this task force. I was told to operate as any other soldier and observe. I never hurt anyone. I just fed information to the cult, I swear!"

"Yet, like all of the Nephilim's slaves, you would have shed blood when the allotted time arrived. If I hadn't exposed you before the inception of the abolition, you would have stabbed every one of your teammates in the back!"

Blye shifted his horrified gaze away from Auzlanten. His eyes met the emerald irises of Daphne Wainwright who was looking on with dread. "Not all of them." He muttered.

Arodi saw the yearning in Yen's eyes and he understood. "Her? The Nephilim promised you her? You would sacrifice your Scourge oaths, the cradle of Templym, and all that is sacred in the eyes of God, for a woman?"

"Yes... For the woman I love."

At this point Auzlanten's hands were engulfed in blinding red flame. He crossed them over his chest, not even searing his robes. "Daphne, if Templym fell and everyone you care about was murdered as a blood sacrifice to the Nephilim, is that something you could live with?"

"No." The Bride said, her lashes wet with overbearing emotion. "And I could never love a man who contributed to such an atrocity."

Blye's head sank in sorrow. His spirit was utterly and completely broken. Arodi Auzlanten crouched onto one knee to get level his face with Yen's. "Greater love has no one than this, that one lay down his life for his friends, John 15:13. You claim to love this woman, yet were willing to destroy everything she cares about to acquire her. What the Nephilim promised you wasn't love. You would have enslaved her, broken any semblance of free will, eliminating any possibility of real love. You are a selfish, damnable fool." The flame shrouding his hands flickered away. He placed a hand on Yen's shoulder pad. "You are lost. You have fallen from Grace by the honeyed words of the Nephilim. You fell to the temptations in your heart, you were exploited. Repent... forgiveness is possible."

Blye did not respond with a plea. The only logical thing to do in this circumstance was to accept the olive branch and beg for redemption. Instead, Yen Blye drove his two short swords into Arodi Auzlanten. The Master of Templym did not confiscate his weapons from him before coaxing out his confession...because even armed, the Expurgator posed no threat. The two light steel blades slammed into Auzlanten's chest. The tips ground into folded ends, as if he had just stabbed a solid wall of flaksteel. Arodi Auzlanten did nothing to avoid the attack, knowing that it would be harmless. The futility of the murderous attempt was lost on Blye as he continued to drive his short swords into Auzlanten repeatedly to no avail. He eventually stopped after thoroughly blunting his blades and looked to Arodi with absolute disgust.

"You have taken everything from me. My one chance to have my Bride's hand and you ruined it! I have nothing to repent. I would gladly see Templym crumble beneath the Nephilim's throne a thousand times over to make her mine!"

Auzlanten struck Blye with the back of his hand. He could have easily broken the Expurgator's neck with the force but pulled back. He stood and shook his head slowly. "I gave you an opportunity to repent. I see now that you are forever outside of God's grace because you have chosen to neglect it. This treachery cannot go unpunished."

"So what now, warlock?" Yen spat with a venomous tone. "You're going to kill me without a trial just like Bog Mama, or Resinous, or Knox Mortis, or any other in our family that you deemed unfit to live. I accept my fate among the martyrs of the Nephilm's faithful. If it is my destiny to lay my life down for my brothers, then so be it!"

Arodi Auzlanten chuckled. It was a dry and humorless laugh, likely a response to the revelation of the spy's true nature. "And that, Yen Blye, is love... a pity your passion belongs to the antichrists of the world." Blye spat at Auzlanten's feet in disgust. He felt the desire to do so as well, but kept his stalwart demeanor. "No blood will be shed in my sanctum."

Arodi swung his fist upwards. Then the traitor was gone. There was no bright flash of light or clap of thunder. It was as though he was never there to begin with. Auzlanten was standing alone, the other seven standing off to the side in shock.

"Where is he?" Daphne broke yet another period of silence.

"Somewhere he will not survive." Auzlanten answered bluntly. "The details are unimportant. Just know that he betrayed you all and paid for his treachery with his life. This will go indelibly for the entire cult of the Nephilim. They are fanatics who will fight to the death for the dark accolades the Idolacreid promised. Are we in agreement that they must be stopped?" The question was greeted with a number of slow nods and worried gazes from S-6319. "Good, because like it or not, you're a part of this war. I'm going to return you to Bastion Prime. It is currently seventeen twenty-two, Verrick

24th. Sleep, eat, do whatever you must to reinvigorate yourself. Tomorrow morning, we disembark on our next mission."

"Which would be what exactly?" Bethel asked.

"I'm giving you your next quarry, Invictus Illuromos."

CHAPTER 40

Arodi Auzlanten escorted S-6319 out of the marble dome structure via another portal into the Frankish capital of Parey. This time they were significantly less nauseated by the transition. Perhaps it was due to this being their second shift, or because it was less rushed, or because of the flurry of distractions rushing through their minds. Bethel suggested not returning to Bastion Prime. If they were hunting the Regent, it would be wisest if he did not know they were free from the clutches of Mortis. Instead, they checked in to a hotel a few miles from the fortress in Parey.

A few hours of rest was a welcomed change to the nonstop adrenaline rush of the last day. Under normal circumstances, they would be elated to have access to proper plumbing, soft beds, and food that wasn't moisture preserved. However, the tension created by the stressful events yesterday and the ones looming on the horizon spoiled any opportunity of proper leisure.

A period of general recreation among a team was normally jovial. The strenuous events seen in the last day lingered in their minds. There was a significant amount of information to swallow. The impact of the encounter with the Grave Gluttons was already massive, but coupled with what happened in Auzlanten's sanctum...even the psychological conditioning they were equipped with couldn't keep them stalwart. The encounter with the young girl, no, the Imago Tumor'at, quickly followed by the exposure of Yen Blye's betrayal left much to be comprehended.

"So where do you think he sent Blye?" Vandross was smoking a bundle of Caribbean tropic leaf and reclining on the lounge room's velvet sofa. This was the first time he was bringing up what had happened, and it was only because the relaxant herbs were dampening his senses.

A number of befuddled scowls met the Inquisitor. "I don't see how that's relevant." Volk responded.

"Come on, aren't you curious? Auzlanten said some place that he couldn't survive. There are so many options! The bottom of the ocean, the heart of a volcano, a thousand feet in the sky..."

"Stowe it Vandross, you're high." Adastra snapped coldly at his partner recognizing the immense discomfort his rambling was causing Bride Wainwright.

"I...that's a decent point. Sorry, I just really need to take the edge off."

Daphne walked over to the couch and snatched the pipe from him. "You're not the only one." She took a single pull from the granite pipe. She hocked up a puff of sweet scented smoke before handing it back to the Inquisitor. "Goodness, that's awful."

"That's his special blend." Adastra said with bitter irony. "He keeps it around for high stress situations, course he loses his chivalry whenever he smokes it."

"I suppose this qualifies." Daphne said instantly feeling her heartbeat slow. "You know, I always knew Yen fancied me. I thought it was cute, like a grade school romance, but I never took it seriously. I certainly never thought he'd...that he'd..."

"Whore himself out to the Nephilim to get you?" Oslin finished the thought with significantly less kindness than Daphne ever would put it.

"I hate to be curt," Jude said swirling a crystal of mead in his hands, not actually sorry about changing the topic. "But we have to prepare for our next mission. I understand you've got a lot of emotions regarding these past events, but you've got to shelf them for now. Yen's treachery just further proves that the Nephilim has rooted its cult into our beloved Scourge."

"So now we assassinate the Regent?" Downey said with a shrug. "I think it's pretty clear that the lines of loyalty have been thoroughly faded. How do we know that this isn't the imposter Auzlanten? What if that was just the Nephilim sacrificing one of his servants to sell a story? What if Illuromos is genuinely loyal and this is a trick to fool us into doing its dirty work?"

"There is no imposter." Adastra said.

"And that's exactly what an imposter would want you to believe." Vandross responded.

"So dumb." Ram's Horn grunted while polishing his fist plating.

"I agree." Downey responded. "This used to be simple. We find villains, take them out, and move onto the next. It was so much simpler when we had one job, punish the wicked."

"Last I checked our lives weren't intended to be easy." Bethel said with his standard cold logic. "Christ warns that we are sheep among wolves. Our enemies prowl in shadow, stalking us in search of the best time to sink their fangs into our throat. The wicked are simply growing more cunning, but that changes nothing for us. We are the Scourge. We are duty bound to locate evil and terminate it. I trust that still rings true in your hearts, even if you find sympathizers in short supply."

There was a period of brief silence. As usual, the High Conservator spoke with words as honed as a flaksteel blade. His optimism, given the grimness of their current situation, was refreshing. His message implied an unspoken truth that they had all acknowledged. There would be time to sort out questions after this was over. Now was the time to focus on the next mission.

"Rumor has it that Invictus Illuromos is Auzlanten's son." Du'Plasse broke the pause. "I'm not a father, but I can't imagine ordering the assassination of one's own child could be an easy thing to do."

"We're really doing this?" Bride Wainwright said nervously biting her lip. "We're about to overthrow the most powerful man in the world?"

"You assume Auzlanten isn't a man." Bethel said. "Yes. Invictus must die. I've witnessed his treachery firsthand. He looked me dead in the eye and lied to me...in a Veritas chamber of all places. He's probably some breed of black host or witch. We're going to need the Master of Templym if this is going to work. Let me give you a brief synopsis of what I know."

Bethel produced a few leaflets of parchments. They were local maps of Parey acquired from tour stops around the urban that Jude had marked with an ink pen. "The Regent has four safe houses around the city that are kept Alpha classified. He's most likely operating out of one of them."

"Why not Bastion Prime?" Adastra asked. "He could have the full resources of the Scourge to serve his dark lord."

"If he's one of the Nephilim's generals then he'll be well connected. He'll know that Mortis is dead and the Idolacreid is lost to them. That means he'll avoid the first place we'd look. Those safe houses offer the optimal resources and secrecy."

"Should we contact the other primes?" Downey asked. "If the Prelate and the Magistrate are with us than we should call in as much aid as we can get."

"I agree, but I can't. Auzlanten was very particular in his instructions. I'm not to make contact with anybody in the Scourge. I trust he'll deal with it."

"Probably because you're dead," Blackwell said. "Or at least, the Regent thinks you are. I bet you'd like to keep it that way."

"Correct. The less the Nephilim and his peons know about our forces, the better. I don't know what to expect from tomorrow. Rest up, pray, do whatever you need to get ready. Tomorrow, the Regent dies."

They awkwardly disbanded after that sentiment. The seven meandered away from the room they had gathered in to their respective bedrooms to rest for the night. Some were set easier by the disgraced High Conservator's words, but not all of them. The Nephilim was no doubt shrouding the clarity of open loyalty. This veil of confusion was clearly an elaborate construct to distract away from the abolition.

Herald Du'Plasse had a knot in his stomach that he couldn't work out. He had stripped his battle plate and undone his intricate hair in an effort to sleep. Such rest didn't find him, just like back in his home of Hrimata during the Monk interrogations. This always happened whenever he yearned to discover something hidden. There was something gnawing at the back of his mind. It was as if there was an internalized itch that he desperately yearned to scratch.

Bethel forged this task force and assigned him as the stenographer specifically. He thought it was primarily because of his lineage to Grigor Du'Plasse, one of the twelve generals of the Reclaiming Crusade. He preferred to think it was because of his thorough investigative abilities and zeal for absolute truth. Ultimately, this mission offered a unique opportunity to lift his suspension and regain his reputation. It had since evolved into something far more crucial than just his public appearance. This created an even greater desire in the young Herald to perform as thorough a job as necessary.

After a full hour of laying in darkness restlessly, Oslin picked up his historian's tablet. The light of the holographic display filled the small bedroom with a faint green light. His intent was to delve deeply into his comrades' backgrounds. There was something off about someone in his team. He would stay up all night, rifling through the Scourge data well as deeply as his Epsilon clearance would allow him to go.

He placed the pyramid in an ossuary etched with thousands of warding sigils. Once inside, the engravings glowed with ghostly blue light indicating a proper seal had been established. Then a lid weighing as much as an entire continent was placed on top. Even after the coffin was closed, the muffled whispers continued assailing Arodi Auzlanten's mind. He figured it was a side effect from when he lifted it out of the sands of Budapest. He was learning to drown it out with other thoughts.

The Idolacreid was locked away securely in a hyper-dense structure and sealed with blessed runes. He turned away from the glossy black ossuary. He hoped that he would never see it again. He walked a specifically geometric path to avoid the traps inlaid around the chamber. Upon exiting it and returning to his sanctum, the wall closed in behind him. The thin outline indicating the existence of an antechamber fused into the marble wall, vanishing from sight. It would take a diviner to even know of its existence, let alone break in.

In the downtime between dispatches to find the Idolacreid, Arodi had been constructing this vault. Over five hundred hours of complex construction were invested into this prison for one purpose, to lock the Idolacreid away for the remainder of time. He considered purging the memory of the vault from his own mind to ensure the wicked tome would never be utilized, perhaps after the Nephilim was defeated. Perhaps he still would, but there was a matter that had to be handled before destroying his adversary.

Invictus Illuromos, his indomitable nullifier, his son, had to die. He had been tasked with this weighty responsibility months ago by the Triune God...and disobeyed. The shame draped over his mind like a wet blanket of shame. He was grateful that his status as prophet had only been temporarily revoked and even then most of his powers hadn't been taken. Tsadaqiel had reiterated this message during their most recent visit and he once again swore that he would vindicate the offense against the Lord. There was no excuse to avoid his task any longer. It was time to put his traitor son to death.

"Arodi." It was her, the blonde woman. He had been staring at the empty space of the wall for several drawn out moments. He had been dreading putting Invictus to death and playing out sweet nostalgia in his mind, torturing himself as a means of distraction. Her glacial blue eyes were sparkling with crystal tears. He regarded her with admiration where the mortals from earlier looked at her with indifference. To them, her features were plain and unappealing. Auzlanten saw an image of quintessential beauty wrapped in a fine sculpted shell. It took mental effort to suppress resentment to the others for the apathy they bore towards her.

"What troubles you?" He asked with genuine care while taking her hand. "This should be a time to celebrate. We've crippled the Nephilim with what we've achieved."

"I don't mean to discourage you or belittle your accomplishment..."

"Our accomplishment." He corrected while wiping a tear away.

"I have troubling news to share with you."

"You're referring to your diagnosis?" Auzlanten asked her to analyze the door containing Tumor'at and determine what caused it to open. He had assumed that the demon had been amassing energy over the centuries, portioning off minute fragments to use when an opportunity to escape presented itself. That is undoubtedly how it morphed into the form of the child. Was it powerful enough to open up the door halfway?

"That and more I'm afraid. The results were indeed disturbing, but I think I should tell you the other discovery first. I regret to inform you that Prelate Greyflame and Patriarch Betankur are both dead."

"I feared as much." Arodi sighed pessimistically. "Invictus must have desecrated the bodies. What of your analysis of the vault?"

"I... don't really know how to explain. I can assure you that the anomaly did not originate from inside the cell."

"This is both troubling and assuring." Auzlanten said while stroking his beard in thought. "This means that the energy siphons are still functional without any leaking. Tumor'at continues to shift in an effort to fool us into releasing it, but that is the extent of his control. That insufferable beast will exploit all that is sacred to worm out of that prison."

"I'm thankful that he only has enough power to morph and nothing else. But that raises a more disturbing question, one which I may have an answer for."

"Judging by your mood, I take it your deduction is grim."

She swallowed as her breathing increased, then bade Auzlanten follow her. "I have no doubt that the source was from the outside. I ran four different analyses hoping to find a malfunction in the locking mechanism or a surge of power. There was none."

Arodi let out a deep sigh. "Which means someone opened it. You think it was one of our guests." The woman began leading him down the corridor.

"Perhaps Blye was a wielder of unclean magick." She suggested knowing it was a vain attempt at optimism. "He could have recognized the locking sigils and the wardiron alloy."

"No. I would have seen that. The taint of the Idolacreid was lingering in his mind, but nothing more. Where exactly are you taking me?"

The woman said nothing. She stopped in front of an empty display cube, a crystal structure that was not supposed to be empty. Auzlanten felt his body fill with arctic blood as the shock hit him. This crystal was forged of metamorphic ballistic diamond. It was keyed to the silver leaflet ring on his right hand, otherwise the plates wouldn't move. It could withstand over a dozen direct blasts from a rocket lancer before as much of a chip was made in the surface. This case was supposed to contain the keystone used to enter Tumor'at's prison cell.

"So that's how the door opened." Arodi said with a trembling voice.

"Yes." The woman responded with an equal level of distress. "Someone was able to lift the key to the vault from its casing. I suppose they tried to release Tumor'at after acquiring it, but didn't know how to properly use it. There wasn't any real risk of it getting out of the cell. The key would only open the outermost barricade."

"That's not my concern. Somebody took the keystone without either of us knowing it. Even worse, they knew how to use it." Auzlanten placed one hand on the pommel of his sabre and the other gripping his temples. "How could we let this happen?"

"This doesn't make any sense." Arodi continued musing in disbelief. "Two things must be true. We let something powerful enough into the sanctum undetected and we let it get away with an arcane artifact. It would take a being of immense power to accomplish such a feat."

"As powerful as Mortis at least," The woman continued dabbing tears from her cheeks in quiet panic. "I'm a failure. I couldn't even detect a trespasser in our most sacred haven."

"You stop that. I need you to remain focused. We are in a critical state right now and I can't have you breaking down." He interlocked his hands and nervously began pacing between the various display cases. "Something came into our home uninvited and stole from us. There are only two possible ways it could have infiltrated. It could have jumped into the portal when I opened it in Budapest or..." Auzlanten stopped himself, the horrific words stopped in his throat before they could leave his mouth. The implications were nigh blasphemous.

His companion finished the thought for him. "Or S-6319 has another traitor in its ranks... and this one far more dangerous than the first."

Verrick 25th in Parey was as pleasant as a summer's day could be. Fluffy white clouds decorated the blue canvas of sky over the artesian structures and cloudtouchers of the Frankish capital. Children played in courtyards and neighborhoods, dynamically enjoying their recess from school until classes resumed the coming Evangelon. Workers went to their respective jobs around the city in search of making their crowns for the day to keep food on the table for their families. The citizens of Templym were blissfully unaware of what the day's events would yield.

Task force S-6319 sat around a wooden table in their hotel dining room. The smell of fresh coffee and sizzling breakfast graced the air as they began fueling their bodies for their upcoming mission. Such a display of well prepared food in a peaceful environment would spark exchanges of light hearted conversation, but their moods were solemn. Even the particularly jovial Volk and Vandross were uncharacteristically quiet. This was no ordinary quarry hunt or cult dissolution. This was a kill strike, an assassination. There was no other way to put it. Their target was the Regent of the Scourge, Invictus Illuromos. Not all of them had made peace with the fact that Yen Blye was a traitor. Now, they were assisting in the death of the head of the organization.

Four safe houses were currently being scouted out by independent Scourge militias. Speculation was that Invictus was holed up in one of these places. At Bethel's discretion, the militants were kept unaware of their true quarry being told only of suspected heretic cells, classified with Bride Wainwright's Beta seal. Their part was merely to identify the Regent's location. One by one, the squadrons would raid their target safe houses at Warden Downey's order, and then withdraw upon discovery of the target. Arodi would get to the appointed location and kill the Regent. Most of them wondered what part they played outside of orchestrating the spotting.

The breakfast table was barely alive with dreary activity. The soldiers slowly consumed their first meal of the day or performed routine checks on their equipment. Effectively, they were killing time before the Master of Templym arrived. Auzlanten would be arriving any moment now and his arrival would signify the start of the strike mission. In reality, and it was one that wasn't lost to them, it was a sleep job more than anything else. The Scourge was always a brutal force unafraid to do that which was grimly necessary, but killing its leader was something else entirely. No mutiny of such a scale had ever occurred since the Strife.

One member of the squadron was absent from the table. Herald Du'Plasse was apparently spending a longer period of time in his private quarters than usual. It wasn't unusual that he was the last to arrive. Of them all, nobody spent more time privately arranging their hair into finely groomed patterns than Oslin. However if there was a time to disregard cosmetics, it would be before such a critical mission.

Bethel was laying out the plan for the task force after deciding he had waited long enough. His scarred blue battle plate had a fresh mark from where the marauder chieftain stomped on his back. Auzlanten had fused the rend so the armor was fully functional, but left a sizeable imprint on the plates, putting the several other scratches to shame.

"Auzlanten assured me that he will be handling Invictus." He said seriously over a hot ebon cup of coffee. "His detachment of Centurions will likely be corrupt as well, so we're going to have to handle them. We need to give him as much space as possible to handle the Regent."

"What kind of resistance are we looking at?" Adastra asked bluntly.

"The usual Centurion guard consists of a dozen men at least. All are chosen by the Regent personally and their names are Alpha classified. I never thought much of their identities personally before this all broke out. I doubt the current intel I have is reliable."

Oslin Du'Plasse lulled his way into the dining room. He looked just as he always did, his platinum colored hair mirroring Auzlanten's and his family ascot hugging his neck. He was carrying something in his hand that looked like a small package.

"Nice of you to join us Herald, I was just going over the details of the strike." There was a bitter undertone to Bethel's words. He despised tardiness and expected better of a third tier warrior like Du'Plasse.

"Apologies, I was just prepping something for the mission," he replied, sounding his usual posh self. He lifted the contents of his hand to show it to the other six. It was a bomb made of the clapshock Bethel had kept in his armor but since removed. Exposed metal wiring and circuits were jutting out of the plastic explosive. "Our bullets or weapons won't do a thing against the Regent. His battle plate is the best in all of Templym. Five pounds of explosives might not be enough to kill him, but it'll certainly hurt."

"Our focus will be the Centurions, Auzlanten will handle our primary quarry."

"Well then, I guess we won't need this." Oslin tossed the bomb in the middle of the dining room table, knocking over a few drinks with the thud and shaking some of the weapons strewn atop it. The flippancy with which the bomb was handled made all the others flinch.

"God Oslin, handle that thing with a bit more care!" Vandross snapped. "And maybe don't throw it right where we're eating."

"You're right, I'm sorry." Du'Plasse said as he revealed the trigger gripped in his other hand. "We wouldn't want this going off now would we?" He said with a wry grin as his thumb pressed down on the activator.

CHAPTER 41

Clapshock detonates with a namesake crackle of air before a sharp sonic boom. The resulting explosion creates a rippling shockwave with enough force to easily buckle steel into a crumpled mess. A single ounce of the ordinance could capsize a chariot or kill anyone within a small radius. This material was often used by the Scourge for high profile cases when large quantities of force were necessary. Each one of them was amply familiar with the killing potential of the bomb staring them in the eye. It did not detonate.

Oslin's thumb was pressed down on the trigger, a defiant look in his eye. All eyes were locked onto him as he began striding around the table. All faint traces of humor were snuffed out in that moment. Everyone was familiar with the mechanism in his hand, a cadaver's trigger. This switch would trigger the bomb should he remove his thumb.

"Oslin," Bethel said with forced calm and suppressed rage. "What is the meaning of this?"

"One wrong move and I'll send us all to Judgment." Du'Plasse said seemingly ignoring Jude's question. "I figured that you wouldn't quite mind the bulk of us dying, but I don't suppose you'd like to miss the abolition would you?"

It was unclear who Oslin was speaking to. He was stepping around each chair carefully, his battle plate humming as its mechanisms turned. His gaze never fully focused onto one person, nor was his speech direct. His words implied a single subject however.
"Os," Volk said between heavy breaths. "Blye's gone. He was the traitor, nobody else."

"And how certain are you of that?" The Hrimatan snapped. "Would you wager your life on that bet?"

"It seems you've placed yours on the table," Adastra grunted coldly. "Yours alongside all of ours, how charitable of you."

"You've got our attention." Vandross said with a bit more sympathy. "That's what this stunt was for right? Scare us, put on a show so we can talk about there being another turncoat in our task force? Mission accomplished, you've brought the matter to light, there's no need for the bomb."

"I'm afraid there is a need." Oslin continued strolling around his allies. "The only thing keeping the Nephilim's spy from killing us all is that bomb. I'd prefer it off as well, but it's an unfortunate necessity."

"We're listening," Daphne said cautiously. "Make your case."

"Thank you Miss Wainwright." Du'Plasse said with a humorless smile. "I can't help but bring myself back to what we witnessed in Lord Auzlanten's sanctum. I haven't a doubt in my mind that the child we saw was a powerful Imago trying to weasel its way out of a sacred prison. A question concerning the matter keeps prodding at my mind. How did that door open?"

"Perhaps Blye opened it." Bethel suggested, coming to terms with the madness at hand. "He saw a potential ally of great repute and aimed to stage a rescue."

"A rather dismal attempt, don't you think? Inquisitors, what did you make of that door?"

"It was made of wardiron, or some variant of it." Adastra bellowed. "I estimate a foot and a half thick, enough to keep a Class A+ at bay."

"The runes looked Coptic," Vandross added. "I'd seen similar etchings on 2nd century temples in Judah during an excavation. Well, I saw them in pictures during my studies. The early church believed that they would summon the Holy Spirit and keep demons away."

Oslin began to speculate aloud. "Assuming the door was made of pure wardiron, approximately twenty feet high, ten feet wide, a foot and a half thick, that door must have weighed twenty-one tons. Without heavy duty machinery, opening that door would require supernatural power of a vast scale."

"And why doesn't Yen qualify?" Daphne asked, biting back her bitterness. "We worked together for two years and I never suspected a thing. I'll never know if his devotion was genuine in the first place or if he was corrupt from the beginning. It's hardly a leap of faith to say that he could call upon black magick."

"And that very thought crossed my mind many a time. Perhaps he could call upon enough dark power to account for the door's weight, but not the inscribings. If he wasn't strong enough to conceal his loyalty from Auzlanten, I doubt he could crack that kind of seal."

"So you conclude one of us?" Downey scoffed, offended at such an accusation.

"Correct." Oslin said, shifting the trigger in his grip. It was a slight motion meant only to adjust his hold, but enough to cause his task force to hold their breath for a moment. "One of you is not who they claim to be."

"I assume you have a suspect." Bethel said, his eyes darting between the Herald and the bomb. "You wouldn't be making such a lavish display if you didn't have a place to stick your accusatory finger."

"In fact I do. It wasn't easy narrowing it down. I'll admit, there isn't much information I'm basing this on. I'd be humiliated to present any of my findings to a court based on their slimness. However, I found evidence to base an accusation against you all."

"This is absurd." Vandross laughed with his gallant charm, seemingly ignoring the obvious threat. "If you wanted to bring this to light you could just ask. There's no need to arm a couple of pounds of clapshock to force the information out. What could you possibly be basing these accusations on?"

"For instance, Mr. Blackwell, less than two years ago your wife was executed for demonic fraternization and attempted child sacrifice. How do I know the same taint that reached Annabelle did not also infect you?"

In less than a wink, the wardiron bastard sword that was lying across the tale was in Vandross' hand and the tip inches away from Oslin's neck. The previous display of lightheartedness was instantly swept away at the mention of his dead wife, replaced with the wild gaze of rabid anger. His dark eyes were bright with the fire of rage as he pointed his sword within killing distance of the Herald.

"Hold your tongue or I will cut it out." He growled. "If you so much as say Annabelle's name I will end you!"

Du'Plasse did not flinch. His grip on the cadaver's trigger didn't falter. "This pain you feel is genuine." He observed. "You won't kill me if for no other reason that your friends will die alongside you. I don't think you're the traitor. So sit down and put that thing away before you get everyone here killed."

Vandross grunted before retaking his seat, keeping his sword in hand. Oslin continued his speech, taking care to stop behind each member when he spoke of them. "Daphne Wainwright, Yen Blye was under your tutelage. How an acclaimed Expurgator became enticed by the Nephilim is beyond me. Perhaps he was simply mimicking his mentor." The Bride bit her tongue in order to resist a venomous response, trying to keep the situation calm.

"Adastra Covalos, you were raised by a coven of witches until you were seven years old. I pray you don't remember what you were exposed to. What if you relish in those experiences though? What if you follow in your witch mother's footsteps?"

"You'd better pray that bombs kills us all, Oslin." The Inquisitor growled, not tolerating his assault on him and his friends. "If it doesn't I might strangle you."

"Charming," Oslin smiled ignoring the remark, confident that it was a bluff. "Jude Bethel, you were in the company of seventeen different marauder tribes, many of which were practitioners of pagan worship. Perhaps one of their faiths stuck with you."

"You think I practice marauder Imago worship?" Bethel's scarred face was scrunched into a scowl. "You think I took after my slave holders?"

Herald Du'Plasse ignored the slight, continuing with his

presentation. "Volk Downey, you were governor of Glaswey for twelve years before its annexation into Templym. Then you were out of service for a full year after your injury during the Civil Strife. That's a lot of time and a lot of exposure to demonic forces."

"That's a stretch if I've ever heard one." The Warden responded.

"I'll admit you're right in that respect." Du'Plasse continued, surprisingly giving credence to the slight. "Of course, I'm not accusing most of you. I'm simply laying out the facts that were troubling me last night. I spent hours combing over all of your backgrounds looking for some schism to break through, some detail you forgot to omit that would expose you for the traitor you are. I sifted as far as my clearance would take me and became experts on the lot of you before I realized the most glaring error in my judgment." Oslin paused and turned his head towards the table, his eyes meeting that of his suspect. "I spent hours researching every member of this team, utterly overlooking you."

With his empty hand, Du'Plasse pointed a golden immotrum coated finger across the table. Each head swiveled around away from the Herald to stare at the accused with quizzical glares. A scattering of breaths ranging from utter disbelief to humorless offense was the only noise that appeared as all eyes in the room fell to Retriever Ram's Horn.

"Me?" Ram scoffed from inside his flaksteel carapace.

"Yes." Oslin spoke grimly. "You're a turncoat to the Scourge, a spy for the enemies of Auzlanten, and a wielder of unclean magick. How do you plea?"

"This is ridiculous." Vandross said half laughing. "There's no way he's betrayed us."

"Interesting that you think that, now ask yourself why. Is it because Ram's Horn has followed every order without question? Is it because of his straight forward attitude and simple approach? Perhaps you think he's too dull to concoct such a genius plan. In all of your theories there is one commonality. Surely, Ram can't be a traitor."

He was met with silence aside from a quiet growl coming from the horned helm Ram's Horn was donning. There was truth to what the Herald was saying. Every one of them internally scoffed at the idea of him being a betrayer and as they realized the consensus among them they were disturbed. Oslin proceeded with his case. "What better guise than that of a silent oaf? Ram's Horn came from the uncivilized jungles of Uzbek, the last of the Steel Skin tribe, a group of marauders that's conveniently undocumented. Yet, nobody was bothered by this. Nobody had ever cared about his questionable past or inquired about his time outside of Templym."

"This is outrageous!" Warden Downey retorted angrily. "I've worked with Ram for years now. There's nobody else in the Scourge I trust more than him. I'd lay my life down for him in a heartbeat and I know he'd do the same for me!" Next to him, Ram's Horn was gripping onto the arms of his chair, audibly straining the wood between his fingers.

"Yes, and his past is no more damning than half those in this room. However, I do bring one additional piece of evidence that supports this point."

"What could you have?" Volk snapped. He was the only one speaking to the plaintiff, everyone else acting as jury and contemplating the presentation. "Ram's the most loyal Retriever I've ever worked with. He never so much as back talked an order. He never did anything outside of a direct order."

"Really? I don't recall anyone ordering him to kill Palladium."

Du'Plasse left the final thought hang. From the horrified looks coming from the others, he knew that his case was made. The realization that Oslin might very well be correct was beginning to sink into their minds. Daphne and Vandross appeared to be at the point of nausea, the same revulsion painting their faces that they wore when Blye's betrayal was exposed. Adastra and Jude were dourly brooding as they calculated conclusions based on the evidence, conflict raging behind their tortured eyes. Only Volk remained in contest to Oslin's accusation, but he was taken aback by the evidence recently presented to him. Presumably, Ram's Horn was glaring at the Herald behind those eye slits.

"Our investigation in Jaspin ended with the death of the Apotheosis cell and their cult leader, Regulom Palladium." Oslin announced to a silent audience. "As some of you may be aware, the Arch Formulator had a cerebral data well that digitally stored his memories. Memories, like when Thomas Monk informed him about the Venetian medical equipment. That data well was destroyed by a single bullet expelled from Ram's tangle barrel. Imagine how brief our time in Hrimata would have been if we knew beforehand that Monk was the man we were looking for. We would have found Mortis sooner, perhaps as much as six weeks."

"That..." Downey stuttered, doubt flushing over his face. "That doesn't prove anything. Palladium was an obvious threat. If I had a round left I would have shot him myself."

"No you wouldn't have. The machine, while a heretical abomination, was just a massive tide processing unit. He presented no immediate threat. You and I both knew that. Yet everyone in Jaspin brushed off the kill so nonchalantly, hell even I did despite it obviously torpedoing our investigation. Don't you find it odd that not one of us questioned the decision? It was an obvious destruction of vital evidence and none of us so much as mentioned the recklessness of it."

"Dear God," Vandross gasped. "He's right. I never even thought about that." He turned his sickly gaze at the accused Retriever. "Did you... have you?"

"He's been playing with our minds." Oslin said defiantly. "Ever since the beginning he's been manipulating our perceptions. We've never once questioned him, to the point that we've ignored an overt slight against Scourge protocol. Imagine how many more he's done without our knowledge."

"Oslin has a point." Daphne said, doing nothing to conceal her shock. "I remember reading the Jaspin report. Any normal 5th tier would have been reprimanded for killing a prime suspect in an investigation like that. It never even occurred to me how wrong that was."

"Black magick explains everything." Adastra said coldly. "A few simple spells could dissuade us from paying attention to the finer details of his actions and mask his "taint", whatever that means. But he'd have to have witchcraft comparable to the sorcerer lords of the Haigon Empire to have bested the vault's inscriptions."

"And if that were the case, why is this bomb even a threat to him?" Volk said desperately trying to convince the others of the Retriever's innocence. "If he's this great and powerful wizard then why hasn't he knocked that cadaver's switch out of your hand and killed us all? Wouldn't it be more practical to just waste us all?"

"That's a fair point Warden." Oslin stated. "But let me retort with an old adage from my forefather Grigor Du'Plasse. You all know it, don't you? It's his most famous saying."

Bethel broke a strenuous moment of silence. "Never trust a man that won't show his face." It was a common saying throughout Templym, even more common in the ranks of the Scourge. While nearly every suit of battle plate contained a helmet to cover one's head, they were never donned during peace times.

"What kind of a man won't show his face to his own team?" Oslin inquired, confident that he had won. "In the past four months, have any us seen Ram's Horn's face? The wisdom of Grigor is ingrained in all our minds and yet we've excused this man for violating his simplest command."

Volk's face sank. His weathered features seemed to collapse as he became overwhelmed with grief. His eyes, both the clear and clouded one, were filled with a fiery hatred at the accusations flying at Ram's Horn. Now they were flushed with overbearing grief at a horrific realization. He couldn't even stand to look at him and he was sitting right next to him. He muttered something inaudibly.

"What was that Volk?" Oslin asked.

He let out a deep sigh of defeat. "I've never seen his face. Three years and I've never so much as seen your face." He drew a Reisinger which he stuck in the Retriever's direction. Tears began pooling in the corners of his eyes. "I never once thought that strange. Barely talking, never showing your face, building up a disguise so you can spy on us for the Nephilim. How long have you been playing me Ram?"

"Liar!" Ram's Horn grunted as the arms to his chair splintered and cracked apart.

"You've lost, traitor." Oslin said confidently. "You are exposed. When Auzlanten gets here, we're going to turn you over to him." He could tell that the others were agreeing with him now. The brashness of his approach had worked just as he anticipated. "I'm sure he'll be eager to find yet another of the Nephilim's pawns. How do you think he's going to pry every drop of information out of you?"

"Alright, we're in agreement." Vandross said pointing his pistol at the brooding Retriever. "Now for the love of God Os, can we get rid of the bomb now?"

A general air of relief was beginning to drape over S-6319. It was a shaky feeling of peace. The realization that an immediate threat was over, but replaced by the exposure of one that had been among them for so long. It was not a hopeless feeling. Auzlanten would fix this. He could glean every secret from the spy's memories and cut deeper into their enemy's plans. What faint glimmer of hope they felt was snuffed out as quickly as it began.

The sound of metal hands clapping together filled the room. It was backed by metallic sounding laughter, a dry humorless chuckle coming from behind a cobalt mouth grille. Ram's Horn was laughing at them.

"I would be more amused if you weren't such a hindrance, Oslin." Ram's Horn growled. It was the first time any of them had heard him speak a line of dialogue greater than two words. "I was minutes away from luring Auzlanten into his grave. Then there would be nothing to stop the abolition from reaching its kill quota. But because of meddling from the stuffed shirt, loud mouthed, arrogant, inbred, fop of the party, my plan was foiled. Oh it was perfect, too. I would have dug into his chest from behind with these hands, wrenching whatever mechanism that functions as a heart from his putrid body. That was going to be the last thing you lot ever saw before Templym crumbled to ash beneath my rule."

Weapons were slowly gathered up as Ram's Horn made his petty speech, uncaring of the guns and blades being pointed in his direction. The Retriever just sighed and continued. "Here I was thinking I calculated for every possibility. I placed Blye there as a distraction while I made my real move. His entire purpose was merely to die as a distraction so I could steal that bauble unnoticed. Imagine my glee when I found Tumor'at's cell. With further commotion, I thought I might be able to worm my way out with Yen's head still on his shoulders. Pity, but his was an acceptable loss, one I had planned for. All that remained was to kill Auzlanten. Then the abolition would fuel my throne and none could oppose me. I regret underestimating your tenacity Oslin."

"It's over," The Herald said defiantly. "You've lost."

Another metallic chuckle gurgled from beneath his helmet. "Oh surely not, I suppose I can salvage this yet. Instead of Arodi coming here to lay out his genius plan to kill his baby boy, he'll just be coming to investigate your deaths."

Ram's Horn flicked a single finger upwards. There was no spectacular explosion or rush of supernatural energies. Instead, Oslin's thumb was suddenly pushed off of the cadaver's trigger. The removal of the pressure activated the trigger mechanism to detonate the bomb.

The task force swiftly ducked beneath the table at the sound of the bomb's single alarm, a single high pitched screech indicating the activation of the trigger mechanism. At this close of range, cover beneath the table would matter little as it would be reduced to burning shrapnel once the clapshock detonated. However, there was no pop or clap of air as they had anticipated. Instead, there was a brief flush of sparks that spurted out of the bomb's circuits, harmlessly sputtering in a small deluge of electricity. Herald Du'Plasse dropped the trigger and had drawn his battle banner from its back holster, a cocky grin painted across his face.

"Seems you've underestimated me once again." Oslin said pridefully.

Du'Plasse had planned to ready his banner to be in a defensive position, but Ram's Horn was on him too quickly. The armored Retriever had leapt out of his seat and across the table. Using a swift *nightmare strike* across his jaw, Oslin was knocked down to the ground unconscious. A curb stomp to the head would have killed the Herald instantly. Warden Downey intervened with a bevy of shots with his pistol discharged into his former friend's back. The force of the bullets at such a close range punched through his battle plate, shredding flaksteel and causing streams of blood and ballistic fluid to leak from the resulting hole. It should have killed him. All it managed to do was throw him off balance to a degree where his raised foot would only grind the floor beneath it.

Turning with his tangle barrel revolver in hand, Ram's Horn had his sight set on Volk's head. A single slug buried into his breastplate before Adastra slammed into him with his shoulder, knocking the hand cannon away. He swung his guillotine axe in a heavy downward slice with the hope of slicing him open. Ram's Horn caught the blade with his gauntlets and brought a knee up to his chest. The force of impact produced a sickening crack in his torso indicating his ribcage fracturing. No human should have been able to produce such a level of force. Adastra considered the pain a worthy sacrifice as he was giving his partner an opening.

Vandross Blackwell connected his sword to a hip joint in his battle plate. The softer material was easily separated by the honed wardiron blade. The affected flesh sizzled as if the sword was molten and Ram's Horn grunted in pain, a clear indication of Imago presence. Vandross had hoped to plant the barrel of his pistol in the parallel joint, but Adastra's greataxe was flung in his path. The Inquisitors collapsed on top of one another and it was unclear whose blood splashed up on the marauder's armor.

Ram turned to face his newest threat, Bride Wainwright, who thrust forward with her rapier. He angled himself in such a way that the blade chinked off his torso plating, allowing him to close the gap that she was trying to maintain. He grappled her by locking his hands around her wrists. She jumped, planting her boots against his massive chest, an escape maneuver that would no doubt work against a normal opponent. He was not a normal opponent. Ram took all her momentum and used it to pivot the grapple. Warden Downey was charging with his mace, inches away from delivering a lethal blow to the back of his head. Instead the impact struck Daphne in the stomach as Ram's Horn twisted her into an exposed position with abnormal dexterity. A rush of blue lightning sparked off her pearlescent chest piece as it was scorched to match the black flaksteel plating of her armor. The combined force of Downey's mace with Ram's pile drive successfully dislocated both of her arms.

Ram's Horn left his defenses open slightly as he let the disabled Bride fall to the ground, enough for Volk to plant his mace into his chest. The impact buckled his armor, desecrating the nailed shield symbol of his marauder tribe. Volk fought with ferocity like none of them had ever seen, swinging his weapon in rapidly lethal arcs. His tortured gaze was rage incarnate, the offense that could only come from a former loved one.

Ram clearly became frustrated at being unable to land effective strikes. The two exchanged blows and he was gaining no headway against his mentor. The head of the tech enhanced mace glanced off his flaksteel carapace with bursts of electricity, ruining the communications gear in his armor. Ram's Horn had enough of letting Volk batter him around.

Wisps of pulsing green energy shrouded his wrists and his agility picked up. Ram's Horn head connected with Downey's in a *bull crush*. As he lurched back with blood streaming down his face, Ram snapped his arm with a swift crack. The armor broke into bits of metal as the bone beneath splintered and Volk lost his grip on the mace. Before Vandross could rejoin the melee, Ram's Horn punched a cavern into the Warden's breastplate.

Vandross engaged his Natandro style sword and pistol style to maintain a safe distance, recognizing the use of magick. A stream of crimson fluid dripped down his face as he parried and shot, exchanging a furious level of lethality with Ram's metal fists. The exchange ended as Adastra brought the blade of his axe into his pauldron. His body should have been thoroughly minced and beyond use, yet he was still fighting.

With a swift backhand to the face, Adastra was knocked back

and his axe flung from his grip. In a second strike he sent a jab in Vandross' direction. The fist did not make any contact, yet the Inquisitor was thrown back as a current of roiling energy slammed into him like a train. The full impact of force flung him back several meters, planting him into the plaster wall behind him. With no immediate threats to his person, Ram's Horn turned his attention to the closest, most vulnerable target.

Daphne Wainwright was left prostrate on the ground. Her useless arms disallowed her to crawl out of harm's way, though that didn't stop her from trying to worm out of harm's way. She had made it a couple feet away before Ram's Horn came trundling her way. The turncoat interlocked his glowing fingers, poising himself for a *hammer blow* unlike anything they'd ever seen. It was obvious that the force could easily collapse her chest in. Adastra Covalos would not let that happen.

As Ram's Horn brought his interlocked, magickally charge strike downwards, the Inquisitor intercepted. Deflecting the strike with his axe would allow him to absorb the blow and continue largely unscathed. His weapon had been tossed several feet away and he did not have the time to retrieve it and intercept, so he used his hands. The paint of his flaksteel gauntlets seared off under the assault of boiling energies and the muscles of his arms began to strain, even beneath the protection of his battle plate. He could feel the heat burning through to his hands and blister his palms. Ram's Horn swept Adastra's legs out from beneath him with a kick to the shin. He recapitulated and angled another jab towards Daphne who was hopelessly prone. The already bright fiery energy sheathing his arm glowed even brighter as he wound up for a more devastating strike.

As stubborn as always, Adastra refused to let him kill her. He threw up his left arm to absorb the strike in her stead. Ram's Horn's supernaturally charged fist tore through the flaksteel of his armor and clean through his forearm, amputating his hand. Adastra screamed and fell to the ground writhing in pain, a singed stump replacing his hand, adjacent to the similarly exposed Bride Wainwright. Ram's Horn now had two equally exposed targets at

The spy was inexplicably talking through perforated lungs and a pinched trachea. "Your threats do not shake me. Destroy this body and I'll resurrect even faster than your Messiah, stronger than ever before."

"Why can't I read you?" Auzlanten spat through clenched teeth. "I have the Idolacreid, I've seen the taint on Mortis' aura, I should be able to identify one of your lord's fanatics with ease. Yet, I see nothing like that from you, just a blank slate, nothing special at all. Now you claim to be able to rise from the dead. What are you?"

He spat a mouthful of blood before giving a wet chuckle. "You still haven't figured it out? It seems I over anticipated your intelligence." His guttural laughter was stifled by increased pressure from Auzlanten's hand, now flickering with fire. Ram would have pulled at his grip if his arms were functional. It didn't stop his bragging. "Come on Arodi, you know what I am. Think about it. What being is wise enough to wield arcane artifacts, yet subtle enough to infiltrate your secret lair without your realization, and still possess the strength to stand against you?"

The fire decorating Arodi's robes died down. The wild glare of anger was replaced with something more distressing, even more anathema to his character than rage. Fear.

"The Nephilim...you're the Nephilim."

Ram's Horn twisted his mouth into a bloody, toothy smirk. The Nephilim, the author of the Idolacreid and mastermind of the most imminent threat to Templym, was here. The spirit who had corrupted Invictus Illuromos was literally in Auzlanten's palm. He did not think. He did not calculate the optimum course of action or take time to process the weight of the situation. He killed. With a snap of his wrist, Arodi wrenched the Nephilim's neck to the side, snapping the spinal cord. He proceeded to incinerate what was left with holy fire, enough to scorch his very soul if it still remained. Once he was naught but a smear of ash on the wooden panel, Arodi fell to his knees.

He knew that the Nephilim was not dead. He could feel its spirit leave the body of Ram's Horn, who he deduced was long since dead when it took occupancy of his body, yet he did not leave this world. The Nephilim fled his broken vessel in favor of another one. Where would it go? What was it going to do with the keystone? When was the abolition? All of these questions assailed Arodi Auzlanten's mind, yet one projected louder than them all. "How could I have been so blind?"

He didn't pay attention to how long he sat there in shock. With respect to ancient Hebrew tradition, he had been smearing the ashes of Ram's Horn into his face in mourning. He had an opportunity to end the abolition before it began and he failed because he lusted for revenge. He pried his hand from his face to see the nervous gazes of S-6319, their fear and grief even more obvious than his own.

They all stood now, healed of the wounds given to them by the Nephilim. Cuts had been healed over, bone fractures sealed, even Adastra's stump at the end of his arm had been sutured. One of them wasn't standing. Jude Bethel stood with a tortured gaze, shifting panicked looks between Auzlanten and the prostrate Volk Downey. He whimpered. "He's not breathing."

CHAPTER 42

Spaiden Vorg was the shaman of the Grave Gluttons. He was the prophet of the Nephilim and acted as the intermediary between their lord and their chief. During his communion sessions, the Nephilim sowed seeds of inexplicable wisdom into his mind. He gleaned so much from being in the presence of such an intellect. The specifications of the abolition were revealed to him, the birth of the meld of spirit and flesh, and a glimpse at his mighty throne were but a few of the secrets Vorg now carried like a priceless trove.

The most miraculous and impactful revelation the shaman was gifted was the Nephilim's dual prophecy. One was true and one was a lie, the burden of discerning which was on Vorg. Both prophecies thrilled Knox Mortis. First, he was told that he would be the slayer of the great warlock. Arodi Auzlanten would die to the chief of the Grave Gluttons. The second was that at the time of the abolition, Knox Mortis would become one with his newest patron. This was cryptic, but the thought of fusing with an unholy being of such magnitude titillated Mortis to his core. Vorg did not tell Mortis one of those was a lie.

When Auzlanten came to Budapest, desolating half of the Grave Gluttons' numbers and their chief, Vorg knew which prophecy would be true. He had been speculating for months, but now had all the evidence he needed to know that the second prophecy was the truth. The dead legion could not be swayed from their path so easily. He let his wicked faith guide his mind.

Vorg gathered the remains of Knox Mortis from where he was slain. The giant's head and hands were severed from his dilapidated corpse and a massive hole penetrated entirely through his shredded breastplate. The remains were sprawled out on a slab of broken building decorated with withered marsh lilies, sacred inscriptions, and his own blood. He had been crouching in the ash for thirty-two hours with his lanky palms lifted towards the heavens, supplicating the Nephilim with incantations in a pitiable display of desperation. His heretical prayers were not in vain.

Miles away, Auzlanten destroyed the Nephilim's vessel. Instantly, the corpse of Knox Mortis began to twitch. The torso began to spasm as it was wracked with unnatural force. Sinewy tangles of veins shot out of the orifices carved into Mortis' flesh. The tendrils hooked onto the detached hands and neck, pulling them back into their proper place with a wet smack, vanishing as suddenly as they spawned. Vorg began laughing as he saw wounds sealing over with new skin. Fresh nerves in his chief sparked to life as he revivified, creating further twists in the body. Mortis sat upright as his empty eye sockets filled with two balls of green fire which formed searing eyeballs. He began screaming as his destroyed lungs became alive and functional. His makeshift teeth of glass and nails popped out of his rotten gums as lines of dagger sharp tusks took their place. The transformation was completed as thorny spines of boney carapace shot out of his body, punching through the armor Mortis still donned in death. His arms became lined with ivory spear heads, his head sprouted two twisting horns, and a pair of spindly draconic wings emerged with a sickening crack.

Spaiden Vorg stood aghast, in awe of the glorious transformation he had just witnessed. He had never seen anything more than a projection of the Nephilim, and he had just witnessed the reincarnation of his latest vessel. He fell prostrate in the ash as his patron lifted himself from the slab of ruin he had been displayed on, worshipping with insipid shrieks of ungodly joy.

The Nephilim, having transformed the once dead body of Knox Mortis into an even more deadly being, towered over the shaman. His dozens of crooked teeth curled up into a devious grin as he relished in his loyalist's veneration. "Knox Mortis is dead." The

Nephilim spoke in a smooth boastful voice free of the raspy sickliness the vessel once possessed.

"All hail the Nephilim!" Vorg replied, facing the giant with tears of joy streaming down his gaunt face.

"Rise, my prophet." The Nephilim motioned after basking in the fanatic's groveling for a short time. "The time has come. You still have the power source?"

"Of course, my liege," The shaman reached into his tattered cloak and revealed a smooth figure made of slate tiles, the keystone the Nephilim stole from Auzlanten. "The Grave Gluttons are scattered, but the teams stand ready to lay waste to their allotted targets."

"We begin forthwith." With one hand the Nephilim took the keystone and with the other gripped onto the hem of Vorg's robe. "Come." A swirling ball of green and purple flame swallowed the two, disintegrating their bodies. A similar flame appeared hundreds of miles away which reconstructed their bodies. They had traveled from the Carthonian wastes of Budapest to the caves buried beneath the Uzbek forest.

Vorg fell to his hands and knees, desperate to regain his bearings. He had never experienced teleportation before and he did not find it pleasant in the slightest. He was blind and his skin bore faint patches of burns. He dry heaved as he gripped onto a nearby stone to hoist himself to his feet. He blinked rapidly, clearing tears from his eyes before he could see where they had gone.

The Nephilim was on his throne, clearly unabated by the translation of reality. The throne was not a traditional seat of precious metals set with gemstones. It was an engine of legend. The structure was made of material similar to blackened gunmetal. Its sharpened prow was like a spearhead and its flanks were spiny plates like segments of an exoskeleton. The Nephilim, who was a giant of a man, appeared miniscule perched behind the massive helm. The chariot-like structure was a quarter mile long. Its bony wings seemed to compliment the arrangement of unholy etchings on the savage metal siding. Seventeen pikes were displayed on the deck, each impaled with the hundreds skulls of those that attempted to betray the new king of the Earth. The demonic looking vessel, covered in thorns multiple meters in length, gave the impression of a snarling starving beast. It caressed the vehicle like it was a beloved steed while wearing a twisted grin. Spaiden Vorg was struck breathless at the sight of the Nephilim's throne.

"The blood is the key," The Nephilim purred while walking across the deck of his throne. "Two hundred years of careful construction, the most specific arcane components, and an endless army of Auzlanten's wretched faithful cut down. Everything culminates here. It's all led up to this moment, to this infallible creation. All that is required now is the blood of a million innocents. Once we have that, I will grind all of Templym beneath the treads of my throne."

The Nephilim's massive fingers twisted the keystone's tiles with impossible deftness. The geometric figure arranged into a bowl shape upon which he placed some kind of control panel, substituting bone chips for buttons and ivory horns for levers. It continued to muse. "I should have had more time. If I had just another few months to establish my following, my army would have been double its current size. Sufficient blood would be harvested with great ease that way. But the damned cur, the great warlock, has meddled in my affairs. I wanted more time, but Arodi Auzlanten forced me to accelerate. This should have been a moment of lavish ceremony, the moment my reign on this Earth begins. Instead, he milled it down to a hasty execution. For that he will suffer."

"He will?" Vorg dared to voice with concern. "Lord...we gave him the Idolacreid. We gave him the chieftain's life, all so you could kill the warlock before the abolition. Were you...unsuccessful?"

Vorg did not live long enough to regret the question. Instantly, his skull was pulverized by an unseen force. His brain was vaporized into superheated gas which detonated his skull from the inside. The Nephilim did not tolerate doubt among his faithful.

The Nephilim ran his, or rather Mortis', finger across the rim of the bowl. One million innocents was a sizeable quota to fill. The power source would fade in twenty-four hours if improperly fueled. One day, one million souls to reap, one cult to do it. The Nephilim had confidence in his following. The more time wasted between the inception of the abolition was more time Auzlanten had to do more damage to the cult. No more waiting. With a single drop of its own blood drawn into the power source, the abolition began.

Volk Downey was dead. His heart wasn't beating, not a single neuron in his brain was firing, and his soul was torn from his body. This did not stop Arodi Auzlanten from trying to revive him. He stood over the bloodied corpse, pumping cascades of golden light into it. He tapped into his nerves and desperately attempted to get them firing again. It was futile.

Vandross sat on the broken remnants of the couch, hat removed, and a horrified stare frozen in his eyes. Uncharacteristically, his granite pipe was still stowed in his satchel. Jude Bethel spoke with Oslin Du'Plasse, calculating a course of action and mulling over the situation at hand. The Herald of course apologized for the scare with the false bomb, but nobody seemed bothered by that anymore. Adastra Covalos was seated in one of the few chairs that weren't shattered in the conflict with Ram's Horn. Daphne Wainwright was crouched next to him, wrapping the stump at the end of his left arm in gauze. She held back tears, acknowledging that the time for mourning had to be postponed. Now was the time for focus.

"That's twice now," Daphne said to Adastra bitterly as she continued wrapping his wound to prevent infection, even though it appeared sufficiently patched.

Adastra turned his gaze toward the Bride away from Auzlanten. "What do you mean?"

"You've saved my life twice in just as many months." She was referencing how he orchestrated her rescue from Thomas Monk in Hrimata last month. "Now, you've lost a hand. It's not fair that you should suffer for acting such kindness."

"I'm right handed." He said, seemingly neutral about his

crippled limb. He looked over to the still form of Warden Downey. His eyes, even the clouded one above the bullet embedded in his skull, had always been so full of vigor. Now they were frozen in an empty stare, regardless of the life giving energy Arodi was pumping into him. "It could have been much worse."

"Volk was a good man." She sighed.

"He is a good man." He replied, bitterly emphasizing the word 'is'."The Lord has called him home. He simply isn't here anymore."

"And that would have been me." Daphne said as she severed the final band of gauze. "If you hadn't thrown your arm in front of Ram's Horn, he would have killed me."

"We can't have that. We still need you." She blushed slightly as the Serbian smiled ever so slightly. It was refreshing to see some glimmer of joy amidst the darkness enveloping the task force. Daphne needed this reassuring, for she knew that they weren't out of this storm yet.

Auzlanten lowered his arms to his side. In all of history, no apostle had been able to perform the feats that he had in the past centuries. Yet, he could not perform the miracle which they were most famous for. He could not revive the dead. The wound perforating his chest had been sealed, but it didn't make a difference. He had only repaired a corpse. This feeling of helplessness, of uselessness, was alien to him. It was an oppressive dread similar to the pitfall sensation of losing a loved one. It was something he had not felt in a long time.

Considering the death of Warden Downey was not the fiercest assault on his mind. He had lost Scourge officers in the line of duty before. What perturbed him more than anything was the Nephilim. What kind of beast was so adept at subterfuge that he would be sophomoric enough to welcome it into his sanctum? It made a fool of Auzlanten and he was going to suffer for it. What purpose did it have for the keystone? What foul machination did it play a part in that it was vital enough to sacrifice the likes of Mortis and the Idolacreid in order to ascertain it?

Auzlanten had dusted the ash off of his head. His act of mourning was emotionally charged and the presence was a somber reminder of his failure. The time to mourn would come later. Now was the time for action.

"Arodi?" Bethel had approached Auzlanten and the Master of Templym didn't even notice. He realized also that he spoke to him earlier and hadn't registered the sentence. He was too deep in thought.

"I'm sorry Jude, could you repeat yourself?" He asked Bethel without removing his gaze from Volk's body.

"I asked you what our next course of action is. Our squad is down two members, but you just killed the Nephilim. Will we still go after the Regent? Has nothing changed in that respect?"

"Everything has changed Jude. The Nephilim is not dead. It was occupying the corpse of Ram's Horn, a spirit inside of an empty vessel. I destroyed that body, but the Nephilim will no doubt have another prepared. That creature can transfer between willing vessels. I haven't seen this kind of magick in over a century, and that was in a Class A Imago."

"It was planning to assassinate you." Bethel said bluntly. "It was waiting for you to arrive and ambush you."

"A logical step. With me dead, the Nephilim could finalize its dubious plan with the preeminent threat neutralized. Now that its persona has been destroyed and its plans have been exposed, it will accelerate the final stages. The abolition is imminent."

"He mentioned a quota." Oslin said joining into the conversation. "He wanted you out of the way so the abolition could reach its kill quota."

Auzlanten pondered this new information. "The abolition is a harvest. The Nephilim needs to kill a certain number of people. I suppose the keystone it stole could be reconfigured to function as a power source. *'An ocean of blood will be spilled. Their life will bear a great titan anew. A crop of corpses will fertilize the fires of war.'* The Nephilim is going to fuel some kind of unholy device to grind Templym to dust."

"Its throne?" Vandross asked while placing his hat back on his head.

"I think so. I can't be certain as to the specifications, but if it requires an 'ocean of blood' to power it then it could devastate Templym, even before reaching full power."

"Do you think we could be looking at another Purus?" Bethel asked.

"No. Something of this magnitude can't be stopped by anything in my arsenal. It would take divine intervention to halt it. If the Nephilim successfully gathers enough blood, I will be forced to helplessly watch my great nation be crushed in its wake. There won't be a crusade, just a massacre."

"Then we can't let that happen." Blackwell said angrily. "We need to stop the abolition from succeeding."

"There is hope." Auzlanten mused. "If configured to act as a power source, the keystone would deteriorate. Its half-life was kept at bay by the stasis container, but exposed to the elements it will be decaying as we speak. If not fueled properly, the relic would become inert within a day of activation."

"So, we just need to keep them at bay until then." Bride Wainwright speculated. "Once the abolition begins we need to prevent the Nephilim's cult from reaching its quota."

The conversation was silenced by a small alarm from a nearby communication receiver. A single red light flashed on and off while producing a high pitched whining. All attention was locked onto this radio. It was a signal from one of the reconnaissance teams scouting the safe houses in Parey. One of the Scourge militias was signaling their team in request for reinforcements.

"That's from the Crimson Saints," Bethel said picking up the small radio box. "That's the Inquisition militia we sent out to scout the Regent's safe house in the Terracotta district. They weren't supposed to contact us unless they engaged a heretic threat."

"Invictus," Auzlanten said, deducing the cause of the alarm. He was becoming exasperated with the amount of imminent threats impending on him and his society. "It's time."

The task force began assembling their weapons in hurried fashion. Even Adastra, unable to wield his favored weapon, holstered a pistol to continue to fight. Arodi Auzlanten raised a hand slightly to wave them off. They were taken aback slightly at his rejection of their aid, but they understood when they saw the way he stared at Volk's corpse.

"I must do this alone." He said plainly, placing a hand on Leagna's hilt. "Having you join me will create liabilities. I will be too focused on keeping you alive than..." He seemed to choke on the words. Auzlanten could barely vocalize the need to kill Invictus Illuromos, even now.

"We won't just standby." Jude growled eager to fight.

"No, you won't. The Nephilim is going to accelerate its plans. The abolition could strike at any given moment. Get on every communicator, broadcast from every wavelength, warn every station on the tide, and spread the word by any and all means. The abolition is coming. From there I want you to move into the city and rally as many troops as you can muster. Protect the innocent. Parey is one of the most populated urbans in Templym so it won't be spared bloodshed. When it begins, I want you all in the front lines. If the Nephilim wants an ocean of blood, it's our duty to dam the flood."

CHAPTER 43

The Crimson Saints were not a famous militia. Other strike forces in the Scourge like Typhoon of the Beacon or Blitzkrieg of the Shackle were more likely to grab the public eye. The Crimson Saints had no yearning for fame or any form of acclimation. They were simply content to serve the Scourge. Perform a task, move on to the next, this was their ideology. It was.

Acolyte Samuel Clint was left on his knees, chained at the feet of some mockery of a Centurion. His brother and the militia's leader, Exarch Victor Clint, scanned some activity inside the suspected heretic outpost. Orders were to hold position and await further instruction, but when motion began Victor gave the order to breach and detain. It was a standard operation, or so it seemed. Bride Wainwright would have forgiven them for going beyond orders in order to acquire the quarry. The Crimson Saints grossly underestimated the mission.

Upon breaching the abandoned cathedral in Parey's Terracotta District, they were captured. An ambush by men dressed as some strange variant of the Regent's security regiment. The black accents of their armor were violet stains and all Scourge insignias were replaced by some jagged flower. These couldn't be real Centurions. Not only because of how they appeared as a mockery of the gallant soldiers, but because the Saints were still breathing. Surely if this was the Regent's guardsmen they would not have been captured. Then Invictus Illuromos arrived.

There was no impersonating the Scourge's leader. He was a giant among men, clad in the blackest armor conceivable. The spike whips on his pauldrons were replaced with cuirasses of jagged purple crystal. It seemed that even more spiked chains clanked off the jet flaksteel to the point it blanketed most of the smooth armor carapace. The most strikingly chilling feature was the massive maul he slung over his shoulder. This hammer's head was a snarling mass of grinding blades and glowing metal. Just looking at the weapon gave the sensation that it was a hungry entity of seething hatred, stirring fear into whoever glanced at it. This was the only Scourge soldier with Alpha Magnus authority, the representative of Arodi Auzlanten. What happened to him?

There was nothing unusual about Invictus donned up to his neck in his armor. His entire head was plated. His philosophy of only ever wielding a weapon only at times of war finalized all hints that he was ready to go to battle. Something was terribly wrong.

He never spoke once. The Regent of the Scourge just strode among the captive Inquisition militia staring at them in quiet contemplation. The Centurions did likewise, not even audibly breathing. Exarch Clint was the only one with the gall to voice the Saints' concern.

"To hell with the chain of confidentiality already Invictus!" Victor spat with immense venom in his tone. Nobody in the Scourge would ever speak so disrespectfully to the Regent, especially not a starch warrior like Victor. Clearly there was rancor billowing inside him, but Illuromos showed no sign of caring. "I demand answers this instant! We are Scourge! You are duty bound to lead us. That requires disclosure of information directly involving us!"

Samuel was distressed by his brother's outburst. Victor was always such a serene character, never so much as raising his voice against his parents during their youth. Now he was seething with rage, his face nearly the color of his battle plate. Invictus didn't care.

The traitor Regent tuned the ranting out several minutes ago, though if he focused he could still draw the information out. Invictus was still in awe at the amount of detail he could perceive. He could deduce the exact decibel of every crack in Victor's voice, though that was not the most intriguing thing he could discern. Several other Crimson Saints were offering hopeless prayers to the

Heavens. He heard pathetic whimpering of names. Spouses, children, parents, siblings, he made note of these names. Their blood would please the Nephilim.

Krakatoa growled in his grip. It was analogous to the gurgling of intestines craving nourishment. It hadn't killed in weeks, not since the Prelate. The spirits quaked inside of his new weapon, desperate for feeding. 'Soon', he communicated telepathically to the entities inside his hammer, 'soon'.

In the pastime, he listened to the rhythm of his captives' heartbeats. Paired with the steady pulse of adrenaline being pumped into their systems, their very bodies created a symphony of glorious fear. A decision would need to be made soon. The Crimson Saints were stationed at Bastion Prime and their absence would be noticed soon. It would be easy enough to send false signatures to the Scourge data wells, but scrounging together reliable imposters would be impossible on such short notice. Their blood could contribute to fueling the Nephilim's throne, but only once the abolition began. This was the Regent's predicament. Kill them now and eliminate witnesses, or pray the abolition comes soon enough to give them meaningful deaths? The latter came true.

Tails of smoke began whipping around Invictus. The sweet smelling vapor curled around the traitor's heads as though they were caressing them. This was simply a byproduct of the Nephilim's communion. He was reaching out to the leaders of his cult, Invictus being one of the foremost. Inside the thin snaking tendrils of smoke, a voice whispered to him. "The abolition has begun. Kill all that you can." It was the Nephilim. His patience was proven to be just. Now, he and his brothers in the cult had only twenty-four hours to murder a million citizens of Templym. There was no time to waste.

Upon the mist subsiding, Invictus Illuromos turned towards Victor Clint. He had been yelling and screaming frantically. He didn't care for what he was saying. "Answer me!" The militia commander yelled. The Regent obliged this request.

With impossible speed, he brought Krakatoa down on the militia leader's head. His snarling face of offense was reduced to a puff of red mist. Samuel Clint wanted to scream in horror and grief, but he couldn't. The Centurion looming over him had impaled him with his spear. The Crimson Saints were cut down within seconds, covering the terracotta tile of the abandoned cathedral with a carpet of arterial fluid. The demonic maw of the hammer grinded its gears like snapping jaws as it noisily gulped down the Exarch's flesh and bone.

Their corpses hit the ground with a lifeless thud echoing through the chamber. It was preceded by a steady deep chuckle emanating from inside of the Regent's helmet. Thirty-two of a million killed already, right at its inception. The fatted calf of Templym was far from slaughtered, but this was an amusing start. Turning a dial on his wrist com, Invictus opened the secure wavelength all of his rebels in the Scourge kept an ear to. With a voice containing far too much sinister relish, he spoke to hundreds of double agents waiting to be activated. "The abolition has begun, my brethren. Go forth. Kill all in your path."

The job of warning the masses fell to S-6319. While Auzlanten went to the Terracotta District to confront the Regent, they spread the news as expeditiously as possible. The time for subtlety had ended. It didn't matter if the Nephilim's cult got wind of their progress. All that mattered was that everyone learned of the coming abolition. Arodi was adamant that the massacre was imminent, that the cult was ready to pounce onto the unsuspecting citizens of Templym. A state of emergency needed to be issued.

The Scourge possesses a specialized wavelength for emergency broadcasts. This low frequency radio wave was intertwined into every machination with a tide connection, but had to be ratified by supervising agents. In order to send out an emergency, one needed only to submit a warning which would then be sent out to five anonymous Scourge officers. If three of those five, who were scattered all throughout Templym, could validate the honesty of those claims then the emergency signal would be sent out.

Upon emergency protocols being enacted, citizens would escape to one of several Scourge bastions or private bunker. Scourge warriors would then arm themselves and establish these safe-zones or meet the threat head-on. The tactics were perfected by Auzlanten himself after accounting for fourteen Purus Crusades and a Strife. This meant every area of heavy populace was locked down as well as the establishment of several strategic choke-points and kill-zones in every urban across Templym. Once that signal went out, it would be nearly impossible for any civilian to be caught in the resulting conflict. It would have saved thousands of lives if it had gone out.

The administrators of the emergency broadcast had identities that were Alpha classified. This meant that only the primes had access to that information, the primes and the Regent. In preparation for the abolition, Invictus had gradually reassigned the duties of oversight of the emergency wavelength. The responsibility was shifted to his loyalists. When the task force called in the threat to be broadcasted to every ear in Templym, the warning was snuffed out immediately.

Thankfully, Jude Bethel was thorough. In addition to a meaningless report to the emergency wavelength, he petitioned his peers to communicate with the major urbans and their respective Arcaes.

Levi Pearl was stationed in Golgotha, the Arcae of Jerusalem. He was on Shackle disciplinarian leave. Six months prior, he had been censured for excessive use of lethal force on a quarry hunt. Now, he was forced to operate the communications relays of Golgotha under the command of the most notorious Archon in all of Templym.

Pearl was on his fifteenth consecutive hour of wavelength oversight. In addition to being disciplined by creeds of the Scourge, his wrist was also being slapped by Crucifix himself. A bitter, impatient attitude does not mesh well with the terse opinionated personality of the Archon. His unceasing vocalization of petty issues was met with a double portion of a job he already despised. It was at this juncture that he received the warning.

"Gospel," Levi groaned, requesting the call-sign from one side of the communications station.

"Palm leaf," Bride Wainwright responded with the proper summons. "This is Bride Wainwright, Beta clearance with urgent information for Archon Crucifix."

"Please wait one moment while I verify your identity." Pearl grumbled as he began striking keys to go through the chain of command.

"Didn't you hear me? This is urgent!" She snapped back. "We have pressing details regarding an imminent threat to Golgotha. I need to speak to Crucifix posthaste!"

Levi's eyes perked up at the realization of something outside of the normal bureaucratic bilge. "The Archon is in the middle of an interrogation at the moment, but I'll gladly pass on the..."

Daphne cut the officer off, stressfully relaying the information as quickly as possible. "All prisoners affiliated with the Nephilim or the Idolacreid must be secured immediately. Expect all traitors exposed by the prime's edicts to be orchestrating an assault on Jerusalem. A state of emergency has been issued. Enact Creed Eighteen on a mass scale if necessary."

"Slow down ma'am, do you have evidence of this allegation?"

"The Scourge emergency wavelength will be relaying this message across all of Templym. There's no time to elaborate further, I have seven other Arcaes to alert in the next hour. Can I trust you to give this message to Archon Crucifix?"

"Um, yes, I'll let him know."

"Repeat the message back to me." She said swiftly.

"Initiate lockdown protocol, discriminate all prisoners under the Idolacreid conspiracy, and scout for a potential urban invasion."

"Good, get the message out right away, In Nomine Veritas." She broke the connection and moved on to her next call.

Levi Pearl adjusted the wavelength of his audio wire. He requested Archon Crucifix to come to the communications center immediately. His blunt request was met with grunts from the zealous leader of Golgotha. One does not pull him away from an enhanced interrogation without consequence. Those ramifications didn't matter now.

Archon Crucifix stormed into the relay, his metal feet fracturing the ceramic he was walking on. One couldn't see his face past the angular helmet he donned, but by the lurching of his shoulders and clenched fists, it was obvious he was furious.

"What is the meaning of this?" His mechanical voice growled. "I was just about to get something out of one of those traitors! You'd better give me an explanation as to why you pulled me off of that dog!"

Pearl swallowed, nervous not to provoke the Archon's ire. "We just got an urgent message from Bride Wainwright." He stammered.

"Am I supposed to know who that is?" Crucifix scoffed lividly. "The hell did she want?"

"Urgent medical update, she demands a detailed report on the prisoners' conditions."

"She wants to know how the prisoners are." The Archon said in disbelief. "You pulled me away from vital information extraction, so I could tell some Bride how the traitors are feeling? You do see the utter ridiculousness of that statement right?"

"Beta clearance sir," Levi says concealing a devious grin. "She has demanded to speak to you personally on the matter."

"Bloody smoking..." He cursed. "Damn HR is probably trying to nail me for unethical conduct again. Give me that."

Crucifix unlocked the seal of his helmet. As aggressive an individual he was and as barbarically jagged his armor was, one might expect the former Cardinal Wick to resemble a marauder more than anything else. In truth, he was unusually handsome with well kempt ebony hair. He pulled Pearl's audio wire off his head and placed it on his own head.

"Archon Crucifix," He grunted into the microphone. He expected some shrill voiced politician on the other end of the wavelength, but was greeted with silence. "Wainwright, are you there?"

Silence. "You pulled me out of interrogation, so this had better be an emergency." More silence. "Smoke, Levi you killed the connection."

He swiveled his body around to chew out the man, disciplining him further for his ineptitude. He was silenced when he realized that Levi had drawn his Reisinger. It was trained on the Archon's exposed head.

Ice flowed through his veins. Moments before, during the interrogation of one of the traitors exposed by Bethel's edict, he was on the brink of a possible lead. The prisoner, who had absorbed substantial punishment, had mentioned something of other traitors still walking in the halls of Golgotha. That convict laughed at the sentiment that the trap would be sprung and the Nephilim would rise from an ocean of blood. Crucifix just flogged him further for his audacity. Surely, all of the traitors had been weeded out, it wasn't possible that any of the cultists were still engrained in his Arcae. The horrific realization that Levi Pearl was one such turncoat and that he had walked right into his trap was the final thought that passed through mind. A single bullet tore through the only exposed flesh on his body and blew his brain out through the back of his skull.

With the Regent's order, the sleeping agents in the Scourge would begin their rebellion. Bethel and Greyflame may have caught a fair number of the Nephilim's faithful, but only the pawns. Those experienced enough to have been blessed to read a page of the Idolacreid gained enough power to surpass the influence of the Veritas Chambers. Those wise enough to stay hidden were waiting for Invictus to give them the word to begin harvesting the blood of the innocent. Now the abolition had begun and the wait was over.

Over the past few weeks, the Regent had been systematically redirecting the prisoners to four Arcaes. Jupiter, Golgotha, Blackfang, and Pluto were the prisons of the most densely populated urbans in Templym. He had forged four small armies out of the primes' edicts. Those not imprisoned would release the captives, arm them, and storm the cities. It would be happening within moments of the signal being transmitted.

Invictus was still relishing the thought of his Archons and guards rising up to stage this glorious coup. He chuckled as Krakatoa continued lapping up the remains of the soldiers he had just slain as he dwelt on the upcoming revolution. Once the throne was ready, he would have more power than he ever came close to having as Regent of the Scourge.

The Centurions lined up behind their Regent. They paid no head to the corpses scattered at their feet. Their chrome boots were already painted with a crimson sheen. By the end of the day, they'd all be up to their necks in gore. Each one of his squadron was armed with antoniat tipped spears and modified laser carbines, only the finest for the Regent's personal armed forces. Invictus Illuromos had his armor outfitted with additional ordinance. Extra spike wire coiled around automatic cannons integrated into his cuirass on the pauldrons. With a demon infused maul in hand, he would surely head the slaughter.

At his command, the Centurions began to march out of the cathedral. Parey possessed a bevy of high traffic areas. There was an ongoing mightfall game at Abnett Stadium. The fifty thousand seat arena would be filled to the brim. Further North was the Purus Monumental Park, a tourist trap regularly entertaining twenty thousand citizens at a time. That would be the rendezvous point for the renegades led by Archon Grim breaking from Jupiter after culling through Brazen Market. After those targets were cloven down, their combined forces would meet and march through the Frankish capital harvesting as much blood as possible. Similar harvests would be happening in over a hundred other settlements simultaneously.

Sixty Centurions would be a formidable strength. Coupled with the public's trust in the Scourge, which would mean little resistance against the Nephilim's loyalists, they would bring this portion of Templym to its knees. Once Parey and Rushmore and Venice Primus and Jerusalem were in flames, the fires would consume the rest of Templym.

Marching in perfect unison, Invictus and his troop sounded like a battalion of Hekatons storming through the baked tile halls of the dust caked citadel. Any crowd in Templym would be tempted to stop and bask in awe at the impressive sight of grandiose military power.

Doing so would be understandable, but a grave error in judgment. Any bystanders in their line of sight would be instantly slaughtered.

The cathedral was sealed with a triplet door of lead paneling, a style of architecture popular during the early 25th century. This cumbersome style offered a highly defensible bunker which made the cathedral an ideal location for a Scourge safe house. Once those heavy metal sheets were cast aside, the most lethal squadron of the Nephilim's faithful would be unleashed like a pack of ravenous hounds. As Invictus and his platoon were fifty feet away the doors began sliding open. The Regent ordered the Centurions to halt. He was not the one commanding this door to open.

Invictus Illuromos suspected that the Crimson Saints might have backup. He did not expect the Master of Templym.

Just the thought of him caused the demons inside him to swell and surge with bloody rage. It had been months since he looked into those glossy blue eyes. They had been so full of sadness when last he looked into them. Those same cerulean irises were now flecked with fury. The Regent believed he would never be as excited again as when he sold his pitiful sob story to so great an "intellect". He had hoped this confrontation would happen after the abolition, once Auzlanten's utopia was naught but ash.

Krakatoa snarled with an exhale of oily smoke as its blade maw turned with a roar. It was eager to kill this beacon of putrid holiness, though not as eager as Invictus. Auzlanten couldn't see his face beneath the thick jet helm, but he knew his mouth was perked into a sadistic grin.

"Father," The Regent's metallic voice growled, venom in his breath.

"Son," Auzlanten responded as he summoned Leagna from its scabbard.

CHAPTER 44

The first hour of the abolition was sheer, bloody chaos. Dozens of different militant cultist simultaneously triggered their traps across the globe. The crystal blue morning in Carthonia became stained red with blood and black with smoke. The serene still night in the UPA smashed into a nightmare as thousands of death shrieks broke out at once.

The Jerusalem cult flooded out of Golgotha and into the streets. Armed to the teeth with jagged blades and assault rifles, they began hacking away indiscriminately. The dead were piled into grotesque heaps of carved flesh to be feasted upon after the coming of the Nephilim. Corpses were nailed into twisted effigies which were raised as cultic banners to rally the cult, inspiring wanton bloodshed.

Venice Primus began crumbling as structures collapsed. The Nephilim's cult in the region had infiltrated several cloudtouchers, planting bombs in preparation for this moment. Once the call went out, several tons of clapshock cracked open support beams. Plumes of rubble shot up like massive grey geysers, backed by screaming as seven different structures were felled. The cultists began harvesting stragglers, bursting from the fog of powdered rock in mad rushes before any civilian could comprehend what was happening.

It was the middle of the night in Rushmore. With the aid of the traitor Archon, the prisoners slithered into the streets under the cover of darkness. In silent guerilla fashion, unsuspecting families were slaughtered with hushed efficiency. Throats slit, skulls caved in, innards spilled, and many more methods of death were inflicted upon the citizens of the UPA. Half of the dead were not awake to see their killers.

These urbans were the sights of the most obvious massacres. Dozens of other cities were victims to similar slaughter. The nuclear reactors of J'kier were splintered and radioactive sluice cascaded on the streets. Those that died in the initial disaster did not suffer as much as the thousands infected with rad poisoning. An EMP in Jaspin deactivated necessary generators and life support systems, leaving them vulnerable, crippled, and in several cases dead. There was carnage across Templym and, according to the cult of the Nephilim, would continue until a million were murdered in the course of a day.

Leagna normally radiated brilliant color. This light was a reflection of Auzlanten's own emotions and internalized thought processes. This was a result of the intimate attunement Arodi had with the weapon. It did not shimmer at all now. While the blade itself was made of multicolored stained glass material, there was no light coming off of it. It was an accurate reflection of the bleak necessity of the situation, Arodi's grim realization of what he was about to do. Or perhaps it was due an overwhelming influx of dissident feelings that the sabre couldn't possibly display, defaulting to nothing.

He could now see what Invictus had become. The Regent no longer needed to conceal his allegiance to fiendish powers. Arodi could see the demons churning inside of him. Dozens, perhaps as many as a hundred, of Mundus Imago were roiling inside of his supernaturally muscled body. He saw the increased flow of nutrient rich blood into his swollen muscles and heard the pounding thrum of his heartbeat harmonizing with the snarling of the dark spirits inside of him. His armor had been outfitted with additional totems and decorum sacred to the cult of the Nephilim, distinguishing him as elite among the heretics. The aura of roiling black magick, invisible to those without Auzlanten's insight, was like a torrent of sentient smoke. And the maul, the wretched hammer he carried, was almost as evil as the man wielding it.

"I had hoped to meet you after the slaughter." Invictus laughed. His stoic, regal voice was now filled with avarice.

"What happened to you?" Auzlanten said, keeping an eye on the Centurions who were breaking from march formation into assault pattern. "What tale did the Nephilim plant in your mind? What promise was powerful enough to seduce you to such a dark power?"

Invictus Illuromos raised a spiked gauntlet as a means to command a halt, which they enacted instantly. "No lies. That's what you preach. In Nomine Veritas after all. That is the creed in which you instilled in the Scourge. You went so far as to make lying an executable offense in our own ranks. What irony then, that you are the greatest liar of them all." The Regent changed languages. He was speaking the guttural tongue of the damned. "Move into the city, I will join you later."

Arodi Auzlanten spoke the profane language. He understood the command and its implications. The abolition must have been declared. That would mean the massacre would be inciting all over Templym. This was no time for pretentious formalities, now was the time to use his powers for their intended purpose. It was time to kill.

Auzlanten stuck Leagna into the clay tile. From out of it, a flood of javelin sharp spears of light shot out from the impact. There was one for every heretic standing in that chamber. The spears of light skewered Centurions, ripping out jagged pieces of flaksteel from their battle plate and producing a thick bloody mist in the air. The stench of boiling metal accompanied the thud of nearly fifty bodies smacking against the clay tile floor in unison.

Invictus was utterly unaffected. The light spear stuck into his thick ebon breastplate without so much as scratching the plate. A few of the Centurions were able to pivot their bodies around in time to avoid the impaling spears, suffering superficial flesh wounds but still standing. Auzlanten's intent of the attack was to dispatch the grunts and leave him and his son alone.

Arodi knew that the spike wouldn't penetrate his armor. He

crafted that suit especially for him. Each of the flaksteel plates were atomicized, meaning each individual plate acted as a single molecule. The inside was decorated with warding runes and glyphs to keep supernatural powers at bay, apparently even his own. He never considered the possibility that he would be fighting Invictus. He made it resilient against himself. Getting through the inches of metal would be impossible without a catastrophic nuclear reaction and his powers would have a severely dampened effect. The only hope of landing the kill would be to undo the magnetic locks keeping the armor sealed and attack the exposed flesh.

Invictus used his empty hand to wrench the light spike from his chest, not even flinching. Arodi could see his choler rising to new levels of hostility he never expected from an individual as sober as he had been. He heard gears grinding inside of the demon maul, the creatures possessing him hissing and laughing with vile glee, and the inertia pack concealed beneath his immotrum cloak heating up. With a burst of superheated gas, the Regent charged at Arodi Auzlanten.

Krakatoa could have split a cloudtoucher in half with the concentrated force it barreled down with. The attack was faster than anything of such bulk could naturally travel. Auzlanten brought Leagna up, catching the hammer before it crashed into his head. Arodi thought he knew exactly how strong his son was. Nobody would look at the giant of a man and think him weak, but the pure force he carried was unbelievable. Invictus was stronger even than the literal giant Mortis. Arodi buckled beneath the force of the impact, shattering the tile beneath his boots.

Just as Auzlanten taught him to, he followed up his downward blow with a swift uppercut. Regent Illuromos was foolishly using the techniques that were taught to him against his mentor. There was no elegance to his rapid assault, no focus, no discipline to his attacks. There was only rage. Every arc of the snarling maul was fueled by his unadulterated anger. A scissor pattern cross meant to shatter shoulder bones, a leg sweep powerful enough to rip a femur off one's hip, downward strikes meant to pulp skull and brain matter, all of his rapid attacks were deflected or dodged. Auzlanten flawlessly parried away the assault which would instantly slaughter any lesser man.

Amidst his defensive dance, Arodi wielded Leagna more like a club than a sabre. The plates of his armor were far too thick to have any hope of being cut through. Even the mesh bodysuit beneath the battle plate was atomicized and therefore immune to lacerations. Instead, he aimed his sword towards the vital magnetic joints of the suit. If he could land a strike powerful enough on a vital area, the armor segment would come detached, leaving the monster beneath vulnerable. But Invictus was too swift. Even clad in nearly two hundred pounds of metal, he was almost as swift as him. The sabre then served only to throw the Regent off balance, making his already wild attack all the more reckless. Such a tactic should have been effective as the traitor Regent subtly lost composure with every swing. He should have been vulnerable to a quick stab to a magnetic seal. However, the Imago guiding his body made him too quick to fall prey to such a tactic.

A straggling few Centurions tried to join in with the skirmish to keep their master alive. Arodi cut them down in a backswing or with a surge of energy, not breaking from the engagement at hand. Tails of spiked chains began shattering as Leagna struck the flaksteel carapace. Invictus was able to land a few blows using modified armor spikes during the closer grapples between the two of them. The jagged angular spikes should have shredded him to rags, but Arodi kept fighting as if he too was clad in atomicized flaksteel.

The remaining Centurions assembled like a pack of wolves around the skirmish. They poised their spears, ready to strike in unison when an opportunity presented itself. Invictus continued to bombard Auzlanten with furious blows from Krakatoa, which slobbered molten metal from its grinding blade maw. A coordinated assault from his bodyguards could deal serious damage to the Master of Templym. Arodi would not let this happen.

The abolition was underway. Every fraction of a second wasted would be lost lives and fuel for the Nephilim. Invictus was effective, if not as a combatant than as a distraction. The Imago hosts empowering his reflexes worked in tandem with his inertia pack, giving his limbs speed that rivaled Auzlanten's. Breaking his stance to focus on the Regent's menials could result in him facing a devastating attack. If there was a time to unleash the full potential of his might, it was now.

Amidst the whirling dervish of defense, Arodi began calling on the power gifted to him. The wind began whipping around him. Tails of vapor swirled in a violent ellipse around the skirmishing juggernauts. The cloaks and plumes of the Centurions began bending at the force of barreling wind and unbalancing their poised stance. While he and Invictus were at the eye of this concentrated hurricane, the other traitors surrounding them were not so fortunate. Howling wind and every horrendous roar of the demon maul was backed by the screaming of traitors as they were thrown off their feet.

Bright fiery sparks flying off the colliding weapons were immediately quenched by the violent winds. Yet Invictus thrashed Krakatoa in wild killing arcs, just as disregarding of the gale as Auzlanten. There was such contempt in his motion, such hatred. His finely crafted battle stance was slowly collapsing into rage-fueled flailing. Arodi thought him a more capable warrior than this, more disciplined than this childishly sloppy assault. If it weren't for the Mundus Imago fueling his physique, this fight would have ended already.

His body began surging with unholy fire as he fought with more and more ferocity. That fire was quenched by the tides of wind enveloping them. Once the gale had conjured enough force, Arodi redirected its direction. The hurricane swept past Auzlanten, sending his braided hair into a wild furl. Invictus was assaulted by a massive gust. The supernaturally charged wind carried enough weight to crack buildings. The Regent was blown back by the storm, but surprisingly held his ground by digging his heels in.

Invictus trundled against the wind. His hate would only be sated once he stood triumphant over the corpse of Templym's founder.

Every demon in his body screamed for blood and Krakatoa roared hungrily. His dark patrons demanded the prophet's life, but that was not his incentive to fighting his father. He needed Auzlanten dead. His unadulterated loathing for the man fueled his motive to lay waste. He would not succeed.

The Centurions swept up by the wind began plowing into his black carapace. The traitors hit with the velocity of a cannonball. Their bodies shattered against the Regent's bulk, splintering into indistinguishable shreds of metal and viscera. His armor absorbed the first impact, causing little more than a buckle in his already unsteady posture. Then a second with more effect, then a third, a fourth, until the fifth and final human projectile brought him down.

Invictus tumbled back deep into the cathedral. Wooden pews were brought up in the gale. Auzlanten redirected the wind so the dust caked timber struck him just like his menials. The Regent crushed through a porcelain mosaic, his spiked armor embedding into its walls. He was jammed into the stone with no hopes of any movement. Pews struck against him like a salvo of missiles. Two tons of solid oak crunched against the helpless Regent, their added impacts in succession began to fracture the skeleton of the man beneath the armor. For no matter how much magick was infused in him, no matter how many demons he welcomed into his coil, he was still a man. Men are breakable.

The howling wind subsided after there was nothing left to assail him with. Without the storm pinning him to the wall he lost his stake and collapsed onto the floor. Invictus growled a murderous snarl and tried to muster the strength to pull himself up to continue the fight. He could not.

His allies abandoned him. After hearing of what Auzlanten did to Knox Mortis and then seeing the might of the Lord firsthand, the Imago knew to fear him. After absorbing dozens of killing blows and recognizing that Invictus Illuromos had no hope of salvaging this fight, they left. Shunting themselves into the spiritual realm, they left their black host an empty vessel. An empty, abated, meager vessel.

Invictus desperately tried to summon the strength to pull himself to his feet. He could not muster the energy to support the armor encasing him. He was left to lay on his stomach, prostrate, entirely at the mercy of Arodi Auzlanten.

The Master of Templym stepped over to the Nephilim's general. Where the Regent's armor was scuffed and dented after being bombarded with his own soldiers and the contents of his safe house, Auzlanten was unscathed. His cerulean robes and platinum half-crown were just as pristine as when he appeared, not even as much as a drop of cooled metal on his skin.

Even the maul, which had earlier been alight like a scalding furnace, was still and cold. Invictus had nothing now. He snorted and roared trying to embolden his limp muscles. Arodi ignored his primitive threats and began removing his helmet. The gale served more than just the purpose of swirling around projectiles that ultimately led to Invictus's crippling. The dust flushed into the cracks of his armor combined with the flush of supercharged static, which interfered with the magnetic locking mechanisms of the battle plate's seals. It damaged the neck area enough that Auzlanten could pop the black casing off with a firm twist.

Pressurized air escaped as the atomicized helmet was taken off of the Regent's head. Invictus Illuromos only vaguely resembled the man known to Templym as the mortal leader of the Scourge. His tanned skin was corpse gaunt, the color of blanched ash, pulled taut over his skull. Dark purple veins bulged as oozing blood pulsed through his body. His stormy grey eyes now resembled spheres of pure mercury with black pinpricks, the only thing distinguishing them as eyes. Arodi Auzlanten didn't see just the monster lying at his feet like a wounded animal. He could see the many faces his son wore over the past.

He saw the orphan boy rescued from the brink of human sacrifice at the hands of an Imago cult. Sandy blonde hair draped over stormy grey eyes flushed with fear, the first time Arodi met the boy. He saw the rebellious teenager, heart alight with anger with no place to put it. He saw the eager young warrior, rising through the ranks of the Scourge. He saw the grieving father, whose wife and daughter had died as collateral in the 14th Purus. He saw the stalwart leader, discerning and brave, leading the Scourge by phenomenal example.

Then he saw the beast he had become. The mutant fiend that had fallen from Grace, away from all that was good in favor of a hellish, self-serving ideology. That truth cut deeper than Leagna ever could.

Auzlanten scowled as he looked down on the snarling animal that had once been his son. He quietly hovered the tip of his sabre a hair's length from the Regent's forehead. With one word, he offered up the most important opportunity he was capable of. Arodi abhorred the thought of damning his foster child to the Pit. He had to extend this one, final choice. "Repent." He stated with bleak melancholy.

Invictus mustered up every ounce of his strength to crane his neck upwards. He pressed his head into the tip of the sword, drawing viscous blood from between his eyes. His lip trembled as if he were about to weep. Then his countenance immediately twisted into wild rage. With gurgling bile in his throat he growled, "No."

It had been centuries since he had felt such a twisted wrench of pain in his chest. He just witnessed his son blatantly reject the salvation offered up on the Cross. There was nothing more that could be done to save him. If Invictus was willing to turn away Grace at his most vulnerable, he would never repent.

So Auzlanten kept the commandment given to him months ago. If nothing else, he could make it swift. Arodi turned his wrist, looping his sword around to a killing posture. The sabre came down in a sharp descent slicing through the Regent's skull. The blade rammed through his brain cavity before jutting out of his jaw and burying into the terracotta below, impaling his head on the length of the blade. It was as merciful a death as one could deliver.

The Nephilim was wetting its own palate, exercising his new bone spikes upon the inhabitants of the American Hinterlands. A mass of peaceful marauders fell victim to his assault. The magick it possessed meshed with the absurd strength of Mortis' body beautifully. With every graceful motion of his hands, tribesmen of the largely passive marauder people screamed in a chorus of slaughter. A deluge of blood sloshed with an upward flick of his salient talons, the wet crack of bone triggered by the scything spikes of his arm, and entrails were spilled with every foul motion. He laughed at the carnage he wrought.

Then a minor chill lifted over him. It had been entirely focused on harvesting blood for the throne-chariot, until a sense of loss struck him. The Nephilim halted in its wild murder masterpiece to focus on the connection that was severed. The connection it shared with one of the cult's foremost champions.

Invictus Illuromos was dead. "Auzlanten." The thought of the wretch nauseated it. The Regent played a vital role in the massacre in Frankon. Now, his position was left vacant. With overwhelming demonic energy, the Nephilim stomped a clawed foot on the ground, summoning a blight of crackling green lightning that singed the inhabitants of the pathetic marauders. It wanted so desperately to relish the slaughter, to hear screams that no-one else in the world would ever hear. It would seem now it could not. It needed to focus on Parey.

Arodi froze with his hand around Leagna's hilt. He stared at what he had just done. In its hundreds of years of use, this sabre had never once taken the life of a good man. He was unsure if that was still true. Invictus was a good man before...before all this. That man was dead for certain, but for how long had the hero Regent been dead? He pulled the lightless blade out of his son's head. He wanted to collapse to the ground and weep for his fallen child. There was no time for that.

He returned his glassy sword to its holster. With a deep sigh, he turned on his heel to make his way out of the cathedral. With this dreadful mission accomplished, Auzlanten began running thousands of calculations through his mind. First, he needed to undergo a threat assessment by scrutinizing areas of highest population density, but he could not spend much time on that. He would need to systematically extinguish the most imminent threats.

As he rushed through the numbers, he came to a woeful realization. There was nothing he could do. If the cult of the Nephilim was as ingrained as he believed it to be, summoning all of the strength in his arsenal could not topple the abolition. He could theoretically sacrifice his own soul as a means to power some overwhelming display of final might, but doing so would leave Templym to an even greater number of threats. What means did he have to prevent this? What spell, what ritual, what artifact, could possibly quench this rebellion before enough lives were garnered for the Nephilim's dark whim?

Genesis Chapter 22 came to mind among this flurry of data. It seemed appropriate given the circumstance. Much like Abraham, Auzlanten was commanded to kill his son. The difference being that Isaac was an innocent child and that Arodi's hand was not stayed. A specific verse came to mind as his complex thought process was shunted off by a flash of vibrant light, verse 14, "the Lord will provide".

Beneath the shroud of glimmering golden light was a figure clad fully in battle plate. This armor was a base of midnight with a blend of silver and stardust. A rich surplice that flowed like milk draped over a face with a gold sun visor. Two alabaster gauntlets as thick as marble columns were crossed over the figure's breastplate.

"Yours is a welcome presence Tsadaqiel." Auzlanten said with a slight bow.

"I was told to bless you." The angel's chorus voice could not hide his contempt of the Master of Templym. "You have fulfilled your command, albeit not in a timely manner."

"You know I haven't the time for your petulance!" He growled, suppressing a great deal of rage. "I have less than a day to purge an Imago cult from this world. If you are not going to provide aid, then quit this plane!"

"I shall be brief." Tsadaqiel said bluntly. He reached one

pearlescent hand into his cloak. From seemingly nowhere, he produced a large, clear gemstone. It was like a diamond or finely polished zirconium, hewn into an icosahedron roughly the size of a human head. "Channel your energy into this. It can reproduce and spread your attacks across the whole globe."

Auzlanten was silenced by this revelation. With widened eyes, he took the gem from the celestial. He was surprised at how lightweight it was. "Thank you." He stammered.

"I am an instrument of the Lord's will, nothing more. Attune yourself to the crystal. Stamp out the Nephilim's cult. Do not delay in this order like the last."

"It will be done." Auzlanten said seriously. "That process will take nearly an hour. What would God have me do in that time?"

The celestial shifted slightly to look at the corpse of Invictus Illuromos. Arodi grimaced as he too looked back at what was left of his son. "You've done that which you initially refused. Perhaps you should do so again."

The glimmering flare of light vanished just as immediately as it arrived. Auzlanten was left in the abandoned cathedral with his new diamond artifact, a literal gift from God. He needed to study this device further, but was confident he could determine its exact use in a matter of minutes. The attunement process was what would be painfully lengthy.

He looked back to the fallen Regent. He saw the gaping wound in the cap of his skull which punctured all the way out of his chin. Viscous black ooze dripped out of the orifice. Auzlanten thought of what twisted information had seeped into Invictus' mind that would make him make such a dramatic change of loyalty. With that query, Arodi realized what Tsadaqiel's final sentiment was referring to. He knew what he needed to do next.

CHAPTER 45

The Scourge responded to the abolition's declaration as quickly as it could, albeit in disorganized packs. The response time would have been significantly lesser but there seemed to be an all too convenient level of technical difficulties in the communications relays. Entire regiments dispatched themselves to quash the various rebellions plaguing urbans and preying on innocent lives. The amount of bloodshed was staggering.

Storm drains welled up with blood and bullet casings. Nearly every major city in Templym was the sight of a brutal combat. The thunderous staccato of gunfire echoed in unison with the screams of innocent civilians. There were froth mouthed cultists brandishing every weapon imaginable chasing after wailing women and children. This was a time when it would be immeasurably beneficial to have the Bulwark again, one to fight and one to protect. The Scourge scrambled to fill both roles.

A battalion of Hekatons were hijacked in Rutuba Kalkhan and marched onto the city Ahldorain. Swifts swept through highly populated areas, cleaving through civilians with their multi-weapon limbs. Larger Ursine class titans of war strayed on the outskirts of the city laying down artillery fire. Even a ten-story tall Everest Hekaton fell prey to the control of the Nephilim's faithful. The heavy Beacon population, under the command of Magistrate Walthune himself, responded with rocket lancers as they desperately tried to discern which engines were theirs.

The rural satellites of Templym were easy prey for vile marauder tribes. Attacks from barbarians were common enough, but for the first time in decades, once warring tribes coordinated scorched earth raids of small towns. Their savagery was met with militias of common civilians armed with picks, scythes, butcher knives, and any other impromptu weapon they could muster if they didn't have firearms. All they had to do was hold off long enough until Scourge cavalry arrived. It would not. They were preoccupied with the more densely populated urbans.

Telemachus Evangelon was Auzlanten's ninth general during the Reclaiming Crusade, hence why the ninth month of the year was named after him. After the establishment of Templym, he created a great mausoleum in what would later become Parey, named for the crusaders that gave their lives. Much like the ancient crypt of Halicarnassus, the tomb was an architectural masterpiece of fine granite plinths, Corinthian style marble columns, and master crafted headstones. While the general himself never named the tomb, which spanned several acres, it was later named Evangelon's Necropolis. It made a fine defensive point.

Blitzkrieg, under the command of Warden Alexandarius Carthage, shepherded as many civilians into the Necropolis as they could. Its massive underground tombs were inlaid with several feet of solid stone, giving it the durability of a military bunker. The crypt itself had only a singular entrance, meaning the Shackle strike force could bottle-neck any attempts to get at the innocents.

Blitzkrieg had spent the past two hours scouring the city for panicking civilians to chorale them to the Necropolis to keep them safe. While half of his team was out recovering civilians, he and the rest of his militia fought tooth and nail, wave after wave, of slobbering fanatics armed with pikes and civilian quality firearms. Their chests, shoulders, and faces were emblazoned with a symbol that Carthage recognized as the holy symbol of the Nephilim. He deduced that the abolition he learned from the traitor Creel and his heretic allies had come.

Alexandarius was immensely out of his element. Blitzkrieg specialized in overwhelming attack, a common breach and clear strategy. That was why the Shackle was founded. *Kynigi et Kako*, pursue the wicked, that was the mantra by which he lived. For his entire life, even during the Civil Strife, he had been chasing after the scum of the Earth. Now. he was holed up in a graveyard, defending a flock of innocents. This was not his specialty.

Evangelon's Necropolis had been sculpted with smooth alabaster stonework. It was meant to be a place of peace, acknowledging that death was not the grim hopeless tragedy thought of by a godless worldview, that there was the hope of Heaven through the Cross. Its serenity was meant to realize that the fallen crusaders were now at peace in Eternity. It no longer appeared as such.

Carthage had unintentionally turned this work of architectural splendor into the backdrop of an overwhelmingly violent conflict. Obelisks and prayer boards were riddled with gnarled chunks blown out from where bullets had torn into stone. Grenades and light rockets dug craters into the ground and lit topiaries aflame. Smooth, once beautiful sculptures were nothing more than dusted rubble. Evangelon's attempt to give the graveyard a sense of bliss was ruined beyond recovery.

The percussive ringing of gunfire filled the once silent memorial. A thick fog of powdered granite and vaporized gunpowder mingled with a thin morning mist to create an eerie, atmosphere. Warriors clad in electric blue flaksteel battle plate ducked behind felled columns exchanging fusillades. A band of cultists donning yellow Arcae bodysuits consistent with Jupiter were pressing a vile advance, trying desperately to claw their way into the underground crypts to slaughter the civilians within.

Retriever Julian Frigate slammed another drum into his rifle. The barrel of his rifle was starting to glow red with exhaust heat. The RK-12's stock pounded against his shoulder as he spat a burst of bullets at another clot of escapees. From there, he commanded Anchor squad to pull back towards the primary mausoleum structure where the entrance to the crypt was. It was a means to communicate panic to their foes. They fell for it.

Seeing Blitzkrieg retreat, the Nephilim cultists advanced. Their nonsensical whooping and guttural chanting was just as boisterous as their undisciplined gunfire. They were too thrilled at the idea of laying waste to so many innocents to realize their mistake, too thrilled to look inside the other mausoleums. This realization did not occur until they heard a boisterous war cry, "Urah!"

Carthage charged headlong into the traitor squadron alone. One head was crushed from the impact of his Key before they even saw his blue flaksteel plate. Another turned to stick a pike in the Warden's chest but was greeted with a swift uppercut to the jaw before even pulling it back. Two shots from a Reisinger plinked off against his breastplate from one cultist as Alexandarius blew another cultist apart with an electrically charged burst from the battering ram. He fired a brief burst of hollow points into that one's torso from a handheld carbine. His concentration on this final cultist distracted him from focusing on the one he had just recently felled. The prisoner with the broken jaw scooped up a sawn-off Blakavit shotgun before Carthage realized he was still kicking. A sharp crack and a barrage of steel pellets burst into the face plate of his helm. Electric blue paint and bits of metal flung off of the impact crater, but the Warden would not fall. He only got one shot off. The Key pulverized the final member of this wave of heretics in a puff of red fluid and blue lightning.

Alexandarius spat a hunk of metal out with a mouthful of blood after ripping his ruined helmet off. The headpiece absorbed the lethal brunt of the force but shredded its impact springs and comms. . The green plume atop the helmet was blackened by soot and now shredded by shot. It was basically just a piece of loose metal obscuring his vision, so he cast it aside.

His helmet was not the only damaged portion of his plate. His breastplate was riddled with dents and welts. The strobe globes on his pauldrons were blown out and the ribbons he sealed onto them were tattered shreds of velvet. His chainmail cloak had been shot and stabbed apart leaving nothing but a few straggling links dangling off his back. There was more raw flaksteel than electric blue finish covering his body. He didn't care.

This was sheer chaos. As an agent of the Scourge it was a

Warden's duty to be a bastion of order in that chaos. If his body was shorn and his armor splintered, that was a fate he could live with. Carthage had to keep up Blitzkrieg's momentum. There were around two hundred civilians cowering in the crypts beneath Evangelon's Necropolis and more were being corralled in between waves of madmen. He had no means to contact Bastion Prime or any other squadron outside of his militia, so this mission is where his focus would lie. He would beat his knuckles down to the bone as long as he still drew breath to keep the Nephilm's fanatics at bay.

Wiping bloody grime off his chin with the back of his hand, he approached Anchor squad as they recuperated. Frigate noted how his half shorn golden hair was a stark contrast to the bleak fog lulling in the graveyard. "Losses?" Carthage asked, the gallant playfulness disturbingly absent from his voice.

"Thomlin took a round in the shoulder." The Retriever reported. "The artery was severed. If we don't get him to a hospitaller soon he's going to lose that arm."

Carthage looked past to the prone Guardian. His skin was flushed of all color aside from the crimson splashes on his half-plate. He was seventeen years old, barely a man by legal standards. "Stanch the bleeding and stick him in the crypt with the civs. Give him an adrenal pack... then put a gun in his working hand."

"He's on guard duty?" Frigate gasped. "The kid can't even keep his head up. He needs a doctor or he's going to be..."

"Don't give me that!" Alexandarius snapped at his lieutenant. "You think I don't know I'm condemning him to the life of a cripple? We don't have time or numbers enough to spare a team to fetch a surgeon. We need every soldier operating at full capacity if we're going to keep this grave from gaining a few hundred new occupants. Get Thomlin in the crypt and get back out here to secure the perimeter."

Under normal circumstances, Julian Frigate would protest such a heartless order. The hurt was obvious in his Warden's voice. His amber eyes didn't glow with their typical fiery passion. Carthage had no desire to give such a command, but this was a desperate situation. Desperate actions would have to be taken to keep the innocents in the tombs alive. He gave a curt nod and followed through with the order.

Alexandarius proceeded to perform a routine comms check, on his wrist unit now that his helmet was shredded. He began by checking to see if there were any other Scourge wavelengths active in the area. Much like the last dozen times he checked, he was still isolated to the short range squad wavelength. He then checked in with the surrounding squads. Mastodon and Bullet were out of range gathering more civilians in the city to bring them to the Necropolis. Anchor remained outside of the immediate perimeter around the mausoleum. Gladius was patrolling the outskirts keeping reconnaissance up. Barb was...gone. Carthage continually had to remind himself. Retriever Creel and his squad were corrupt, among the heretics roaming the streets sowing terror. He hoped he would get a chance to perform a delayed execution to quench the burning desire for vengeance in his heart. That didn't seem likely given he had left Ichabod in Blackfang, on the other side of the planet.

One of the Blitzkrieg medics applied a dose of suturant to the Warden's face to stop the minor bleeding from his abrasions. He scowled coldly as he mentally assessed the situation. They were coming in waves, about fifteen at a time. In an hour they had already repelled three waves. If they continued losing soldiers at the current rate...they'd all be dead by noon.

"Warden Carthage," one of the members of Gladius squadron said trotting towards the Cyan Bullet. Each dogged breath brought a small puff of steam.

"Speak, lad." Alexandarius said plainly.

"A small Scourge battalion is requesting entry into the Necropolis." Since there was mass confusion, it was crucial to vet all that through. "High Conservator Bethel and a Shackle task force."

Carthage flashed a smile. "Finally some bloody good news. Get them here posthaste!" The spark inside of the Warden was rekindled. In his mind, Blitzkrieg just went from surely doomed to only probably doomed.

Long range communications relays were cut off shortly after the abolition's beginning. The Regent's agents within the fabric of the Scourge were saboteurs, several of which crippled every network and wavelength used to speak across large distances. Once Bethel and S-6319 abandoned their impossible task of spreading Auzlanten's warning, hoping that the message was at least somewhat received, they took to the streets. Parey would surely fall prey to the cult of the Nephilim, so they needed to go out and prevent the grisly harvest. Jude and Oslin performed a strategic analysis and had the same idea as Carthage. While they weren't expecting to find Blitzkrieg stationed here, it was a welcomed surprise.

The five of them, Jude Bethel, Adastra Covalos, Vandross Blackwell, Oslin Du'Plasse, and Daphne Wainwright, had to fight their way through a mob of escaped prisoners over the course of the three mile trek to the Necropolis. Their battle plate was already splashed with blood and soot.

Gladius squad did not escort them in, rather they let them pass, trusting they could find the mausoleum on their own. Jude looked as battle ready as ever leading the troupe. His longcannon Venator was strapped to the back of his scarred armor, a cold serious stare in his eyes. The Guardians and Chaperones of the militia gave the Scourge heart-rip salute at the sight of their High Conservator. Warden Carthage just stood cross armed with a gallant grin on his face.

"Alexandarius," Jude spoke, his voice like a blade being unsheathed. "I'm pleased with your progress here. I'm glad to see that you were ready to..."

Bethel was cut off when Carthage grabbed the man in a hearty brotherly embrace. He squeezed hard enough for his plate to start belching black vapor as its impact pistons engaged. "Enough with the formalities Jude, you're a light in the dark if I've ever seen one!"

Alexandarius released the Shackle's prime from his grip and looked past him. There were four others. Two Inquisitors, a Herald, and a Bride, their addition would help weather this storm even further. The tall pale one had gauze wrapped around a stump on his arm where a hand should have been, but he was still wielding a pistol as though nothing were awry. At first he didn't recognize them, but after a second of thought Carthage recognized them all. He raided an Apotheosis warehouse in Jaspin with them, he advised them on a Dilictor hunt in Hrimata, ... Downey's task force. The grim realization of his friend's absence shunted away the warmth brought into his chest by the hope of salvation when he saw his friend was absent.

"Where's Volk?" He asked, feeling coldness wash over him.

"The Nephilim murdered him." Bethel responded with his typical curtness. There was no way to deliver this message kindly, so why waste time dampening the blow?

"Ram too?"

"The Nephilim was masquerading as Retriever Ram's Horn. It was a ploy to get close to Auzlanten and kill him before the start of the abolition."

"Demon filth masquerading as one of our own? Heresy! How long was this Imago filth walking in Ram's flesh?"

"I have no idea. Days, months, years, who can say?"

"We don't have time to speculate on the specifics." Inquisitor Covalos cut in. "The Nephilim aims to reap a specific number of innocents to fuel its throne, whatever that means."

"We've got to stop that from happening." Herald Du'Plasse said, shifting the grip on his battle banner. "Logically, the best thing to do is to preserve as much life as possible."

"What's your situation right now?" Daphne asked, her hand on the pommel of her rapier.

"Last report I got from Bastion Prime was that Jupiter has been compromised." Carthage replied, his mood even bitterer than before. "Blitzkrieg was en route to recapture the escaped convicts. We weren't expecting them to be outfitted with military ordinance so we were caught off guard. When we saw them mowing civilians down in flocks instead of pursuing anything of strategic value, I assumed this was the abolition I'd heard too much about. Ever since, I've been shepherding as many I can into the crypt. It's practically a bunker and there's only one entrance. Somewhere around two hundred inside right now and my militia is operating at about seventy-five percent. Two squads roaming the urban for more innocents and the other two standing guard."

"That's good work, Warden," Bethel said calmly. "Put us where you need us, you've got the helm on this operation until comms get back up."

Normally such an accolade would cause Alexandarius to perk up with pride at such an honor. There was no joy in his heart and his bleak, matter of fact demeanor showed that. As Bethel said that, the audio wire on his wrist chimed to life. The feed was muffled by static and Carthage couldn't determine if this was a result of the injury to his helmet or from something on the other end.

"Retri...Lonestar...Arc...traitor!" There was a wash of background noise, but Carthage could tell who it was. Retriever Daniel Lonestar, lieutenant of Bullet squad. The fact that he was within comms range meant he was at most a mile out.

"Lonestar, repeat last." Carthage barked back.

"Archon Gri...leading a mob..." The background noise became more distinguishable as the sound of screaming and gunfire. "Coming fo...cropolis get ready for..." The feed became nothing but a static haze. Carthage heard a fluid filled cough before the transmission went totally dead.

Archon Grim of Jupiter Arcae, that's who Lonestar was talking about. If the prisoners from Jupiter had escaped, the Archon shouldn't have lived to continue fighting let alone leading a mob. Carthage had to conclude that he was a traitor...and that he was coming.

"Bullet squad is down," Carthage said adding an extra layer of despair to an already miserable situation. "Gladius fall back on the mausoleum, Anchor prepare to brace against another assault." Alexandarius checked the bullets in his Kimlock and the charge on his Key then shifted his attention to S-6319. "Bethel, take up an oversight position on the roof, target the most imminent threats, the rest of you on me. We'll weather this storm yet."

Archon Grim, once Groom Bertrand Vivect, was among the first corrupted by Invictus Illuromos. Grim was in charge of the largest Arcae in Templym, in one of the most densely populated urbans, so he possessed a certain strategic advantage. One gaze at the Idolacreid and after seeing his heart's dark desires made manifest, his soul belonged to the Nephilim. He led a detachment of around eighty convicts, most of whom were former Scourge warriors who were not clever enough to avoid the primes' prowling, in a massacre of outlandish proportions.

The Lord General Illuromos, but more importantly the Nephilim, would be pleased with the slaughter they wrought in the streets of Parey. He had just pulled his crescent scythe from the back of an arbiter captain when they saw the bright blue armor of the Blitzkrieg squad, escorting a small band of civilians to the South. As they were gunned down with Zeduacs and carbines, Grim swore he heard the Retriever leading the band yell to the unarmed innocents to make for the Necropolis before his blood was harvested for the great throne.

He mused for a moment. Evangelon's Necropolis could be fashioned into a moderately defensible position. It was on their course towards Invictus. After a brief communion with his Imago tutor, who confirmed the presence of much blood to be taken, Grim commanded his band of cultists to make for the graveyard.

"I have a visual," Bethel yelled from atop the mausoleum. If the communicators were functioning properly he would have whispered. "Multiple contacts, unknown count, they're using the graves as cover."

"Ready for war, Blitzkrieg!" Carthage yelled as he charged up the Key, blue lightning sparking off of it. He turned to the task force, who were likewise readying for the coming fight. "The Nephilim killed our brother Volk. No mercy!"

Shots began ringing out. Venator was the first firearm to spit out a shot. An alkali-packed round buried into a cultist with a rocket lancer, turning the tattooed man's head into a red flower. From there, bullets began flying in a chaotic hail from both sides. A cloud of rubble from impacted marble and granite filled the air. Suits of armor and prison bodysuits ducked behind once pristine structures to hide from the blizzard of bullets.

Clumps of dirt were thrown up as grenades detonated. Shards of broken rock were turned into lethal shrapnel at the force of massive explosions. The loyalist Scourge force was encased in fine battle plate, equipped with higher grade weaponry and disciplined training. However, there was at least a four to one ratio, favoring the cultists. Strategy and strength would not prove to be as vital as endurance.

Blitzkrieg fired concentrated bursts at the wild prisoners, firing their limited ammunition conservatively. Brass casings fell in unison with bloodied corpses. In response, the Nephilim cultists sprayed their bullets wantonly with little aim. Their voracity could be sated only by blood and it mattered not whose was spilled.

Carthage fought as he always did, from the front with furious indignation. Even without a helmet or his strobe pauldrons, he was the most obvious threat on the battle field. After expending the last of his ammunition reserves, he charged into the flock of assailants. He had taken a handsaw from a cultist he pulverized and used it in tandem with his battering ram. Every swing of his arms saw one traitor felled to the ground as a broken skeleton wrapped in charred flesh or as a corpse void of blood and entrails. He killed with furious efficiency, never once relishing in a single life taken. He killed so that others might live.

Carthage didn't realize it at the time, but Jude Bethel saved his life a number of times. From atop the mausoleum he strategically eliminated foes with his longcannon, neutralizing several targets that were seconds away from taking the Warden's life. His sharpshooting had to be flawless. Venator's cybernetics could hardly compensate for the dozens of factors produced by this hectic combat, but he didn't need much technological assistance at this range.

S-6319 fought with as much zeal as they could muster. Adastra Covalos abhorred being forced to stay back, but with only one hand he could not wield his greataxe, so he opted for a Reisinger. It was remarkable he was still fighting at all. Oslin Du'Plasse kept his banner high as a rallying point. He brought the flag down only to use the spear tip end to bring another cultist to judgment. Vandross Blackwell kept his sword and pistol in hand, exercising his full expertise of the Natandro style. Daphne Wainwright kept her rapier drawn at all points, gracefully outmaneuvering every foe in her wake and painting her pearlescent battle plate red. Their combat prowess and dexterity was the quintessential display of Scourge militarization.

The combat showed no sign of dissipating nor was there any indication of either side gaining advantage over the other. For every soldier of Blitzkrieg that fell, nearly ten cultists met their end. Yet, for every fanatic killed there was, without fail, another two to take its place. Men and women of corrupt soul fought indiscriminately with the hopes of simply overwhelming their foes. Their bulging bloodshot eyes were filled with a gruesome cannibalistic hunger, inspired by the promises of their unholy lord.

They were closing in. Inch by inch, the cult pushed closer to the central mausoleum. If they made it inside, the civilians hiding in the crypts would be slaughtered. The Scourge was to act as the protector of the people, but primarily as the punisher of the wicked. They would kill the Nephilim's cult or die long before letting them through.

Carthage roared as the battle continued. His tech enhanced battle plate kept feeding adrenaline into his bloodstream to keep him dynamic. The Key and his commandeered handsaw met traitor skin with every swing. One of his famous "Urah" cries was cut off by a scream of pain.

Archon Grim had quietly skulked through broken tombs and shattered graves with the hopes of taking Carthage's blood for the Nephilim. Were it not for a last second twist of his body, Grim's scythe would have been buried inside of the Warden's head instead of his shoulder. The energized scythe glowed black and hissed as Alexandarius' blood boiled on contact with the crescent blade.

Bethel shot once at the traitor Archon, but he did not fall. This battle plate was on par with that of the primes. Its ebon sheen was accented with the dark violet of the Nephilm's cult. His head was capped in a helmet shaped like skull. A bullet landed at his center of mass, the ballistic fluid and impact springs absorbed the lethality of the blow but made him stagger backwards. The scythe lurched out with him as he stumbled back, shredding the tendons and collarbone and rendering Carthage's left arm useless.

Grim ordered a salvo of rocket and bullet fire at the top of the mausoleum. Bethel ducked behind thick stone cover, unable to line up another shot. He wouldn't be an effective sniper if he was dead. The Archon shifted his attention back to Warden Carthage. Alexandarius was already being escorted back to the cover of the main structure by Herald Du'Plasse, keeping the army at bay with wide arcs of his battle banner. Grim's voice gurgled mechanically through his toothy mouth grille in demonic tongue. Upon doing so, the cultists rushed after the two, recognizing that if the Cyan Bullet fell it would deal irreparable damage to their foe's morale.

Vandross Blackwell rushed to help, but struggled to cut through the cultists fast enough to keep pace with Archon Grim. Du'Plasse thrust his banner spear, aiming for sensitive unarmored joints. Grim side stepped and sliced his banner in two at the pole, leaving it as no more a weapon than a length of pipe. That didn't make it useless, but it certainly threw Oslin off balance, opening his body up for a deadly strike. Grim was but a moment away from bringing both of them to their bloody end. His scythe came down like a hooked guillotine blade but instead of digging into his target, it was redirected by Bride Wainwright's rapier.

Daphne landed two attacks that would have killed any unarmored man before Grim was able to respond to her attack. Her sword was designed to inject liquid argon into the body, which would be lethal if it could pierce the thick layer of flaksteel coating the traitor Archon's body. Instead, the blade only coated the thick plates with a thin layer of hoarfrost. Grim responded with absurdly powerful blows with his scythe. The weapon hissed past the Bride as she deftly dodged the massive hooked blade.

Grim could have overpowered Wainwright given enough time. The only advantage Daphne had over the Archon was in evasion, being far nimbler than the hulking man. She wouldn't be able to avoid or deflect every slash of the scythe. Adastra saw this. Using his handless arm as a prop to steady his Reisinger, he emptied the pistol when he saw an opening. Three rounds buried into his breastplate.

The impact made Grim stagger, but it would be mere seconds before he could recover and continue his assault on Wainwright. She had to act swiftly. Bethel's explosive round hit around the same area where Adastra's salvo landed. There was a miniscule rend in the main plate which wept ballistic fluid. This tiny flaw could be exploited.

With all her bodyweight, Daphne stabbed the end of her rapier into the crack. The blade stuck into the breastplate. Near absolute zero fluid rushed into the armor. The ballistic fluid beneath solidified instantly. The crystallized liquid expanded, breaking from its internal casing and destroying the armor's tech enhancements while simultaneously immobilizing the Archon. A pitiful grunt came out of Grim's skull helm and Bride Wainwright knew she had him. As he fell to his knees Daphne circled around his back. With one hand she pushed Grim's head forward, twisting his neck to reveal the undersuit beneath the Archon's battle plate. With the other, she brought her sword into his neck, severing his spinal cord and puncturing his throat. Archon Grim died instantly.

The cultists' assault began dissipating after seeing their leader fall. With no commander to rally them, they fell apart. Half of the remaining murderers fled while the others stayed, only to be mopped up by the warriors defending the Necropolis.

Bethel walked over to the edge of the mausoleum's room after reemerging from cover. He took inventory of the dead. About half of Carthage's militia was immobile on the ground, riddled with bloody wounds. Another third, including the Warden himself, were injured but still standing. There was no way to take stock of resources from this distance and with Alexandarius so crippled the rest of the squad would need a leader on the ground. So he made to climb down from the Necropolis' main structure and back to the ground.

He was not allowed.

When Bethel turned to walk down the staircase, there was a monstrosity standing behind him. It was a giant. Pallid flesh was pulled taut over swollen musculature and decorated with plates of spike and bone. Empty eye sockets were filled with balls of sickening green flame. Its mouth, curled into a devious smile, was filled with daggers. A pair of bony wings and curled horns like those of a ram defined this monster as an unholy Imago fiend.

Before Bethel had any moment to react or to consider how such a monster snuck up behind him and all of his teammates, the beast attacked. Bone claws the size and shape of meat hooks dug into Jude's breastplate, cutting through the flaksteel like paper. The force of the impact hurled the High Conservator from his feet and over the edge. Bethel plummeted three stories, tumbling down the marble stairs and to the feet of his team below.

The squadron gawked in terror at the sight. They were too frozen in terror to even check if Bethel was alive as they stared at the titan towering over them. The few remaining cultists stopped their onslaught, dropping their weapons while planting their faces into the ground. The spiked monstrous man lumbered over the edge. Its green fire eyes were filled with demented glee. He raised his clawed hands in an elaborate somatic motion as tongues of violet flame danced around his spiny body. After the giant finalized the unholy spell a column of nauseating light shot up like a geyser. The beam of hellish energy struck through the main structure of the Necropolis. The mausoleum imploded, huge chunks of stone collapsed in a boisterous rubble strewn dust storm. The structure was directly atop of the crypts where the civilians were hiding.

A thick white cloud swept over the Scourge. They stared horrified at the massacre so causally brought by the giant. The monster flew on gangly wings where the mausoleum once stood. The

Nephilim loyalists still drawing breath screamed and chanted with excitement at the sight of their lord. The giant raised a single bone clad fist in the air to signal their silence and spoke with a deep, eerily familiar voice. "All hail the Nephilim."

In 2159, the brink of the Age of Anarchy, affiliation with Mundus Imago cults was surprisingly common. Even worse so, the demonic fiends roamed the Earth, combing the wastelands for souls to prey on. The devils rallied cults demanding sacrifice of all manner of egregious debauchery. There was once an infernal creature that ruled a portion of the world in that time. Its name among its worshipers shifted throughout time and sect, Az'druat, Mephos'loze, Baal'zerub, but at this time it was known as Tumor'at.

Tumor'at demanded flesh sacrifices from its following. Not of the cannibalistic desires for flesh as most demons. Worse. Tumor'at demanded young, unblemished women that it may violate their flesh, quenching the most fulsome of sadistic desires. Its cult took this practice with the utmost reverence. So, when one of the Imago's victims conceived, they perceived it as a child of promise.

Six months later, the child tore its way out of the mother's womb. The wild infant clawed and chewed through the mother's flesh, devouring her from the inside out. Tumor'at's cult sang songs of praise at the sight of the son of promise which they called Bar-Tumor'at. In truth, it was unclear if their lord cared, or was even aware of what it had fathered.

The cult taught Bar-Tumor'at, educating him in the ways of dark magick and Imago communion. He learned faster and of higher complexities than most mature adults. It developed physically within a much narrower time frame, reaching peak bodily function at age five and staying there for years to come. It was a greater intelligence, more attuned to the dark spirits they idolized, a more talented practitioner of black magick, and a far greater athletic spectacle than any other man living at the time. Bar-Tumor'at was not satisfied with being the student of a cult. He wanted more. He craved power.

Bar-Tumor'at began demanding worship. Wielding a potent blend of sorcery and witchcraft, he killed all who opposed him. He asserted himself as a divinity, annexing dozens of other marauders into his following. When he had a sufficient number of servants to make great power strides throughout the wastelands, he decided to redefine himself. His studies and communions revealed new information to him and he decided to solidify his standing. He learned what he was and demanded to be addressed properly. At the time they called him Thamortalis but in modern temple-tongue he would be called the Nephilim.

The Nephilim ruled as an attempted tyrant until 2174. Its short reign was lost to history as just another marauder conflict among the hundreds during the chaotic era. Why did his violent expansion halt? If the Nephilim had continued its rise as a false god, it could have dominated a large swath of land and competed for expansion among the dictators of the Tyrranis Period. It knew of what was coming, it knew of the imminent Reclaiming Crusade.

Through dark divination with a score of different patrons, the Nephilim foresaw the coming of Arodi Auzlanten three hundred years before his arrival in Carthonia. It was aware of its own inability to stand against him successfully. If the Nephilim established itself as a god amongst men, it would be obliterated just like the other tyrants.

So it hid. That thirsting desire for power could not be sated with anything less than an entire continent beneath its foot. Knowing through supernaturally acquired information that Auzlanten would destroy everything it built, it began pursuing immortality. It could live for eons by cleaving the tie between soul and body. The bond of the physical and immaterial aspects of the Nephilim's body was ended, allowing its spirit to roam the Earth from body to body.

Over the next hundreds of years, it planned its uprising. It needed ordinance. So it made one. Through a number of pacts with Class A+ Imago and craftsmanship using exotic materials, it made its throne. Throne was a formal title, more accurately it was a war engine. A vehicle nearly a quarter mile in distance, inlaid with magickal artifacts, and lances of overwhelming might. This throne could easily topple a Gigarobus Hekaton with its firepower. But the engine needed a power source.

So the Nephilim plotted, scouring its dark nether of informants for an answer. Acquiring the knowledge of the battery kept within Auzlanten's sanctum took as much time as construction of the throne. The plot continually grew more elaborate as it concocted a devious scheme to infiltrate its adversary's lair and harvest an ocean of blood to power its throne.

He saw it all. He saw the Nephilim transferring its spirit from body to body. The most recent of which was that of a marauder who sacrificed his entire tribe simply to gain his patron's attention. That marauder was Ram's Horn and the Nephilim hollowed out his body and used it as the vessel to infiltrate the Scourge. That was not all he saw. He saw how the Nephilim nurtured its following into fruition. He saw the scores of fanatics brought into its following, everyone from the lowliest madman to the IX Regent Invictus Illuromos. He saw the hybrid's authorship of the heretical tome, the...

Auzlanten slammed his hands together. His pupils were dilated, his breath a cold mist, and legs trembling. He struggled to stay propped up in his oaken seat. His assistant stood at a distance, eyes wide with terrified concern, but forbidden to walk closer. Arodi was suffering internally, his very soul assaulted by unholy secrets, but a thin smile appeared beneath his beard. The Idolacreid told him exactly what he wanted to know.

CHAPTER 46

Templym continued to be ravaged by the Nephilim and its cult. Civilians died in droves as slobbering fanatics mowed down innocents with bloody rapaciousness. The throne's power source was welling up. With every citizen slain, a single drop of blood spawned in the bowl shaped fuel cell. The unnatural contraption was already halfway filled and only four of the twenty-four hours had passed.

The Scourge fought back in a desperate effort to quell this uprising, but it was an exhausted effort. The Regent's sabotage had practically left the entire military blind and deaf, leaving naught but small factions to fight the unnaturally coordinated cult army. Tiny groupings fell, but they fell with dull blades and empty guns. Thousands of names in and outside of the organization would be listed among the dead, that much was obvious. But would it be the million that the Nephilim required?

The geyser of unnatural energies was hot enough to vaporize stone and powerful enough to quake the very Earth. It was like one of the mythical satellite lasers from the Cybernetic Revolution and just as devastating as the epics detailing them. The Nephilim unleashed an assault so overpowering, yet so instantaneous. The civilians inside were dead. The Nephilim had casually lulled in the air, its tusked mouth twisted into a devious grin, its engorged frame sprawled out in an ignoble display. S-6319 was too mortified to tear their gaze from what would surely be their demise.

The giant began laughing as it lowered its bulk to the ground. The sound was a sickening mash of deviant maniacal cackling and the shrill screams of dying children. The ominous tone was broken by a wet, pained-filled cough coming from below. Jude Bethel survived his massive fall, but was crippled by this massive mutant.

"You are a tough bastard, Jude," The giant said as its feet touched the rubble dusted ground. "I could have sworn I dug into your chest."

Bethel coughed and flecks of blood spurted out of his helmet's mouth grille. "You missed." He grunted painfully, making no effort to get off his back.

The Nephilim's wicked smile, melted away into a pinched rage. "Ever the gall, I suppose that's why the great warlock chose you to rally his peons. Pathetic."

"You're dead," Du'Plasse stammered at the sight of the giant.

"If you are referencing Knox Mortis, yes he is dead. I have taken his body as my latest vessel. A suitable host for the amount of blood I must reap." The Imago hybrid's fanatics hollered in celebration as it boasted loudly to the crowd.

Those unholy, flaming eyes leered over the Scourge soldiers and the twisted grin returned. "Come friends," the monster said coyly. "Are you not pleased to see your old friend Ram's Horn?"

"Shut your bloody trap!" Inquisitor Blackwell barked, disinterested in hearing any more taunting. "We all know you've a time limit to kill as much as possible. Quit toying with us and just end it already!"

"That is correct, but you clearly underestimate the efficiency of my faithful. We are operating with far greater capacity you could possibly conceive. I have ample time to drink in my victory... to play with my food."

A shot rang out in the air. Vandross fired the final shot chambered in his Reisinger. The wardiron bullet dug into the Nephilim's chest. The wound seeped a dribble of liquid fire before sealing over. The typically quick witted Inquisitor was caught speechless for the ineffectiveness of shot. The goliath did not even seem to notice the injury.

"I will remember you lot fondly as Templym is ground beneath the iron treads of my throne. Perhaps, I will decorate it with your bloodied corpses after I skewer you on a collection of pikes. After all, you came so close to ruining everything. Auzlanten was supposed to be dead by now, but I am pleased he has done nothing to significantly abate the abolition."

"Invictus Illuromos is dead," Bride Wainwright said in retort, praying that Arodi Auzlanten had succeeded in his mission. "The loss of one of your most senior generals hardly seems negligible."

The Nephilim gave another demented chuckle in response. "Yes the Regent was a valuable asset, but he served his purpose. Perhaps if Auzlanten had taken his life weeks ago it would have made more of an impact. He didn't." The Nephilim tapped its bony claws together in devious glee. "Enough chatter. I aim to enjoy this moment by giving each and every one of you an excruciating end. I'll start with you, Du'Plasse, since you saw through my cover. I think I'll skin you and turn your tanned hide into a pair of boots as a reminder that I came out on top."

There seemed to be no hope. To one side a band of remaining cultists freshly rallied by their immortal lord on the other. Escape was not an option. Death was inevitable. There was only one reasonable thing to do. As the Nephilim began prowling closer to the Scourge warriors, they shut their eyes and prayed.

The Lord answered.

The sky began illuminating. Where a fog of rubble and smog laid over Evangelon's Necropolis like a blanket, the dreariness of the graveyard seemed to be lifted. Motes of light began piercing through the veil of vapor, casting the bleakness away. The Nephilim and its cultists gazed quizzically into the air, confused as to how or why this shift in the atmosphere was taking place. The Nephilim quite enjoyed the ominous feel and was irritated that something had sullied it. The truth was much more devastating.

The glowing motes began slicing through the air. Arrows composed of pure starlight barreled through the fog. The light javelins began sticking into the Nephilim cultists, stabbing through them with the force of a longcannon shell. The Nephilim itself was stuck with a number of the spears, but it pulled them out as if they were nothing but sewing needles. The Scourge was completely untouched by the divine fusillade.

The Nephilim's destruction of the Necropolis opened a gap in the fog that opened up to the sky. It was early afternoon still, not a cloud in sight, but there were stars. Impossible stars danced through the stratosphere faster than aerial chariots. It was as though a meteor shower was entering the Earth, creating an astrological wonder. This storm was nothing natural. The Nephilim measured up the paths of the stars. They were spreading over all of Templym, each at supersonic velocities, and they were targeting its following. "What breed of magick could produce such catastrophe?", the monster thought to itself...but not for long.

"Arodi," the Nephilim hissed, his throat full of bile and hatred. Its body fizzled into a cloud of green and violet fire, which swirled away into the sky like a flaming twister. The giant left Evangelon's Necropolis, speeding away like a cancerous meteor among the swarm of white stars. With that, the monster vanished.

The storm of light lances subsided in the graveyard, leaving still bodies all around. However, the shooting stars were still darting in the sky. Nobody moved until after an awkward pause when Inquisitor Covalos spoke. "What just happened?"

Arodi Auzlanten stood in the Sinai Peninsula, using his gift from God with miraculous efficiency. The icosahedron diamond channeled angelic might which blanketed over the world. The Master of Templym crafted javelins of celestial energy which were refracted by the gemstone. Arodi's hands and eyes glistened like an active furnace as he channeled his might into the diamond floating before him. His fingers danced over the space above the artifact as though he were conducting a symphony of seraphic heraldry.

He could see them all. Through his study of the contraption, he realized that it could be used to target any number of individuals. Through isolated divination, he could see everyone carrying the Nephilim's taint. Careful study of the cult leaders' auras, especially those of Mortis and Illuromos, created a clear picture. It was as if the gemstone operated as an infrared radar in which each Nephilim cultist was a bright spark on a black canvas. It could also duplicate a single missile into a blizzard of projectiles that sought out their target across vast distances. With the Lord's blessing, Auzlanten was conducting the end of the abolition.

The Sinai Peninsula was a strategic location. It was as close to the center of Templym as possible, allowing an even distribution of arrows for the optimum rate of attack. There was also a sacred, almost poetic aspect to this setting. This was the desert where Moses led the Exodus, a prophet escorting his people to salvation. It seemed appropriate. There was also a necessary confrontational thematic. Hebrew society taught that the desert is where dark spirits dwelt. Christ Himself confronted the Adversary when isolated in such a place. This was the best place to confront the Nephilim.

The Imago hybrid was clever. Its admittedly brilliant machination was coming dangerously close to destroying Templym. It was clever enough to follow the traceries of star spears to their origin point. It would be only a few minutes after beginning his cleanse of his society before the Nephilim would come for him. It was the only logical step lest it risk its cult being obliterated and halting the harvest. Arodi gave the Nephilim this ultimatum with the assurance that it would come for him.

Auzlanten conducted his symphony of destruction for twenty minutes, during which time he had killed over a thousand cultists. The artifact itself was a nebulous explosion of brilliant energy spears that stretched miles into the sky before spreading out and enveloping the entire world. The radiant white light reflected off of the white gold pattern sewn into his cerulean robes and his platinum half crown. His black braids whipped with the twists of his body as he summoned the death of the Nephilim's cult. Then their lord appeared.

A column of fire, which was nauseating to even look at, struck into the dust flat. The Nephilim emerged from the flame, warranting Auzlanten to still his hands and the light dimmed from his eyes. He instantly recognized the body of Knox Mortis, but with an entirely different entity walking around inside of it. Thick ridges of bone formed crescents around its pallid flesh creating multiple jagged weapons composed of gnarled organic matter. Arodi could see bits of flesh and blood decorating it. He could distinguish the skin tones of dozens of different humans who had fallen before him. The energy surging through his body quelled as he readied to confront his foe, but the gemstone remained suspended where he left it.

The Nephilim glared at the Master of Templym as he gripped onto Leagna's hilt. Its head and shoulders limbered its stolen body into a fighting stance. Where Auzlanten was clean, well kept, and calm, the Nephilim was slobbering, covered in the filth of battle, and seething with vehemence.

"Ever the splinter in my side, Auzlanten." Its voice was guttural yet raspy, as though it was gargling nails. Blood and sludge dripped from its tusks where Mortis' glass teeth once were.

"You seem surprised, Nephilim," Auzlanten spoke defiantly as he began pacing around the gem in a circular pattern. In stalking fashion, the giant mimicked his motion and leveled pace with him. "I'm disappointed. I would have expected an intellect as great as yours to have accounted for resistance."

"I did. You should have been dead before the abolition even began."

"You'll find that things rarely occur as we anticipate." Auzlanten chuckled dryly. The Nephilim cocked its horned head in confusion. "You still think I am a fool, don't you?"

"There are a plethora of slurs that apply to you, worm, but I'll admit that fool isn't one."

"Then you continue to underestimate me, your continual downfall." Auzlanten stopped in his tracks, turning to stare down the giant. "Why haven't you attacked me yet?"

Green fire drenched its gangly talons. The Nephilim growled like a starving predator, but it did not pounce. A half-smile appeared on Arodi's lips. He continued his speech. "Knox Mortis was driven by an insatiable bloodlust and a greed for power. He would have charged alone into an army if he thought he could win. Invictus, his flaw was his vitriol. His personal vendetta against me blinded him to the impossibility of victory. You. You are much smarter than they."

"I am aware of this." The Nephilim said boastfully.

Auzlanten ignored it. "When you tried to kill me, you used subterfuge and infiltration to catch me off guard. Upon failing, you accelerated your plans. You knew that you could never best me in single combat. Even now, you didn't come to kill me but to stall me long enough that your wicked harvest might have a sliver of a chance of succeeding. I will kill you...and you fear this."

"I am immortal!" The Nephilim retorted without actually rebutting Auzlanten's theory. It was roaring at this point, riled by the accusation before it. "Death has no hold over me. If you break this body I will move on to the next and the one after that! No wait is too long. No plan is too tedious if the end is everything you love dead by my hand!"

Auzlanten's eyes shifted down towards the Nephilim's clawed feet. It was a brief glance, but it was telling. When the Nephilim saw this quick change in its foe's gaze it came to a horrid realization. It had fallen into a trap.

The Nephilim had hoped to rocket into the sky on its wings, but it couldn't react fast enough. A ring of blue fire had spawned around it. The fire itself was cold, unnaturally sucking all heat out of the desert air. Runes were emblazoned into the sand, magick runes. The Nephilim could feel its spirit being shackled by dark energies, as though frozen chains were wrapping around its very soul. Then the fire snapped away as quickly as it was created, but the loathsome feeling of the strangling sensation of Auzlanten's soul snare remained.

The Nephilim gasped as it immediately realized what had happened. It had spent decades perfecting its immortality using only the keenest of spells. Auzlanten had just undone it, trapping its once mobile soul into the body it now occupied. Arodi could not have possibly done so without knowing the exact specifications of the magick rituals used to enable its fail-safe. There was only one way he could have done so this quickly.

"You read the Idolacreid." The Nephilim stammered, baffled by the revelation.

"Once again, Bar-Tumor'at," Arodi said with confidence, "You underestimate the lengths I will go to preserve all that is holy. If I must sully my own hands by using your own blasphemous tome against you, so be it."

There would be no hesitation. No rationing of power. The Nephilim had to die here and now. Arodi Auzlanten attacked. A cascade of blinding energy, like that of a quasar, shot from his finger tips. The flood of energy smashed into the pallid giant's chest.

The Nephilim was pushed back, but held fast. It had to flee, which it knew was futile, or to fight. It retaliated. The beast spread its razor sharp wings and took flight, spinning around the beam as it charged. Two scythe bones came down onto Auzlanten, but Leagna flew into his hand and deflected the blow. Sparks flew off of the red glowing blade.

The Nephilim couldn't use conventional combat tactics. Riding its own inertia, the Nephilim hooked its talons beneath the hem of Arodi's robe, scooping him off his feet before slamming him into the ground. Sand and dust was kicked up in the impact, but Auzlanten came up along with it. Rebounding from the attack, he darted up the length of the Nephilim's spiked arm. He stabbed his sabre once into its shoulder and then propelled himself off its bulk.

Arodi slashed his sword sideways as he flew mid-air. A slash in reality spawned a dozen light javelins that barreled at the Nephilim. The giant brought its arms up to block the salvo, just as Auzlanten wanted. With its meaty arms over its face, the Nephilim couldn't see the column of stone shooting up beneath its feet. A stalactite of sandstone smashed into its jaw, cracking its ivory teeth.

The Nephilim countered with magick. A screeching explosion of overwhelming noise shot out of its hooked fingers. The sonic boom swallowed Auzlanten and his body absorbed a large portion of the assault. He was brought to one knee after the explosion of screams. He was receiving visions of his children being torn to shreds by hell hounds. He ignored the thoughts as best he could, the pain, the unholy forces clawing at his soul. The Nephilim would serve as a beacon on which his wrath would be focused.

Auzlanten stomped his boot into the sand, kicking up a fog of thick gas. This was the same venom that he used when he toppled the UNACs centuries ago. It was a thick soupy texture, impossible to see through, and it would prove poison to the Nephilim. As the cloud drifted over it, its lungs cried out in pain, but it ignored the acrid sting. The giant stormed through the cloud, dispersing the gas with rapid motion of its bony wings. Arodi's hope of using the selective poison as cover was thwarted as the Nephilim attacked.

The giant melted down the sand surrounding them. The molten glass was then snaked through the air and lashed out at Auzlanten. They were tentacles of molten silica that burned ugly yellow, snapping at Arodi as if sentient. With one hand he parried away the molten glass, with the other he froze the liquid tentacles into bulbous solid masses. The Nephilim used this opportunity to skulk around with the hope of flanking him. A potentially lethal blow from its claws was blocked when Auzlanten sloshed a gobbet of the liquid glass onto its hand.

The swarm of fluid ceased and the remaining tendrils solidified into brittle pillars. The mass on the Nephilm's hand cooled, coating its claws in a sheet of ugly black crystal. Auzlanten saw a brief opening in its defenses, a brief window where Leagna could pierce the giant's heart. He leapt through the air, sword arm out, barreling towards the giant's exposed chest. But he miscalculated the Nephilim's reflexes. It side swiped Arodi out of the air, shattering its solid glass fist against him. Auzlanten skidded across the desert like a stone across a pond.

He flipped over onto his feet to begin the next attack, but the Nephilim was on him before he could recuperate. It had seized the diamond Arodi was earlier using to smite its cult. Now the giant wielded the artifact as a much cruder weapon. Auzlanten's face absorbed blow after blow from the gem. Arodi struggled to break the grapple as talons dug into his skin and the crystal slammed into his skull. Auzlanten decided not to escape, but to take advantage of the Nephilim's misguided confidence.

Through the splitting pain, Arodi mustered his power. Channeling his celestial power into the artifact, he created a devastating torrent out of the crystal. It was just like his attack on the international scale, but concentrated onto a single target. A bright column of deadly light burst out, piercing the Nephilim's stolen flesh with hundreds of lances. This flung the beast back into the sky, punctured with an overabundance of projectiles.

The Nephilim plummeted to the ground like a bird riddled with buckshot, but its unholy body began knitting itself back together. Boiling blood dripped from the wounds before suturing over. Auzlanten had noted its healing ability. It was slowing.

Auzlanten pressed on even more rigorously. He swung Leagna in furious upwards arcs, spawning a massive blast of force each time. The cascading energy tore the ground asunder as the columns charged at the fallen Nephilim. It took flight, weaving between the geysers with more agility than possible for an organism of such bulk. It weaved deftly through the air, darting past the erupting masses as it tore through the air towards Auzlanten.

The Nephilim's magick charged through its arms, spilling out of its excess of bone blades in the form of nauseating green energy. It swung the full length of its swollen arms in furious *nightmare strikes* and *hammer fists,* Steel Skin tactics gleaned from the mind of Ram's Horn. Arodi's feet buckled beneath him as he struggled to block the massive force from each terribly lethal assault. The two traded blows with lightning speed and raw fury. Leagna and the magickally charged hooks attacked so rapidly, so cacophonously, that the very atmosphere shuttered as if pained by their furious interchange.

Auzlanten's face began to twist into a mask of anger. His stone visage collapsed as he let his choler rise. Normally Arodi shut out such primal feelings, believing that such emotions dampened the objective judgment needed to efficiently execute his swordsmanship or wield his celestial might. Now was a unique occasion. There were benefits to allowing rage into his mind: a certain drive to disallow loss, excess power behind his attacks, heightened focus on a singular target. Or perhaps that was just what he told himself. In reality, Arodi Auzlanten had become exceedingly enraged at the Nephilim for everything it had done. Perhaps this was a self deception to excuse the allowance of such a flood of human emotion.

His sabre struck at the Nephilim with a preternatural power of its own. The crimson sheen of the blade matched the lividity inside of Auzlanten. Sparks flew off the edges of the Nephilim's arms as they met Leagna. As his temper rose, bits of bone began chipping off the sparking weapons as each swing was filled with more and more hatred. He attempted a feint maneuver to open up the giant's defenses to stick the length of the sabre into its neck. It was a bold tactic that would leave him exposed for a brief moment, but it would be worth the risk if a killing blow was landed.

Arodi Auzlanten side stepped and spun as if going one way before ducking down and going in for the final blow. His rage had clouded his judgment. The Nephilim was quick enough to react to the intentional opening. A hook talon slashed across Arodi's face, knocking him off balance and killing his momentum. As he winced back in pain, the Nephilim stuck a shoulder spike into his back.

The giant took full advantage of its success. It brought a knee onto his chest, pinning Auzlanten into the sand with its full weight. Talons swarmed his torso and neck. Mats of black hair were ripped from his head and inexorably resilient skin began tearing. Arodi frantically grabbed for his sword, but it was nowhere to be found. A guttural laugh came from the tusk filled maw of the Nephilim after dealing enough damage to kill a hundred men.

"Never best you, will I?" The giant laughed pridefully. Arodi's hands clutched at the weight on his chest to relieve the massive pressure. Its fire eyes stared longingly at its prey. "Die with the knowledge that God has abandoned you."

The Nephilim took Auzlanten's head in one of its bulky hands and his torso in the other. Spines pierced his flesh and dug into his body as his fingers tightened. It was killing him in a multiplicity of ways. Arodi's skeleton was being crushed by immense pressure. His organs were being ruptured with bony spines. His spine was being twisted and cracked. The Nephilim was sucking out the oxygen out of his blood while injecting virulent poison in its place. Magick energy surged through his nerves destroying neurotransmitters and blocking brainwaves.

But he refused to die. Arodi Auzlanten's body fought back against the debilitating injuries as expeditiously as they were dealt to him. Celestial power surged through his body, undoing all the harm that the Nephilim was doing to him. The Master of Templym did not, could not die here in the Sinai desert. There was a place for martyrs and their sacrifices, but this was not such a place and Auzlanten was not a martyr. God chose him to deliver the world from the clutches of the Mundus Imago. The responsibility of delivering Templym from massacres such as the Nephilim's heretical rebellion fell to him. Arodi could not give up and die.

As the Nephilim continued to strangle the life out of Auzlanten, he was continuing to work against the giant. He shared a special connection with his sabre Leagna. The Nephilim had kicked the sword away before pinning him to the ground. He called it.

The sabre shot out through the air like a rocket from its lance. The blade spun into the air before landing tip first into the base of the Nephilim's neck. It spasmed as its spinal cord was cut and it clutched at its back, dropping Auzlanten from its coiling grip. The giant fell to its knees as desperately trying to wrench the sword out. Arodi leapt over the Nephilim's head. He grabbed the hilt of his sword and yanked it down the full length of its back. Leagna ran down every one of its spiked vertebrae, spewing thick gore out of the stolen body.

Its eyes widened in terror at the injury, primarily in pain, but mostly in terror. The Nephilm's magickal healing was thoroughly spent. Auzlanten saw this too as he ripped his sabre from the monstrous giant's back. He didn't allow for any break in its punishment. Just like when he killed Mortis the first time, Arodi summoned a spike of stone from the ground at its feet. The stalactite dug into the pallid meat of the Nephilim's chest. Auzlanten leapt around to stand on the spike, but instead of decapitating this body once again, he shot the rock into the ground. Now it was pinned to the sand and Arodi Auzlanten was on top.

The Nephilim, in its last desperate attempt to survive, swung up its broken hand to gore Arodi's neck with its talons. In response, Auzlanten stabbed his sword through the hand and pinned that to the ground, fusing the sand into glass with the heat of the impact. Arodi Auzlanten was now free to vent the rage that had been building up over the past three months. He grabbed one curled horn with one hand and pulled its massive head in close. With the other, Arodi beat the head until it was little more than a mask of pulped bone and bruised skin.

Auzlanten's own visage was wildly irate. He too had suffered a great deal of punishment and that only furthered the boiling fury in his heart. This was an unkempt coalescence of the Master of Templym and untamed ire. He didn't care. He had earned the right to vent his frustrations.

Auzlanten didn't want to inflict any actual pain onto the Nephilim. There wasn't any true methodology behind his assault. Arodi could kill it and be done with the whole abolition at this point. He had won...but he craved vindication.

Arodi continued to beat the Nephilim's head until every last razor tooth and curled horn was naught but chips of bone. Auzlanten stared down at the Nephilim and the monster gave a toothless grin when it saw that its adversary's cheeks were wet with tears.

"Invictus Illuromos was my son," Auzlanten growled. "He was one of the most loyal, most disciplined, and most accomplished children I ever fostered. Never have I had a child fall so far from Grace as him. How?" Arodi grabbed the one in tact horn and pulled the Nephilim's head close. He whispered, "How did you corrupt him? What lie did you fabricate? What promise was powerful enough to seduce Invictus to a life of sin?"

The Nephilim sputtered a cough full of blood and teeth. It was unclear if the noise was a pained moan or a pathetic attempt at laughter. "What makes you think I lied?" It managed to say with a surprising level of eloquence given the level of punishment it had endured.

"In Nomine Veritas, vermin. The Scourge upholds truth above all else. So I ask again, what fabrication did you feed into the mind of my son that would cause him to turn his back from that notion?"

"I confess Arodi, I told a number of lies to bolster my following, but Invictus joined me on a truth."

"Why would I ever believe that?"

"Because you know of the truth I speak, warlock...I told him what you are."

Auzlanten froze and dropped the Nephilim's head. This hybrid had a formidable intelligence, but could it possibly know such a secret? Arodi Auzlanten was a mythic figure shrouded in mystery, just as he wanted to be. His exact origin was so intimately secluded that he was certain only the Lord and His angels were aware of them. How could this beast have possibly known?

That same gurgling noise, now obviously laughter, gargled out of the Nephilim's throat. "Even though my abolition is thwarted and today is the day I embrace the Pit, I can safely say it was all worth it. Nothing I have experienced in my centuries of existence has ever been as sweet as the sight of you sniveling in terror. I shall eagerly await your arrival in Hell."

Auzlanten refused to hear any more. Leagna flew into Arodi's hand. He stabbed the sabre through the Nephilim's skull, burying sword so deep the hilt stopped at its bloody forehead. What nerves still functioned in its stolen body twitched and lurched one final time as its brain was severed. He finished by beating his hand against the pommel of the sabre, sending a surge of energy directly through the blade. In a flash of blinding white energy, the giant's already desecrated head detonated into a smear of black soot.

It was done. The Nephilim was dead and its spirit cast to Judgment. Never again would the disgusting creature steal a body and extend its life on this Earth. Never again would it found a cult or plot a global uprising. Its magick engine of war would never be used and Templym would remain intact.

The victory was not enough to calm Arodi Auzlanten. The questions still haunted him. Did it really know? If it knew, then how? Were there others that knew his secret? Was this really the knowledge fed into his son that caused him to fall and betray?

Auzlanten shunted the irksome thoughts from his mind. There would be time enough to mull on this information later. There was still a job to do. He turned on his heel and walked back towards the artifact. Leagna dug itself out of the ground and soared back into Arodi's hand where he returned it to its scabbard. He shut his eyes, let out a deep sigh, and continued to conduct his symphony of light.

CHAPTER 47

The death of the Nephilim devastated its cult. The warlocks devoted to the abolition were instantly cut off from their source of magick and rendered useless. They were defenseless to Auzlanten's international assault. The sight was spectacular. Such displays were historical turning points written about in ancient epics.

For the next three hours, light arrows blanketed the Earth targeting the shattered remnants of the abolition. The fanatics that weaseled away from the miraculous swarm were mopped up by the Scourge. Even if cultists were able to take cover from the javelin barrage, these missiles would act as beacons which exposed them in their hiding holes. The Nephilim spent decades assembling its following, the abolition lasted about nine hours, and the founder was killed in fifteen minutes.

The dead were beyond the count of grief. One hundred-two different colonies and urbans fell prey to the abolition and an unrecorded number of marauder tribes were decimated. The bullets, shrapnel, and weapons discarded in every street would continue being swept up for years to come. Blood tainted several water supplies and required enhanced filtration, though the more densely populated cities carried a disturbing metallic tang from its taps. The Scourge's tasks for the next several days were to properly dispose of the mountain of corpses. It was an austere and disparaging job, but far preferable to prolonging the war that was just wrought.

The citizens of Templym needed to be addressed. Word of the Idolacreid and the Nephilim had been kept Upsilon classified, so the general public was largely unaware of anything before the abolition.

A conference was held Verrick 28th, three days after the abolition. A public hearing was organized at the front gates of Bastion Prime. Journalists and broadcasters gathered at the granite and steel dais that served as the Scourge's announcement platform. It was the same stage where the IX Regent's treachery was discovered back in Nyvett when he was supposed to announce his resignation.

Magistrate Averrin Walthune and newly reinstated High Conservator Jude Bethel flanked the black podium awaiting the speaker. Walthune had led the counterstrike against the Hekaton assault in Ahldorain. His white beard was disheveled and his eyes were bloodshot from lack of sleep. Bethel sustained heavy skeletal damage when the Nephilim tossed him off the top of the mausoleum in Evangelon's Necropolis. Until today, he had been on a regiment of bed rest and bone growth supplements. The support mechanisms of his battle plate were keeping him standing.

The journalists muttered nervously among themselves. They already anticipated a somber announcement, but they were expecting it from the Regent. Little had been officially confirmed, but rumors of his death had been circulating over the past few days. When the Centurion guard were absent from the stage, the sickening truth became obvious.

Arodi Auzlanten took the stage. He stepped out from behind the tungsten walls of the Scourge capitol fortress. His jeweled hands were crossed behind his back, his azure robes rippling in a gentle breeze. This was not a sight the citizens of Templym were accustomed to. The Regent was the liaison between the Master and his constituents and as such only the direst of circumstances warranted his presence. Every broadcaster held their breath as Auzlanten took position behind the podium.

Arodi sighed deeply. He did not want to reveal this painful truth to the citizens of Templym, but it was necessary to do so. Rumors and misinformation would fester like a cancer. The truth had to be revealed, no matter how intolerable it proved to be.

Auzlanten did not introduce himself. His considerable reputation was matched with his unchanging presence. He spoke to the crowd without technological aid, speaking as resonantly as if he were wired to a sound system.

"Verrick 25th, 2722, much like Huron 18th, is a day that will live in infamy for the remainder of Templym's life. Three days ago, our fair nation was violently and mercilessly assaulted by dark forces of the Adversary. A beast called the Nephilim executed a deliberately ingrained plot with the intent of murdering as many innocents as possible. Through the Grace of God and the dedication of the Scourge, the Imago fiend was thwarted."

Arodi ran a hand through his mane. He desperately loathed what was to come next. "Several urbans and settlements came under attack, which will henceforth be known as the Nephilim's Abolition. Chief among them were Parey, Rushmore, Jerusalem, and Venice Primus, the most heavily populated cities in Templym. We grieve for the dead, all five hundred thousand, most of whom were noncombatants. No doubt rumors have spread of who lie among them. I regret to inform you that several chief Scourge operatives were lost. Patriarch Arodus Betankur and Prelate Terran Greyflame were both assassinated before the outbreak of this grievous assault. Foremost in the Scourge was the life of the IX Regent. Invictus Illuromos was also killed."

Several gasps broke out among the hundreds of reporters. This shock was the reaction that Auzlanten anticipated. This was not the news he dreaded sharing. "The Nephilim infiltrated our ranks, planting spies and saboteurs to undermine our military operations to better further its hellish agenda. Chief among the traitors...was Invictus Illuromos." He paused once more to allow the terror to ripple through the crowd. "Without his subterfuge, the Nephilim's Abolition would not have claimed so many innocent lives."

Auzlanten saw so much pain in the crowd, nearly as much turmoil he saw when the initial news broke. The idea of the Regent betraying the doctrine of the Faith and of Templym was appalling. This was still not the news that nauseated him to his core.

"The treachery of the Scourge's general is unfathomable. This betrayal was so unthinkable that not even I comprehended it." The Magistrate and the High Conservator did not flinch until that point. The news that even Auzlanten himself had doubts made them shake their heads in surprise. "In the days leading up to this attack, I received divine revelation. I was told to execute the Regent months before and I refused."

No gasps of terror, no pained weeping came from the crowd. Silence. There was nothing but eerie silence and wide eyed stares at the Master of Templym. Many thought Auzlanten infallible, this had proven them wrong. In truth the silence was more distressing than if it were screaming and booing. "I confess my sin to you, the people of Templym, for two reasons. Firstly, it is to keep myself accountable. While I am ashamed of my mistake, it is more vital that I do not falter in this way again. If my name is to be dragged through the mud because of my lapse in judgment, so be it. I am your leader and I must be put in check. My transparency is more important to me than my popularity. 'For all have sinned and fall short of the grace of God', Romans 3:23."

Only the sounds of cameras click-capturing images and the reels of tidecasters were audible in the crowd. He continued. "The second reason is to open myself up to you, to make myself vulnerable. Too often, I am deified. There are sects who claim that I am the Messiah, regardless of my consistent denials. Your hope should not be placed solely upon me. Your hope should be place in Christ above, not to mankind below."

Such a priestly acclaim would normally be met with cheers and praises. Though often it would be at the echoing of someone like the Prelate, Terran was gone. "I do not know for certain what difference I could have made. I do not know how many lives were lost at the Nephilim's Abolition because of the extra time Invictus Illuromos was granted. Take my failure to heart and look to my example that you should heed the Lord's commandments and execute them to the best of your ability. I hope you can find it in your hearts to forgive me."

A collection of half-hearted claps started breaking out through the crowd. Small patches of individuals began cheering. It was a step in the right direction, but not the ovation he had hoped to gain. He ignored the apathy and moved on. "This is a time of mourning. We cannot split into factions and begin arguing amongst ourselves. We must unite to comfort the orphans and widows, to reconstruct our cities, to bolster our defenses against the next assault by the wretched Mundus Imago."

Auzlanten tucked his hands behind his back again and began moving across the stage. "I have made my failure known, but where I failed the Scourge has succeeded. Before deliverance came, the brave men and women of the Scourge kept the Nephilim and its cult at bay. Through military genius and masterful discipline, your bulwark against evil ensured that the Abolition was ultimately a failure."

Arodi walked over to Magistrate Walthune and placed a hand on his golden pauldron. "Averrin Walthune fought a traitor battalion of Hekatons in Ahldorain. His usage of the city's power plants as electromagnetic weaponry disabled the massive ordinance. Magistrate, your actions prevented the total annihilation of the Kalkhanian capital, and the greatest stronghold of the Beacon."

Auzlanten clasped his forearm and moved over to where the High Conservator was standing. "Jude Bethel was the first brought to light on the conspiracy. His tenacity brought him to rooting out traitors and preparing the Scourge for the inevitable assault. Though the Nephilim's traitors did significant damage to Templym, Bethel ensured that damage was lessened."

Arodi grabbed Bethel's hand and shook it before returning to the podium. "One squadron of soldiers in particular showed great involvement in the Nephilim's Abolition. A Shackle task force, drafted by High Conservator Bethel, was instrumental in the downfall of the Nephilim's plot against us. With the aid of task force S-6319, several high ranking members of the cult were neutralized and a plot to assassinate me was foiled. Herald Oslin Du'Plasse, Inquisitor Adastra Covalos, Inquisitor Vandross Blackwell, and Bride Daphne

Wainwright are the surviving members of this task force. I'd like to call them to the stage at this time."

The four survivors marched onto the stage in full battle plate. As they positioned in a line behind him, Arodi Auzlanten continued to speak. "This squadron went to the fullest lengths to capture their quarry, going so far as to enter the Hellpit of Budapest. At their inception, there were more members. Retriever Ram's Horn and Expurgator Yen Blye, were traitors in this conspiracy. The original leader, Warden Volk Downey, gave his life in service to stopping the Nephilim's Abolition before it began. But without fault, they spent the past three months overcoming every obstacle in their path to acquire their target. For that, they deserve public acclimation."

From beneath the podium, Auzlanten claimed a small wooden box made of polished wood. "Today I am creating a new honor, the White Pinion, awarded exclusively to those who act in a manner of bravery that prevents global catastrophes or acts of genocide. Were it not for them, the Nephilim would have killed me and pre this horrendous coup may very well have succeeded. For that, I am personally granting all four of them this reward."

Arodi Auzlanten opened the box on its hinges as he walked over to the squad. They were each locked into the Scourge's salute with their fists at their hearts. Inside, they could see red velvet lining and six alabaster tokens. The medals were gossamer white pennants made of pearl, shaped like an unfurled angel's wing. The medallion possessed a magnetic seal on the underside that could affix to flak-steel or immotrum.

This was an extraordinary occasion for them all. To be granted an award by Arodi Auzlanten himself, let alone one that had just been created, was a privilege few experienced in their lifetime. It is said that receiving a gift from Templym's founder changes one and never for the worse, as though the Scourge accommodation were just a physical symbol of an immaterial gift given.

Auzlanten went down the line, beginning with Herald Du'Plasse. Oslin's chest swelled as he pulled his hand down from his chest in a heart ripping motion. Arodi fastened the White Pinion to his breastplate so the diamond colored wording wasn't concealed by it. Arodi smiled faintly as he grasped the Hrimatan's wrist. "It's an honor, Master Auzlanten." He said happily.

Arodi leaned in close to him, reducing his voice to that of a hushed whisper. "You're a good man Oslin, albeit a bit prideful. I know of your conflict with your family." Oslin's smile was wiped away. "Your mother has made you the target of her animosity. She will never forgive you. As painful as it may be to hear, you need to move on with your life. And please, learn to humble yourself."

A small pool welled up in Oslin's eyes. He swallowed the rock in his throat and forced down the tears. This was something he realized a long time ago, but finally hearing it from someone of such wisdom helped the message set.

Next in the line was Inquisitor Blackwell. He swiped his hand off his chest and removed his hat. Auzlanten planted the Pinion onto his crimson bulletproof vest. Vandross shook Arodi's hand rigorously. "God bless you, Master Auzlanten." The Inquisitor said through a wide grin.

Arodi leaned in and whispered again. "Vandross, Hugo already lost his mother. He needs his father in his life." Vandross winced at the statement. Once again, Auzlanten had given out a piece of painful, but much needed wisdom.

He moved onto Inquisitor Covalos. There was nothing fancy from him. He just moved his arm and Auzlanten pinned the token at his chest, the same side of his body beneath the blue and gold Urim on his shoulder guard. "Thank you my liege." He grunted in gratitude.

"Your body is a temple Adastra. Your continual self-flagellation is neither healthy nor productive. I speak from experience. There is no need to torture yourself as penitence, Jesus paid it all."

Adastra nodded quickly, requiring no further reprimand. "All to Him, I owe." The two clasped hands, then Auzlanten moved on to the final person in the line, Bride Wainwright.

With fluid motion, she gave the salute and placed her hands at her sides. He placed it on an ebon portion of her mostly white plate so it would show. It fit in well with the ornamental flower pennants. "I thank you for this honor, Master." Her slightly musical voice whispered.

"The honor is mine, Daphne." Like the others, they clasped forearms. "Do not think yourself a lesser woman because of what someone did to you years ago. I know you crave companionship, but you believe to be tainted because of what happened to you. That is nonsense. Pursue the relationship you desire."

Daphne smiled at Auzlanten. Somehow he knew of the internal struggle she had been grappling with for the past twelve years. It should have come as no surprise that he also knew what exactly to say. He wasn't done giving his advice yet.

His eyes darted back between Bride Wainwright and Inquisitor Covalos. "He feels the same way." Auzlanten spoke ever so slightly louder. Not nearly enough for anybody other than the two of them to hear. He spun on his heel and returned to the podium. Adastra and Daphne, holding their posture exchanged a brief peripheral glance. They said nothing, but their cheeks became flushed with pinks as they fought back smiles.

Arodi took to the podium once more, raising the volume of his voice to project to the audience again. "Warden Volk Downey will be awarded the White Pinion posthumously for his dedication in this endeavor. High Conservator Jude Bethel has also earned this accolade. However, I will not be adorning his current suit of battle plate with it. Jude, will you kindly approach the podium."

Excited whispers began echoing out from the crowd. The members of S-6319 smiled, but not nearly as obviously as Magistrate Walthune. If the High Conservator was excited, he showed no indicator. Everyone knew what was coming next.

"The Scourge needs a leader and I need an envoy. Considering the acts of heroism and demonstration of your investigative prowess during the buildup to this massacre, I believe that to be you. Jude Bethel, will you take up office as X Regent of the Scourge?"

"I accept." Bethel's cold voice was audible only to the first few rows of reporters and everyone on stage. The pink scarring around his mouth seemed to perk up as his mouth rose into a shallow smile. He took a knee in front of Auzlanten.

"Do you swear, to uphold the laws of Templym and the doctrine of the Faith above your own personal interests?"

"In Nomine Veritas." Bethel said in response.

"Do you accept the responsibility of the safety of its citizens and the sanctity of its populace? Do you swear to enact my will, but more importantly in the interest of your constituents?"

"In Nomine Veritas."

"*Kynigi et Kako, Diatro Agape, Kyrie Eleison, Monimos Alitheia*?"

"In Nomine Veritas."

"Then as Master of Templym and Voice of the Lord, I anoint you Jude Bethel, X Regent of the Scourge." Auzlanten raised a hand in front of Bethel's face. A brief fire pattern in the shape of an X beneath his eye appeared. The searing pain hurt, but Jude had suffered far worse than that. He did not flinch. When the fire died down, the X was forever branded into Jude Bethel's tanned skin.

"Let history show that Templym refused to back down in the face of adversity. Let the Mundus Imago know that we have survived every onslaught they have ever mustered. Let the Adversary know that no matter how many of our own he turns against us, we will have even greater warriors to take their place and that we will endure. We are God's nation and as long as He is with us, no foe of this plane or the next can ever stand against us!"

Finally, the crowd began cheering. The typical uproar of thunderous applause that Arodi Auzlanten had grown fond of pounded the walls of Bastion Prime like artillery. The new Regent stood on his feet and his companions on the stage with him rushed to congratulate him. The temptation to bask in the glory of such gratuitous admiration was intoxicating, but Auzlanten resisted. There was much work that needed to be done to rectify the damage done. At least for now, Arodi Auzlanten could acknowledge that Templym was in a period of peace.

EPILOGUE

"Drink this." Auzlanten and the newly appointed Jude Bethel had retreated to the privacy of the Regent's quarters of Bastion Prime. Invictus' personal items had been removed leaving only the blackwood desk and the four burning braziers. Arodi handed Jude a silver chalice inlaid with rubies and ivory. It was filled to the brim with liquid that was red like wine but had the consistency of milk.

Bethel didn't question the ceremony or necessity of this situation. He took the drink in with a single draw. He expected it to be too sweet for his taste and it was. Consuming the fluid gave no sign of change and his confusion showed. "I feel no different."

"That will continue for the next five years." Auzlanten replied. "I've frozen your body's natural aging process. Every five years I will ask if you wish to continue to operate as my Regent and if you accept I'll give you another dose."

"So this is how you've kept the Regent young over the centuries?" Jude queried with a slight grin. Unconsciously, he rubbed at the new brand beneath his eye.

"The mark of the Regent is permanent." Auzlanten said ignoring his question. "It's a brand of identity, immortalizing you in this position. It won't be heal or scar over anytime soon. If you'd like I can take care of the others for you."

"You already know I don't want that." Bethel retorted as he took a seat at his new desk. "My scars may not define me, but they show what I've been through. Each one tells a story of a hardship I overcame. This brand is the latest trophy I've acquired over the past three months." Bethel shifted his gaze from Auzlanten to the doorway into his new office. Magistrate Walthune was outside, waiting to meet with his new boss. "What should my first action as Regent be?"

"I leave that in your hands, Jude. As Regent it is your duty to act in my interests, though not as a mindless automaton. There is much to be done to rebuild the Scourge's ranks and Templym's infrastructure. I trust your judgment."

Arodi took a seat in front of Bethel's desk, his eyes falling onto the Scourge's mantra mounted to the front. He then looked up at the new Regent. "I have more for you."

"Is the new position and immortality not enough?" Jude said, surprised at the treatment he was receiving.

"You need a new suit of battle plate, something befitting the leader of greatest military to exist on God's Earth. I'll begin atomocizing flaksteel and have it done for you by the end of the week. There is also another gift I think you will appreciate. Tradition has it that I give a gift of knowledge to the Regent upon the conclusion of a great accomplishment. Seeing as this is your inauguration, I will grant you the answer to any question you may have."

Bethel leaned forward. To be given this opportunity was certainly a privilege. Many questions fluttered to the forefront of his mind, most of them concerning Arodi Auzlanten and the supernatural world. Perhaps he would ask about Malacurai and the Civil Strife or the Reclaiming Crusade or one of the Purus Crusades or being in the presence of the Lord. These were all questions that common citizens had, but Jude had seen far more than the ordinary townsfolk.

His exposure to Auzlanten's world had raised several questions that burned at his mind. Why was he the first to be trusted with the news of Regent Illuromos' betrayal? How did the Nephilim corrupt him? His thoughts consistently came back to Arodi's private sanctum. Why did he have an A+ Imago imprisoned there? Who was the blonde woman? What did he do with the Idolacreid? How did he kill the Nephilim permanently? What became of its throne?

Bethel stroked his scarred chin in deep contemplation. He could spend some time speaking with his comrades that went through the same things. He wanted to ask something that nobody else could conceive of. Then he thought back to the conversations they had shared in his sanctum. Then he remembered a modicum of information he caught that he believed most of his team didn't catch.

"The girl, who was she?" Jude finally asked.

Auzlanten leaned back and stroked his beard. "You're referring to my assistant?"

"No." Bethel said to Arodi's surprise. "When the prison door cracked open, the Imago locked within took the form of a little girl. You said that it had taken that exact form dozens of times. So, who was she to you?"

Auzlanten pinched his chin in contemplation. He gave a shallow smile, acknowledging Bethel's observation skills and realizing that he made the right choice for Regent. That didn't make sharing the answer any easier.

"The Imago Tumor'at has tried exploiting people from my past to trick me into releasing it. The one you saw, a six year old girl, was the girl that should have been." He expected Bethel to ask for additional elaboration, but he was honed in on his words with laser focus. So Auzlanten continued. "Her name should have been Lydia."

Arodi pictured the child in his mind and smiled. He saw her freckled cheeks, black ponytails, and glittering brown eyes. She had a wide grin and a sweet innocent voice. "She should have been born in the Western Glaswegian coast. Lydia should have become a nurse and then a cardiologist. She should have married at age twenty-one and had four children. She should have raised three impactful evangelists and a military mastermind. She never did."

Auzlanten's smile faded as he dwelt on the 'should' aspect of his regret. "Lydia should have been born February, no Decathys 23rd...but she never was. She should have been born."

Bethel broke his silence. "But who was she to you?"

Arodi Auzlanten paused and Jude swore he saw glint of a tear in the corner of his eye. "She should have been my daughter."

The Regent stopped agape. His answer was telling. First, it told that Arodi Auzlanten was human, or at least he used to be. Second, he let it slip just how old he was, he had been human and had a family at some point in time when the second month of the year was called February and not Decathys. Jude had never heard that name before, but surely Beacon historians had record that would allude to his age.

"I think I've said enough for now." Auzlanten stood up from his seat and nodded at his new Regent. "I will be in touch with special protocol after I finish revising it. For now...get to work." He gave a brief half-smile and was gone.

Bethel sat alone in his new office. He blinked as he processed the information that he just gleaned from his superior. There was no need to be told that this information was Alpha Magnus classified. So he tucked this data away in the back of his mind and proceeded with his new responsibilities. Then he buzzed in the Magistrate.

Averrin Walthune stepped inside. His bright teeth starkly contrasted the darkness of his skin. He carried what looked like an animal horn in his hand as he quickly approached the desk. "Regent Bethel," his deep voice boomed as he saluted his former equal. "The title suits you."

"At ease, Averrin," Jude responded humbly as he motioned for him to sit. "Do me a favor and drop the formalities for the first few weeks."

"Of course, I got you something." Walthune slapped the horn onto the blackwood desktop. Bethel lifted it up to inspect it. It was actually not from any beast, it was made of flaksteel and sapphire stained enamel glass. "What's this?"

"That is a horn from the helm throne of the *Azure Claw,* the only Everest class Hekaton that turned traitor at Ahldorain. We boarded it after disabling its mechanisms and killed the fanatics inside. This horn was the lever controlling one of its nuclear cannon arms. I have the other. We'll each keep one as a reminder that we are the two primes that survived this horrific massacre."

Bethel's scarred mouth rose in a grin. "You're a true friend, Averrin. I'll get a stand for this. You raise a good point, which I think needs to be handled first. My first action as Regent needs to be replacing the vacancies in the Scourge's positions of authority."

"Yes," Averrin said taking his seat and becoming more serious. "With your promotion, I am the only active prime in the Scourge. We need a new High Conservator, Prelate, and Patriarch. Do you have any candidates in mind?"

"Yes, I believe I have the Veil's replacement and I know of a few good Conservators that could replace me. I am at a loss for Cardinals though. I'd like your input."

The Magistrate seemed to wince slightly. "If I may, when selecting the new primes you must heavily consider the public opinion when choosing. I feel Auzlanten's confession will erode trust with the public."

"Agreed, we've put him up on a pedestal for so long, news of an admitted failure will shake the public trust of him. We're going to have to build it back up." Bethel paused and pondered for a moment. "Let's take a more active role in reconstruction. Dig up old Trench reconstruction tactics and devote large portions into renovating the lost urbans."

"I have a few ideas, may I use your computer?"

"Please do," Bethel turned the monitor around and slid the rune keys towards Magistrate Walthune. "I'll call some coffee up. I hope you didn't have any plans for the afternoon, we're going to be here for a while."

Oslin Du'Plasse finalized his last stenographer's report. Tapping on the projectum keys of his tablet, he finalized the last report detailing the work of task force S-6319. His back was to a locker and his battle plate was removed. The suit was on its holster in his clear glass locker. He found his gaze constantly falling onto the White Pinion on his breastplate and losing his train of thought.

Herald Du'Plasse was happy. Not just because the horrific events of the last few months were over, but also because his suspension was surely about to end. Maybe people would finally forget about the Senator. He doubted history would do justice to the record, but as Auzlanten had reminded him, he needed to remember to be more humble.

"How about you, Os?" Vandross asked him. Du'Plasse didn't even notice Inquisitor Blackwell and Covalos enter the locker room. He was so enthralled in his thoughts, or perhaps he was just too exhausted to notice.

"I'm sorry, what was that?" Oslin asked the pair, ignorant of their conversation.

"We've been given a month of paid leave." Adastra said as he struggled out of his breastplate. Having only one hand hampered his ability to perform simple tasks and he would have to learn to adapt. "How do you intend to spend it?"

Oslin thought for a moment. He had heard they were being granted a brief recess, but he hadn't put much thought into it. "I'm off to Rio Epiphanies," Vandross said while adjusting his hat, the one constant of his wardrobe. "Auzlanten suggested something that should have been obvious. I'm spending the month with my son."

"I see, Auzlanten gave us all some sage advice." Oslin said. "I suppose the only plans I have are in attending Warden Downey's memorial in Glaswey. Afterwards, I suppose I'll just return to Hrimata, perhaps reconnect with my sisters. What about you Adastra?"

"No real plans beyond this week. I've got a dinner with Daphne tomorrow evening, but no plans after that."

Vandross cocked his eyebrows upwards. "A dinner with Daphne, eh?"

"Well, yes. We were planning on this evening, but apparently Regent Bethel has requested her presence. I think he's planning on making her the new Matriarch of the Veil."

Vandross ignored the plan and kept staring at his partner with a smile. He couldn't possibly conceal his ear to ear grin as he eyed his partner. "You're courting that girl, aren't you Adastra?"

Adastra chuckled, but his pale cheeks turned pink for a moment. "It's just a dinner with a friend. It'll be nice to have some food with her that isn't in a preserved food pack."

"Right, it's just a dinner." Vandross said ironically then decided to drop the subject. As a romantic and a gentleman, he respected his friend's right to be modest. "If there's nothing else going on tonight, how about a drink then?"

"God knows we've earned one." Adastra said. "I'm in. Oslin, would you care to join us?"

"Oh, I don't think so," Oslin responded. "I've got to finish this last report. I am the stenographer after all."

"Wrap it up, Du'Plasse," Vandross said playfully. "I think you owe us a round for that stunt you pulled with the bomb."

Oslin scoffed at the Inquisitor. "Well alright, but I think you owe me a round for saving Auzlanten's life."

"Deal," Adastra said. "Let's hit the bar down on Dubari street."

"I'll be with you in a moment," Oslin said tapping away on his pad. "Let me finish this last page and I'll meet up with you, fifteen minutes?"

"It's a date," Vandross said as he stuck his pipe in his mouth. "See you there, Os."

The two Inquisitors took their leave. Du'Plasse could hear the two exchanging gests back and forth as they left Bastion Prime. The Herald chuckled to himself. He wasn't particularly fond of them, or any member of his squad, when he first met them in Rexus. He was thankful that he managed to make good friends out of them.

He was nearly done with the report. After completion, he would submit the report to the Shackle's interim prime and S-6319 would be officially disbanded. The mission was a success, end of story. In truth, Oslin could probably submit the report right now and put the Nephilim conspiracy to rest. That was not Oslin's style. He submitted a report only after every loose end of a case was tied up. There was something still nagging at him.

Du'Plasse was rolling through old interrogation footage. He had already combed through Diogo Numerri and Nuoli Lamiash. He kept coming back to Thomas Monk. Hrimata's Dilictor Ignotum had said something that hadn't settled in his mind yet and he kept going over the records of the investigation. This would be the last time he went through the video log.

Thomas Monk: "If I tell you everything I know. Will you shoot me here and now? I won't risk being captured by the Mortis. He scares me more than you."

Oslin Du'Plasse: "That can be arranged. It depends on what you tell me."

Thomas Monk: *Swallows.* "There isn't much more to tell. It seems as though you figured out most of what I know."

Oslin Du'Plasse: "What did I miss?"

Thomas Monk: "Knox Mortis is the name of one of the Nephilim's three generals, the only one I'm aware of. We all indirectly report them who relay relevant information to it. I reported to him through one of his personal lieutenants, a marauder named Fel Maul."

Oslin Du'Plasse:"A marauder of what tribe?"

Thomas Monk: "I don't really know, they only referred to themselves in their...*Stop. Rewind.*

Oslin Du'Plasse: "What did I miss?"

Thomas Monk: "Knox Mortis is the name of one of the Nephilim's three generals, the only one I'm aware of. We all indirectly report them who relay...*Stop. Rewind.*

Thomas Monk: "...the name of one of the Nephilim's three generals, the only...*Stop.*

Oslin stopped the footage and placed a marker on the time line. That same segment kept gnawing at his mind. He never really acknowledged it much when Monk was alive and the Veil from the Solace were all too eager to put him in the ground so he didn't get a chance to elaborate. As far as he could tell, there was nothing left to investigate for the moment. He stamped this portion of the tape with a marker to indicate an incompletion.

1. Knox Mortis (*confactus*)
2. Invictus Illuromos (*confactus*)
3. ?

Arodi Auzlanten stood in quiet contemplation in his private sanctum. His hands were tucked behind his back. Leagna sat in its scabbard at his hip. The icosahedron the Lord had blessed him with sat in a new display a few meters behind him. The Nephilim's throne had been located and dismantled, the pieces disintegrated, and the ashes scattered. The Idolacreid was locked away in its own cell, hopefully never to be read again.

He was staring at the prison door, its contents the focus of his meditation. Many problems would be solved by the death of Tumor'at. Many more would be created if it died. This arrangement would have to do.

Was the truth out? Did the Nephilim actually know what he was? Was this the information used to corrupt Invictus? He shuttered at the thought. If this knowledge was circulating, many more could exploit that information. These thoughts and millions of others bombarded Auzlanten's mind in a cascade of overwhelming uncertainty. Perhaps this was just the beast's dying ploy. The Nephilim delighted in creating fear and distress by means of informational warfare. It was reasonable to assume that it wanted one last lie planted in the mind of its most hated foe before damnation. Telling himself that made him feel better.

"Arodi?" The woman, still dressed in the same dull grey Scourge uniform approached. Her eyes, as icy blue as they were, were warm and comforting. Auzlanten pushed the cloud of thought from his mind, deciding to deal with them later. "Might I suggest you take a Sabbath? You haven't relaxed in over three months. Even God rested on the seventh day."

"Death toll?" Auzlanten asked, dryly ignoring her recommendation.

"Five hundred sixty-two thousand-four hundred-eleven citizens of Templym were killed in the Nephilim's Abolition. What won't be recorded by the Scourge is the two hundred three thousand-nine hundred-eighty-six marauders that were also killed in the Hinterlands and other unofficial territory."

Arodi continued his bleak extrapolation. "The keystone required the blood of a million innocents. The Nephilim was less than a quarter million away from its goal. At the rate the slaughter was proceeding, its quota would have been reached within an hour if I hadn't intervened."

"But you did intervene." The woman grabbed his hand, tenderly caressing his jewel clad fingers. "By the Will of the Triune God, you destroyed the Nephilim and its cult. Nobody but you could have done so. Only you, with your vast powers, had the capability to stop the slaughter from reaching irreparable levels. You saved Templym. You're a hero."

Arodi stared at her delicate fingers as they danced around his. They were so soft, so warm. Her loving touch was not enough to distract him from his loathing. "Did you run the theoretical I asked you to?"

She turned his head to force him to look directly at her. He hadn't even realized he wasn't making eye contact. "There's no way to know for certain what would have been different. If you killed Invictus when you were first commanded, the Nephilim would have adjusted its plans to compensate for the loss."

"Did you make the calculations?"

She sighed deeply. "Assuming identical timing and circumstances as the actual abolition, which I sincerely doubt would occur if the Regent was killed three months prior, the Scourge would have been better equipped to repel the assault. Invictus and his following sabotaged every Scourge wavelength and central data wells, hindering their coordination and response ability. If that were not a factor, the Scourge would have been able to preserve an additional one hundred thousand lives."

Auzlanten stared blankly as he struggled to come to terms with what she told him. She saw his turmoil and immediately offered council. "That is a highly unlikely scenario. There is no way of knowing exactly what would have been different. There are hundreds of different paths the Nephilim could have taken to retaliate, each resulting in an equal number of deaths. For all we know, your delay could have actually saved lives. There's just no way of knowing for sure."

"I'm a failure." Auzlanten said bitterly.

"No you're not." She responded, her ancient Glaswegian accent keeping its soft charm despite her stern tone. "God had placed you in this position knowing that you are suitable for the responsibilities. You delivered the world from the Tyrranis Period, through the Purus Crusades, the Civil Strife, and most recently the Nephilim's Abolition. You are a hero and your humility here shows what a man of noble character you truly are."

Arodi had never felt such support from his assistant. Warmth and comfort replaced the icy feeling of dread that had once occupied his mind so heavily. He was so grateful to have such a companion in his life he did something senseless.

He pulled her in close and kissed her. As two lovers embrace one another, Auzlanten pressed his lips against his assistant's. She seemed to enjoy the romantic gesture just as much as he did. It had been years since they had kissed and Arodi had missed the sensation. Her lips were so soft, so warm...so real.

She seemed so human. So much so, that Auzlanten forgot. Upon ending the kiss, he placed his chin on her shoulders and whispered into her ear. "Thank you, Joyce."

The woman pulled back, looking at Arodi with a puzzled expression. "Sir, I'm not supposed to let you call me that."

He remembered again and the pain of the memory crept back into his heart. He expressed his grief the only way a sensible man could. He cried.

Auzlanten buried his head in her shoulder as water streamed from his eyes. He cried for the sorrow of disobeying his Heavenly Father. He mourned the loss of those who died in service to the Scourge like Betankur, Greyflame, Downey, and thousands others who he knew by name. He sobbed for the fall of Invictus Illuromos and what he was forced to do because of his traitor son. He wept for the thousands that were killed by the cult of the Nephilim, more so for the hundred thousand he now believed should have been saved. He cried for the girl who should have been. He cried for the woman that was.

Arodi Auzlanten wept bitter tears of agony for hours. The blonde woman did not interrupt him; she did not even attempt to console him. She simply provided the shoulder on which he could cry. No man could be exposed to centuries of anguish and not break down every so often. He had earned the right to mourn.

All the while, a vague noise permeated the sounds of weeping. From inside of the prison chamber something stirred. The multitudinous voice of a dark spirit reached out from behind the thick wardiron vault. The barely audible chorus was not distinguishable as any kind of speech. The captive inside wasn't even attempting to communicate with anything outside of its cell. Somehow, Tumor'at knew that Arodi Auzlanten had broken down his stoic façade, exposing the true tortured soul within, and it was laughing.

CPSIA information can be obtained
at www.ICGtesting.com
Printed in the USA
FSHW010821070321
79251FS

9 781977 23874